Steam Highwayman

Volume III

The Reeking Metropolis

by

Martin Barnabus Noutch

Illustrated by

Russ Nicholson

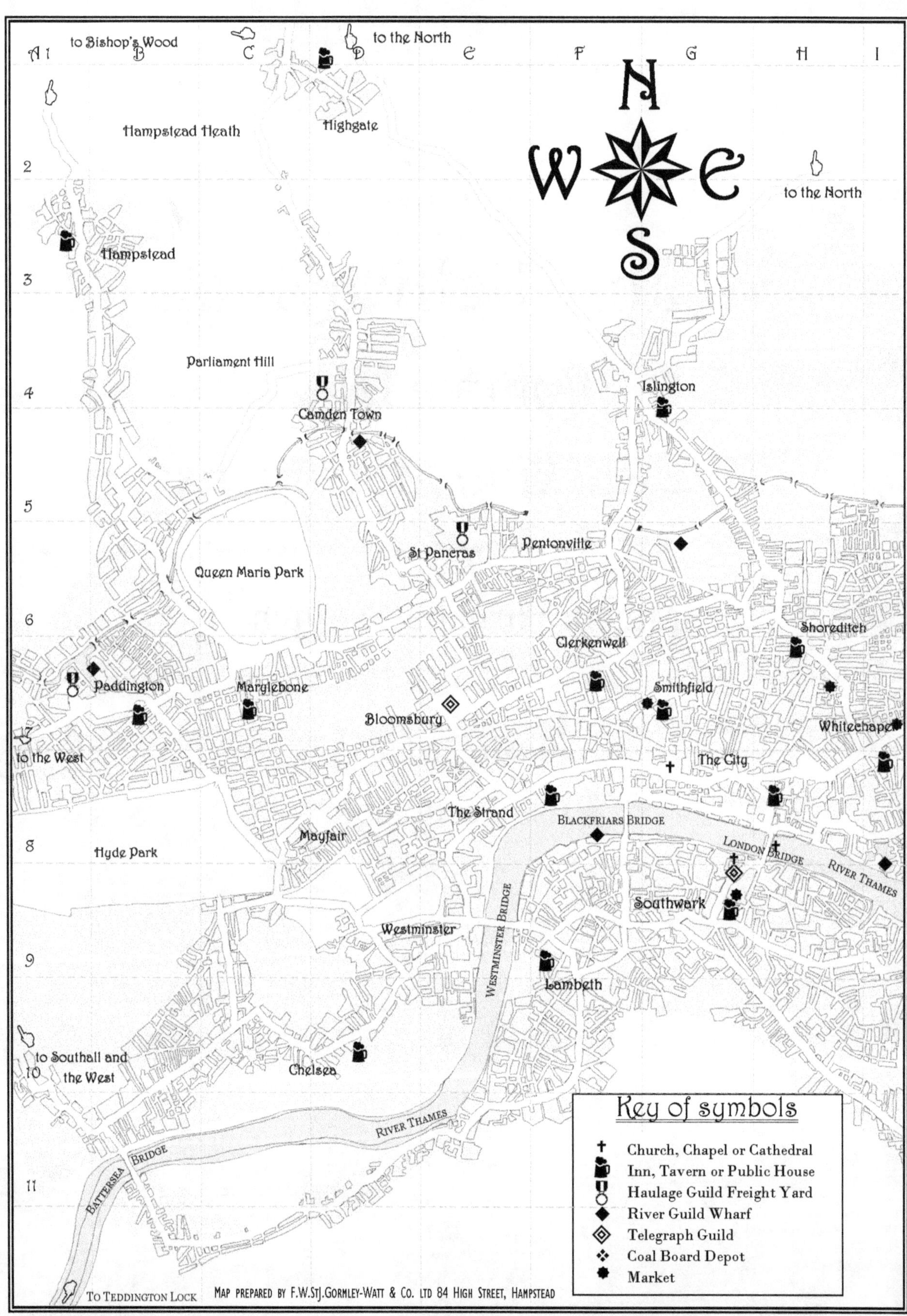

to Bishop's Wood
to the North
Hampstead Heath
Highgate
N
W E
S
to the North
Hampstead
Parliament Hill
Islington
Camden Town
St Pancras
Pentonville
Queen Maria Park
Shoreditch
Clerkenwell
Smithfield
Paddington
Marylebone
Whitechapel
Bloomsbury
The City
to the West
The Strand
Mayfair
Blackfriars Bridge
London Bridge
Hyde Park
River Thames
Southwark
Westminster
Westminster Bridge
Lambeth
to Southall and
the West
Chelsea
River Thames
Battersea Bridge
To Teddington Lock
Map prepared by F.W.St.J.Gormley-Watt & Co. Ltd 84 High Street, Hampstead
Key of symbols
Church, Chapel or Cathedral
Inn, Tavern or Public House
Haulage Guild Freight Yard
River Guild Wharf
Telegraph Guild
Coal Board Depot
Market

The Reeking Metropolis

LONDON

During the Reign of His Imperial Majesty Charles III

illustrating famous taverns and public houses, Telegraphic Guild Stations, Haulage Guild Freight Yards, the King's Canal, various River and navigation wharves, places of worship, etc.

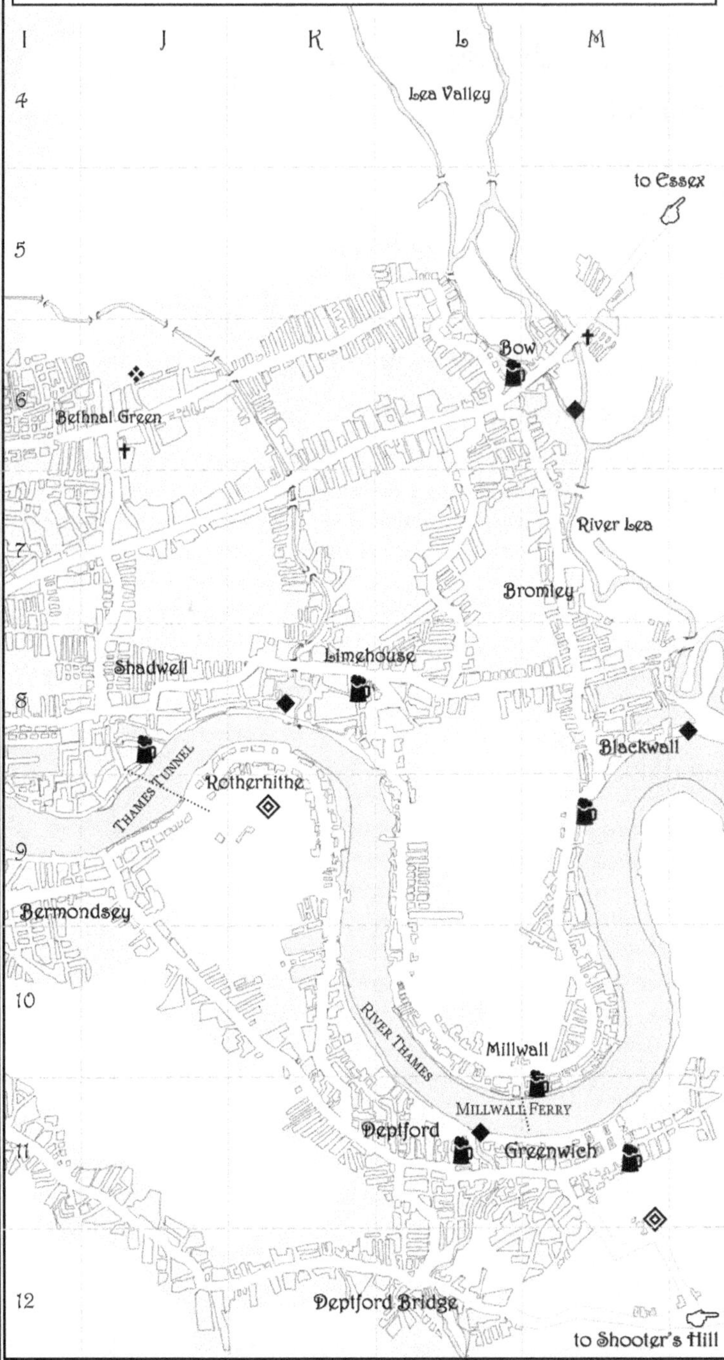

BERMONDSEY M8
House of St Katharine

BETHNAL GREEN J6
St John's Church
Coal Board Depot

BLACKWALL I9
East India Dock
The Gun, Public House
Sugar Warehouse
Building Supplies Yard

BLOOMSBURY E7
The British Museum
The Royal College of Surgeons
Telegraph Station
Bloomsbury Hotel
Guberstein's

BOW L/M6
Bird Alley Chapel
The Young Prince, Public House
Three Mill Wharf
High Way House
The Metropolitan Sewerage Cpy.

BROMLEY M7
The Ash Heaps

CAMDEN TOWN D5
Camden Brewery
Camden Wharf
North London Steam Omnibus Cpy.
Haulage Guild Freight Yard

THE CITY G/H8
Lightfoot's Oyster Bar
St Thomas Abridge
Brewer's Hall
The Exchange
The Bank of England
The Tower of London
The Monument
St Margaret's Court
The College of Arms
Newgate Gaol
St Katharine's Dock
St Paul's Cathedral

CHELSEA D10
HMS Spartan, Public House
Kent Mansion
Sussex House
Hough's Piscatorial Purveyors

CLERKENWELL F7
St Gorgonia's Court
Foundling's Home
The Horn, Public House
M.L. Frobisher, Dentist

DEPTFORD L11
The Unicorns, Public House
Deptford Wharf

DEPTFORD BRIDGE L12
The Unicorns, Public House
Deptford Wharf

GREENWICH M11
The Plume of Feathers, Pub. Hse.
The Royal Observatory (Telegraph
   Station)
Ferry

HAMPSTEAD A3
The Holly Bush Inn, Public House

HAMPSTEAD HEATH B2
The Heath
Ken Wood

HIGHGATE D2
The Flask, Public House

HYDE PARK B9
The Great Exhibition

ISLINGTON F/G4
Canonbury Tower
Laycock's Lairs
The Compton Arms, Public House
Remus Wine Merchants

LAMBETH F9
Crafton's Cookshop
Fresher & Sons, Clockwork
   Mechanics
The Pineapple, Public House

LIMEHOUSE K8
The Grapes, Public House
Dr Smythe's Surgery
The King's Canal Dock

MARYLEBONE C7
Nestor's Bakery
Swithin Arcade, Clothing
The Imperial, Public House

MAYFAIR D8
Derwent House
Hendon Mansion
Tort Manor

MILLWALL M11
The Ship, Public House
Shipyards
Engineering Workshops
Ferry

PARLIAMENT HILL C4
Atmospheric Union Airfield

PADDINGTON A7
Haulage Guild Freight Yard
Paddington Basin Wharf
The Brunel Arms, Public House
Imperial Western Railway Terminus

PENTONVILLE F6
Battlebridge Basin
Forsi's Ice Warehouse

QUEEN MARIA PK C6
The Zoo

ROTHERHITHE K9
Telegraph Station
Cary's Chandlery
The Thames Tunnel

SHADWELL J8
The Prospect of Whitby, Pub. Hse.
The Thames Tunnel

SHOREDITCH H7
Spitalfield Market
The Old Blue Last, Public House
The Old Nichol slum

SMITHFIELD G7
Smithfield Market
The Yard, Public House

SOUTHWARK G9
Borough Market
St Saviour's Church (Telegraph
   Station)
Bargehouse Wharf
The George, Public House

ST. PANCRAS E6
Haulage Guild Freight Yard
Burrage Assembly Hall

THE STRAND F8
The Leopard, Public House
The Lyceum Theatre
Blucock Publishing House
Coulter's Bank
Somerset House

WESTMINSTER E9
The Houses of Parliament
Street Market
St. Eanswythe Hall
The Gentilesse
St. James' Palace

WHITECHAPEL I7
Whitechapel Market
Whitechapel Bell Foundry
The Grave Maurice, Public House

Travellers are minded to be wary of the following locations, as known haunts of highway robbers: Shooter's Hill, Old Kent Road (between Southwark and Deptford Bridge), Essex Road north-east of Bow, Bishop's Wood and the Southall road west of Chelsea. Hyde Park can also be dangerous at night.

❧Introduction ❧

Who is the Steam Highwayman?

You are the Steam Highwayman. Whatever brought you here, you now stand on the verge of an exciting adventure. Within this book you can explore a world of different choices and consequences, puzzles, mysteries and quests, discovering your own story as you turn from passage to passage. You will need a pencil and eraser to mark your adventure sheet at the back of this book to track your progress and two dice to help calculate the effects of chance in your tale. Your decisions will be matters of life and death, not just for yourself, but for many others too.

Options

From the very first passage in this book you are presented with choices: where to travel; how to answer a challenge; to kill or to spare a villain. Choices presented beneath a passage's main text are optional; instructions within a passage must be followed to maintain the narrative: this allows you the freedom to make choices but also means you are subject to their consequences. To make a choice, simply turn to the passage indicated and continue to read from there...

Conditional Options

Options followed by a price, item or codeword in brackets are conditional options: you can only choose these if you possess the **money** in your purse, item noted on your **Adventure Sheet** or have ticked the relevant codeword. You should remove money spent in this way immediately, but you will be told when to remove items or codewords. Options preceded by an empty box may only be chosen once that box is ticked. Options preceded by a crossed box may only be chosen once: after choosing this option, you should cross it out with a pencil.

Tickboxes

Some passages include tickboxes which track your progress. You will be instructed to tick them with a pencil when you encounter them and either read on or proceed to a different passage. When the time comes to restart your adventure, you will need to erase any ticks before beginning afresh.

Codewords

As you travel throughout the realm you will learn many secrets, hear many rumours and experience strange and wonderful adventures: codewords allow the book to track this. When you gain a codeword, tick that codeword in the back of the book. When you are asked if you have a particular codeword, check to see if it is ticked in your codeword list. Some options are only available if you have a certain codeword, indicated by a codeword in brackets after that option (*Crisis*). When travelling to another book in the series, retain your codewords, but if you restart your adventure you will need to erase all the codewords you have collected.

Your Adventure Sheet

Abilities

Your adventure will require you to use a diverse set of skills, which the following list represents:

RUTHLESSNESS   How threatening you seem, both in appearance and reputation
ENGINEERING   Your skill with pneumo-mechanics and steam machinery
MOTORING   The knowledge of road lore and the art of handling an engine
INGENUITY   Your ability to solve problems
NIMBLENESS   Your physical quickness and agility
GALLANTRY   The appeal of your manners, words and deeds

To make an ability roll you must **roll two dice and add the total to the appropriate ability score**, plus any modifiers. If the total score is **greater than** the difficulty, you have succeeded.

Bonus Skills

During your adventure you may gain additional specialist skills such as **animal friendship**, **legal knowledge**, **explosives expert** or **medical training**. When you learn one of these, you will gain a **level** in this skill and should note it on your **Adventure Sheet**. Possessing a level of **animal friendship** or three or more levels of **legal knowledge** may help you with specific ability rolls or may allow you to access unique quests and adventures.

Possessions

You will collect, find and buy many items as you travel the land. You may carry up to 12 possessions in your inventory (representing your saddlebags) at any time. In addition, you may carry 12 small items in your **jewellery pouch**. These may only be small objects that would fit within the hand, such as **keys**, **rings**, coiled **necklaces** or similar. Flat objects, such as **punchcards**, **tickets**, **notebooks** or **posters** may be carried in your **satchel**, which can hold 12 paper or card items. If in doubt, act like a Steam Highwayman. Remember - this is intended to be a fun adventure, not a lesson in inventory management!

Many items modify your Ability scores. These modifiers are cumulative as long as the items are unique. For example, your ENGINEERING score of 4 could be improved by possession of a **pneumatic manual (ENG+3)** and an **adjustable wrench (ENG+1)** to total 8, but could not be improved by two adjustable wrenches. Some options are only available to you if you possess a certain item, indicated by a bracketed item (**grappling iron**). If these do not indicate that you should discard or use up the item, you may retain that item for later. Limited use objects have a number of tickboxes beside them which you should tick on each use: bonuses conferred by these objects to Ability scores are temporary and will revert after a single fight or skill check. After the final tick, erase the object from your Adventure Sheet. You may also be asked for your **unmodified ability score** (ie your Ability unchanged by possessions).

Money

The realm uses the Imperial monetary system - pounds (£), shillings (s) and pence (d). You will normally deal only in shillings, but when making deposits at the bank or expensive purchases you will need to do a little maths: there are 20 shillings to the pound or sovereign, and 21 shillings to the guinea. Paper money is normally only used by the wealthiest and is not always easy to exchange. A bundle of notes such as **thirty guineas in notes** may not be spent as normal - you will need to find someone to accept it as a deposit or exchange it for hard money (sometimes at a discount). Paper money does not take up a possession slot in your inventory.

Bank Deposits

Should you wish to deposit your money in a bank account, you will need to subtract amounts in multiples of ten guineas (**£10 10s**) from your purse and write this amount into the account space on your **Adventure Sheet**. If you travel to another book, write this number onto the new **Adventure Sheet** as your account will be available at other branches of the bank, where you may withdraw it with the same restriction.

Within the text you will be asked to note a certain **passage number** on your **Adventure Sheet**. Shortly after this you are likely to encounter an instruction that indicates that you should turn to your **noted passage**. This should be your most recently **noted passage number**, as you will never be required to note more than one passage number at a time.

Hidden Links

Not every choice in *The Reeking Metropolis* is marked with an option: keeping your eyes peeled and learning from the adventures you encounter may lead you to making leaps of faith from one passage to another. In general, these will involve making calculations based upon the **passage numbers**, so you are advised to calculate carefully and to keep note of the passage you are leaving in case you need to return there.

Weapons

Shooting Guns

Each gun has an ACCURACY rating (e.g. **blunderpistol (ACC 6)**). To shoot, roll two dice and add the score to your gun's ACCURACY together with any other modifiers. A score **greater than** the difficulty is a success. Of course, should you lose your firearm, you should not choose any option that would require you to take a shot.

Fighting enemies

Combat proceeds in rounds, and in each you have an opportunity to wound your opponent before they have a chance to hurt you. When the number of **wounds** you have inflicted is equal to your opponent's TOUGHNESS, or when you have **five wounds**, the fight is over. To calculate whether you wound your enemy, roll two dice and add the score to your NIMBLENESS, together with any modifiers. If the total is **greater than** your opponent's PARRY, you will succeed in wounding them.

Your opponent then has the same chance: the roll of two dice is added to their NIMBLENESS and if the total is **greater than** your PARRY then you gain a **wound**. Your PARRY score is the total of your NIMBLENESS plus the PAR value of your weapon. Note that if your opponent has a weapon with modifiers, these have already been added to the NIMBLENESS, PARRY and TOUGHNESS scores printed. You make take your opponent's weapon if you win.

Wounds

A highwayman's life is a dangerous one: you may be wounded in single combat, shot at by angry Constables or hurt in a road accident. Keep track of each **wound** on your Adventure Sheet, as normally your fifth **wound** will incapacitate you and may hasten the end of your adventure. You are able to treat your **wounds** in a safe location either through rest or paying for medical treatment, which will normally result in your **wounds** converting to **scars**.

Scars

The normal process when a wound is healed is to erase the **wound** from your Adventure Sheet and add a **scar** to your scar tally. Sometimes you will be prompted to roll two dice and a score of 11 or 12 will result in an **intimidating scar (RUTH+1)**, which should be noted in your **Other Modifiers**.

Velosteam

Your velosteam is your most prized possession: a finely-tuned and carefully engineered two-wheeled road engine of unsurpassed mechanical beauty, it runs on readily available coal-gas and can achieve considerable speed. However, it can be damaged by accidents or risk-taking. Keep track of any **damage points** on your Adventure Sheet, along with any customisations that you manage to fit. You must take care! Your velosteam can sustain three **damage points**, but should you suffer the fourth your machine will be **beyond repair**. At this point you will be forced to abandon your adventure on the road - so ensure you know a trustworthy mechanic who can help you repair your velosteam before that stage.

Reputation

As you proceed about your lawless way you are bound to make enemies as well as friends. Record your notoriety (for example, **Wanted by the Coal Board**) and your friendships (for example, **Friend of Diana Derwent**) on your Adventure Sheet. These will decide your fate at many a turn.

Great Deeds

Some adventures may result in you becoming known for your **great deeds**. Note these on your Adventure Sheet: they will influence your eventual fate when you come to retire from this life. They may also influence those around you, as your legend precedes you in the land.

Solidarity Points

The common people of Britain are oppressed and disenfranchised: their poverty enables the wealth of the landed, the gentry, the industrialists and the political classes. Some of your choices may result in you gaining **solidarity points**, which indicate whether the poor of the land know you as a saviour or as an oppressor. Should you gain 50 or more **solidarity points** you will be known as the **People's Champion**. However, you may lose **solidarity points** for participating in the oppression of the common people. It is not possible to have a negative number of **solidarity points.**

Retirement and the End of your Adventure

Once you have fully explored the world of *The Reeking Metropolis*, you may adventure on into the other books in this series, riding airships, fighting for Cornish independence or riding the Great North Road.   However, your good fortune cannot last forever and when you decide to settle down and retire from the road you will be invited to turn to the **Epilogue**. Several important factors will decide the happiness and security of your later years: the number of **friendships** that you have made, the amount of money you have banked with Coulter's Bank, the number of **solidarity points** and **great deeds** that you have collected and your health, represented by the number of **scars** you bear. All of these will also help you calculate a score to share with other riders of the midnight road, or to better in another adventure.

✤ 1 ✤

The city lies before you, smoking and stinking with life. Here on Highgate Hill you can peer through the dirty dusk from the saddle of your Ferguson velosteam and survey the capital of the British Empire, the greatest city in the world. London. Countless chimneys reek. Unnumbered fires burn. But where there's muck, there's brass, and that coin calls to you.

How did you come to be here?

"I swam ashore from a hulk."	**147**
"I want recognition for my inventions."	**224**
"I used to carry despatches for the guilds."	**338**
"Childhood stories of chivalry inspired me."	**453**
"An orphan must fight to survive in this city."	**575**
"My people lost their land to the Coal Board."	**698**

✤ 2 ✤

The inhabitants of Hampstead like that their village is separated from the city by green fields, but this is also a setting-off point on the road north. You should find rich pickings close by: Bishop's Wood is not far to the north-east.

The nearby Heath is not trusted at night: the little woods and dells hold all manner of threats and secrets. Locals are far more likely to be found in the busy warmth of the Holly Bush Inn, while hauliers sup in the yard outside.

Visit the Holly Bush...	**61**
Head west onto the Heath...	**22**
Steam south towards Queen Maria Park...	**83**
Take the road to Marylebone...	**35**
Steer for Bishop's Wood...	**49**
Leave this region...	**50**

✤ 3 ✤

The landlord takes one quick look at the Camden Brewery contract and shakes his head. "I wouldn't have thought you'd be doing their business," he says. "Trying to squash out all the independent tradesmen."

If you want to try to back up the offer with a threat, make a RUTHLESSNESS roll of difficulty 10, adding 1 if you are **Wanted by the Constables**.

Successful RUTHLESSNESS roll!	**20**
Failed RUTHLESSNESS roll	
or did not attempt...	**12**

✤ 4 ✤

The design for the 'line of assembly' looks like it would transform the way manufacturing of large machinery happens. By breaking down the various tasks into simple, repetitive actions, a manufacturer will rely less on skilled labour, increasing output and lowering costs. What the result will be for the workers is another question.

With your considerable skill in understanding engineering and processes, you commit what you can to memory and later sketch out the **assembly line plan** on a piece of paper. You should be able to find a buyer for information like this.

Turn to...	**noted passage**

✤ 5 ✤

The guild keep long records of those who have offended them, for they are entitled by Royal Charter to imprison and punish on their own behalf. You have been unwise enough to allow your own name or likeness into their files and now several Constable velosteams appear from nearby hiding places: you must flee!

Ride east...	**410**
Head west...	**421**
Steam south...	**445**

✤ 6 ✤

☐

If the box above is empty, tick it and read on. If it is already ticked, turn to **41** immediately.

Another colossal flash overpowers your vision at the same moment as an intense pain shoots through your body - a pain like scalding heat, somehow transmitted through your very bones. The electrical force throws you from the velosteam and you hit the ground hard.

As you carefully pick yourself up and check yourself, you are amazed to find that, other than a freakish red welt running the length of your body, you seem unharmed. Your **hat**, if you possessed one, has been ruined, and if you were carrying anything electrical or magnetic, it too should be removed from your possessions. However, you can add **struck by lightning** to your **Other Notes** section of your **Adventure Sheet**.

Your velosteam has not fared so well. The gutta-percha handles and the heavy rubber tyres are steaming: some of the bodywork is hissing. It is now **critically damaged** and you only just manage to get it moving again. You had better make your way out of the storm and towards a repair shop as swiftly as possible.

Ride towards Hampstead...	**2**
Ride towards Highgate...	**28**

❧ 7 ❧

☐ ☐ ☐ ☐ ☐

If any of the boxes above are empty, tick one and read on. If they are all already ticked, erase the ticks and turn to **33** immediately.

You should put some distance between yourself and your victim. Which direction will you ride?

South...	**741**
East...	**151**
South-east to the Strand...	**139**

❧ 8 ❧

A man's body lies in the gutter. He is dead and cold and his mouth full of vomit. Something about him seems familiar: have you seen him before, somewhere else in the reeking metropolis of London?

If you are entirely without shame, you can take **2s** and a **deck of marked cards** from his pockets. His body is too heavy and soiled to carry - even if you had somewhere decent to take it. The Constables will be along eventually, and they are unlikely to be pleased to find you nearby. Remove the codeword *Critical*.

Ride away...	**noted passage**

❧ 9 ❧

Around the brazier, figures warm themselves, chatting about the mud on the Great North Road, the tolls and the Guild's water prices. Note passage number **61** and roll a dice to see whom you meet among the travellers in the Holly Bush Inn yard:

Score 1-2	Actors...	**1318**
Score 3-4	Guildsmen...	**1338**
Score 5-6	Long distance travellers...	**1360**

❧ 10 ❧

"Oho! These, my friend, are the Highgate horns! Take the Oath, kiss the horns, and you'll be a Freeman of Highgate, with all the privileges that entails."

"What privileges?"

"Oh, plenty, plenty of privileges. You will never want for a place to sleep in Highgate, nor a drink to wet your gorge. There is a fee - a nominal, a nominal fee."

If you wish to take the oath, cross out the option and turn to the passage indicated. If it is already crossed out, you must simply return to the parlour.

⊕ Take the oath...	(**£1 1s**)	**32**
Return to the parlour...		**12**

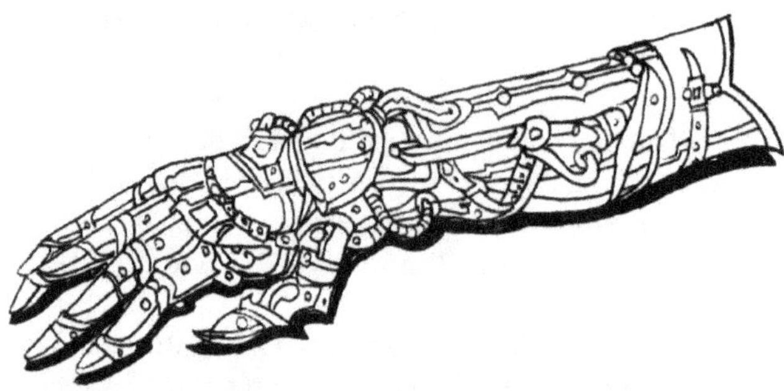

❧ 11 ❧

"I don't think I'm worth the waste of your time," you tell the railwayman, who is now blocking your exit. "I'm just a despatch rider. Perhaps I resemble someone you know."

Make an INGENUITY roll of difficulty 10, adding 1 if you possess a **top hat**.

Successful INGENUITY roll!	**64**
Failed INGENUITY roll!	**13**

❧ 12 ❧

The Flask stands behind a yard full with road engines. Steamsmen shout as they manoeuvre wagons, bow to lift ladies into passenger compartments, jostle for tips and argue over parking and watering rights. Inside, the parlour roils with people. Haulage Guild medallions are worn proudly here by prosperous hauliers and a row of smoke-blackened coats hang at the door. A particularly fine set of deer horns hang down over the bar.

In one side-room, hauliers strike deals to carry this or that cargo to Bedford, to Birmingham or to Sheffield. In another, a trader buys odds and ends and puts ready cash in these men and women's hands. You too can buy or sell here - but the walls themselves have ears, so take care. Near the bar, a knot of dangerous-looking rogues offer their protection services for travellers on the Great North Road - perhaps something you could also offer.

Jewellery	To buy	To sell
gold necklace	-	£3 4s
gold ring	£3	£1 18s
silver necklace	£2 5s	£1
silver ring	-	8s
pocket watch	£3	£2 4s
ten guineas in banknotes	-	£5 5s

Buy a drink at the bar...	(**2s**)	25
Drink with the men-for-hire...	(**2s**)	70
Ask about the horns...		10
Talk to the landlord... (**publican's contract**)		3
Consider the rumour you heard... (*Chatty*)		96
Leave the Flask...		60

ᕲ 13 ᕲ

Securely bound and heavily manhandled by several Constables, you are brought before an officer who cranks his portable telegraph into life and scans the most-recent bulletins for your description. What happens next will depend on your record: after all, the punishment must fit the crime. If you have the codeword *Crisp*, turn to **1065** immediately. Otherwise, check the options below and total the number of points indicated by relevant conditions.

If you are **Wanted by**...	Points
the Constables...	5
the Haulage Guild...	4
the Atmospheric Union...	4
the Telegraph Guild...	4
the Coal Board...	4
the River Guild...	2
the Wallingford Town Guard...	1
the Locobus Co-operative...	1

If you are...	
the **People's Champion** or a **Famed Lawbreaker**...	4
a **Member of the Compact for Workers' Equality**...	3

If you possess...	
a **convict's ticket**...	2
a copy of **Jensen's statement**...	3
any **explosives**...	2

Any **weapons**, **explosives** or paper money (**guineas in banknotes**) will now be taken from you - remove them from your **Adventure Sheet** - but you can hold onto other **possessions** and up to £10 of your **money**. Any more you possess is confiscated.

If your charges total **20 or more points**...	504
If your charges total **15-19 points**...	407
If your charges total **5-14 points**...	312
If your charges total **0-4 points**...	153

ᕲ 14 ᕲ

If you have the codeword *Chaff*, turn to **566** immediately. Otherwise, read on.

A train of Haulage Guild wagons painted in red and gold are leaving the freight yard as you weave through the gates. Here you may deal for tools and repairs for your velosteam, as well as listening to the gossip of the people of the road. A smith can even melt and cast metal for you. Note passage **64**.

Clothing	To buy	To sell
mask	4s	-
cloak	£1	10s
dungarees (GAL-2)	£2	£1
Tools	To buy	To sell
shovel	8s	4s
heavy wrench (ENG+1)	£1 15s	13s

Repairs	To buy
Per **damage point**	£2 12s

Deliver a package... (**rattling package**)	800
Talk to the smith...	105
Listen for rumours...	116
Leave the freight yard...	64

ᕲ 15 ᕲ

If you have the codeword *Conglomerate*, turn to **94** immediately. If not, but you have the codeword *Credit*, turn to **66**. Otherwise, read on.

The Camden Brewery is a massive complex of oasthouses, tall iron silos, sheds and cellars. Its own cable-powered railway trucks trundles backwards and forwards, down to the canal and over to the Freight Yard. Hundreds of people work here.

The Director is keen to meet ruthless and efficient individuals like yourself. He explains that the brewery is trying to expand its reach into the pubs of London, not just supplying their beer, but owning them outright. If you can convince the various publicans to sign a contract with the Camden Brewery, he will pay you ten guineas a time.

"Which pubs do you mean?" you ask.

"Well, any of them who will consider it," says the Director. "Chiefly those in the west and north. If I could get my hands on any of them, the Ship in Chelsea and the Compton Arms in Islington would probably be the most profitable." If you decide to help with the expansion of his empire, take a copy of his **publican's contract** in your satchel. You will need to note which innkeepers sign it as you read.

Leave the brewery... **84**

❧ 16 ❧

The rentman is used to rough language and threats. How will you ensure he gives you the information you are looking for? Make a RUTHLESSNESS roll of difficulty 12.

Successful RUTHLESSNESS roll... **69**
Failed RUTHLESSNESS roll... **85**

❧ 17 ❧

"Oh, there's always work. You should try the Freight Yard at Paddington, or Blackwall."

Another haulier interrupts. "But if you want to join the Guild, you'd best go see Director Short just east of Maidenhead."

Leave the guildsmen... **noted passage**

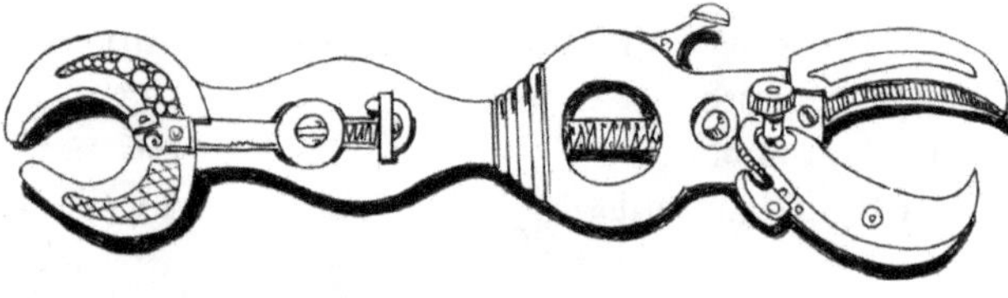

❧ 18 ❧

You steam on down the old river, eventually reaching Teddington Lock just as the water begins to shine under the rising moon dusk. "Best tie up," advises your mate, who proceeds to check the boiler and slowly release the pressure.

Morning comes with the croak of a nearby heron and the echo of men's voices at the quay. A mist has risen from the river and you will have to stamp the cold out of your bones. You certainly never felt so chilled astride the Ferguson.

Turn to... **364**

❧ 19 ❧

You climb away from the city and past a row of half-built villas. If you have the codeword *Anhedonic*, turn to **279** immediately. Otherwise, note passage **2** and roll a dice to see what you encounter as you ride up the hill towards Hampstead.

Score 1-2   A drunk...   **481**
Score 3-4   Nothing of interest...   **2**
Score 5-6   Chimney sweeps...   **1458**

❧ 20 ❧

You get a reaction from the landlord, but not one of fear. He takes down a heavy blunderbuss from behind the bar. "I've had enough of you and of these threats," he says. "I can look after myself here. Be off with you - or you'll be picking buckshot out of your teeth for the next fortnight."

Leave the Flask for now... **60**

❧ 21 ❧

Note passage **71**. A crow croaks and flaps down to land on a bundle of rubbish in the gutter; a desperate-looking girl tries to net it as you speed past. If you have a **black eye**, turn to **122** immediately. Otherwise, roll a dice to see if you encounter anything:

Score 1-2   Beggars...   **217**
Score 3-4   Nothing of note...   **71**
Score 5   A bent Constable...   **254**
Score 6   The Waterside Boys...   **143**

❧ 22 ❧

The Heath is a confused place, pocked with unregulated sand-digging pits, dotted with variable springs and ponds claimed by various corporations and guilds. The height of the heath has long been coveted by the Telegraph Guild, for a new Telegraph tower that would flash their messages north, and the Atmospheric Union, who currently make do with a cramped landing field at Parliament Hill to the south. Squatters live by the glassworks in Hatch's bottom and the poorest inhabitants of the nearby villages find firewood here.

Yet on a sunny day, riding across the open hillside or beneath the beeches, you can forget for a moment that you are within the bounds of London.

Prepare an ambush here... **72**
Steam to Hampstead village... **2**
Cross the heath to Highgate... **36**

❧ 23 ❧

There are several clothing shops here in Marylebone, all catering to high society and offering expensive tailoring.

Clothing	To buy	To sell
cloak	**£1 10s**	**15s**
dark cloak (RUTH+1)	**£5**	**£3 5s**
jewelled eyepatch (RUTH+1 GAL+1)	**£5 2s**	**£4**
golden monocle (GAL+2)	**£10**	**£6**
wide-brimmed hat	**£1 10s**	**£1**
silk scarf	**£3**	**£1 10s**
bow tie (GAL+1)	**£1 10s**	**£1**
top hat	**£2**	**£1**
lady's wig	**£1 5s**	**8s**
fur coat	**£4**	**£3 5s**
silk waistcoat (GAL+1)	**£4**	**£3**
lace shawl	**18s**	**12s**
fencing gloves (NIM+1)	**£8 15s**	**£6 10s**
dancing shoes (GAL+3)	**£24**	**£12**
dinner jacket	**£5**	**£2**

Ask about the pearls... (*Charred*)	**1248**
Return to Marylebone...	**47**

❧ 24 ❧

If you have **tally stick 391**, turn to **39** immediately.

When you show the publican the contract, he whistles. "I'd be more than happy to put my name to this," he replies, "But I've just done a deal for my next year's beer with Perkins at the station."

"You could tear up the contract," you suggest.

"Ain't no contract," he says. "Just account on tally. But say you got that tally back off him... Why, then I'd be free to sign this here doccyment." Gain the codeword *Contradict*.

Return to the parlour...	**86**
Leave the Brunel Arms...	**64**

❧ 25 ❧

The beer at the Flask is brewed down in the city. You are poured a pot of strong, murky beer, sweet with unfermented sugars and laced with a sandy-coloured head. It seems popular here: they call it the Dark Haulier's Draught. Note passage number **12** and roll a dice to see what you hear:

Score 1	News from the North...	**559**
Score 2	Crafton's cookshop...	**1067**
Score 3	Prize fighting...	**883**
Score 4	A guild rivalry...	**1013**
Score 5	A gang of young ruffians...	**958**
Score 6	Bright stones...	**1099**

❧ 26 ❧

Note passage **47**. The villas of Crawford Street peer down as you weave between a delivery van and a hay cart: then, suddenly, you are forced to brake to a stop. What has blocked the road in front of you? Roll a dice:

Score 1-2	A robber dashing away...	**644**
Score 3-4	Actors on their wagon...	**1434**
Score 5-6	Just a cat...	**47**

❧ 27 ❧

Camden Wharf is a busy place. Steam hammers smash down on plate iron, thinning it out into patches for the hulls of hard-working barges. If you have a water craft, you can fit it out with several customisations here. Note that you can only have one boat at a time.

Customisation	To buy
cargo crane	**£18 5s**
Perkins Machine	**£25**
(allows you to carry refrigerated cargoes like Ice and Frozen Meat)	
strengthened screw	**£12**
butty boat	**£32**
(allows you to carry three more units of cargo)	

Type of boat	Cargo	To buy	To sell
Small skiff	1 unit	**£20**	**£10**
Medium launch	2 units	**£28**	**£17**
Large barge	3 units	**£40**	**£32**
Tug	-	**£45**	**£30**

If you buy a boat, give it a name and note that it is **moored at Camden**. If you sell your boat, don't forget to remove it (and any remaining cargo) from your **Adventure Sheet**. Customisations cannot be removed or sold here - you would simply have to pay to have them removed.

Board your boat... (**moored at Camden**)   1033
Return to Camden...   **84**

❧ 28 ❧

The village of Highgate straddles the high road running north out of London, providing a place for thirsty hauliers and travellers to refresh themselves. A Haulage Guild Tollhouse controls the highway and the innkeepers charge tolls of their own. Many travellers stop at the Flask to hire protection from the dangers of highwaymen before continuing their journeys north. Bishop's Wood is known to be haunted by robbers...

Visit the Flask Inn...   **12**
Ride towards Bishop's Wood...   **49**
Ride to Parliament Hill...   **58**
Cross the Heath to Hampstead...   **22**
Ride down towards Camden Town...   **34**
Strike out for the North... *The Great North Road 8*
Take the road to Islington...   **151**
Leave this region...   **50**

❧ 29 ❧

"Oh, right, then. You must be one of them despatch riders, right? After all, the Guild can't be sending everything by Telegraph. There's information those green beggars can't be allowed to read."

"Like what?" asks a younger haulier.

"Well, like the opening of the new Chesterfield tunnel. If the Telegraphers knew that it was almost finished, they'd be claiming rights to run their own engines through it. But what they don't know, they can't do, can they?"

Information like this could be valuable to someone in the Telegraph Guild. Perhaps they would even pay for it. Gain the codeword *Chesterfield*.

Before you leave, the hauliers are happy to offer a fellow guildsman what help they can. Replace any single **wound** with a **scar**, and remove a **cold, fever** or **stiff back** if you have them.

Leave the guildsmen...   **noted passage**

❧ 30 ❧

If you are **Wanted by the Telegraph Guild**, turn to **76** immediately. Otherwise, read on.

You are poured a pint of Imperial Champion Ale in a stoneware pot. Whatever your feeling about the company here, the beer is brewed to keep everyone drinking happily. It is a strong, dark, sweet brew, starting nuttily and moving through a toffeeish flavour to finish with a strong boozy roar. Note passage **53** and roll a dice to see what you overhear in the bar.

Score 1   The King's Woman...   **984**
Score 2   Parliamentary blades...   **1075**
Score 3-4   A gang of young ruffians...   **958**
Score 5-6   A guild rivalry...   **1013**

❧ 31 ❧

You show the contract and explain the Director's offer. The landlord scratches his chin. "Maybe it will be worth it all," he says, "And maybe not. I might need some thinking time."

If you want to push him, make an INGENUITY roll of difficulty 12, adding 3 if you are the **Brewer's Friend** or the **Friend of Louise Standler**.

Successful INGENUITY roll!   77
Failed INGENUITY roll
    or did not attempt...   **90**

❧ 32 ❧

A crowd gathers for the ceremony of the horns. You are bedecked with a wreath of prickly holly hung around your shoulders ("'Tis our Highgate bush," explains a tipsy 'official') and the horns themselves are brought down from behind the bar.

"Now," instructs the Master, "Speak after me. I swear never to eat upon brown bread while I can get white, except that I like brown better. I swear never to drink the small beer while I can get the strong, except that I like the small better. I will not kiss the maid while I can kiss the mistress, except the maid be prettier, but sooner than lose a good chance I will kiss 'em both."

He leads you through some 'symbolic' actions, concluding with the kissing of the horns, and a great cheer goes up. You are now a **Freeman of Highgate**.

The exact details of the privileges and rights of this ancient rank are these: while in Highgate, should you ever be in want of shelter, you are entitled to kick a pig out of a ditch and take its place, although should you find three pigs in the ditch, you may only kick out the middle one and take its place. Should you ever be thirsty here in Highgate, and penniless, you can take free drinks for yourself and your friends, but should anyone confess their thirst to you, then you are bound to buy a round of drinks for them and their friends.

Gain a GALLANTRY point.

Return to the parlour...	**12**
Leave the pub...	**28**

ᤌ 33 ᤚ
Too many times have you struck at the populace here! The Constables are beginning to look inefficient - and that, they cannot abide. They have prepared a squadron of velosteam riders to catch you and bring you to justice. Which way will you turn?

Ride east...	**410**
Head west...	**421**
Steam south...	**445**

ᤌ 34 ᤚ
About halfway down Highgate hill, just past a newly-built brick church, you pass the buffers and switching lane of the cable tram, which runs all the way down to Camden Town. Note passage **84** and roll a dice:

Score 1	A broken cable!	**274**
Score 2-4	A quiet road...	**84**
Score 5-6	A fortune teller's booth...	**282**

ᤌ 35 ᤚ
The evening is breezy and strangely clear. It looks set to be one of those rarest things in the capital, a moonlit night. If you are **Wanted by the Atmospheric Union**, turn to **137** immediately. Otherwise, note passage **47** and roll a dice to see what you encounter as you ride south towards Marylebone.

Score 1-2	A gang of decorators...	**1488**
Score 3-4	Nothing of interest...	**47**
Score 5-6	Moonlight wanderers...	**1511**

ᤌ 36 ᤚ
The weather worsens as you ride out across the heath. Dark clouds approach from the west. You feel the first few drops of what will surely be a downpour.

Shelter in Ken Wood...	**57**
Continue across the heath...	**75**

ᤌ 37 ᤚ
The Freight Yard is the strict preserve of the Haulage Guild. If you are **Wanted by the Haulage Guild**, note passage **84** and turn to **507** immediately. Otherwise, you steam cautiously in, between a red and gold Carocall engine with its articulated trailer and a small yard shunting engine.

Inside you can arrange repairs and customisations for your velosteam, as well as trading in certain tools and possessions. You might even hear a rumour or two among the drivers and engineers. Note this passage (**37**) before making a decision.

Clothing	To buy	To sell
top hat	-	**£1 10s**
fur coat	-	**£3**
hair matches (RUTH+2) ☐ ☐ ☐	**£2**	-
Tools	To buy	To sell
rope ladder	**15s**	**7s**
axe	**10s**	**8s**
brass flange joint	**8s**	**6s**
copper pipe	**6s**	**2s**
high pressure valve	**18s**	**15s**
measuring line	**10s**	**4s**
plaster of paris	**5s**	**1s**
chimney brushes	**£3**	**£1 8s**
Other Items	To buy	To sell
pair of golden candlesticks	**£8**	**£5 4s**
miniature Bible	**£2**	**18s**
Coal Board Accounts book	-	**£4**
box of cigars	**£2 2s**	**£1 1s**
Velosteam Customisations	To buy	
muffled exhaust	**£5 10s**	
double headlamp	**£10 10s**	
gas pressuriser	**£15 15s**	
Repairs	To buy	
Per damage point	**£4**	

Listen for rumours...	**116**
Return to Camden...	**84**

ᤌ 38 ᤚ
Three strangely dressed women are huddled around a cooking pot, obviously trying to prepare something to eat despite the rain. They call to you as ride by.

"All hail, Steam Highwayman! All hail, Steam Highwayman, that shall be a Member of Parliament hereafter!"

How very odd.

Continue on to Highgate...	**28**

ᔥ 39 ᔥ

You give the landlord **tally stick 391**, which he immediately snaps across his knee. "There we go. Out with the old, in with the new. Pass me that there contrack!"

Gain the codeword *Conglomerate*.

Leave the pub...   **64**

ᔥ 40 ᔥ

An old-timer at the bar hears your order and over-rides it. "What you want, youngster, is a cup of this. Come on, woman, look lively!" He insists she draw you a glass of Griffin Pale - a treacly, golden pale ale with a smooth and balanced flavour, building steadily from the first fragrance of its pouring to the final lingering bitterness of Goldings hops. "That went down quickly," says the elderly drinker. "You'll probably need another."

If you have a **publican's contract**, turn to **31** immediately. Otherwise, note passage number **90** and roll a dice to see what rumours you overhear in the low, smoky parlour.

Score 1	A fence...	**175**
Score 2	Crafton's cookshop...	**1067**
Score 3	An untrustworthy landlord...	**1135**
Score 4	The King's Woman...	**984**
Score 5	Prize fighting...	**883**
Score 6	The price of oysters...	**396**

ᔥ 41 ᔥ

They say that lightning never strikes the same place twice. But with a massive crack, a bolt tears down from the cumulus above and shoots through you. Gain **three wounds** and add **two damage points** to your velosteam. If your velosteam is now **beyond repair**, turn to **1111**. If not, but you now have **five wounds**, turn to **999**. If you have somehow survived, you had better leave this dangerous, storm-wracked place as swiftly as possible.

Ride towards Hampstead...   **2**
Ride towards Highgate...   **28**

✥ 42 ✥

Your journey from Cutthroat Wood takes you largely along broad, well-maintained Guild roads - except where you take detours to avoid tolls or trouble. The closer you get to the city, the noticeably dirtier the air becomes,. It has been a long journey

Ride to the Imperial at Marylebone...	**53**
Head for the Brunel Arms at Paddington...	**86**

✥ 43 ✥

Shouts, cries and the uneven throb of propellers warn you of an airship struggling to stay aloft. While you watch, its gondola appears through the cloud, and then the long bulk of its gasbag and wide stabilising fins. With a thump softened by distance, it crashes heavily into the Heath. The crew seem torn between throwing cargo overboard to keep it aloft and grappling for anchorholds.

See if you can collect some cargo...	**101**
Help with the skyanchors...	**115**
Continue on your way...	**28**

✥ 44 ✥

You wait for a steam vehicle to approach, readying your Ferguson and your weapons. Roll a dice to see what comes your way, adding 2 if you possess a **telescope** or **binoculars**.

Score 1-3	Nothing approaches...	**22**
Score 4	A local businessman...	**1448**
Score 5	The Hampstead Locobus...	**1414**
Score 6+	A private steam carriage...	**1349**

✥ 45 ✥

You steam past the old church of St Pancras beneath its ungainly planes trees. They lean over the street like so many mournful grey elephants. If you have one or more **wounds**, turn to **243** immediately. Otherwise, note passage **107** and roll a dice:

Score 1-2	Chimney sweeps...	**1458**
Score 3	An accident...	**626**
Score 4-6	Nothing extraordinary...	**107**

✥ 46 ✥

As you head over to the exit and your parked velosteam, a couple of burly railwaymen in bowlers look you over. If you are **Wanted by the Railway Guards**, read on. Otherwise, turn to **64** immediately.

"'Aven't I seen you somewhere," begins one of the railwaymen, reaching for your shoulder.

Make a dash for it...	**33**
Talk your way out of the situation...	**11**

✥ 47 ✥

Marylebone is a district of tall red brick, considering itself somewhat more refined than the nearby industrial streets. There are fine houses here, cake shops and women's outfitters. A pub bedecked with flowers stands on one corner: the Imperial.

Visit the Imperial...	**53**
Enter a bakery...	**76**
Look at the clothing shops...	**23**
Steam west to Paddington down	
Crawford Street...	**64**
Take Euston Road to St Pancras...	**71**
Ride towards Camden Town...	**65**
Cross Oxford Street into Mayfair...	**750**
Steam towards Hyde Park...	**741**
Ride north into Queen Maria Park...	**83**
Leave the north-west region...	**50**

✥ 48 ✥

The landlady gets her daughter down to read the contract aloud for her. She opens a bottle of her special damson wine to share with you while you wait for her answer. It is very sweet, tart and slightly smoky, with distinct almond notes.

"It all sounds above board," she says. "I could do with a fixed price for beer. I've been cut up many a time down at the Freight yard. I'll sign."

She makes her mark on and her daughter witnesses it. Gain the codeword *Conglomerate*.

Leave the Imperial...	**47**

✥ 49 ✥

The road through Bishop's Wood is long overdue a modernisation. Despite its proximity to the city and its importance to long-distance hauliers, the Haulage Guild have not yet graded or surfaced it. Consequently it is a rutted, steep-sided holloway, often flooded and perfect for an ambush.

Plan an ambush here...	**68**
Head south-west to Hampstead...	**2**
Steam east to Highgate...	**28**

❧ 50 ☙

The roads from north-west London can take you anywhere you choose to go: it is simply a matter of the way you turn your machine.

Head south towards Hyde Park...	**741**
Steam south-east into the City...	**544**
Ride through town to Whitechapel...	**555**
Cross the city to Bow...	**570**
Strike out west for Wycombe, Marlow and Reading... **(10s)**	**1091**

❧ 51 ☙

The rain comes pouring down in steady sheets. Roll a dice, adding 2 if you have a **cloak** of any kind, to see whether you suffer any result of the exposure.

Score 1-4	Catch a bad **cold (RUTH-1 ING-1)**...
Score 5+	Just a sniffle...

The rain shows no signs of stopping, so you had better find somewhere warm and dry to shelter.

Ride over the Heath to Hampstead...	**2**
Ride over the Heath to Highgate...	**28**

❧ 52 ☙

If you are **Wanted by the Haulage Guild**, turn to **507** immediately. Otherwise, read on.

The Freight Yard at St Pancras is not a natural place for an avowed road-pirate to be found. Who knows, but one of your many victims may recognise you here, remembering some robbery in a dark wood, far away down a long road. Nonetheless, if you are discreet, you may find a paying job, or perhaps do a little trading.

Clothing	To buy	To sell
goggles (MOT+1)	£3	£1 18s
engineer's gloves (ENG+1)	£4	£2 10s
engineer's gauntlets (ENG+2)	-	£5 5s
wide-brimmed hat	£1 5s	15s
Tools	To buy	To sell
rope	4s	2s
lantern	8s	3s
axe	10s	8s
copper pipe	6s	2s
grappling iron	-	12s
net	5s	2s
tarpaulin	5s	2s
telescope	-	£4
Weapons	To buy	To sell
club (PAR 2)	6s	2s
sabre (PAR 3)	£2 15s	£1 10s
rapier (PAR 4)	-	£3
gamekeeper's shotgun (ACC 10)	-	£8
Other Items		
ten guineas in banknotes	-	£9
twenty guineas in banknotes	-	£20
thirty guineas in banknotes	-	£31
pair of ferrets	£1 1s	-
Velosteam Customisations	To buy	
off-road tyres	£6	
enlarged tank	£6 10s	
pump and filter	£7 5s	
Repairs	To buy	
Per **damage point**	£3 10s	

Speak to the local Guild Chairman...	**74**
Leave the yard...	**71**

❧ 53 ☙

There is a distinct separation inside the Imperial. Telegraph Guild officers in their green tunics sit in the saloon drinking imported wines. Their men drink beer raucously in the parlour behind a glazed partition over in the public bar. This seems to be their pub of choice, locally, so you had better tread carefully if you have any history with the Telegraphers.

Buy a drink... **(2s)**	**30**
Speak to the landlady... **(publican's contract)**	**48**
Leave the pub...	**47**

❧ 54 ☙

Spotting walkers approaching a thicket, you raise pressure and accelerate towards them on your velosteam. It is the perfect chance to snatch something as you pass: make a MOTORING roll of difficulty 11, adding 1 if you possess **improved brakes**.

Successful MOTORING roll!	**1507**
Failed MOTORING roll!	**1437**

❧ 55 ☙

The house's most popular drink is the locally brewed Westburn, which, the landlord is pleased to tell you, takes its water from that nearby river. It is a nosy bitter, its fragrant nose betraying a blend of English hops in the early and mid brew. Drinkable and fairly light-bodied, it finishes with a spicy bitterness. Note passage **86** and roll a dice to see what you overhear.

Score 1	Barricades and blunderbusses...	**1150**
Score 2	Forging documents...	**1181**
Score 3	An ambitious brewery...	**1196**
Score 4	For the tourists...	**1206**
Score 5-6	An investment opportunity...	**556**

✤ 56 ✤

The roads out of Camden are narrow and clogged with traffic. It takes some weaving and risky steering to get out of the jam and on your way. What is your destination?

Islington...	**62**
Highgate...	**28**
Marylebone...	**47**
St Pancras...	**21**
Pentonville...	**45**
Travel further afield...	**50**

✤ 57 ✤
☐

If the box above is empty, tick it and turn to **79** immediately. If it is already ticked, read on.

As you bump into the shadow of the beeches of Ken Wood, the heavens open and the rain begins to pour down. If you have a **cloak** of any kind, it will prevent you from getting a chill. Otherwise, you should roll a dice as below.

Score 1-2   Catch a bad **cold (RUTH-1 ING-1)**
Score 3+   Just a sniffle

Eventually the rain eases off.

Ride on to Highgate...   **28**

✤ 58 ✤

If you are **Wanted by the Atmospheric Union**, turn to **5** immediately. Otherwise, read on.

The Atmospheric Union's airfield here is their major depot serving the capital. Long iron-framed sheds hold their ships, ready or under construction. There is a slender launching ramp running obliquely across the grassy slope and five tall mooring posts, each clustered with airships like strange bulbous branches on alien trees, stand in a ring around the field. In the centre is a terminal building where passengers wait, freights are stored and loaded and Union passenger vehicles are parked. Everywhere men and women in grey and blue uniforms scurry about. Here and there stalks the occasional haughty airship captain, attended by a gaggle of staff.

| Look for work... | **97** |
| Leave the station... | **83** |

✤ 59 ✤

"Tower? Lessee now. Well, there's a Warden of the Tower goes about riding in his carriage - you'll recognise it by a big crest - and he's in charge of the place. Oh and lions. Lions in the moat, there is, so take care around feeding time. The crown jewels is up in a tower on the north side, so I hear, and guarded pretty well, but the King gets in without a bother, of course. And then there's the prisoners inside. Like Marshal."

"Who's Marshal?"

"Oh, that chap what tried to set up his own country on some sea-fort somewhere. Fabulous rich. All the ideas in the world. Dreamer type. But they banged him up on account of trying to claim Imperial territory. Yes, that's about all's I can remember for a shilling."

"What about getting in and out?"

"I imagine folks use the door. Hur hur hur."

Leave the street-sweepers...   **139**

✤ 60 ✤

If you have the codeword *Chirrup*, turn to **81** immediately. The busy yard of the Flask contains many sharp-eyed roadsters. Someone here is in the pay of the Constables, and many are members of the Haulage Guild. If you are not hunted by either of these two factions, you can leave unmolested and untroubled by the attention of the Flask's customers, and should turn to **28** immediately. However, if you are **Wanted by the Constables**, turn to **33** immediately. If not, but you are **Wanted by the Haulage Guild**, read on.

Some of the drivers and engineers peer at you closely. Have you been recognised from one of your previous exploits? As you are returning to your Ferguson, you become aware of a burly Haulage Guild thief-taker approaching with his club. You must fight him to get away!

Attacker	Weapon: **club (PAR 2)**
Parry:	9
Nimbleness:	7
Toughness:	4

Victory!	7
Defeated!	**113**

✎ 61 ✐

Several engines stand in the narrow street, their crews warming their hands at an open firebox and preparing for long journeys. Wagons are piled high, covered over with canvas and tarpaulin and lashed down tight against the fingers of the wind and the thief. Engineers work on the couplings and linkages, tightening massive nuts and repairing roadside damage. They are more than happy to share their tools and their expertise, so if you wish to repair your velosteam, note this passage **61** before making your decision.

Enter the parlour...	90
Repair your velosteam...	1300
Stay in the yard and talk with the crews...	9
Leave the inn...	2

✎ 62 ✐

The streets between Camden and Islington are home to a thousand tiny businesses; craftsmen and pieceworkers labouring away in workshops open onto the roadway. Note passage **151** and roll a dice:

Score 1-2	Fruit sellers...	**859**
Score 3-4	Little to interest you...	**151**
Score 5-6	A desperate boy...	**1374**

✎ 63 ✐

If you have a **Telegraph Guild Codebook**, turn to **975** immediately. Otherwise, read on.

As you enter, the hall is in revolutionary fervour, crammed with men and women enthralled by the speaker's voice. "Would you work your life long, only to have your children enslaved as you are?"

"No!" comes the roaring reply.

"Would you see your sweat gilded on the coaches of your employers?"

"No!"

"Will you take your part in a new order - a new society - in which all who labour are given a fair share of possession - a fair share of wealth - a fair share of life?"

The room erupts in a roar. It seems that the Compact will enlist many more members this evening.

"Every honest son and daughter of the land is welcome to participate - to take their share," continues the speaker. "But the parasite, the usurer, the tax-collector, they will be cast out into the street! Come forward and make your pledge - a pledge to one another, and to our agreement, that we shall not rest, no, not until we have torn down the old order and built this land anew!"

Join the Compact...	**964**
Leave the hall...	**71**

✎ 64 ✐

Paddington is a centre for transport here in the west of the city, where the mighty arches of the Imperial Western Railway Terminus cover a full eight platforms, and the King's Canal broadens into the Basin managed by the River Guild. The pubs hereabouts are full of navvies, engineers, porters and enginemen. The air is filled with coal smoke from a thousand sooty boilers.

Board your barge...	
(moored at Paddington Basin)	**99**
Step inside the Brunel Arms...	**86**
Investigate the Terminus...	**73**
Investigate the Freight Yard...	**14**
Take Crawford Street towards Marylebone...	**26**
Steam south towards Hyde Park...	**741**
Leave this region...	**50**

✎ 65 ✐

You cut through the gates of Queen Maria Park just as a warden is rolling them closed, and steam up the long avenue of horse-chestnuts. Note passage **85** and roll a dice:

Score 1-2	Constables...	**1427**
Score 3-4	Beggars...	**1496**
Score 5	Travellers...	**1379**
Score 6	A fortune teller's booth...	**282**

❧ 66 ❧

After all your efforts to expand the Camden Brewery's empire, business is flourishing. Drays of machine-made beer trundle out of the East and West Yards constantly, off to the Compton Arms, HMS Spartan and all the others. Perhaps you have helped a business grow more profitable, making the jobs of its employees more stable, and improved the reliability and cleanliness of the beer drunk across the capital as well. Or maybe you have become part of the process of mechanisation, squeezing the independent businessperson and ironing away the diversity of product - of beer. It's all a matter of perspective. But one thing is sure - there are no more rewards or work for you here. Everyone is too busy.

Leave the brewery...   **84**

❧ 67 ❧

A sleek Union airship is flying low over Park Crescent. You speed on beneath, heading west. Note passage **47** and if you are the **Friend of Lord Dashwood**, turn to **261** immediately. Otherwise, roll a dice:

Score 1	An accident...	**626**
Score 2	A light-fingered lady...	**1466**
Score 3	A gang of decorators...	**1488**
Score 4-6	Nothing in particular...	**47**

❧ 68 ❧

Note passage **7** and if you have the codeword *Clarify*, turn to **93** immediately. If not, but you have the codeword *Chuffing*, turn to **1396**. Otherwise read on.

Fallen leaves swathe the road here in amber and yellow, but the dense branches that hide you also give you little chance of spotting what is coming. A **telescope** or **binoculars** will not help: luck decides your encounter! Roll a dice to see what approaches:

Score 1-2	A private steam carriage...	**1373**
Score 3	The Coal Board...	**1301**
Score 4	The Telegraph Guild...	**1400**
Score 5	The Atmospheric Union...	**1421**
Score 6	The Haulage Guild...	**1444**

❧ 69 ❧

You learn from the rent collector that he has no idea who he collects rent for: he simply gathers the money, shilling by clipped shilling, and deposits it, less his commission, at Coulter's bank on the Strand. Gain the codeword *Commission*.

Leave the pub...   **308**

❧ 70 ❧

The men standing at the bar may claim to offer protection for travellers, but they seem just as likely to rob their employers. They stop their laughter to look you over as you approach. If your RUTHLESSNESS score (including modifiers) is 5 or greater, read on. Otherwise, they will dismiss you and you should turn to **12** immediately.

The ruffians see that you are as rough and ready for trouble as they are, so they make space in their circle for you. It seems that they have several semi-regular customers who hire them one-by-one or as pairs to accompany dangerous journeys, and while they wait, they drink here in the Flask. They plainly supplement their earnings in other ways, such as thieving from the wagons they protect, as one proudly shows off some goods that 'fell off the wagon' he rode here.

A driver approaches, looking to hire a guard for a trip out of town. There is plainly a seniority amongst the ruffians, but if you want to challenge for the job, make a NIMBLENESS roll of difficulty 11 and arm-wrestle the leader of the gang.

Successful NIMBLENESS roll!	**1071**
Failed NIMBLENESS roll!	**1087**
Not interested in the job...	**12**

❧ 71 ❧

The area to the north of Euston Road is occupied by a massive Haulage Guild yard - one of the largest in the land. A local railway line also terminates here, but it is the road engines and their trains of road wagons that carry the vast majority of both cargo and passengers. Decades of Guild influence in Parliament have prevented the railwaymen from expanding, and the Hauliers have made good on their opportunity.

The nearby coalgas works and countless small factories mean that this is a working district, although there are also rows and rows of tenements and fine old houses rented room by room to house all the bodies that haul on the levers and shovel the coal. The

Burrage Assembly Hall stands behind a statue of that noble philanthropist, its stage taken hourly by speakers and committees.

Enter the Assembly Hall... (**passdisc 32**)	**63**
Steam into the Freight Yard...	**52**
Head for Camden Town...	**84**
Steam west down Euston Road...	**67**
South to Bloomsbury...	**114**
Ride into Pentonville...	**107**
Leave this region...	**50**

❧ 72 ❧

The Heath is crossed by a rough and bumpy track, with few steam vehicles coming this way. However, there are also several pedestrians whose pockets might be worth investigation. Note passage **7** before making your choice.

Wait for a carriage...	**44**
Rob someone on foot...	**54**

❧ 73 ❧

If you are **Wanted by the Railway Guards**, turn to **561** immediately. If not, but you have the codeword *Cricket*, turn to **426**. Otherwise, read on.

Paddington Station is the headquarters of the Imperial Western Railway. Although Parliament will not endorse the building of an entire network, the parts that have been built have proven to be very profitable indeed. Beneath a handsome set of steel arches, broad-gauge engines prepare to take their passengers out to the west - to Maidenhead, Bristol, and even as far as Okehampton, in Devon, and Barmouth, in Wales. No wonder the Haulage Guild hate the railways so much.

Buy a ticket to Maidenhead... (**£1 4s**)
Smog and Ambuscade 594
Buy a ticket to Reading... (**£2 10s**)
Highways and Holloways 297
Buy a ticket to Henley... (**£2 2s**)
Highways and Holloways 547
Buy a ticket to Okehampton... (**£3 10s**)
Princes of the West 454
Buy a ticket to Barmouth... (**£5 5s**)
Dark Vales and Dark Hearts 200

Plan a small conflagration...	**106**
Discuss beer prices... (*Contradict*)	**413**
Leave the station...	**64**

❧ 74 ❧

The local Guild Chairman - there is one for each region - is interested in your reputation. "I have heard you are the ruthless type," he says. "Act against our rivals and I will reward you."

"Whom do you mean?" you ask.

"The River Guild are trying to overtake us - fat chance - in freight tonnage. Their docks at St Katharine's are far too profitable. What if the gates failed and the tide flooded their warehouses? And the bleeding Imperial Western Railway have been licensed to carry cargo west from Paddington station. Anything you can do against them will please the honest Haulage Guild."

✇"The River Guild docks have been destroyed." (*Collapse*)	**89**
✇"Paddington station has mysteriously burnt down." (*Cricket*)	**104**
Leave the yard...	**71**

❧ 75 ❧

You ride over the crest of the heath just as the first brilliant lightning flash erupts above you. An immense peal of thunder splits the sky and torrents of water begin to fall. Roll a dice to see what you encounter:

Score 1	An airship in trouble...	**43**
Score 2-3	Strange figures on the heath...	**38**
Score 4-5	A soaking...	**51**
Score 6	Struck by lightning...	**6**

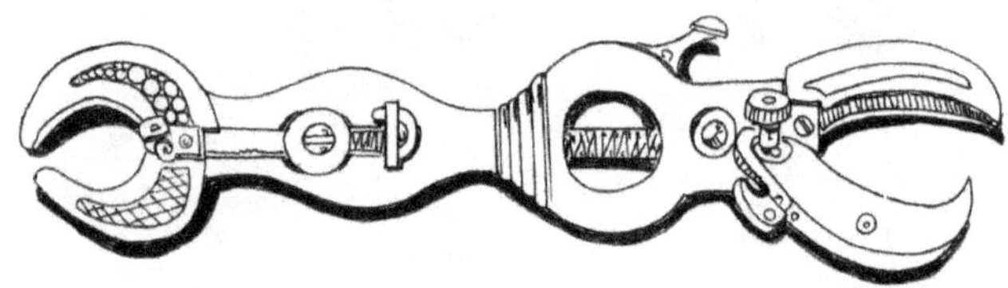

❧ 76 ❧

A posse of green-jacketed Telegraphers spot you at the bar. They have been briefed to look out for enemies of the guild - and you top the list. You must fight them to have any hope of getting away.

Guildsmen	Weapons: **sabres (PAR 3)**
Parry:	10
Nimbleness:	7
Toughness:	4

Victory!	**47**
Defeat!	**999**

✎ 77 ✎

You continue to outline the benefits of the contract and after a while, the landlord starts to nod his head. "I see your point," he says. "Perhaps it'll be worth my while. Show me where to sign."

Gain the codeword *Conglomerate*.

Leave the pub... **2**

✎ 78 ✎

"You are enjoying that drink," says the man with the pencil moustache. "I can see that."

Whether you admit the truth of his observation, he continues, chattering with the manner of a rabbit taking bites out of the air in front of him. "Stout goes better in a pewter pot anyway. China. Pink china is best for a bitter. But stout goes best in a pewter pot."

He begins scribbling in his notebook again. "You might consider me rude," he says. "Interrupting you about your refreshment. But I am drawn to characters such as yourself. Travellers. Ones unaccustomed to the conventions of the city. Of the time. You are almost a person out of time. As, I feel, I am." He stares at the wall for a moment.

"Do you ever feel that you are being watched? Not briefly, but constantly? By a big... brother of some kind. Staring at you from behind every hunting print on the wall... From every window?"

He is plainly somewhat paranoid. He takes your pause for frustration, swallows his own beer and walks out into the fog.

Drink up... **186**

✎ 79 ✎

You turn the Ferguson through the pelting rain and plough into the wood, seeking shelter from the storm. You bump over a ditch and fight to keep the heavy machine upright in the mud.

Suddenly, you come face to face with an armed man draped in a sack blocking the path. He raises his carbine. "Stop there, gorger," he says imperiously. "You're trespassing."

You have come across a gypsy camp here in the heart of Ken Wood. Behind the guard you can see a circle of steam caravans.

Another man appears, puffing on a long pipe despite the rain. "Ain't no musker," says the newcomer. "Cushty machine, stranger. Come on to the fire and dry yourself."

Within a few minutes you are sat drinking sweet tea in the headman's caravan. His family are cramped in around you, the children staring at the newcomer, his mother knitting in the chair and his wife handling hot griddle cakes on the stove. They are private people and have no need to know your business, but your host is clearly intrigued by your machine.

Offer to show him your Ferguson... **1146**
Discuss mutual friends... (**Friend of Barsali**)**1155**
Pay for the meal... (**2s**) **1162**

✎ 80 ✎

Your room at the Holly Bush is kept clean and ready for you: there is a small fire burning and the sheets exude a rare scent of clean linen. What a relief after your days and nights in the mud and murk of the road!

You can leave possessions here, writing them into the box below and erasing them from your **Adventure Sheet**, to collect them later.

One of the maids from the parlour knocks at the door with a jug and bowl for you to wash away the stains of your journey.

If you want to treat your **wounds** or open a **strongbox** (if you have one), note the current **passage** (**80**).

Open a **strongbox**... **331**
Treat your **wounds**... **500**
Leave your room... **98**

✎ 81 ✎

Since you dealt with the previous landlord of the Flask, no-one here dares to inform the Guilds or the Constables. You are free to come and go in peace.

Leave the Flask... **28**

❧ 82 ❧

You have been recognised by the Bank Guards, who quickly attempt to surround you. You must fight them to escape!

Bank Guards	Weapons: **sabres (PAR 3)**
Parry:	9
Nimbleness:	6
Toughness:	6

Victory!	**278**
Defeat!	**1500**

❧ 83 ❧

Queen Maria Park is named for George IV's wife, for whom he constructed the pleasure gardens and the zoo. Wardens at each entrance maintain the peace inside and a horde of gardeners keep the arboretum, lawns and collections of plants in trim. The common people of London come here to stroll and breathe clean air, if they can afford the time, but there is a charge to visit the animals.

Atop nearby Parliament Hill, airships swarm like elephantine bees. They discharge their passengers into fast steam cabs and locobuses, taking them to the city.

Head up to Parliament Hill...	**58**
Ride into the Park...	**95**
Head south towards Marylebone...	**35**
Ride north towards Hampstead...	**19**

❧ 84 ❧

Not long ago Camden was a village with green fields between it and the city. Then the steam revolution came, with the King's Canal, the freight yards, the workshops, the stables and the goods sheds. Now it is one of the most densely-built and hard-working districts, with every possible nook crammed with tenements and cottages rented by squeezed families. Above the buildings, a dense network of cableways carry messages and machinery, half-finished goods, parcels and pies. These busy streets are home to some of London's big industries, including the Camden Brewery and the North London Steam Omnibus Company.

Visit the Brewery...	**15**
Head to the wharf...	**27**
Ride to the Freight Yard...	**37**
Approach the Omnibus Depot...	**92**
Leave Camden...	**56**

❧ 85 ❧

The rent collector calls his mates in from the parlour. "This son of a gun thinks I'm for pushing around," he says. "Let's show him how things are handled round here." You will have to fight them to escape!

Thugs	Weapons: **knives (PAR 1)**
Parry:	7
Nimbleness:	6
Toughness:	6

Victory!	**308**
Defeat!	**999**

❧ 86 ❧

The Brunel Arms is a modern, steel-framed building with an impressive terrace cantilevered out over the street and a footbridge leading directly into Paddington Station. It is the haunt of railway clerks, porters and stationmen, as well as offering refreshment and business news to the Imperial traveller. A mechanical ticker mounted in the saloon relays share prices direct from the city, all handled automatically by the licensed telegraph mounted on the roof.

Talk to the landlord... **(publican's contract)**	24
Buy a drink...	**55**
Leave the pub...	**46**

❧ 87 ❧

You pause on your journey to the city in a little village, hoping to top up your water tank and splash some water on your own face. No-one comes out of their homes to speak to the traveller: they stay safely shuttered up inside. Soon you are on your way again, down the long road to Paddington.

Steam on to Paddington...	**64**

❧ 88 ❧

The rentman from the Old Nichol slum told you that he made his deposits here, but it will not be a simple matter to discover whose account they are paid into. If you are a punchcardsman and you have acccss to a computing engine somewhere in the city, you might be able to 'slice' out that information with the right set of punchcards. Otherwise, your best bet would be to try to bribe - or befriend - one of the bank tellers.

Choose a teller to approach...	**155**
Leave the bank for now...	**139**

✎ 89 ✎

"My goodness me," says the Chairman, rubbing his hands. "So it was true, what I heard! However did you manage that?"

He gives you ten guineas (**£10 10s**) and a treasure of the Guild: a **pneumatic manual (ENG+3)**.

Leave...   71

✎ 90 ✎

The locals drink inside the Holly Bush, with the dismounted nobility who take their final fortifying draughts before wrapping up against fog and damp. Several boys are kept busy ferrying drinks and food.

The landlord has a room to let here and for a payment of **two guineas (£2 2s)** you can reserve it. If you so choose, remove the money from your **Adventure Sheet** and tick the option below. He warns you that there may be further charges to pay.

Buy a drink...   (2s)   40
☐ Visit your room...   80
Head to the yard outside...   61
Leave the pub...   2

✎ 91 ✎

You press on through the dripping leaves of Ken Wood and come the clearing where the Lee family vardos stand. Lee looks up from some piece of whittling and greets you warmly.

Lee's mother will treat any wounds or other ailments you may have.

Medical items	To buy	To sell
bandages	3s	-
cough medicine	5s	-
soothing lotion	2s	-
bottle of chloroform	£2	£1 5s
Medical treatment	To buy	
Treat a **wound**...	£1	
Treat a **black eye**...	18s	
Treat a **fever**...	10s	
Treat a **burn**...	6s	
Treat a **stiff back**...	12s	

Head towards Highgate...   28
Ride up to Hampstead village...   2

✎ 92 ✎

The Camden Omnibus Depot is the hub of north London's busy steam locobus service. Garages and sheds stand around a cobbled yard. Countless drivers and mechanics in their yellow-striped uniforms saunter around. A giant clock surmounts the complex, its gears timed to gates and pipework and lines, all designed to keep the locobuses running on time.

If you are **Wanted by the Locobus Co-operative**, turn to **1144** immediately.

Take work as an omnibus driver...   1118
Return to Camden...   84

✎ 93 ✎

You remember that the manufacturers you met were planning to head north along this road, and sure enough, you see their carriage approaching up the rutted holloway. Remove the codeword *Clarify* and make a your choice: to stop the carriage you should make an ACCURACY roll of difficulty 16 or a RUTHLESSNESS roll of difficulty 14.

Successful ACCURACY roll!   1263
Successful RUTHLESSNESS roll!   1276
Failed either roll!   1446

✎ 94 ✍

Tick the box of any pub that has agreed to sign the Camden **publican's contract**. If they are now all ticked, turn to **108**.

The Brunel Arms, Paddington	☐
The Imperial, Marylebone	☐
The Holly Bush Inn, Hampstead	☐
The Yard, Smithfield	☐
The Compton Arms, Islington	☐
The Horn, Clerkenwell	☐
HMS Spartan, Chelsea	☐

The Director is very pleased to see you. "Well done indeed," he says, chortling. "Camden Beer will soon be the biggest in the entire city." He gives you **ten guineas in banknotes**: remove the codeword *Conglomerate*.

Leave the director...	**84**

✎ 95 ✍

The Park is busy with well-to-do sightseers, strolling among the roses and ponds. Just inside, the Zoological Gardens are popular with the gentry and the commonfolk. You can go and watch the antics of the golden-haired monkeys, see a crocodile tear a rotten leg of lamb to pieces, or observe a lion do very little but yawn. And then there is Jumbo the elephant - the greatest land beast alive! Or so his poster proclaims. He is marched around in a circle for the amusement of children and ladies, his eyes dull with fatigue and homesickness. A much smaller notice at the side indicates that help is wanted handling the animals.

Enquire about work at the zoo...	**162**
Steam to Camden Town...	**84**
Leave the park by the southern gate...	**47**
Ride north towards Hampstead...	**19**

✎ 96 ✍

You have been told that the landlord here passes information on to the Constables - but what does that mean for you? You can simply keep a low profile, or you can try to find proof of his treachery and punish him.

Keep your mouth shut...	**12**
Watch for suspicious behaviour...	**1130**

✎ 97 ✍

The Union is looking for help with various engineering problems - the sort of that you will need access to a computational engine, together with knowledge of how to use a variety of punchcards, to solve. Then there is the steady work of carrying luggage back and forth - not dignified, but hardly difficult either.

Offer your calculating abilities...	**599**
Become a luggage porter...	**627**
Report destruction of Haulage Guild vehicles... (*Cabal*)	**216**
Leave the place...	**58**

✎ 98 ✍

The maid returns as you are preparing to leave your room. "There's four shilling to pay," she says, "For the fire, sheets and service."

If you are unable or unwilling to pay the **4s**, then you must erase everything from the box in passage **80**: the landlord will take it in lieu of payment. Then turn to **90** immediately, where you should erase the tick in the box. If you do pay, simply remove the money from your **Adventure Sheet** and roll a dice, adding 1 to the score for each **Wanted Status** you possess.

Score 1-6	**61**
Score 7+	**103**

✎ 99 ✍

At Paddington, the King's Canal reaches the Haulage Guild Freight Yard and the terminus of the Imperial Western Railway. It is a busy, smelly corner of the city, where loitering gangs look for a chance to make a few coins, honestly or otherwise.

	To buy	To sell
Charcoal	-	£22
Furniture	-	£24
Machinery	-	£28
Pottery	-	£22
Cotton	-	£3
Woollen Cloth	-	£16
Coal	£20	£12
Beer	£18	£15
Wheat	-	£9
Malt	£10	£6
Frozen Meat	-	£15
Ice	£11	£10

If you wish to purchase **Ice**, you will need a **Perkins**

Machine. If you wish to moor here, write **moored at Paddington Basin** on your **Adventure Sheet** and turn to **64** immediately.

Steam west along the King's Canal...	**977**
Steam east through north London...	**944**

❧ 100 ☙

You strike up a conversation with the man, implying that you too have to deal with the ungrateful and unreliable inhabitants of the Old Nichol slum. To convince him to open up, make an INGENUITY roll of difficulty 14, adding 1 for each **£1** you spend on drinks, to a maximum of 4.

Successful INGENUITY roll!	**69**
Failed INGENUITY roll!	**85**

❧ 101 ☙

You ride along in the airship's wake, watching to see what falls. Roll a dice to see what you can come across:

Score 1-2   a **strongbox**...
Score 3-4   a **steam accordion**...
Score 5-6   some **welding tools**...

Ride on out of the storm...	**28**

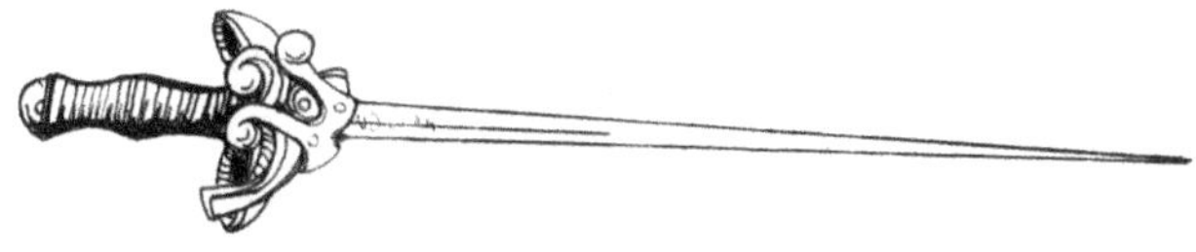

❧ 102 ☙

You ride towards the knot of troublemakers and scatter them. The gentleman thanks you, tossing you a florin (**2s**), and curses the boys noisily.

Turn to...	**noted passage**

❧ 103 ☙

As you ready yourself to journey on, it becomes plain that there are eyes watching. That man over by the doorpost, leaning on a stick... That open window across the street. You kick your Ferguson's friction starter and the furnace flames, but even as you accelerate over the cobbles, you hear the approaching bell of Constabulary velosteams.

Flee...	**33**

❧ 104 ☙

The Chairman begins to laugh uproariously. "Let us see if their board can recover from *that*!" He gives you fifteen guineas **£15 15s**) and a **calculating engine (ING+3)**. "Take care of that machine," he says.

Leave the yard...	**71**

❧ 105 ☙

There is a smith working over a furnace at one side of the yard, melting iron in a crucible for some urgent casting. "Can you melt gold or silver in that?" you ask. If you are **Wanted by the Haulage Guild**, turn to **507** immediately.

"Course I can. But not on Guild time - and not with Guild coke."

For a flat fee of **£1** to buy his time, his fuel and his silence, the smith will convert any number of pieces of gold or silver jewellery into small, anonymous ingots. What you do with these is then up to you.

gold bar   any **six** gold items
          (**gold ring, gold bracelet, gold
            necklace, golden candlesticks** etc)
silver bar any **six** silver items
          (**silver ring, silver bracelet,
          silver necklace** etc)

If you have **Stolen the Crown Jewels** among your **Great Deeds**, turn to **133**.

Return to the freight yard...	**14**
Leave the freight yard...	**64**

❧ 106 ☙

Were this proud edifice to burn down, the Imperial Western Railway would be in some serious trouble. Their share prices would plummet, for example - and their rivals would be very pleased indeed. To set about such an act of arson, you will need to identify spots in the building where a fire can take hold undetected. You will need to make an ENGINEERING roll of difficulty 16, adding 1 if you have a **measuring line** and 2 if you possess a **lantern** or any **hair matches**.

Did not attempt ENGINEERING roll...	**64**
Successful ENGINEERING roll!	**124**
Failed ENGINEERING roll!	**160**

❧ 107 ❧

The streets of Pentonville swirl with a greasy, brown smog. Steamcabs and locobuses trundle past, their forelamps blurred and their wheels rattling on tramline and cobble. Terraces of tiny worker's dwellings cluster around low courts between the city streets, and behind the high-fronted warehouses and offices, poverty rules this parish.

Enter the Guild of Chimney Sweepers... **825**
Ride to Battlebridge Basin... **129**
Steam up Upper Street into Islington... **151**
Head down Rosoman Street into Clerkenwell...**144**
Take Euston Road to St Pancras... **71**

❧ 108 ❧

The Director is astounded. "My, my! What a very persuasive individual you have proven to be! You have assisted us in forming quite an Empire." He calls in some of his staff and begins planning how to roll out his new, machine-brewed beer, to profit the most he can from the new public houses.

You have indeed learned a great deal in your wheelings and dealings. Add 1 to your INGENUITY score. The Director gives you a generous payment of **twenty guineas in banknotes** and shakes your hand. Remove the codeword *Conglomerate* and gain the codeword *Credit*.

Leave the Director... **84**

❧ 109 ❧

Perhaps keeping that key all this time has paid off... It does not fit the lock of your cell, but one evening, as the warden opens the door to collect your bucket, you take the chance and launch yourself at him. You quickly overpower him and set off at a run.

You dash through corridors, almost at random, and emerge in the outer bailey. A nearby shed contains, wonder of wonders, your velosteam, just as it was when it was confiscated. You clamber aboard, light the burner and steam out to the gatehouse.

It is the dead of night, and nobody is expecting a vehicle to approach from inside the tower. You have just enough time to fit the key in the lock and turn it before someone spots you. Remove the **Tower Key** from your **possessions**, but add **Escaped from the Tower** to your **Great Deeds**.

Ride towards London Bridge... **1000**
Ride to Whitechapel... **356**

❧ 110 ❧

You step off your Ferguson into the thick London mud. It isn't like country mud. It is black, foul-smelling and sticks to everything, being composed of stone-grits, horse-dung, and abraded iron. No wonder the gentlefolk pay to have their road-crossings swept.

The sweepers are fiercely territorial, sticking to their patch and building relationships with the regular pedestrians, but in truth the total of their earnings is a meagre twelve or fifteen shillings a week. They are amongst the poorest working men and women of the city. However, they also have their ears open - if you are willing to tip them a coin.

Ask about the Tower of London... (**1s**) **59**
Leave the sweepers for now... **139**

❧ 111 ❧

The long journey down the Thames passes slowly and without the work of handling the boat or paying for tolls you have little to do. Roll a dice to see how you spend your time:

Score 1-2   Gambling: gain **£2 3s**...
Score 3-4   Fishing: gain a **large pike**...
Score 5-6   You catch a **cold (RUTH-1 ING-1)**...

Eventually the cruiser reaches the heart of London. A crewmember helps you wheel your velosteam off the deck, giving you a suspicious look as step ashore.

Arrive at the wharf... **273**

❧ 112 ❧

Careful reconnaissance of Somerset house, its yards, jetties and gates, gives you clues to a likely route for secret entry. Then you wait for dark to fall. If you have a **winged harness**, turn to **163** immediately. Otherwise, read on.

Leaving your velosteam carefully hidden nearby, you make your way down onto the silt and mud of the riverside. Up a rusted ladder onto one of the less-used jetties, onto a small quayside and between a series of sheds and you come to the rear of the grand mansion at the heart of Somerset House. Once a nobleman's palace, this place is now given over entirely to the law. The Constabulary is run from here with the assistance of famously powerful computational engines and the devious mind of Lord Hadrian Beaufort. A vast network of information flows into these buildings through the telegraph tower standing in the yard, manned by a special detachment of Telegraph Guild officers. Countless smaller optical telegraphs stand on the rooftops and windowledges of various departments. One, high up on the mansion roof, must belong to Lord Beaufort's suite: it remains quiet for long periods, but after clattering out short messages, every other telegraph begins to shuffle and dance in response. You will need a **rope**, a **grappling iron** and a **crowbar** if you are to gain access to his rooms from here.

Begin the climb...
    (**rope**, **grappling iron** and **crowbar**) **179**
Retrace your steps...   **139**

❧ 113 ❧

Gravely wounded though you are, the Constables are not about to lose a potential conviction. They haul you upright, strip you of all your **weapons**, **possessions** and **money** and carry you away.

You awake briefly to considerable pain. A Constabulary doctor is treating your wounds: remove a **wound** and replace it with a **scar**. Unable to fight the exhaustion and pain, you collapse back into darkness again.

Turn to...   **13**

❧ 114 ❧

You have to weave down a mews or two and even bump over steps to avoid the obvious Constabulary posts between Pentonville and Bloomsbury, but even then you can't quite guarantee that you'll avoid the boys in green. Note passage **400** and roll a dice:

Score 1-2	A newspaper boy...	**307**
Score 3-4	Evening's quiet...	**400**
Score 5	Constables!	**1427**
Score 6	Moonlight wanderers...	**1511**

❧ 115 ❧

One of the anchors swings above your head. You leap from the saddle and catch its fluke, before looping it around the trunk of a sturdy oak. The crew then manage to lodge the others and bit by bit, the leviathan is winched to the ground and out of the wind.

The captain comes to the equator rail to thank you, yelling through the storm. "Really very good of you. The Union knows how to reward those who help them." He tosses you a small bag containing **£5**.

Ride on to Highgate...   **28**

❧ 116 ❧

The men and women of the road are a close-knit bunch. Make a MOTORING roll of difficulty 10 to see whether you can win their trust and get them talking.

Successful MOTORING roll!   **128**
Failed MOTORING roll!   **141**

❧ 117 ❧

You are poured a Panther's Pelt Stout, brewed here at the Leopard. Raising your glass to the gas lamp, you find the beer utterly opaque: not a glimmer of light passes through. The open and pale head whispers away quickly, leaving you to enjoy a smooth, creamy pint. If you have **Mrs Petty's note**, turn to **700** immediately. Otherwise, note passage **165** and make a choice from the options below.

Talk to the landlady... (**publican's contract**) **177**
Report to Mrs Petty... (*Citrate*)   **756**
Listen for rumours...   **148**

❧ 118 ❧

The slick mud of the fields churns like filthy butter beneath your wheels: you come crashing down to the ground and, before you can relight your Ferguson's burner and regain pressure, a Constabulary airship is hovering overhead. They turn a powerful beam lantern on you and dazzle you into submission.

Raise your hands...   **1500**

❧ 119 ❧

The beggars are not impressed by your generosity - but then if you expected something in return, were you really being generous?

"On to Crafton's," you hear one of them say. "Lambeth-a-hoo!"

Ride on...   **noted passage**

❧ 120 ❧

You explain how the Director of the Camden Brewery is looking for pubs to sell his beer, but the landlord shakes his head. "I don't know if it would suit my customers round here. They're dreadful set in their ways." Make a RUTHLESSNESS roll of difficulty 11 or an INGENUITY roll of difficulty 10.

Successful RUTHLESSNESS or INGENUITY roll! **142**
Failed RUTHLESSNESS or INGENUITY roll! **126**

❧ 121 ❧

You pass through Canonbury, passing villas built for the burgeoning bourgeoisie. Despite the fog, the place feels cleaner than much of the city. Note passage **151** and roll a dice:

Score 1-2	Chimney sweeps...	**1458**
Score 3	Empty roads and fog...	**151**
Score 4	A robber...	**644**
Score 5-6	A wandering cow...	**1348**

❧ 122 ❧

Your luridly bruised eye catches the attention of a lady shopkeeper, who sends her burly son to sweep you on your way. If you knock him down, you risk losing a GALLANTRY point on a dice roll of 1-3, but you can continue to your **noted passage**. Otherwise, roll a dice to see where you end up.

Score 1-3	A sidestreet...	**63**
Score 4-6	Back the way you came...	**84**

❧ 123 ❧

The Lyceum is one of the finest theatres in the city. The King himself keeps a box there, as do several other noblemen and ladies. Gilt lettering shines over the door, reflecting lime light and flickering oil flames. Opera capes and top hats are much in evidence. Actors and patrons are all as flamboyantly dressed as one another. Whether you stand out or blend in depends on what you have chosen to wear for a night at the theatre...

Head around to the stage door...	**511**
Return to the Strand...	**139**
Ride north to Bloomsbury...	**400**

❧ 124 ❧

☐

If the box above is empty, tick it and read on. If it is already ticked, turn to **195** immediately.

After surreptitiously surveying the station, you set a few smouldering lantern wicks where they will not be noticed. Each one should burn away until the middle of the night, when they will catch the hay, sawdust, scraps of oil-soaked cloth and other rubbish that you have collected. Then you withdraw and wait.

It is shortly after one o'clock, when the clocks of the city have chimed their gloomy tones, that the glow of fire first shows through the glass of the station. You, of course, have been waiting for it, but to the station staff it is a complete surprise. No sooner do they begin to grapple with the fire beneath the wooden platform supports than another is discovered in the roof, and a third near the goods shed, and another and another. Despite the approach of the local extinguishing machine, there is little they can do, and by dawn the sky is lit, with the sun rising in the east and another glorious blaze of fire in the west. The arches of the wide, wide roof tilt, crack and fall. Paddington station is completely destroyed. Gain the codeword *Cricket*.

Ride away...	**64**

❧ 125 ❧

Your raven knows the tower and its inhabitants well. It was already a ruthlessly smart bird before you began to train it, but now it understands several instructions and can recognise specific objects... including keys.

So it is no surprise when, late one evening, she drops a key with a tinkle through the high arrow-loop in your cell. It opens the heavy door and you are out. along the cold corridors and out onto the ramparts, where the raven greets you with a croak of recognition. Then you follow the bird to a shed that seems to have caught its attention.

Enter the shed...	**529**

❧ 126 ❧

Smithfield Market is a sight indeed. The modern glazed halls are built on the ancient site of the cattle fair, just outside the London Wall, and in the open ground herds of Lincolns, Herefords, Red Devons, spotted country bullocks, scores of black-faced and white-faced mutton sheep are penned, auctioned and sold. The slaughterhouses steam with hot blood and the cobbles are stained with the iron of life. Mechanical cranes lift and swing carcasses through the market to be hung up in front of bidders and then swung away again and loaded onto steam wagons. This is the stomach of the city, where beef becomes fuel for the millions.

Smaller butcher's shops, specializing in this or that aspect of the trade, line the streets either side, along with the allied trades of skinners, apron-makers, basket-weavers, hook-turners, scalesmen, cutlers and grindsmen and such. A game specialist might be a profitable place to sell anything you have caught. Here and there amongst the crowds, you spy a porter with a red button in his lapel. This, then, must be a Compact stronghold.

If you have the codeword *Baron*, turn to **1100** immediately.

Food and Drink	To buy	To sell
rabbit	6s	4s
pheasant	10s	5s
large pike	£2	£1
deer carcass	£4	£2 10s
wheel of cheese	£2	£1 5s
pork pie	2s	1s
picnic hamper	£4	£2 10s
Clothing	To buy	To sell
mask	1s	-
dungarees (GAL-2)	£1 10s	15s
engineer's gloves (ENG +1)	£3	£2 10s
Tools	To buy	To sell
lantern	6s	3s
axe	8s	6s
shovel	8s	6s
billhook (PAR 2)	12s	10s
scissors (PAR 1)	10s	8s
wirecutters	12s	9s
net	6s	4s
tarpaulin	4s	2s
measuring line	6s	4s
Weapons	To buy	To sell
club (PAR 2)	3s	-
sabre (PAR 3)	£2 10	£1 5s
blunderpistol (ACC 6)	-	£3 5s
Medical items	To buy	To sell
bandages	3s	-
Other items	To buy	To sell
clockwork bird	-	£2
revolutionary poster	1s	-
sketchpad □ □ □	3s	2s
flute	£1 5s	£1

Visit the Yard...	150
Talk to someone about the Compact...	184
Steam north into Clerkenwell...	144
Head into the City...	210
Ride west to Bloomsbury...	400

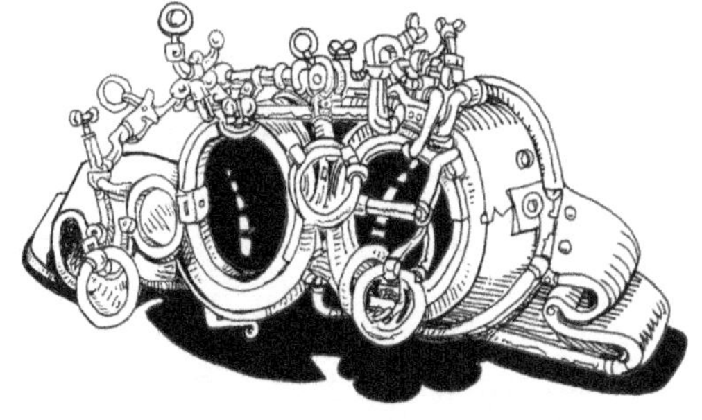

⤳ 127 ⤳

The boys don't take long to whip away the gentleman's purse, watch and handkerchief, and then swing off down the alleyways. It will take a MOTORING roll of difficulty 12 to follow them.

Successful MOTORING roll!	191
Failed MOTORING roll!	**noted passage**

⤳ 128 ⤳

An engineer is roasting chestnuts on a shovel in the firebox of his Aubrey engine. You are welcomed into the fold, where scents of oil and tobacco mingle with the sweetness of the morsels. Roll a dice to see what you hear:

Score 1-2	The Dover Road...	**309**
Score 3-4	Up to Essex...	**321**
Score 5-6	Bishop's Wood...	**333**

⤳ 129 ⤳

Barges are clustered in the basin edge below the cranes where massive blocks of straw-strewn ice hang from pincers. On the western side, along the road towards Islington, Barret's Foundry rings with the blows of a steam hammer.

Enter the ice warehouse...	1125
Board your boat...	
(moored at Battlebridge Basin)	1218
Ride into Islington...	151
Pentonville...	107

⤳ 130 ⤳

Your florin buys you a pot of pale, weakly-bubbling ale. It has a strong scent that tells you it has had flavours added after brewing, as well as the raw finish of a quickly-fermented commercial beer. You spy a barrel labelled 'Mager's Fast-Brew'. That must be its name. If you are **Wanted by the Haulage Guild**, turn to **766** immediately. Otherwise, note passage **176**: with your pot in hand you head to a table in the middle of the room and open up your ears and eyes in search of useful information. Roll a dice to see what you hear:

Score 1	Grave robbers...	**1019**
Score 2	The Compact...	**1060**
Score 3	Parliamentary blades...	**1075**
Score 4	A street gang...	**1113**
Score 5	Bright stones...	**1099**
Score 6	False papers...	**1159**

❧ 131 ❧

A narrow wooden building stands in the narrow alley running parallel to Bow High Street. Beside it is a cobbled yard faced with several short terraces of some slum-lord's domain.

This is Bird Alley Chapel. Reverend Highrun and his wife minister to the poor and the downtrodden here, preaching the Word of God and doing what he can to bring about a heavenly kingdom in east London.

Speak to Reverend Highrun...	**517**
Stay to hear a sermon...	**530**
Visit the rectory...	
(Friend of Reverend Highrun)	**547**
Leave the chapel...	**471**

❧ 132 ❧

You use every ounce of power that the Ferguson can give you and manage to gain and sustain a lead. Night falls and the bells of the Constables fade away - after all, they are charged with keeping the city's peace. Once you have been chased away, their job is done.

As for you, you are far to the west. If you want to put the city behind you, you could now take the road towards High Wycombe. Otherwise you must conserve your fuel and water and ride carefully back towards Hampstead.

Head for Hampstead...	**2**
Steam towards High Wycombe...	
Smog and Ambuscade 561	

❧ 133 ❧

"And what about something more... delicate?"

The smith grunts. "If there's metal in it, it'll melt. That's all I care about."

For a flat fee of **£5** - the higher price to cover the increased need for discretion - the smith will convert any of the following items into bullion for you.

golden sceptre	two **gold bars**
sword of state	a **gold bar**, three **sapphires** and a **handful of small diamonds**
pearl armills	two **gold bars** and a **bag of perfect pearls**
ruby-studded gauntlets	a **bag of fine rubies**
sapphire coronet	a **gold bar** and three **sapphires**
diamond crown	a **gold bar**, a **bag of fine rubies** and a **handful of small diamonds**
ceremonial mace	three **gold bars**

Return to the freight yard...	**14**
Leave the freight yard...	**64**

❧ 134 ❧

The boys recognise you, of course, and wave you a combination of secret signals. They finish their game without raising any suspicion and come over to see you.

"'ello guvner," says Jerry. "You've found us abaht our work. You ain't got somefink to eat, as yer?"

The boys will swap some of their recent loot for various items of food.

Item	Exchange for
pocket watch	**tin of fruit**
gold bracelet	**tin of fruit** or **pork pie**
silk scarf	**pork pie**
jewelled eyepatch	
(**RUTH+1 GAL+1**)	**picnic hamper**

Turn to...   **noted passage**

❧ 135 ❧
☐ ☐ ☐

If any of the boxes above are empty, tick one and read on. If they are all already ticked, erase the ticks and turn to **182** immediately.

For now you are untroubled by the attention of Constables. Perhaps you have got away with your crime? Will you remain in the area or speed off towards other, unplundered areas?

Ride towards Camden Town...   **84**
Hide yourself in the City...   **213**
Take Old Street towards Shoreditch...   **308**
Head for along Shaftesbury Avenue to Mayfair... **750**

❧ 136 ❧

When you whisper that you have information vital to the King's safety, the Constable at the desk narrows his eyes, but he decides to take the chance and brings you to a fat officer in a rear office. His eyes widen at the **note** (remove it from your possessions). It will plainly bring him favour with his superiors.

"Well done, citizen. Should you come across any more such information... Letters from the woman in question, anything in her handwriting that confirms our suspicions."

"What suspicions?"

"She is almost certainly an agent of the dangerous Compact for Worker's Equality," replies the officer. "We suspect that she assists with the distribution of seditious literature."

"And you think these papers are...'"

"Possibly stored aboard her cruiser, moored downstream from Westminster Bridge." The officer walks to the window and peers out. "There! The *Gentilesse*."

As payment for the information, the officer makes sure you receive a small purse of coin (**£2 10**) and also offers you a fine pair of **fencing gloves (NIM+1)**.

Leave Somerset House...   **139**

❧ 137 ❧
☐

If the box above is empty, tick it and read on. If it is already ticked, erase the tick and turn to **5** immediately.

You pause for a moment as a wagon laden with sacks of feathers pulls out from a yard, and as you do, a poster plastered onto the rough bricks catches your eye. It informs you that there is a Reward of One Hundred and Fifty Guineas for the Capture of that dreaded rogue, the Steam Highwayman.

With the right friends, you could stage manage a good profit out of a false arrest, as well as humiliating the Union. Will you try it?

Take the poster to Flat Billy...
     (**Friend of Flat Billy**)   **619**
Take the poster to Crafton...
     (**Friend of Crafton**)   **629**
Ignore the poster...   **noted passage**

❧ 138 ❧

You turn out onto the long road west, overtaking engines and their loads, crashing through gravelly puddles and bumping over heavy ruts. Noise of your pursuers behind you continues and the sound of an airship overhead throbs down through the clouds.

Cut across country...   **149**
Strike out west...   *Smog and Ambuscade* **218**

❧ 139 ❧

The Strand is in the busiest part of London. There are countless steam-cabs chuffing through the fog, weaving in and out of the printers' drays piled high with tomorrow's newspapers. Bowler-hatted swells escort their ladies across the street to the gas-lit theatres, their paths swept by forelock-tugging sweepers desperate for a copper. Here, your velosteam is just another machine to be manouevred through the mass.

The gold-spotted sign of the Leopard Inn swings over the street opposite St Mary's le Strand, blackened by every passing funnel and fume. Further down,

Coulter's Bank stands on the corner where the Strand becomes Fleet Street. In turn, Fleet Street becomes Ludgate Hill and leads to the steps of St Paul's and the city.

On the southern side, the gleaming stone of Somerset House belies the dark business of the Constables inside. Their own Class-B telegraph tower stands in the courtyard and their river launches are moored at the quay. It is a place to be careful - very careful indeed - if you have any sort of criminal deed to your name.

Enter the Lyceum Theatre...	**123**
Visit the Leopard Inn...	**165**
Enter Coulter's Bank...	**173**
Approach Somerset House...	**284**
Speak to the street sweepers...	**110**
Steam east up Fleet Street towards the city...	**201**
Ride west into Mayfair...	**750**
Cross Oxford Street into Bloomsbury...	**400**
Ride down towards Westminster...	**721**

❧ 140 ❧

Remus Wine Merchants is a narrow, strangely shaped building at the meeting of two streets. Every shelf inside is crammed with bottles - from the newest, machine-processed wines, to ancient muddy vintages priced for collectors.

Food and Drink	To buy	To sell
bottle of gin	15s	-
bottle of wine	10s	-
bottle of champagne	£1 10s	-
bottle of whisky	£1	-
bottle of Quinta de Vesan	£55	£35

Leave the shop...	**151**

❧ 141 ❧

Your manner and looks convince the company that you are an informer from the Constables, trying to inveigle your way into their fellowship. They pelt you with lumps of coal: roll a dice to see the outcome.

Score 1-2	a **stiff back (NIM-2)**
Score 3-4	a **black eye (ACC-2 GAL-1)**
Score 5-6	a **missing tooth (GAL-1)**

Leave the freight yard...	**noted passage**

❧ 142 ❧

The landlord eventually comes round to your way of thinking. "I'll keep some of what I've got on tap, though," he says. "A bit of variety is good for business." Gain the codeword *Conglomerate*.

Leave the pub...	**126**

❧ 143 ❧

A posse of young street turks are bamboozling a wealthy pedestrian in an attempt to pick his pockets. It shouldn't be too difficult to scare them off - or to follow them after they succeed. If you are the **Friend of the Waterside Boys,** turn to **134** immediately.

Scare them off...	**102**
Let them succeed and follow them...	**127**

❧ 144 ❧

You are in the district known as Clerkenwell. Brick warehouses stand side by side with ancient walls, medieval jettied dwellings and countless tiny craftsmen's workshops. The Horn Inn stands waiting for custom, the street outside cluttered with tables and stools to cater for all the drinkers. A massive enamel tooth hangs over one shopfront, advertising a dentist. Through a gothic arch is the mysterious St Gorgonia's Court, home of the Noble Brotherhood of Self-Denial. You are also only a short distance from the shouts and smells of Smithfield, just within earshot to the south.

Visit the Horn Inn...	**176**
Take a look at the dentist's shop...	**193**
Investigate Smithfield Market...	**126**
Enter St Gorgonia's Court...	**1131**
Ride north into Pentonville...	**170**
Take St John Street Road to Islington...	**151**
Head east along Old Street to Shoreditch...	**157**
Steam along Great Ormond Street into Bloomsbury...	**400**
Follow Farringdon Road into the city...	**201**

❧ 145 ❧

The hungry boy grabs the proffered food greedily. "Yer the Steam Highwayman, encha? Fort so. Lissen, not a lot o' people know this. But Lord Beaufort 'as been takin' money off've Flat Billy. Regular meetin's on the monnyment at midnight an' all." He scampers off down a side-street.

Ride on...	**noted passage**

146

The company are keen to see your skill and one fellow stands up to oppose you. The wager will be a simple round of drinks. You take three feathered points and toe the line. The house board rewards accuracy and balance: make three NIMBLENESS rolls in sequence and total the points:

Score less than 30...	Lose: pay **16s** for a round...
Score 30 to 49...	Win a free drink! Note passage **474** and turn to **422**.
Score 50 or higher...	Win in style: roll two dice and subtract 2. If the total exceeds your NIMBLENESS, increase it by 1.

If you are unable to pay for a round of drinks, the company will strip you of all your **possessions** and dump you in the street.

Leave the Grapes... **474**

147

Whatever accusation brought you to imprisonment in the hulks, justified or not, your crime and your sentence are long forgotten, like the shackles dropped into the filthy Medway stream. Long you have known the Constables' pursuit, their bloodhounds, informers, traps and schemes. Outrunning them has become your normality.

Here in the city you will surely be able to disguise your trail once and for all. Perhaps the forgers of St Margaret's Court, or friends in one of the Guilds will be able to get you a new Citizen Identification Number. Perhaps you can claw your way out of the poverty trap and gain some sort of respectability - or become so feared that the Constables never bother you again? Perhaps at last you can take vengeance on the Chief Constable and destroy his happiness as he did yours.

Your ability scores are:

RUTHLESSNESS	6
ENGINEERING	4
MOTORING	3
NIMBLENESS	4
INGENUITY	2
GALLANTRY	2

You have in your possession a **blunderpistol (ACC 6)**, a **sabre (PAR 3)**, a **mask** and a **telescope**.

Turn to... **1200**

148

Roll a dice to see what you hear:

Score 1	Something for the tourists...	**1206**
Score 2	An investment opportunity...	**556**
Score 3	A religious revival in Wales...	**573**
Score 4	Men for hire...	**1193**
Score 5	Somewhere to stay...	**928**
Score 6	Recognised!	**664**

149

There is a coppice of trees a short distance to the north. Dusk is falling and if you can cover the ground unseen, you may be able to hide up until morning and avoid your pursuers. Make a MOTORING roll of difficulty 13, adding 2 if you possess **off-road tyres** and 2 if you possess a **muffled exhaust**.

Successful MOTORING roll!	**229**
Failed MOTORING roll!	**118**

150

The pub is bright, well-lit and modern, presumably built along with the new market buildings to serve the drovers and butchers who trade here at Smithfield. It takes its name from the steelyard that hangs in every slaughterman's shop - the slide-weighted lever that can measure a whole carcass to the very ounce.

A party of long-distance drovers sit at the bar, swapping stories of the roads they have travelled and the country they have passed through. Their patient, long-haired droving dogs loll beneath the stools. Men like these are good sources of information about what is happening in other parts of the land.

Buy a drink... (**2s**)	**198**
Talk to the drovers...	**724**
Speak to the landlord... (**publican's contract**)	**120**
Leave the pub...	**126**

151

Upper Street runs almost due north through Islington, bringing the herds of cattle and sheep in to the city for slaughter. It is a busy district, with workshops in every yard and chimneys belching out thick forge-smoke. The lairs on the west side of the road are livestock stalls owned by a local businessman named Laycock, who has made a fortune providing for the drovers and their stock. There are several pubs, including the intriguing Compton Arms down a side-street, and a well-reputed wine merchant. A little to the east stands old Canonbury Tower in its grounds - the home of Baroness Dimlight.

✎ 152 ✑

If you are the **Friend of Richard Pierce**, turn to **158** immediately. Otherwise, read on.

Mr Richard Pierce is the proprietor of the Horn and he is proud to consider his inn one of the finest in the city. He takes out his eyeglasses and reads through the contract carefully. "I can see the benefits," he says, "But I'm hesitant to stake my business on this."

"What do you want?" you ask.

"The Worshipful Guild of Brewers are choosing a new Chairman. Get me elected and I'll sign." Gain the codeword *Corrupt*.

Return to the parlour...   176

✎ 153 ✑

The Constables are far from impressed with you. They consider you an unimportant vagrant - little more than a beggar. They confiscate any **keys**, **tools** or **jewellery** you still possess (remove them from your **Adventure Sheet**), patch up the worst of your hurts (remove one **wound** and replace it with a **scar** without checking for **intimidating scars**) and send you on your way. You can also remove a single **Wanted Status**, if you possess one.

"Consider yourself fortunate," says the officer who releases you. "Do not cross our paths again or you will be treated much more harshly. Find yourself gainful employment, Citizen."

Roll a dice to see where you are released:

Score 1	Highgate...	28
Score 2	Clerkenwell...	144
Score 3	Southwark...	631
Score 4	Whitechapel...	356
Score 5	Bow...	471
Score 6	Lambeth...	647

✎ 154 ✑
□ □ □

If any of the boxes above are empty, tick one and read on. If they are all ticked already, turn to your **noted passage** immediately.

"I'll pay your fine," you say, stepping off your machine and standing in front of the greedy constable. He narrows his eyes and looks you up and down. If you are **Wanted by the Constables**, turn to **236** immediately. Otherwise, the constable will shrug and take your money. The costermonger is appreciative: roll a dice to see what you receive in return for your selflessness.

Score 1	a **solidarity point**...
Score 2	the codeword *Compassionate*...
Score 3-4	a **melon**...
Score 5-6	a **pineapple**...

Ride on...   **noted passage**

✎ 155 ✑

You spend some time studying the appearance and behaviour of the bank's employees. They are all dressed the same way, all men aged between eighteen and forty, and all equally keen to impress their employers. However, tiny differences speak volumes if you can interpret them. One of the younger men wears a waistcoat of an older style, discreetly mended once or twice. Perhaps he has inherited it, along with his position. He will be far too loyal to the bank to consider taking a payment for information. You are looking for someone in need of money...

One of the other tellers is well-dressed, sports shiny, macassared hair and has an air of frantic keenness. A quick glance at his desk shows that he has a personal letter - from a lady - on his desk. You wait nearby until the bank shuts up, and then approach this nervous clerk as he trots homeward in the gloom.

"Who are you?" he cries, as you place a hand on his shoulder.

"A friend. A benefactor."

You explain that you need to know who is receiving the rents from the Old Nichol. He seems rather frightened, but cheers a little when you mention payment. Make a GALLANTRY roll of difficulty 12, adding 1 for each **£4** that you offer him, to a maximum of **£20**.

Successful GALLANTRY roll!   169
Failed GALLANTRY roll!   185

❧ 156 ❧

The Dimlight family have held Canonbury Tower since it was confiscated from a religious order during the reformation. It is a strange, ramshackle old place, with a stubby brick tower and a large private orchard.

Ask for an audience with the Baroness

(Letter of Introduction)	**567**
⊕ Make a delivery... **(Tillson's hot sauce)**	**542**
Hand over the document...	
(lineage transcript)	**1198**
Return to Islington...	**151**
Leave the area...	**167**

❧ 157 ❧

Note passage **308**. The streets here wind and bump unevenly, forcing you to wrench your heavy machine to and fro across the roadway. Wives and children with pails jump out of the way. Roll a dice to see what you encounter:

Score 1-2	The Waterside Boys...	**143**
Score 3	A fight!	**1452**
Score 4-5	A drunkard...	**481**
Score 6	A sailor...	**1339**

❧ 158 ❧

Pierce welcomes you warmly. "Ah, my friend! Come and share a bottle of something special with me." He has put on weight since being elected by the Worshipful Company of Brewers. "Business is good," he says, "Very much thanks to you."

Pierce will let you a room here at the Horn as an appreciation for your work. You can leave belongings and money here safely (write them in the box below) and take the time to recover from your adventures. He will also allow you to work on your velosteam in the yard, if you need to do any repairs. Note **this passage (158)** before making any further choices.

Tend your wounds...	**500**
Open a strongbox...	**331**
Repair your velosteam...	**1300**
Return to the parlour...	**176**

❧ 159 ❧

The cobbles over Thornhill bridge are uneven, loosened by the iron wheels of a thousand engines. A glimpse down at the canal shows you an argument between bargee and wharfwoman. Note passage **167**. If your velosteam is **damaged**, turn to **209** immediately. If not, but you are **Wanted by the Atmospheric Union**, turn to **137**. Otherwise, roll a dice to see what you encounter:

Score 1-2	A hungry boy...	**432**
Score 3-4	Badly-cobbled streets...	**167**
Score 5-6	A broken cable...	**274**

❧ 160 ❧

You are accosted by a porter as you go about placing the tinder and rubbish you hoped to burn. Wherever you had chosen to place it was obviously far too conspicuous.

You drop the incriminating bundles and dash for your velosteam. Note that you will now be **Wanted by the Railway Guards**.

Ride away!	**50**

❧ 161 ❧

The recommended beer at the Compton Arms is a soft, creamy draught stout called the Drowned Moon. It goes down well - very well - in a fine pewter pot, carved with the name of the pub.

A man with a pencil moustache looks up as you raise your drink and begins scribbling in a notepad. Is he some sort of informer? Note passage **186** and if you have the codeword *Compassionate*, turn to **1213** immediately. Otherwise, roll a dice to see what you hear:

Score 1-2	The moustachioed man talks...	**78**
Score 3	Bright stones...	**1099**
Score 4	The King's woman...	**984**
Score 5	Prize fighting...	**883**
Score 6	Parliamentary blades...	**1075**

❧ 162 ❧

After a short series of questions by a stern and moustachioed Keeper, you are issued with a uniform, shown a hayloft where you can sleep, and put straight to work shovelling manure. Roll a dice to see what you encounter during your work here:

Score 1-2	Bitten by a camel...	**192**
Score 3-4	Befriend an elephant...	**183**
Score 5-6	Make a discovery...	**172**

❧ 163 ❧

A quiet wool warehouse along the river provides you with a suitable launching point. Diving off the highest door-trap, you extend the mechanical wings and swoop down towards Somerset House. The flight is brief and tricky, but you manage to slow yourself in time to grab at a windowsill beneath Lord Beaufort's personal telegraph.

If you have the codeword *Commensurate* or *Currently* turn to **202** immediately. If you have the codeword *Constable*, turn to **1460**. Otherwise, you must roll a dice: whether the suite is empty depends entirely on luck.

Score 1-4	A risky endeavour...	**211**
Score 5-6	Possible interruption...	**315**

❧ 164 ❧
☐

If the box above is empty, tick it and read on. If the box is already ticked, erase the tick and turn to **473** immediately.

You pull over to the kerb to check your direction and top up your water tank from a water fountain, and are surprised to hear a baby's cry in the gutter. An abandoned infant lies partly swaddled in a dirty piece of cotton and covered with a sack. At this time, no-one else is on the street.

Ride on regardless... **noted passage**
Try to find someone to care for the child... **174**

❧ 165 ❧

The Leopard is always busy. The landlord owns a rare thing - a day-and-night licence - as a result of some favour to the Constables or the Licensing Board, and so sweepers and night watchmen come here in the early morning, steamcab drivers at all hours, traders after closing up their shops, lonely, grey-faced women at the start of the day. You will have to shoulder your way through the smoky mass to the bar to order a drink.

Order a drink... (**2s**) **117**
Leave the pub... **139**

❧ 166 ❧

You cut across the busy junction at Lower Charles Street and past a sewerage wagon pumping waste out from one of the many Corporation urinals. Note passage **144** and roll a dice:

Score 1-2	Only alley cats...	**144**
Score 3-4	A bundle...	**164**
Score 5-6	A wandering cow...	**1348**

❧ 167 ❧

From Islington, the roads run in every direction. The city lies to the south, but from here you can strike out for the Great North Road and the country beyond.

Take the Great North Road... *The Great North Road 8*
Steam west towards Camden Town... **84**
Head towards Pentonville... **107**
Ride down St John Street Road to Clerkenwell... **166**
Take the road out towards Bow... **570**

❧ 168 ❧

"You're looking for the Commissioner, no doubt," says your contact. "You need to head down to the sugar warehouse at Blackwall. That's where all the preparations are being made."

"Preparations?"

"Yes, preparations. For the uprising."

He gives you **passdisc 820**.

Return to the market... **126**

❧ 169 ❧

The clerk agrees to get you the information you require. The next day, he slips out of the bank to pass you a handwritten note, naming Hortensia Duploye, the Duchess of Kent and bearing the **Duchess's account number**. You now need to decide what to do with this information - confront her at her house in Chelsea? Or perhaps there is another way to even things up. Remove the codeword *Commission*.

Leave the bank.. **139**

❧ 170 ❧

Farringdon Road is full of traffic, so you slip through the backstreets up towards Pentonville. You weave through Clerkenwell Close, up past the hovels of Lock's Gardens and Chapel Row and bump over the uneven cobbles of Margaret Street. If you have the codeword *Certain*, turn to **342** immediately. Otherwise, note passage **107** and roll a dice to see what you encounter.

Score 1	A street sweeper...	**346**
Score 2	A drunk...	**481**
Score 3-4	Quiet streets...	**107**
Score 5	A bundle in the gutter...	**164**
Score 6	An urchin...	**432**

❧ 171 ❧

The Telegraph Guild Tower at Bloomsbury is a marvel of modern technology. It stands twice the height of the surrounding mansions, topped with a double bank of shutters and hung with many more subsidiary arrays on the sides. The entire tower can rotate under the power of steam, and the flashing and clattering continues through the day and the night.

There is a busy office, handling the communications of businesses and even branches of government, as well as a depot for the Guild's road trains, which carry in a ceaseless stream of supplies and personnel. A dedicated bay with an automated steam-shovel unloads the Coal Board's wagons that arrive every hour.

If you have the codeword *Crestfallen*, turn to **196** immediately. If not but you possess the **Bloomsbury package**, turn to **194**.

Try to see a Telegraph Guild Officer...	**241**
Leave the tower...	**400**

❧ 172 ❧

☐

If the box above is empty, tick it and read on. Otherwise, turn to **192** immediately.

While working at the zoo cleaning the enclosures, you come across a **diamond brooch** that has been dropped by a wealthy visitor. The discovery prompts you to head on your way again.

Leave the zoo... **95**

❧ 173 ❧

Although Coulter's is really a regional bank, with its headquarters on the High Wycombe marketplace, there is a branch here on the Strand among the other banks and financial offices of the city. If you are **Wanted by the Constables**, turn to **82** immediately. If you have the codeword *Commission*, turn to **88** immediately. Otherwise, read on.

Here at the bank you can deposit or withdraw money in multiples of ten guineas (**£10 10s**) from your account. Write your new balance into the space on your **Adventure Sheet** before leaving. This can be accessed at any branch of the bank, but it will also be vital to have a healthy balance if you wish to retire to a more respectable life, or if you wish to move in high society. You can also exchange any **banknotes** or **gold** or **silver bars** for coin here.

Items	To buy	To sell
ten guineas in banknotes	£10 10s	£10 10s
gold bar	-	£30
silver bar	-	£8

Return to the Strand... **139**

❧ 174 ❧

Local people shake their heads when you ask them about the baby. All are overstretched anyway, and some find it difficult to understand why you are bothering them.

One suggests you take it to Maggie Laine's, in Shoreditch. She is a baby farmer, who can arrange a wet-nurse and raise children out of their infancy in return for a fee. Your other options are very limited.

Go direct to Maggie Laine's...	**197**
Visit Doctor Smythe...	**207**
Take the baby to Princess Alexandrina...	
(*Childless*)	**219**
Steam to High Way House... (*Caritas*)	**233**

✎ 175 ✎

You come across a one-eyed man doing business in a corner of the bar. This is Sidney Hardbutt, the fence. He will buy certain items from you, at what he claims is the best price.

Food and Drink	To buy	To sell
bottle of gin	18s	15s
Jewellery	To buy	To sell
pocket watch	-	£1 5s
gold ring	-	£3
gold bracelet	-	£3
gold necklace	-	£4
silver ring	-	15s
silver bracelet	-	£1 10s
silver necklace	-	£2
sapphire	-	£12
emerald	-	£9
Other items		
accordion	£3	£2 10s
assembly line plan	-	£5
pair of golden candlesticks	-	£8

Turn to... **noted passage**

✎ 176 ✎

Another smoky, dirty tavern stands here under the sign of an old hunting horn swinging in the street. The bar staff are harried and over-worked: at times you can barely even see the bar for the mass of bodies trying to make their order.

Buy a drink... **(2s)** 130

Talk to the owner... **(publican's contract)** 152

Ask for the woman in the red suit... (*Chaff*) 551

Head to your room...
  (Friend of Richard Pierce) 158

Leave the parlour... 144

✎ 177 ✎

The landlady is brusque. "I've got no interest in making money for another brewer," she says.

"It could be profitable..." you begin.

"Now listen, sunshine. I said no and I mean it. If you're thinking of trying anything, well, look around you. This ain't the place for funny business or rough behaviour. You won't come out of it well."

Return to the parlour... 165

❧ 178 ❧

This time the porter scowls at you. "We've got all the meat we need," he says. "We don't need you traipsing around here any longer. Be off before someone gets nosy."

Turn to...   400

❧ 179 ❧

The Constabulary never sleeps, even if you can spot individual Constables dozing at their desks and at their posts, and to make your rooftop journey even more fraught, a Constabulary airship approaches and hovers overhead. You are forced to hunker into the shelter of a chimney-stack until the airship finishes loading and chugs off to the east.

Eventually you come to the rooftop near Lord Beaufort's telegraph. Your crowbar helps lever open a maintenance hatch and you drop into a dark attic. Light shines through the cracks between boards: you are directly above Lord Beaufort's offices. If you have the codeword *Commensurate* or *Currently* turn to **202** immediately. If you have the codeword *Constable*, turn to **1460**. Otherwise, you must roll a dice: whether the suite is empty depends entirely on luck.

Score 1-3	**211**
Score 4-6	**226**

❧ 180 ❧

Doctor Smythe keeps a small surgery on Rose Lane. He will patch up wounds and sell you treatments for various diseases. He prefers payment in guineas - and his prices are not cheap.

Medical items	To buy	To sell
bandages	3s	-
cough medicine	5s	-
soothing lotion	2s	-
bottle of chloroform	£2	£1 5s

Medical treatment	To buy
Treat a **wound**...	£3 3s
Treat a **black eye**...	£2 2s
Treat a **fever**...	£3 3s
Treat a **burn**...	£2 2s
Treat a **stiff back**...	£2 12s

Return to Limehouse...   474

❧ 181 ❧

The woman laughs as you count out the cash. "I knew you'd see sense. But I'm surprised to see you carry so much money on you. London is a dangerous place for those unprepared to defend themselves." She nods to her massive companion, who leans forwards and wrenches part of your velosteam off, tossing it aside with a clang. Remove one **customisation** or receive a **damage point**.

"Remember us, Steam Highwayman," she menaces. "Don't cross our path again."

They climb into the steam van and drive off, leaving you to coax your velosteam back into action. If your velosteam is now **beyond repair**, turn to **1111** immediately. Otherwise, remove the codeword *Certain* and continue on your way - if you can live with the indignity of being robbed in the street.

Ride on...   107

❧ 182 ❧

You are deep in the city, with miles of urban streets on every side of you. Your best chance of a getaway from the Constables, whose bells are clanging as they approach, might be to steam for the outskirts.

Ride northwest...	**421**
Make for the east...	**950**
Ride for Upper Street...	**868**
Head for the river...	**858**

❧ 183 ❧

You are tasked with caring for Jumbo, the giant elephant. His previous keeper left as a nervous wreck and you have to try and build a rapport with this massive beast.

Over the first few days, he is wild and antagonistic, barely letting you approach, but with patience you are able to get closer to him. He suffers badly from having to stoop inside his shelter and his previous keeper kept him happy with bottles of liquor. However, you manage to calm him and soon speak to the Zookeeper about Jumbo's shelter.

"It's a matter of money," he says. "We can't afford to build a taller shelter."

"What about digging out the floor?" you suggest. "Jumbo can help."

The Zookeeper is delighted with the idea and soon you have remedied another of this dark city's injustices. Gain a level of **animal friendship** if you have fewer than three already, as well as the codeword *Callused*.

You cannot stay here forever and the road calls you. Besides, the hayloft and the company of the other keepers are far from comfortable. You announce your intention to leave, say a sad farewell - or arrivederci - to Jumbo, take your owed pay of **£3 10s** and climb aboard the velosteam once more. The elephant will always remember you: elephants never forget.

Leave the zoo...   **95**

❧ 184 ❧

The red-buttoned men are very wary of talking to you, but you find one more voluble than the others. If you are already a **Member of the Compact for Workers' Equality**, turn to **168** immediately. Otherwise, read on.

"So, you too recognise the cruelty of the landed gentry? How those with capital oppress and deceive the workers, who are the true wealth-creators? It sounds like the Compact is the place for you, friend. If you want to join, take this to the assembly hall in St Pancras. There's a talk there tonight."

He gives you **passdisc 32** - a small, circular piece of brass punched with a complex, machine-coded pattern.

Return to the market...   **126**

❧ 185 ❧

The teller agrees to help you (accepting any money you offered him), but when you return the next day, the Bank Guards have been warned about you. They firmly refuse you entry to the bank. To gain the information you need, you will have to try again - or come up with a different approach.

Leave the bank...   **139**

❧ 186 ❧

The Compton Arms is situated down a cobbled side-street behind an ornate chapel. Its low, dingy parlour is almost as smoggy as the street outside. It is frequented by drivers, locobus mechanics, foremen and shopmen. There is nothing in the way of food to be had here - only the beer itself, drunk and drunk in quantity.

Buy a drink...   (2s)   **161**
Leave the pub...   **151**

❧ 187 ❧
☐ ☐ ☐

If any of the boxes above are empty, tick one and read on. If they are all ticked, turn to **178** immediately.

You bring your gruesome bundle to the rear door of the Royal College of Surgeons. The porter there is anything but surprised. "Butcher's delivery?" he smiles. "Wait here."

A few minutes later, a gentleman surgeon appears. He asks you to unwrap the body and appraises it before making an offer. Roll a dice to see how much he will offer you:

Score 1-3   Poor condition: **£2 2s**...
Score 4-5   Worthy of dissection: **£6 6s**...
Score 6   A unique specimen! **Ten guineas in banknotes**...

Remove the **body** from your **possessions** if you choose to accept the offer.

Ride away...   **400**

❧ 188 ❧

Blackfriars Bridge spans the Thames in several graceful, iron-framed arches. As a construction, it could not be more different to the ancient London Bridge a few hundred yards downriver.

The surface is broad and smooth, inlaid with tracks for steam trams, and the traffic streams across in both directions. Down below, the filthy river swirls in eddies: it is slack tide.

Cross the bridge into Southwark...   **631**

❧ 189 ❧

The streets here are lined with tall mansions and lawyers' offices. Nonetheless, the streets are free and you could meet anyone at all here. Note passage **144** and if you are carrying a **deer carcass**, turn to **306** immediately. Otherwise, roll a dice to see what you encounter:

Score 1   A light-fingered lady...   **1466**
Score 2   Chimney sweeps...   **1458**
Score 3-4   Nothing of note...   **144**
Score 5   A robber...   **644**
Score 6   A worried nobleman...   **1358**

❧ 190 ☙

The publican of the Compton Arms is unsure about the brewery's offer. Make a RUTHLESSNESS roll of difficulty 12 or an INGENUITY roll of difficulty 14 to convince him.

Successful RUTHLESSNESS or INGENUITY roll **199**
Failed RUTHLESSNESS or INGENUITY roll!   **186**

❧ 191 ☙

The boys keep up an impressive turn of speed, leaping steam-carts, dashing over plank bridges and making their way towards the heart of the old city. Wrenching your machine this way and that, you just manage to keep up with them, and come to Upper Thames Street, where some of the boys disappear into the heights of an old warehouse and others scatter onto the silt and scum of the riverside.

Approach the boys...   **288**
Leave them be for now...   **273**

❧ 192 ☙

The one job that you try to avoid while working as an under-zookeeper is grooming the camels. They are cantankerous, vicious beasts that take a sadist's pleasure in kicking or biting their keepers. Unfortunately, you are caught out at last, and receive a sharp bite on your shoulder. Gain a **wound**.

Your overseer is not impressed: he blames you for treating the animal too roughly. You are dismissed with your pay (**£2 4s**) and a bottle of **soothing ointment**. If you now have **five wounds**, turn to **999** immediately.

Leave the zoo...   **95**

❧ 193 ☙

A giant enamel tooth hanging outside M.L. Frobisher, Dentist, identifies the place you are looking for. Inside you can buy some basic medical supplies, as well as having replacement teeth fitted, should you have any missing.

Tools	To buy	To sell
plaster of paris	4s	3s
jeweller's loupe (ING+1)	£4	£1 15s
Medical items	To buy	To sell
bandages	3s	-
soothing lotion	2s	1s
bottle of chloroform	£2	£1 5s
white pills (ING+2) ☐ ☐ ☐	£3	-
false teeth	£1 2s	10s
gold tooth	£2	10s

Medical treatment	To buy
Replace a **missing tooth**...	10s
Replace a **missing tooth** with a **gold tooth**...	10s and **gold tooth**
Treat a **toothache**...	£1 8s
Treat a **black eye**...	15s

Leave the dentist...   **144**

❧ 194 ☙

The officer receiving the parcel turns up his nose at the mud-spattered figure in front of him. If you have passed fewer than **30** passages since collecting the parcel at **1057**, turn to **655** immediately. Otherwise, the officer will take the **Bloomsbury package** (remove it from your **possessions**) and give you **10s** for the delivery.

Ride away...   **400**

❧ 195 ☙

What ardent pyromania has possessed you to return to the scene of your previous crime? Sure enough, you manage to set a fire, but the far warier staff of the still partially-rebuilt station are on high alert, desperate to find and extinguish any unauthorised flame. They chase you out of the station, forcing you to dash for your velosteam. You are now **Wanted by the Railway Guards**, if you were not already.

Ride away...   **50**

❧ 196 ❧
☐ ☐ ☐ ☐

If any of the boxes above are empty, tick one now. If they are all ticked, erase the ticks and turn to **214**. Remove the codeword *Crestfallen*. A Colonel of Signals chortles as you report how you impeded the Coal Board. "Very good," he smirks. "Those moles need to be kept in their place." Roll a dice to see how you are rewarded, adding 1 for each ticked box above.

Score 1-3   **£5** and a **silver ring**
Score 4-5   **£8**
Score 6+   **duelling pistols (ACC 7)**

Return to the compound...   **171**
Leave the Guild compound...   **400**

❧ 197 ❧

Maggie Laine turns out to be a woman of normal enough appearance, living in just another of the many terraced houses. "Whose is it?" she demands.

"That is unknown," you are forced to reply.

"Hmm. Could be carrying something infectious. My girls don't want to catch something themselves."

"Have you got a nurse for the child?"

She grimaces. "Could have. Depends." She explains the cost of nursing a baby to health and spells out your options.

Pay for the best treatment...
            (£10 10s or **ten guineas in banknotes) 205**
Pay for the essentials...   **(£3)**   **510**
Take the child to the Foundlings Home...   **526**

❧ 198 ❧

"Moisten your chaffer with that," says a sassy bar-girl. You are poured a long glass of Drover's Draught, a deeply caramel, bubbly beer with little head and a sharp, awakening finish to its flavour. Intended as a refresher for these hard-walking men and imported to the city from along the droving roads, it has become popular with some of the butchers too.

If you have the codeword *Additive*, turn to **711** immediately. Otherwise, note passage **150** and roll a dice to see what you hear:

Score 1-2   News from the North...   **559**
Score 3   Revival in Wales...   **573**
Score 4   Revolution in Belize...   **586**
Score 5-6   A Guild Rivalry...   **1013**

❧ 199 ❧

You manage to convince the landlord to sign the contract. He makes a scratchy signature on the bottom and heads away to check his barrels. Gain the codeword *Conglomerate*.

Leave the pub...   **151**

❧ 200 ❧
☐ ☐ ☐ ☐

If any of the boxes above are empty, put a tick in one and read on. If they are all ticked, turn to **581** immediately.

The boys are raring to go and pinch something. Roll two dice to see what your share is:

Score 2-5   A bad day: rain and a fight...
Score 6-7   a **silk scarf** and **15s**...
Score 8-9   **£3 4s** in coins...
Score 10-11 a pair of **golden candlesticks**...
Score 12   a **melon** and **£1 8s**...

Leave the boys...   **252**

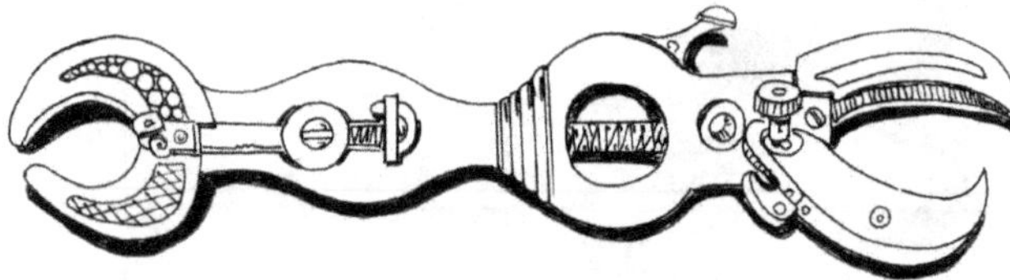

❧ 201 ❧

Ludgate Hill is busy with steam wagons laden with the evening's newspapers. You are at the boundary of the ancient City of London itself, and St Paul's Cathedral is only a few yards up the gently-sloping street. If you are **Wanted by the Constables**, turn to **289** immediately.

Visit Blucock Publishing House...   **1322**
Ride up to St Paul's Cathedral...   **215**
Steam north up Old Bailey...   **210**
Head towards Blackfriar's Bridge...   **252**
Steam west down Fleet Street...   **139**

❧ 202 ❧

Jerry and the Waterside Boys were certain that Lord Beaufort was away from his headquarters for a while: you are confident that you can slip into his suite without being caught. No-one else amongst his staff will dare enter, surely?

Climb down into his suite...   **211**

❧ 203 ❧

The guards let you into the prison, then take the **release order** out of your hands and arrest you. You have been recognised! Hoping to walk in and out of a prison with a record like yours was really not a prudent way to behave.

Turn to...   **13**

❧ 204 ❧

Since the flooding and destruction of the docks here at St Katharine's, the whole area has been redug and rebuilt. The collapsed warehouses are being used to flatten the ground and new buildings with iron frames are being erected as you watch. The River Guild must have lost a huge amount of money, but they are making the most of the opportunity to rebuild with even more capacity.

Ride towards the Tower...   **290**
Ride towards Shadwell...   **380**

❧ 205 ❧

The woman pockets the money greedily and takes the baby from your hands.
    "How can I come and check on the child?"
    Maggie looks confused. "Check on it?"
    "That's right. To see how healthy it is."
    "Come and ask here, I guess," she says.
    There has to be a better way than this.

Ride away...   **144**

❧ 206 ❧

☐

If the box above is empty, tick it and read on. If it is already ticked, turn to **269** immediately.

    You spend several hours in stud books and pedigree charts, identifying the strains of past race-winners and tracing their line down to modern horse racers. Of course, there are always new fillies on the field, new bloodlines coming in, but some knowledge of the horses of yester-year will help you place a good bet. Gain a level of **racing information**.

Return to the library...   **269**
Leave the Guild...   **210**

❧ 207 ❧

When you reach the surgery in Limehouse, Dr Smythe shakes his head. "Another abandoned infant? I wonder what we can do. Only true desperation provokes a mother to overcome her instinct and do this - desperation or the hardest of hearts, hardened by drink and need." He agrees to find the infant a wet nurse. "Can you provide any money," he asks, "To pay the woman who will feed him? She will need a good diet, and time, for the only women I trust have babes of their own and must be recompensed."

Make a donation... (**£2**)   **242**
Unable or unwilling to help...   **474**

❧ 208 ❧

You pause at the north end of London Bridge. A long queue of wagons and vehicles wait for the paddles to indicate the hourly change in direction for traffic. All manner of men and women wait about, chattering, puffing on pipes and cheroots, looking each other's machines over and watching their pressure gauges. A short distance away stand the sites of the old city: the Monument, towering over the houses, the fishmarket at Billingsgate, the Tower a short way to the east.

Gossip with the waiting drivers...
    (**improved burner**)   **247**
Head towards the Monument...   **264**
Ride west into Allhallows the Less...   **273**
Cross onto the bridge...   **1000**
Ride east towards the Tower...   **290**

❧ 209 ❧

Your damaged velosteam has begun to make a worrying grinding noise. You have left it unrepaired too long. You must pull over and repair at the roadside, or you will incur further damage. Make an ENGINEERING roll, adding 2 if you possess **welding tools**.

Score 10 or less   Gain another **damage point**...
Score 11 or more   Prevent further damage...

If your velosteam is now **beyond repair...** **1111**
Otherwise...   **noted passage**

❧ 210 ❧

You are in the north-eastern corner of the ancient City itself. The old towers and walls still run along the streets here, semi-ruined, built about with hovels and houses and chapels and minor telegraph posts. This is a corner of old overshadowed Guilds, of pensioners and holdings and shared livings, of medieval names and medieval customs. Looming over Old Bailey are the sooty stones of Newgate Prison: a dark place indeed.

Visit Brewers' Hall...	**228**
Ride up to Newgate Gaol...	**253**
Ride to Smithfield...	**126**
Steer down to Ludgate Hill...	**201**

✎ 211 ✎

You creep into the suite and carefully look around: there is no-one here. You have the opportunity to help yourself to a few choice possessions from his desk, including a **Constabulary logbook**, a **gold ring** and a **release letter**. There is also the terminal to his telegraph, if you know how to use it, giving you the opportunity to send a crucial message clearing your name. Otherwise, you can use the remainder of the night's darkness to retrace your steps.

Remove your **Wanted Statuses**...	
(**telegraphy**)	**257**
Leave Beaufort a taste of revenge...	
(**bottle of poison**)	**271**
Return the way you came...	**295**

✎ 212 ✎

Riding ahead of the speeding tram, you manage to get a heavy rope strung between two lamp-posts. It twists the posts out of the ground before snapping, but manages to absorb enough of the cabletram's momentum that it can be brought to a stop. "You probably saved our lives," says a grateful passenger. "Can we have a momentary collection for this brave individual?" They pass around a hat, and you are **£1 3s** richer for your good deed.

Ride on...	**noted passage**

✎ 213 ✎

You steam towards the ancient heart of the metropolis itself. Crows and ravens stand on the gables watching you ride. A Constabulary post stands on the corner of the Minories. If you are **Wanted by the Constables**, turn to **278** immediately. Otherwise, choose where to steer your velosteam.

To the Tower...	**290**
To the Monument...	**264**
To the Bank of England...	**244**

✎ 214 ✎

Your campaign of harassment and plunder against the Coal Board has earnt you some respect amongst the Telegraph Guild. They arrange for you to begin an apprenticeship in the dark arts of telegraphy: add **telegraphy** to your **Other Skills**. You have also changed: you may attempt to improve any one of your skills by 1 point. To succeed, roll two dice and score higher than your current score.

Return to the compound...	**171**

✎ 215 ✎
☐

If the box above is empty, tick it and turn to **230** immediately. If it is already ticked, read on.

You halt at the foot of the massive edifice of St Paul's Cathedral, on the busy thoroughfare known as Ludgate Hill that runs into the heart of London. Nearby shops specialise in ecclesiastical supplies and church clothing, and their keepers stand at the door like hungry birds, strangely at odds with the absent-minded air of worshippers, pilgrims and churchmen wandering across the street.

Food and Drink	To buy	To sell
bottle of wine	10s	8s
picnic hamper	£4	£2 10s
Clothing	To buy	To sell
dark cloak (RUTH+1)	£5	£3 5s
cassock	£5	£3 5s
Jewellery	To buy	To sell
silver ring	10s	-
gold ring	£3	-
gold necklace	£5	-
pectoral cross	£9	£6
Other items	To buy	To sell
flute	£1 5s	£1
miniature Bible	£1 10s	£1

Ride west down Ludgate Hill...	**201**
Cross Blackfriar's Bridge...	**188**
Head north towards Smithfield Market...	**210**
Head further into the city...	**244**

<h3 style="text-align:center">➻ 216 ❧</h3>

The Atmospheric Union's hatred of the Haulage Guild is well known: their rivalry over freight and carriage means that the Union have been known to reward, discreetly, those who have harassed Guild road trains.

In your case, it will depend who is on duty and how sympathetic they are to your report. Roll a dice to see how you are treated:

Score 1   Arrested! Turn to **13** immediately...
Score 2-3   Paid **£2 2s**...
Score 4-5   Given a **pocket watch** and **£1 1s**...
Score 6   Paid **ten guineas in banknotes**...

Remove the codeword *Cabal*.

Return to the station...   **58**

<h3 style="text-align:center">➻ 217 ❧</h3>

You come across some beggars wearing the remnants of Imperial uniform. "Take pity on old soldiers," they cry. "Suffered on the plains of Valencia, fighting King Charles's war." They will sell you a set of **false teeth** for **4s** if you like.

Ride on...   **noted passage**

<h3 style="text-align:center">➻ 218 ❧</h3>

Taking on a single constable should be within your ability: it will be another matter if he can manage to escape you and call for help.

Constable	Weapon: **sabre (PAR 3)**
Parry:	6
Nimbleness:	3
Toughness:	3

Victory!   **540**
Defeat!   **1500**

<h3 style="text-align:center">➻ 219 ❧</h3>

You quickly recall Princess Alexandrina's plight. Having recently lost her baby, surely a woman like her would be swift to do what she could for this helpless child. You wrap the infant inside your coat and tear off towards St James' Palace.

The sentries are reluctant to let you through the gateway until you reveal your **purple brooch**. You are taken to Princess Alexandrina's apartments and find her there, reading a book at the window. The marks of her recent sorrow are still etched on her face, but she looks up with a smile. "Ah, my protector returns," she says. "But what is so very urgent today?"

You unbutton your coat and reveal the crying child. "For one as small as this, your Highness, hunger and loneliness are urgent indeed." You explain how and where you found the baby, what is at stake for him, and how grieved you have been at the Princess's loss. "Perhaps you two can be each other's healing."

She takes the child from your arms. "A boy? You might have been my Leo's twin." She calls for a shawl and puts the babe to her breast, and immediately her face betrays the strength of his suck. First pain and then ecstasy flash over her visage and, for the first time since you have known her, she looks happy.

"Steam Highwayman, you have done a noble thing indeed," she says. "And a kind one. I may not have much influence in the family, and perhaps I will always be scorned by my uncle and unknown in the nation, but I know that in you I have a true subject. And in me you have a grateful friend." You are now the **Friend of Princess Alexandrina**. Remove the codeword *Childless*.

Leave the palace...   **721**

<h3 style="text-align:center">➻ 220 ❧</h3>
☐

If the box above is empty, tick it and read on. Otherwise, erase the tick and turn to **278** immediately.

You will not go long unnoticed here in the heart of the old city itself. Even in the fog, the smoke and the filth of the city, there is a semblance of order. The Constables patrol the streets regularly and it will not be long until they come across evidence of your criminality. You should get away directly.

Head for London Bridge...   **208**
Ride towards Clerkenwell...   **144**
Steam up Whitechapel Road...   **356**

<h3 style="text-align:center">➻ 221❧</h3>

A ragged horse chestnut tree drips into the puddles of St Margaret's Court. A few cramped tombs and faded gravestones stand alongside the church Shuttered windows keep the occupants and their occupations secret. A water pump stands in the yard: perhaps this would be a good place to see to your velosteam. Note this **passage number** if you wish to make any repairs.

Repair your velosteam...   **1300**
Return to the city...   **244**

✨ 222 ✨

The cabletram careers past, leaps out of its rails at a curve and crashes into a shopfront. There was nothing you could do.

Ride on...   **noted passage**

✨ 223 ✨

If you have the codeword *Capital*, turn to **246** immediately. The moustachioed owner of the Oyster Bar is drinking a mournful glass of gin in his empty restaurant. "No-one wants oysters," he says. "Not since the cholera scare. I can't sell 'em fur tuppennies."

"So oysters carry cholera?"

"What? No! Oysters is good clean food, prime nutrition fur nursin' mothers and wurkin' men, full of nutrients and the like. But some bleeder has been about, tellin' folks that the cholera down in Bermondsey was all doo to some bad oysters. And that's it fur my livelihood."

"Will nothing remedy your situation?"

"Why, if the King himself were seen eating oysters, I might be back in business. I can't see anything less 'avin an effect." Gain the codeword *Contactless*.

Owen Lightfoot will gladly sell you some of his stock, seeing as no-one else wants them.

	To buy	To sell
a dozen of oysters	6s	-
bottle of Tillson's Hot Sauce	3s	-

Head on your way...   **264**

✨ 224 ✨

Your years of hard work in the workshops and factories of the North saw you learn many techniques and create many intricate mechanisms. Everything you did, however, only served to profit your masters. They sold your inventions and they profited from your sweat. But that time has passed. You scrimped and saved and bought a badly-damaged wreck of a velosteam from a scrap merchant, and then rebuilt it to your own specifications. Complete, it became your ticket to freedom, and since then you have travelled the roads of the land working for your keep and riding on in search of adventure.

What will the city hold for you? Certainly, hundreds of thousands here are trapped, as you were, indentured for their labour, slaving away to make others rich. Will you be the one to cut their shackles or free their minds? Will you sell your designs to the Haulage or Telegraph Guild, finding the wealth and security you crave? Maybe you will even set up your own workshop and have your machinery displayed at the Great Exhibition in Hyde Park, earning recognition and fame? The factories and shipyards of Millwall are said to provide all the employment an engineer can need.

Your ability scores are:

RUTHLESSNESS	3
ENGINEERING	6
MOTORING	4
NIMBLENESS	2
INGENUITY	4
GALLANTRY	2

You have in your possession a **blunderpistol (ACC 6)**, a **sabre (PAR 3)**, and a **mask**. Your velosteam is customised with an **improved burner**.

Turn to...   **1200**

✨ 225 ✨

The Royal College of Arms is a dusty, poorly-maintained place. The historians and heralds care far more for their books, charts and trees than for anything as humdrum and worldly as keeping the building in repair. You manage to slip inside an unlocked door, and find yourself in a hallway piled high with leather-bound tomes.

"Yes?" asks a voice, "Are you the butcher's boy?"

"Who runs this place?" you ask, bluntly.

"Why, I do. Lord Lieutenant Andrew Carl Fitzgerald deBurnham Scott King of Arms."

"Then you're the one I'm looking for," you reply. "A lady sent me with a query about her grandfather."

Threaten him...		**1353**
Bribe him...	**(£20)**	**1371**

✨ 226 ✨

Lord Beaufort is holding a meeting in his suite. Despite the late hour, you can see several high-ranking officials and officers through the cigar-smoke. The few snatches of conversation you hear concern their attempts to locate the headquarters of the Compact for Workers' Equality. A woman called Mrs Petty is explaining her efforts to work with informers. Do you recognise her?

The meeting goes on and on. If you stay here too long, you will not have enough darkness to make it back over the rooftops: there is nothing you can do but retrace your route through the hatch and over the tiles.

However, you are part-way down a particularly steep mansard when another airship approaches. Its searchlights sweep around and a cry goes up over the throb of the steam engines: you have been spotted! You must get away as quickly as possible: make a NIMBLENESS roll of difficulty 12.

Successful NIMBLENESS roll!	**237**
Failed NIMBLENESS roll!	**256**

❧ 227 ❧

"Welcome to the Tankard! Come to drink, or to do business, or to make a bet?" You are welcomed by the massive figure of the Tankard's ex-pugilist landlord, Terence Loose. He has no need of bouncers or heavies to keep his customers in check: his own reputation is enough for them that know, and his fists for them that don't!

Buy a drink...	**(2s)**	**245**
Gamble with the other customers...		**270**
Leave the pub...		**264**

❧ 228 ❧

If you are the **Friend of Richard Pierce**, turn to **238** immediately.

The Brewers' Hall is the home of the Worshipful Company of Brewers, one of the ancient City Guilds founded way back in medieval times. You join a small crowd who have gathered for a tour and follow a pimpled young man who effuses about the building, the Guild and the antiquated traditions they keep. "Every month, three quarts of stout are poured onto the foundations as rent to the building itself. The roof there is made of eighty-five oak trees. But we also have some of the most up-to-date methods in the City. We have a powerful calculation engine which handles much of our information and our library. Right now, it is calculating the results of our recent Chairman election."

He takes you round to see the machine in its side-room. The keeper is oiling its parts assiduously.

⊕ Return at night to break in...	**294**
Leave the hall...	**210**

❧ 229 ❧

You reach the cover of the copse and douse your velosteam's burner by withdrawing the Gruber valve. With a hiss, the mighty machine quietens, and you pull down a fir branch, heavy with needles, to cover you both.

In the falling darkness, the Constables miss your trail and head on up the road, believing you have struck out for the west. You leave your hiding place at first light.

Leave the little wood...	**1022**

❧ 230 ❧

No-one is about. The breath of your mighty machine trails over the cobbles and swirls into the morning mist.

You brake to a gentle stop beneath the towering facade of Wren's masterpiece. An old woman in rags shakes herself awake and gawps up at you from her step. "Lord 'elp us all! Spare tuppence to feed these birds, yer 'onour?"

"Take this for the birds, and this for yourself." **(1s)**	**260**
"What will we get then? Fat birds!"	**215**

❧ 231 ❧

"What, the jewel-thieving lady out of Mayfair?" The boys set off into the city. If you have the codeword *Crisp* or are the **Friend of Lady Diana**, turn to **1419** immediately. Otherwise, read on.

"She's at home," says Jerry. "Derwent Mansion in Mayfair. Alf climbed up onto her balustrade and watched her at her dressing table, the cheeky beggar."

Return to the hideout..	**581**
Leave the boys...	**252**

❧ 232 ❧

Ruben Tutling is led up from the condemned cells in chains. He looks just like his brother - apart from his handsome, unbroken nose and his massive physique. He is clearly a dangerously powerful man. You take a moment to show him **Fat Billy's thumbprint** while pretending to inspect his manacles, which elicits a massive wink and a most co-operative manner.

"So I'm off to see Lord Beaufort, am I?" asks the murderer. "Sounds fine to me. I've been hoping someone important would pay some attention to my case."

"This man is dangerous," says the Warden. "I would be happier if you took some of my men as an escort."

"That won't be necessary," you reply. "Even this animal will respond to reason if his life depends upon it." You address Ruben. "Convict, Lord Beaufort has the power to grant a full pardon you if co-operate and name all of your accomplices."

"Certainly," begins Ruben. "I can start right now. There's Chilly William up at the Fox, to begin with..."

A blow to the head quietens him. He is plainly far too simple to trust with any sort of subterfuge. You haul on his chain instead. "Save your prattle for Lord Beaufort," you reply. He looks utterly confused, but you flash the little blue thumbprint again and drag him out into the street towards your velosteam.

Ruben doesn't fully understand, but you pause your journey part-way across town and remove the manacles and chains. Then you ride on, through the fog, to meet up with Flat Billy.

Ride on to Whitechapel...　　　462

ଓ 233 ଔ

One place will certainly take the baby in, care for her and find her a nurse - you have made sure of that. You steam for Bow as quickly as ever you can and bring your burden to the Matron of High Way House. She is a kindly woman, despite the connotations of her title, and she quickly takes the child away to be fed and properly clothed. Gain a **solidarity point**.

Ride away...　　　471

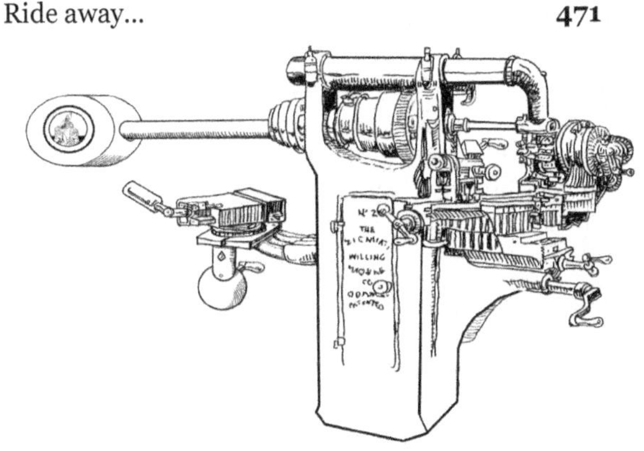

ଓ 234 ଔ

Your money buys you passage downriver to London aboard a dusty waste-barge. The voyage is slow, and you have time to pick up plenty of information, such as the location of a reliable dentist in Clerkenwell, the state of rivalry between the Haulage Guild and the Imperial Western Railway, the lawlessness of Whitechapel Market and the difficulty of finding honest work that isn't filthy or dangerous.

Eventually, you are put ashore at Battersea Bridge, in the Southwest of the city.

Turn to...　　　1132

ଓ 235 ଔ

The boys take the coins and tear off to handle the business. You settle down amongst their rags and broken furniture with some of the youngest and entertain them with tales of your adventures.

Early in the misty morning, the gang reassembles. Aldwin, a gawky young burglar, proudly carries **Prishaw's sword**, which he hands straight to you. There follows a celebratory breakfast with sausages and mustard, and the boys settle down to sleep through the day as you head out into the city.

Leave the hideout...　　　252

ଓ 236 ଔ

A glimmer of recognition appears in the Constable's eyes. He dashes for an alarm post, intending to set the bell ringing in its tall frame. How will you respond?

Mount your velosteam and ride for it...　　　402
Attack him...　　　218

ଓ 237 ଔ

There are men on the jetty and the tide has come in, so you look for another way out. You swing down your **rope** to the ground, but don't have time to untie it: remove it from your **possessions**.

The street is slick with fog and dew, but you race across to where your velosteam is hidden and jump aboard. From here, you will be pursued through the city: you must choose your route very carefully! Which way will you steer?

North...　　　841
South...　　　858
West...　　　882

ଓ 238 ଔ

Richard Pierce greets you as you walk in. "Welcome," he says. "I suppose you're practically an associate member now. The Guild is at your disposal." Note **passage 238**.

Ask to use the computational engine...　　　255
Read in the library...　　　269
Leave the building...　　　210

❧ 239 ❧

☐ ☐ ☐ ☐

If any of the boxes above are empty, tick one now. If they are all ticked, erase the marks and turn to **288**.

The thick, silty mud captures all manner of flotsam and jetsam. There are families who depend on their children bringing home scavenged coal, rope or bone. These are the mudlarks. Sometimes one finds something precious and a fight breaks out. To try your luck, roll a dice, adding 1 if you possess a **net**.

Score 1-3   Nothing of value
Score 4-5   a **constable's whistle**
Score 6-7   a **gold tooth**

Climb the stairs to the street...   **273**

❧ 240 ❧

Once inside the silent building, you are free to look around and take what you can. A **pair of candlesticks** is ready for lifting. In a display case hangs a fine **gold necklace**. In its side room the computational engine stands quiet and ready. Note passage **210** before making a choice.

Take a look at the computational engine...   **255**
Leave the building...   **210**

❧ 241 ❧

Note passage number **400**. You will have to wait a long time to speak to someone here - or push your way to the front of a queue - and the officers will only permit you to speak to someone important if they genuinely believe you have something they want.

Offer information about the Coal Board...
    (**coal board accounts**)   **291**
Offer information about the Haulage Guild...
    (*Chesterfield*)   **258**
Offer to design machinery for the guild...
    (**improved burner**)   **1325**
Leave the office...   **400**

❧ 242 ❧

Smythe takes the money gladly. "Good. This child will have a better chance of surviving. Though it will still be battling the odds, poor mite." He raises the child's eyelid and peers at the baby's sclera. "Hmmmm. We will see." Gain the codeword *Compassionate*.

Ride away...   **474**

❧ 243 ❧

A stinging pain in your open wound forces you to stop for a while in Old St Pancras churchyard. While washing in a municipal fountain, you find a silver tin lying on the rim. Opening it, you find some **pink pills (NIM+2)** ☐ ☐ ☐ .

Continue on your way...   **107**

❧ 244 ❧

Now you are in the heart of the ancient City of London. Gents in bowlers steam past on monocycles, rushing between important meetings. The Bank of England, protected by its own uniformed guards, looms over the junction at Threadneedle Street and Cornhill. Standing opposite is the massive edifice of the Exchange, where investors and speculators deal in shares, futures and bonds, trading across the world from their position at the centre of a net of telegraphy.

Two B-Class towers stand atop their respective buildings, flashing and flickering constantly by day and night. St Margaret's Court is one of the many courts and yards hidden behind the cramped, ancient banks, churches and terraces crammed together here.

Enter St Margaret's Court...   **221**
Enter the Exchange...   **403**
Head towards the Monument...   **264**
Steam east into Whitechapel...   **356**
Take the road west to St Paul's...   **215**
Ride towards the Tower of London...   **290**

❧ 245 ❧

You are poured a finely balanced medium bitter, clear and bright copper in colour, but creamy to the palate, without a strong hop flavour, but cleanly malty from fore to after-taste. It is called Caughton's Copper Number 4.

If you have the **Andrea Rathbone's Letter**, turn to **285** immediately. Otherwise, note passage **227** and roll a dice to see what rumour floats your way:

Score 1   A Guild rivalry...   **1013**
Score 2   Flat Billy...   **873**
Score 3   Barricades and blunderbusses...   **150**
Score 4   An ambitious brewery...   **1196**
Score 5   Oyster prices...   **396**
Score 6   An investment opportunity...   **556**

✎ 246 ✎

Since the King's public repudiation of the oyster scare, business has returned to Lightfoot's. The place is filled with a lunchtime crowd of ladies, painters, thinkers and society folk. Owen Lightfoot welcomes you with a wave and bustles over. "Seems that the King likes oysters after all," he says. "Came just in the nick of time, too. I thought we was goin' under."

	To buy	To sell
a dozen of oysters	8s	-
bottle of Tillson's Hot Sauce	6s	-

Leave the restaurant... **264**

✎ 247 ✎

"That's an interesting amendment there," says a woman in the brown livery of Norton Bros. "Never seen a burner quite like that on a Ferguson. My mate used to ride one of these. Powerful, isn't it?" Note passage **208** and roll a dice to see what you hear among the drivers and engineers.

Score 1-2	The Dover Road...	**309**
Score 3-4	Up to Essex...	**321**
Score 5-6	Bishop's Wood...	**333**

✎ 248 ✎

"I see," says the pale old man with the quivering hands. "You were simply toying with me." How has he recognised you? "Well now you must take by force what you demand." You may take **£4 5s**, a **Coal Board accountbook** and a **gold ring**. Remove the codeword *Anhedonic* and gain *Crestfallen*. You will also now be **Wanted by the Coal Board**.

Ride away... **noted passage**

✎ 249 ✎

The Warden is not impressed. Something has caused him to smell a rat. He orders his guards into the room and they remove your **weapons**, **Fat Billy's thumbprint** and the **release order**. Then you are marched into another room of the tower.

Turn to... **13**

✎ 250 ✎

If you already have a **pet raven**, turn to **276** immediately. Otherwise, read on. The ravens of the Tower of London are famously intelligent. Using your knowledge of bird calls, you gain the attention of one and it flaps over to investigate. To gain the bird's trust, make an INGENUITY roll of difficulty 16, adding 1 for each level of **animal friendship** you possess and 2 if you have a **rabbit**.

Successful INGENUITY roll!	**292**
Failed INGENUITY roll!	**275**

✎ 251 ✎

"Made yourself a tidy little profit there?" asks a slimy character leaning against the wall beside your velosteam. "Flat Billy will be 'appy to take his cut."

"Of course."(**15s**)	**266**
"I haven't sold anything here, creep."	**280**

✎ 252 ✎

Upper Thames Street runs between Blackfriars Bridge and London Bridge. Quays and wharves abut its southern side, and here and there stairs of weedy steps cut between the tall warehouses down to the silt of the riverside. An ivy-decked building stands grandly half-way along the street: the Royal College of Arms - the vault of many an nobleman's lineage. A sidestreet cuts past it towards the dome of St Paul's, a short way north from here.

Visit the Royal College of Arms... (*Canvey*)	**225**
Take a look at St Paul's Cathedral...	**215**
Head to Blackfriars Bridge...	**188**
Ride towards London Bridge...	**208**
Steer to Allhallows Wharf...	**273**

✎ 253 ✎

If you have **Flat Billy's thumbprint**, turn to **272** immediately. Otherwise, read on.

The walls of Newgate prison loom through the fog, towering over the hot-potato woman at her stall, over the panting locobus with its flickering advertisement mosaic, over the line of patient sons, daughters, wives and mistresses awaiting their allotted times with their imprisoned menfolk. Inside are murderers and debtors, fraudsters and vagrants, impersonators, forgers, burglars and thugs. Among them some must be innocent - the laws of statistics demand it - but the laws of the land forbid any judge consider it. Once within Newgate, a debt must be paid, with coin, years or strong hemp rope.

Leave the prison for now... **210**

❧ 254 ❧

A Constable with his chargebook open is talking to a protesting costermonger. "You can see the bleedin' licence on me barrer right 'ere," says the street vendor. "Valimated this last January!"

The Constable tugs at the brass licence disc, tearing it from its linen strap and dropping it into the gutter. "This one? Should be kept clean, legible and prominently displayed at all times."

"It were until your dirty 'ands were laid upon it!"

"Now, now," says the constable. "Do you want me to write you up for abusing 'is Imperial Majesty's authorised lawkeepers as well? You owe two pound, right now."

Offer to pay the fine...	(£2)	**154**
Teach the constable a lesson...		**218**
Ignore the abuse of power...		**noted passage**

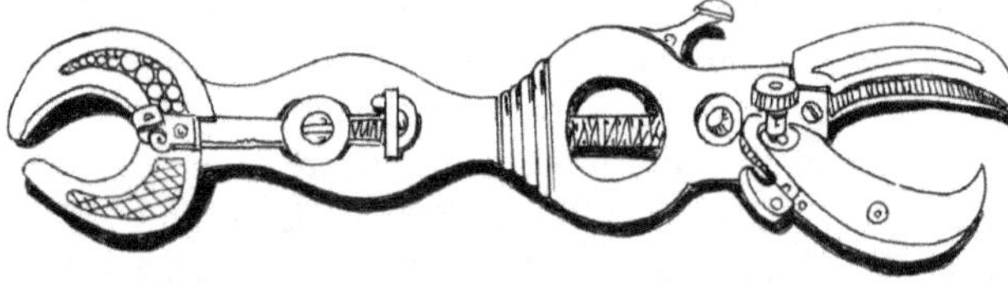

❧ 255 ❧

Here in the side room, the massive brass and steel computational engine squats, ready to receive instructions. Its hopper is unlocked, the wooden veneer brightly polished There is also a punchcard machine here, allowing you to convert your own sets of **blank punchcards** into working programs - if you possess the secret. Knowledge like that is not easy to come by, even in this city.

Create some **punchcards**...	
(**blank punchcards**)	**348**
Leave the engine...	**noted passage**

❧ 256 ❧

A misjudged foothold sends you crashing to the cobbles. There is a nasty crack as you land: gain a **wound** and a **sore back (NIM-2)**. If you now have **five wounds**, the Constables will have to pick you up off the street: turn to **113**. Otherwise, you can hobble to your velosteam and climb aboard. It is certainly time to put some distance between you and your pursuers. Which way will you steer?

North...	**841**
South...	**858**
West...	**882**

❧ 257 ❧

A coded message from Lord Beaufort's own telegraph will be sure to exonerate you. Who would dare go against the Chief Constable's direct orders?

You sit at the terminal and begin to laboriously program out a message, using scraps of commands and instructions lying about on the desk as templates. Then you code the command into the machine, and all those hours of work learning the skill of telegraphy have come in useful at last.

You pull the initialisation lever and the telegraph begins to flicker its message. Remove any **Wanted Statuses** on your **Adventure Sheet**.

What now?

Leave Beaufort a taste of revenge...	
(**bottle of poison**)	**271**
Return the way you came...	**295**

❧ 258 ❧

You find a Major of Signals and tell him what you have heard about the Chesterfield Tunnel. He grins slowly, then leaves the room for a short time. When he returns, he hands you a **Letter of Introduction** and shakes your hand. "The Telegraph Guild are grateful," he says. "Head down to our Greenwich depot and our mechanics might be able to help you with your machine." Remove the codeword *Chesterfield* and gain the codeword *Clockwork*.

Leave the compound...	**noted passage**

❧ 259 ❧

This patch has been completely swept clean by the Waterside Boys. You won't find anything of value here - unless you enjoy the shimmering colours of the silt, the flints and half-bricks, the rust and weed and smoothed-out glass, the smell of rot and river, the gleaming piles and the quiet.

Return to the wharf...	**273**

❧ 260 ❧

As soon as you scatter the crumbs, a flock of starlings descends and begins to peck them up out of the crevices between the paving slabs. The old woman shakes her head in glee. Several of the birds hop onto your head, shoulders and outstretched arms. "They ain't scared o'you!" she says. Gain a level of **animal friendship**.

Leave the birds...	**215**

✎ 261 ✎

A familiar silver steam car approaches: it is Lord Dashwood, driving the Wagtail. He catches sight of you, pulls over and leaps out. "My friend! How very good to see you!" He postpones his business while he drags you to a nearby pub and orders a slap-up meal.

"I had no idea you were in town. Little enough to race up here, eh? Traffic, smog and delay on every side. I tell you, I keep away from the city as far as I am able."

For old times' sake, he writes you a **Letter of Introduction**. "This should get you in with some friends of mine in Mayfair," he says. "Picky people. Or perhaps you could go and see my aunt, the Baroness Dimlight, who lives at Canonbury Tower?"

Eventually, the table is empty and Dashwood is forced to be about his business. "Dashed fine to see you," he says, shaking your hand. "Dashed fine."

Ride on...   **noted passage**

✎ 262 ✎

The boys stand around in awe of the beautiful pie. "Is it... for us?" asks Runt.

They eat it in reverent silence, passing around the greaseproof paper and tracking every dropped crumb. They finish by sniffing their fingers and inhaling the delicious scent. Remove it from your **possessions**.

Jerry is very grateful. "You really care about us, doncha? Well, anyfink we can do for you, we will. Just let us know, right?" You are now the **Friend of the Waterside Boys**.

Turn to...   **252**

✎ 263 ✎

"'Ere! What are you doin' on my roof?" A voice cries out as you work around a dormer window towards the gables of Brewers' Hall. You have been spotted and have no option but to scramble down to the ground and tear back to your velosteam. Unfortunately, once in the saddle, you find that you are being pursued! You must weave your way through the City to escape!

Make a break for it...   **278**

✎ 264 ✎

The Monument is a single Doric column of Portland stone topped with a flaming golden urn. It was built to remember the Great Fire, some two hundred years ago, and stands around two-hundred feet high. Many days its summit is hidden in the London fog. A woman lives in the base and is licensed to charge a shilling to let visitors climb to the top.

Just across the street stands the Tankard: a pub known for its ex-prize-fighter landlord, Terence Loose. The benches outside are plain but clean, the glass in the windows bright and clear. A brass tankard stands above the door. On the opposite side of the street are the striped windowshades of Lightfoot's Oyster Bar, equally as smart and emanating a salty, maritime smell.

Climb the monument... (**1s**)   **281**
Enter the Tankard...   **227**
Investigate Lightfoot's Oyster Bar...   **223**
Towards the Bank of England...   **244**
Towards London Bridge...   **208**

✎ 265 ✎

You quickly overtake the stolen carriage, leap from your saddle and grapple with the thief. You knock him out, haul on the brakes and jump down. "Thank you," puffs the owner. "Thank you. Here, take these." He presses some **goggles (MOT+1)** into your hands in gratitude.

Ride on...   **noted passage**

✎ 266 ✎

The slimy fellow is Canter Dorkins, one of Flat Billy's lieutenants. He pockets the coins and gives you a foul-toothed grin. "Glad to see you know which side yer bread's buttered."

Return to the streets of Whitechapel...   **356**

✎ 267 ✎

Your ride from the Tower into the old city takes you through the busiest streets of London. You are forced to weave between horse-carts, steam-gurneys and carriages, manouevring around hastily-trestled-off trenches for pipes, through puddles and slicks of manure and over bumpy cobbles. There is a Constabulary post here, manned by sharp-eyed city Constables. With their mechanically-augmented oculars and their printofit wallets, they will be certain to identify any approaching criminal. If you are **Wanted by the Constables**, turn to **278** immediately.

Ride towards the Monument...   **264**
Head for the Bank of England...   **244**
Steer for London Bridge...   **208**

❧ 268 ❧

There is no glamour to the work of sweeping chimneys. It is long, filthy work. You are paid **10s** for sweeping the flues, but you also pick up a nasty **burn (NIM-1)** from a still-hot flue.

Working in the house, you hear about the owner - a lady called Diana Derwent who holds the title Lady Serene. She is a traveller, a socialite and a lover of jewels.

Leave the house...   **750**

❧ 269 ❧

The library is very well-stocked, not just regarding the brewing of alcohol and the growing of hops, barley and brewer's barm, but also on many matters regarding modern technology. Then there are the papers, which will tell you all you wish to know about current affairs.

Read about computational engines...   **1291**
Read about horse breeding...   **206**
Leave the Guildhall...   **210**

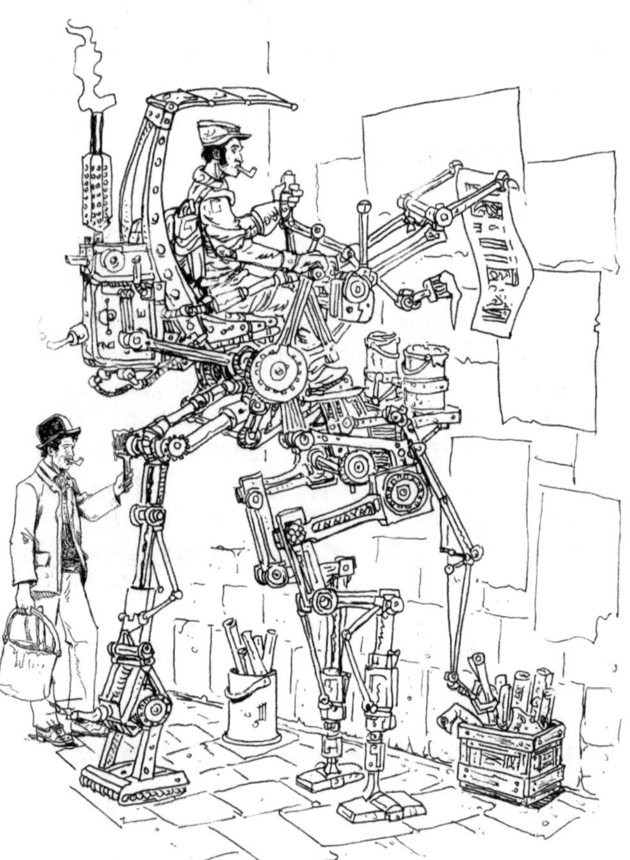

❧ 270 ❧

If you want to gamble on the sporting news with the clientele, you can be sure to find someone here to wager with. Decide your stake (between **5s** and **£5**) and roll a dice, adding 1 for each level of **racing information** that you possess.

Score 1-2   Lose all your stake...
Score 3   Lose half your stake (rounded up)...
Score 4   No gain or loss...
Score 5   Gain half your stake (rounded up)...
Score 6+   Double your stake...

Return to the parlour...   **227**
Leave the Tankard...   **264**

❧ 271 ❧

There is a glass tankard sitting on Lord Beaufort's desk. You smear a little of the deadly poison onto the base of the glass. It may not be the most honourable way of dealing with the commander of the Constables, but he has proven himself to be far from honourable in his manners and dealings. Gain the codeword *Currently*.

Send a message...
  (**Telegraphy**)   **257**
Return the way you came...   **295**

❧ 272 ❧

After asking around, you discover that Ruben Tutling is being held in the condemned cells under a sentence of death. Apparently he broke the necks of two street girls with his bare hands.

It won't be easy to get access to him. Perhaps with a Bishop's **cassock**, you could impersonate a priest come to shrive him, had you sufficient confidence in your GALLANTRY. Otherwise, if you could get hold of a **release order** signed by Lord Beaufort, the Chief Constable, you might be able to spring Ruben more subtly. A **Constables' logbook**, a **skeleton key** and tools for opening doors would be useful in either case.

Impersonate a priest... (**cassock**)   **293**
Use Beaufort's authority... (**release order**) **305**
Take time to prepare your plans...   **210**

❧ 273 ❧

You have come to Allhallows Wharf on the north bank of the Thames. A series of alleys run past warehouses and manufactories to Upper Thames Street and the narrow, overshadowed lane called Waterside runs parallel to the river. Stairs dripping with weed step down to the silt and mud, where you can see children mudlarking for oddments.

Head out mud-larking on the flat...   **239**
Ride towards the north end of London Bridge... **208**
Steam onto Upper Thames Street...   **252**

❧ 274 ☙

A cabletram full of terrified passengers comes tearing down the street in the wrong direction. "Cable's gorn!" yells the brakeman, heaving fruitlessly against the brake lever. If you have a **grappling iron**, turn to **212** immediately. Otherwise, make an ENGINEERING roll of difficulty 13 if you want to try to stop the runaway tram.

Successful ENGINEERING roll!   **212**
Failed ENGINEERING roll or did not attempt... **222**

❧ 275 ☙

The Tower itself stands before you. Once the palace and keep of Kings, it is still an intimidating emblem of the Crown and a seat of power. The wide moat and curtain walls surround the ancient White Tower, where traitors and the most feared criminals are imprisoned. In the moat prowl lions, kept since ages past as a living deterrent to escapers and attackers alike. If you have **Marshal's letter**, turn to **1230** immediately.

Call a raven... (**animal friendship**)   **250**
Leave the tower...   **290**

❧ 276 ☙

Your raven hops up onto your shoulder and caws in recognition at its friends. Then it takes off with a heavy beat of its wings and disappears towards the tower. Roll a dice to see how it returns.

Score 1-2   Pursued by Constables: turn to **278**.
Score 3-4   Carrying a **Tower Key**...
Score 5-6   Carrying a **pork pie**...

Turn to...   **290**

❧ 277 ☙

"'Oo are youse anyway," asks a spotty little runt. "The Steam 'ighwayman or somefink?"

"Garn," says another. "'E ain't real. 'E's made up, 'e is."

"The Steam Highwayman is real," you reply. "And

stands before you."

The boys are very impressed. They come to finger your clothes, to feel for themselves. The youngest simply stands there speechless.

"We're the Waterside Boys," says their leader in the hat. "And on behalf of all of us, I would like to welcome you to London and officially extend you our hand of friendship. Please, come and dine."

The boys lead you under jetties and up forgotten stairs to a warehouse attic . The gathered sacking and occasional stolen horse-blanket tell you that they have made this their home. They feed you with some half-burnt sausages and iced buns. Jerry, the leader, decides that this is a special enough occasion for a celebratory drink and sends one of the youngsters to whip a bottle of beer to share together. He returns with a delightful Suffolk Stout, and drinks half from the bottle alongside you. He is twelve and the leader, lawyer and father of the group.

"What would be nice right now," says Jerry, "Is a nice pork pie."

"Oooh," sigh the hungry children.
"Fink of that pastry," says one.
"The jelly!"

Unwrap a **pork pie**...   **262**
Bid them farewell...   **298**

❧ 278 ☙

The city is a busy place, night or day, and you must ride quickly or risk capture by the dreaded Constables.

Hide in Spitalfields Market...   **991**
Head for Islington...   **868**
Make for Smithfield...   **897**
Head for the docks...   **1006**

❧ 279 ☙

A black steam carriage approaches. Something about it is familiar... It is indeed the carriage of the blind man you met, long ago, in the woods north of Marlow. It pulls to a halt near where you are waiting.

Rob him...   **248**
Let him go...   **538**

❧ 280 ☙

The ruffian changes his manner immediately. "Don't know 'oo you might fink you are, matey," he says, flicking open a knife, "But round 'ere, it pays to keep Flat Billy happy." Suddenly you realise that there are others around you - at least two of them - and that you have found yourself outnumbered and surrounded. This will be a very unfair fight: for each attack you make, your opponents will manage to make two consecutive attacks.

Flat Billy's Men	Weapons: **knives (PAR 1)**
Parry:	8
Nimbleness:	7
Toughness:	6

Victory!	**302**
Defeat!	**999**

ᔧ 281 ᔬ

From atop the Monument you can peer over the roofs and chimney-tops of smoky London town. Each telegraph tower makes a prominent dent in the skyline and over your head throb dozens of airships and skycraft. If you have a **black oilcloth packet**, turn to **708**. Otherwise, you must be on your way.

Descend the stairs...	**264**

ᔧ 282 ᔬ

A wheeled booth and a woman with an eyepatch stand beside the road. She catches sight of you and calls out: "The rider on the steel steed! The time has come! Pray enter my booth and I will tell you all that will befall thee."

Stop and have your fortune told... (2s)	**297**
Ride on...	**noted passage**

ᔧ 283 ᔬ

An angry crowd are marching along the road, waving placards and protesting about high rents and absentee landlords. If you are a **Member of the Compact for Workers' Equality**, you can address them and convince them to support the cause, gaining the codeword *Clavicle*. Otherwise, you simply ride on by.

Turn to...	**noted passage**

ᔧ 284 ᔬ
☐

If the box above is empty, tick it and turn to **537** immediately. If it is already ticked, simply read on.

A row of Imperial velosteams stand in the street beside the iron gates to Somerset House. Constables mill around, escorting prison-wagons through the arches and attending to their machines. What could possess a vagabond and criminal such as yourself to seek entry here?

Offer the Constables information...	**554**
Attempt to break into Lord Beaufort's suite (NIMBLENESS 6 or more)...	**112**
Return to the Strand...	**139**

ᔧ 285 ᔬ

Armed with **Andrea Rathbone's letter**, you go looking for a banker called Ennis. Having read the short note over and over since you received it from the priest in Ibstone, you can tell that the girl's existence as a scullery maid was miserable in the extreme. Despite trying to put a brave face on her experiences, the limits of her expectations and her acceptance of harsh treatment show how very hard her life must be. There are also hints of something worse: of the unwelcome attentions of male staff and members of the household. If you can find her, perhaps there will be some respite for her.

The drinkers in the Tankard know Ennis well. Under the pretence of having an important and profitable message for him, you are directed to tall house in Mayfair where he resides.

Knock at the front door...	**304**
Knock at the tradesman's entrance...	**324**

ᔧ 286 ᔬ

Flat Billy sinks to the ground. His remaining lieutenants will surely brawl among themselves for control of his territory, probably causing his empire to disintegrate. You can take **twenty guineas in banknotes**, a **silk scarf** and a **bottle of gin**. Gain the codeword *Churl*, three **solidarity points** and add **Defeated Flat Billy** to your Great Deeds!

Make a swift retreat...	**377**

❧ 287 ❧

How long have you been carrying that fish around for? Far too long, you realise, when you give it a sniff. Discard the **large pike** immediately.

Turn to...   **noted passage**

❧ 288 ❧
☐

If the box above is empty, put a tick in it and read on. If it is already ticked, turn to **259** immediately.

"What you doin' ere, then?" calls a truculent youngster. He is barefoot but sporting a battered old top hat. Behind him, a gang of mudlarks and ragamuffins are fingering stones picked from the river. "This is our patch!" If your GALLANTRY score is 5 or less, the boys will give you a chance to talk, and you should turn to **277** immediately. Otherwise, they will take you for a slumming toff and pelt you with stones. Roll a dice to see how badly they hurt you:

Score 1   Gain a **wound**
Score 2-3   Lose a **tooth (GAL-1)**
Score 4   You gain a **stiff back (NIM-2)**
Score 5-6   Just some bruises

If you now have **five wounds**, turn to **999** immediately. Otherwise you can choose how to proceed.

Talk to the boys...   277
Leave the mudflats...   273

❧ 289 ❧

There is a checkpoint here at the entrance to the old City, manned by several armed Constables. They have seen your approach and identified you from the printofit description circulated to all their posts. Glancing about, you realise that officers have already begun to take up position on each of the surrounding streets, several astride their Imperial model velosteams. At least in such a populated area, they will be slow to use their firearms, surely!

You must make your getaway as swiftly and discreetly as possible. What direction will you take?

North...   841
South...   858
West...   882

❧ 290 ❧

You pause at Tower Hill, where an empty gibbet seems to beckon troublemakers like yourself. The open ground here has long been used for assemblies and gatherings, executions and rabble-rousing speeches. For now, it is empty. A short distance to the east are the buildings of St Katharine's Docks, walled off from the itchy fingers of the populace and piled high with goods from around the world.

Approach the Tower...   275
Steam west onto Great Tower Street...   267
Ride up the Minories to Whitechapel...   356
Head for London Bridge...   208
Cross over to St Katharine's Docks...   341

❧ 291 ❧

When you are eventually shown to one of the higher-ranking officers and show him the accounts, you are ushered to the commander of the station. He takes the book from you (remove it from your **Adventure Sheet**) and authorises a payment of **ten guineas (£10 10s)**. You have also found the favour and gratitude of the Guild and are told about the workshop in Greenwich where you can access their engineering expertise. Gain the codeword *Clockwork* if you do not already possess it.

Leave the compound...   **noted passage**

❧ 292 ❧
☐ ☐

If either of the boxes above are empty, tick one and read on. If they are both ticked, turn to **326** immediately.

The raven is flattered with your attention. She flies off to bring you a gift from the tower. Roll a dice to see what she returns with:

Score 1   An **emerald**...
Score 2-5   A horse-chestnut...
Score 6   A guinea **(£1 1s)**...

Leave the ravens...   275

❧ 293 ❧

Dressed in your robes, you step through the postern of Newgate gaol and smooth-talk your way to the Warden's suite. He demands to know your business and you explain that you have come on a mission of mercy, to talk to the prisoner Ruben Tutling and to try to save his soul from certain damnation. The Warden is unsure whether to trust you: make an GALLANTRY roll of difficulty 13, adding 1 if you possess a **pectoral cross** and 2 if you have a **Bible** of any kind.

Successful GALLANTRY roll!   **311**
Failed GALLANTRY roll!   **327**

❧ 294 ❦

Leaving your velosteam hidden under some sacking in an alleyway off St Bartholemew's Court, you head over to the Brewers' Hall for a little burglary. Entry from the roof of a neighbouring house will probably be easiest, but you will have to tread quietly. Make a NIMBLENESS roll of difficulty 13, adding 1 if you possess a **grappling iron**, 1 for a **crowbar** and 1 more if you have some **lockpicks**.

Successful NIMBLENESS roll!   **240**
Failed NIMBLENESS roll!   **263**

❧ 295 ❦

A few moments spent wiping down surfaces will prevent anyone from picking up your fingerprints, in case you give any other reasons to suspect a forced entry. Then you return to the attic, the roof and eventually, the street and your hidden velosteam. The dawn light is a dirty pink over the uneven roofline of London Bridge and a distant steamship hoots.

Start your velosteam...   **139**

❧ 296 ❦

The first Aramanth punchcards are quickly read and the machine is prepared for use. What do you want it to do?

Fix the Brewer's election for Pierce... (*Corrupt*) **515**
Create some **calculated patterns**...   **1170**
Solve the Leviathan's engine
     problems... (*Cabin*)   **839**
Hack into Coulter's Bank... (*Commission*)   **532**
Nothing for now...   **noted passage**

❧ 297 ❦

If you have a **rabbit's foot charm**, turn to **314** immediately. The woman takes your palm and peers into it. "Oh, violence in the past and violence in the future. I sense much suffering in these hands. Your line of life... is short. Your line of family..." She gulps. "But the line of wealth..."

"Yes?"
"Is indistinct. You are an unlucky soul, it seems."
"Oh dear."
"You are right to be worried. But I can sell you a charm. It will help you in situations where you must depend on chance." If you wish to buy the **rabbit's foot charm**, it will cost you **4s**.

Leave the fortune teller...   **noted passage**

❧ 298 ❦

"If you want to come find us again," says Jerry, "Come to the secret stairs off the wharf."

To do this, when you are nearby, turn to a passage that is exactly double the number of the passage in which you find the phrase *children mudlarking for oddments*. This will bring you back up the secret stairs to the Waterside Boys' hideout.

Head onto Upper Thames Street...   **252**

❧ 299 ❦

You attach an output pantograph to the engine and feed in your desired parameters. Before long, the machine begins to sketch a four-legged, ambulatory pachyderm. This machine will be the wonder of the world - if you can build it! Gain the **mechanical elephant design**.

Turn to...   **noted passage**

❧ 300 ❦

A steam carriage tears past you on the road, weaving dangerously from side to side. A glance at the driver tells you that he is not the owner: he is far too reckless and not even wearing goggles. A man puffs towards you. "Stop that man! Stole my carriage!"

To give chase, make a MOTORING roll of difficulty 12, adding 1 if you possess an **improved burner** or a **gas pressuriser**.

Successful MOTORING roll!   **265**
Let him go or failed
     MOTORING roll...   **noted passage**

❧ 301 ❦

The family make good company on the slow voyage to the city. As good as their word, they pay every river toll on the way, and also contribute to your fuel costs. In your evenings, you learn a little more of their sad history, as well as a few of their family tunes. Nonetheless, your mate isn't comfortable with the children running along the gunwale and the mother sitting smoking on the prow, and he breathes a sigh of relief when they wave you farewell from the lockside at Brentford. "I'm not sure they haven't stolen my best cap," he mutters. Gain a level of **musicianship** and a **solidarity point.**

Turn to...   **952**

✌ 302 ✌

You have managed to out-fight three of Flat Billy's most feared enforcers: he will hear of this for sure. So will the common folk of Whitechapel, and you'll enjoy a certain grudging respect as a result. Don't expect to be able to return to Whitechapel Street Market with impunity, though. Gain a **solidarity point** and the codeword *Cutthroat*.

Leave the market...   **356**

✌ 303 ✌

☐

If the box above is empty, tick it and read on. If the box is already ticked, turn to **313** immediately. The actors are impressed by your performance and offer you a part in their production of *Every Gentleman's Obligation*, a society farce written by one of their number - a curly-haired man called Charlie.

Following a week or so of rehearsals, you spend a month or two performing every night, acting out the artificial role of a member of high society - a false impression of a false set of mores and manners. Still, it teaches you something of how to move among the upper classes: increase your GALLANTRY by 1.

Eventually the run finishes. You are paid your wages (less bed and board at the actors' hostel) of **£15 4s** and told that your contract is finished. It is none too soon - the open road calls.

Ride to Hyde Park...   **741**
Ride to Hampstead...   **2**

✌ 304 ✌

A butler opens the door warily. "Can I help you?" he asks. Make a GALLANTRY roll of difficulty 11 to convince him to let you in to see the master.

Successful GALLANTRY roll!   **340**
Failed GALLANTRY roll!   **324**

✌ 305 ✌

Flourishing the **release order**, you hammer on the doors of the prison and demand to see the Warden. If you are **Wanted by the Constables**, turn to **203** immediately. Otherwise, read on.

You are shown up to the Warden, who reads through the document carefully. "Well, it seems in order," he says sceptically. "If Lord Beaufort wants the dog, then he's welcome to him. And you're to escort him?" Make an INGENUITY roll of difficulty 15 to convince the Warden, adding 3 if you have a **Constables' logbook**.

Successful INGENUITY roll!   **232**
Failed INGENUITY roll!   **249**

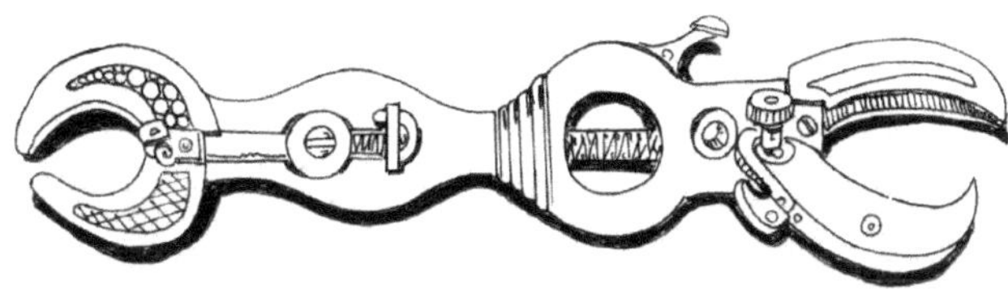

✌ 306 ✌

A large wolfhound appears from nowhere and launches itself at the **deer carcass** tied across your velosteam's bonnet. The dog manages to break it free and drags it away down an alley before you can dismount and give chase. Remove it from your possessions.

Ride on...   **noted passage**

✌ 307 ✌

A boy riding a tottering contraption is crying the news and selling penny papers. If you have the codeword *Crisp*, turn to **318** immediately. Otherwise, roll a dice to see what he tells you:

Score		
Score 1-2	Election at Brewers' Guild!	**867**
Score 3-4	Boxing Champion in Deptford!	**784**
Score 5-6	Flat Billy's Cousin Arrested!	**765**

✌ 308 ✌

Shoreditch bustles. The streets are clogged, both with the busiest of craftspeople and shopkeepers, trading from drays and shopfronts beneath the bells of Old St Leonards, and with the poorest of the poor. You are only an alleyway away from one of the most notorious of all of London's slums, where the fiercely insular,

semi-criminal inhabitants of the Old Nichol tear at one another in desperation and want. Every corner has its pub, catering to its own class, and every jinnel and alley is lined with tightly-fit terraces, paying rent, rent, rent for their absent landlords.

and speculators and builders have thrown up iron-framed tenements in long rows, keen to cram in every possible rent-payer. The Coal Board has their regional depot here too, where a tall fence guards the mountains of coal that keep the city fired.

❧ 309 ❧

The drivers are discussing a Guild delivery to Dover that will take them up Shooter's Hill. "Nasty place," says one. "All them overhanging branches and the like."

Listening carefully, you can work out exactly when to intercept them. Gain the codeword *Chosen*.

Leave the gossipers... **noted passage**

❧ 310 ❧

Bethnal Green is strung out along the road, smearing the original village into a long row of taverns, mills and sweatshops. The tall spire of St John's Church still marks the original settlement, but land is cheaper here

❧ 311 ❧

"Well, I don't know whether you'll have much success, but I daren't prevent you, your holiness. Never have I seen a man more sure of damnation than this Ruben Tutling," says the Warden. He escorts you down to the condemned cells and has the gaoler unlock a heavy door. "Simply knock when you've finished your efforts."

Inside you find a huge, crop-haired convict sitting on a bare bunk. His face is the image of his brother's - apart from the nose. Ruben Tutling's nose is aquiline and well-formed, and presumably hints at what Flat Billy's used to look like.

"They've sent me a parson fer breakfast," says Ruben brightly. "Well, I ain't killed anyone for some time and if I'm about to hang anyway..."

When you explain that you've come to help him

escape and show him **Flat Billy's thumbprint**, Ruben looks a little disappointed. Then he shrugs. "Alright," he says. "So what's the plan?"

"You take care of the gaoler and I'll get us
    through the doors." **339**
"I'll drug the gaoler and we'll use his keys."
    (bottle of chloroform) **357**

❧ 312 ❧

You are clearly a dangerous criminal. The Constables take you to Newgate Gaol, where you will remain until you have paid your debt to society through hard labour and imprisonment. You are not chained, but you are watched very carefully. If you have the **Newgate prison keys**, turn to **317** immediately. If not, you may still have an opportunity to escape.

Among the inmates, there is a sort of black market for the few possessions that you might have managed to bring with you. Several of the guards are ready to take advantage of their prisoners by 'lending' them money on the security of a ring or pocket watch, and a few are even prepared to sell tools that can be turned into escape equipment. The prices are, of course, deeply unfair - but who are you to argue?

Tools	To buy	To sell
rope	£2	-
grappling iron	£3	-
Jewellery	To buy	To sell
locket	-	1s
pocket watch	-	15s
silver ring	-	2s
silver bracelet	-	5s
silver necklace	-	15s
gold ring	-	£1
gold bracelet	-	£1
gold necklace	-	£2
Medical items	To buy	To sell
gold tooth	-	3s
Other items	To buy	To sell
chess set	£4	-
box of cigars	-	10s
pair of golden candlesticks	-	£3

Plan to break out...
    (grappling iron and **rope)** **397**
Bribe the guards... **(£10)** **483**
Endure the ordeal... **475**

❧ 313 ❧

"Oh, welcome back," says Charlie. He has written a new play with a small part for you: roll a dice to see how it goes.

Score 1-2   The play is a failure: no pay and a **black eye (ACC-2, GAL-1)** from thrown fruit...
Score 3-4   Moderate success: paid **£4**...
Score 5-6   A modern classic: paid **£10**...

You cannot hide away here in the theatre for long. Eventually you need to smell the open road again.

Ride to Hampstead... **2**
Ride to Hyde Park... **741**

❧ 314 ❧

"Hello again," you greet the one-eyed fortune teller. "Now this charm. Absolute waste of my money. It hasn't helped me in the slightest."

The woman draws in her breath. "Ooh, now. You must have some powerful bad luck, my friend. It's worked for everyone else. That was my uncle Alf's lucky foot." She rustles in a bag. "Now, maybe you need something stronger. What about a nice dried frog?"

You can buy the **dried frog** for **10s** if you want.

Leave the fortune teller... **noted passage**

❧ 315 ❧

The window succumbs to your quick fingers and you leap in over the sill, folding your flight machine behind you.

A startled cough causes you to look around. The amazed figure of Lord Beaufort himself, commander of the Constabulary, stands in the doorway. However, it is only a moment before he draws his sabre and lunges at you.

Lord Beaufort	Weapon: **sabre (PAR 3)**
Parry	9
Nimbleness	6
Toughness	5

Victory! **334**
Defeat! **113**

❧ 316 ❧

"Yer a mighty fine looking figure on that machine," says the old woman. "I knows you got coin." She is obviously looking to sell stolen goods.

Clothing	To buy	To sell
dancing shoes (GAL+3)	£8	-
Medical items		
white pills ☐ ☐ ☐	£1 10s	-

As you prepare to leave, a shadow flits across the doorway. Make a RUTHLESSNESS roll of difficulty 12.

Successful RUTHLESSNESS roll!	**354**
Failed RUTHLESSNESS roll!	**344**

❧ 317 ❧

Since you already possess the keys to the cells, which you have presumably been keeping against such an eventuality, it is simply a matter of choosing your moment to escape. In the dark of the night, when the least reliable guards are on duty, you unlock your cell door and creep out.

Another key fits the door from the courtyard to the street, but jams in the lock - you are unable to remove it. Just then, the Warden appears: you abandon the precious keys (remove them from your **possessions**) and dash to the shed where your velosteam is waiting. You should add **Escaped from Gaol** to your **Great Deeds** before going any further, and then it is time to make your getaway!

Which direction will you ride?

To Chelsea...	**794**
To Bow...	**471**
To Highgate...	**28**

❧ 318 ❧

"Read oooorlll abaht it!" yells the boy atop his machine. "Crawn jools lifted! Aynchunt sanctitee of White Tower despoiled!"

His paper describes the work of a jewel thief who has broken into the Tower of London itself and stolen a share of the treasure inside. Apparently the Constables have several good leads and are even now pursuing their chief suspects.

Turn to...	**noted passage**

❧ 319 ❧

The Old Blue Last is named after the wooden form used for shoemaking, a popular trade hereabouts. Presumably a previous landlord wished to advertise his artisanal roots, but since then the pub has been rebuilt in a modern style and does a roaring trade among the shopkeepers and local residents. It is also known as a place where musicians gather, and there is always someone interested in making a few bob trading a fiddle or suchlike.

If you have a **mortar sample**, turn to **372** immediately.

Buy a drink... (2s)	**332**
Buy the band a round... (14s)	**361**
Leave the pub...	**308**

❧ 320 ❧

Despite the dreadful situation, you manage to elicit some sympathy from one or two of the warders, impressed by your reputation, your kindliness to the common people and the tales of your adventures. Through them you are able to arrange for deliveries of hot food and a few luxuries that may make your 'stay' more survivable.

How to spend your time is another question. Without distraction, you are like to go mad.

Plan an escape...	**516**
Write a book...	**528**
Befriend the frog...	**536**

❧ 321 ❧

There is set to be a Guild convoy up into Essex before long. The drivers are discussing the route they will take, meaning that you are able to calculate exactly when and where to intercept them. They will pass Bow and head up the road to the north-east. Gain the codeword *Chapter*.

Leave the guildsmen...	**noted passage**

৯ 322 ৶

☐ ☐ ☐ ☐ ☐

If any of the boxes above are empty, tick one and read on. If they are all already ticked, erase the ticks and turn to **347** immediately.

With all the crime here in the east, you have a chance to breathe before any Constabulary will be despatched in your pursuit. Still, discretion is the better part of valour, they say. Well, some say that.

Ride into the City... **213**
Steam east up Bow Road... **471**
Make your way towards the Thames Tunnel... **373**
Steer a route towards the docks... **341**

৯ 323 ৶

With the Selladore punchcards in position, you are ready to give the machine your instructions.

Repair a **torn manifest**... **535**
Predict stock prices... (at least two different
    share certificates) **328**
Nothing for now... **noted passage**

৯ 324 ৶

You hop swiftly down the steps and open the kitchen door. There, despite it being the middle of the day, you find the cook weeping into her hands. She looks up in panic. There is something primal, hurt and broken in the look she gives you.

By instinct, you head over to a high shelf and take down a bottle of cooking brandy and pour her a glass. She drinks it slowly, splutters, and dries her face.

"I'm looking for a scullery girl called Rathbone," you say.

"Oh, poor Andrea!" wails the cook, and she begins crying again.

Eventually you calm her and coax out what you least wanted to hear. Ennis is a predator of the worst kind, exercising his privilege as a wealthy man to have his way with any and all of his female servants. Andrea Rathbone was simply one in a long line of maids he treated in such a way - as well as the cook herself.

"What can I do?" she weeps. "If I leave without a character, I'll not get another position. I've children at home needing my wage. I can't run away like the girls did."

"Did Andrea run away?" you ask.

"No, poor mite. She's run where the monster can't get his hands on her. She wasted away and coughed her lungs out in the attic bedroom. Buried her six months ago."

There is no doubt that Ennis deserves punishment. Will you be judge, jury and executioner? The Constables will not pay any attention to an accusation from a cook or a road-wanderer. In fact, they are more likely to side with the wealthy banker.

Confront Ennis yourself... **739**
Leave the house... **750**

৯ 325 ৶

The young woman leads you into a low room in Nichol Court where a crowd are drinking gin and sour beer. You are poured a pint of Nichol Ale, which frankly tastes raw, badly fermented and faintly reminiscent of the farmyard. Nonetheless, the company are playful and garrulous, keen to hear the stories of your adventures and your deeds. Until you indicate that you will leave. The young woman leads you back out towards your velosteam, but the night has fallen now and the alleyways are entirely unlit.

Blunder back to your velosteam... **344**

৯ 326 ৶

The raven seems to have taken a liking to you and decides to accompany you on your adventures. Note on your **Adventure Sheet** that you now have a **pet raven** amongst your **Other Notes**. She cannot be lost when your **possessions** are taken from you: she will fly along as you explore the roads and come to roost when you rest. Who knows when such an intelligent and cheerful bird will come in use?

Leave the tower... **290**

❧ 327 ❧

The Warden is far from impressed with your efforts. He doesn't doubt that you are a clergyman, but he won't let you get anywhere near the condemned criminal. He has his men see you back out of the postern gate.

Try to arrange the man's release...
(**release order**)   **305**
Leave the prison...   **210**

❧ 328 ❧

The engine swallows all the data you can give into it, inferring the number of shares (remove the **shares** from your **possessions**), their price variations, the dates of significant changes, the number of purchasers and much more besides.

Then it makes its predictions. The most likely outcome, it says, is a slow rise in prices across the board, with a massive crash in values in the near future, triggered by a minimum of four different holdings reaching their lowest figures. However, it then makes some more specific predictions. Use the table below to replace any of the appropriate codewords: if you possess one in either column, erase it and replace it with the opposite codeword.

Catiline...	Replace with...	*Chipped...*	and v.v.
Cricket...		*Egret...*	
Crumb...		*Carling...*	
Depth...		*Driven...*	
Fatal...		*Forgo...*	

Turn to...   **noted passage**

❧ 329 ❧

As soon as the first Livingstone punchcards are read by the machine, it pauses and begins a subtle rearrangement, better suited for the analysis of complicated instructions.

Analyse a set of **Aramanth A punchcards**... **684**
Take back your punchcards...   **noted passage**

❧ 330 ❧

Here in Whitechapel Street Market, you can buy and sell just about anything, as long as you aren't going to upset the status quo. No-one is going to worry whether your goods are stolen, but they might worry whether Flat Billy knows what you're doing. If you have the codeword *Cutthroat*, turn to **434** immediately.

Clothing	To buy	To sell
mask	1s	-
cloak	£1	15s
green coat	-	15s
goggles (MOT+1)	£2 15s	£1 15s
eyepatch (RUTH+1)	15s	6s
golden monocle (GAL+2)	-	£6
wide-brimmed hat	£1 10	£1
silk scarf	£3	£1 10s
top hat	£2	£1
lady's wig	£1 5s	8s
airship officer's cap	-	£1 10s
fur coat	£4	£3
lace shawl	18s	12s
dancing shoes (GAL+3)	£21	£12
sprung leg braces (NIM+3)	-	£15
dinner jacket	£3	£2
Tools	To buy	To sell
scissors (PAR 1)	10s	8s
adjustable wrench (ENG+1)	£1 8s	£1 2s
grappling iron	12s	9s
tarpaulin	4s	2s
lockpicks	6s	3s
telescope	£4 10s	£3
roll of oiled silk	£6	£4 2s
bolt of cloth	£8	£5 10s
Jewellery	To buy	To sell
locket	10s	4s
pocket watch	£6	£2
silver ring	£1	8s
silver bracelet	£2	15s
silver necklace	£6	£2 5s
gold ring	£6	£2 5s
gold bracelet	£7	£3
gold necklace	£8	£4
Medical items	To buy	To sell
bandages	3s	-
cough medicine	5s	2s
poison	£1	10s
Other items	To buy	To sell
deck of marked cards	-	6s
parasol	£6	£3
box of cigars	£4	£1 8s
revolutionary poster	3s	-
pair of golden candlesticks	£12	£6
flute	-	£1
fiddle	-	£2
accordion	-	£3
dog-eared Bible	3s	2s

Leave the market...   **251**

❧ 331 ❧

To open the **strongbox**, you can either make an ENGINEERING roll of difficulty 16, adding 1 if you have a **crowbar** and 3 if you possess **welding tools**, a **steam fist** or a **mechanical arm**, or an INGENUITY roll of difficulty 16, adding 1 if you possess some **lockpicks**.

Successful ENGINEERING or INGENUITY roll!	**560**
Failed ENGINEERING or INGENUITY roll!	**noted passage**

❧ 332 ❧

Your florin buys you a dark ruby red beer scented with dried fruit and almonds. They call it Shore Ditchwater, by way of a joke. Roll a dice to see what you hear:

Score 1-2	Recognised!	**664**
Score 3	Flat Billy...	**873**
Score 4	Barricades and blunderbusses...	**1150**
Score 5-6	Contraband!	**706**

❧ 333 ❧

The drivers are talking about a route the guild runs through Bishop's Wood, north of Highgate. Listening carefully, you are able to work out exactly when to strike to intercept a road train. Gain the codeword *Chuffing*.

Leave the hauliers...   **noted passage**

❧ 334 ❧

Lord Beaufort clutches at his bleeding wounds as he slumps against his desk. "Bettered by a burglar," he spits. "I know not who you are, but rest assured of this: you will be found and punished..."

You can take his **sabre (PAR 3)**, a **release order** lying on his desk and a **gold monocle**

(GAL+2) fallen from his brow. You also gain the codeword *Currently*. However, a sudden ringing bell and the sound of feet on stairs inform you that guards have been alerted. You jump to the window and launch yourself out on your wings once more as Constables charge into the room. You are now **Wanted by the Constables**, if you were not already.

Down in the street below, you race to your velosteam as the sound of Imperial pistons start up. You will have to ride for your life! Which way will you steer?

North...	**841**
South...	**858**
West...	**882**

❧ 335 ❧

Here in the Tower you have, at least, the privacy of your own cell, and a little daylight runs down from the ancient arrow-loop high above your head when the smog clears and the sun shines. Sparse furnishings include a desk and a low bed with a straw mattress: it is more comfortable by far than many of your bivouacs and resting places.

The walls are covered in scrawled notes from previous inmates, cursing various wardens, unfaithful wives, treacherous partners-in-crime, deceitful contacts and God himself. In the dampest corner, there is a frog in a small pool, who blinks at you, unimpressed.

If you have **fifteen or more Solidarity points**, turn to **320** immediately. Otherwise, read on.

For an indomitable spirit like yours, imprisonment chafes far more than manacles or foot irons. You get no sympathy from your warders, who bring you food, remove your bucket for emptying every evening, but otherwise have nothing to do with you. You are isolated, ignored and forgotten. Roll two dice to see how you fare, subtracting 2 for each **wound** you currently possess.

Score 0-4	Gaol fever: lose 2 from your NIMBLENESS, INGENUITY and MOTORING...
Score 5-8	The poor diet weakens you: reduce your NIMBLENESS by 2...
Score 9-10	The isolation touches your mind: reduce your INGENUITY by 2...
Score 11-12	Relative stability: your sentence passes eventually.

Turn to...   **398**

✥ 336 ✤

If you have the codeword *Gripe*, turn to **368** immediately. If not, but you possess the codeword *Charley*, turn to **534**. Otherwise, read on.

Eyes are watching as you steam out of the alleyway. The mood of the inhabitants is unpredictable and your fame or reputation outside the Old Nichol has no consequence here. A bold and barefoot boy approaches you, before taking a slap round the head from a young woman. He dives into an open doorway and the woman calls over to you. "Come and join us for a drink, and let's hear all about you. Have an ale."

Across the street, a toothless old woman beckons. "Got a couple of shillings? I might have something you like."

Talk to the young lady...	**325**
Approach the old woman...	**316**
Follow the boy...	**399**

✥ 337 ✤

The vicar appreciates your gift. "This will help us alleviate the sufferings of the poor souls in the asylum," he says. "They are kept like animals, poor creatures."

Return to Bethnal Green...	**329**

✥ 338 ✤

Life as a despatch rider has been hard and thankless. Your payment, when you could get work, was sometimes good, but the guilds are loathe to trust outsiders with their secrets. And more and more is being coded up and sent by Telegraph, nowadays.

For you, the end came when you were accused of tampering with a despatch that displeased the recipient - a clear case of blaming the messenger for the message. You were left unpaid after a string of difficult jobs, with repairs to make on your velosteam and money owing to various inns and hostelries along your wonted routes. But if the upper classes are so free to rob the men and women they depend upon, then why shouldn't you rob them in turn?

Since then you have done what you can to establish yourself as a feared road thief. Preying on the rich is not only fair - it's good business sense. In the city of London you'll find many more opportunities for good business, perhaps using your skill and knowledge of the roads to join the outriders who work out of Highgate, or on Shooter's Hill on the Kent road where generations of highwaymen have terrified the gentry.

Your ability scores are:

RUTHLESSNESS	4
ENGINEERING	4
MOTORING	6
NIMBLENESS	2
INGENUITY	3
GALLANTRY	2

You have in your possession a **blunderpistol (ACC 6)**, a **sabre (PAR 3)**, a **mask** and some **welding tools**.

Turn to...	**1200**

✥ 339 ✤

The gaoler returns at the sound of your knock and begins to sort his keys. Ruben waits at the door-jamb and, at the moment the iron-shod door begins to swing, wraps his hands around the man's head and twists it with a sickening crack. He throws the body to the floor without hesitating and bursts out into the corridor. It is left to you to grab the **Newgate cell keys** and dash after the brute.

Follow him...	**390**

✥ 340 ✤

You are greeted by a handsome and warm man dressed in formal morning wear. Leonard Ennis is a successful banker in his thirties and has all the privilege and opportunities that money can buy a man in this age. "Good day," he greets you. "I don't believe I recognised the name. How can I help you?"

You spin a story about private investments, colonial income and hopes for a position with a bank, all the while watching Ennis and keeping your eyes and ears open. He recommends the Boulter's Lock Hotel as a place for quiet and relaxation, just a short distance from the city. "I go there all the time." In your presence he does and says nothing out of the ordinary, but he becomes increasingly suspicious as you talk.

"I feel that there is some other reason for your visit," he says. "Please be frank."

"I promised a family that I would enquire after their daughter. A Miss Andrea Rathbone. They believed she had found employment here."

"The name isn't familiar. You might have to ask my housekeeper, but she isn't here at the moment, as she is visiting her aunt in Chelsea." Ennis's lie is smooth, but as a practised liar yourself, you can easily spot the untruth.

He quickly tires of the pretence and the interview and makes an excuse, heading upstairs and leaving the butler to show you out. Now you must decide whether to drop the matter.

Leave the house...	**750**
Leave and sneak into the kitchen...	**324**

❧ 341 ❧

If you have the codeword *Collapse*, turn to **204** immediately. Otherwise, read on.

St Katharine's Docks are the most important and most profitable possession of the River Guild, who gained control here through still much-resented political means. High walls surround the oddly-shaped polygonal quay, which is crammed with steamships from across the world. To get inside, you will require some sort of pass, or a very good story.

Only a short distance away stands the Tower of London - the palace, fortress and prison that guards the Crown Jewels, high-profile prisoners and many of the Crown's secrets. Tower Hill is still a place for demonstrations, meetings and executions.

Enter the docks... (**bargee's badge**)	**376**
Climb into the docks by night...	**385**
Investigate the Tower...	**290**
Ride through the district towards Shadwell...	**380**

❧ 342 ❧

Continuing up through the alleys towards Pentonville, you turn onto the uneven surface of Spring Street, a narrow, gloomy terrace that should bring you to Kings Cross Road. The end, however, is blocked by a steam van, so you turn about to return the way you came.

Suddenly, just as you are about to turn right, another steam van lurches out ahead of you, blocking the road. You brake hard, but still slam into the bodywork of the heavy vehicle.

A thin woman in brown appears beside you. She is dressed in a tunic and breeches, like an aeronaut or a velosteamer, but she has the poise of a high class lady.

"We hear you have been selling diamonds," she says, without preamble. "We even know how much you sold them for. But they weren't yours to sell."

"Who are you?" you reply.

She smiles. "We are the Company. You stole a pouch of diamonds from one of our salespeople. We are on our way to getting them back. But you..." She leans towards you, her smile gleaming. "You don't seem to realise with whom you are dealing. So the first thing we want is the money you got for them."

Give her the full price... (**£262 10s**)	**181**
Stall for time...	**485**

❧ 343 ❧

Hibbert is glad to see you out and on your feet. "Why, the last time I saw you was when you dragged yourself to the farm," he says. "You were pretty close to death right then."

He hasn't visited Hard-to-Find Farm himself for some time. "Too much to do here, what with the sewers and the Wheatears trying to gain their majority in Parliament. But you're welcome to stay there whenever you need."

Remove the codeword *Ambulatory*.

Leave the sewer works...	**471**

❧ 344 ❧

A mighty blow on your head knocks you to the ground. Gain **two wounds** immediately, or **one** if you are wearing a **hat** of any kind. If you survive, you must fight!

Cosh-carrier	Weapon: **club (PAR 2)**	
Parry:	8	
Nimbleness:	6	
Toughness:	4	

Victory!	**358**
Defeat!	**999**

❧ 345 ❧

If you have the codeword *Churl*, or the codeword *Carrier* and do not possess **Lord Beaufort's note**, turn to **503** immediately. Otherwise, read on.

The Grave Maurice is the heart of the criminal East End. You are running a risk simply by entering the place: everyone here is armed and the majority answer directly to Flat Billy. The parlour falls quiet as you step in through the ornate doors. If you have the codeword *Cutthroat*, turn to **428** immediately.

Buy a drink...	(1s)	359
Head to the upstairs parlour...		
	(**Friend of Flat Billy**)	370
Leave the pub...		356

❧ 346 ❧

A street sweeper stops to watch as you ride past. He waves to grab your attention and comes scurrying over. "Watch out. The Chief Constable 'as 'eard about you. They're lookin' for you right now." You are now **Wanted by the Constables**, if you were not already.

Turn to...   **noted passage**

❧ 347 ❧

With the Constables on your tail, you must make swift and sharp decisions. Begin by deciding which direction you will ride in an attempt to lose them.

West...	404
South...	1006
East...	995

❧ 348 ❧

Discard the blank punchcards. To punch your own set of cards you must possess the appropriate codeword and then make an INGENUITY roll of difficulty 16. With a successful INGENUITY roll you can add the appropriate set of punchcards to your possessions - but only one set for each set of blank punchcards you have! A failed INGENUITY roll means that your time and blank punchcards have been wasted.

	Codewords needed
punchcards (Aramanth A)	*Chirp or Entertain*
punchcards (Habbukuk K)	*Busybody or Fireside*
punchcards (Selladore V)	*Collector or Dexter*
punchcards (Livingstone M)	*Coaxial or Faucett*

Turn to...   **noted passage**

❧ 349 ❧

With the punchcards in the hopper and the feeder wheel idling, all you have to do is to decide exactly what you want the machine to compute. The Habbukuk routines are effective at creating a whole variety of physical structures and designs.

Design a better bridge...	633
Calculate an airship's buoyancy...	792
Calculate a demolition...	
(**plan of St Katharine's Docks**)	1227
Design a **mechanical elephant**...	229

❧ 350 ❧

You steam up Whitechapel Road and turn left just after the Albion Brewery, accelerating up Cambridge Road, towards Bethnal Green. The slow traffic is easily outmanouevred and you reach the corner by St John's Church in moments.

Turn to...   310

❧ 351 ❧

□

If the box above is empty, tick it and turn to **360** immediately. Otherwise, read on.

The owners of the bell foundry are busy modernising their methods. They are keen to buy any **blueprints**, design documents or pieces of machinery you might possess.

	To buy	To sell
blueprints	-	**£4 5s**
assembly line plan	-	**£10**
plan of St Katharine's Docks	**£12**	**£6**
pneumatic manual (ENG+3)	**£18**	**£12**
heating blueprints	-	**£3 2s**
airship buoyancy calculation	-	**£1 8s**
improved bridge design	-	**£2 8s**
chart of the lower Thames	**£1 10s**	**£1**
calculated patterns	**£5 15s**	**£2**

Leave the foundry...   356

❧ 352 ❧

Spitalfields Market stands in the centre of a busy district of craftspeople and workshops. Half of the market is given over to machinery, tools and intricate metalwork. Market Guards stand at every entrance, watching the deceitful errand boys, vagrants and strangers like yourself.

Clothing	To buy	To sell
mask	1s	-
dungarees (GAL-2)	£1 10s	15s
goggles (MOT+1)	£2 15s	£1 15s
engineer's gauntlets (ENG+2)	£5	£4 10s
eyepatch (RUTH+1)	15s	6s
hair matches (RUTH+2) ☐ ☐ ☐	£2	-
sprung leg braces (NIM+3)	-	£15
Tools	To buy	To sell
rope	4s	2s
waterproof paint	6s	-
lantern	6s	3s
billhook (PAR 2)	12s	10s
scissors (PAR 1)	10s	8s
wirecutters	12s	9s
adjustable wrench (ENG+1)	£1 8s	£1 2s
grappling iron	12s	9s
tarpaulin	4s	2s
measuring line	6s	4s
brass flange joint	8s	7s
copper pipe	6s	5s
high pressure valve	18s	15s
pneumatic tyres	£4	£2
titanium alloy	£4	£2 10s
ultra-tensed wire	£2 10s	£1 10s
jeweller's loupe (ING+1)	£2 2s	£1 15s
binoculars	£3 15s	£2 10s
pneumatic manual (ENG+3)	-	£8
Weapons	To buy	To sell
club (PAR 2)	3s	-
sabre (PAR 3)	£2 10	£1 5s
blunderpistol (ACC 6)	£4	£3 5s
duelling pistols (ACC 7)	-	£10
Constable's carbine (ACC 8)	-	£10
Medical items	To buy	To sell
stethoscope	£1	12s
catling knife (PAR 1 NIM+2)	-	£3 5s
Other items	To buy	To sell
ivory fan	-	£2 2s
clockwork bird	-	£2
punchcards (Aramanth A)	£10	£8
punchcards (Habbukuk K)	£15	£12 10s
punchcards (Selladore V)	-	£18 10s
punchcards (Livingstone M)	-	£22 10s
flute	£1 5s	£1
fiddle	£4	£2
accordion	£4	£3
steam accordion	£6	£4 10

Head north to Shoreditch... **308**
Ride south to Whitechapel... **356**

Head north to Shoreditch... 308
Ride south to Whitechapel... 356

❧ 353 ❧

The band invite you to sit in and play their next set. The music is fast and challenging, but with a couple of drinks in, you to loosen you up. With the sweat flying, you catch the gist of their tunes and give your best.

"Well played, well played," says the leader.

The new tunes and the stretching musicianship have sharpened you up considerably: you can gain either a **level of musicianship** or improve your INGENUITY by 1.

Return to the pub... **319**
Leave the pub... **308**

Return to the pub... 319
Leave the pub... 308

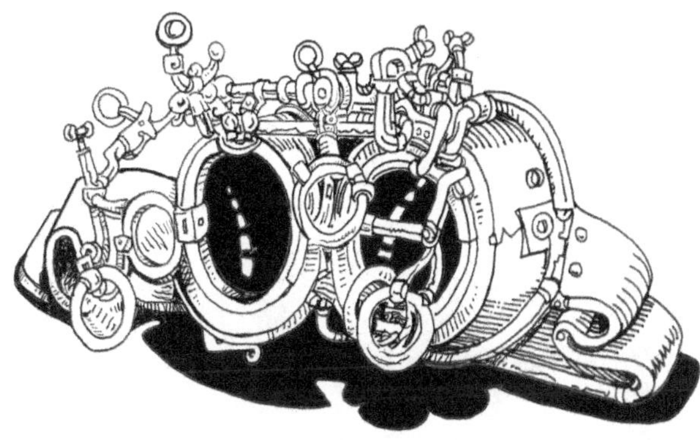

❧ 354 ❧

You have managed to escape the Old Nichol - unlike its many inhabitants. Predatory gazes flicker, but no-one dares act on their naked avarice. For now. This is a dangerous place.

Head up Gosset Street... **310**
Slip out an alleyway... **308**

Head up Gosset Street... 310
Slip out an alleyway... 308

❧ 355 ❧

Mrs Roberts narrows her eyes. "You want me to do something about the oyster scare? Yes, it must be quite tragic for the fishmongers of London. I suppose you think the King eating oysters will put them back in business. What do you gain from it, then?"

"I am simply an emissary of truth," you reply. "There is no link between the cholera and a few oysters." If you have **St Katharine's brooch**, turn to **394** immediately. Otherwise, make a GALLANTRY roll of difficulty 16, adding 3 for each piece of **gold jewellery** (such as a **gold bracelet** or **gold ring**) you want to give Mrs Roberts as a sweetener.

Successful GALLANTRY roll! **394**
Failed GALLANTRY roll! **476**

Successful GALLANTRY roll! 394
Failed GALLANTRY roll! 476

❧ 356 ❧

Whitechapel is never quiet. Here in the east, industry and low-class rented tenements are jammed side-by-side, downwind from the more affluent areas of the city. Consequently, this is one of the first places for immigrants to settle, only a short distance from the docks where they arrived seeking their fortunes. The Constables are always busy here, breaking up fights between gangs and generally throwing their weight around amongst the newcomers. However, the real power around here belongs to Flat Billy.

❧ 357 ❧

As the gaoler puts his head through the door, you clamp a choloroform-soaked pad onto his face. He struggles for a moment and then falls to the ground. You drag him into the cell, put him beneath the rat-nibbled blanket and take his **Newgate cell keys**.

❧ 358 ❧

The tables are turned and your assailant is at your mercy. He is a rough, ill-dressed man, clearly preferring the attack from behind to a fair fight. Out of the corner of your eye you spot the young woman who lured you here hovering in the gloom.

❧ 359 ❧

The beer at the Grave Maurice is not exceptional. They serve a cheap, machine-brewed ale called Elstons No.3, which is a mild, almost flat bitter with a simple yeasty flavour and a sweet finish.

❧ 360 ❧

As you ride between the gateposts of the Whitechapel Bell Foundry, you hear a colossal clang and a riot of shouting erupting from the sheds. A bell has been dropped, trapping one of the workers under a half-collapsed wooden frame.

You rush over and quickly appraise the situation. Make an ENGINEERING roll of difficulty 12, adding 1 if you possess a **rope**.

❧ 361 ❧

In a corner of the pub are a quartet jamming along contentedly - a guitar, a steam accordion providing the hiss and pulse of the rhythm, a violin and a chap playing a selection of to-hand percussion. They nod, but keep playing as the girl brings them a tray of drinks.

After finishing their set, one comes over to thank you. "Musician yourself?"

❧ 362 ❧

You coast to a halt on a sidestreet near the entrance to the Thames Tunnel, meaning to carefully check the lie of the land before proceeding. However, you have already been seen and a thin man in brown appears from a doorway and walks over. "So have you got them with you? The diamonds you took from us? I trust I don't have to tell you how seriously we are taking this. So this will be your final chance to hand them over - or their value."

❧ 363 ❧

You accelerate ahead of the boy's pursuer, swerve behind him and haul him up onto the seat in front of you. The shopkeeper's indignant cries fade as you churn through the hubbub of Shoreditch and then, at a good distance, you come to a stop and set the boy down again.

"Cor, fanks!" says the lad.

"Hungry, then?"

"You bet I am."

"Don't your family feed you?"

"Oh, somewhat, somewhat." He proudly tells you that his father is a cosh-carrier - a violent criminal who ambushes strangers in the streets around their slum, stealing what he can and revelling in the protection of this isolated, insular community.

Leave the Old Nichol...	354
Talk to the boy's father...	384

❧ 364 ❧

Teddington Lock is the last lock on the Thames - or the first, depending the direction of your voyage. Downstream from here, through those heavy tarred gates, the river obeys the moon and swills out to sea twice a day. When the tide is out, great swathes of mud and silt line the banks, filthying every boat and boot.

There are several goods merchants here who profit from the transhipment of cargo from the smaller river craft to the London lighters. If you wish to carry your cargo further into the city, you can, but you may not be able to find better prices.

	To buy	To sell
Charcoal	£17	£16
Furniture	-	£27
Machinery	£29	£27
Pottery	-	£21
Cotton	-	£3
Woollen Cloth	-	£12
Coal	£20	-
Beer	£21	£19
Wheat	£7	£6
Malt	£9	£8
Frozen Meat	£15	£11
Ice	£8	£6

If you wish to purchase **Frozen Meat** or **Ice**, you will need a **Perkins Machine** fitted to your craft.

Pass downstream through the lock...
 (**2s** or a **Bargee's Badge**)   580
Head upstream towards Maidenhead...
 (**£1** or a **Bargee's Badge**)

Smog and Ambuscade 672

❧ 365 ❧

Remove the **music box** or **clockwork bird** from your possessions. Mr Fresher goes to work and soon makes his promise good: he has improved the responsiveness of your brass fingers and the tightness of the grip you control. Increase your ENGINEERING and MOTORING scores by 1.

Mr Fresher refuses any payment. "Oh no. I have been amply paid by what I have learnt from this excellent machinery. Hmm." A glint comes into his eye. It shouldn't surprise you if Fresher and Sons soon become specialists in mechanical prosthetics. Perhaps business is on the up.

Leave the shop...   647

❧ 366 ❧

☐ ☐ ☐ ☐

If any of the boxes above are ticked, tick one and read on. If all the boxes are already ticked, turn to **392** immediately.

The Keymaker is a skilled locksmith who works for the criminal gangs of the East End. He can turn the **impression** of any key into a key for a single payment of **£1** - for example, if you have an **impression of a rusty key**, he can turn it into a **rusty key**. He mentions that he learnt his trade from a man in Maidensgrove, a tiny and well-hidden village south of Pishill in the Chilterns. "It's not an easy place to find," he chortles as he works. He describes the route up the hill from Pishill Chapel. Now that you know the route, you will need to add 50 to the passage number in which you find this landmark in order to find the secret way up to Maidensgrove. "But I won't be working here much longer. The Constables have been asking around. I'm sure they's onto me."

He will sell you some essential breaking and entering tools and buy any old keys you happen to have. "Old keys is the most interesting," he says. "I can allus learn a thing or two from an old barrel key."

Tools	To buy	To sell
lockpicks	15s	-
plaster of Paris	6s	-
skeleton key	-	£2
spare key	-	4s

Return to the parlour...   345
Leave the Grave Maurice...   356

❧ 367 ❧

"Well, it's a good day to join a club. I'm the regional membership officer, and I can see you're an ideal candidate. Meet me when I get off my shift and I'll enroll you."

He talks you through the Compact's aims and methods and hands you **passdisc 820**. You are now a **Member of the Compact for Workers' Equality**. "Come and attend a meeting in Blackwall," he says. "Try the sugar warehouse."

Leave the foundry...   356

❧ 368 ❧

Where the infamous streets of the Old Nichol once stood there is now only blackened rubble. Nelson Street, Mead Street and the pit that was Nichol Court are all obscured with mounds of burnt brick and timber. The shoddy billysweet and the collapsed courses of half-fired clay lie in mounds, burying tales of suffering, sorrow and want.

Most of the inhabitants have dispersed, but a few of the most desperate cling on to their old lives here. If you want to distribute some money, remove **£4** from your purse and gain the codeword *Compassionate*.

Ride away...   308

❧ 369 ❧

The Church of St John stands in the centre of Bethnal Green between some fine modern gardens. A small churchyard planted with roses (reserved exclusively for the better-off parishioners) has at least one fresh grave, but seems largely there for show. The vicar is known to be a busybody and a do-gooder, always running bunsales and doing his best for the local poor. He is also a frequent visitor of the neighbouring lunatic asylum.

Make a donation to the poor work... (**£2**)   337
Leave the church...   310

❧ 370 ❧

Recognising you as one of Flat Billy's trusted henchmen, his door watchers let you pass up the stairs. He is seated in an armchair hearing the petition of a local shopkeeper, but nods as you arrive. If you have **Lord Beaufort's note**, turn to **383** immediately.

Offer to do a job for Flat Billy...   493
Leave the Grave Maurice...   356

❧ 371 ❧

You check your pressure and the level in your coalgas reservoir before preparing to take a longer journey across the city. The Ferguson's pistons long for a good run.

Head west towards Queen Maria Park...	**95**
Head towards Hyde Park...	**741**
Head to the City...	**213**
Take a ride east to Blackwall...	**425**

❧ 372 ❧

The rentman is a portly fellow in a greasy buff waistcoat. He will probably have a commission agreement with the owners of the Old Nichol slum - whoever they are - so it is in his interest to have every tenant pay up and pay right. Despite looking like a violent sort himself, you have heard that he brings a couple of hardened brawlers with him on his Friday rounds, to make sure every farthing owed is paid.

To get him to reveal who is ultimately responsible for the buildings of the Old Nichol, you can either choose to try to terrify him, relying on your RUTHLESSNESS skill, or to wheedle the facts out with flattery and false friendship without raising his suspicions, using your INGENUITY.

Terrify him...	**16**
Trick him...	**100**

❧ 373 ❧

The Thames Tunnel was dug by four hundred men working behind an iron shield to protect them from flooding, collapse of the treacherous clay, and bad air. Much to the Haulage Guild's frustration, it is privately owned, and every vehicle is charged a toll, making the owners fabulously rich despite the immense construction cost. If you have the codeword *Certain*, turn to **362** immediately.

Pass through the tunnel... (**1s**)	**656**
Turn around...	**380**

❧ 374 ❧

"I should have known it," cheers the bellmaker. "Next meeting, you'll be chaired in, so you will. You know where we meet? In the sugar warehouse at Blackwall?" He gives you **passdisc 820**. "This'll get you inside," he assures you.

Ride away...	**356**

❧ 375 ❧

You are poured a tall glass of dark, strong ale, brought down by wherry from the Norfolk coast where it is brewed in an old windmill. "That's our Windmill Super," says the barmaid. "Very popular." It is a finely balanced, very drinkable dark ale, particularly suited to the toasted cheese that stands on the bar as a snack for drinkers. Note passage number **389** and roll a dice to see what rumour reaches your ever-open ears:

Score 1	A street gang...	**1113**
Score 2	An untrustworthy landlord...	**1135**
Score 3	Barricades and blunderbusses...	**1150**
Score 4	Forging documents...	**1181**
Score 5	An ambitious brewery...	**1196**
Score 6	For the tourists...	**1206**

❧ 376 ❧

The badge you wear shows you to be a paid-up member of the River Guild, with your own craft and your commitment to paying the fairly-priced tolls that the Guild set. Presuming that you have a craft moored inside the docks, the gateman lets you through with a wave.

Board your boat...	
(**moored at St Katharine's**)	**387**
Explore the docks...	**408**

❧ 377 ❧

Whitechapel Road runs north-east out of the city, on towards Bow and Bethnal Green. However, you are still within the metropolis proper and streets bounded with warehouses and terraces run in every direction. You can even set out further and cross the City from here. Which way will you turn?

Towards Shoreditch...	**308**
Ride for Spitalfields Market...	**352**
Steam to Bethnal Green...	**350**
Ride up to Bow...	**412**
Ride towards Limehouse...	**474**
Head for the Tower...	**290**
Ride down New Road to Shadwell...	**380**
Leave this region...	**371**

❧ 378 ❧

Despite your help, by the time the bell is lifted, the poor foundryman has passed away. One of his friends tosses a chip of wood angrily at the office windows. "It's a death trap here. Bosses won't even notice. There'll be a whip-round for his widow, but only amongst the men." If you want to contribute to the whip-round, remove **£5** from your purse and gain the codeword *Compassionate*.

Ride away...   356

❧ 379 ❧

The Coal Board Depot is not simply several mountains of coal piled in a yard - although it is that. There are overhead conveying belts, chain diggers, automated weighbridges and dozens of steam engines loading and unloading - enough to supply the whole metropolis with coal. If you are **Wanted by the Coal Board**, turn to **347** immediately.

There are also offices, where members of the board scheme how best to outmanoeuvre their rivals, the Telegraph Guild, and workshops where tools and supplies can be had.

Tools	To buy	To sell
lantern	6s	3s
wirecutters	12s	9s
adjustable wrench (ENG+1)	£1 8s	£1 2s
grappling iron	12s	9s
tarpaulin	4s	2s
high pressure valve	18s	15s
binoculars	£4	£2 10s
Weapons	To buy	To sell
sabre (PAR 3)	£2 10	£1 5s
blunderpistol (ACC 6)	£4	£3 5s

Arrange a coal delivery to your workshop...
    (**£4 10s**)   696
Report to the Board...   393
Leave the depot...   310

❧ 380 ❧

Shadwell is dominated by the tall warehouse blocks standing around the London Docks. There is a distinctly maritime flavour to some of the buildings, which seem to have been built out of repurposed ship's timbers.

Visit the Prospect of Whitby...   389
Look for the sailor's house... (*Carpet*)   690
Approach the Thames Tunnel...   373
Make your way west into the Docklands...   341
Ride east to Limehouse...   474
Head north towards Bethnal Green...   310
Steam to Whitechapel up New Road...   356

❧ 381 ❧

Before Ruben can lose his patience, you twist the skeleton key in the doorlock and make your way out into the exercise yard. So far, nobody has noticed your breakout. However, you are still dressed in your cassock, so you motion for Ruben to stay well behind and breezily approach the front gate.

"I say," you begin. "I seem to have taken a wrong turning."

The door guards scratch their heads at the sight of a bishop crossing their yard. If you have a **Constabulary logbook**, turn to **417** immediately. Otherwise, you must make an INGENUITY roll of difficulty 14 to get the guards to unlock the door and then to distract them long enough for Ruben to nip out.

Successful INGENUITY roll!   409
Failed INGENUITY roll!   424

❧ 382 ❧

It takes very little effort to ride up alongside the little squeaker and haul him off his feet by the collar of his ragged shirt. He kicks and spits, but you turn about and dump him on the cobbles outside the grocer's. The shopman grudgingly tosses you a florin (**2s**) and takes his turn to grab the boy's collar.

Leave the shop...   308

❧ 383 ❧

Flat Billy orders everyone else out of the room. He peers at the note - remove it from your **possessions**. "That's a list of requests there," he confides. "Folks what he'd rather have beaten up by my boys than by his. An agreement about certain times and places when his bogies won't be marching around. Pretty incriminating, was anyone else to read it."

He gets up and walks over to a cupboard. "He must have taken the money off yer, an' it must 'ave been the right amount, so I suppose yer pretty honest." Flat Billy rewards you with a powerful **gamekeeper's shotgun (ACC 7)**, a forged **Letter of Introduction** and **fifty guineas in banknotes**.

"I might 'ave more work for yer soon," he says.

Leave the Grave Maurice...   356

❧ 384 ❧

You ask the man directly. "So is this your trade? Cosh-carrying?"

"Well, around here I'm one of a few fortunates practising such a line of work. But that's just the way life is in the Old Nichol, see? Swell folks who have what we haven't, why, they're not easily convinced to hand it over."

You talk some more and he educates you about the Old Nichol, about the unfair rents and dilapidated buildings, the desperation of families without work or hope. When you take a look at the streets of houses without doors, of half-lit basement rooms housing a family of nine, of crumbling brickwork and subsiding walls, it is obvious that the landlords, whoever they are, permit the dilapidation here as a way of keeping their tenants utterly dependent and desperate.

"These ain't built proper, anyway," says your guide. He shows you what they call billysweet - the mortar that should hold the brickwork of the houses together. It can be raked out of its courses with a fingernail. "When they put these up, they saved money on the mortar, didn't they? And on the drains. And on the roofs."

"Who owns these streets?" you ask.

He shrugs. "Ain't never known. Just pays our rent to the rent man on Fridays at the Old Blue Last."

If you are interested in pursuing the landlords of the Old Nichol, take a **mortar sample** from the walls to have tested, or to confront them with. Whether you will be able to get conditions improved, or justice done, is unlikely in this city of such inequality.

If you wish to distribute some money (**£5**) before you go, then gain the codeword *Compassionate*.

Leave the Old Nichol...   **354**

❧ 385 ❧

You have to wait until the early hours of the morning for the dockside streets to empty. Nothing stirs but the fog and the shadow of a climber attempting to get over the steeply-battered brick wall. If you have a **rope** and a **grappling iron**, turn to **411** immediately. Otherwise, you must make a NIMBLENESS roll of difficulty 11 to get in.

Successful NIMBLENESS roll!   **411**
Failed NIMBLENESS roll!   **418**

❧ 386 ❧

You aim to confuse your pursuers by heading west, into the city, winding between the wharves and factories of Limehouse. If you can reach the mouth of the Thames Tunnel ahead of them, you may be able to get away.

Shooting down Narrow Street along the Limehouse waterfront, you see glimpses of the river over your left shoulder. You ride past the mouth of the King's Canal and come to the end of Narrow Street. Are the buildings unfamiliar? Which way should you turn?

Left...   **401**
Right...   **391**

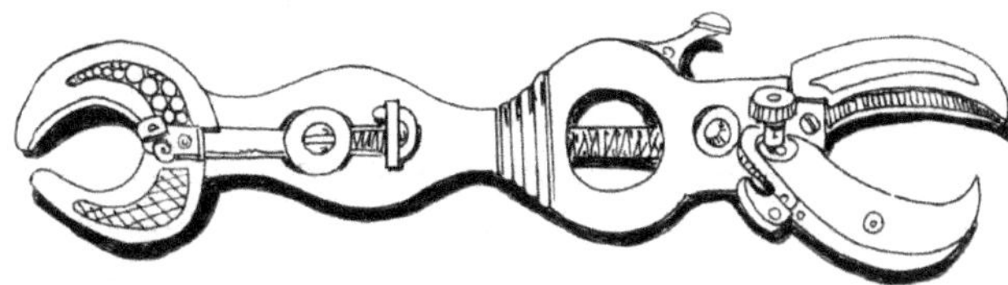

❧ 387 ❧

St Katharine's Docks are clogged with ships and smaller craft taking on and unloading cargo. You will have to be patient to pass through the lock onto the river itself. Your **bargee's badge** allows you to buy and sell here, as well as to moor and to pay for improvements.

	To buy	To sell
Charcoal	-	£18
Furniture	-	£32
Machinery	-	£30
Pottery	£25	£23
Cotton	-	£9
Woollen Cloth	£10	£10
Coal	£10	£8
Beer	£20	£20
Wheat	-	£7
Malt	-	£6
Frozen Meat	£15	£15
Ice	£10	£9

If you wish to purchase **Ice** or **Frozen Meat**, you will need a **Perkins Machine**. If you wish to moor, mark **moored at St Katharine's** on your **Adventure Sheet**.

Customisations	To buy
Perkins Machine	£25

Moor here...   **408**
Head through the lock onto the river...   **478**

✌ 388 ✍

You quickly improvise a powerful lifting engine using your velosteam's drive pistons and a nearby crane arm. Carefully cranked, it lifts the two-ton bell enough for the foundryman to be dragged clear. One of his colleagues shakes your hand. "We'd be paying for his funeral if it weren't for you. You're plainly a friend to the working man. Tell me - have you heard of the Compact for Workers' Equality?

"Of course." (**Member of the CWE**)	**374**
"I'm keen to join."	**367**
"I've no interest in these political groups."	**356**

✌ 389 ✍

The Prospect hangs over the tide like a beggar leaning over his lunchtime soup: the jettied stories stretch out to make the most of the building's narrow plot. To one side, Prospect Stair runs down to the foreshore, although when the tide is in, all you can see are little dirty waves slapping and spitting against the brickwork.

This is place for the sailors of London town, for deals of cargo-carrying and ship-broking. Under the moody glow of oil lamps, matelots and rovers wet their whistles and wait for the Blue Peter to call them away.

Buy a drink...	(**2s**)	**375**
Leave the inn...		**380**

✌ 390 ✍

You pass through several doors with the gaoler's keys but come to a door into the main gateway that you cannot immediately open. Ruben eyes it impatiently, obviously tempted to do something sudden and violent. If you have a **skeleton key**, turn to **381** immediately. Otherwise, read on.

Unable to wait any longer, Ruben grabs the door handle and begins to wrench at it noisily. You try to calm him, but he only becomes more angry and rough. After driving his shoulder into it several times, it bursts open and you rush into the men's exercise yard. However, several prison guards arrive from different directions, giving you only one route out - upwards!

You dash over to a heavy drainpipe and begin to climb. Ruben follows you and the pipe rattles worryingly. If you have a **grappling iron**, turn to **405** immediately. Otherwise, make a NIMBLENESS roll of difficulty 12 to make it onto the roof of the gaol.

Successful NIMBLENESS roll!	**405**
Failed NIMBLENESS roll!	**452**

✌ 391 ✍

The right turn takes you away from the river and onto Broad Street, which continues west behind the wharves. You turn left again, just by the reek of the Fish Market, bump over the cobbles onto Wapping Wall, flash past the Prospect of Whitby and in no time you are at the Thames Tunnel.

The barrier man is just letting a haulage guild locomotive through, so you accelerate alongside and zoom into the echoing chamber of the tunnel. When you emerge, the trail has gone cold.

Leave the tunnel...	**649**

✌ 392 ✍

The Keymaker has fled. You will no longer be able to buy keys from him here. Can you remember what he told you about his master in Maidensgrove?

Return to the parlour...	**345**
Leave the Grave Maurice...	**356**

✌ 393 ✍

"Yes?" asks a haughty clerk. "What do you have to tell us?"

⊕ "The Telegraph station at Rotherhithe is destroyed."	(*Crazed*)	**470**
"I have been harassing Telegraph Guild supplies."	(*Chipped*)	**520**
"Nothing, I suppose."		**379**

✌ 394 ✍

Mrs Roberts agrees to help, and several days later, the newspaper boys of the city are crying the King's preference for oysters and his confidence in their healthy, disease-resistant properties. Remove the codeword *Contactless* and gain the codeword *Capital*.

Return to the river...	**847**

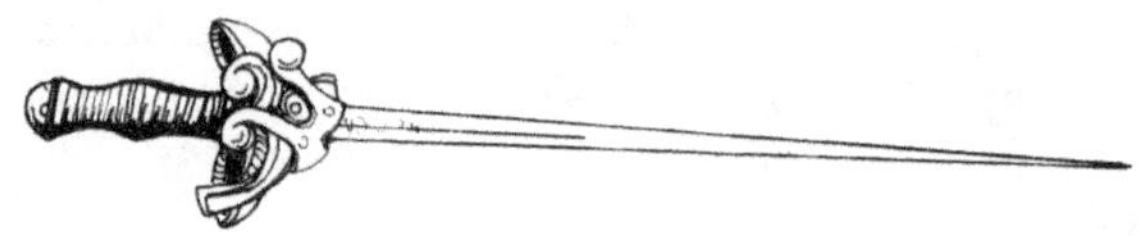

✌ 395 ✍

The thug is carrying nothing but his **cosh** and, on a chain around his neck, a cheap **silver ring**. You leave him in the gutter, where he doubtless belongs.

Leave the area...	**354**

❧ 396 ☙

A blue-suited speculator is complaining to his friend about the low price of his Colchester Oyster Collective shares. "It's this dratted cholera rumour," he says. "Depressing!"

"You bought them far too high," says his friend.

"Rubbish! They could climb a lot higher. The poor man's dinner, oysters. Everyone eats them."

"Not anymore, apparently."

"It'll pass. It has to pass."

Gain the codeword *Contactless* if you do not already possess it.

Finish your drink...	**noted passage**

❧ 397 ☙

It is far from simple to get out from Newgate Gaol. Through much patient grinding at the mortar of a window sill, you manage to loosen the iron bar and make a space through which you can squeeze. Down you climb, into the street outside (remove the **grappling iron** or **rope**) from your **possessions**, before heading to the shed where you have heard your velosteam is being kept. There is no regaining anything else that was confiscated, but then you have avoided the far more serious consequences of long imprisonment.

You should add **Escaped from Gaol** to your **Great Deeds** before going any further, and then it is time to make your getaway. Which direction will you ride?

To Chelsea...	**794**
To Bow...	**471**
To Highgate...	**28**

❧ 398 ☙

One day, far past your ability to count, the door to your cell is opened and you stagger out. "Time to leave," says the warden. "We need this cell for a real criminal."

Any **money** you yet possessed is long gone, spent on minute improvements to your diet and conditions, and any **wounds** have healed and turned into **scars**: for each one, roll two dice, and convert it to an **intimidating scar (RUTH+1)** on a roll of 11 or 12.

You are issued with a **convict's pass** and led, surprisingly, to your velosteam. "Find some honest employment," you are told sternly. "If we catch you again, you won't be treated so well." You may also remove any **Wanted Statuses** that you possess.

Steam off...	**275**

❧ 399 ☙

You watch as the lad cautiously prepares to steal what he can from a nearby grocer. He waits until the shopman's back is turned, then makes a grab for a box and a bag and launches off down the road. It will be a simple matter to catch up with him on your machine - or to obstruct his pursuer's path.

Catch the boy...	**382**
Protect the boy...	**363**

❧ 400 ☙

Bloomsbury is a fashionable district where the servant classes are kept hidden away in their own streets and courtyards, leaving the roads free for the gentle classes to promenade. The Central London Telegraph Tower stands here in one of the squares and the Imperial Museum of History fronts Bloomsbury Square itself. Tucked away down one sidestreet is the Royal College of Surgeons, where scientific discoveries about anatomy seem to be made every day. There are also many hotels for travellers among the fine white terraces. While their prices are high, they are places where a room, a bath and a meal can be had.

Approach the Telegraph Tower...	**171**
Visit the Royal College of Surgeons...(**body**)	**187**
Take your discovery to the museum... (**treasure trove**)	**429**
Ride towards the Lyceum Theatre...	**123**
Head to the Guberstein Club...	**1506**
Take a room at a hotel... (**£3**)	**1313**
Cross Oxford Street towards the Strand...	**139**
Head north towards St Pancras...	**71**
Ride west into Mayfair...	**750**
Head up Theobald's Road to Clerkenwell...	**189**

❧ 401 ☙

The left-hand turn takes you down several shallow steps, until you emerge between Phoenix Wharf and the Koop lumber yard. In front of you, the Thames laps at the steps of Ratcliff Cross Stairs. It is a dead end. As you turn around to retrace your steps, the Constables appear on their Imperials, cutting off your escape.

Turn to...	**13**

❧ 402 ☙

The direction you now take will depends upon your most recent **noted passage**: if it is less than **500**, turn to **50**. If it is more, turn to **614**.

❧ 403 ❧

You are on the trading floor of the Exchange, the noisy home of that despised class of parasites, the speculators, who gather at the break of day, grinning stupidly at their gains and gurning at their losses, imagining that their hunches and gambles are a solid day's work. A flickering mechanical pricechart tallies the rise and fall of each business, as telegraphs are added into the complex welter of records.

The table below shows the value of the shares you can buy and sell here. Unlike with regular goods, their prices depend upon the codewords you may possess at any particular time. You may buy or sell any number of **share certificates** and keep them in your satchel. If you have three or more of the codewords in the central column, turn to **527** immediately.

	Base price	Low price	High price
Colchester Oyster Co-operative	£2 10s	£1 4s (*Contactless*)	£4 (*Capital*)
Delevinne Engineering	£4 15s	£3 2s (*Depth*)	£8 5s (*Driven*)
Imperial Seal Oil	£4 15s	£3 2s (*Fatal*)	£8 5s (*Forgo*)
Northern Grain Milling	£3 9s	£1 8s (*Crumb*)	£6 2s (*Carling*)
Atmospheric Union	£8 17s	£6 4s (*Catiline*)	£10 5s (*Chipped*)
Imperial Western Railway	£2 10s	19s (*Cricket*)	£5 6s (*Egret*)

Leave the Exchange...   **244**

❧ 404 ❧

You cannot enter the old City of London itself, for the ancient walls and gates are still patrolled by the Constables, so you turn up Commercial Road and power through Spitalfields towards Shoreditch. Your pursuers are still following, aided by a Constabulary airship hanging overhead, so you must choose which way to go now.

Hide in Spitalfields Market...	**991**
Head for Islington...	**868**
Make for Smithfield...	**897**

❧ 405 ❧

You and Ruben make it up onto the roof, despite the hue and cry and, with the skirts of your cassock flapping, you skitter over the rain-polished tiling. Ruben pushes past you and leaps across an alleyway onto a lower roof, leaving you no option but to grit your teeth and follow. Then through a dormer window, a tenement, over a cobbler's table and down several flights of stairs and you emerge into Old Bailey, a few yards from where you left your velosteam. Ruben clambers on behind and you roar away into the merciful fog!

Steer for Whitechapel...   **462**

❧ 406 ❧

Flat Billy grimaces. "You just don't care 'oo you pester, do yer? Right then. I'll 'ave to teach you a lesson meself."

He draws out a massive club and swings at you without warning. Watch out - in the following fight, Flat Billy will have the first attack.

Flat Billy	Weapon: **club (PAR 2)**
Parry:	10
Nimbleness:	8
Toughness:	7

Victory!	**286**
Defeat!	**999**

❧ 407 ❧

A criminal of your standing can only be taken to the Tower. You are led in chains to an iron prison-wagon and driven across the city. The gates swing open, the drawbridge is lowered, and you are inside.

The Warden of the Tower comes to greet you.

"At last. The so-called Steam Highwayman. Now you will pay for your crimes: there is no escape from the Tower of London. Your adventures are over."

Turn to...   **335**

❧ 408 ❧

Bales of sisal, hemp, wool, cotton and straw. Barrels of rum, tar, turpentine, paint, molasses, burgundy wine, gutted haddock, salted cod and vinegar. Crates of beer, machine parts, pottery, stoneware. Sacks of coffee beans, tea leaves, dried fruits, grain, fertiliser. It is all here, stacked on the dock, labelled with punchcards and watched by the beady-eyed stevedores.

Try to steal some goods...	**466**
Deal destruction... (**explosives**)	**488**
Agitate amongst the dockers...	
(**Member of the Compact for Workers' Equality**)	**494**
Board your boat...	
(**moored at St Katharine's**)	**387**
Leave the docks...	**341**

❧ 409 ❧

You awe the two guards with a genuine-sounding impression of a high churchman and make some absurd promises about seeing that their sons are educated. They dash inside their lodge to fight over

pen and paper to write down the names of the boys while you motion to Ruben, who reappears from the shadows and helps you unbolt the gate. Over the lower sill and you are a short dash from your parked velosteam. Ruben clambers on behind and, with a quick kick of the friction igniter, you are off into the city mist!

Ride for Whitechapel...	**462**

❧ 410 ❧

Your journey through the streets of the metropolis leaves a trail of chaos: crushed chicken coops knocked from steam lorries, freed chickens, smashed eggs, splashed puddles, tumbled-down piles of deliveries, toppled butcher's tricycles. Anything you do in damage is only compounded by the velosteams of the Constables charging along behind you, utterly focused on their prey.

Turn up into Islington...	**868**
Head south towards the City...	**897**
Continue eastwards...	**907**

❧ 411 ❧

The night-time docks are guarded by watchmen and many of the moored ships have their own lookouts, but the deep shadows and high walkways are perfect for an outlaw like yourself to get around. Under the cover of darkness, you have a surprising amount of access.

Try to steal something...	**466**
Set explosives... (**explosives**)	**488**
Survey the dock... (**measuring line**)	**506**
Leave St Katharine's Docks...	**341**

❧ 412 ❧

You steam past the tenements of Whitechapel and on towards Bow. The buildings become seedier yard by yard, it seems.

Roll a dice to see what you encounter:

Score 1-2	An urchin...	**432**
Score 3-5	Nothing of note...	**471**
Score 6	A street sweeper...	**346**

❧ 413 ❧

Finding Perkins the beer agent doesn't take long. You let yourself into his little glass-fronted office on Platform 12 and close the door.

"I'll just be a moment," he says, punching at the keys of a card-biter.

Will you try to intimidate him into surrendering the contract, or will you wheedle and bribe your way to a compromise? To intimidate him, make a RUTHLESSNESS roll of difficulty 12, or to convince him with words and coin, make an INGENUITY roll of difficulty 14, adding 1 for every **£2** you are willing to pay.

Successful RUTHLESSNESS roll!	**430**
Successful INGENUITY roll!	**447**
Failed either roll!	**64**

❧ 414 ❧

You loiter near the churchyard until night falls. If you wish to dig up the freshly-interred body in the name of science, you will need a **shovel** and a **lantern**, and, ideally, a customer in mind. You cannot carry a body about with you for long without exciting suspicion.

Dig up the grave... (**shovel** and **lantern**)	**448**
Leave the churchyard...	**310**

❧ 415 ❧

You take a firm grip on Ennis and drag him towards the window. His heels scrabble on the parquet floor and he begins to yell and squirm... and suddenly, with a tearing of his fine jacket, he escapes your grasp and dashes down the stairs.

Pursue him...   446

✎ 416 ✎

The Young Prince is anything but grand. Cracked and dirty windowpanes and dust on the oxblood-hued glazed brick tell you all that you need to know about its proprietor and his customers.

Several men and women are doing business over at one of the tables: they will buy and sell items without troubling themselves about their origin.

Clothing	To buy	To sell
mask	1s	-
golden monocle (GAL+2)	-	£7
top hat	-	£2
lady's wig	£1	8s
fur coat	-	£2 15s
lace shawl	-	18s
dancing shoes (GAL+3)	-	£7
dinner jacket	-	£1 10s
Jewellery	To buy	To sell
locket	10s	4s
pocket watch	-	£2
silver ring	£1	10s
silver bracelet	£2	16s
silver necklace	-	£3
gold ring	-	£3
Other items	To buy	To sell
ivory fan	-	£2
clockwork bird	-	£1 5s

Buy a drink...   (1s)   436
Leave the Young Prince...   471

✎ 417 ✎

"I intended to return this," you say, waving the logbook. "It looks important."

The guards are very interested. Each one argues that he should take it up to the Warden, as there will obviously be a considerable reward. You politely offer to mind the gate while they both climb the stairs in the tower. Remove the **logbook** from your possessions.

Ruben reappears and together you lift the postern off its hinges and dash out into the fog. It is only a few yards to your velosteam and you mount up, cassock skirts flapping, and ignite the coal-gas with a kick of the friction-starter.

Head for Whitechapel...   462

✎ 418 ✎

Your clumsy attempts to get over the wall do nothing but attract the attention of the Watchmen. One appears on a lookout post and another in the street, so you will certainly hear the bells of the Constables before long. You had best be off!

Look for a hiding place at Spitalfields Market... 991
Ride for Bow..   973

✎ 419 ✎

"You wasn't quite so wary of a fight when you took on my chaps," says Flat Billy. "Listen, I've got another offer for you. Just some delivery work I'd normally trust to Canter. Do this for me and we'll forget how you've inconvenienced me."

"Just delivery work, right?"   465
"It's still a no."   406

✎ 420 ✎

The Constables have located you. They are determined to pursue and capture you: you will need all your knowledge of the city and its streets to escape them now. Which way will you ride?

Into the docks...   1006
Towards the tunnel at Shadwell...   386
Towards Islington...   868

✎ 421 ✎

Good riding and gaps in the traffic have brought you to Harrow Road. Out here, the buildings begin to thin out a little, and you can see the banks of the Grand Junction Canal on your left. However, the more open road also favours the Constables with their powerful Imperials. If you manage to break away from them out here, you will have left the city far behind. Make a MOTORING roll of difficulty 15, adding 1 for each velosteam **customisation** you possess.

Successful MOTORING roll!   132
Failed MOTORING roll!   1010

✎ 422 ✎

Stepping up to the bar, you are poured a glass of the house beer as soon as you show your shillings. It is a very pale, small beer with a fair head and a wheaty, biscuity flavour. They serve it cool, rather than cold, and in a slightly larger than pint-sized glass. "Dockside Ale," says the busy barmaid. Note passage **449** and if you have an INGENUITY score of 7 or greater and do not possess the codeword *Coaxial*, turn to **1394** immediately. Otherwise, roll a dice:

Score 1-2	A fence...	**175**
Score 3	A blind man...	**480**
Score 4	All about oysters...	**396**
Score 5-6	Contraband...	**706**

❧ 423 ❧

☐

If the box above is empty, tick it and read on. If it is already ticked, turn to **501** immediately.

Flat Billy got his name from the shape of his nose, which some past event has spread across his face in a grotesque and irregular manner. He holds court here in the private upstairs parlour, dispensing his versions of justice, clemency to the poor and even charity. But there is no doubt that he is a ruthless and violent man.

"So yer a rum one," begins the crime lord. "Not shy of action but a thinker too. I need someone to help Ruben out of the clink. He's doing time in Newgate."

"What will you give me?" you ask boldly.

Flat Billy chortles. "Gratitude, fer a start. I got friends 'igh up. Yer want someone bumped off? Yer looking for a favour? I'm a powerful feller."

Whether Flat Billy is the sort of ally you are looking for is hard to tell. Either way, the prospect of a gaol-break would do no harm to your fame. If you want to take on the challenge, Flat Billy will give you his thumb-print inked on a scrap of paper: **Flat Billy's thumbprint** is as good as his word, and with it, you'll have no problem gaining Ruben's trust.

Head on your way... **356**

❧ 424 ❧

Something about your disguise attracts the guards' attention. "Just where exactly are you bishop of, your eminence?" asks one. The other spots Ruben lurking in the exercise yard and pulls an emergency alarm chain. Within a minute, heavily armed guards surround you. Remove **Fat Billy's thumbprint** and any **weapons** from your possessions.

Turn to... **13**

❧ 425 ❧

Iron masts tower over the streets of Blackwall like metal trees along dingy boulevards. Ships and barges moor right amongst the buildings, although many are kept behind the high walls of the Company's private docks. The Gun stands at the riverside beneath its faded sign offering food, drink and rooms for sailors, across the street from a tall sugar warehouse. There is a broad Haulage Guild yard where cargoes of stone and timber for construction are transshipped. Where so much money is to be made, the Guilds work side-by-side with other, less public, organisations.

If you have **passdisc 820**, turn to **455** immediately.

Visit the Gun Public House...	**469**
Enter the Building Supplies Yard...	**443**
Enter the sugar warehouse... (*Cheered*)	**427**
Ride to the dockside...	**461**
Ride towards Millwall...	**431**
Steam for Bromley...	**460**
Head towards Limehouse...	**474**
Journey further west...	**435**

❧ 426 ❧

Since the mysterious conflagration at the station, much rebuilding work has begun. However, the station is still far from safe. A reek of burnt and sodden wood hangs in the air and tottering pillars of brick and steel come crashing down every day. Certainly no train will leave these platforms for a long time.

Return to Paddington... **64**

❧ 427 ❧

The watchman at the gate of the sugar warehouse opens the gate at the sound of your velosteam. "Welcome, Comrade."

Turn to... **489**

❧ 428 ❧

"So you're the one 'oos done such a bruisin' to me friends," says a deep voice. You turn to see Flat Billy, the crime lord, standing at your side. He waits for a response.

"Yes," you say.

"I like your brass," says Flat Billy. Fancy doin' a little rough work for me while Canter's restin' up? I've a team of fellers headin' down the docks tonight to remind them dockers to get their dues in sharpish. It'll be quite a brawl. Might want to bring a beater."

"I'm not getting involved in your enforcement."	**419**
"I'm always up for a fight."	**465**

❧ 429 ❧

The Director is utterly enthralled by what you have found. "This is incredible, mmm, incredible," he repeats to himself. After hearing the story of how you found it, he takes the artefact over to a powerful mechanical microscope and begins to look at it in detail. You cough to catch his attention.

"You're still here?" he asks.

"I expected some sort of payment."

"Payment? What for? This is property of the Crown. Be off with you." The Director has already rung for three heavily armed guards who appear from a small door and escort you out. Remove the **treasure trove** from your **possessions**.

Leave the museum...   **400**

❧ 430 ❧

You lean over the desk and haul Perkins to his feet. "Listen here," you snarl. "I've heard about you and your contracts. You're going to do exactly as I say - or face the consequences."

He gives in immediately, stutters a vague apology (since he has no idea who you are or how he has earned your wrath) and offers to make things right. He finds the record of his agreement with the Landlord of the Brunel Arms, **tally stick 391**, and hands it over directly. Remove the codeword *Contradict*.

Leave the station...   **64**

❧ 431 ❧

Millwall is named for the embankment along the curving riverside, topped with steam-mills that pump out water and hammer out iron plate. The yards here are famed for building some of the biggest ships afloat, such as the mighty *Leviathan* on its slipway.

There are several vacant workshops here that you can lease. If you want to take possession of one, it will cost you ten guineas - **£10 10s** - and the agent will accept bank notes. You can then tick the option below and have it as an available choice. If you have the codeword *Chariot* and a blunt weapon (a **club, blackjack** or similar), turn to **454** immediately.

Visit the shipyards...	**439**
Visit the Ship Inn...	**498**
☐ Head to your workshop...	**1308**
Take the ferry across to Greenwich... (**3s**)	**863**
Steam up to Blackwall...	**425**
Steam towards Limehouse...	**474**

❧ 432 ❧

"You got anyfink to eat, trav'ler?" The voice belongs to a small boy wearing a cut-down, worn-out, bare-threaded jacket.

Give him something to eat...

    (**pork pie**, **tin of fruit** etc)   **904**
Ride on by...   **noted passage**

❧ 433 ❧

You force Ennis to sit at his writing desk while you dictate a confession for him to write. He takes up a piece of notepaper from the Boulter's Lock Hotel and his ink pen and begins to write. Initially he complies, but suddenly he leaps up, throws a pot of ink into your eyes and dashes away.

Pursue him...   **446**

❧ 434 ❧

As you weave between the stalls, you notice the gaunt figure of Canter Dorkins limping towards you with a heavy shotgun in his hands. He has obviously heard of your reappearance and is eager to exact a repayment for his humiliation at your hands. This isn't the time or place for a fight, so you make your way prudently back to your velosteam and ride away.

Turn to...   **356**

❧ 435 ❧

The roads from Blackwall could lead you a long way indeed. Where are you headed?

Whitechapel...	**356**
The Tower of London...	**290**
Clerkenwell...	**144**
St Pancras...	**71**
Westminster...	**721**

❧ 436 ❧

The ale the girl pours you is surprisingly good. It is a small beer, malty, bitter-sweet and very refreshing. They simply call it by the name of the house: the Prince.

While enjoying your glass, you hear about the goings-on of the region and the city around you. Note passage **416** and if you have the codeword *Compassionate*, turn to **1213** immediately. Otherwise, roll a dice to see what rumours tickle your ears:

Score 1	A street gang...	**1113**
Score 2	Crafton's cookshop...	**1067**
Score 3	An untrustworthy landlord...	**1135**
Score 4	Oysters...	**556**
Score 5	An ambitious brewery...	**1196**
Score 6	A distant revolution...	**586**

✦ 437 ✦

The man behind the bar narrows his eyes at your request. If you are a **Famed Lawbreaker** or have a RUTHLESSNESS score of 10 or higher (including any item bonuses), then you will be deemed important enough to meet Flat Billy: turn to **423** immediately. Otherwise, you will be turned out of the Grave Maurice.

| Leave the pub... | **356** |

✦ 438 ✦
☐ ☐ ☐ ☐ ☐

If any of the boxes above are empty, tick one and read on. If they are all already ticked, erase the ticks and turn to **420** immediately.

Leaving your victims behind, you take to the road once more. Which way will you turn?

| Ride west for Bethnal Green... | **310** |
| Steam towards Millwall... | **431** |

✦ 439 ✦

The Millwall shipyards are engaged in one of the greatest engineering projects in the world: a massive steamship, the Leviathan, stands here on a slipway. It is aptly named, for its size is simply monstrous. The iron hull towers above the sheds of the yard. The paddlewheels have a diameter greater than the length of many whole road steamers.

The chief engineers are looking for help to complete their dream. They are hiring engineers to make components offsite, in their own workshops. You will be handsomely paid: everything about the project is done on a lavish scale.

| Take on the project... | **524** |
| Leave the shipyards... | **431** |

✦ 440 ✦
☐

If the box above is empty, tick it and turn to **486** immediately. If it is already ticked, read on.

Your room here at the Gun is low and awkward, jettied out over the river and roughly furnished. However, it is a place you can rest and regain your strength. From a side window you can just see your velosteam, parked at the side of the inn.

If you wish to leave any possessions here, write them into the box below. You can collect them when you return here again. There is even a hiding place up the narrow chimney for valuables. Note this **passage** before choosing from the options below.

Tend your wounds...	**500**
Open a strongbox...	**560**
Leave the room...	**499**

✦ 441 ✦

Bromley is certainly among the poorest parts of the city. The streets are narrow, cheaply-built terraces, sharing water pumps and lavatories. The few shops are dingy and display cheap goods and basic foodstuffs, offering short credit to their desperate customers. To the east, the ash heaps, symbols of the city's profligacy and waste, tower over the slate roofs.

Visit the ash heaps...	**459**
Steam down to the East India docks...	**425**
Ride north towards Bow...	**471**

✦ 442 ✦

You ask around and, with patience and discretion, manage to eventually come face to face with the man you are looking for. He sits at a desk piled high with all manner of documents, certificates, even half-finished banknotes.

"He-hee," chuckles the old forger. "I can use this old paper for all manner of work. You got any old documents - anything legal or monetary?"

	To buy	To sell
Letter of Introduction	£15	£10
Constables logbook	-	£4 10s
Coal Board accounts book	-	£6 3s

Ask about removing **Wanted Statuses**...	1115
Discuss forging banknotes...	1167
Commission a **release order**... (£25)	1249
Forge some incriminating material...	
(**£10, love note,**	
and **Jensen's statement**)	1093
Leave the garret...	221

❧ 443 ❧

The builder's merchants has a tall fence. An incongruous, dusty villa sits in the middle of the yard, surrounded by heaps of stone and timber, now the foreman's offices.

Tools	To buy	To sell
rope	4s	2s
waterproof paint	6s	-
shovel	8s	6s
explosives	£1 4s	-
welding tools	£2 2s	£1 10s
grappling iron	12s	9s
tarpaulin	4s	2s
measuring line	6s	4s
plaster of paris	4s	3s
brass flange joint	8s	7s
copper pipe	6s	5s
high pressure valve	18s	15s
ultra-tensed wire	£2 10s	£1 10s

Arrange for a shipment of stone... (*Caraway*)	571
Leave the yard...	461

❧ 444 ❧

Once aboard the *Tiger*, a posse of sharp-faced rogues quickly appraise the value of your clothes and possessions and decide to relieve you of them. They cut off your retreat back to dry land and lay their hands on heavy belaying pins. You will have to fight to get away!

Sailors	Weapons: **clubs (PAR 2)**
Parry:	9
Nimbleness:	6
Toughness:	6

Victory!	425
Defeat!	1106

❧ 445 ❧

You charge through the gates of Hyde Park before the keepers can ask you your business, and tear over the lawns, weaving between families of tourists picnicking in spite of the cold. Bells ring out as the Constables approach: they seem to be coming from all sides. To get away you will have to head into the exhibition itself.

You steam through the open gates of one of the mighty glasshouses, scattering tourists, guides, salesmen and awe-struck children. Make a MOTORING roll of difficulty 14, adding 3 if you possess **improved brakes**.

Successful MOTORING roll!	457
Failed MOTORING roll!	463

❧ 446 ❧

As you leave the house at a run, you see Ennis disappearing down a Mayfair mews. A patrol of six Constables comes down the street between you and your quarry. Once they have passed, the trail will be cold, but you cannot attract their attention here in the heart of Mayfair. Ennis has escaped you - for now. Where might he flee to? Remove **Andrea Rathbone's letter** and gain the codeword *Charged*.

Ride away...	750

❧ 447 ❧

"How much do you stand to gain from the Brunel contract? Personally?"

Your question jerks the man's head up from his punchcard machine. "Eh? Well, that's my own business. Entirely my own business."

"Is it? If I tell you that you are missing out on a better profit by not taking the contract?"

His beady eyes glitter. Soon he hands over **tally stick 391**, the official record of the transaction. Remove the codeword *Contradict*.

Leave the station...	64

❧ 448 ❧

Your shovel hits the top of the coffin with a hollow thump. A gruesome task follows, but you manage to lump the corpse into a sack and haul the **body** out to your velosteam (add it to your **possessions**). After refilling the hole and doing your best to erase all the traces of your presence, you sneak away.

Turn to...	**noted passage**

✤ 449 ✤

Inside the Grapes, a gang of dockers and their friends fill the parlour and the saloon. This is one of the recruiting points where foremen come to find workers for the day: those unlucky enough to be left unchosen drink on credit and waste away their time. If you have the codeword *Chaldean*, turn to **1068** immediately.

Buy a drink... (**2s**)	**422**
Join a game of darts...	**146**
Hire some casual labourers...	**965**
Leave the pub...	**474**

✤ 450 ✤

The road to London is long and dirty. You have been splashed by countless heavy wagons and soaked by the rain. Your tyres need repressurising and you need rest, but at last you are approaching the metropolis. Roll a dice to see what you encountered on the way:

Score 1-2 Get a **cold (RUTH-1, ING-1)** unless you possess a **cloak**

Score 3-4 Find a **mask** on the roadside

Score 5-6 Remove **18s** from your purse, if you have it, as the cost of food and drink on your way. If you do not possess so much, you will simply be arriving in the city hungry and cold.

Continue on to Southall...	**1022**

✤ 451 ✤

The Metropolitan Sewerage Company are excavating massive new underground tunnels to carry the effluvium and waste of the city out to the east. Their brick arches have brought them this far - but they still have a long way to go before the project will be complete.

Look for work...	**1215**
Look for Mr Hibbert...	
(**Friend of Thomas Hibbert**)	**467**
✚ Ask for a donation... (**donors' list**)	**545**
Return to Bow...	**471**

✤ 452 ✤

You slip and come crashing to the ground, bringing Ruben with you. The guards quickly pounce on you both and wrap you in chains. As they haul you off, you see **Fat Billy's thumbprint** lying in the gutter, soaking in the rain. Remove it from your possessions immediately.

Turn to...	**13**

✤ 453 ✤

Those authors have a great deal to answer for! The tales of adventuring knights and brave wanderers sank deep into your childhood imagination and you were never going to be content with a sedentary, humdrum life. Your privileged background became a stale prison and the prospect of steady employment - perhaps as a clerk, or a teacher - gnawed at you. For a few years, you tried it. But it could not satisfy the deep hunger for adventure. So, selling what you owned and bidding your few friends a secret and sudden farewell, you set out for a life altogether different - altogether new! You will create a new legend and a new hero. Like Ivanhoe, or Robin Hood, or Don Quixote, or any other of your inspirations, you will fight for justice and defend the weak!

Your ability scores are:

RUTHLESSNESS	3
ENGINEERING	2
MOTORING	2
NIMBLENESS	3
INGENUITY	5
GALLANTRY	6

You have in your possession a **blunderpistol (ACC 6)**, a **sabre (PAR 3)**, a **mask** and a **Letter of Introduction**.

Turn to...	**1200**

✤ 454 ✤

You find a motley gang of Flat Billy's men loitering near the shipyards. Each is armed with a nasty-looking club or a heavy truncheon. The plan is to jump the labourers leaving one of the shipyards where a stand has been made against paying Flat Billy's protection rates. You are given a place at the front and then off you march.

You arrive at the gates just as the hooter sounds for the end of the shift. The gates open and a chatting group of ironworkers appear - and then pause at the sight of you. With a yell, Flat Billy's men charge into them, swiping left and right with their clubs. Whether you mean to stay apart or not, you are quickly drawn into the violence as a pair of rivetmen come rushing at you with hammers: you lay them both to the ground.

It is a short and uneven battle. The ironworkers are laid out on the ground or forced to flee. Flat Billy's men head towards a nearby inn to refresh themselves. Lose a **solidarity point** and remove the codeword *Chariot*.

Return directly to Flat Billy...	**472**
Travel elsewhere...	**431**

✤ 455 ✥

You ride cautiously up to the gates of the sugar warehouse where a watchman chews a mouthful of tobacco and show him the token.

"Very interesting," he mutters, turning it over and over and giving it a rub. "Looks like I should be opening the gate for you."

You ride in, over cobbles and iron rails, between barrels and barrels of part-refined sugar, molasses and rum, and come to a halt where a man in overalls is reading from a long list at a desk. "Welcome, Comrade," he says. "The Compact for Workers' Equality are preparing for the coming revolution, right here in the heart of the capitalist machine. This is our territory. And I am Comrade Tate."

He takes you by the arm and shows you the weapon stockpiles, the printing presses and the library. "The printed word is the Compact's greatest weapon, and education the greatest freedom." Remove **passdisc 820** from your **possessions** and gain the codeword *Cheered*.

Turn to...   **489**

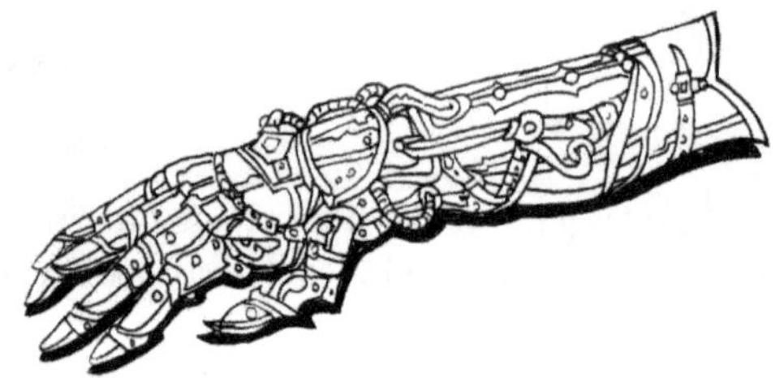

✤ 456 ✥

Fortune is smiling on you: amongst the tiny pieces of cinder and unburnt coal, you find a dirty guinea! Add **£1 1s** to your purse.

Leave the ash heaps...   **441**

✤ 457 ✥

You haul on your brakes and skid the heavy velosteam to a halt in front of the central fountain. Casting around for a way out, you see a service ramp heading into the undercroft. Your Ferguson's mantled bonnet smashes the simple barrier aside and you plunge down into the gloom, through a wide carriageway, past store-rooms and tanks, and up into the fresh air of Hyde Park. Your pursuers are nowhere to be seen.

Turn to...   **718**

✤ 458 ✥

The pot of strong, Kentish ale you are poured is called Gun Smoke. It is a rich chestnut colour, smelling of roast and berries to the nose, rich, fruity and bitter on the tongue. Note **passage number 425**. If you have the codeword *Compassionate*, turn to **1213** immediately. Otherwise, roll a dice to see who you encounter here at the Gun.

Score 1	A blind man...	**480**
Score 2	A fence...	**175**
Score 3	An investment opportunity...	**556**
Score 4	Hear about a forger...	**1181**
Score 5	Prize fighting...	**883**
Score 6	Men for hire...	**1193**

✤ 459 ✥

The ash heaps are mountainous piles of waste from the countless fires and furnaces of the city. Cinders and soot are brought here before being sorted and reused. Men women and children, the poorest of the poor, sift through the heaps, selecting pieces of broken brick, shards of metal or wood, bits of glass and anything of value, with scraps of cloth over their mouths and noses and rags around their hands.

Take work as a sifter...	**468**
Leave the ash heaps...	**441**

✤ 460 ✥

This end of the city is dominated by the dirty trades: tanning, soap-making, brick-making, and anything that stinks. You steer between a knacker's cart piled high with bones and a nightsoil wagon. Note passage **441** and roll a dice to see what you encounter:

Score 1-2	A fight in the street!	**1452**
Score 3-5	Nothing but a bad smell...	**441**
Score 6	Something sparkly...	**896**

❧ 461 ❧

You can weave your velosteam along the quay between countless stacked cargoes and past children cadging treats and women catching eyes. A small iron-hulled steamer named the *Tiger* is tied to the final pier.

Up the *Tiger's* gangplank... **444**
Board your barge... (**moored at East India**) **1069**
Leave the docks... **425**

❧ 462 ❧

The streets of the city flash by. Ruben, for once, seems intimidated by the speed and suddenness of his journey, pillion on the Ferguson. The fog thickens and you are forced to intensify the beam of your lime-lantern to see more than a few feet at a time. Then you come to Whitechapel and the Grave Maurice.

Ruben jumps off as you apply the brakes. He hops up the steps to the entrance of the pub and walks right into his brother's massive fist.

"You great lummock," says Flat Billy to his prone sibling lying in the street. "What did you go and kill them birds for? What can you do now every bogie in the entire blooming reeking metropolis is looking for you, eh?"

It might be prudent to stay out of this family disagreement. Flat Billy notices you and nods. "I appreciate that," he says brusquely. "When you're in a spot of bother, let me know and I'll do what I can. Now give me that print back." You return **Flat Billy's Thumbprint** and he tosses you a bag of coins, containing **£8** and two **silver rings**. You are now **Friend of Flat Billy**.

Leave the pub... **356**

❧ 463 ❧

You haul on the brakes but it is too late: your velosteam ploughs into the fountain at the centre of the glasshouse, throwing you into the water. Note that your velosteam is now **critically damaged**.

A hand helps you out of the fountain, and then claps a set of clock-cuffs onto your wrists. You have been taken by the Constables.

Turn to... **13**

❧ 464 ❧

The broad road east out of Bow is far less congested than the streets of the City. You open the regulator and lean back into the Ferguson's saddle, weaving around the horse-drawn drays of costermongers and the slow lumber-wagons. Three Mill Island, Stratford Broadway, the long straight up to Ilford and then, suddenly, you are in the countryside. Orchards and open fields line the roadside.

Prepare an ambush here... **482**
Return to London... **484**

❧ 465 ❧

"Good," says Flat Billy. "Lay your hand on summat heavy and blunt and meet me down Millwall. All's well, I might just fergit about what you done to poor ol' Canter." Gain the codeword *Chariot*.

Leave the Grave Maurice... **356**

❧ 466 ❧

Not only will you have to try to avoid being seen, but here in the docks, there is a great deal of competition. Everyone seems to be making off with bulges under their jacket, or tossing packages over the wall to accomplices. Make an INGENUITY roll.

Score 2-7   Caught! Turn to... **508**
Score 8-9   **two pineapples**...
Score 10-11 **two bottles of whisky...**
Score 12-13 a **net** and some **binoculars...**
Score 14-15 **two boxes of cigars...**
Score 16+   Leave empty-handed...

Get away... **341**

❧ 467 ❧

If you have the codeword *Ambulatory*, turn to **343** immediately. Otherwise, read on.

Thomas Hibbert is striding about the works with a roll of plans in hand. He is overseeing the engineers and seems very glad to see you. "It won't be long now until a flood of waste comes sluicing down these tunnels," he says. "And you have to remember that

that's a flood of waste that won't be sluicing directly into the Thames."

He is more than happy to help you make progress here in the city. He will write you a **Letter of Introduction** or make you a small loan. Cross out the options below once you have received his assistance.

⊕ **Letter of Introduction**
⊕ **£20** in coin

Leave...   471

❧ 468 ❧

The work is filthy and slow. The hope of finding something valuable amongst the ash and cinder may have been entirely unrealistic. Roll two dice to see whether anything turns up.

Score 2-3   Something glittering...   456
Score 4-9   A taste of dry dust...   491
Score 10-12 A fight breaks out...   479

❧ 469 ❧

Inside the low parlour of the Gun, rivermen and dockside porters swill their beer and sell whatever they have taken from the many 'spilt' loads at Blackwall dock. The gun itself, namesake of the house, is an old and rusted four-pound cannon standing on end at the bar. Local legend says that it was taken from the famed *Centurion*, but it is as likely to be the discarded and outmoded armament of some broken-up Indiaman. Back stairs head down to the river and a thin strip of grey silt is revealed at low tide.

As well as liquid refreshment, the owner of the Gun has rooms to rent. If you wish to take a room, you should pay **£3** and tick the box next to the option below.

Food	To buy	To sell
dozen of oysters...	6s	-
bottle of gin	10s	4s
bottle of whisky	12s	5s
Tools		
grappling iron	5s	2s
bolt of cloth	£3	-

Buy a drink... (**2s**)   458
☐ Take a room...   440
Board your boat... (**moored at East India**) 1069
Leave the inn...   425

❧ 470 ❧

A slow smile spreads across the clerk's face. "That will put a spanner in their works... Let me go and fetch the Senior Manager."

Several of the important Guild officers appear, keen to hear the story of your exploits. They laugh and clap in a most bloodthirsty manner, utterly delighted at the damage you have caused their rivals.

You are rewarded with an **autogauge (MOT+3)**, a finely calibrated automatic measuring device that will allow you to tune your velosteam and optimise its speed, as well as a purse of **£5** in coin.

Leave the offices...   379

❧ 471 ❧

Bow stands on the western bank of the River Lea, which flows south to become Bow Creek. Once its own little world, it has now been entirely swallowed by the metropolis, surrounded by brick terraces and iron-framed factories. Everything dirty and laborious is made here, near the river and the thousands of eager hands: oilskins, soap, glue, coalgas, building timbers, rivets, bricks, caustic lime, stoneware bottles and their glazes. At a short distance stands the Haulage Guild's asphalt works, where the tarmacadam for the city's roads is produced, and the massive excavations of the Grand Sewer run east from here.

Enter the Young Prince public house...	416
Ride over to the sewer excavations...	451
Head to Bird Alley Chapel...	131
Steam to Three Mill Wharf...	487
Visit High Way House... (*Caritas*)	987
Leave Bow...	495

❧ 472 ❧

"So, they's all done in, are they? The other yards will put their dues in much more quickly, I fancy. Now that's done, I reckon I've another job for you. Interested?"

"I suppose so."   423
"Not in the slightest."   406

❧ 473 ❧

The bundle of rags is stained with a mixture of someone's bodily fluids. It contains nothing but more rags. You angrily cast it back into the gutter, but before long a hot flush, an ache in the head and a nauseous lurching in the belly tell you that you have caught some kind of fever. Add a **fever (NIM-1 ING-1)** to your **Adventure Sheet** until you find some way to recover from it.

Turn to...   **noted passage**

❧ 474 ❧

Here you are amongst the terraces of Limehouse, cut through by the broad Commercial Road. The King's Canal joins the Thames here in an over-crowded dock, where an engine-powered gantry grabs cargoes recognised by their punched tickets and hauls them over to another vessel, or onto the quay.

Visit the Grapes tavern...	**449**
Enter Dr Smythe's Surgery...	**180**
Board your barge...	
(**Moored at King's Canal Dock**)	**912**
Ride for Shadwell...	**380**
Steam towards Bow...	**471**
Head to Blackwall...	**425**
Ride to Millwall...	**431**

❧ 475 ❧

Your sentence is long, with many petty unfairnesses and sufferings. The inmates are violent and ruthless, brawls are common, food is poor, disease is rife and hope precious hard to come by. Any form of distraction is welcome. To see what you experience during the remainder of your stay, roll two dice, adding 4 if you possess a **chess set** and 1 for each **£1** you can spend on improving your living conditions. However, you should subtract 2 for each **wound** you might still possess.

Score 1-5   A debilitating disease: lower your NIMBLENESS by 3...

Score 6-8   Your reputation suffers: lower your RUTHLESSNESS by 2...

Score 9   Set upon by a gang: you have **lost a hand (NIM-2, MOT-2)**...

Score 11-13   Your friends forget you: remove the two **oldest Friendships** you possess...

Score 14+   A good opponent and frequent games of chess improve your mental agility: improve your INGENUITY by 1...

Eventually any **wounds** you have will heal: replace each one with a **scar**, rolling two dice and gaining an **intimidating scar (RUTH+1)** on a score of 11 or 12. Remove any remaining **money** (all spent on bribes, morsels of more nourishing food or laundry).

Turn to...   **1498**

❧ 476 ❧

Mrs Roberts is frankly insulted by your crass attempt to flatter her. "Get out," she says. "Before I toss you in the Thames myself."

Return to your boat...   **847**

❧ 477 ❧

The beer served at the Ship is, unusually, not brewed locally. It is brought down the coast from the North country. Dark reddish-brown, with a mighty head of foam that persists even as you drink, it has a nutty flavour, somewhat reminiscent of sunlight on freshly-ploughed ground. This Sutherland Champion is the sole reason for the establishment here: with access to a beer this good, the landlord needed to borrow money to fund his licence and set himself up in business. Note passage **498** and roll a dice:

Score 1-2	Grave robbers...	**1019**
Score 3-4	A fence...	**175**
Score 5-6	False papers...	**1159**

❧ 478 ❧

Just east of the Tower are the lock gates to St Katharine's Docks - the headquarters of the River Guild here in the city. You will only be able to pass through and enter the dock if you possess a **bargee's badge** - as well as considerable patience, as the gates are busy and the queue substantial.

Enter St Katharine's docks... (**bargee's badge**)	**387**
Steam on upriver...	**1009**
Steam downriver towards Limehouse...	**968**

❧ 479 ❧

A fight breaks out among the other sifters: the overseer insists that one has hidden something from the ash heaps in his clothing.

Help the overseer...	**496**
Help the sifter...	**505**
Get out of the fight...	**441**

❧ 480 ❧

The man across the table from you is blind. He has a long staff leaning against the settle beside him and a filthy bandage across his brow. He shifts as you approach. "Eh? Who's there? Pity on an old man, a sailor in King George's wars, God bless 'im, lost 'is eyes in the service of 'is country, such as it is."

He tells you of the war against Denmark and the iron ships of King Augustus, of battles on the German Ocean and drownings in the fog. He tells you of shipwrecks and storms and shipmates fighting one another for the final place in a boat. He tells you of losing his eyes and much of his face to a raking broadside of splinter-shells and how he has scratched a living ever since. "Like a poor old crow, I am, hobbling along and goin' fer scraps."

Give him money...	(£2 2s)	490
Return to the parlour...	**noted passage**	

❧ 481 ❧

If you have the codeword *Critical*, turn to **8** immediately. Otherwise, read on.

A man sits at the side of the road, dressed in a torn shirt and fumbling at an empty leathern bottle. He catches your eye. "What I need is another drink," he says. "You got any pity for a drunk like me? I'll give yer this ring?" If you have a **bottle of wine** or another alcoholic drink, you can swap it for the **gold ring** he offers you and gain the codeword *Critical*.

Leave him be... **noted passage**

❧ 482 ❧

You are on the Roman Road at place known as Seven Kings: note passage **438**. A Haulage Guild watering station stands a short distance away. If you have the codeword *Chapter*, turn to **1396** immediately. If you have a **telescope** or **binoculars**, turn to **492** immediately. Otherwise, roll a dice to see what you encounter.

Score 1-2	A private steam carriage...	1373
Score 3-4	The Telegraph Guild...	1400
Score 5-6	The Haulage Guild...	1444

❧ 483 ❧

You spread your gold about among the guards (remove it from your purse now) and quickly discover which of them is the most vulnerable to avarice. You must then do what you can to convince him to actually overlook the lock on your cell one night. Make a GALLANTRY roll of difficulty 14, adding 2 if you have more than **15 solidarity points**, 2 if you are the **People's Champion** and 1 for each **£1** you can afford to add to your bribe.

Successful GALLANTRY roll!	**497**
Failed GALLANTRY roll!	**475**

❧ 484 ❧

Your ride back towards the city comes as the sun sinks ahead of you. Gas street lamps are lit in Stratford. At Three Mill Island the late shift is rung in and the day shift is released from the foundries and the factories. You brake the heavy velosteam, ride over Bow Bridge and slow to the pace of the city traffic.

Ride into Bow... **471**

❧ 485 ❧

"If you think I carry that much money around with me, then you're a fool," you counter.

"You're a fool if you can't lay your hands on it quickly," snarls the woman, drawing a sharp knife and pointing it at your throat. She moved with a smooth suddenness that gave you absolutely no chance of protecting yourself. "Bring the money - or the pouch of diamonds - to the north entrance of the Thames Tunnel before the end of the week. If you don't, we will find you and we will kill you."

She climbs back into the van, along with her companion, and drives off.

Carry on to Pentonville... **107**

❧ 486 ❧

The landlord takes you up a flight of stairs and shows you the room. "Pretty nice hideaway for one such as yourself," he says. "Good view of the river. See every sail from here. No-one need know you're here." He winks and rubs his hands together as if they are cold.

For a one-off fee of three guineas (**£3 3s**), he promises to keep your presence here a secret from the Constables and anyone else who comes asking. If you choose to pay him, remove the money and gain the codeword *Considerate*.

Turn to... **440**

❧ 487 ❧

The wharf at Three Mill Island is busy but there is just enough room to roll through the gates and down to the quayside. A vast paper mill uses the water of the river Lea to hammer rag into fine paper for the city trade, and a grain mill churns flour from wheat. The third mill saws away, night and day, producing lumber. Barges unload corn and machinery.

Tools	To buy	To sell
measuring line	6s	2s
net	4s	2s
rag paper	10s	6s

Go aboard your barge...

(moored at Three Mill Wharf)	1001
Leave the wharf...	471

❧ 488 ❧

The docks at St Katharine's could be destroyed, given time and the skilful use of explosives. The lock gates, once broken apart, could release the destructive force of the tide into the dock, and where the buildings are close to the edges of the quay, they could be encouraged to topple into the water, releasing a destructive wave. But the risks are great - both to you and to many others. If you wish to go ahead, and you have a **demolition sequence** calculated by computational engine, turn to **502** immediately. To calculate such a thing, you would require at least a general survey of the docks, measured secretly by night or found in some other way. Otherwise, make an ENGINEERING roll of difficulty 20 or leave the challenge for now.

Successful ENGINEERING roll!	502
Failed ENGINEERING roll!	519
Did not attempt ENGINEERING roll...	408

❧ 489 ❧

The sugar warehouse swarms with grim-faced men and women. Some, it is true, are ferrying hundredweight sacks of raw or processed sugar to and from, but many more are working at the presses, attending lectures on Ambrose's *Principles and Purposes*, crafting weaponry and explosives, or scheming in alcoves. If you have the codeword *Anteater*, turn to **1092** immediately.

While here, you have access to the Compact's resources. They will sell supplies to you and buy without question. You can also seek out medical treatment if you are wounded or unwell.

Clothing	To buy	To sell
mask	2s	-
cloak	£1	15s
goggles (MOT+1)	£2	£1 15s
eyepatch (RUTH+1)	10s	6s
Tools	To buy	To sell
adjustable wrench (ENG+1)	£1 8s	£1 2s
grappling iron	12s	9s
tarpaulin	4s	2s
lockpicks	6s	3s
telescope	£3	£2
explosives	£2	-
Jewellery	To buy	To sell
silver bar	-	£10
gold bar	-	£35
Medical items	To buy	To sell
bandages	3s	-
soothing lotion	2s	1s
bottle of chloroform	£2	£1 5s
poison	£1	10s
white pills (ING+2) ☐ ☐ ☐	£2 10s	-
pink pills (NIM+2) ☐ ☐ ☐	£2 10s	-
Other items	To buy	To sell
revolutionary poster	1s	-
Jensen's Statement	£1	-

Medical treatment	To buy
Treat a **wound**...	£1 10s
Treat a **black eye**...	15s
Treat a **fever**...	10s
Treat a **burn**...	6s
Treat a **stiff back**...	12s

Contribute towards the Revolution!	919
Speak to the High Council... (*Catastrophe*)	1149
Leave the warehouse...	425

❧ 490 ❧

When he feels the cold coin in his hand, the blind man seems overcome with gratitude. "What goodness you show an old sailor," he stutters. "Now, friend, I have shipmates still. Aboard the *Tiger*, docked nearby, you'll find recompense for your generosity."

Leave the man... **noted passage**

❧ 491 ❧

You find nothing amongst the dust and ashes other than a pervasive dryness that later turns into a hacking cough. You are paid **1s** for your day's work and dismissed.

Leave the ash heaps... **441**

❧ 492 ❧

With the benefit of your lenses you will be able to see the approaching traffic in good time and choose your target carefully. What will you take as your prey?

A private steam carriage... **1373**
The Telegraph Guild... **1400**
The Haulage Guild... **1444**
The Coal Board... **1324**

❧ 493 ❧
☐

If the box above is empty, tick it and read on. If it is already ticked, turn to **501** immediately.

"It ain't widely known that I've come to an arrangement with the Constables," says Flat Billy. "But Lord Beaufort and I... Well, he's been taking my money for a good while now. Which is nice, because if anyone ever finds out, he'll be for the chop, won't 'e?"

"What do you want me to do?"

"Just our regular handover. You take this bundle over to the top of the Monument and give it to Lord Beaufort. In person. Normalwise, this is Canter's job, but 'e ain't feelin' that well. 'Is nobility will give us a little list of requests in return. Bring it back sharpish."

Flat Billy hands you a **black oilcloth packet**. "You open that and I'll skin yer," he says happily. Gain the codeword *Carrier*.

Head on your way... **514**

❧ 494 ❧

You can gather a crowd of the dockers fairly easily, but to convince them, you must assure them that you are cut of the same cloth. This you cannot do if your GALLANTRY is too high. If your GALLANTRY score (including modifications) is 6 or higher, turn to **408** immediately. Otherwise, make an INGENUITY roll of difficulty 14, adding 2 if you possess a **revolutionary poster**.

Successful INGENUITY roll! **522**
Failed INGENUITY roll! **408**

❧ 495 ❧

The streets of Bow lead in all manner of directions. You might even choose to steam up and take a longer ride across town from here.

Ride to Whitechapel... **356**
Head south towards Bromley... **441**
Steam to Bethnal Green... **310**
Turn towards Limehouse... **474**
Up towards Essex... **464**
Go west to Camden Town... **84**

❧ 496 ❧

You take up the cause of the authority. If the sifter is paid to work here, then anything he finds must be turned in to the owners of the ash heaps. Note whether you decide to take on the sifters with a bladed weapon (**sabre**, **rapier** or similar) or a blunt weapon (**blackjack**, **club** or your **fists (PAR 0)** before you engage in the combat.

Sifters	Weapons: **clubs (PAR 2)**
Parry:	8
Nimbleness:	6
Toughness: 4	

Victory!	**512**
Defeat!	**999**

❧ 497 ❧

Somehow, through promises of future favour, flattery, false friendship and good hard cash, you manage to convince one of the cell-keepers to arrange your escape. He leaves your cell unlocked one night and leaves his post early, but manages to land the blame squarely on the warden on the next shift. You slip out and climb first onto the roof, then over onto the slates of a neighbouring biscuit manufacturers, down to the ground, and then regain your velosteam from the shed where it is stored. You should add **Escaped from Gaol** to your **Great Deeds** before going any further, and then it is time to make your getaway. Which direction will you ride?

To Chelsea...	**794**
To Bow...	**471**
To Highgate...	**28**

❧ 498 ❧

The Ship is barely more than a private dwelling with a licence pasted onto the door-lintel. It is the local den of the shipwrights' mates and the stevedores. While you stand in the doorway a boy of no more than six squeezes past carrying a jug of beer for his parents at home.

Buy a drink...	**(2s)**	**477**
Leave the Ship...		**431**

❧ 499 ❧

A maid is sent to collect payment for your bed, board and fire here. Roll a dice to see what you must pay her.

Score 1-3	**3s**
Score 4	**6s**
Score 5	**10s**
Score 6	**£1 10s**

If you cannot pay the rent, the landlord will remove any **possessions** from the box in passage **440** (erase them now). If you have no possessions for him to confiscate, he will change the lock on the room: erase the tick in the box in passage **469**.

Finally, before you depart, you should take care to see whether anyone has been watching your room. Roll another dice and: add 2 if you were unwilling or unable to pay the maid; add 1 for each **Wanted Status** you possess; add 1 if you are a **Member of the Compact for Workers' Equality**; subtract 5 if you have the codeword *Considerate*.

Score 0-5	Nobody knows...	**425**
Score 6+	The Constables await!	**420**

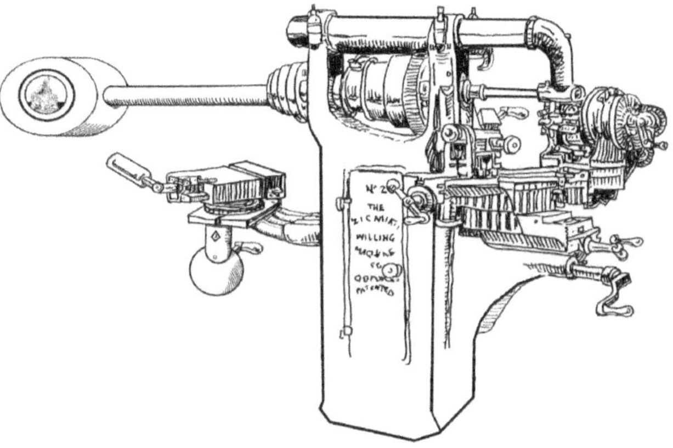

❧ 500 ❧

Now that you are in a quiet and sheltered place, you can set about treating the damage of your adventures. To treat one or more **wounds**, you will need **bandages** or a **cloak** of any kind to staunch the bleeding. Remove this from your possessions and make an INGENUITY roll, adding 2 for each level of **medical training** you possess and 1 if you have a bottle of **soothing ointment** (which you should also remove).

Score 0-9	A problematic injury: the **wounds** remain...
Score 10-14	Healed: replace one **wound** with a **scar**
Score 15	A dramatic result: replace one **wound** with an **intimidating scar (RUTH+1)**...
Score 16-18	Healed: replace two **wounds** with two **scars**...
Score 19	Healed: replace three **wounds** with three **scars**...
Score 20 or more	Healed: replace two **wounds** with a single **scar**...

You may also treat the following ailments:

a **fever** take a hot bath, drink a bottle of **whisky** and take three **white pills**

a **burn** use a bottle of **soothing ointment** and any piece of **clothing**

a **cold** drink a **bottle of cough medicine**

a **stiff back** a bottle of **soothing ointment** and a tightly-wound **bandage**

a **black eye** a poultice made from a **bandage** and a cold **meat pie**

Remove any **possessions** you have used and erase any successfully-treated ailments from your **Adventure Sheet**.

Turn to...   **noted passage**

❧ 501 ❦

"Simple little job," says Flat Billy. "Take these explosives down to Lambeth. The landlord of the Pineapple will look after them and give you a payment in return. Alright?"

Add the **explosives** to your possessions.

Head on your way...   **377**

❧ 502 ❦

To obtain an avalanche effect, in which each destructive catastrophe triggers another, you must place your precious explosives with particular care. Working under the cover of darkness, you pack them beneath the pillars supporting the larger warehouses, around the sluices of the great lock gates, and over the air vents of the boiler house. Once the little clockwork timers are set ticking, you retreat to the roof of an overlooking warehouse to observe the destruction.

The first crack of gunpowder destroys several warehouse supports and the building above them crashes to the ground, cracking the arches of the quay and setting the dockwater rippling. Boats crash into one another, amplifying the shockwaves, and then the quay itself collapses into the water, bringing down another warehouse with a crash. Barrels of rum and spirits split and burst, then flash into flame as the vapours ignite. Another explosion sends the chimney of the boiler house crashing down onto the gates, and another loosens their hinges and releases a surge of tidal water through the sluices. The mighty iron gates groan, twist and surrender to the high tide, which rushes in, raising boats up above their mooring bollards and slamming them against one another, holing some,

overturning many, and bringing down even more of the warehouses.

Cries go up - the shouts of the trapped dockers and sailors - but you are already making your escape. You slip down a drainpipe and swing yourself into the Ferguson's saddle, kick the friction igniter and accelerate away. Remove the **explosives** and gain the codeword *Collapse*. Having learnt a great deal from this escapade, you should also add a level of **explosives expert** to your **Additional Skills** on your **Adventure Sheet**. Note that you are now **Wanted by the River Guild**, and if you were foolish enough to leave a boat **moored at St Katharine's**, it and all its cargo should be removed from your **Adventure Sheet**.

Ride off!   **290**

❧ 503 ❦

A group of ruffians emerge from the Grave Maurice. "You should've known better than to come back here," says their leader. "Let's scrag this beggar, lads."

Gang	Weapons: knives (PAR 1)
Parry:	12
Nimbleness:	11
Toughness:	2

Victory!	**356**
Defeat!	**999**

❧ 504 ❦

The officer leaps up when he recognises who he has in front of him. "Men, bring a ball and chain! This dangerous criminal must not get away!"

You are hooded, chained and hustled into an iron carriage. A jolting ride comes before being hauled down and stumbling, shambling and tripping behind your chain. Eventually the rough hood is torn off, your chains removed and a door slammed behind you.

"Where am I?" you ask.

The warder laughs through the hatch in your door. "These are the condemned cells in Newgate Prison. Where did you expect to end up? You're to be hanged in the morning. Mr Fazerlacky is coming up from Woolwich to do the job. Should draw quite a crowd. settle down. Don't want to lose control of your emotions. Or your bowels. Happens all too frequently on the stand, and then who has to clean that up, eh?"

Can you sleep, as the candles are dowsed in the corridor and your cell is plunged into darkness? A tiny grill allows a thin ray of moonlight in, together with, in the very middle of the night, the sound of twelve strokes of a handbell and a mournful voice. "Consider your sins and crimes. Consider the eternal torment of damnation that awaits and turn to your Saviour in sorrow and repentance! Justice will be done upon your body - flee from the punishment of your soul!"

Turn to...   **828**

❧ 505 ❧

The overseer is shocked to see the workers ganging up to protect the sifter and he draws a long knife as well as his club. The others hang back, unsure how to proceed. You will have to deal with him yourself.

Overseer	Weapon: **knife (PAR 1)**
Parry:	8
Nimbleness:	7
Toughness:	5

Victory!	**525**
Defeat!	**999**

❧ 506 ❧

It takes you three nights to loosely plan out the docks, the moorings and the quayside, but you succeed in drawing a **plan of St Katharine's docks.** Quite who this will interest is, in itself, an interesting question.

Leave the docks...   **341**

❧ 507 ❧

You have been recognised. Whether it is your unique velosteam or the written description that has been circulated among the drivers, you are unable to simple turn about and leave. A posse of men and women accustomed to hard fighting begin to form around you, spurred on by the prospect of a reward. Individually, they may not be your match, but together...

Make a break for the gates...   **521**
Talk your way out of trouble...   **531**

❧ 508 ❧

A shout goes up: you have been spotted pilfering! The guards give chase, forcing you to clamber onto bales of cotton and leap over the wall. You are now **Wanted by the River Guild** (if you were not already).

Mount your velosteam...   **341**

❧ 509 ❧

Your efforts have not been stealthy enough: you are discovered by a guard and felled with a blow to the head from a wooden truncheon. They take your few **possessions** from you - enough to identify you as a potential assassin - and toss you into the deepest available cell in one of His Majesty's prisons.

Turn to...   **335**

❧ 510 ❧

"Well for that money," says Maggie Laine, "We'll have to see how the little one does. There's a lot of abandoned babes in this awful place. And not many of them are strong enough to live." She takes the baby from you and closes the door.

There has to be a better way.

Ride on to Clerkenwell...   **144**

❧ 511 ❧

Behind the gilt and glamour, the stage door of the Lyceum reveals the tawdry reality of the world of the theatre. Two actors lean against the unpainted bricks, sharing a raw cigarette. They eye you suspiciously. Are you an informer for the Constables? A thief looking for a way into the building? A pirate of plays, hoping to swipe a script and have it printed?

Chat with the actors...   **564**
Ask about auditions...   **576**
Ride down to the Strand...   **139**
Steam north to Bloomsbury...   **400**

❧ 512 ❧

The owners of the ash heaps appreciate your help in keeping order amongst their employees. "It's them dratted Compact everywhere stirring up trouble," you are told. "People ain't got no respect for law and order no more." If you are **Wanted by the Constables**, remove that **Wanted Status** now, as the owners put in a good word and have your record cleared. If you won the fight using a **bladed weapon**, lose a **Solidarity Point**.

Leave the ash heaps...   **441**

❧ 513 ❧

You chug steadily downstream, making a few minor trades that allow you to pay the river tolls on the way. Nobody pays any attention to another river haulier -

they are all far too busy making money and carrying on their own business.

Eventually you approach Teddington lock - the final lock across the Thames - and the furthest reach of the tide. From here on, you will be sailing on the brackish water flushed upstream twice a day.

Turn to... **364**

✧ 514 ✧

Of course, you carefully untie the packet as soon as you are out of sight. Inside are **two hundred guineas in banknotes**.

You have several courses of action open to you now. If you want to simply steal the money, remove the **black oilskin packet**, add the paper money to your **possessions** and continue your adventures. However, you had better steer very clear of Flat Billy in future.

Alternatively, if you possess **two hundred guineas in forged banknotes**, you could replace them for the real ones. If you can do this now, or can make the exchange later while you still possess the **black oilskin packet**, then make a note of its new contents on your **Adventure Sheet**.

If you choose to leave the money where it is, then you can simply take it to the rendezvous.

Head directly to the Monument... **264**
Continue on your adventures for now... **356**

✧ 515 ✧

You connect the machine to the Brewer's Guild database, and the engine swiftly records an alteration in the vote, indicating a clear majority for Mr Richard Pierce. With this mischief complete, you reset the machine and take back your **punchcards**.

Late the next day, you head over to the Horn at Clerkenwell, where Pierce is celebrating the outcome of the election. "I was appointed Chairman this morning! This is my dream come true. Do I have you to thank?"

When you explain what you did, he laughs, reaches into his pocket and gives you **£10 10s**. "A small appreciation. Come and have a drink with me here when you can and I'll show you my gratitude." You are now the **Friend of Richard Pierce**. If you have the **publican's contract** he will also add his signature and you can gain the codeword *Conglomerate*. Remove the codeword *Corrupt*.

Ride on... **144**

✧ 516 ✧

An escape from the Tower will be a challenge indeed - or a legend in the making. From your cell and armed only with any meagre possessions you have managed to slip past the guards, you will need to break through yards of solid stone, lower yourself down steep ramparts, escape guards, tripwires, traps and even lions.

If you have a **pet raven**, turn to **125** immediately. If not, but you have the **Tower key**, turn to **109**. Otherwise, you must set to work. First, to break through the wall and prepare an exit, make an ENGINEERING roll of difficulty 18, adding 2 if you possess a **mechanical arm** or **steam fist**, 2 if you have a **skeleton key**, 1 if you have any **lockpicks** and 1 if you have a **grappling iron**, **crowbar** or **rope**.

Successful ENGINEERING roll! **529**
Failed ENGINEERING roll! **568**

✧ 517 ✧
☐

If the box above is empty, tick it and turn to **565** immediately. If it is already ticked, read on.

"So you return," says the Reverend. He doesn't seem sorry to see you, but he looks thin and overworked. If you have the codeword *Clearly*, turn to **935** immediately.

"I need to confess my sins." **579**
"I have a contribution towards your work." **589**

✧ 518 ✧

You slip into the river near Peddlar's Acre, at the eastern end of Westminster bridge. The filthy water is chilling and the tide is about to turn: the river itself will carry you downstream to your target, if you are careful.

Make a NIMBLENESS roll of difficulty 15 to make the swim successfully.

Successful NIMBLENESS roll! **539**
Failed NIMBLENESS roll! **533**

❧ 519 ❧

You place your explosives where you think they have the best chance of creating an avalanche effect (remove them from your **possessions**), light the fuses and retreat.

A colossal explosion shakes the ground and one of the warehouses slumps as its pillars give way. Waves ripple out across the water, rocking the moored ships, but you have failed to set off a destructive chain. As the dust settles, voices cry out and dockers and stevedores come running. They spot you in your hiding place and give chase. You must be off! Note that you are now **Wanted by the River Guild**.

Ride away...   **278**

❧ 520 ❧

The clerk listens to your report and takes down some notes. He disappears into a backroom before returning with the reply of his superiors. Remove the codeword *Chipped* and roll a dice to see how you are rewarded.

Score 1   Reported: you are now **Wanted by the Constables**
Score 2-3   **£2** in cash...
Score 4-5   **£3 10s** in cash...
Score 6   a **Letter of Introduction**...

Leave the offices...   **379**

❧ 521 ❧

The gates are already being swung shut and a net readied to entangle you. Make a MOTORING roll of difficulty 11, adding 2 if you possess a **ramming beak**.

Successful MOTORING roll!   **noted passage**
Failed MOTORING roll!   **541**

❧ 522 ❧

The dockers come around to your way of thinking fairly quickly. They disperse, muttering about how to form their own cadre and appoint their own officials. Note passage **408** and turn to **1133**, where you should tick the box marked **Dockers Radicalised.**

❧ 523 ❧

The box below is for any items you are unable to carry while on the Compact's mission; write them here, and if you survive, you may be able to collect them again.

Turn to...   **noted passage**

❧ 524 ❧

A man in a stovepipe hat comes over to see you. "Rum sort of engineer, you make." He has parts of the engine that still need milling, but their exact dimensions must be calculated carefully - probably using a calculating engine and the correct series of punchcards - before being fabricated at a workshop. "I will pay thirty guineas for good work," he says. Gain the codeword *Cabin.*

Leave the shipyards...   **431**

❧ 525 ❧

Your final blow knocks the overseer to the ground and you and the accused sifter make off, sharply. You help him onto the back of your velosteam and ride between the lines of steam lorries and locobuses into the smog of the city. "Drop me off in Clerkenwell," he says. "I can fence this there." He shows you a **gold ring** that he found amongst the rubbish. "That's a month's eating for my three little ones." If you want to buy the ring from him for **£3**, add it to your **possessions** and gain the codeword *Compassionate.*

Turn to...   **144**

❧ 526 ❧

You have no choice but to take the baby to the Foundling's Home. Your knock at the gate provokes a sharp response from the warder and then, when they see the baby, the question.

"Whose is it?"
"I have no idea."

"Not yours, is it?"

"No."

The child is grudgingly admitted. As you hand it over, small, pink and wheezy, barely awake to its own life and with barely a hair on its head, you are forced to confront the utter unlikelihood of the child surviving to maturity and happiness. This is the city in which you find yourself.

Leave the Foundling Home...   **144**

✵ 527 ✵

Something is happening on the purchasing floor... Share prices are tumbling. Steady stocks are flickering, as shareholders on the telegraph network get the news and begin to sell. Now the traders themselves are off-loading their portfolios in a desperate attempt to avoid the worst losses.

As you watch, the values of everything on the board drop to their lowest value.   It is a vast depreciation - and surely a harbinger of much economic difficulty to come.   Remove any of the codewords in the box to the left and tick any in the box to the right that you do not yet possess.

Remove these codewords	Tick these codewords
Carling	*Crumb*
Chipped	*Catiline*
Egret	*Cricket*

Turn to...   **403**

✵ 528 ✵

With paper, pen and the occasional candle, you set about writing. Has this been a dream of yours, or is it the act of desperation? One thing is sure: you will be blessedly free of interruption here.   What are you writing?

A novel...   **550**
A political manifesto...   **569**
Your adventures...   **582**

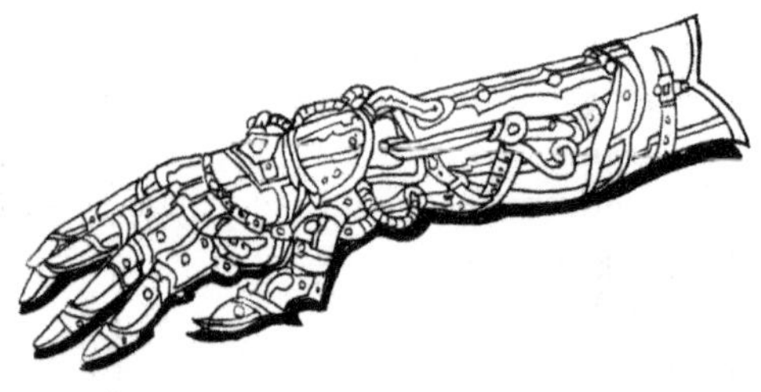

✵ 529 ✵

You have found your faithful Ferguson again at last. Apart from dust, she bears no further damage or markings of interference. You keep watch through the door of the shed, waiting until the guards open the gate and lower the drawbridge for some arrival. You mount up, kick the friction igniter, and accelerate through the gate and out into the city.

You had better add **Escaped from the Tower** to your **Great Deeds**.

Ride towards London Bridge...   **1000**
Ride to Whitechapel...   **356**

✵ 530 ✵

You sit yourself in a rough wooden pew near the back. Outside, the gas lamps of Bow High Street light themselves with a flash and the congregation dribbles in for the evening service.   The Reverend Highrun greets some of his regulars, then heads to the pulpit and leads the singing of several hymns. There is no accompaniment to the rough accents of the working people: some voices are passionate and energetic, others tired, lacklustre or bored of the same words they have sung before.

A woman hobbles up to lead prayers for the city and for people known to the congregation. Then the Reverend begins to speak.

"My text is the sixty-eighth Psalm." He reads in a fine, carrying voice, choosing to repeat a verse he wants to emphasise. "A father to the fatherless, a defender of widows, is God in his holy dwelling." He looks up.

"Many of you know of my vision of a Foundling's Hospital here in the city - a place for orphans and abandoned children to find health, home and a path to adulthood.   But do you know that the spirit of orphanhood preys upon more than those without parents? It possesses all those who protest that they need no help, who insist upon earning for themselves instead of receiving gratefully. It is the voice that says, 'I will owe nothing to any man. I will make my own way.' It dominates our national attitude of the mind, for somehow we believe that God helps those who help themselves."

He pauses to look around. "But that is not what Jesus taught about our heavenly Father. 'Suffer ye the little children to come unto me,' he said. 'You must be like little children,' he said. 'God is our refuge and our help,' we sing. If we are too proud to call ourselves children of the most high God, we will always be striving, always be stuck in a place of poverty, no matter how rich we make ourselves."

Some of the congregation are muttering angrily to one another. Presumably they dislike being called proud for wanting to stand on their own two feet, or perhaps they are convicted in their spirits. Gain the codeword *Childlike*.

Heckle the minister...	**805**
Slip away...	**471**

❧ 531 ❧

"Wait, wait!" you cry. "Yes, it is true that I have stolen from the Guild - but only in the name of the poor and the downtrodden!" You will have to work hard to convince the crowd: make a GALLANTRY roll of difficulty 10, adding 2 if you are a **Member of the Compact for Workers' Equality**.

Successful GALLANTRY roll!	**noted passage**
Failed GALLANTRY roll!	**541**

❧ 532 ❧

To remotely access the bank's account database, you encode a query as though it originated from within the bank itself. The powerful alternate-possibilty testing routine of the Aramanth punchcards allows you, eventually, to extract a name and address associated with the account: Hortensia Duploye, the Duchess of Kent.

What you choose to do with this information is up to you. Perhaps you will pursue her at her house, Kent Mansion, in Chelsea?

Remove the codeword *Commission* and gain the **Duchess's account number**, which the engine helpfully stamps out for you. Before you leave, you collect the **punchcards (Aramanth A)** and reset the machine.

Turn to...	**noted passage**

❧ 533 ❧

The Thames is not a friend to the unwary swimmer: you head downriver towards the mooring, keeping low in the water and hoping for sleepy guards. Then, out of nowhere, a heavy log jettisoned by some lighter comes sweeping along with the current and cracks into your head. If you have the codeword *Catastrophe*, read on. Otherwise, turn to **1106** immediately.

The blow is sharp enough to concuss you: together with the loss of blood, it is enough to leave you floating facedown in the river for as long as it takes you to drown.

Turn to the **epilogue**...

❧ 534 ❧

Bit by bit, the Old Nichol is being rebuilt. The inhabitants are wary of their landlady's motives, sure that she will raise rents and force them to leave their tightly-knit community. Perhaps they don't realise that the rent-collectors and enforcers had already inflated their rents to the highest in the city. Either way, progress is slow, but the first of the worst tenements built with the evil billysweet mortar have been knocked to the ground and the foundations for fine, well-lit, gracefully tiered dwellings put in their place.

Ride up to Bethnal Green...	**310**
Turn towards Shoreditch...	**308**

❧ 535 ❧

The computational engine does the impossible: it takes the information from the **torn manifest** and posits exactly what the full cargo of the airship should have been. Tiny levers flick backwards and forth from an inkpad, stamping out a new, complete version of the document. Remove the **torn manifest** and replace it with a **repaired manifest**.

Turn to...	**noted passage**

❧ 536 ❧

You have little to offer the frog, but the occasional dead fly caught whizzing over your bucket seems welcome, and with little else to occupy you, you manage to build some sort of companiable inter-dependence, if not a true friendship. Gain **two levels** of **animal friendship**.

Wait for your release...	**398**

❧ 537 ❧

Just as you approach Somerset House, a bell begins to clang over an archway and a fast steam-carriage comes charging out. Constables hanging from the running boards beat the crowd aside with their truncheons and through the glass you spot the handsome, dark-haired face of Lord Hadrian Beaufort, Chief Constable.

A street sweeper sees you spit in disgust and comes to offer her perspective. "I fancy, like many, you've no high opinion of his excellency Lord Beaufort. We of the streets would be happy to see him gone."

"Oh yes?"

"But you'd have to get close to do the deed." She isn't wrong: even if you were to aim at some other method than murder, hoping to destroy his reputation and see him exiled or imprisoned, you would need to get into his company to find out more.

"What does he want?" you muse aloud.

The street sweeper laughs. "That's simple. He want Maria Roberts brought down from her position advising the King. Anyone who can bring him information against her is welcomed with open arms."

"Maria Roberts?"

"The King's mistress, of course. The actress that caught his eye."

Leave Somerset House for now...	**139**

✎ 538 ✐

Somehow he recognises you. "Twice you have stopped me, and twice you have shown mercy," he says. "I thank you. Should you travel as far as Caernavon, seek me out there. I will have work for as considered a road thief as yourself." Remove the codeword *Anhedonic* and gain the codeword *Caernavon*.

Turn to...	**noted passage**

✎ 539 ✐

Despite the current and the constant barrage of jetsam - including a log that almost strikes you in the head - you manage to reach the mooring chain of the *Gentilesse* without being spotted. Climbing aboard is your next challenge: if you have a **grappling iron**, turn to **549** immediately. Otherwise, you must make another NIMBLENESS roll of difficulty 15, adding 1 if you possess a **rope**.

Successful NIMBLENESS roll!	**549**
Failed NIMBLENESS roll!	**533**

✎ 540 ✐

The Metropolitan Constabulary will not take your ruthless assault on one of their officers lightly: you are now **Wanted by the Constables** if you are not already. However, there is some reward to having defeated one of the hated enforcers. Roll two dice to see what you receive.

Score 2-3   Gain a **solidarity point** as news of your deed spreads

Score 4-6   Loot a **constable's whistle** and **14s**

Score 7-8   Take a **cloak** and **pocket watch**

Score 9-12   Take a **lantern** and **£1 8s**

Turn to...	**402**

✎ 541 ✐

The gathered crowd tear you from your velosteam and mete out their rough justice: any enemy of the Guild suffers the same as a violent warning and a punishment. You hand is held against a block and a heated shovel blade used to take it clean off. Hot tar cauterises the stump: note that you now have **lost a hand (NIM-2 GAL-2)**. But the Guild consider your debt paid. They could not imagine you would continue to offend them after such a horrific ordeal. You are no longer **Wanted by the Haulage Guild**.

Turn to...	**noted passage**

✎ 542 ✐

You are admitted to Baroness Dimlight's salon. "Oh, you have it?" she asks. She grabs at the bottle of **Tillson's hot sauce** (remove it from your **possessions**) and cracks it open. She takes a big sniff and smiles. "Excellent." Then she whips off her boots and socks and begins to smear it between her toes.

"The money is in that pouch over there. Good

trustworthy gold, not that paper rubbish."

The leather pouch contains fifty guineas, as she promised: **£52 10s**. How much of it will reach the orphanage?

Leave the mad Baroness...   **151**

❧ 543 ❧

The series of cables and cams within the tower that govern the flapping panels are complex, but twisted and jammed correctly, they can themselves put enough tension into the structure to tear the telegraph apart. With a few carefully placed chocks and wedges, you set the structure groaning. Gain the codeword *Crazed*.

In a few moments, a catastrophic failure will send the tower to the ground - but how will you get down? If you have a **winged harness**, turn to **1298** immediately. Otherwise, make a NIMBLENESS roll of difficulty 14, adding 1 if you possess a **rope** or **rope ladder**.

Successful NIMBLENESS roll!   **1204**
Failed NIMBLENESS roll!   **1169**

❧ 544 ❧

The piston rods whirr in their steady rhythm as you steam past freshly-built terraces of dirty yellow brick. Your Ferguson, though heavy, is responsive enough to your bodyweight to loop round slower vehicles and maintain momentum. The Telegraph Tower on Bloomsbury Square is directly ahead, looming over those terraces and the far grander mansions of Seymour Street. Note passage **400** and roll a dice to see what you come across:

Score 1-2	An accident	**626**
Score 3-4	Nothing of note	**400**
Score 5-6	A robbery	**644**

❧ 545 ❧

"For the orphanage? Reverend Highrun's building project? Absolutely. Wait here."

A few minutes later, Mr Hibbert returns with an envelope. It contains **twenty guineas in banknotes**. "There you are. No need to mention my name."

Leave the sewer works...   **471**

❧ 546 ❧

You find the hidden stair after a few mistaken and slippery turnings under the jetties. Over the missing boards and past the thumping printing presses, you climb to the attic hideout of the Waterside Boys. If you are the **Friend of the Waterside Boys**, turn to **581** immediately.

⊕Give them a **pork pie**...   **262**
Return to Upper Thames Street...   **252**

❧ 547 ❧

The Reverend Highrun and his wife are happy to see you. "We can talk a while," says the minister. "But I must complete my sermon preparations..." Yet he seems unwilling to leave your company.

Mrs Highrun will offer you medical aid, and you may convert any number of **wounds** to **scars**, rolling for **intimidating scars (RUTH+1)** as normal.

Leave the rectory...   **471**

❧ 548 ❧

Your attempts to frighten the Duchess are miserable. "Get out of my house!" she shouts, reaching for a heavy lamp and advancing on you. You tumble down the steps and clamber onto the Ferguson. From the south comes the sound of ringing Constable bells...

Make your escape...   **770**

❧ 549 ❧

If you have the codeword *Catastrophe*, read on. Otherwise, turn to **1088** immediately. Once aboard the *Gentilesse*, you must carefully find your way to the King's cabin. You head forward carefully, listening out for guards and staff.

The furnishings become more and more opulent: eventually you come to a passageway ending in a door that can only lead into Maria Roberts' private cabins that she shares with her royal lover. Standing at the railing, just opposite, a young man armed with a repeating carbine looks out through the drifting river fog. You will need to disable him before you proceed. If you have a **bottle of chloroform**, turn to **557** immediately. Otherwise, make an INGENUITY roll of difficulty 13, adding 2 if you have a **truncheon**, **blackjack**, **club** or other blunt weapon.

Successful INGENUITY roll!   **557**
Failed INGENUITY roll!   **509**

❧ 550 ❧

A good novel must draw on the manners and deeds of realistic characters and will depend upon your ability to have first observed, and now remember, the behaviour of a wide range of people you have encountered. Make a GALLANTRY roll of difficulty 18, adding 1 for each **Friendship** you possess.

Successful GALLANTRY roll!   **981**
Failed GALLANTRY roll!   **590**

❧ 551 ❧

☐

If the box above is empty, tick it and read on. If it is already ticked, turn to **577** immediately.

The woman in the red suit is drinking wine in an inner room. She looks up. "That was good work," she says. "I do hope you weren't too much hurt." She gives you your payment of **ten guineas in banknotes**.

Return to the parlour...   **176**

❧ 552 ❧

Mrs Roberts has not heard of the Reverend Highrun or his project. "There are always people trying to raise money for this or that charitable aim," she says. "What is so special about this one?" If you have **St Katharine's brooch**, turn to **604** immediately. Otherwise, make a GALLANTRY roll of difficulty 16, adding 3 for each piece of **golden jewellery** (for example, a **gold bracelet** or **gold ring**) you offer her as an appreciation.

Successful GALLANTRY roll!   **604**
Failed GALLANTRY roll!   **672**

❧ 553 ❧

Looking back over all your adventures is a rather reflective exercise in itself, but the process of putting all your experiences into words is therapeutic, pleasant and entirely absorbing. You manage to stave off any sense of isolation or mental oppression as you retreat into your memories, and at the end you have produced a hefty **memoir manuscript** that might even be welcomed by a publisher on Ludgate Hill. Who knows - it could even add to your reputation!

Wait out the rest of your sentence...   **398**

❧ 554 ❧

You talk your way into a waiting room in the Constable's headquarters. If you are **Wanted by the Constables**, turn to **13** immediately. Otherwise, read on.

If you intend to give the Constables information, it had better be good. After choosing an option below, cross it out.

⊕ Offer them the **love note**...   **136**
⊕ Offer the **annotated manifesto**...   **1089**
Make something up...   **1101**

❧ 555 ❧

It is a long way across the city to Whitechapel. You pass through many of the quieter districts, keeping to narrow streets to avoid traffic and the Constables, and see into uncurtained tenements where women weep, narrow pubs where men drink and wait for employment, derelict yards where no fire burns in the furnace and tumble-down stables that were once ringing with the sound of hooves.

Reach Whitechapel...   **356**

❧ 556 ❧

"You look like a fore-sighted hindividual," says a greasy -haired fellow at the next table. "The future is 'ard to tell in this city, I'm sure you'll hagree. But I 'ave 'eard certain things. Ever go down to the Exchange on Threadneedle Street? Trade in stocks or shares, much?"

"Why do you ask?"

"Well I 'ave these 'ere share certificates in a certain firm. I can't get down there myself as I 'ave to be leaving town forthwith. But their value is on the up-and-up, and you're sure to make a profit."

The fellow will sell you two **Imperial Seal Oil certificates** for £4 10s each - or just one, if that is all you want to risk.

Turn to...   **noted passage**

❧ 557 ❧

Once the door guard is despatched, you turn your attention to the lock of the suite. If you have a *Gentilesse* key, turn to **562** immediately. Otherwise, you will have to do your best to break in. Make another INGENUITY roll of difficulty 15, adding 1 if you have some **lockpicks** or 3 if you have a **skeleton key**.

Successful INGENUITY roll!	**562**
Failed INGENUITY roll!	**509**

❧ 558 ❧

"The Member for Southampton is one of us," says Commissioner Timms, to the visible surprise of the others. "He is reliable and no-one suspects the connection. After all, even my fellow members of this Council did not know his true allegiance."

It is decided that the Member will begin the process of introducing an Abolishment Bill, dismantling the monarchy and holding Charles responsible for the injustices in the land, with a penalty of death. "One must die that the land may live," says Comrade Feaver. "Our time has almost come."

You spend several weeks with the Council, making preparations, intimidating unconvinced members, helping in the disappearance of several of the more troublesome opponents. In the end, the Council are left waiting at a Telegraph terminal for a message to be relayed back to you. Roll two dice to see the outcome:

Score 2-7	The Bill fails...	**607**
Score 8-12	The Bill is passed!	**574**

❧ 559 ❧

You hear about the revolt under the Duke of Chester, and how he holds York against the King. He is one of the old nobility, furious at the privileges given to the guilds at his expense, and with the support of his estates and manors he has been able to raise troops and capture the city.

"Bloodshed and fire," says one drinker. "Since the army have laid siege. And the countryside around is sown with salt."

"They're well-supplied, though. The Duke'll hold York as long as he pleases - and probably drub the King's men into the bargain if you ask me."

Finish your drink...	**noted passage**

❧ 560 ❧

The strongbox surrenders to your concerted effort. Roll a dice to see what it contains:

Score 1	Turn to...	**587**
Score 2	Turn to...	**622**
Score 3	Turn to...	**638**
Score 4	Turn to...	**717**
Score 5	Turn to...	**820**
Score 6	Turn to...	**915**

❧ 561 ❧

The Railway Guards are not about to let a criminal of your ilk into their station. As soon as you are spotted, they send out an armed posse and contact the constabulary. You have no choice but to flee!

Ride away...	**33**

❧ 562 ❧

The door opens, silently, and you slip into the suite. There, on a four-poster bed the size of a common man's parlour, sprawls His Majesty Charles III, Emperor and King. Of his mistress, Maria Roberts, there is no sign.

This is the moment of truth, for the man - and he is no more than a man - is utterly at your mercy. His snores easily cover the sound of your footsteps and there is no-one here to protect him. If you have a **knife**, **razor** or any **bladed weapon**, turn to **578** immediately. Otherwise, you must make a RUTHLESSNESS roll of difficulty 20 to smother him.

Successful RUTHLESSNESS roll!	**578**
Failed RUTHLESSNESS roll!	**572**

❧ 563 ❧

This confrontation has been a long time. "Are you Hortensia Duploye?"

The woman in the carriage is middle-aged, plump and very, very rich.

"I... I..." she is plainly terrified. "What do you want?"

"You own land everywhere. You probably don't have time to actually be responsible for it. I'm sure you employ people to do that for you. But let me ask you this, before I am forced to hurt you. How many rooms are there in that mansion behind you?"

"I... I don't really know."

"You live in a house with more rooms than you can count. And over in Shoreditch, your tenants live eight or ten to a room in damp, cholera-ridden tenements built without foundations and with substandard materials. Ever heard of *noblesse oblige*, Madame?"

"Who are you? What do you want?" she repeats.

"I want to open your eyes."

Despite her struggles and protests, and with her driver and footman looking on in horror, you drag her from the carriage and bundle her onto the velosteam in front of you. "Have you ever even seen the Old Nichol slum, madam? Well, let me take you on a tour of your estate."

Your ride across town is particularly hair-raising - you can't resist putting more fear into the woman - and when you reach Shoreditch she is almost gibbering with fright and desperation. You help her down with a mocking bow. "Madam. Your estate - the Old Nichol."

She pulls herself together and begins to look around. "My god," she blurts. "My god. What is this place?"

Insulated from the reality of the source of her rents and utterly ignorant of the ways of the world, the Duchess of Kent has allowed herself to imagine that her money is honest. Now, after your harsh intervention, she can hide from it no longer. The woman would be a hypocrite or a devil to return home and do nothing about it.

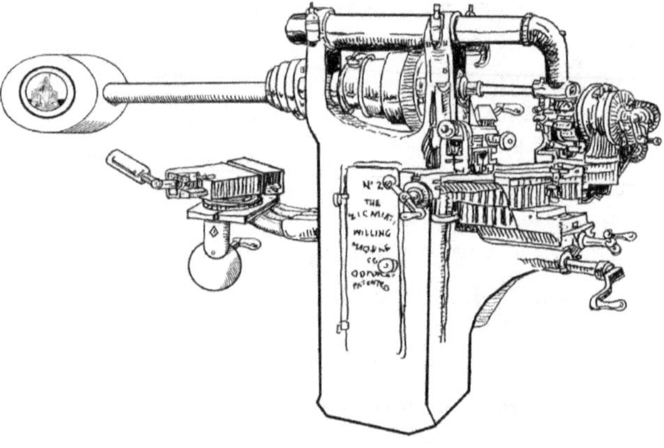

Sure enough, over the next weeks the inhabitants of the Old Nichol are gathered by the Duchess' agents. She identifies those most in need and sets to work rebuilding the worst of the tenements.

Your part in it is done now. If you return to these parts, you are more likely to be recognised with a smile, but you might still be coshed and robbed. The inhabitants of the Old Nichol are not about to changes their ways of life so quickly. Remove the **Duchess's account number**, and gain **three solidarity points** and the codeword *Charley*.

Ride to Shoreditch... **308**

⚬ **564** ⚬

If you have **20 or more Solidarity Points**, the actors will consider you entirely trustworthy: turn to **584** immediately. Otherwise, make a GALLANTRY roll of difficulty 10 to get them to open up, adding 2 if you possess a **pack of cigars** or a **bottle of gin** or **wine**.

Successful GALLANTRY roll!	**584**
Failed GALLANTRY roll!	**597**

⚬ **565** ⚬

The Reverend invites you into a bare study in the adjoining cottage, grandly called the rectory. "Visitors are always welcome here," he says. "Especially travellers. One never knows whom one will be called upon to host."

He explains what he is doing here in Bow. Called by God, he believes, to this part of the city and desperate to help alleviate the suffering of the very poorest, "It was when I first saw a dead, abandoned, new-born child that I really reconsidered what I have been doing. By comparison, even the poorest of my congregation are rich: they have life. The little boy I found at the side of the river did not even have that."

He wants to build an orphanage and foundling hospital. "It will take a great deal of money. Perhaps a thousand pounds, just to begin with. I have intended to call upon the great and the good here in the city and convince them to contribute, but my duties keep me here. I have written letters, but it is really the face-to-face appeal that works." He looks at you.

"Are you asking me to do this?"

He smiles. "Perhaps that is why you are here. I do not believe in coincidences."

If you want to help the Reverend, he will give you his **donors' list**. It names a number of individuals who might give to the work - if you can convince them, one way or another.

Donors' list

His Majesty King Charles III, St James' Palace
Princess Alexandrina, St James' Palace
Baroness Dimlight, Canonbury Tower
Thomas Hibbert, Metropolitan Sewerage Company
Lord Chislebry, Duke of Griston, Oakham
Herbert Shut-Proply, Industrialist, Caernavon
Antony Friston, Industrialist, Camelford

"This is just my start," he says. "You may well find others who feel as we do, and are willing to put their hand in their pocket."

"Not many of these are likely to keep their cash in their pockets," you say. "But I am confident I can get pledges from some of them."

Head on your way...   **471**

❧ 566 ❧

The Freight Yard is still a smoking ruin after the explosion. All freight has been diverted for the time being to Camden.

Return to Paddington...   **64**

❧ 567 ❧

The Baroness is a grand old lady, little used to venturing out. She is rich, opinionated and proud. "This little note of yours," she begins, waving the **Letter of Introduction** (which you should remove from your **possessions**) "Recommends you as an individual of resource and determination. Perhaps I can do something with you... Or can I help you?"

"Will you donate to the founding of
    an orphanage?"   (**donors' list**)   **592**
"I am at your service."   **635**

❧ 568 ❧

Your attempt to escape goes badly wrong. Before you can exit your cell, you are discovered. Any **possessions** or **money** that you still possess are confiscated and your food ration is cut even more as a punishment. Together with the chains on your ankles, this succeeds in wearing down your strength of body and mind: you contract a **fever (ING-1, NIM-2).** Your confidence is also badly affected: reduce your RUTHLESSNESS by 2.

Wait out the remainder of your sentence...   **398**

❧ 569 ❧

Surely you have opinions - opinions about the problems with the society around you, the inequality, the poverty, the stagnant, polarised political debate? Well, now is the time to explore your solution. Make an INGENUITY roll of difficulty 17, adding 3 if you are a **Member of the Compact for Workers' Equality** and 3 if you are (or have been) a **Member of Parliament.**

Successful INGENUITY roll!   **994**
Failed INGENUITY roll!   **590**

❧ 570 ❧

The cobbles of St Paul's road are spattered with horse manure and thick, black mud. You weave past the cars of the Islington and Hackney Cable Tram, accelerate past a row of half-built villas and continue eastwards through the smoke-stained terraces. Eventually you reach the Lea valley and turn south, riding past a continuous procession of factories beside the canal. The streets are less regular here, shaped as much by the irregular meanderings of the sluggish river as by the hand of man. Then, over the unfinished Great Sewer and past the Fairfield match factory, and you see the spire of St Mary's, Bow ahead of you.

Note passage **471** and roll two dice to see if you encounter anything on your ride.

Score 2-5   A bundle in the gutter...   **164**
Score 8-12   A quiet road...   **471**

❧ 571 ❧

If you have the codeword *Blended*, then you have no further need of building stone, and should return to **461** immediately. Otherwise, your half-built mansion at Shiplake requires drastic rebuilding. A stone dealer will arrange for a shipment of fine Portland stone to be taken up the Thames to your house - for a price of **£40**. If you choose to pay the fee, gain the codeword *Clapper*.

Leave the yard...   **425**

❧ 572 ❧

Summoning your courage and your strength, you take a pillow and climb onto the bed. The snoring King coughs, splutters and begins to choke as you press down onto his face. Then his brawny arms reach out and grab you: he is a massive man and desperation lends him might. He tosses you backwards and you crack your head on a decorated chair. Momentarily dazed, you are lifted up and bodily thrown into the river by the roaring monarch.

Bleeding and half-conscious, you will not survive this encounter. If this is your end, at least you can be confident that the Compact will try again: the Revolution may be delayed, but it cannot be prevented.

Turn to the **epilogue**...

✎ 573 ✎

One traveller is telling about his recent trip to Wales. "'They're all in a religious frenzy," he says, shaking his head. "Think the world's about to end or something. I tell you, it's hard enough to get a strong drink in many of those towns. Beer, maybe, but whisky... impossible. It sells for pounds a bottle."

Turn to...   **noted passage**

✎ 574 ✎

The passing of the Abolishment Bill is a massive shock to the metropolis, the Empire and the world. What Godless nation would do such a thing? In France, where the Bourbons still reign in power, anti-revolutionary measures will be pushed even further. In Spain, where the Anarchist War continues, there will be cheers and solidarity for the people of Britain. But now, there will be only chaos...

"A storm," says Tate to his fellow councillors, "A tempest. We must ride it out: we must call the Compact to arms and take up our position at the helm." You, Tate, Feaver and a team of the most loyal comrades meet the Member for Southampton, who has become the de facto leader of the Progressives, in Westminster. Plans are afoot for a quick court hearing and an immediate execution, on Tower Hill, where the people can be witnesses to the righting of this most ancient of wrongs.

The King himself makes a pitiable prisoner, and he is handed into the care of the comrades of the Compact for Workers' Equality, rather than the undecided Constables or the frankly royalist lobsters of the Parliamentary Guard. A trial takes place behind closed doors, the very same day, with an unsurprising result: Charles Hanover, citizen, is found guilty of crimes against the people, and sentenced to death.

Turn to...   **676**

✎ 575 ✎

Is there a sadder or more desperate tale than the urban orphan? Your birth is entirely unknown to you, your parents less than shadows. The only family you have ever known are the unreliable knot of thieves, ladies-of-the-night, street-sweepers and bridge-sleepers who taught you how to feed yourself, to pick pockets and to lie whatever lie would give you a chance to get away. Your sympathy for the poor of the streets has only grown since then: the city is riven with orphans, like the gang of mudlarks who live in the warehouse attics down by Upper Thames Street. How can you better their lot?

It was a good day indeed when you took the machine from outside a north London inn. How many times you had watched and noted the riders' motions, building the flame, adjusting the valves, controlling the pressure, until at last you had the confidence to do it yourself. A desperate chase followed, but you are not in the clink, nor in a shallow grave, so what regrets can you have?

Now with the city before you and the powerful engine of the machine beneath you, you will be able to do more than simply survive. Will you fake and trick your way to the very top of the ladder? After all, you have always had a talent for deceit and impersonation. With the right clothes, you could fit in anywhere.

Your ability scores are:

RUTHLESSNESS	3
ENGINEERING	2
MOTORING	2
NIMBLENESS	4
INGENUITY	6
GALLANTRY	4

You have in your possession a **blunderpistol (ACC 6)**, a **sabre (PAR 3)**, a **mask** and a **skeleton key**.

Turn to...   **1200**

✎ 576 ✎

You can audition for a part in the company, if you wish, but it will require considerable skill in mimicry and performance. Make a GALLANTRY roll of difficulty 15, adding 3 if you possess a **lady's wig** and 2 if you have a **cloak** of any kind.

Successful GALLANTRY roll!   **303**
Failed GALLANTRY roll!   **123**

❧ 577 ❧

The woman in red no longer comes to the Horn. "Where did she come from?" says one of the servers. "Didn't she arrive out of the west, one day?" His colleague nods. "On a strange carriage. From somewhere in the revolt. You know. Cornwall."

Return to the bar... **176**

❧ 578 ❧

It is the work of a moment. One moment, the room is inhabited by a monarch and his subject: the next, by a murderer alone.

You disdain to take anything from the suite, but collect yourself and cautiously make your way onto the deck. The murder will be discovered by the morning, by which time you and your allies must be ready.

With a splash, you dive into the water of the filthy old river and strike out towards your rendezvous, filled with a fresh energy. The Revolution approaches! Soon it will all be overthrown - the hegemony of the nobility, the corruption and control of the Guilds, the unjust laws and the inequality. Soon the common man will be free to profit from his own labour, and to own a share in his own land, the birthright of every individual in the nation. Soon!

The comrades who agreed to meet you help you ashore at Pelican Stairs and one sets off to send the news of your success to the Compact Headquarters. You will be warmed, dried, and clothed again, but with the dawn comes an entirely new challenge: not that of an independent, roadside thief, but the responsibilities and dangers of a revolutionary!

Note passage **650** and turn to **523**, where you can collect any possessions written in the box.

❧ 579 ❧

"This is not a Roman chapel," explains the Reverend, "And you are not required to confess to me. But I appreciate that you may feel the need to lighten your spiritual burden and I am happy to hear and pronounce absolution, if you are truly repentant. But that is exactly what this depends on: are you repentant? More than merely sorry for whatever hurts you have done to others and to your Father in heaven - are you willing to change? Or to try to change?"

Whatever your intentions and whatever you choose to mention to the Reverend, his response will be the same: "'I tell you who hear me: Love your enemies, do good to those who hate you, bless those who curse you, pray for those who ill-treat you.' I know very little

about you, but you seem to be one of those convinced of your need to get, to gain and to take at the expense of others. The world may seem to run on those terms, if we forget that God reigns."

Leave the chapel... **471**

❧ 580 ❧

You are chugging along the Thames River between Teddington and Brentford Locks. The tidal mud tells you that you have entered the Lower Thames, and from here westwards, the influence of the sea will only increase. While the banks are still green, dotted with browsing cattle and lined with dry cow-parsley, the horizon is grey and heavy.

Pass through Brentford Lock...
    (**2s** or **Bargee's Badge**) **952**
Head on downriver... **979**
Head upriver towards Teddington... **364**

❧ 581

"What's new, Toby?" asks Jerry. "Anyfink 'appening?"

Send them out stealing... **200**
Set them looking for something... **1021**
Get them to follow somebody... **605**
Leave the hideout... **252**

❧ 582 ❧

A good memoir will depend on your ability to spins stories from your adventures. For each **Great Deed** you have on your **Adventure Sheet**, gain 3 points. For each **Friendship** or **Additional Skill**, add 1 point. The total will decide your success:

Total 15 or more... **553**
Total 14 or less... **590**

❧ 583 ❧

Considering your position within the House, the Council are happy for you to propose the Bill. They have had clerks, lawyers and judges work on it for months now: it simply needs passing into law.

You return to your chambers in Westminster for what may be the last time: if the King goes, so too may all of this. The structures and hierarchies that seem to have defined the land for so many centuries are all about to come tumbling down... If you succeed.

The most radical of your Progressive allies gather and share the Compact's plan. It comes as no surprise to you that many of your colleagues are also comrades and privy to the Compact's long-term plan, but some are terrified by the prospect. Between you, however, you manage to get something like agreement to propose the Abolishment Bill as it has been written.

Now for the Bill to pass the house, you will need to muster up all of your skill and ability. Make a GALLANTRY roll of difficulty 19, adding 2 for each level of **legal knowledge** you possess.

Successful GALLANTRY roll...   **600**
Failed GALLANTRY roll...   **593**

✎ 584 ✐

You make a joke about directors and their need for approval, which certainly appeals to the actors. They offer you a drag on their shared cigarette. What will you ask them?

"Where did Mrs Roberts come from?"   **612**
"How can I get a part in a play?"   **632**

✎ 585 ✐

"Somebody high up in the Constabulary is taking payments from Flat Billy in the East End. It's the only explanation for what's been going on. I want you to infiltrate Flat Billy's gang, gain his trust, and find out who is in his pay. When you have hard proof - I mean documents, or signatures, not simply rumours - bring it to me here. I'll clean up this force whether my superiors want me to or not."

Leave the Leopard...   **139**

✎ 586 ✐

"Where on God's good earth is Belize?" you hear a meat porter cry.

"'Tis over in the Caribees. Where the cotton comes from, you fool."

"Ain't that all Confederacy?"

"No. Belize is Imperial. Well, it was. From all I hear, there's a dreadful revolution afoot there. Fire and revolt and that sort of thing."

"God keep it from these shores."

"Well we ain't got slaves 'ere, 'ave we?"

"I'm not so sure about that," says a drinker darkly. "Been down the Whitechapel tailoring yards recently?"

Turn to...   **noted passage**

✎ 587 ✐

Inside the iron casket you find a drift of golden coins. Together, they total **£124**.

Turn to...   **noted passage**

✎ 588 ✐

The key in your possession will be the answer to this. Looking at it carefully, it seems likely that it does indeed open the massive lock on the main gates.

Your comrades agree to begin a diversionary assault on the northern corner of the moat: they suffer losses, but it gives you the chance you need to approach the gatehouse. There you fit the huge iron key into its keyhole and turn it...

Open the gates...   **617**

✎ 589 ✐

Add whatever you are contributing to the box below. This is not a bank and you cannot withdraw money from your donations. However, once you have helped the Reverend Highrun raise certain amounts towards his orphanage, you may choose further options. Once you have raised the required amount, turn to the relevant passage: each can only be chosen once.

Total Raised

⊕ **£50** raised   Speak to Rev. Highrun...   **821**
⊕ **£1000** raised   Visit the orphanage...   **955**
Leave the chapel...   **471**

✎ 590 ✐

Try as you might, you simply cannot seem to order your thoughts and get them down on paper. Is it an internal pressure and a need to succeed that cripples you? Or is it the cold, the low diet, and the lack of stimulation? Either way, your screwed-up sheets end up burnt and your pen broken and tossed through the arrow loop.

The ordeal is mentally exhausting. Reduce your ENGINEERING and your INGENUITY scores by 1.

Wait for the end of your sentence...   **398**

✎ 591 ✐

Your clumsy attempt draws the attention of the Guildsmen in their cabin. At the sound of sabotage, they burst out and chase you further up the tower, far more nimble on the rickety framework than you. If you have a **winged harness**, turn to **1298** immediately. Otherwise, there is no way past them other than a certain-death drop to the ground. You are taken prisoner and handed over to the Constables. Note that you are **Wanted by the Telegraph Guild**, if you were not already.

Turn to... **13**

✌ 592 ❧

The Baroness listens to your account of Reverend Highrun's cause. "It sounds worthy," she says. "Write me down for fifty guineas."

"Thankyou, milady."

"But do an old woman a favour first. There is a brand of sauce I have been trying to get my hands on. I've just run out. Tillson's Hot Sauce. Nothing like it. Bring me a bottle, and I'll make the donation."

Head on your way... **151**

✌ 593 ❧

The proposal is a disaster. Shock and anger meet the very opening of your speech and you are unable to proceed far before the indignation rises to a boil in the chamber.

"This is outright treason and anarchy!" cries the Chancellor. "Arrest the member for Portsea immediately!"

Hands reach out to grab your collar, and, despite the protestations of your allies, you are hurried away. You did not have the support you thought you did, it seems.

The House invokes extraordinary measures to strip you of your position: you are no longer a **Member of Parliament**. Instead, you are charged with treason, sedition, anarchy and a range of other heinous crimes, found guilty in a swift and silent trial, and thrown into the deepest cell that can be found. All of your **weapons** and **possessions** will be confiscated, although you may keep your **money** and anything in your **jewellery pouch**.

Discover your cell... **335**

✌ 594 ❧

A strangely familiar figure steps into the hall: a lady you saw, once before, at the Duke of Beverley's Cliveden Ball. A lady who wore burnt roses in her hair, and dropped one in the room where you attempted to steal the Dervish's Eye.

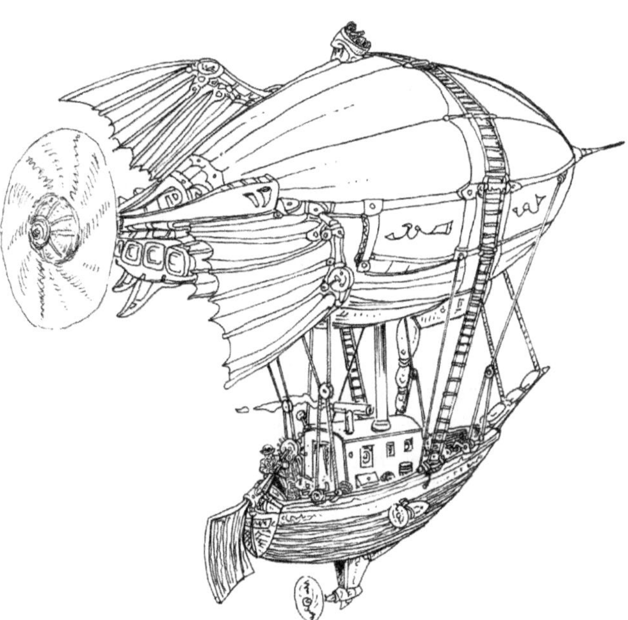

"Madam," you begin. "Have you come here to fence... or to get me in trouble again?"

She stops, poised, and looks into your face. Then she recognises you and laughs. "My word! The jewel thief!"

"The would-be jewel thief," you return, through gritted teeth.

"Ha, yes, rather a better description. Say, are you still in business, as a thief? Or are you simply a fencing master now?"

"That rather depends...   "

"On what I mean to steal. Come and let me tell you all about it."

"Where?"

"Derwent House, in Mayfair."

"But the lesson..."

"Some other time."

Turn to... **760**

✌ 595 ❧

The steam-winch huffs and begins to raise the portcullis, but it also brings the guards back into the room. They draw their sabres and prepare to attack.

Soldiers	Weapons: **sabres (PAR 3)**
Parry:	10
Nimbleness:	7
Toughness:	4

Victory!	**617**
Defeat!	**648**

❧ 596 ❧

It takes a few days for you and Lady Diana to prepare your scheme. She takes the lead, with a conceit so audacious that it will go down in history. "We will impersonate the King and his mistress," she says. "Nobody can deny dear old Charlie a peep at his own jewels, can they? And if he wanted to bestow a few on a niece of his, whose business would that be?"

"Impossible. Mimic both of them?"

"The King could keep his face shrouded, of course. And his 'niece' could have a nice wax mask... I know a lady in Millwall who does these charming likenesses."

"You'd have Mrs Roberts' emnity for ever!"

"Well," smiles Diana, "There won't be much left for me to steal after this. Not in these islands. I rather fancy a little trip round the world. Mrs Roberts can vent her fury however she likes."

"And the King?"

"We all know he hasn't long left, my dear. Between the rebels in the west, the Duke of Chester in the North, the progressives in Parliament, the Compact in Blackwall... I'm not too worried about him. The thing that will convince them is a message from St James, properly encoded with the King's personal cipher."

"That sounds like something I can do."

(telegraphy)	615
"Tell me what I need to do..."	652

❧ 597 ❧

The actors are convinced that you are a spy, whether from the Constables or another company, and they refuse to talk to you. When you persist, an accomplice from the floor above tips a bucket of water out the window, drenching you. A short while after leaving the theatre, a sniffle confirms that you have caught a **cold (RUTH-1 ING-1)**.

Ride north to Bloomsbury...	400
Ride south to the Strand...	139

❧ 598 ❧

You choose a high warehouse gable on the south river bank as your launching point. After the city's clocks have struck one, you launch out over the dirty water, gripping the control orbs of your wings tight and fixing your eyes on the Tower ramparts opposite.

You swoop down onto a towertop, directly into the path of a soldier emerging from a stairway. You must fight him - with your normal NIMBLENESS score reduced by 2, on account of the ungainly, unfolded wings strapped to your back.

Soldier	Weapon: **carbine and bayonet** (PAR 5)
Parry:	9
Nimbleness:	4
Toughness:	3

Victory!	**665**
Defeat!	**648**

❧ 599 ❧

☐

If the box above is empty, put a tick in it and turn to **1501** immediately. If it is already ticked, read on.

"Yes?" asks Desk-Captain Survit. "Do you have something for me, after all? I thought you were some sort of engine magician?"

⊕ Show your **airship buoyancy calculation**...	803
⊕ Hand in the **repaired manifest**...	817
Return to the station...	97

❧ 600 ❧

There is shock when the Speaker announces the proposed Bill, and indignation when you stand to read it. However, your allies are numerous, committed, and influential. It seems clear that the tide has turned at last, and that many of the politicians are keen not to be caught on the wrong side of history. You begin to see nods of agreement and support where you least expected it. Members stand to talk about redressing ancient injustices, and the rights of the common man. It is as though the ground itself is moving beneath your feet...

When the eventual vote comes, it is a landslide. The King must die.

Take the news directly to the Compact...	**574**

✎ 601 ✎

You find Mr Wright - a tall, distinguished gentleman with his boots up on a chair and the Wheatear and Cog of the Progressive party in his hat.

"So. You are the one I was told about. Come and have dinner with me and my friends and we will make you an offer."

Turn to...   **630**

✎ 602 ✎

You coast to a stop at the east end of Westminster Bridge. Green-coated Constables guard the crossing, leading as it does to the seat of parliamentary power. On this bank of the river, a massive embankment is being constructed, restraining the Thames beyond a great stone wall. Steam cranes claw at the mud, heaping it, and a row of engines tip their loads of waste and rubble.

Cross the bridge to Westminster...   **634**
Head south into Lambeth...   **647**
Ride into Southwark...   **631**

✎ 603 ✎

Old Kent Road continues on towards Deptford Bridge. The city is beginning to peter out, and the gaps between buildings have become coppices and orchards. The road is busy enough to warrant an ambush, if you think you can get away from any pursuers.

Plan an ambush here...   **628**
Ride to Deptford Bridge...   **814**

✎ 604 ✎

Mrs Roberts smiles. "Let me see what I can do." Gain the codeword *Clearly*.

Leave the *Gentilesse*...   **847**

✎ 605 ✎

"Yer 'appy to pay expenses?" asks Jerry.

"Reasonable ones," you reply. "Plus sausage allowance, of course."

"Alright," the boy replies happily. "'Oo are we lookin' for, then?"

"Lord Beaufort."   (£3 10s)   **618**
"Lady Serene."   (£2 5s)   **231**
"Mrs Roberts."   (£4 3s)   **1463**

✎ 606 ✎

The heavy cable splits with a single stroke of your axe and the portcullis rattles up. Guards dash in through the opposite door, but you are already out and down the stairs.

Greet your comrades...   **617**

✎ 607 ✎

The news of the failure of the Bill is far from encouraging, but the grimly determined members of the High Council simply sit back and fold their arms.

"Now, perhaps, you will consider my view," says Comrade Feaver.

"Yes. I will assassinate the King."   **1097**
"We must prepare before trying again."   **669**

✎ 608 ✎

The streets of South London are places of desperate poverty and dirt. You roar past the terraces, the never-quiet foundries, the potteries, and on towards Bermondsey. Roll a dice to see what you encounter:

Score 1-2   A bundle...   **164**
Score 3-4   Nothing of interest...   **668**
Score 5-6   Beggars...   **1496**

✎ 609 ✎

Old Kent Road leads north-west up into London, running along past the market gardens and the stables, the little terraces and the remaining copses of trees between strawberry fields. Ahead, the smog hangs over the city, but this is the last remnant of the Kent countryside, and here is your final opportunity to ambush passing traffic before you reach the bounds of the metropolis.

Prepare an ambush here...   **628**
Continue towards Southwark...   **624**

✎ 610 ✎

☐ ☐ ☐

If the boxes above are empty, tick the first and turn to **1004** immediately. If the first is ticked, tick the second and turn to **1418**. If two are ticked, tick the third and turn to **556**. If all three are ticked, read on.

While enjoying your beer, you are approached by a woman trying to sell her jewellery to make ends meet.

Jewellery	To buy	To sell
locket	3s	-
silver ring	4s	-
silver bracelet	6s	-
silver necklace	£1	-

Turn to...   785

❧ 611 ❧

Fresher & Sons gleams with brass, but the excited look on the shopkeeper's face at your entrance tells you that, despite all the polish, business is poor.

Tools	To buy	To sell
wirecutters	12s	9s
adjustable wrench (ENG+1)	£1 8s	£1 2s
lockpicks	6s	3s
brass flange joint	8s	7s
ultra-tensed wire	£2 10	£1 10s
jeweller's loupe (ING+1)	£2 2s	£1 15s
binoculars	£4	£2 10s
telescope	£6	£3
calculating engine (ING+3)	£30	£9
Jewellery	To buy	To sell
locket	6s	4s
pocket watch	£3	£2
Other items	To buy	To sell
Constable's whistle	-	3s
clockwork bird	-	£4
fine clock	£8	£2 4s

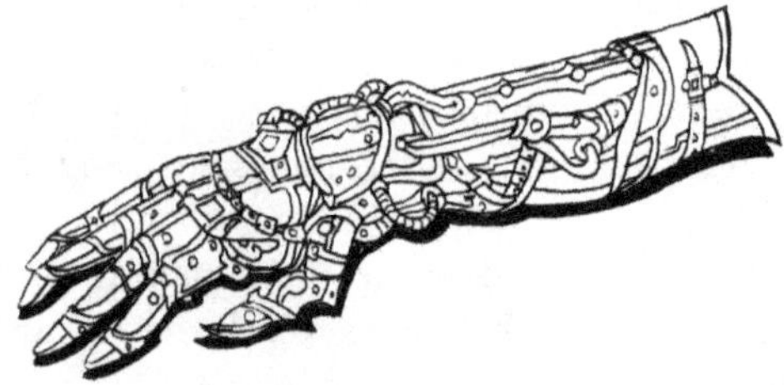

If you have a **mechanical arm**, turn to **639**.

Ask about clockwork birds...   623
Leave the shop...   647

❧ 612 ❧

"Mrs Roberts? The King's femme-du-jour? The great floozy? Yes, she was onstage here. You worked along o' her, didn't you, Maude?"

"I did, back when she first arrived. But a beauty like her, it was only a matter of time before someone plucked her off the stage and up into their private box. But the King weren't the first, you know?"

"No?"

"Not at all," replies Maude, licking her lips at the taste of her own gossip. "She was bedded by the Duke of Sussex at first." She rustles around in her sleeve. "In fact, I happen to have one of their old love-notes right here. You can have it - for a guinea." If you want to buy the **love note** for **£1 1s**, add it to your **possessions**.

"An interesting tale."   123

❧ 613 ❧
☐

If the box above is empty, tick it and read on. If it is already ticked, turn to **603** immediately.

As you ride down the hill, you pass a man trudging ahead of you, carrying a wooden box on his back. You stop to offer him a lift, which he accepts gladly.

He is a computational engineer, heading to the Telegraph Guild compound near Greenwich. "Did you know that you can hire their engines there?" he asks. "It's far from cheap, but for a feller like me what has to be satisfied with running my cards on other folk's engines, it's not too bad."

"Do you profit?"

He licks his lips. "Oh, yes. I has to pay out to test the cards, but I can sell what I punch for good prices." If you are interested, he offers you a set of **punchcards (Habbukuk K)** for only **£10**.

You drop him off at the foot of the hill and make your way into Deptford.

Turn to...   603

❧ 614 ❧

With the Constables behind you and the maze of Southwark's streets ahead, you must choose a direction to escape your pursuers. Riding at random will only lead you into the Constable's grip, or into the river!

Head for Crafton's... (**convict's pass**)   689
Make for Blackfriar's Bridge...   736
Disappear into Deptford...   716
Race for Rotherhithe...   702

❧ 615 ❧

High in the attic of Derwent House is a powerful computational engine that Lady Diana keeps for her own machinations. It is linked to her personal telegraph terminal - all licensed by the Guild, of course. Seated at the controls, you begin by analysing some intercepted personal messages of the King's .

Make an ENGINEERING roll of difficulty 16, adding 4 if you possess some **punchcards (Aramanth A)** or the codeword *Chirp* or *Entertain*.

Successful ENGINEERING roll!	**686**
Failed ENGINEERING roll!	**712**

⚘ 616 ⚘

As soon as you show the proof of your imprisonment, room is made for you at the tables. "That ticket may mean shame elsewhere," says Crafton, as he ladles a hearty stew into your bowl, "But here it enters you into an exclusive brotherhood. I've been inside, and so have all these here, and we know how folks simply want to write you off as a bad'un. It ain't easy to get back on your feet. But here - well, you can stay here as long as you like, until you're ready to move on."

Crafton shows you to a tiny room, sparse but clean, where you can stay and keep your possessions, safe from the raids of the Constables or the fingers of thieves. "We all look after each other, see?" You can rest here and tend any **wounds** or sores you may have as well. Note this **passage** before making a choice from the options below.

Crafton's charity extends even further: he will furnish you with a **cloak** and a **hat** from clothes donated for the relief of the poor, should you want them.

Hire some men...	**1185**
⊕ Find an apprentice... (**workshop**)	**1513**
Tend your **wounds**...	**500**
Repair your velosteam...	**1300**
Leave the cookshop...	**647**

⚘ 617 ⚘

A massive tide of revolutionaries comes rushing through the gateway. They spread out and begin to fight, tooth and claw, using tools, posts, cobbles, snatched sabres, Compact-issued carbine-butts and clubs. The garrison fell many of your comrades, but they are overwhelmed.

Raise the flag!	**719**

⚘ 618 ⚘

"What, the Chief Constable hisself? 'E could be anywhere. 'E could be at his country estate, or in Somerset 'ouse or up at St James Palace wiv the King."

"You can find him," you reply.

The boys depart about their various ways, scurrying through the city bothering bogies, as they call the Constables, street-sweepers, tramps and shopkeepers. The Chief Constable is a busy and important man - exactly where he is will be hard to establish, and he might use one of the many modes of transport at his disposal to leave or return to the metropolis unexpectedly. If you have the codeword *Currently*, turn to **640** immediately. Otherwise, roll a dice to see what the boys tell you on their return.

Score 1	**640**
Score 2-4	**660**
Score 5-6	**671**

⚘ 619 ⚘

Later that day, you reach Whitechapel and Flat Billy in his parlour above the Grave Maurice. He rubs his hands together as he hears your scheme.

"Excellent. Money fer nothing, right?" He agrees to a fifty-fifty split and arranges to have a posse of his more presentable gangsters to take you up to Parliament Hill. There, they will hand you over, in handcuffs, receive the reward, and promptly turn around and rescue you.

The first part goes entirely to plan. It's when Bradley 'The Rat' Terrigan should be slipping you the key to your cuffs that it starts to seem off. Too late, you realise their intentions: he and his men receive the reward and then clear out, leaving you at the famously cold mercy of the Atmospheric Union. They strip you of your **money**, **possessions** and velosteam before handing you over to the Constables.

You are no longer the **Friend of Flat Billy**.

Turn to... **13**

✎ 620 ✎

A gaggle of gentlemen approach you at the bar. In their hats are the Wheatear and Cog - the symbols of the Progressive party. They are Members of Parliament.

"It is you, isn't it?" stammers one. "The Steam Highwayman! Friend to the poor, enemy of the unjust!"

Before you can make an excuse and your exit, another grasps your sleeve. "We need your help. The nation needs your help." He realises that he has gone too far and looses his grip. "Ah, my apologies. Will you accompany us to dinner in the Salon and allow us to explain our predicament?"

"Get out of my way."	**647**
"I will dine and listen to you."	**630**

✎ 621 ✎

"Well this is what I am thinking so far. With a set of mechanical wings like I've been hearing about, we fly into the Tower on a moonless night, crack into the tower where the jewels are kept, collect exactly what we wish, and then fly away again."

"Mechanical wings." Is that disbelief or scorn in your voice? "Do you have much experience with these wonders?"

She laughs. "I rather hoped that you did."

"And otherwise it would be a simple smash and grab?"

"Not my most elegant plan, but refreshingly daring."

"I happen to possess such things."	
(winged harness)	**1011**
"Where can we get hold of these wings?"	**1061**

✎ 622

The strongbox has several hidden drawers and pockets. It contains three **gold rings**, a **golden necklace**, a bottle of **poison**, a **golden monocle (GAL+2)** and a faded bouquet of dead flowers.

Turn to...	**noted passage**

✎ 623 ✎

"Clockwork birds, eh?" Mr Fresher leans forward excitedly. "I can tell what I know. So for sure, they're some of the finest brasswork I've ever come across. If you've seen one, you know what I mean. Twitching, pecking, even singing. Normally they have little hidden winding sockets beneath the tail. Very popular with children and ladies."

"Where do they come from?"

"Ah, well. I'm fairly certain they're made by a chap in Oldham, up the Great North Road. But they're more than playthings. Several of them that I've seen have code printed on the underside of their wings. Why, and what it does, I can't tell you yet. But it's certainly some sort of machine code. A good computational engineer might be able to work it out, but I can't afford those sort of friendships."

Mr Fresher buys any such machine he comes across, in order to use the fine workmanship in projects of his own, adapting another maker's handiwork to achieve his own ends.

Thank him...	**611**

✎ 624 ✎

☐

If the box above is empty, tick it and turn to **681** immediately. Otherwise, simply read on.

The road gets busier as you approach Southwark. Soon you are forced to slow your velosteam to little more than a crawl. Whatever can possess people to leave the clean air of the countryside to dwell here, among this murky, unbreathable din?

Ride into Southwark...	**631**

✎ 625 ✎

☐ ☐ ☐ ☐

If any of the boxes above are empty, tick one and read on. If they are all already ticked, erase the ticks and turn to **614** immediately.

South of the river has always been lawless and rough. Perhaps that is why your actions have gone unpunished... for now. Where will you turn?

Towards London Bridge...	**699**
To Blackfriars Bridge...	**680**
Head for Westminster Bridge...	**602**
To the Thames Tunnel...	**656**
Down to Deptford Bridge...	**814**

❧ 626 ❧

A locobus has collided with the last wagon of a Telegraph Guild roadtrain and turned over in the road. Traffic is still trying to pass the scene, while passers-by are running around in panic.

Look for loot to pick up...   **643**
Help the passengers...   **662**

❧ 627 ❧

The daily work of carrying luggage is dull and tiring. You are paid **2s** for the work, as you are expected to receive some tips. Roll a dice to see what else you receive:

Score 1-3   Nothing...
Score 4-5   **3s**...
Score 6   **10s**...

However, no work is without its risks. Roll a dice to see what else you experience.

Score 1   Accused of theft: you are now **Wanted by the Atmospheric Guild**...
Score 2   Gain a **burn (NIM-1)** from a hot engine...
Score 3-6   No other effects...

Leave the station...   **83**

❧ 628 ❧

Amongst the smallholdings and strawberry farms, there is still green country between you and the smoky city. You wait for dusk and prepare your trap: note passage **625**.

If you have a **telescope** or **binoculars**, turn to **653**. Otherwise, you should roll a dice to see what approaches.

Score 1-2   The Haulage Guild   **1444**
Score 3   An independent haulier   **1381**
Score 4-5   A private steam carriage   **1391**
Score 6   The Telegraph Guild   **1411**

❧ 629 ❧

Crafton takes some convincing, but when you tell him that the Atmospheric Union are pursuing you for crimes committed long ago, and for which you have already been punished, he is convinced to join you in your endeavour. He is no friend to the great Guilds and their powerful magnates and is as ready as any to relieve them of what he considers unfairly gained wealth.

So with Crafton and a mate in long coats and some disguise, you make your way up to Parliament Hill and the Atmospheric Union station. The ruse goes without a hitch: you are handed over, seemingly tightly bound, and Crafton takes the bag of coin. Then you cut the cords on your wrists with a thumb-blade and trip the Union officers grasping your shoulders. A roll, a dash, a leap through the door as Crafton tumbles a beam across it and you are back astride your trusty velosteam, with a pair of passengers hanging on grimly behind you. You take quiet streets and cross the river well to the west, returning to the cookshop in the early hours of the morning, when the streets are empty but for wisps of river fog and stray tomcats. Crafton laughs, despite his aches, as he dismounts, and he counts out **£75** in coin as your share. "The rest," he says, "Will help many a poor soul fleeing injustice."

Leave the cookshop...   **647**

❧ 630 ❧

Around the laden table in the Private Salon of the Pineapple, the gentlemen introduce themselves. Mr Andrew Wright, the Member for Allington, Sir Dustin Hurtbridge, the Member for Short Loughton, and Mr William Wheelhouse, the Member for Fingley and Fangley.

"Our situation is this," begins Wright, ladling a hearty game soup into his bowl. "You have heard the cry in the streets, no doubt. 'Reform or Revolution', they shout."

"God keep us from bloody revolution!" splurts Wheelhouse.

"Quite. There must be Parliamentary reform. Do you know, the six hundred thousand inhabitants of Manchester are represented by only a single member, and he a shamefaced lackey of the most entrenched privilege?"

"Intolerable!" continues Wheelhouse.

"However, although we have increasing influence in the House of Commons, and may even have the sympathy of our enlightened Sovereign himself, whenever a motion is to be brought for debate, our opposition in the so-called 'Establishment' camp disable our efforts in the most scandalous way. You know that Members are immune from arrest? Well, we are also 'privileged' to engage in duelling without reprimand, and the Duke of Hereford and his friends repeatedly bring about deadly encounters with our members, with terrible effect."

"We are being decimated!" coughs Wheelhouse.

"What is my part?" you ask.

"We must have a champion amongst our ranks: someone who can meet the Orthodox duellists like the Duke of Hereford and defeat them, allowing our members to make the case for Reform and bring about change before Revolution, with all its horrors, falls upon us."

"But only a Member of Parliament could participate in such a duel."

"Yes," continues Wright, "And although it would be entirely against our principles, we would be willing to have such a person elected within a friendly borough, entirely without parliamentary responsibility, in order that they might be a champion on the lawns of Westminster. What do you say?"

"How might a dangerous character like myself be elected?"	**659**
"I will have nothing to do with it."	**641**

৯ 631 ৵

Southwark is one huge market. Goods brought in from the south are sold on here at Borough and Hays markets. Every second passerby trundles a steam-lift or carries a sack. Children dash backwards and forwards with freight tickets in their hands, or leap to hook them onto bundles and crates being craned onto the overhead rails that run along the streets. Even the old church of St Saviour's has been topped with a Telegraph Guild station. Still, if you look, you can find vestiges of the old city. Down a sidestreet stands the George. Its galleried courtyard is filled with horses and wagons and the velosteams of despatch riders.

Food and Drink	To buy	To sell
bird's eggs	-	6s
pheasant	10s	5s
deer carcass	-	£2 10s
tin of fruit	4s	2s
wheel of cheese	£2 10s	£1 8s
bottle of wine	10s	8s
bottle of whisky	15s	10s
pork pie	2s	1s
picnic hamper	£4	£2 10s
Clothing	To buy	To sell
hair matches (R+2) □ □ □	£2	-
silk scarf	-	£1 10s
top hat	£2	£1
lady's wig	£1 5s	8s
airship officer's cap	-	£1 10s

Tools	To buy	To sell
rope	4s	2s
axe	8s	6s
billhook (PAR 2)	12s	10s
fishing line	1s	-
snare	2s	-
net	4s	2s
shovel	8s	6s
pneumatic manual (ENG+3)	-	£8
calculating engine (ING+3)	-	£9
Jewellery	To buy	To sell
locket	6s	4s
pocket watch	-	£2
silver ring	-	8s
silver bracelet	-	15s
silver necklace	-	£2 5s
gold ring	-	£2 5s
gold bracelet	-	£3
gold necklace	-	£4
Medical items	To buy	To sell
bandages	3s	-
cough medicine	5s	2s
soothing lotion	2s	1s
Other items	To buy	To sell
box of cigars	£2 2s	£1 8s
ivory fan	£2	£1 15s
punchcards (Aramanth A)	-	£8
punchcards (Habbukuk K)	-	£12 10s
pair of golden candlesticks	-	£6
sketchpad □ □ □	3s	2s
fiddle	£4	£2
dog-eared Bible	3s	2s

Visit the George Inn...	674
Head to St Saviour's Church...	673
Board your barge...	
(Moored at Bargehouse Wharf)	922
Leave the area...	695

৯ 632 ৵

"Why, audition! You might want to brush up on your pronunciations, tho." They describe how a high GALLANTRY score, a **lady's wig** or a **cloak** can come in handy.

"If you find it hard to break in here," says one, "You might try up the Great North Road. I'm not saying that standards are lower there... but it might be a nice place to begin."

Leave the actors...	123
Leave the stage door...	511

❧ 633 ❧

The calculation engine is perfectly suited to this kind of work. A pantograph begins to draw a crossing in which the roadway hangs on a series of cables from tall towers. Gain a **computed bridge structure**.

Leave the machine...   **noted passage**

❧ 634 ❧

Has earth anything to show more fair? Ships, towers, domes, theatres and temples all lie before you. The sky, however, is thick with fog and coal-smoke. You would have to be dull indeed to pass this sight by without realising how dirty and degraded the glory of the metropolis is. Looking downriver, you can see the shape of the *Gentilesse* moored at the apex of the river's curve, and many other boats, lighters and launches besides. On the western bank stands the old Palace of Westminster, the seat of the Imperial Government, and beyond it the park and palace of St James. There too hang dark clouds.

Slip into the river... (NIMBLENESS 6+)   **518**
Cross the bridge...   **721**

❧ 635 ❧

"Very good," says the Baroness. "Listen well. There is a jumped-up johnny running matters down at the College of Arms on Upper Thames Street. He made the astonishing claim that my grandfather was illegitimate. Publically. Go and get him to retract that nonsense. Get me some sort of proof."
    "Do you mind how I do it?"
    "Bribe him. Scare him. He isn't important ."
    Gain the codeword *Canvey*.

Leave Canonbury Tower...   **151**

❧ 636 ❧

Crafton's Cookshop is a meeting house, hostel and canteen rolled into one. Edwin Crafton, the proprietor, is a convicted felon who served his time for violent crimes. Reformed and full of pity for the men he encountered inside, he has somehow created a stable business in feeding and sheltering the poor of Lambeth. He has a particular soft spot for anyone who has come off the worst with the penitential system. If you have a **Convict's Pass**, turn to **616** immediately.

Hire some men...   **1185**
Leave the cookshop...   **647**

❧ 637 ❧

The young man is expecting, or maybe unwisely hoping, to be challenged to a duel in the process of pursuing his beloved. He needs coaching in the basics of footwork, attitude and sword-grip.
    "The sword is like a bird," you explain. "Hold it too tightly and you choke it. Too lightly and it flies away." He pays ten guineas (**£10 10s**) for his lessons. You have not suffered a scratch, of course.

Turn to...   **760**

❧ 638 ❧

The box seems to have belonged to an officer of some kind. It contains a **rapier (PAR 4)**, a **dinner jacket**, a **dark cloak (RUTH+1)** and **thirty guineas in banknotes**.

Turn to...   **noted passage**

❧ 639 ❧

Your mechanical arm catches the eye of the Mr Fresher. "May I take a look?" he asks politely. "What fine work. But if you would allow me, I believe I can make an improvement. The parts I need can be found in one of those clockwork birds - or perhaps a music box. I am sure that I can give you a significantly improved grip."

⊕ "Go ahead."
    (**music box** or **clockwork bird**)   **365**
"Not now."   **647**

❧ 640 ❧

Jerry brings you the boys' report. "No-one ain't seen 'im fer a while," he says. "In fact, rumour is that 'e ain't very well. Dangerously ill, in fact." Gain the codeword *Currently* if you don't already have it.

Return to the hideout...   **581**
Leave the attic...   **252**

❧ 641 ❧

Mr Wright and his friends are disappointed. "I see there is no way to convince you," he says. "Perhaps you are no more than the robber and thief they say you are. Enjoy what you will of the table - this is no company for us. Come on, Mr Wheelhouse. Mr Wheelhouse!"
    They leave. Remove the codeword *Chertsey*, but you may add a **pair of golden candlesticks** from the table, if you have no scruples about taking them.

Leave the pub...   **647**

✥ 642 ✥

You take a winding street towards Rotherhithe, running east over the low and marshy ground. Note passage **649** and roll a dice to see what you encounter.

Score 1-2	A crooked Constable...	**254**
Score 3-4	Nothing extraordinary...	**649**
Score 5-6	Travellers...	**1379**

✥ 643 ✥

You root among the spilled cargo and see what there is of value. Roll 2 dice:

Score 2-3	A **strongbox**...
Score 4-6	A set of **chimney brushes** and a **green coat**...
Score 7-9	Some **bandages** and a bottle of **poison...**
Score 10-12	Four **blunderpistols**...

As you look up from your looting, you spot the figure of a Telegrapher watching you from the road engine further up the street. You are now **Wanted by the Telegraph Guild.**

Ride on...	**noted passage**

✥ 644 ✥

"Stop, thief!" cries a lady. A figure is dashing away down the street, clutching a bag.

Toss a tin at the figure... (**tin of fruit**)	**661**
Let them go...	**noted passage**

✥ 645 ✥

On entering your bolthole at St Eanswythe Hall, it is very plain that you have been raided. Your possessions have been confiscated: you must erase everything written in the box in passage **760**. Even worse, the Constables have posted watchers waiting for your return: even now, cries go up. You must clamber aboard your velosteam and get away! Remove the codeword *Chinstrap*.

Head for Hyde Park!	**882**
Ride for Blackfriars Bridge!	**858**

✥ 646 ✥

This revolution will find you in the water again, then. You prepare by greasing up, leaving most of your belongings behind the barricades, and drinking half a bottle of brandy. Then into the midnight water it is...

One of your comrades hands you a **blackjack (PAR 2)**. Apart from this, you will not be able to use any of your **possessions** until the assault is over.

The Thames is no republican's friend: it is a monarchist's river. The Thames himself is a King of sorts, but a wild, unadvised one. The current is flowing strongly, but there are eddies and backdraughts along the wharf-edges.

If you have a NIMBLENESS score (unimproved by any **possessions**) of 6 or less, turn to **533** immediately. Otherwise, you push hard and eventually come to the Water Gate, the famous entrance of traitors and the doomed. There is a guard here, but you are able to creep up behind him and give him a turn into the river.

Dash for the gatehouse...	**665**

❧ 647 ❧

Streets of brick cottages are interrupted here in Lambeth by the sprawling park of Lambeth Palace - the London seat of the Archbishop of Canterbury. At the other end of the social spectrum, the local trade is clockwork: in the attics and parlours of a hundred terraces, men and women work with brass, creating the tiny pieces that come together to power the computational engines of the great guilds and corporations. You can buy and sell such things in Fresher & Sons, Clockwork Mechanics. Nearby stands the Pineapple public house, and down a darkened row, Crafton's Cookshop, which is run for the benefit of the poor and most needy.

Visit Crafton's Cookshop...	**636**
Enter the Pineapple...	**651**
Look around the Fresher & Sons...	**611**
Head to Westminster Bridge...	**602**
Head towards Southwark...	**631**
Ride for Battersea Bridge...	**1132**

❧ 648 ❧

Your body lies on the ground, unheeded by revolutionary or counter-revolutionary. Many are the corpses of the fallen in this time, and you can only hope that your final sacrifice will speed the people's victory.

Turn to the **epilogue**...

❧ 649 ❧

Rotherhithe Street runs between the River and a vast acreage of docks and pools. Along it, like dirty knots on a cable, are strung chandleries, forges, wharves, sawmills, a short terrace here and there, dry docks and slips. Accessed only from the river, or at either end over swing bridges, Rotherhithe is almost a nautical village cut off from the rest of London.

At the western side of the docks, the Thames Tunnel has been dug all the way under the river itself: passage through is but a few shillings, and a huge transhipment yard has been built beside the entrance, over the rubble of countless demolished dwellings. Progress goes on.

Visit Cary's Chandlery...	**682**
The Thames Tunnel...	**656**
Rotherhithe Telegraph Station...	**692**
Bermondsey...	**668**
Deptford...	**816**

❧ 650 ❧

With the King dead, the stage is set for the revolution to begin. It is not only the Compact for Workers' Equality who have been waiting for this moment, but every gang, movement, guild and collective will come out in force to muscle their way to the front. The Compact's advantage is fore-warning, together with the people's support.

"We take and hold the Tower," says Commissioner Timms. "It will be powerful sign, and a gathering point."

It also holds weapon stores and the crown jewels, you reflect.

"I will infiltrate the fortress."	
(**Tower Key** or *Click*)	**688**
"We must assault it directly."	**703**

❧ 651 ❧

The Pineapple is a high-class establishment, decorated and bedrizzled with pendant lamps, leather armchairs, frosted glass, carved wood finials and a hundred other unnecessaries. It is known as the preferred haven of the Wheatears - the opposition Members of Parliament who are campaigning for electoral reform and a fairer system. If you have some **explosives** among your **possessions**, turn to **683** immediately.

Buy a drink...	(**2s**)	**667**
Ask for Mr Wright...	(*Chertsey*)	**601**
Leave the pub...		**647**

❧ 652 ❧

Lady Diana, as well as being an accomplished thief, has studied the art of telegraphy. When you ask her whether that was with the Guild's permission she simply smiles.

In an attic, high in Derwent House, she has a computational engine and, like many of the nobility, a private telegraph terminal. Unlike the majority of the nobility, she is able to use it to intercept and decode the King's signals.

She shows you how to work the levers and dials of the terminal, inputting an outgoing or incoming message into the engine which can complete a complex encoding, disguising an important message as an unimportant one, or using a cipher that only the most experienced telegrapher can understand. Roll two dice, and if you roll equal or less than your current INGENUITY score (including bonuses), you can add **telegraphy** to your **Additional Skills** if you do not already possess it.

With your assistance, Lady Derwent takes several messages she has intercepted, each marked with the King's personal callsign, and proceeds to attempt to crack their code. Make an ENGINEERING roll of difficulty 16, adding 4 if you possess a set of **punchcards (Aramanth A)** or the codeword *Chirp* or *Entertain*.

Successful ENGINEERING roll!	**686**
Failed ENGINEERING roll!	**712**

❧ 653 ❧

With your ability to scour the road ahead, you have the liberty to ambush whatever traffic you choose. Only dense fog or armed guards can trouble you now. For whom will you wait?

The Haulage Guild...	**1444**
The Telegraph Guild...	**1411**
The Atmospheric Union...	**1421**
An independent haulier...	**1381**
A private steam carriage...	**1391**

❧ 654 ❧

The sudden and violent appearance of a snarling madman on a powerful velosteam throws the crowd into panic. They dive aside as you accelerate over the roadway, some even throwing themselves into the river! A moment later and you are across, and quickly weave your way into the narrow streets of old London, leaving your pursuers far behind you.

Turn to...	**252**

❧ 655 ❧

The officer is quite impressed. "You have kept quite a pace across the metropolis. You plainly know this city well." He pays you **£10** in coins and offers you some advice. "You are plainly a character of great resource. We at the Guild are engaged in something of a power struggle with the Coal Board. Their monopoly on fuel means that they think they can control us. So we really wouldn't mind if they suffered a few setbacks... if their wagons were robbed. Or damaged. Or their depot shut down for a while. Hmm? Come back here when you have done something along these lines and we will have further rewards for you."

Leave the tower...	**400**

❧ 656 ❧

You are at the southern mouth of the Thames Tunnel. Behind the gate, the black maw gapes like a hungry monster. The keepers raise the barrier for each road-train that trundles through, as if saluting those about to embark on a journey to the underworld. After, of course, charging a hefty toll on each.

Ride through the tunnel... (**1s**)	**380**
Head to Bermondsey...	**668**
Head to Rotherhithe...	**649**

❧ 657 ❧

The officer is already a fair swordsman. You practice sabrework with him and help him to develop some combinations of footwork and bladework that will give him an edge on the battlefield, or in a duel. He pays you ten guineas (**£10 10s**) for the lessons.

Score 1-3	Unhurt
Score 4	An old **wound** re-opens: replace a **scar** with a **wound**
Score 5	A nasty scratch: gain a **wound**
Score 6	Badly cut: lose a NIMBLENESS point

If you are **Wanted by the Constabulary**, gain the codeword *Chinstrap*. If you now have **five wounds**, note passage **760** and turn to **500** immediately.

Turn to...	**760**

❧ 658 ❧

"Well, if they're not for me, what on this good earth are you doing bringing explosives into my pub? Get out before I call the Constables!"

Leave the pub...	**647**

❧ 659 ❧

Seeing that you are warming to the idea, Wright eagerly leans over the skeletal remains of his guinea-fowl. "We would furnish you with a new name, of course. The election is a simple matter." He waves to Sir Hurtbridge, so far a quiet presence behind the beef.

"It is my borough in Portsea," says Hurtbridge. "We can have you representing the twelve voters within a week."

"Will you do it?" asks Wheelhouse. He spears a sausage and dips it into the mustard pot. "Someone must stand for the commoners!"

Wright interprets your silence as thoughtfulness.

"There is one other way. Slower and less sure, but also putting yourself rather less in the limelight. Perhaps you would agree to coaching some of our members in duelling? You would be well-paid."

"I will represent this rotten borough for you."
    (NIMBLENESS 8+)   **677**
"I will teach your Progressives to fight."   **685**
"I would not enter into such an endeavour
      for any reason. Good day, gentlemen."   **641**

❧ 660 ❧

Jerry returns to the hideout whistling. "I got news for yer, Toby. Beaufort's gone north to hunt traitors. 'e's off to York for a while." Then he turns to the other members of the gang. "Breakfast's ready boys. 'oo wants some nice tasty kidneys?" Gain the codeword *Commensurate*.

Return to the hideout...   **581**
Leave the attic...   **252**

❧ 661 ❧

It takes a moment's calculation, but the tin of fruit sails through the air and cracks into the back on the thief's head, flooring her instantly. Pedestrians applaud. You return the lady's bag to her. Remove the **tin of fruit** and roll two dice: if you score higher than your unimproved NIMBLENESS score, you can improve it by one point.

Ride on...   **noted passage**

❧ 662 ❧

You do your best to help the victims of the accident. Roll two dice, adding 3 if you are the **People's Champion**, 1 for each level of **medical training** you have and another 1 for each of the following that you possess: **bandages**, a **bottle of whisky** or a **stethoscope.**

Score 2-4   Unable to help anyone...
Score 5-8   Save a passenger's life: gain the codeword
           Compassionate...
Score 9-11 Help a trapped woman; rewarded with a
           pocket watch...
Score 12+ Save the day: gain a **solidarity point**...

Ride on...   **noted passage**

❧ 663 ❧

You come across a starving beggar and pass him a morsel of food. "There used to be some nuns what would bring us food of an evening," says an old beggar. "But not recent."

"What happened to them?"
He shrugs.
Asking around, you are directed to the house used by the Sisters of St Katharine. Nobody answers your knock, but you climb the gate and peer in through the back window.
A horrible sight meets your eyes. The emaciated body of a woman lies on the floor. Entering through the rickety door and keeping a cloth clamped over your face, you explore the house and find four more sisters, all dead, plainly after considerable suffering. What dreadful disease did they catch? Typhoid fever? Cholera? There are any number of such things borne on the fogs and miasmas of the district. You back out quickly. Gain the codeword *Charity*.

Return to the streets of Bermondsey...   **668**

❧ 664 ❧

There is a hubbub in the room. One drinker nudges another, and then another, and soon the whole room is turning to look at you. If you have the codeword *Compassionate*, turn to **1213**. Otherwise, read on.

There could well be a reward on your head, and many of these desperate people would be quick to claim it, if they could. What will happen next depends on how popular you are.

If you possess fewer than 15 **solidarity points**... **691**
If you possess 15 or more **solidarity points**...   **707**

❧ 665 ❧

Now you weave through stairways and along passages, moving as quickly as you can but freezing at any sound of movement. Eventually you arrive at the guardroom above the gatehouse. By some stroke of luck, it is empty! A lever here unlocks the gate, and a steam-winch raises the portcullis.

Start the winch...   **595**
Cut the counterweight rope... **(axe)**   **606**

❧ 666 ☙

Remove the **explosives** from your **possessions** and add **£5** to your wallet. The landlord gives another massive wink and carries his parcel downstairs.

Return to the parlour...	**651**
Leave the Pineapple...	**647**

❧ 667 ☙

The beer you are served is poured in a tall, many-faceted glass etched with the name of the inn. It is a pale, crisp, bubbly brew, artificially carbonated with a new industrial process. The brightly citrus flavoured beer has an almost pine-like aroma, followed by a cloudy, indistinct bitterness and an earthy finish. They tell you it is called a Ladybird Pale. If you are the **People's Champion** but not a **Member of Parliament**, turn to **620** immediately. Otherwise, note passage **651** and roll a dice to see what you hear among the drinkers.

Score 1	Grave robbers...	**1019**
Score 2-3	The Compact...	**1060**
Score 4-5	A street gang...	**1113**
Score 6	Flat Billy...	**873**

❧ 668 ☙

The laws of the metropolis have outlawed all the noisome and foul industries to the edges of the city and so Bermondsey, along with housing its countless inhabitants in terraces of particular squalor and filth, is home to a dozen great tanneries, each responsible for a cloud of awful stench. Incredibly, it is also a centre of food canning and home to a massive complex of biscuit manufacturing. Yet despite all these employers, work is intermittent and unstable, the people poor and desperate. A few brave souls have set up their missions here, but even these struggle.

Explore the streets of Bermondsey...	**663**
Ride towards Southwark...	**631**
Steam on to Rotherhithe...	**642**
Head for the Thames Tunnel...	**656**

❧ 669 ☙

"We have waited until now," you argue.

"Every day sees more of the people's blood pressed from them, like cheese in the whey-press," says Snell.

"Wait we must," says Commissioner Reel. "Go out and tip the balance in our favour - although this set-back will certainly scare some of the less dependable Members of that accursed Parliament."

Note passage **425** and turn to **1133**, where you should tick the box marked Abolishment Bill Unsuccessful.

❧ 670 ☙

A Constable peers at you through thick lenses. A glimmer of recognition flashes across his face - but his memory is easily bought.

Bribe the Constable... (**£1**)	**252**
Unable or unwilling to pay...	**278**

❧ 671 ☙

"Beaufort's 'ere in London," says Jerry. "e'll be in 'is suite up on the Strand at that big Somerset 'ouse, makin' plans and such-like."

"Very helpful, boys," you reply. "May I join you for breakfast?"

This morning it is kippers. Runt, Aldwin, Rupert, Jerry and the entire gang sit around munching on the smoked fish and then wipe the paper they came wrapped in with several crusts of stale bread. They joke and laugh and make their plans for the day.

"Maybe I'll take a trip on the river," says Jerry. "'oo's coming along?"

"I will," says Runt. "We gonna pinch a rowboat again?"

Return to the hideout...	**581**
Leave the attic...	**252**

❧ 672 ☙

Mrs Roberts has grown tired of your efforts. "Oh, do go away," she says. "I cannot always be carrying petitions."

Leave the *Gentilesse*...	**847**

❧ 673 ☙

St Saviour's Church has stood here for many centuries, but in the recent years the chapterhouse has come to some agreement with the Telegraph Guild, who have erected a noisy telegraph atop the tower. Perhaps they have made their house of prayer into a den of robbers, as the press have cried, but they have found a use for their tower and a new income stream while they are at it. If you have the **Southwark package**, turn to **743** immediately.

Leave St Saviour's...	**631**

❧ 674 ❧

A steam engine and its wagons stand in the yard at the George while its crew take on provisions for their journey. Several mechanics and hauliers mill around drinking while they tinker with machinery. You dismount and brush the dust from your clothes. Note this passage (**674**) before choosing an option.

Buy a drink... (**3s**)	**687**
Mend your velosteam...	**1300**
Return to Southwark...	**631**

❧ 675 ❧

"Where did you get this, then?" asks a Captain of the Constables. "Looks like seditious material."

"If you look closely, you might see annotations..."

"Is that right. In your hand?"

"No. Have it looked at. They will be recognised... it is significant."

The Captain puts the book away. "There is a small bounty paid on seditious material." He digs out a shilling and tosses it over the desk. "Be on your way, now." Remove the **annotated manifesto** from your **possessions** and gain **1s**.

Return to the Strand...	**139**

❧ 676 ❧

Tower Hill has never seen such crowds: it seems the whole metropolis has turned out in celebration, in awe and in shock. A platform, complete with block, has been built in full view of the whole crowd. You accompany the men and women bringing the chained prisoner to his doom.

"Where is the Tower executioner?" cries Commissioner Tate. His axe is here, but the man cannot be found.

"You do it," says Comrade Feaver, with a sly look. "You're the most committed of all of us, surely. You take this honour."

"I will not do it."	**704**
"I will gladly carry out this just punishment."	**734**

❧ 677 ❧

No sooner than you have given your hand in agreement to Mr Wright and his Progressives than telegraph messages are sent at once to Portsea, where ballots are prepared. It is only a matter of a few days before the results of the 'election' are reported, during which time Mr Wright coaches you on your role within the party.

"You'll be given all the privileges of a Member of the House," he reassures you. "Chambers, remuneration and so forth. And you will have to attend a certain number of the debates in the Commons. But chiefly we need you to fight. To challenge, fight and defeat three of the most deadly swordsmen of our age, each of whom is an Establishment Member of the House."

"And they are?"

Mr Wright counts them off on his fingers. "The Honourable Francis de Lankey, he's killed three of our fellows and put several out of action. Then there's the Duke of Innishmore, a very dangerous character. And last, but quite the most dangerous, is the young Baronet Dressley. Now he put two of our Wheatears under the turf just last week."

The electors unanimously choose you to represent them on Portsea. "It is exactly this sort of thing that we must change," says Mr Hurtbridge, apparently without irony.

Note that you are now a **Member of Parliament**.

Make your way to the house...	**806**

❧ 678 ❧

An engineer sees you riding in and hurries out to meet you. He takes the **Rotherhithe package** from you (remove it from your **possessions**) and looks at his watch. If you have passed through **12 passages or fewer** on your way here from the Greenwich station (passage **1057**), he will pay you **£8** as a bonus. If not, you are paid **10s**. "I imagine you're in quite a rush," he laughs. "Off you go."

Do not forget to continue to tally the number of passages you read if you are continuing to deliver the Guild's parcels.

Turn out of the gate...	**649**

❧ 679 ❧

If you have a **burnt rose**, turn to **594** immediately. If you have **Lady Serene's calling card** or the codeword *Curly*, turn to **1030**. Otherwise, read on.

A glamorous travelling lady would rather learn to defend herself than to pay for bodyguards, while making her world tour aboard the *Verne* airship. She has a few days to improve her ability with a blade before she departs. Roll a dice to see the result.

Score 1-3   A bad cut to the calf: gain a **wound...**
Score 4-5   Gain a **stiff back (NIM-2)...**
Score 6   You are unhurt...

She pays you six guineas (**£6 6s**) before waving you adieu.

Turn to...   **760**

❧ 680 ❧

You come to Blackfriars Bridge and begin to ride across. At the half-way point stands a Constables' post, where watchers check amongst the traffic for criminals, out-of-date licences and dangerous engines. If you are **Wanted by the Constables**, turn to **670** immediately. Otherwise you can cross with impunity.

Head for St Paul's Cathedral...   **215**
Steer towards the Strand...   **139**
Ride onto Upper Thames Street...   **252**

❧ 681 ❧

You come across a man jauntily walking along the road, whistling a tune. He has just returned from the horse races, where he has won several good bets. He chats excitedly about this season's winners and good prospects. Gain a level of **racing information**.

Ride on...   **631**

❧ 682 ❧

The chandlery deals in supplies for ship-owners and sea-captains, but the staff will sell to individuals too. They specialise in hardware and weaponry: ship crews know the value of a good blade.

Tools	To buy	To sell
rope	2s	-
waterproof paint	6s	-
lantern	4s	1s
axe	8s	6s
heavy wrench	18s	12s
explosives	£1 4s	-
welding tools	£2 2s	£1 10s
grappling iron	12s	9s
fishing line	1s	-
net	6s	4s
tarpaulin	4s	2s
measuring line	6s	4s
telescope	£4 10s	£3

Weapons	To buy	To sell
club (PAR 2)		2s	-
sabre (PAR 3)	£2 10	£1 5s
rapier (PAR 4)	£10	£5
blunderpistol (ACC 6)	£4	£3 5s
duelling pistols (ACC 7)	£15	£10
Constable's carbine (ACC 8)	-	£10

Return to Rotherhithe...   **649**

❧ 683 ❧

The landlord notices what you are carrying and sidles over. "I've been waiting for a delivery from Flat Billy," he says with a wink. "That looks about right. I've got five sovereigns here waiting."

Make the exchange...   **666**
Refuse to part with your **explosives**...   **658**

❧ 684 ❧

The routine in the Livingstone M punchcards is powerfully analytical: it demonstrates the workings of the Aramanth program, allowing you to understand how you could create punchcards of your own from a blank set. Remove the **punchcards (Livingstone M)** and gain the codeword *Chirp*.

Turn to...   **noted passage**

❧ 685 ❧

Mr Wright arranges the hire of a small hall down a Westminster backstreet and you collect the necessaries. Your first client is a panicked, portly rabbit of a fellow: Jermyn Hyss, the Honourable Member for Lincoln. "I've received a challenge from this de Lankey chap," he tells you. "I've never so much as crossed his blessed path! He's writing nonsense about me honour and claims about where I spend me evenings - things me wife needn't know. Can you teach me to fight?"

"How long have we got?"

"If I don't fight him by the end of the week, me career will be over. And me wife will kill me unless I contest those accusations."

A week. This won't be possible. Perhaps you had better simply teach the man to parry, and how to accept a flesh wound with the least danger.

Teach him how to survive...   **694**
Teach him to fight dirty...   **758**

✎ 686 ✎

"See here," you show Lady Diana. "The encoding for each of these messages changes every time, but the one stable feature is the final phrase: 'Long Live the King!' Cracking that is the key to the King's code.

Working with the engine through the night, you manage to narrow down the possibilities until, in the early morning, Diana calls to you from behind her binocular stand at the high window. "The palace is signalling! King's code!"

"This is our chance," you reply.

She immediately begins inputting the movements of the telegraph with the levers at her side. You set the computational engine whirring with the decoding program clicking through on its fresh punchcards. A punch begins to click, tapping out the text of the message:

> 1ST LD IMP. AETH. CPS REP IM STJA. ADDIT.FRESH SARDINIAN TRUFFLES FLORIAN'S FACECREAM LONG LIVE THE KING!

Lady Diana grins as she looks over at the transcript. "Congratulations," she says. "He is in our hands. Long live the King!" Add the **King's code** to the satchel in your **possessions**.

Continue with the plan...   **742**

✎ 687 ✎

The beer here is brought in from Kent, on particular steam-drays, and it is worth the cost. Foregate Pale Ale is brewed on a spring water drawn from the Kentish hills, rich with malt and bitter with the distinctive whiff of Murfin hops. Roll a dice to see what rumours you hear:

Score 1-2	A place to stay...	**928**
Score 3-4	Recognised!	**664**
Score 5	The Compact...	**1060**
Score 6	Parliamentary blades...	**1075**

✎ 688 ✎

If there is a way into the Tower, you will find it. The moat, with its prowling lions, is out, and the garrison will be on high alert. If you have the **Tower Key**, turn to **588** immediately. Otherwise, read on.

Your time inside the Tower of London is what you will have to depend on. You recall the layouts of passages and rooms that you saw within the walls, relentlessly pursuing an answer. There are two options: an entrance through the water gate, or an aerial approach.

Swim through the water gate...	**646**
Fly in... (**winged harness**)	**598**

✎ 689 ✎

You race through the streets towards Crafton's Cookshop. A young girl has to dive out of your way when she steps out from behind a coal delivery engine, but otherwise you manage to reach Lambeth without accident. The bells of the Constables' Imperials are still ringing, though, as you pull into Crafton's yard.

"They just don't let us get back on our feet, do they?" Crafton huffs angrily. "Ride on into this shed here. You can come in and get something to eat. We'll all swear you was here all day."

Accept Crafton's protection...   **616**

✎ 690 ✎

While here in Shadwell, you have the opportunity to accept the invitation of the sailor you helped down in Deptford. You find the tiny terraced cottage where his wife and children live, close by the wall of the docks and overshadowed by a tall water tower.

The sailor is at sea, but his wife shows her appreciation by laying out her best tea: a mixture of poor man's groceries, stolen goods from the nearby docks and far-eastern delicacies brought by the sailor.

The meal - and the chance to rest by a small coal fire and doze - is a welcome break from the hard life of a road thief. When you awake, you find she has laid a blanket over you in the chair. Any **aches**, **pains** or **ailments** (other than **wounds**) have disappeared.

Remove the codeword *Carpet*.

Leave the house...   **380**

✎ 691 ✎

A group of determined men decide that this is their opportunity to claim the Constables' reward on your head. They gather clubs and chair legs and attack you.

Drinkers	Weapons: **clubs** (PAR 2)
Parry:	10
Nimbleness:	8
Toughness:	6

Victory!	**noted passage**
Defeat!	**1500**

✎ 692 ✎

If you have the codeword *Crazed*, turn to **697** immediately. Otherwise, read on.

The Telegraph Station stands behind high fences. Its four towers clatter incessantly, carrying the coded messages of a thousand businesses. If you have the **Rotherhithe package**, turn to **678** immediately.

Attempt to put the station out of action...	**1084**
Leave the Telegraph Station...	**649**

✎ 693 ✎

The foreigner is a man of power and privilege from the continent. He is unused to the etiquette of fighting in this land. You teach him how to comport himself. Roll a dice to see the result.

Score 1-4	You are unhurt...
Score 5	A cut reopens: replace a **scar** with a **wound**...
Score 6	Drastic injury: lose a NIMBLENESS point...

The foreigner pays you with **ten guineas in banknotes** and heads on his way.

Turn to...	**760**

✎ 694 ✎

Teaching a gentleman like Jerymn Hyss is not straightforward: he is remarkably stubborn and unwilling to take instruction - even when his life depends on it. You flatter him and soothe his panic the best you can, while trying to anticipate the attacks most likely to kill him. He does improve slightly, as you clatter backwards and forwards across the boards of the dusty hall, and seems to believe you when you teach him that he can block a sabre-cut with his forearm. Better a severed tendon than a sabre-point between the ribs! Roll a dice to see how he fares in the eventual duel.

Score 1-3	Bad news...	**802**
Score 4-6	Other bad news...	**811**

✎ 695 ✎

The streets spread out from Southwark like the strands of a great web. Haulage Guild engines head south-east, along the road to Deptford Bridge, while others wait for the hourly change of direction on London Bridge.

Cross London Bridge...	**699**
Cross Westminster Bridge...	**602**
Cross Blackfriars Bridge...	**680**
Head for Lambeth...	**647**
Steam towards Bermondsey...	**668**
Take the road to Deptford Bridge...	**613**

✎ 696 ✎

It is a simple matter to arrange for a load of coal to be delivered to your workshop in Millwall - after all, this is the Coal Board's entire business. It is more expensive than fetching it yourself by river, however.

Tick the box marked ☐ **Coal delivery** in passage **1129** before making your next choice.

Return to the depot...	**379**
Leave the depot...	**310**

✎ 697 ✎

The ruin of the station swarms with builders, guildsmen and craftspeople, anxious to rebuild the tower you destroyed. There is no way in for you here!

Leave the Telegraph Station...	**649**

✎ 698 ✎

It was only a few days' notice you were given to leave your cottage - the cottage your family had held the tenancy of for generations. But like the rest of the little village where you lived, you had no choice but to leave. The Coal Board's massive, steam-powered excavators began ripping through the common and the vegetable gardens without any mercy. You saw a chance to get some sort of revenge and stole the velosteam from a Coal Board rider.

Your family bid you go and seek a better life. Ailing and heartbroken, they did not last long once separated from their ancestral holding. Perhaps you are the only one left.

Now you have the city before you, where all the wealth of the land is concentrated in the hands of the guilds, the nobles and the crown. Here you may be able to strike a blow for the little people of England - the forgotten villagers and dispossessed smallholders.

Your ability scores are:

RUTHLESSNESS	3
ENGINEERING	2
MOTORING	3
NIMBLENESS	6
INGENUITY	5
GALLANTRY	2

You have in your possession a **blunderpistol (ACC 6)**, a **sabre (PAR 3)**, a **mask** and a **grappling iron**.

Turn to...   1200

❧ 699 ❧

The signals indicate that traffic is currently flowing in your favour, from south to north across the bridge. It would be a long wait otherwise. You edge out between the wagons of a Coal Board road train and ride onto the ancient bridge. If you are **Wanted by the Constables**, turn to **714** immediately.

Onto the Bridge...   1000

❧ 700 ❧

"The first thing I want to know," says Mrs Petty calmly, "is the location of the Compact's headquarters here in London. If you have that information, I want it now. If not, go and get it for me. Do this and I will have your slate wiped clean."

Tell her what you know... (*Cheered*)	726
Leave the pub...	139

❧ 701 ❧

The bell rings cheerily as you push through the door. Inside, you can find a mind-boggling array of rods, baskets, nets, hooks, lures, baits, clothing and everything else that you might imaginably need to spend a day sat beside a flowing stream.

Food and Drink	To buy	To sell
large pike	-	£2
bottle of whisky	15s	10s
picnic hamper	£4	£2 10s
Tools	To buy	To sell
lantern	6s	3s
fishing line	1s	-
net	6s	4s
tarpaulin	4s	2s
ultra-tensed wire	£2 10s	£1 10s

Leave the shop...   794

❧ 702 ❧

The powerful velosteam accelerates as you let more steam into the pistons. You must choose the longest stretches of road you can: once moving quickly, the Ferguson has a wide turning circle, although it also has the weight to knock many obstacles out of the way. You rattle over round-headed cobbles and splash through the puddles alongside the Neckinger brook. You come to Bermondsey Wall, right where East Lane stairs climb up from the river. Which way must you turn towards Rotherhithe?

Turn right...	735
Turn left...	752

❧ 703 ❧

The Compact has prepared and even trained for this moment, but the great rabbleous mob of Londoners know nothing of the ways of war. Your part is to try to prevent them from throwing their lives away, and turn their angry energy into useful progress. Barricades across Tower Hill are soon erected, watchmen posted on rooftops, caches of equipment collected and distributed. Then, as night falls, leaders gather to plan the assault.

There is no overall commander, as many of the revolting citizens are wary of the Compact, but Commissioner Timms holds sway with his talk of tactics and siege. His plans are adopted and the fight begins.

Gunfire begins to crackle out from the barricades, aiming at the ancient crenellations and arrow-loops of the Tower, trying to provoke return fire, giving some guess at the defenders' strength. Then squads begin to move forward behind makeshift shields: iron plate swinging doors taken from the dockyards or nearby warehouses.

An explosion of shattered metal, cobbles, earth and the torn limbs of men echoes through the square: the defenders have begun to fire their artillery on the mob. The squads get closer and closer to the moat, but more and more artillery fire pounds into them. The mob behind the barricades becomes restless. "When do we charge?" asks a butcher waving a sharp cleaver. "When do we gut 'em?"

One large squad has made it over the first bridge to the gatehouse. They shelter behind their makeshift protection as defenders toss down burning timber, rocks and sharpened iron stakes. Sharpshooters, dotted along the rooftops, target the defenders, trying to buy time for the assault.

Consult the revolutionary checklist in passage **1133**: if the Comrades are trained in using explosives, turn to **729** immediately. Otherwise, read on.

The premature explosion of a charge blows the gate party asunder: their bodies fall into the ditch, where the Tower lions leap at them. Without a gate entrance, the losses of the mob will be much higher, but their blood is the price of freedom.

A roaring cry and a raised flag announces the full assault. The mob rises from behind the barricades and dashes towards the shielded parties. They tumble down into the moat, or toss in bundles of seized goods, and begin to erect the ladders.

The slaughter from the defenders' gunfire is terrifying. Shot after shot of artillery splits the crowd. Carbine and musket-fire ring on the stones. Splinters, tossed grenades and bullets whizz backwards and forwards. Despite it all, the mob raise their ladders, and the first, most death-defiant, comrades climb up towards the ramparts.

The fight continues through the night, first as the ramparts are taken, then through and into the grounds of the tower. The people do not have the weaponry or the training of their enemies, but they are powered by the pressurised rage of generations, heated by a furnace of today's injustice. They are unstoppable.

Raise the flag! **719**

❧ 704 ❧

"I knew it," says Comrade Feaver. "Remember this moment, comrades! I will not flinch from my duty." Gain the codeword *Chary*.

Small though she is, she raises the immense executioner's chopper high above her head. The crowd goes silent - and in a flash, the King is dead. His head tumbles to the ground and rolls beneath the platform.

Turn to... **650**

❧ 705 ❧

If you have **Hendon's letter**, turn to **720** immediately. Otherwise, read on. The landlord considers the contract but shakes his head. "The only thing that would convince me to sign this," he says, "would be the say-so from the Duke. He owns the place."

"Which Duke?"

"Why, Duke of Hendon, o'course."

"Where do I find him?"

"Well, at his place in Mayfair. Or at his club. But I don't think he'd be speaking to the likes of you very often."

Gain the codeword *Craven*.

Leave the pub... **794**

❧ 706 ❧

"Got some spoiled goods from the docks here," calls a man to the assembled drinkers. "All ruined, like, and hence the low prices."

The goods are not spoiled at all - they are stolen from a bulk shipment in the manner common to the dockers. However, the entrepreneur is also interested in buying trinkets of yours - so long as he believes he can make a profit on them.

	To buy	To sell
pineapple	5s	-
bottle of whisky	8s	-
silk scarf	£1	-
silk waistcoat (GAL+1)	£3	-
locket	-	6s
pocket watch	-	£2 10s

Turn to... **noted passage**

❧ 707 ❧

"Drinks on the house!" calls a voice. You are feted and celebrated by the drinkers, every one of whom wishes to shake your hand. The people of this city are desperate for a hero to represent them and to stand up for the needy. A trio of musicians begin to play and the company dance and drink into the early morning.

Turn to... **noted passage**

❧ 708 ❧

Lord Beaufort is not a tall or an impressive looking man. His fine pelisse of blue wool and seal fur, however, is heavily brocaded with gold and he wears a mechanically-focusing monocle of custom design. His posture and the characteristic quiet of the man indicate intelligence and patience, but there is also something rash in the glint of his eye and the devil-may-care puff he gives his cigar. If you are **Wanted by the Constables**, turn to **733** immediately. Otherwise, read on.

"You aren't the normal fellow," says Lord Beaufort. His left hand rests on the hilt of his basket-hilted sabre.

"I have your normal packet, though," you reply.

He takes the **black oilskin packet** (remove it from your **possessions**) and fastidiously unties the knotted string. He makes no attempt to hide the bundle of banknotes from you.

"Yes, this looks right," he says. "Here. Take this note to our, hmm, mutual friend. Some of this needs immediate attention."

He hands you **Lord Beaufort's note**, but it is written in some sort of code. There are plainly names in a list and presumably punishments or deals written opposite them.

The Chief Constable tosses his cigar butt off the Monument, clearly careless to the irony of throwing smouldering ashes from a memorial to the greatest fire the city has ever known, and makes his way down the stairs. After a prudent pause, you do as well.

Turn to...   264

❧ 709 ❧

You drive off the ruffians and approach the woman. She calms down from her panic and you realise that you have just saved Princess Alexandrina, the King's niece, from a dreadful fate. She is heavily pregnant and seems to be in some pain.

Clearly you must act decisively. Her driver is still unconscious, but you make sure that he is out of danger before helping the Princess onto your velosteam. It is only a short distance to St James' Palace, where she has a set of apartments, so you set off through the mist once more.

The guards make way and a lady-in-waiting comes to help the Princess up the stairs. For a moment you are celebrated by the sentries, then welcomed into a kitchen for a hot drink, where you hear more about the Princess and discover why the Palace staff have such pity and affection for her.

"She's never been a favourite of her uncle's, on her father's account. But then she found a good man in her husband, the Duke of Corrigan, before he was killed outside Valencia last year. So she's kept here, a young widow, with all her hope in this child and not a friend in the palace."

"Why is she so unpopular with the King?" you ask.

A cook tops up your hot drink. "Well, his brother wasn't one to keep quiet when he saw his Majesty acting wrong. And milady Princess Alexandrina even spoke up once or twice too. They never liked the way he treated his wife, for a start."

The lady-in-waiting reappears to thank you and bring a message from the Princess. "It may have been just in time," she says. "The baby is coming. The Princess wanted me to give you this, so that you can return and she can thank you properly in person." You are given a **purple brooch** and for this good deed you will also gain a **solidarity point**.

Leave the Palace...   721

❧ 710 ❧

A few stalls line the narrow street, standing between slime-filled gutters and piles of refuse. A church hall stands boarded up and the stallholders look hungrily at your purse.

	To buy	To sell
Clothing	To buy	To sell
Dungarees (GAL-2)	£1 2s	15s
top hat	£3	£1
lady's wig	18s	12s
fur coat	-	£2 15s
lace shawl	-	18s
dancing shoes (GAL+3)	-	£7
Jewellery	To buy	To sell
locket	10s	4s
pocket watch	-	£1 10s
silver ring	£1	15s
silver bracelet	£2	£1
silver necklace	-	£2 5s
gold ring	-	£2

Leave the street...   721

❧ 711 ❧

Something about the boy weaving his tray between the tables looks familiar to you. Catching his face in one of the massive mirrors, you recognise Braddins, the boy you redeemed from the workhouse in Marlow, who then ran away from the butcher in Cookham. He is startled to see you here, but assures you that he is treated well and glad to be in the city. "I 'as my own little room 'ere, under the stairs, and I gets to save all the sparrers these 'ere customers gives me fer carryin' their drinks, so what I don't spend on smokes and pies, I'm saving. I'm going to have my own barrer, that's what I want, selling hot pies, and then a cookshop, like on the corner. I'll marry meself a wife and raise a family. No indeed, the city is a fine place!"

If you want to contribute towards Braddins' savings, remove **£4** from your purse and gain a **solidarity point**. Erase the codeword *Additive*.

Return to the Yard...   150

✎ 712 ✎

The work to crack the code is long and arduous. Together, you and Lady Diana spend several days inputting the intercepted messages into the computational engine. Fragments of sense appear here and there, but you cannot achieve a complete deciphering.

"What now? Call it off?" you ask.

"Oh no," says Lady Diana. "This was merely to help with our credentials. On we go: we must set about our disguises."

Turn to...   **742**

✎ 713 ✎

If you have a **razor**, turn to **334** immediately. Otherwise, you must fight Lord Beaufort himself. If you are still breathing after five rounds, and thinking the better of your rash assault, then you can attempt to flee, leaving Beaufort alive.

Lord Beaufort	Weapon: **fine sabre (PAR 3)**
Parry:	10
Nimbleness:	7
Toughness:	5

Victory!	**334**
Defeat within five rounds!	**113**
Flee after five rounds...	**1514**

✎ 714 ✎

A constable raises his hand. "Stop right there! You - the velosteamer!" He begins to flick through his printofit to see whether your face is on the Wanted List. You must make an INGENUITY roll of difficulty 13 to convince him to let you through, adding 1 if you possess a **top hat** and 1 for every **£1** bribe (up to a maximum of **£5**) that you are willing to pay him.

Successful INGENUITY roll!	**1000**
Failed INGENUITY roll!	**614**

✎ 715 ✎

You manage to find the Duke of Hendon at home, but he is far from impressed with you. "What do you want?" he asks, haughtily.

When you explain about the beer contract at the HMS Spartan he becomes visibly frustrated. "This is some sort of commercial discussion? How tiring. Let us make it interesting. A wager. A game of cards to decide the thing. You win, and I write you a letter to

take to the landlord, releasing him from his contract. I win, and you give me, oh, a hundred pounds." If you have a **deck of marked cards**, turn to **885** immediately.

"I'll take your wager."	**1037**
"I don't bet that high."	**750**

✎ 716 ✎

You must quickly plan a route to Deptford that will keep you ahead of your pursuers. You will have to ride wide streets to make the most of your velosteam's power, but you cannot afford to take highways with Constabulary posts.

Make for Creek Road...	**783**
Steer for New Cross Road...	**748**

✎ 717 ✎

The box contains a **pneumatic manual (ENG+3)**, two **high pressure valves**, some **copper pipe** and a **measuring line**. In a leather bag is **£28** in coins.

Turn to...   **noted passage**

❧ 718 ❧

You draw up at the gates at the south-eastern corner of Hyde Park. Tall white Palladian mansions stretch away on either side, hiding their shameful secrets in basements and mews. A pall of smoke rises from the terracotta forest of chimneys, but a steady westerly breeze blows it away.

Head into the Park...   **741**
Steam to St James' Palace... (**purple brooch
    or Friend of Princess Alexandrina**) **775**
Ride into Mayfair...   **750**
Turn towards Westminster...   **721**

❧ 719 ❧

Atop the White Tower, in the centre of the ancient fortress, you gather with the bloodied veterans of the fight to raise the flag of the revolution. Commissioner Timms is nowhere to be found, but Comrades Feaver, Tate and Snell, yourself and Commissioner Reel represent the Compact. The people of London are here too, in the persons of some of the leaders of the assault.

The flag billows out into the dawn: a cross of St George surrounded by a cog-toothed wheel of progress on a green field, edged with scarlet. A new day has dawned and with it, a new age of equality and freedom for the people of the land.

"We still have much to do, Comrades," says Commissioner Reel. "We have heard that there will be a counter-attack tonight. We must prepare the defences and fully arm the people."

While the comrades begin that work, you ride out into the nearby streets. Largely deserted, the roads and lanes echo strangely to the sound of your velosteam's wheels. Parties of revolutionaries are tearing down walls to make barricades along the riverside embankment, across London Bridge, and at other key points.

Then you come across the army moving forwards over Blackfriars Bridge. Armoured road engines and soldiers in steam-powered exoskeletons crunch forward into the city. The citizens have fled, hide in their cellars, or have joined the revolutionaries around the Tower.

You ride back to report on what you have seen. If you have the codeword *Citrate*, turn to **751** immediately.

Turn to...   **759**

❧ 720 ❧

"There you are," you say to the landlord, throwing **Hendon's letter** on the table. (Remove it from your **possessions**). "Now sign the contract."

Hesitantly, he does. Gain the codeword *Conglomerate*.

Leave the pub...   **794**

❧ 721 ❧

Here you are in the heart of the Capital, where the ancient, crumbling palace of Westminster hosts the King's Parliament. Cheek by jowl with these halls of privilege and power huddle some of the darkest, dankest slums, the new riverside embankment built by the Metropolitan Sewerage Company, the broad Westminster bridge, guarded at both ends, and the booths, stalls and shops of countless hawkers and tradespeople. A short way north is the enclave of St James' Park, a royal pleasure-ground fenced off from the populace, and behind that St James' Palace, where King Charles keeps court.

Approach the Palace of Westminster...   **744**
Ride to St James' Palace.. (**purple brooch
    or Friend of Princess Alexandrina**) **775**
Take a look at the stalls...   **710**
Take the road to Chelsea...   **794**
Cross Westminster Bridge...   **738**
Head on towards Mayfair...   **750**
Ride towards Hyde Park...   **718**
Steam onto the Strand...   **139**

❧ 722 ❧

You steam on through Chelsea, heading for the river crossing at Battersea. The houses in this area are palatial - each one a mansion in its garden, a veritable manor in its own estate. Perhaps they provide work for a score of servants each... but how many rooms of glass and glitter are kept for the wealthy owners, when in Shoreditch, eight children share a bed and their parents sleep on the floor? You ride on, past the gas lamps and the wisteria plants, and reach the bridge.

Arrive at the bridge...   **1132**

❧ 723 ❧

The ruffians turn on you instead! However, you quickly knock two down by ramming into them with your velosteam. The remaining two come at you with blackjack and club.

Ruffians   Weapons: **blackjack (PAR 2)**
Parry: 8
Nimbleness: 6
Toughness: 3

Victory!   **709**
Defeat!   **999**

❧ 724 ❧

The drovers can tell you all about the unrest across the land. "Did you know that York is held against the King?" asks one, pointing at you with the stem of his pipe. "The Duke of Cumberland and half a dozen of them big industrialists have all declared for some German Prince they prefer. They won't deal with the big guilds at all."

"Ah, but they don't have to, up there," continues another. "Got they own coals, got they telegraphs and got the heart of the people, too."

"Sounds like they've your sympathy, Macklemore," jests the first drover.

"What they ain't got is real money," comes the reply. "Can't sell 'em beef. They only pay in their own scrip and that ain't no good anywhere else."

Leave the drovers...   **150**
Leave the pub...   **126**

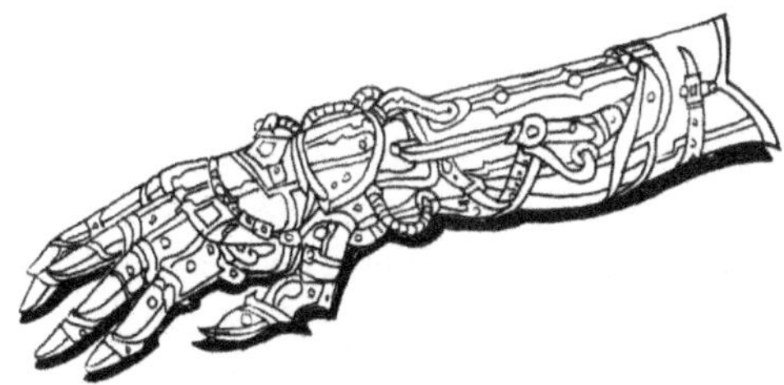

❧ 725 ❧

In a repurposed stable behind Tort Mansion is Professor Prentiss's workshop. He is the genius behind Sir Reginald's business venture, and he fully looks the part. Scraps of wild, white hair project at random like puffs of cotton-plant down from his shiny scalp, and a leather and brass optical magnifier is strapped over his temples. He is peering through one of several lenses suspended above his eye and fiddling with a tiny detail somewhere deep in a machine.

He shows you the keyboard. "It will punch cards exactly as you play, " he enthuses. "Every note, every hesitation, every ritardando and every accelerando. Every flourish. Don't hold back on the emotion, now!"

The quality of the recording will depend entirely on the expressiveness of your playing. Make an INGENUITY or ENGINEERING roll of difficulty 14, adding 2 for each level of **musicianship** you possess.

Successful INGENUITY or ENGINEERING roll... **764**
Failed INGENUITY or ENGINEERING roll...   **772**

❧ 726 ❧

Mrs Petty leans forward over her glass of port. "Excellent!" she hisses, as you tell her about the Blackwall sugar warehouse. "When the time is right..." She crumples a scrap of paper in her hand and tosses it into the fire.

Mrs Petty sends a message out to her connections, instructing them to remove your name from the list of dangerous criminals. You can now remove all your **Wanted Statuses** and gain the codeword *Citrate*.

Leave her for now...   **165**

❧ 727 ❧

Hyde Park is so massive, and in some places, so badly overgrown, that you have a fair chance of getting away with daylight robbery here. However, you will have to make a quick getaway as there are Constabulary posts in every direction. Note passage **730**.

If you have a **telescope** or **binoculars**, turn to **737** immediately. Otherwise, roll a dice to see what you encounter:

Score 1-3   A rich pedestrian...   **54**
Score 4-6   A private steam carriage...   **1425**

❧ 728 ❧

Now Lord Beaufort turns to give you his attention. "You are plainly an individual of some ability," he muses, "to get hold of this." He tosses the book aside.

"I need to get someone inside a gang in the East End," he says. "The thug called Flat Billy who operates out of the Grave Maurice in Whitechapel. He's powerful - far too powerful - and dangerous. Perhaps you can infiltrate his organisation for me."

"How would I do that?"

"He is always looking for ruthless enforcers. Take this little treat I had made." He hands you a **steam fist (RUTH+3)**. "If you make enough of an impression, they will let you get to him."

"And for the book?"

He smiles. "Very well. Do not muzzle the ox and so on." He rewards you with **£12** in coin. "And one more thing. There is a woman about in the city called Mrs Petty. She is another seditious rebel. Have nothing to do with her."

Leave Somerset House...   **139**

❧ 729 ❧

The gate party plant their explosive charges and run for cover. One is shot down as she dashes over the open ground, but a moment later, announced by an almighty crash and a cloud of dust, the gatehouse collapses.

The cheering mob stream towards the breach, waving their flags and thirsting for vengeance. Some will be killed now, particularly as the fight becomes a hand-to-hand brawl inside the Tower, but the Compact's tactics - and your training - have saved many more.

It is the work of several hours - although they feel like minutes - to fully take the Tower of London. Eventually, the revolutionaries have their victory.

Raise the flag!   **719**

❧ 730 ❧

☐ ☐ ☐

If any of the boxes above are empty, tick one and read on. If they are all already ticked, erase the ticks and turn to **770** immediately.

Your ambushes have not attracted the attention of the Constables yet. Nonetheless, you had better raise steam and get moving. The private guards of the wealthy are trouble enough.

Steam north towards Paddington...   **64**
Take the road further into London...   **746**
Head for Westminster Bridge...   **738**
Ride through Chelsea to Battersea Bridge...   **722**

❧ 731 ❧

The innocuous doorway of St Eanswythe Hall belies the wide, well-lit space inside. From the outside, nobody in the street would know that it is here. If you have the codeword *Chinstrap*, turn to **645** immediately.

Enter the hall...   **760**

❧ 732 ❧

The roads west are less busy than the smog-choked, traffic-filled streets of the metropolis, but the signs of the city's growth are everywhere. You pass new terraces for workers, new rows of villas for masters, new garages and stables and workshops, all the way out into the gardens and orchards of the outskirts. There, the road becomes a Haulage Guild highway, chained on either side and posted with markers and milestones, each bearing the Guild's crest. Note **passage 1022** and roll a dice to see what you encounter:

Score 1-2   Actors   **1318**
Score 3-4   A quiet road...   **1022**
Score 5-6   Refugees...   **830**

❧ 733 ❧

"I know you," says Lord Beaufort slowly, drawing his fine basket-hilted sabre and circling around to block the top of the stairs. "Or, shall I say, I recognise who you are. You are the Steam Highwayman, at last."

You indulge yourself in a mocking bow.

"I have been looking forward to dealing with you," says Lord Beaufort. "That machine you ride will be a nice addition to my collection."

Lord Beaufort   Weapon: **fine sabre (PAR 3)**
Parry: 10
Nimbleness: 7
Toughness: 5

Victory!   **1499**
Defeat!   **113**

❧ 734 ❧

The executioner's blade is so sharp, so broad and so weighty that the job of beheading the portly man before you will not be difficult... physically. But never before have you had the task of killing a helpless, chained man in broad daylight, in the full view of thousands.

The blade almost seems to pull itself down in a sweeping arc, and the task is complete. The curly-haired head rolls away from the block, until it is stopped by Comrade Feaver's booted foot. She grins at you with a wicked, thoughtful grin.

Turn to...   **650**

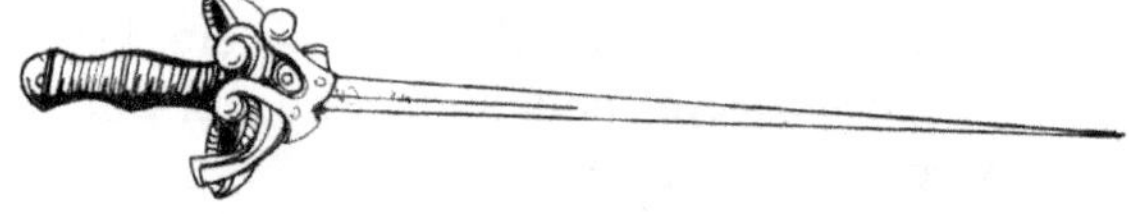

❧ 735 ❧

The sharp right turn sets you running east, parallel to the river, and you swerve past lorry-loads of cargo and countless warehouse cranes until Bermondsey Wall becomes Rotherhithe Street. Now you must see whether you have been quick enough to leave your pursuers behind: make a MOTORING roll of difficulty 14, adding 2 if you have an **improved burner** and 1 if you have a **strengthened boiler**.

Successful MOTORING roll!	**649**
Failed MOTORING roll!	**1010**

❧ 736 ❧

It doesn't take you long to reach the southern end of Blackfriars Bridge. Surely in the alleys of the City on the other side, you'll find somewhere to go to ground.

However, before you get there, you'll need to get through the crowds that churn from one bank to another over the massive Portland stone. If you are the **People's Champion**, the crowds will part for you in awe and admiration, and you should turn to **252** immediately. Otherwise, you must make a RUTHLESSNESS roll of difficulty 8 to terrify the townspeople into making way.

Successful RUTHLESSNESS roll!	**654**
Failed RUTHLESSNESS roll!	**1010**

❧ 737 ❧

With a good hiding place and a sharp glass, you are able to peer over the gravel pavements that criss-cross the Park, spying out potential victims. What will you select as your target?

A rich pedestrian...	**54**
A private steam carriage heading for Mayfair...	**1425**
A private steam carriage heading west.. .	**1391**
An Atmospheric Union vehicle...	**1421**

❧ 738 ❧

The traffic across Westminster Bridge moves freely, most of the time, but sentries of the Parliamentary Guard at either end close it if they detect - or imagine - the slightest threat to Parliament. If you are **Wanted by the Constables**, turn to **747** immediately.

The view from Westminster Bridge is inspiring - when the smog clears enough to see. All around are towers, chimneys and domes. Overhead, dirigibles and airships plough their paths against the wind. The river is thronged with steam tugs, barges and lighters. A short way downstream, the lavishly decorated *Gentilesse* swings at her moorings.

Slip into the river... (NIMBLENESS 6 or more)	**518**
Cross the bridge...	**602**

❧ 739 ❧

You barge your way upstairs and confront the man of the house. "Ennis! You miserable creature! How many women have you destroyed?"

He hesitates, utterly taken aback, and then narrows his eyes. "How dare you come in here making such accusations! Such slander is intolerable!"

You grab him by the scruff of the neck. "You can deny it now, but to the face of a weeping woman? To the parents of a dead daughter? Are you utterly inhuman, man?"

His defiance collapses. "No, I'm just as human as you. I have my impulses, as you do. Yours tend to violence, mine are amorous."

Throw him out of the window...	**415**
Force him to write a confession...	**433**

❧ 740 ❧

Princess Alexandrina looks much better than when you last saw her. She is caring for her adopted son with the desperate devotion of a woman who has found purpose.

"He may not be a prince by birth," she says, "But he will be a prince to me. He will have everything."

"How different his life would have been, if he had been left in the gutter," you muse.

"How short, poor darling," she replies. "How short it would have been."

Princess Alexandrina is willing to help you however she can. Each time you visit her, choose one of the options below and tick the appropriate box. Once all the boxes are ticked, she has used her influence as far as she is able.

Write you a **Letter of Introduction**...	☐ ☐ ☐
Remove a single **Wanted Status**...	☐ ☐
Help the Progressives in Parliament...	☐

(note passage **721** and turn to **850**, where you should correct the Parliamentary Swingometer **one point in the Progressives' favour**)

Give **£50** towards Reverend Highrun's project...(**Donors' List**)	☐

Leave the Palace...	**721**

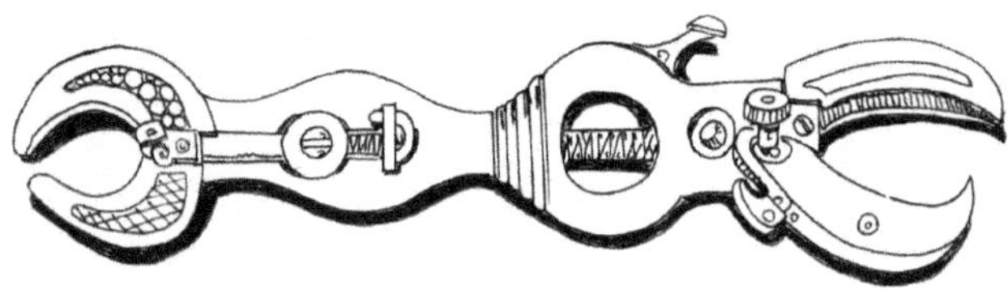

❧ 741 ❧

Even the vast glass and iron construction of the great Crystal Palace, the myriad temporary stalls crowding around it and the vast multitude of visitors cannot fill Hyde Park. The place is huge, and although powered vehicles are forbidden except under licence, the Constables are far too busy with the crowds to enforce the rule. Shadowy lanes and copses form excellent hiding places: when dusk falls, you are sure to have success ambushing rich pedestrians here.

Enter the Crystal Palace...(**6s**)	**780**
Prepare an ambush here...	**727**
Leave the Park...	**798**

❧ 742 ❧

You and Lady Diana travel to the workshop in Millwall she knows. She fancies a ride on the Ferguson, so she wraps up in a muffler and hat and clings behind you. The journey may be a little longer than it needs to be, but when you have the opportunity to fly through the city with a beautiful woman riding pillion, why shouldn't you treat her?

Millwall is a pitiful place. The little terraces of hovels speculated in between mechanical blacksmitheries and guttering merchants are each the workplace of an outworker, making what pennies they can towards the rent. Lady Diana points out one in particular, and you come gently to a halt outside.

The craftswoman you have sought out is a mistress of carving likenesses. When Diana explain what she wants, Mrs Bamber grins cannily. "You're not asking a wee thing, dearie. Mrs Roberts' face..."

"Can you do it?"

Mrs Bamber doesn't deign to answer. She shakes her grizzled hair and patters over to her range, where a battered pot of wax is warming beside the kettle. "What matters in this, it seems to me, is the price. I could spend a night on it, have it ready tomorrow. And that would resemble the naughty woman at a glance. Or I could work on it for longer."

"We want it tomorrow."	**781**
"Spend three days on it." (**£3 10s**)	**791**
"Money and time are no object." (**£10**)	**801**

❧ 743 ❧

You jump off the Ferguson, dash up the spiral stairs towards the telegraph station on St Saviour's tower and hand over the **Southwark package** (remove it from your **possessions**). If you have managed to deliver it quickly, passing **fewer than 20 passages** since passage **1057** to reach here, you will be rewarded with **£5**. If not, you are paid **10s** and sent back on your way.

Do not forget to continue your tally if you are still delivering the Guild's packages.

Ride away...	**631**

❧ 744 ❧

The Palace of Westminster stands on the riverbank in all its crumbled, confusing, gothic glory. Iron railings encircle most of the palace, but you are able to approach the Common Door where the red and gold-suited Parliamentary Guard in their traditional lobster-pot helmets stand on either side handling a queue of petitioners.

If you are a **Member of Parliament**, turn to **755** immediately. If you are **Wanted by the Constables**, turn to **773**. Otherwise, you can wait in the queue to lodge a petition of your own or return the way you came.

Join the queue... (**petition**)	**788**
Leave the palace...	**721**

❧ 745 ❧

A messenger brings news of someone trying to speak to you: it is Flat Billy, grinning hugely, and flanked by his toughest enforcers.

"So the day 'as come, 'as it? We'll be fightin' alongside yer, don't you worry." The Council are unsure, but you have first-hand knowledge of Flat Billy's ruthlessness and violence. He also commands allegiance among many in the East End, and will be a valuable ally.

"We've got some chaps up there in the airships," he says. "I shouldn't worry too much about them, really."

Almost on his word, you see one of the lumbering giants turning towards its fellow: the massive gas bags collide and give. A crack of thunder and a sudden downpour begins. The troops west of the Tower take it as their signal and open fire.

Take cover!	**789**

❧ 746 ❧

London is a vast, sprawling place: a city built of hundreds of connected villages. There are streets built in rows for factory hands, and streets built like stars around ancient wells. There are modern steel-framed towers and medieval hovels side by side. As you ride east, you find just as much variety among the inhabitants.

Into the City...	**215**
Towards Clerkenwell...	**144**
To Whitechapel...	**305**
In the direction of Bow...	**471**

❧ 747 ❧

The sentries of the Parliamentary Guard may look foolish in their antiquated gold and red, but beside their pikes they carry modern repeating carbines. You are halted in a queue while two flip through a printofit catalogue, checking faces. Make an INGENUITY roll of difficulty 12, adding 2 if you have a **top hat** to disguise yourself. Otherwise you will be recognised and arrested.

Successful INGENUITY roll!	**602**
Failed INGENUITY roll!	**13**

❧ 748 ❧

New Cross Road is broad and smooth - difficult for the Constables to block and allowing you to open the Ferguson's regulator fully and get up to your maximum speed. You see the dial reach thirty-seven, thirty-eight, then thirty-nine miles an hour! In no time you reach Broadway, with Deptford Bridge head of you and Church Street to your left.

Cross the bridge...	**804**
Steer left...	**832**
Head right down Mill Lane...	**865**

❧ 749 ❧

You are poured a hoppy pale ale called the Warrant Officer's Ale. It has an unusual combination of toasted foretaste, a resiny middle and a very bitter finish, with a lemony, almost rose-like fragrance. Note passage **785** before making your choice.

Speak to the landlord...	
(**publican's contract**)	**705**
Listen for rumours...	**610**
Return to the parlour...	**785**

❧ 750 ❧

Mayfair is a place of villas, tall houses named for country estates, long cobbled mewses lined with expensive engines, and locked gardens. It is where the wealthiest of the land have their London homes - hardly a place for a road-soiled troublemaker like you.

Investigate Derwent House...	**768**
Call on Sir Tort...	
(**Sir Reginald Tort's calling card**)	**777**
Visit Hendon Mansion... (*Craven*)	**715**
Ride down onto the Strand...	**139**
Steam to Bloomsbury...	**400**
Ride towards Marylebone...	**47**
Head east across the city...	**746**
Skirt St James Park into Westminster...	**721**

❧ 751 ❧

You return to find the revolutionaries in chaos: fighting has broken out within the High Council itself, and Comrades Feaver and Snell are dead. None of the mob have any sense of direction or order. This is undoubtedly the work of Mrs Petty, who has long since infiltrated the Compact with her agents. Who was it among the Council? Tate? Reel? Who can say.

All that you know is that this rabble will have no chance of resisting the professional soldiers coming their way. Your best hope is to get away... far, far away.

But as you mount your velosteam one more time and accelerate out through the gatehouse, you discover it is too late. The army have taken up positions across Tower Hill. A clattering salvo from an automatic revolving gun rips into you and your Ferguson, sending you crashing into a wall.

Turn to...	**648**

❧ 752 ❧

You haul your velosteam around to the left and steam up Bermondsey Wall, but soon realise that you are heading into the city, not away from it. Glancing over your shoulder, you see the Imperial velosteams of the Constables approaching and their riders recklessly knocking pedestrians and carts aside.

Then you come to the high warehouses of St Saviour's dock. The road turns a sharp left again, and around the bend you come face to face with a Constabulary roadblock, formed of an armoured riot-wagon and several commandeered carts.

Turn to...	**1010**

❧ 753 ❧

The streets swirl with fog off the river. Somewhere in the distance, a deep-throated ship's horn sounds. Night approaches, but the City is still thronged with life. Note passage number **721** and roll two dice to see what you encounter.

Score 2-3   Ruffians...   **761**
Score 4-5   A street sweeper...   **346**

❧ 754 ❧

A Constable stands at the post on the corner of Stratford Place. As you approach, he lowers a glass from his helmet through which to study you. If you are **Wanted by the Constables**, turn to **236** immediately. Otherwise, roll a dice to see if you encounter anything as you ride on towards Marylebone.

Score 1-2   Street sweepers...   **346**
Score 3-4   Nothing of interest...   **noted passage**
Score 5-6   A drunk nobleman...   **1358**

❧ 755 ❧

The Parliamentary Guards sweep the wide doors open, sharing a smile with the maverick figure of mystery who has become such a feature of the modern House. "Welcome back, yer 'onour," says one, with a grin.

Head to the Commons...   **795**
Head to your own chambers...   **778**

❧ 756 ❧

If you have **Lord Beaufort's note**, turn to **776** immediately.

"There is a great deal you can do for the authorities," says Mrs Petty. "You are not simply serving me. You are serving the crown! The Compact and their anarchistic friends must be stopped before they tip this nation into bloody chaos!"

Once you have completed each of these tasks, tick the box next to that option, as each mission should only be undertaken a single time.

⊕ Betray the Revolution... (*Catastrophe*)   **793**
⊕ Identify a traitor among the Constabulary...   **585**
Leave for now...   **165**

❧ 757 ❧

Remembering Princess Alexandrina's desire to thank you in person, you manage to make your way up a set of back stairs to the apartment reserved for her in the less-prestigious part of the Palace. There you are met by her sole lady-in-waiting, who recognises you immediately.

"Oh," she says, "The velosteamer. Her Royal Highness has been asking to see you. But... please don't ask about the events following that evening. You might distress her."

The Princess emerges and clasps your hands gratefully. "I have so much, so much, to be thankful for," she says. She is no longer pregnant. She takes some interest in you, but soon seems tired, and returns to her private rooms.

"The child..." you ask her companion.

The lady-in-waiting shakes her head. "A boy. A prince. But he didn't last the night."

Gain the codeword *Childless*.

Leave the Palace...   **721**

❧ 758 ❧

You wheedle and cajole your student until you find his mean streak - and then plan how to exploit it. Thinking over all the dirtiest tricks you have learnt in your adventures across the land, you have him practice slashing at hamstrings, throwing gravel in his opponent's eyes, faking injury and even biting.

"Is this sort of thing acceptable on the grass?" he asks nervously, to begin with.

"All in Quarenboot's *Code of Gentlemanly Recounter*," you reply.

He squints and nods. "I suppose I've rather wasted my reading time. I've never heard of Quarenboot."

Of course he hasn't. Not when you've just invented him. Roll a dice to see whether Jermyn Hyss survives his duel.

Score 1-2   Bad news...   **811**
Score 3-5   More bad news...   **802**
Score 6   A bloody end...   **836**

❧ 759 ❧

As night falls, it seems clear that you yourselves will be under siege now. The streets surrounding the Tower to the west are blocked, and airships hover overhead. The revolutionaries are skittish, falling into arguments. "That's one of ours overhead," you hear one insist. "Don't you regard the colours. Plenty of them airships wearing the King's livery are for us." You can't be so sure.

The armoury has been emptied. Hundreds of defenders are now armed with guns, and many more stationed in the buildings to the north and east are organised into companies. Trained comrades are overseeing the use of the Tower's artillery, and already a few shots have been sent into the army's advance posts. How possible is victory now?

If you are the **Friend of Flat Billy**, turn to **745** immediately. Otherwise, read on.

Thunder rolls in the distance, and a heavy rain begins to fall over the metropolis. As if waiting for the signal, the first bomb comes whistling down from the airships overhead.

Take cover...   **789**

❧ 760 ❧

Here you may continue to give your fencing lessons, earning honest coin from your skill, as well as storing possessions and taking care of yourself. Note passage **760** before making your next choice.

Tend your wounds...	**500**
Open a strongbox...	**560**
Repair your velosteam...	**1300**
Give fencing classes...	**771**
Leave the Hall...	**721**

❧ 761 ❧

☐

If the box above is empty, tick it and read on. If it is already ticked, turn to **796**.

A veil of fog covers Ebury Street. Each droplet reflects your lime-lantern in a dirty dazzle. You slow to a crawl to avoid hitting anything.

A woman's voice cries out in panic. A gang of ruffians have taken advantage of the darkness and are attempting to rob a woman in an open-topped carriage. Her driver lies on the cobbles, motionless.

| Intervene to help her... | **723** |
| Ride on by... | **721** |

❧ 762 ❧

In the queue you get to talking with an old lady who has come to London to ask for her dead husband's criminal record to be expunged. "Y'see, I can't work as a felon's widow. And because 'e died afore finishin' 'is sentence, it's all still to pay."

During the day the queue shuffles forward a few steps. Then, towards evening, the door is shut.

"What now?" you ask.

"Well, I 'aven't anywhere else to go to. I might as well wait 'ere," comes the old lady's reply.

| Come back another time... | **721** |
| Keep waiting... | **788** |

❧ 763 ❧

"Your party? I presume you are of the Wheatears faction." Mrs Roberts is sympathetic to many of the Progressives' ideas, and agrees to do what she can behind the scenes. Note passage **847** and turn to passage **850**, where you should change the Parliamentary Swingometer **one point in the Progressives' favour.**

❧ 764 ❧

Professor Prentiss is very pleased. "Fabulous work," he gushes. "That will really please the buyers. We are going to need more like this."

You return to the laboratory over the next few evenings, each time to play another piece of dramatic, classical repertoire. During that time you learn much about the workings of Professor Prentiss's machines. Add 1 to your ENGINEERING score.

"I always dreamed of creating calculated music," he tells you, one evening after you have performed a

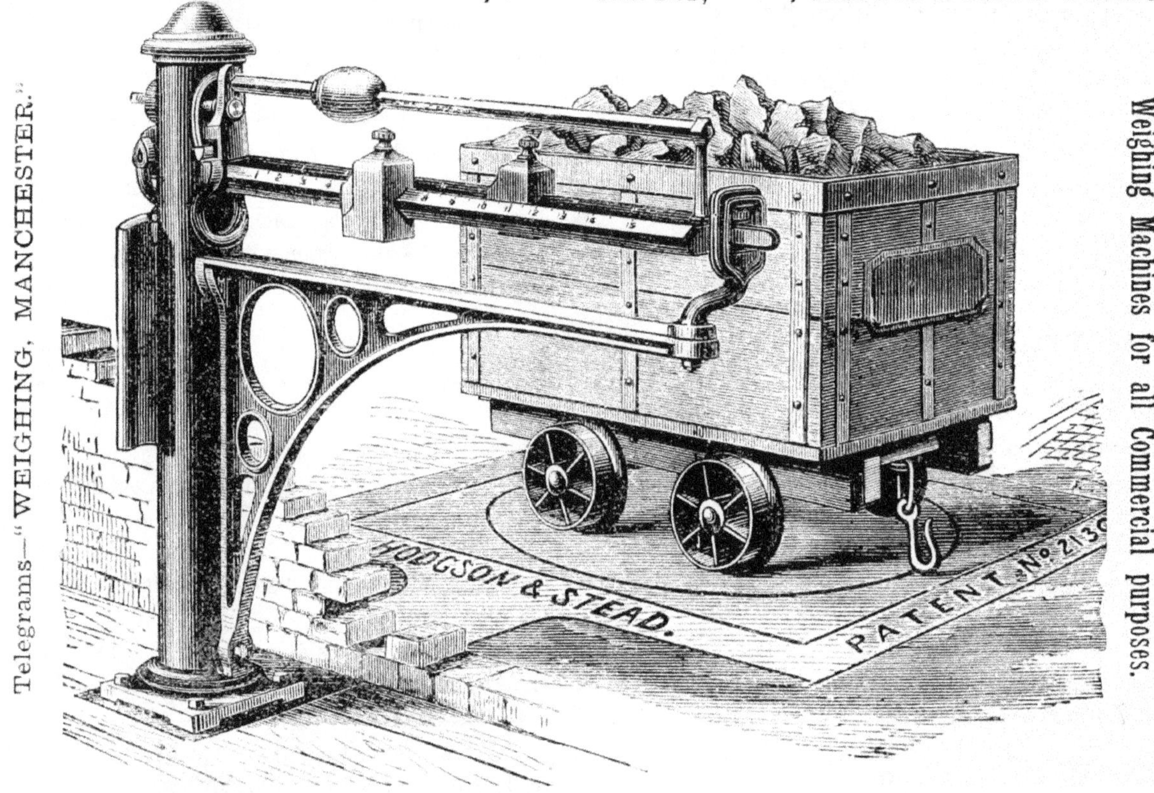

particularly exhausting sonata. "Then we could dial up exactly the sort of expression we desired, without the need for a musician to sweat over the pedals and keys as you do." A glance at his wistful face confirms that he is completely serious.

"Perhaps we could do such a thing together," you suggest. "With my musicianship and your inventions, we must be able to create a set of punchcards that develop patterns, melodies, resolve cadences and so on."

It turns out that you are not far wrong. Over several evenings you and Prentiss write a series of punchcards that are ideal for getting a computational engine to display - or mimic - human creativity. He gives you a set - add **punchcards (Selladore S)** to your possessions. Even better, you have gained the understanding of how to program a set of these yourself: gain the codeword *Collector*. "And of course I cannot forget that you were promised some coins," he says, handing you **£10 10s**. Remove **Sir Reginald Tort's calling card**, if you still possess it.

Bid the Professor farewell... **750**

750

❧ 765 ❧

The cousin of the East London crimelord, Flat Billy, has been sentenced to hang. He murdered two street girls and has been wanted by the Constables for months. Apparently, he is being held in Newgate Gaol, and Flat Billy is livid.

Turn to...   **noted passage**

❧ 766 ❧

☐

If the box above is empty, tick it and read on. If it is already ticked, turn to **1016** immediately.

As you sit down with your drink, you are approached by a woman dressed in a dark red suit. She narrows her eyes and sits down beside you.

"You're no friend of the Haulage Guild," she says. "I know they have a price on your head. You're probably planning to disrupt their plans already. How would you like to be paid to do that?"

"What would I have to do?" you ask, purely out of curiosity.

"Just a small... delivery to one of the Freight Yards."

"Would this delivery be of an explosive nature?"

She feigns shock. "Why would you think that?"

"Who do you represent?"

She smiles. "I represent money. Ten guineas now, ten guineas after planting... delivering the package at Paddington yard. You can collect it here."

If you fancy taking the job, you can take **ten guineas in banknotes** and a **rattling package** from the woman.

Return to the bar...   **176**

✤ 767 ✤

Looking out across the city, you see crowds heading through the streets from the north and the east, marching under revolutionary flags. All those posters you hung, it seems, had their effect: the city has risen up in support.

The military halt their advance upon the Tower as they, in turn, are attacked. Gangs of untrained but savage citizens fall on the soldiers from side-streets and shop-fronts. Comrade Feaver seizes a pikestaff and calls a charge. You and the other revolutionaries stream over the rubble and the chaos and hurl yourselves headlong into the fray. The soldiers' morale collapses. They toss down their guns, or turn and run for Blackfriars Bridge.

The remaining commanders are agreed that they must continue to advance. "We must head west," says Feaver. "We cannot stop until the entire city is taken. Food, water, even these must wait. We will sate ourselves on the blood of our oppressors."

The revolution cannot be stopped...   **813**

✤ 768 ✤

The towering walls of Derwent House are being cleaned by a team of decorators as you approach. Their rags and brushes are transforming it from another soot-blackened Mayfair mansion to a stately palace of Portland stone. If you have the codeword *Curly*, turn to **1237** immediately.

Seek entrance...

   (**Letter of Introduction** and *Cool*)   **1161**

Call on the Lady of the House...

   (**Lady Serene's Calling Card**)   **1180**

Ask for work at the tradesman's entrance...   **1306**

Return to Mayfair...   **750**

✤ 769 ✤

"Stop this immediately!" cries a voice from the archway. It is Princess Alexandrina, her hooded cloak thrown back and her royal features moulded into an expression of furious, imperious command. "Cut the prisoner down!"

The executioner stutters and looks to the Prison Governor. He bows deeply to the Princess. "Your royal highness! You... you want us to withold punishment from this deadly criminal? This enemy of the crown and the realm?"

She marches through the crowd of bowing and stunned Londoners towards the platform. "This individual is an agent working for me. The appearance of criminal behaviour has clearly convinced you and the Constables. Sign a release immediately. My servants stand by to receive the prisoner." She motions to the open archway, where a carriage awaits.

Confused but subservient, terrified of disobedience, the Governor does as he is told, and a very few minutes later you are hustled out of the prison and into the Princess' carriage. There are no servants, no guards, and no chains, only a driver, the Princess and yourself.

"Your highness," you begin. "You have saved my life. And put your own reputation at stake..."

She smiles. "When I heard you were to hang, my conscience would not let it go ahead. I make no pretence that you are a good person, but I know you are not entirely bad either. And I do think that I will have some use for you in time. But for now, you should leave the city."

She makes sure any **wounds** you have are treated by her staff (convert them into **scars**, rolling to see if they become **intimidating scars (RUTH+1)** in the normal way), hands you a purse of **£10** and informs you that your velosteam waits in the palace garage. Then she sets you on your way out of the city.

While you will no longer be **Wanted by the Constables**, your adventure will certainly be discussed. You should add **Famed Lawbreaker** to the **Titles** in your **Adventure Sheet**, as well as adding **Cheated the Gallows** to your **Great Deeds**.

Head west...   **1022**
Ride north...   **167**

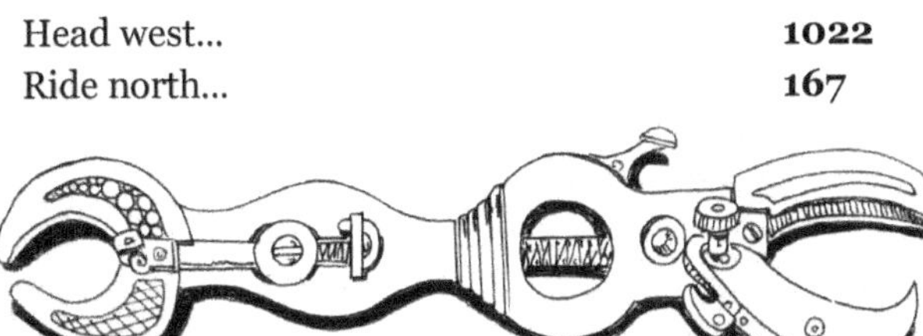

❧ 770 ❧

With pursuit close behind, you accelerate rashly through the streets, punching through fog-banks and trusting in your quick reactions to steer you around the suddenly-appearing wagons that block your path. Choose an escape route - and quickly!

Ride into the city...	**182**
Head north-west...	**421**
Ride out south-west...	**138**

❧ 771 ❧

Once word gets round that you are once more taking students, hopeful duellists from the commons and the gentry are quick to make contact. Whom will you take for a lesson? Cross out each choice you make: only when all have been crossed out, can you erase the markings and choose from them again.

⊕ A young man in love...	**637**
⊕ An officer...	**657**
⊕ An adventurous lady...	**679**
⊕ A foreigner...	**693**

❧ 772 ❧

You try your best but the Professor shakes his head. "This is not expressive enough. Buyers will not invest in our machine if they consider it too mechanical in its sound. Perhaps you should go and work on your musicianship. There are places in this city where you can learn such a thing - maybe in Shoreditch, where the Irish bands gather?"

Leave the workshop...	**725**

❧ 773 ❧

The sentries are quick to recognise you from the daily bulletins. They ring an alarm bell and begin to swing iron gates shut behind you. The queue of common folk begin to panic and get underfoot. You have a moment's grace to try and ram through the gates before you are arrested: make a MOTORING roll of difficulty 13, adding 3 if you possess a **ramming beak**.

Successful MOTORING roll!	**770**
Failed MOTORING roll!	**1500**

❧ 774 ❧

You spend some time watching the comings and goings at Kent House. Eventually, you spot Lady Kent leaving her mansion in her private carriage, and follow at a distance. She rides down towards the river, but before she can reach her unknown destination, you ride out into the road and block her way. Her carriageman throws on the brakes and you march up to confront her. Make a RUTHLESSNESS roll of difficulty 15.

Successful RUTHLESSNESS roll!	**563**
Failed RUTHLESSNESS roll!	**548**

❧ 775 ❧

☐

If the box above is empty, put a tick in it and turn to **757** immediately. If you are the **Friend of Princess Alexandrina**, turn to **740**. Otherwise, read on.

Your privileged access to the Princess manages to get you into the courtyard of St James' Palace itself. Princess Alexandrina receives you in her parlour - she jokes bitterly that it is her audience chamber. She has no official duties and little influence, so her life here is subdued and sad. She asks you to distract her from her sorrow with tales of your adventures.

"I long to see more of my country," she says. "Wales, particularly. I have friends there."

It is plain that a young widow and a bereaved mother like the Princess cannot flourish cooped up here in the Palace. Perhaps you will find some way to assuage her grief on your travels.

Leave the Palace...	**721**

❧ 776 ❧

Initially, Mrs Petty cannot believe your report. Then you show her the evidence (do not remove the **note** from your **possessions**).

"What could possess the man to come to terms with a creature like Flat Billy?" she wonders aloud. "There is more to this than meets the eye. I will get to the bottom of this, sooner or later."

She insists you carry the note back to Flat Billy, to close the loop and ensure that Lord Beaufort's suspicions are not raised. She also rewards you with a small **bag of perfect pearls** - easily portable property of an impersonal and relatively untraceable sort.

Head on your way...	**139**

❧ 777 ❧

A footman lets you into Sir Reginald's mansion and waits, eyeing you suspiciously, while the great man puts down his paper.

"Ah yes, the musician with such a gift!   I remember your playing - such emotion. I'm glad you called - there's something you can help me with."

Sir Reginald tells you about a business venture he has engaged upon with a inventive engineer, building automatic steam organs for churches and fairs. The first models are almost ready, but a keen musician is needed to record the music onto punchcards by playing into a special keyboard. He offers you ten guineas for helping him out. "I might even be able to make a few introductions for you here in the city," he finishes.

Accept the work...	**725**
Leave the mansion...	**750**

❧ 778 ❧

The chambers appointed for the Member for Portsea are luxurious indeed for one used to making do with dirty inns and hasty bivouacs. A fire smoulders in the grate before a maroon velvet chair. A desk, a speaking tube, a small but well appointed washroom and a fold-down bed complete the tidy little nest. If you have the codeword *Blameless*, turn to **826** immediately.

⊕ A challenge...	**1081**
⊕ A letter from a constituent...	**810**
⊕ A challenge...	**1095**
⊕ An invitation...	**1494**
⊕ A challenge...	**1108**
⊕ A letter from a constituent...	**824**
⊕ A challenge...	**827**
Nothing of interest...	**797**

❧ 779 ❧

☐ ☐ ☐

If any of the boxes above are empty, tick one and read on. If they are all ticked, erase the ticks and turn to **770** immediately.

Southall and the west road may seem distant from London, but Constables are constantly patrolling and you cannot risk staying here any longer. You must head on your way. Which direction will you take?

Further west...	*Smog and Ambuscade 218*
Towards Battersea Bridge...	**1132**
To Hyde Park...	**741**

❧ 780 ❧

The enormous palace of prefabricated iron and glass is the first and greatest wonder of the Great Exhibition. For all the years it has been running, the palace has been extended across the park, with new wings, mezzanines, ever-larger domes and lecture halls added year by year. The various realms represented within each show their most advanced technology and mechanisms. There are Confederate milling machines alongside Indian gemwork, railway engines from Russia, boilers from Belgium, something like a bazaar of wild extravagance laid out for Imperial Princes. You are steadily moved along with the crowd, shuddering at the jerky movements of the automatic walkways and rotating stairs. The crowd are rapt by what they see: thirty thousand people are here on this day alone and each is entranced as if by the magic of technology.

Pick a pocket...	**1047**
Stick up a poster... (**revolutionary poster**)	**1090**
Purchase an exhibitor's license...	**1363**
Leave the Great Exhibition...	**741**

❧ 781 ❧

Lady Diana pays a minimum for the work. "It wouldn't do to overpay her," she whispers to you. "She will only attract attention splashing the money around."

The next morning, you ride through the puddles of Millwall to collect **Mrs Roberts' face**.

Return to Derwent House...	**823**

❧ 782 ❧

"A reward? For burgling one of the most important ladies in the land? Why yes, I might be able to find a suitable reward for you."

He hands you over to his men.

Turn to...	**1500**

❧ 783 ❧

The plane trees of Creek Road tell you that Deptford Creek and the narrow swing-bridge are not far away. You can see that the bridge itself is in place, but a Haulage Guild engine is about to cross. To leave your pursuers behind, you will have to ride with the utmost skill at top speed. Make a MOTORING roll of difficulty 14, adding 2 if you have an **improved burner**.

Successful MOTORING roll!	**863**
Failed MOTORING roll!	**969**

❧ 784 ❧

Despite the ban on bare-knuckle boxing, it is reported that there will be a fight in the yard of the Unicorn between Wyndham Jack, the champion pugilist, and an unknown challenger. It could be worth your while paying a visit.

Turn to...   **noted passage**

❧ 785 ❧

The HMS Spartan is named for a famous ship of the line that defeated the flagship of the French Revolutionary fleet in 1822. It stands some distance from the river, but its light and airy parlour is popular with the nobility who occasionally wish to escape their mansions, as well as the workmen who repaint their windowsills and tend their gardens.

Buy a drink... (**2s**)   **749**
Return to Chelsea...   **794**

❧ 786 ❧

A stone whizzes past your face and catches the priest in the eye. He staggers back and falls from the platform. Spinning around, the hangman is caught by a hailstorm of pebbles fired from the accurate slingshots of the Waterside boys, clinging to the tiles of the prison roof. "Yaah, yer black corby," cries little Tobias. "Get yerself some other prey!"

They leap down onto the platform and whip a hood of sacking over the executioner's head, then whip out his feet from beneath him and tumble him into the crowd. The guards, posted around the yard, are still barging their way through the mass of Londoners, half of whom are cheering the drama and half baying in frustrated rage.

"Come on, Toby!" cries Jerry, as he cuts through the noose-rope. "Let's away!" You scramble up a knotted rope ladder anchored by several more of the boys who have remained on the pitched roof, and then follow your short and dirty saviours in a dash from rooftop to rooftop, leaping from gutter to hanging gutter, while the bells of the Constables begin to ring behind you.

Back at the boy's nest, they tell you that they heard of your capture and have been planning to spring you for several days. "Then Sallyboo heard you were gonna hang, and we set to! What a lark, eh?" They have already stolen your velosteam from the Constables and it waits in an alley down the rickety stairs, covered in sacks and rubbish.

You stay with the boys for several days until the manhunt has died down. In the meantime, the boys do what they can to get you back on your feet. If you have any **wounds**, you can replace up to three with **scars**, rolling for **intimidating scars (RUTH+1)** in the normal way. They have also stolen you a **blunderpistol (ACC 3)** and a **razor (PAR-1 NIM+3)** and, for old time's sake, a fresh **pork pie**. "It's no more than what you would do fer us, Toby," says Jerry. "You'se like a Waterside Boy yerself!"

Your escape will not have gone unnoticed. Besides being **Wanted by the Constables**, you should also add the title **Famed Lawbreaker** to your **Adventure Sheet** if you do not already possess it. You can also write **Cheated the Gallows** in your **Great Deeds**. And then, at last, it is time to depart from the hideout. Perhaps you should put this deadly metropolis behind you for a while...

Leave the hideout...   **252**

❧ 787 ❧

The walrus-moustached actor seems happy to see you - but then he is an actor. Remove the **actor's affidavit** and roll a dice to see how the tour has gone, and whether he has any profits to share with you.

Score 1-2   No profit, but gain a **lady's wig**
Score 3-4   **£5 profit**
Score 5-6   **£20 profit**

Ride on...   **noted passage**

❧ 788 ❧

You join the line of petitioners and peasants. Through the length of the day the lobster-potted guards do their best to bully the common folk into leaving or to extract what little money they have from them. Roll a dice to see what happens today:

Score 1-2   An old woman...   **762**
Score 3-4   A meat pie seller...   **819**
Score 5   An opportunity...   **829**
Score 6   Your patience is rewarded...   **809**

❧ 789 ❧

Only after hours of bombardment, when the ancient walls of the Tower are crumbling and breached, do the military begin to advance. Several armoured engines stand out in the open ground, firing their mounted artillery. Troops scuttle forward under the cover of the rain, the night, and the smoke of burning buildings. You take your place on the ruined ramparts with the other revolutionaries and return fire.

Yet despite your efforts, the troops cross the moat and the rubble and the hand-to-hand fighting begins once more. Consult the revolutionary checklist in passage **1133**: if the Revolutionary Posters have been hung, turn to **767** immediately. Otherwise, read on.

You jump up to swing at a trooper charging through the mist. He grunts as you toss a piece of Kent ragstone into his face, then stabs at you with his bayonet. You dodge and give him a backhanded blow, leaving him to tumble off the rampart. It will be a bloody and desperate fight.

Some hours later, as a westerly breeze moves the drifting smoke away, you and the commanders of the revolutionaries are able to take stock of your situation. You still hold the Tower and have managed to repel the military, despite all their advantages, but the loss of life to the people has been colossal. In places, desperate revolutionaries have rebuilt their ramparts with the bodies of their comrades. The riverside has repelled assault after assault of soldier in commandeered lighters and barges, which lie burnt to the waterline and reeking.

Yet the flag still flies.

You find the command post and gather with the remaining leaders. "Now we must press our advantage," says Comrade Feaver. "Advance on Westminster. Burn Parliament to the ground. Burn the palaces. Burn as much of the city as we have to."

The revolution cannot be stopped... **813**

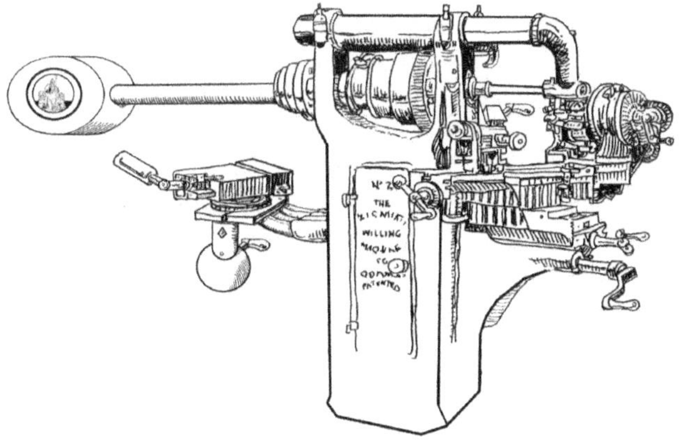

✧ 790 ✧

It will be a serious test of your skill to create a weapon that loads itself after firing - and continues to do so. Remove the **titanium alloy** and **carbine** from your **possessions** (or the box in passage **1308**) and make an ENGINEERING roll of difficulty 16.

Successful ENGINEERING roll!	**1503**
Failed ENGINEERING roll!	**1308**

✧ 791 ✧

The money allows Mrs Bamber to make a fantastically accurate mimicry of the face of the King's mistress. The wax is so lifelike that it feels absurd to see the face lying there on the plain pine tabletop when you return in a few days. Mrs Bamber laughs to see you recoil, before wrapping it up in paper. Add **Mrs Roberts' face (excellent)** to your **possessions**.

Return to Derwent House... **823**

✧ 792 ✧

The machine clatters as it balances the weight of drilled-out iron frames against differing volumes of helium and hydrogen, working steadily through the different permutations of equilibrium. A stippled printout contains the results: you now possess the **airship buoyancy calculations**.

Turn to... **noted passage**

✧ 793 ✧

You explain the Compact's preparations and their readiness to spark the revolution, detailing all that you have seen and heard over the past weeks. Mrs Petty listens intently, making no notes, but growing increasingly grim.

"You have done very well, bringing this to me," she says. "By the sounds of it, any later and we would be overrun by the godless anarchists already." She scribbles a note and goes to the door to hand it to her runner. "We will deal with this now. And as for you... Let me see how I can show my gratitude.

A few hours later, a carrier brings a parcel to the Leopard, where Mrs Petty instructed you to wait. Inside is a miniature **calculating engine (ING+3)**, powered by a simple hand-crank and a **Letter of Introduction**. Remove the codeword *Catastrophe*.

Leave the Leopard... **139**

❧ 794 ❧

Chelsea has kept some of its independence from the city: in the cleaner part of the metropolis, it is favoured by the western winds and a relative paucity of industry. Down by the river are the usual string of workshops and foundries, but along the main road are a bustle of shops catering for the gentry, including an angler's paradise: Hough's Piscatorial Purveyors.

Enter HMS Spartan...	**785**
Visit Hough's Piscatorial Purveyors...	**701**
Look for Kent Mansion...	
(Duchess's account number)	**774**
Look for Sussex House...	
(burglary ballad)	**854**
Steam east into the city...	**753**
Take the road west...	**732**
Head towards Battersea Bridge...	**722**

❧ 795 ❧

If you have the codeword *Converse*, turn to **848** immediately. Otherwise, read on.

The House of Commons is not an exciting place. The two major factions, the Establishment and the Progressives, are locked in a stalemate. No new legislation has been passed for years: business is dominated by a ceaseless argument about the need to reform the boundaries of parliamentary constituencies, and so to represent the people of the nation more fairly.

The Prime Minister, Lord Pfeffel, is a stubborn man, refusing to be swayed to either camp. He keeps his monarch's interests foremost, but he is an absolute stickler for the rules. If the Progressives can gather a majority, he will certainly side with them and see the Reform Bill passed.

While you are here, you are invited to sit with the Progressives, several rows back from Mr Wright and his allies. You may decide to participate in some of the debates, if you can stand the tedium. Once you have done so, cross the box beside the choice to indicate that it is complete and no longer an option.

⊞ Join the debate about wheat prices...	**869**
⊞ Listen to the presentation of the Manufacturing Bill...	**886**
⊞ Participate in the debate about Airship Regulation...	**901**
Head to your chambers...	**797**
Leave the Palace of Westminster...	**721**

❧ 796 ❧

A gang of ruffians are loitering in the street. With your dangerous appearance, they make no attempt to interrupt you, but you overhear some of them haggling over prices. If you want to offload any stolen goods, now might be a good opportunity.

Clothing	To buy	To sell
silk scarf	**£1**	**15s**
top hat	**£1**	**15s**
Jewellery	To buy	To sell
silver bracelet	**5s**	**3s**

Ride on...	**noted passage**

❧ 797 ❧

Here in your chambers you may rest and recuperate or store belongings and money in complete confidence before making your way to the debating chamber. Note passage **797** before making any choice.

Tend your **wounds**...	**500**
Head to the House of Commons...	**795**
Leave the Palace...	**721**

❧ 798 ❧

The streets radiating from Hyde Park can take you in any direction. Choose carefully, however, for Constables patrol streets here in the west, along with locations they wish to keep free from crime - public crime, anyway.

Head east from this region...	**746**
Down towards Chelsea...	**794**
Towards Paddington...	**64**
Into Mayfair...	**750**
Towards Westminster...	**721**

✎ 799 ✎

You are warmly welcomed by the acting troupe. "Haven't seen you since that disaster in Oakham."

"What a night that was!" remembers the leading lady. The actors crack open a few bottles of wine and you share a pleasant few hours reminiscing at the side of the road.

"If you fancy another shot at spear-carrying," the director offers, "I know they're looking for help at the Lyceum."

Turn to...   **noted passage**

✎ 800 ✎

Remembering the instructions of the woman in red, you look for a place to leave the package. Make an ENGINEERING roll of difficulty 12, adding 1 for each level of **explosives expert** you possess.

Successful ENGINEERING roll!   **831**
Failed ENGINEERING roll!   **818**

✎ 801 ✎

Mrs Bamber goggles greedily at the proffered coinage. "Well, milady," she says, a lot more respectfully, "I reckon a week will give me time to do as well as I could."

Outside, Lady Diana stops you as you remount the Ferguson. "Ten pounds is more than that woman will have ever seen in her life," she says. "She probably has no idea how to spend it."

"Nonsense," you reply. "She will pay her debt to the baker and her owed rent, buy some gin, have three days to herself, and then work her fingers to the bone producing the a likeness of Maria Roberts so good that even King Charles would woo it."

Lady Diana smiles. "We'll see."

A week later, you return to collect the work. Mrs Bamber, indeed reeking of gin, hands you a newspaper parcel. You return to Derwent House with **Mrs Roberts' face (excellent)**.

Return to Derwent House...   **823**

✎ 802 ✎

Mr Wright brings you the bad news. "Ah. It seems that the Member for Lincoln was rather ruthlessly cut down by young de Lankey. Took a nasty cut to the neck, severed an artery, and bled out on the grass. That's another loss for the Wheatears, of course. I don't

suppose you could have helped him more than you did: poor Jermyn never really had a chance. Always a bit of a timid, rabbity type."

Note passage **864** and turn to **850**, where you should correct the Parliamentary Swingometer **one point in the Establishment's favour**.

✎ 803 ✎

Desk-Captain Survit is in no better a mood than when you last saw her. She takes the **airship buoyancy calculations** from you with a grim nod and looks them over. "This looks better," she says. "So we can take the ship after all - if we half-fill with hydrogen. Hmm."

"You mentioned a payment?"

She unlocks a box. "I can give you cash... or something a little more unique." Choose either **£25** or a **steam fist (RUTH+3)** as your reward.

"Now there is something else you can calculate for me," says Survit. "The *T909* went down into the Irish Sea last month, with all its cargo. The only copy of its manifest was half-torn up by an idiot clerk and we need to deal with the insurance company. Find some way of working out what should have been on this paper."

"I'm sorry," you say, "But you want me to tell me what should be written on a missing piece of paper?"

"Exactly. I thought that was the sort of magic computational engines were meant to perform, hmm?"

Add the **torn manifest** to your **possessions**.

Leave the office...   **97**

✎ 804 ✎

The Ferguson lurches as you accelerate again, but the bridge ahead is blocked. A line of heavy trestles are laid across near the hut used by the Constables: they must have received a telegraph message telling them of your approach. It is too late to turn now. Your pursuers are close behind. Make a MOTORING roll of difficulty 13 to ram through the trestles, adding 2 if you have a **ramming beak** fitted to your velosteam!

Successful MOTORING roll!   **957**
Failed MOTORING roll!   **969**

✎ 805 ✎

"Are you blaming these people for their own poverty?" Your voice cuts across the small hall. Every head turns to look at you in shock, although some of them nod and seem to agree with your point.

The minister seems quite happy to be interrupted. "I know it can sound like that. I do believe, to a degree, that each of us is responsible for where we find ourselves - but this is the degree: Jesus healed those *who came to him*. He taught those *who would listen*. Where he found people too self-satisfied, too sure of their own rightness, or too closed to the possibility of God really caring, he could do nothing. He said so himself in the thirteenth chapter of Matthew's Gospel, and in the fourth Chapter of Luke." He sighs. "God's love is strong... but stronger yet is a man's heart locked against him. Perhaps you know of this yourself. Speak with me after the service, friend, if you wish."

The Reverend continues to explain what he calls the orphan spirit, teaching from Jesus' parables and example, and eventually the service finishes.

Speak to the Reverend...   **565**
Leave the chapel...   **471**

✎ 806 ✎

You prepare to accompany Mr Wright and his friends to Westminster, where you will be invested as a Member of Parliament and where, all being well, you will be able to represent the Progressive Party with a blade. Unsure as to whether you will be allowed in with your current wardrobe, Andrew Wright provides you with a rich **velvet cape (GAL+2)** to cover your travel-stained clothing, and you set off in time for the evening sitting.

The Old Palace of Westminster is a rambling, historic cacophony of buildings and courts, little towers and stairways, all leaning this way and that around the mighty Westminster Hall, more than seven hundred years old.

Just as archaic and nonsensical are the customs and rules that you must follow: there are gates that must be entered on the left by a Member of the lower House and on the right by Members of the Lords, paving stones that cannot be trodden on, tips and gratuities for every doorman and servant, in careful and traditional proportions, let alone the greetings and florid legalese spoken at every opportunity. Mr Wright guides you through it all, noting that, when the Great Reform is passed, all of this will pass away and be replaced by something much, much more rational.

Then at last you are brought to the doorway of the House of Commons for your investiture. The doors are opened and the Speaker announces you: "The new Member for Portsea."

Eyes turn, particularly from the Establishment benches on the left, and watch you enter in Wright's party. It is not easy for them to sum you up, but you can see several scratching their heads and talking together. Everyone knows that Portsea is a rotten borough in the gift of Wright and his friends - all they are wondering is who has been chosen to join the party.

If you have any **Wanted Statuses**, turn to **838** immediately. Otherwise, you take your seat amongst the Progressive politicians on the right and do your best to follow the business of the day.

Turn to...   **795**

✎ 807 ✎

A murmur and a chuckle runs through the house when the Speaker calls on the Member for Portsea to step forward. You are afforded the floor and have a chance to make your case. Make an INGENUITY roll of difficulty 16, adding 2 for each level of **legal knowledge** you possess but subtracting 2 if you possess the codeword *Converse*.

Successful INGENUITY roll!   **929**
Failed INGENUITY roll!   **913**

❧ 808 ❧

The wharf here dries out with the tide: barges of one sort or another are settled on the silt while men and boys haul their cargoes ashore over gangplanks. On the bank opposite stand the massive holding tanks of the South Metropolitan Gas Works and beside that, the conical mountains of the Coal Board Deptford Depot.

Board your boat... (**moored at Deptford**)   **948**
Leave the wharf...   **816**

❧ 809 ❧

Eventually you are at the front of the queue. You move up to the clerk and present your **petition**.

"What is this?" he asks with a sneer.

You explain about the situation that has led the petitioners to write to Parliament. He scratches some notes onto the precious paper and puts it in a drawer. "It will be passed on," he says. Gain the codeword *Causeway*.

Leave the Houses of Parliament...   **721**

❧ 810 ❧

The letter contains a desperate plea by one of your (unfranchised) constituents, who begs for your support for a new bill to prevent the further enclosure of common land. He writes simply, presuming that you are another career politician with little interest in his daily difficulties, yet choosing to believe that his missive may sway the great affairs of state a little.

Go to your chambers...   **797**

❧ 811 ❧

Jermyn Hyss goes out to fight on the lawns of Parliament the very next Friday morning. It is a private affair, so you cannot watch, but you later hear from your contacts that he was badly wounded by the Honourable Francis de Lankey - something about cuts to both forearms, possibly disabling him for life. Nonetheless, he has survived for now.

Before long, Mr Wright sends another client your way.

Meet your next client...   **864**

❧ 812 ❧

It takes some time to gather your arguments, speaking with various members of the Anti-Corn Law League, the Progressive party and even a few Establishment rebels. You sit up late in your chambers, penning a speech by gaslight, determined to make your mark on the law of the land. Make an INGENUITY roll of difficulty 15, adding 2 for each level of **legal knowledge** you possess and adding 2 if you possess the codeword *Converse*.

Successful INGENUITY roll!   **943**
Failed INGENUITY roll!   **913**

❧ 813 ❧

The march across the city is both grim and strangely celebratory. For many, the prospect of a complete change to the order they have grown up in is exciting in itself. "The novelty will wear off," says Commissioner Reel. "This is only the beginning of the Revolution. We must rebuild from the ground up."

Nonetheless, songs leap into the air - old songs of country love, new songs of defiant fervour - and dancing starts. Across the city you march, past the cathedral of St Paul, on towards Westminster.

If you have the codeword *Callused*, turn to **843** immediately. If not, but you are a **Friend of Princess Alexandrina**, turn to **835**. Otherwise, read on.

The mob press forward, overcoming sporadic resistance from knots of remaining Constables, but in the face of an entire uprisen population, there is nothing that can be done.

Advance on Westminster...   **866**

❧ 814 ❧

The Broadway at Deptford Bridge is a triangle of land where the Kent road meets Church Lane. which runs parallel to the creek. It is a place where engine-drivers pause to rewater, to steady their loads and to do repairs. The nearby Gill Brothers' Engineering Works provides smiths and furnaces, but mostly profits by fashioning the wrought ironwork needed by the countless industries of the city, as well as massive frames for new buildings. This is a prosperous, but dirty, corner of the metropolis, quite distinct from Deptford to the north.

Green-coated Constables stand guard on the wide road-bridge over the creek. The only bridge north of here is the small swing-bridge at the creek mouth, which can only take traffic one way at a time and is often closed to traffic for hours at a time, while this bridge carries the main road to Chatham, Canterbury and Dover.

Mingle with the engine-drivers...	**834**
Ride north to Deptford...	**816**
Head up onto Blackheath...	**852**
Take Old Kent Road into London...	**609**

৯ 815 ৵

The woman looks surprised. "That is all? You came here only to ask that?" She rings a bell and speaks to a servant. You are dismissed and, after a short wait in the antecabin, receive a purse of **£5**.

Return to your boat...	**847**

৯ 816 ৵

You are in Deptford. A gaunt brick pub stands with its back to the filthy creek. The faded sign swings creakily, displaying two unicorns and an indistinct shield. Several lighters are drawn up at the wharf, where listless docksmen dally over their tasks. Most of the local streets are formed of low and dirty cottages, but Creek Street has been recently rebuilt and slender plane trees stand in rows, their bark still smooth and untouched by the pollution and smog. Behind a spike-topped wall stand the naval barracks.

Visit the Unicorns...	**872**
Approach the wharf...	**808**
Steam south towards Deptford Bridge...	**870**
Cross the swing-bridge to Greenwich...	**863**
Take the road towards Bermondsey...	**608**
Make your way to Rotherhithe...	**649**

৯ 817 ৵

For the very first time, you see the Desk-Captain smile. The **repaired manifest** is exactly what she has been hoping for. "I didn't really know if it was possible," she said. "But you are more than you seem." She takes out **twenty guineas in banknotes** and hands them over, together with a pair of **engineer's gauntlets (ENG+2)**. "Our top men developed these," she says. "Integral pockets in the wrist-guards, supple calf's leather in the palms and oxhide on the finger-tips to protect against burns. I use them myself."

Working with the calculation engine has taught you a great deal: increase your INGENUITY by **1**.

Leave the office...	**97**

৯ 818 ৵

You choose the spot that will cause the most destruction and wedge your package between some barrels: gain the codeword *Chaff*. However, your lack of care means that the bomb erupts in flame and smoke before you have left the yard. Debris whirrs about you: roll a dice to see whether you are hurt!

Score 1-2	Receive a **wound** from flying metalwork...
Score 3-4	Receive a **burn (NIM-1)**...
Score 5	Receive a **black eye (ACC-2 GAL-1)**...
Score 6	Escape without injury...

If you now have five **wounds**, turn to **999** immediately. Otherwise, you must mount your velosteam and flee!

Ride away!	**770**

৯ 819 ৵

While you are waiting in line, a pie seller comes along with his tray slung around his neck. "Fine meat pies," he cries. "Premium pig filling! No gaps in the jelly! Just flavour, flavour, flavour!"

"How much?"

"Two shillings. And I'm cutting my own throat to give 'em to you at that price."

	To buy	To sell
pork pie	**2s**	-

Even with the distraction of pies, the afternoon passes slowly. The line crawls forward but, long before dark falls, the gates are shut. "What now?" you ask the nearest lobster.

"Oh, the gents stop work at three," he replies. "Nothing happens now until tomorrow."

Wait another day...	**788**
Leave the queue...	**721**

✎ 820 ✐

The box contains a finely crafted **steam fist (RUTH+3)**, designed to fit over your hand and massively increase your strength.

Turn to...   **noted passage**

✎ 821 ✐

The Reverend is very pleased. "A good start. I hope that my list has been helpful? I will set about hiring an architect and a master builder immediately, now that we can afford their salaries."

He invites you to his rectory for a meal. It is meagre fare by anyone's standards, but at home, the Reverend is cheery company, his wife charming and hospitable. She is amazed to hear of your adventures on the open road, and the couple are far from judgmental. You find yourself opening up and telling the honest truth. You are now the **Friend of Reverend Highrun**.

With Mrs Highrun's attention, you may convert any number of **wounds** to **scars**, rolling for **intimidating scars (RUTH+1)** as normal.

Leave the Highruns...   471

✎ 822 ✐

Since you are in the Telegraph Guild's favour - for now - you are allowed into the workshops, inside the compound itself. Several artificers are clustered around a complex pneumomechanical device and a blacksmith and apprentice hammer out brackets.

You can have your velosteam repaired and customised here, and even hire the use of the Guild's calculating engine. Note this passage (**822**) before making a decision.

Customisations	To buy
muffled exhaust	£5
enlarged fuel tank	£7 2s
double headlamp	£10 10s
gas pressuriser	£15

	Per Damage Point
Repairs	£3 5s

Ask to use the calculating engine... (**£6 4s**)   255
Leave the workshops...   878

✎ 823 ✐

The next part of Diana's plan is straightforward: you arrange for an unmarked steam carriage to collect you in the dead of night, and, dressed as a large man, entirely cloaked and masked, and as a lady whose face occasionally appears through her veil, you set out for the Tower.

Parked at the gates, the carriage's running boy is sent with a carefully-written note to the gatekeeper. If you have the **King's code**, turn to **844** immediately. Otherwise, read on.

The boy returns quickly. "The gatekeeper says 'e 'ain't 'ad no message over the telegraph. 'e begs your nobility's parden, but asks whether you would be so kind as to approach on foot so's 'e can see yer."

Now comes the first trial of your costume and your demeanour. Make a GALLANTRY roll of difficulty 16, adding 1 for each these that you possess: a **cloak** of any kind, a **mask**, a **wide-brimmed hat** and 2 if you have **St Petersburg cologne**.

Successful GALLANTRY roll!   **861**
Failed GALLANTRY roll!   **874**

✎ 824 ✐

"To the new Member for Portsea," reads the letter. "As an elector in your constituency, I feel obliged to warn you against the dangerous influence of Mr Wright and his party within the Houses of Parliament. These so-called 'Progressives' are nothing but anarchists and godless revolutionaries, bent upon such a complete destruction of our land's divinely-inspired system of government that they cannot see the plain truth in front of them. Are you aware that, had they their way, your own constituency will be swept away? The Compact for Workers' Equality could not do more damage to the history and stability of this Eden, this England!"

How you decide to act, having received such a warning, is entirely up to you.

Head to your chambers...   797

✎ 825 ✐

The Worshipful Guild of Chimney Sweepers and Flue Clearers, to give them their full name, revel in the soot-smearings of their trade. Here you can apply to join the guild, which is a simple matter of purchasing a **chimney-sweep's button** for **£2**.

Leave the Guild...   **107**

❧ 826 ❧

You open one letter and find that it is from Letitia Forbury. She is writing to thank you for your part - if you had a part - in having her father's candidate Mr Elfinstone elected for the Whitchurch Constituency. She is so grateful, in fact, that she includes a **Letter of Introduction**, should you need one.

Remove the codeword *Blameless*.

Return to your chambers...   **797**

❧ 827 ❧

Yet another of the opposing politicians has taken a dislike to your face. The letter tells you, in no uncertain terms, that he considers your presence in the Chamber an insult to the nation and to humanity. Nothing will give him greater pleasure than to prove his point on the grass.

So the very next morning, you step out to meet him.

Member of Parliament	Weapon: **rapier (PAR 4)**
Parry:	11
Nimbleness:	7
Toughness:	4

Victory!	**1124**
Defeat!	**1134**

❧ 828 ❧

The morning of your execution dawns, but the pervasive smog of the city diffuses and consumes the sun's light. When you are led into Newgate yard, a crowd of sight-seers drawn from all classes are standing at the foot of the gallows, and more cram in through the open gate, climbing onto ledges and sills despite the Constables' protests.

The executioner, Mr Fazerlacky, is a fussy, small man who chatters at you as he tweaks your position on the trap and tries to smarten your clothes, besmirched by a night in the cells.

The noose is looped about your neck. "Do you wish to say anything?" asks the vicar of St Saviour's church, whose voice you recognise from the midnight warning. This is your very last chance to escape - or the very end of your adventure - and for once, you must depend on somebody else to rescue you. If you are the **Friend of the Waterside Boys**, turn to **786** immediately. If not, but you are the **Friend of Princess Alexandrina**, turn to **769**. Otherwise, read on.

Your final words, however long you have been preparing them, are lost in the babble and chatter of the crowd. The trapdoor opens without warning and you drop an inch or so into the loop of deadly rope. It will be some time before everything goes black.

Turn to the **epilogue**...

❧ 829 ❧

Through the day the queue moves forward and eventually you are standing at the front. The bells have rung five o'clock, though, and the lobsters, as the guards are nicknamed, have been neither regular nor fair in their timings. A large man runs up to the queue with a list in his hands. He mops his brow and turns to you.

"I say, I must deliver this petition today. I beg you, let me take your place in the line - I'll give you a guinea!"

"Wait your turn like everyone else."	**842**
"I'll take your coin."	**856**

❧ 830 ❧

A pitiful straggle of families dragging carts comes up the roadway. They hastily move aside at the steam-horn of a rushing Guild engine, and trudge on in its cloudy wake. A boy hangs back to look at your engine.

"Where are you all going?" you ask.

"London," he replies, with a west country lilt. "They burned down our village."

"Who did?"

"Tellygraphers. Said we was hidin' someone. But we wasn't."

A man calls to the boy and he dashes off.

You catch up with the main party and, when a woman sees the interest in your eyes, you are accosted for help. "You wouldn't have some medicine for aunty here?" A gaunt woman lies on a mattress atop the few remaining possessions on the back of the cart. If you have a bottle of **soothing lotion** to give them, receive the codeword *Compassionate*.

Ride on...   **noted passage**

✎ 831 ✎

You spot a good place to 'deliver' the package. You jam it under the boiler of an engine raising steam and make your exit. You are some distance away when you hear the explosion. Gain the codeword *Chaff*.

Ride away...   **64**

✎ 832 ✎

You tear down Church Lane, jolting over the pitted surface and sending a sheet of water flying over a cloaked woman as you split a puddle. Then you twist through a couple of streets of terraces, emerge by the gasworks, head left and come out onto Creek Road. The bells of the Imperial velosteams are not far behind.

Turn left...   **877**
Turn right...   **783**

✎ 833 ✎

You roar across Blackheath in a cloud of dust. A glance behind clearly shows your pursuers, as well as a Constabulary airship high above you, no doubt transmitting instructions by telegraph. On you ride, down Blackheath Hill, braking hard and bumping over the steam-tram lines. Then you come to the bridge over Deptford Creek, but of course the Constables there are expecting you. If you have **improved brakes**, turn to **845**. They fan out across the road and lower their carbines.

Turn to...   **1010**

✎ 834 ✎

This is not an official Haulage Guild depot, but several Guildmembers are resting while their boys refill the watertanks. There are also independent drivers here, keeping themselves to themselves for the time being. If your RUTHLESSNESS score is 9 or higher, or if you are **Wanted by the Haulage Guild**, turn to **857** immediately. Otherwise, note passage **814** and roll a dice to see what you hear:

Score 1-2   The Dover Road...   **309**
Score 3-4   Up to Essex...   **321**
Score 5-6   Bishop's Wood...   **333**

✎ 835 ✎

In an attempt to prevent further bloodshed, Princess Alexandrina has ordered the army to stand down. She has always been sympathetic to the suffering of her people: if she handles this well, there might be a place for her in the new order after all. As you march west, you come across straggling groups of soldiers, who are welcomed into the column.

On to Westminster!   **866**

✎ 836 ✎

The following week, a runner brings you a message from Jermyn Hyss: using all of your deadly trickery, he managed to defeat his opponent. In fact, he also cut his throat after blinding him with a thrown sod of turf, and Hyss is now accounted amongst the most ruthless fighters in Parliament. Gain the codeword *Clinched*, note passage **864** and turn to **850**, where you should correct the Parliamentary Swingometer **one point in the Progressives' Favour**.

✎ 837 ✎

Shooter's Hill is infamous for roadside danger - hence the name. You find a place to wait as dusk falls. Note passage number **888** and if you have the codeword *Chosen*, turn to **1444** immediately. If not, but you have a **telescope** or **binoculars**, turn to **1481** immediately. Otherwise, roll a dice to see what approaches:

Score 1-2   The Haulage Guild...   **1444**
Score 3   The Telegraph Guild...   **1400**
Score 4-6   A private steam carriage...   **1349**

✎ 838 ✎

"Stop right there!" calls a voice from the back benches of the left. "I know this character! This a dangerous felon, a road-thief and a robber! I demand the arrest of this so-called Member immediately!"

You look up at the red-faced politician pointing his finger down at you. Do you recall ever robbing this man? There have been so many, after all.

Mr Wright stands, calmly. "This is a very serious accusation and a very insulting one for my friend, the Member for Portsea. After all, I am sure that the Member for Goodwood is just as aware as we all are, honourable Members of the House, of the immunity from arrest afforded to all representatives here? God forbid we should become like France, when any servant of the nation can expect to be caught up and disappeared simply because they have offended the current law-makers. Unless, of course, the Member for Goodwood is making a personal challenge upon the honour of my friend here..."

You choose that moment to open your velvet cape and reveal your weaponry, nodding warmly to the red-faced man, who stutters a retraction.

"No... I certainly didn't mean a personal challenge... Not me. No. I am deeply sorry - I believe I may have mistaken you for someone else."

Now there can be no doubt among the House exactly why Mr Wright has brought you along. Remove any **Wanted Status** you currently possess. You have been granted a peculiar amnesty - make the most of this opportunity!

Turn to...   **795**

᧞ 839 ᧞

The engines of the Leviathan must be tuned closely, both to balance the power of the pistons against one another and to maximise the power output.

Each input can be entered onto a brass disc on the engine, positioned to represent a measurement of a thousandth of an inch within the engine. Then the machine sets off, steam whistling through a maze-like weave of fine brass tubing, flicking gates open and shut, setting cogs and cams and screws whirring. The program runs for over an hour, at the end of which the machine punches out a series of calculations on a paper reel. Add the **tuning calculations** to your **possessions**.

Turn to...   **noted passage**

᧞ 840 ᧞

"Yerwhat?" asks Jerry. "Like mechanical wings or summat? Who'd be so stupid? Men ain't birds!"

When you insist that such things exist, he shrugs. "Well, if they'se any in London, we'll find 'em for you."

That evening the boys welcome you back to the loft and toss back a piece of dirty canvas to display their findings. "Got em off a Union airship up Parliament 'Ill. Tez almost went aloft, dincha, Tez? But we got 'im out."

"What do I owe you?"

"New boots all round, Toby. That's abaht right."

A pair of solid new boots for each of the boys will cost you about **£10**. If you want to spend the money, add the **winged harness** to your **possessions**.

Leave the boys...   **252**

᧞ 841 ᧞

Your quick manouevrings bring you up towards Smithfield, where men in overalls are sluicing the streets of bullocks' blood. The Constables have lookouts up on the corners of busy junctions, as well as several observation balloons tethered above their stations, so you should get yourself into the alleyways where it is harder for them to track you. Of course, one wrong turn and it will be all up with the chase.

Continue northwards...   **868**
Ride to the railway excavations...   **887**
Head for the alleys of St Sepulchre's...   **894**

᧞ 842 ᧞

The fat man doesn't give up. He turns to the man behind you, who readily accepts his offer.

"That isn't right!" cries out the man behind. "I've been here for four days!" He tries to take the interloper by the collar but gets rewarded with a heavy shove. The outcome is inevitable - the line quickly dissolves into a brawl, prompting the lobsters to throw you all out of the Palace precincts with lowered pikes. Your time in the queue has been an utter waste.

Turn to...   **721**

᧞ 843 ᧞

A shout from the fore of the march grabs your attention.

"An elephant! A bleedin' elephant!"

It is indeed an elephant. In the chaos, Jumbo the elephant has escaped from the zoo in Queen Maria Gardens and found his way down towards you. He has left a trail of devastation and when you get to him, he is tossing revolutionaries to and fro while they try to control him with ropes.

"Leave him," you cry imperiously, stepping up to the mighty beast.

Jumbo raises his foot - and then pauses. He remembers you and the kindness you showed him. He bows down at the command you taught him and allows you to climb aboard. You rejoin the march atop the biggest bull elephant in the land, who has also joined the revolution, it seems.

On to Westminster!   **866**

৯ 844 ৯

With the knowledge of the King's personal cipher in your hands, you were able to send ahead a message, informing the Tower of the King's desire to visit the very same evening, in the company of a lady, to show her some of the jewels. The gate swings open at your approach, and the gatekeepers are all keeping their faces respectfully averted. You and Lady Diana enter the fortress on foot.

Turn to...   **908**

৯ 845 ৯

The customisations fitted to your velosteam are vital now! A sharp, controlled pull on the brake lever allows you to slew around, sending gravel and dirt into the faces of the waiting Constables. Confused, they let off a wild volley of shots, but you have already opened the regulator and accelerated away. You head up Greenwich Road, dodge left by the tower of St Alfege's, through an open gate and across the churchyard, eventually tucking your machine into the shadows beneath the wharves near the ferry. You climb off and cover up your distinctive machine with a loose tarpaulin, before climbing down to the riverside wait out the pursuit. A steady rain begins, no doubt dampening the Constables' interest, and as dusk falls you relight your velosteam's burner, confident that you have got away.

Ride into Greenwich...   **863**

৯ 846 ৯

You tear down through Greenwich Park, past the Telegraph Guild's depot at the Observatory and make for the swing-bridge over the creek. As you reach it, you can see that a heavy barge is being manoeuvred up the river: the swing bridge hangs to one side. If you want to cross the creek, you will have to make a jump.

There is an old loading ramp at one side that might just give you enough height, if you can get up enough speed. You'll then be able to make your way on to Rotherhithe and put a real distance between you and the pursuers. Make a MOTORING roll of difficulty 16, adding 4 if you have an **improved burner**.

Successful MOTORING roll!   **649**
Failed MOTORING roll!   **969**

৯ 847 ৯

After you have been dismissed, you are left alone aboard the *Gentilesse* for a few minutes. It is not long enough to look around in detail, but you do have a chance to investigate the locks on the cabins. If you have some **plaster of paris**, you may replace it with an **impression of the *Gentilesse* key** before you leave.

Return to your boat...   **922**

৯ 848 ৯
☐

If the box above is empty, tick it and turn to **1459** immediately. Otherwise, read on.

Now that the Progressives have the majority in the House, Lord Pfeffel has had to step aside. Mr Wright has been asked to form a government, and all is in flux and flurry. No debates will happen or legislature will be discussed until some form of stability is found.

Of Wright himself, you are unable to find a trace. He no longer has time for you and has ensconced himself among advisors and allies, organising a cabinet and a programme of reform. There is little for you to do in the House now.

Head to your chambers...   **797**
Leave the Palace of Westminster...   **721**

❧ 849 ❧

You have bitten off more than you can chew this time, and you will pay dearly for it. The surface of the Portland stone parapet is slippy with the mist and fog and you cannot stay upright. With a sickening lurch, the Ferguson slides off the bridge-edge and you tumble into the river.

The fall injures you beyond survival. Even if you had clung onto life, your beloved machine is also destroyed by the descent into the Thames. Your adventure is over.

Turn to the **epilogue**...

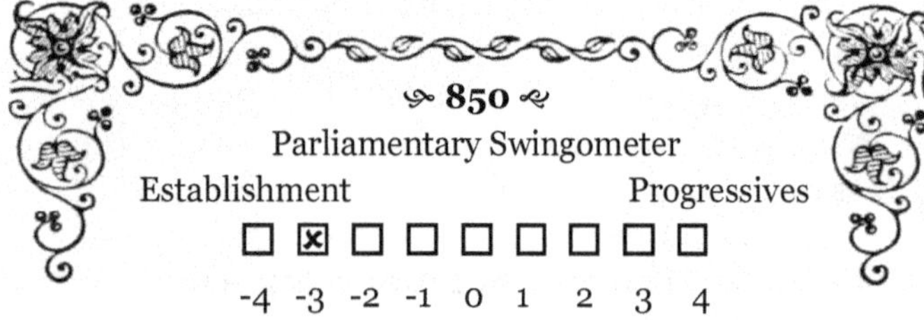

❧ 850 ❧

Parliamentary Swingometer

Establishment   Progressives

☐ ☒ ☐ ☐ ☐ ☐ ☐ ☐

-4   -3   -2   -1   0   1   2   3   4

On your first visit to this passage, mark the Parliamentary swingometer at -3, indicating a majority of 3 in the Establishment's favour. You may need to immediately correct this score, or do so on further visits: if you seek to assist the Progressives in their desire to pass a Reform Bill through Parliament, you must find ways to increase their majority in the House.

If the Swingometer is at 1 or greater, the Progressive party will hold a majority over the Establishment and you should gain the codeword *Converse*. If it falls below 1, you must remove the codeword *Converse*.

Turn to...   **noted passage**

❧ 851 ❧

The barman draws a short pint of his Dolphin Tayl Porter into a freshly-wiped pewter pot and slides it over the bar towards you. The first sip is sweet and rich; it is an old-fashioned flavour brewed to keep the fog out of your bones, almost savoury, with hints of liquorice, rum, raisin and chocolate. If you have a **black eye**, turn to **862** immediately. Otherwise, note passage **872** and roll a dice to see what you hear among the drinkers.

Score 1-2	The King's Woman...	**984**
Score 3-4	Bright stones...	**1099**
Score 5-6	False papers...	**1159**

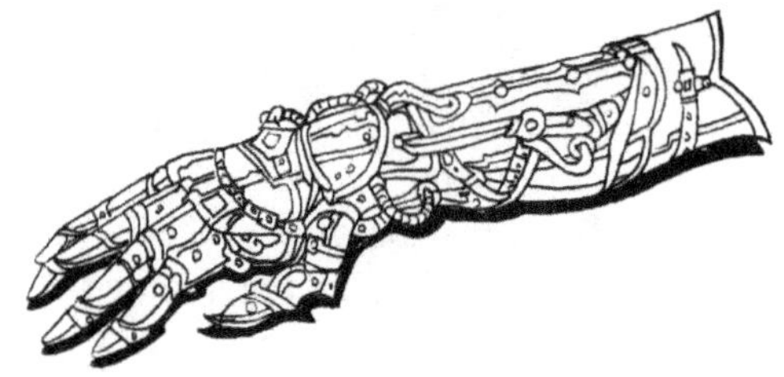

❧ 852 ❧

The road climbs steadily up towards Blackheath. You pass a run-down stables and a dilapidated garment factory. Note passage **891** and roll a dice to see what you encounter:

Score 1-2	Actors on their wagon...	**1434**
Score 3-4	Fruit sellers...	**859**
Score 5-6	Something sparkly...	**896**

❧ 853 ❧

A Major-of-Signals looks you up and down. "I need some urgent deliveries made across the city," he says. "Perhaps you and your machine are what we need."

"We've need of help unloading these barrels of tar," calls one haulier. "Hurry on over here."

Take the delivery job...	**1057**
Lend a hand with the unloading...	**1050**
Return to the compound...	**878**
Leave the compound...	**891**

❧ 854 ❧

You set out to find Sussex House. It is a fine building of the previous century set behind a long garden on a plot running down to the river. Under the guise of a knife-sharpener, you gain access to the rear door, where you charm one of the cooks to tell you the whole story.

"Oh yes, absolutely true. But not like in that there broadsheet. But it was a lady. We all know who it was. For she came visiting not three weeks before. He hadn't taken delivery of the ring, then, the Duke, but she must have known about it somehow. Lady Derwent, that's who it was."

"You're sure?"

The cook pauses, then pulls something out from her apron. It is a rose, its petals crisped by flame and tinged with soot. "She has a liking for these here burnt flowers... There's a great big garden of them at Derwent House in Mayfair."

Gain the codeword *Cool*.

Leave the house...	**794**

❧ 855 ❧

You pause on Shooter's Hill, where the road to Canterbury and Dover rises high over the city. Evening fog lies across the metropolis, glowing where the furnaces, fires and lamps attempt to illuminate the dark city. Out in the countryside it is already dark, touched here and there with pinpricks of light.

Prepare an ambush here...	**837**
Head towards Blackheath...	**891**

❧ 856 ❧

You take the coin (**£1 1s**) from the fat man and step aside. However, you have done nothing but aggrieve those waiting behind you. Regardless of your threatening appearance, the injustice you have done is so great that it sets the others muttering angrily. They hold just shy of attacking you, but you must lose a **solidarity point**.

Leave the Palace...	**721**

❧ 857 ❧

The Guildsmen shy away from your approach and begin muttering together, quite intimidated. One of the other hauliers beckons you over.

"Them dratted Guildsmen think they own the road," he says. "Even the municipal water, like this here tank. But they don't. It's a good system: all you have to do is punch in the number of your employer here, and it credits the cost to your account."

"What's to stop someone putting in a number they aren't entitled to use?" you ask. The haulier stares, and then turns away with a scowl.

Return to Deptford Bridge...	**814**

❧ 858 ❧

You dodge down several alleys, even steering your Ferguson down a flight of shallow steps, heading for the river. Once on Upper Thames Street, you turn left and ride up a builder's ramp to bring you to the level of the road crossing Blackfriars Bridge. It is thronged with locobuses filled with the workers returning to their cheaper lodgings in the south: to make your way through, you will have to steer your machine along the parapet itself. A single slip could be disastrous for yourself and your machine! Make a MOTORING roll of difficulty 15, adding 3 if you have **off-road tyres** and 1 if you have **improved brakes**, to manage this stunt. If you dare not try it, you can simply let the Constables,

never far behind, catch up with you rather than take this deadly risk.

Successful MOTORING roll!	**631**
Failed MOTORING roll!	**849**
Did not attempt the MOTORING roll!	**1010**

❧ 859 ❧

A costermonger has his barrow set out here in the street, selling vegetables and fruits grown on the outskirts of the city. He recognises you. "You're the Steam Highwayman, right? You're on the side of the common people, right? Well, you ought to be doing something about this grave-robbing that's going on. My aunt was lifted out of her coffin, up at St John's Bethnal Green. We buried her Tuesday, she was out by Thursday morning. No good telling the Constables. They aren't any help at all."

He will also sell you some of his wares.

Food and Drink	To buy	To sell
tin of fruit	6s	-
wheel of cheese	£2	-
melon	-	12s
pineapple	-	12s
picnic hamper	£4	-

Ride on...	**noted passage**

❧ 860 ❧

This time the Constables are on your tail - you cannot escape notice for ever! The sound of their bells clearing the road ahead of them are ample warning of their approach up the Dover Road, so you turn about. It is time to steam for your nearest bolthole, or to put water between yourself and your pursuers.

Head for Deptford Bridge...	**833**
Steer for the swing-bridge at the creek mouth...	**846**

❧ 861 ❧

Your regal tread upon the cobbles is enough to convince the doorkeepers that their sovereign approaches. Something about you smacks of royalty - fortunately - and the gates swing open. Your companion nods, giving a gracious glimpse of her face, and the doormen hunker back, whispering, before deciding to risk a low bow. You wave at them to rise, adjust your clothing, and continue into the Tower.

Turn to...	**908**

❧ 862 ❧

"Where d'you cop that mouse?" asks the barman, eyeing your livid bruise. "You a prize fighter? Hey, looks like we've got a brawler here!"

Your replies are interpreted as modesty and the drinkers hustle you out into the yard and into the ring.

Turn to...   **892**

❧ 863 ❧

Greenwich has always been more a place of the sea than the land. Even this far up the Thames, ocean-going ships moor at Greenwich to take on cargo or make repairs. This is also the home of the grand Imperial Naval College, and every pub is thronged with tattooed mariners or their officers.

A busy chain ferry runs across the breadth of the Thames, chiefly to carry the products of the workshops of Millwall across to the naval yards

Visit the Plume of Feathers...	**880**
Cross the river by ferry... **(3s)**	**431**
Head to the Telegraph Guild compound...	**878**
Cross the creek to Deptford...	**816**
Steam up onto Blackheath...	**891**

❧ 864 ❧

The next hopeful seems more likely to bring the Progressives some success: it is the youngest member of the house, 'Boary' Stuart, a passionate sportsman, famed friend of hedgehogs and Member for Penrith.

"You're the fencing chappie, correct?" he says excitedly. "Old Wrighty said I could find you here. Just need a little sharpening up before Thursday. Duke of Innishmore said I was a blaggard half-Scot mongrel and a liar. I don't mind you knowing my grandfather *was* from over the border, but 'liar' is a very dirty, dirty word."

You work hard to keep up with the energetic Stuart. He has a wild and rather unguarded style, depending on his speed and vigour to outpace an opponent. You know that Innishmore is a skilled fencer, however, and do everything you can to train the young man to cover his guard and anticipate counter-attacks.

Roll a dice to see the result of the duel, adding 1 for every 10 scars that you possess.

Score 1-4 No one can do more than their best...	**881**
Score 5+ A blow for the Wheatears...	**893**

❧ 865 ❧

Mill Lane is filled with heavy vehicles loading ironwork from the brewery. You are forced to slow right down to manouevre around them, losing your lead over your pursuers.

Turn to...   **1010**

❧ 866 ❧

In Westminster, pickets and bonfires dot the squares. The Palace of St James burns, but Westminster Palace still stands, sheltering the nobles and members of parliament who have not fled - or joined the revolution.

The lobsters - the parliamentary guard - are quickly overcome and squads are sent into parliament to winkle out those deserving punishment. A scaffold is set up on the western end of the bridge, and before long, the Thames runs red with blood.

This is truly the point of no return - for you and for the nation. What happens now will depend on whether you and the High Council can ride the tide of bloodshed and violence that you have released. But there will be no more midnight rides on your trusty velosteam: you have a responsibility to the people now. If you have the codeword *Chary*, turn to **876** immediately.

In the coming months, the destruction and suffering will increase. Factions trying to re-establish control will arise in parts of the land: a real civil war. However, within the Compact for Workers' Equality there will also be squabbling and betrayal. You are recognised as a true revolutionary - after all, it was by your hand that the King died - but soon you have to make another decision. To prevent the ambitious Comrade Feaver from taking power, you will have to cement the other members of the Compact's leadership into an inner circle - with you at its head. Unless you act, she will eventually eclipse all of you.

Take power for yourself...	**884**
Step aside...	**899**

❧ 867 ❧

According to the newspaper, the Brewer's Guild are in the process of electing a new Guildmaster. Their hall, north of the St Paul's Cathedral and within the bounds of the ancient City itself, is famed for the splendour of its architecture and the wealth of its members. Perhaps it would be worth a visit?

Turn to...   **noted passage**

❧ 868 ❧

You pass the Angel on the corner of Pentonville Road and steam north, up Upper Street into Islington. The wide road here is still the cattle-droving route down to Smithfield, but you are fortunate not to meet any herds of fattened cows today. Instead you have the traffic of the city to worry about: locobuses suddenly pulling out from side-roads, gravel-trucks trundling over the beaten ground, horse-drawn delivery carts standing at odd angles to your journey. All the time, the jangle of the Constables' bells rings behind you, and overhead the throb of an airship threatens. You have one last chance to make a getaway.

Hide amongst Laycock's Lairs...

(Friend of Laycock)	**946**
Take sanctuary at St Mary's Church...	**974**
Make for Abney Park Cemetery...	**985**

❧ 869 ❧

The tariffs on imported corn have contributed to urban poverty for many years, supporting the high price of bread and foodstuffs, while making English landowners rich on the value of their estates. However, it also supports the high wages of the rural poor, whose harvest labour is directly related to the sale price. Mr Wright is a member of the Anti-Corn Law League and longs to see the tariffs abolished. "With cheap imports, the urban population can be fed more cheaply and our cities will flourish. It is only the typical shortsightedness of the Tories that insists we are better off with protectionism."

Wright is simplifying. Many of his own Wheatear friends support the tariffs as they fear a collapse of British agriculture, should free trade swamp the land with cheap American and Russian corn. Others amongst the Establishment hate the Corn Laws as violently as Wright does.

Speak in support of the Corn Laws...	**807**
Argue against the Corn Laws...	**812**

❧ 870 ❧

You turn down the walled canyon that is Copperas Street. High, soot-blackened brick stands either side, painted with the name and telegraph address of the Deptford Manure Works, right next to the Bright Dawn Soap Works. How strange that out of this dark and stinking corner of Deptford comes the soap that lies on the wash-stands of the rich, the powerful and the royal.

Another turn to the left, past where a gaggle of

boys are playing at a water pump, puts you on Knot Street, where the warehouses of Kent Wharf and Normandy Wharf loom over narrow tenements. You pass a busy mission hall, where a man in black stands on the steps beside his texts, the acrid-smelling chemical works, turn a corner and then take a left after a dilapidated creekside inn. The wheatmills of old Deptford Bridge fill the air with the sound of crashing water and the noise of engines raising steam tell you that you have reached the Broadway.

Turn to...	**814**

❧ 871 ❧

You explain who you are to the footmen and they grudgingly let you board. Mrs Roberts remembers you, however. "Oh, the race-car driver. Yes, that was quite a drama, wasn't it? How is dear Dashy? And tell me what he has done with that car. Quite a piece of engineering."

You chat a little longer and then she looks at the clock. "So, is there something I can do for you?"

Turn to...	**917**

❧ 872 ❧

The Unicorns is a ramshackle, leaning old place, nonetheless rammed to the metaphorical gunwales whenever the mariners are given leave from the nearby barracks. The Deptford Moorings are the base of the Imperial Nethundical Corps, as well as a staging post for convoys, so the landlord can be sure of steady trade, although his breakages bill must be considerable.

Buy a drink...	**(2s)**	**851**
Chat with the sailors...	**(4s)**	**890**
Head into the yard...		**900**
Leave the Unicorns...		**816**

❧ 873 ❧

A carpet salesman is telling his friend about a dangerous visit to Whitechapel, where he was showing his sample swatches and found himself in hot water.

"For a start, Whitechapel Street Market? Flat Billy's got that entirely sewn up. You don't pay protection to his fellow, you don't trade there, and that's that. So I got thrown out of the market. Then I thought I'd try a pub, right? Nice looking place called the Grave Maurice. Well. It was like some sort of buster's convention, wasn't it? Magsmen and dippers left and right... Looked like I was the mug, so I did a scoot, quick as I could! Turns out Flat Billy keeps court in the upstairs parlour."

Turn to...   **noted passage**

❧ 874 ❧

You approach the gate with your lady following close behind. You bang stoutly on the door with a gloved fist in what you imagine to be a manner both regal and furious.

"Let me in, by God," you call. "If you value your positions, your freedom and your lives!"

There is argument behind the door, but it does not open.

"There is one more thing we can try," says Diana. "The golden key that opens many a door..."

Pour gold through the talking hatch... (£12 4s) **895**
Turn about...   **906**

❧ 875 ❧

You are allowed aboard by some wary-looking footmen and made to wait in a salon with a fine view of the industrial riverbank. After some time, Mrs Roberts enters and greets you.

"How very enterprising of you to seek me out here aboard my little floating retreat. I presume there is something I can do for you?"

Turn to...   **917**

❧ 876 ❧

It is during one meeting of the now all-powerful council that Comrade Feaver denounces you. "Not all among us are equally committed to the cause. We have within this council one who still sympathises for the monarchs of old."

"What do you mean?" you retort.

"I did not flinch from taking the axe," she says.

"You would not shed 'royal' blood, I remember. We all saw it."

It is enough. In the atmosphere of paranoia and accusation, you are swiftly removed from your position and written out of existence. There never was a Steam Highwayman among the revolutionaries. You will never get to see the eventual fruit of your labours.

Turn to the **epilogue**...

❧ 877 ❧

A line of plane trees flash by. You are now headed towards Southwark: unless you have a hide-away planned, you will find it very hard to escape the Constables in these busy streets.

Ride on...   **614**

❧ 878 ❧

The Royal Observatory has been in the care - or some would say, the grasp - of the Telegraph Guild for as long as they have enjoyed the monopoly on telegraphic communication. The main tower handles all the telegraph traffic to Kent and the continent and is constantly moving. The compound on the hillside comprises a substantial barracks, several training towers, a supply depot for the Guild's engines and a sizeable, noisy workshop. Note this passage (**878**).

If you are **Wanted by the Telegraph Guild**, you will not be able to remain here without being recognised and must turn to **891** immediately.

Head to the workshops... (*Clockwork*)   **822**
Deal in machinery... (**artizan's note**)   **996**
Ask around for work...   **853**
Hire the computational engine... (£12)   **255**
Steam up the hill to Blackheath...   **891**
Ride downhill to Greenwich...   **863**

❧ 879 ❧

The Empire runs on freight - the power of the Haulage Guild and the Atmospheric Union are testament to that. And any invention which speeds up the transhipment of goods from one vehicle to another is bound to be profitable. You can't help but have noticed the punchcard tags used to label many of the sacks and barrels in the Freight Yards you have passed through: if there were a way for a gantry crane to read or register these automatically, think how efficient it could be! You and your workers set to work.

Developing a prototype takes time. Remove the

brass **flange joint** and **copper pipe** from your **possessions** (or the box at passage **1308**) and make an ENGINEERING roll of difficulty 15.

Successful ENGINEERING roll!   **1217**
Failed ENGINEERING roll!   **1308**

❧ 880 ❧

A little, narrow, maritime place, the Plume of Feathers stands on a quiet street somewhat removed from the bustle of the military quay and the wharves. This is a dark place for rendezvous, steady drinking, and the occasional secretive deal.

Join the drinkers...(**1s**)   **898**
Leave the pub...   **863**

❧ 881 ❧

A few days later, you hear about the duel. Apparently 'Boary' Stuart let his guard down and the dastardly Duke of Innishmore slipped his blade between the youngster's ribs. Perhaps the Establishment's grip on Parliament is insoluble? Note passage **905** and turn to **850**, where you must correct the Parliamentary swingometer **one point in the Establishment's favour.**

❧ 882 ❧

You crash through drifts of leaves in Green Park and bump down over the kerb into Wellington Place. Perhaps you can head into Hyde Park and hope to lose your pursuers amongst the noise and bustle of the Exhibition?

Ride into Hyde Park...   **445**
Head further west...   **138**

❧ 883 ❧

You watch a couple of men betting on a game of toss-a-cockle. Another drinker shakes his head. "That's not sport. You want the real stuff to get the blood pumping. Prize fighting."

"It's banned in the city, ain't it?"

"Weeel, mebbe it is. But that don't stop it. There's fightin' down in Deptford too, at the Unicorns, if you've the taste for it."

Drink up...   **noted passage**

❧ 884 ❧

So it is that you align your allies, test your Comrades and make your move. Comrade Feaver and her party are arrested and removed. The others look to you to take the helm - for now, at least - until one of them has amassed enough power and support to replace you. You are Comrade Highwayman - first among equals - and the destiny of the land is yours to decide. But that is another story.

Turn to the **epilogue**...

❧ 885 ❧

The game ebbs and flows, but slowly and certainly it turns in your favour. Hendon throws down his final hand with a laugh. "I'd better write you that letter then, and get rid of you." Add **Hendon's letter** to your **possessions** and remove the codeword *Craven*.

Leave the mansion...   **750**

❧ 886 ❧

The Member for Southwark, the Honourable Russell Barming, proposes a Bill to encourage manufacturing in the city. He wants to remove the limits on coal deliveries, the sizes of furnaces and the amount of water that factory owners can draw from the Thames without a licence. The effect will be drastic, markedly increasing pollution and smog, along with a rise in productivity. The House vote massively in favour - your own opinion is quite insignificant.

Return to your chambers...   **797**

❧ 887 ❧

The tunnelling is still going on apace here beneath Smithfield and you head to one of the navvies' ramps. Workmen dash out of your way, spilling their barrows down the slope, but you keep your balance and head down onto the track. No airborne Constables will be able to spy on you down here! The southbound tunnel is blocked by a stationary passenger wagon, so you only have two options.

Take the westbound tunnel...   **903**
Take the eastbound tunnel...   **936**

✆ 888 ✎
□ □ □ □ □

If any of the boxes above are empty, tick one and read on. If they are all already ticked, erase the ticks and turn to **860** immediately.

The roads around you are quiet. Shrouded in the autumn fog, you are unobserved by the authorities, the guilds and your enemies.

Steam down into Deptford...   **816**
Take the road further into London...   **609**

✆ 889 ✎
"There's the *Gentilesse*," says your mate, pointing out a fashionable several-storied steam barge moored at the side of the channel. "What King Charles' lady keeps on the river for her rendezvouzes. You know, Maria Roberts. Her."

"How do you know about that?" you ask.

"Oh everyone knows about the *Gentilesse*," he replies.

Perhaps you wish to find out for yourself. You will not be allowed to board the *Gentilesse* without something to prove that you will be welcome there.

Seek an audience... (**Letter of Introduction**) **875**
Remind Mrs Roberts of the Spencer Cup...(*Able*) **871**
Depend upon a word in your favour...
    (*Chattering*)   **1319**
Steam on...   **922**

✆ 890 ✎
□

If the box above is empty, tick it and read on. If it is already ticked, turn to **911** immediately.

You get talking to a sailor in a blue peacoat and knitted cap. He claims to be a member of the Imperial Nethundical Corps - the famed and fearless sailors who man the navy's underwater steam attack ships - but he has none of their discipline or hauteur.

"Just married yesterday. And recalled today," he blubs over his liquor. "I was told I had two weeks' leave!"

"Maybe I can convince your Sergeant..."   **926**
"That's a sailor's life, matey."   **872**

✆ 891 ✎
You pause to take in the view from the heath. Due north stands the Class A telegraph tower beside the cupola of the Royal Observatory and below that, the buildings of the Royal Naval College at Greenwich. You can see across the river to Millwall, where the river bank is forested with the smoking chimneys of three dozen iron foundries. Countless masts speak of countless hulls a-building, some iron and some English oak.

But here drifting leaves and the skeined open branches overhang the rutted road. The way to Dover runs eastwards, up towards the famous Shooter's Hill. Westwards the road crosses Deptford Creek, passes the engineering works, market gardens and new terraces, and heads into the metropolis itself.

Ride to the Observatory...   **878**
Roll downhill to Deptford Bridge...   **814**
Head east to Shooter's Hill...   **855**

✆ 892 ✎
□ □ □

If the boxes above are empty, tick the first and turn to **1404** immediately. If only the first is ticked, tick the second and turn to **1443**. If two are ticked, tick the third and turn to **1470**. If all three are ticked, read on.

"There ain't no-one willing to take up your challenge here," says the fixer. "Jim Blackwall, Wyndham Jack and that travelling fellow... You're a real survivor, that's all I can say."

Turn to...   **872**

❧ 893 ❧

Your protégé has done it! 'Boary' Stuart bounds back into the practice hall with a grin and a **bottle of champagne**, which he gives to you. "I'm very grateful," he says. "I was fighting for my life. A really dirty fighter, that old Duke. But he won't bother the Progressive Party any more!" Gain the codeword *Classic*, note passage **905** and turn to **850**, where you should correct the Parliamentary Swingometer **one point in the Progressives' favour.**

❧ 894 ❧

St Sepulchre's Parish is still the knot of medieval lanes that grew up spontaneously outside the city walls, and off St John's Street are a whole variety of hiding places. The archway into Eagle Court is dark and inviting, although you can hear children at play that way. White Horse Alley will lead you towards the industry of Turnmill Street, while Hay and Mitre Court has a wide and wheel-rutted entrance.

Ride into Eagle Court...	**938**
Take White Horse Alley...	**925**
Choose Hay and Mitre Court...	**909**

❧ 895 ❧

The shower of coins does something that your voice never could. The door creaks open.

"'Tis a cold night, doorkeepers," you say with a regal sweep of the arm. "Find something to warm your insides."

"My eyes, the King!" cries one, and reflexively genuflects. The others follow suit, more or less confidently.

"Hush, hush," you say. "I am only a gentleman visitor."

Turn to...	**908**

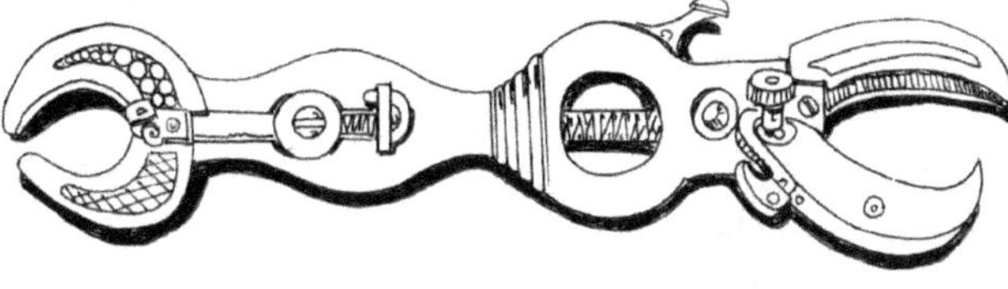

❧ 896 ❧

You find a **pocket watch** lying in a puddle in the roadway. Nobody nearby seems to be looking for it.

Turn to...	**noted passage**

❧ 897 ❧

You swerve down Warner Street beneath the grand Rosebery Viaduct and emerge near Clerkenwell. In this busy part of the capital, you should have plenty of places to hide.

Ride to the railway excavations...	**887**
Head for the alleys of St Sepulchre's...	**894**

❧ 898 ❧

Your pint is poured from a jug, not a cask, into a stoneware pot with a rough lip that supports the delicate foam of the head while you drink. It is served cool, fragrant with the clear, direct call of Suffolk hops, its flavour leaning hard on a malty tone and lingering there, finishing sweet, bitter, and sweet again. Simply to lift the pot is a masterclass in brewing: this is the Plume of Feathers' Eider Pale Ale. Note passage **880** and roll a dice to see what you hear among the drinkers.

Score 1	A forger...	**1181**
Score 2	A street gang...	**1113**
Score 3	Gloves for sale...	**1418**
Score 4	Contraband...	**706**
Score 5	A fence...	**175**
Score 6	Recognised!	**664**

❧ 899 ❧

Others in the Compact are not so patient. Comrade Feaver's supporters move to have her appointed Comrade-in-Chief, and it is a short time until the ideals of the revolution become tainted with dictatorship and autocracy.

You, however, get to see little of that. You meet your end in a secret execution, denounced as a traitor to the Compact and the people. Whatever wishes you had for the people of the land, you can only pray and hope that one day, they will come to pass.

Turn to the **epilogue**...

❧ 900 ❧

The yard sports a dusty, much-beaten-down ring, where bare-knuckle boxers vie for glory and guineas. A fight is about to start - and there is always a little room for a newcomer.

Take up the challenge...	**892**
Return to the parlour...	**872**

❧ 901 ❧

The Members have been debating regulating the size and capacity of airships for some time. Clearly, the Atmospheric Union stand to lose a great deal, and the Haulage Guild, who handle the greater part of the nation's freight by road and are terrified of losing their dominance, have been lobbying hard in favour of the bill.

Several speakers stand and give their perspectives. Mr Wright and his Wheatears lean strongly towards regulation. Will your own history with the Atmospheric Union sway you - or will this be an entirely altruistic decision?

Vote in favour of the Airship Regulation Bill... **1055**
Vote against the Airship Regulation Bill... **1128**

❧ 902 ❧

Steaming westward through the City, you steer between the barges and lighters carefully, your mate standing at the prow, clanging the smog bell. All around, a welter of noise from other craft echoes across the river. Your mate turn and calls back to you. "Sooner we're out o' this unnatural smog, the better, captain."

Eventually you reach Battersea Bridge, where the murk begins to subside. If you want to moor here, marked **Moored at Battersea Bridge** on your **Adventure Sheet**.

Moor here and go ashore... 1132
Turn around and sail back into the city... 922
Continue eastwards towards Brentford... 580

❧ 903 ❧

The tunnel westwards makes for challenging riding: the wooden sleepers holding the rails thump against your tyres. It is also only a matter of time until you meet an underground train carrying passengers into the city.

A side-tunnel offers you a way out of harm's way, but it is closed by a wire-mesh gate. As you bend to take a look at the lock, the sound of an approaching engine echoes down the tunnel towards you. If you have a **skeleton key**, you will be able to open it quickly. Otherwise, make an INGENUITY roll of difficulty 11, adding 2 if you possess any **lockpicks**, to open the gate and avoid a horrific collision.

Possess a **skeleton key** or successful
INGENUITY roll! 932
Failed INGENUITY roll! 959

❧ 904 ❧

The boy munches happily on your gift. He looks at you shrewdly, calculating whether he will profit more from reporting or befriending you. If you have more than 10 **solidarity points**, turn to **910**. Otherwise, read on.

The boy tells you a sad story of want and neglect. When you offer to help him further, he shrugs proudly. "I'm going to head down to the riverside," he says, "And join meself a gang. Mix wiv me own type."

When you next stop, you notice that he has picked your pockets: remove the third object in your **Jewellery Pouch**, or **£1 1s** from your wallet if your pouch has fewer than **three items** in it. Of course, if your wallet is empty as well, how can it become emptier? That would be humiliating indeed - for a street urchin to find nothing to thieve from the Steam Highwayman.

Turn to... **noted passage**

❧ 905 ❧

It is late in the evening when your next client comes to begin her training with you: Lady Eliza Longlym, the Member for Exeter, wishes to improve her swordplay. She has accepted the challenge thrown down by Sir Edgar Dressley, known to be the most dangerous of all the Parliamentary duellists.

However, Lady Longlym is no mean swordswoman herself. It remains to be seen whether you can teach her anything. She means to fight you with untipped blades: the **first to three wounds** will win this bout.

Lady Longlym	Weapon: **rapier (PAR4)**
Parry:	12
Nimbleness:	8
Toughness:	3

Victory! 921
Defeat! 942

❧ 906 ❧

You return to Derwent House, where Diana strips off the veil and the sweaty wax visage and laughs as she pours herself a bumper of cold champagne. "My goodness, your attempt at the King's voice!" It seems to tickle her. "'If you value your position, your freedom and your lives!' You've never met the King, have you?"

"Enough of this. Steal your own jewels." 914
"Perhaps burglary would be better." 621

✤ 907 ✤

You burst out onto Pentonville Road between two locobuses, scattering the queues waiting to board. One of your pursuers has managed to catch up with you and he swerves across the tarmacadam towards your Ferguson. His pillion rider swings a looped pole towards you. Make a NIMBLENESS roll of difficulty 11 to dodge and keep your balance.

Successful NIMBLENESS roll!	**950**
Failed NIMBLENESS roll!	**969**

✤ 908 ✤

"Now let me take the lead," says the intrepid lady. She smiles as two Beefeaters stand aside at your approach and asks one, so sweetly, despite the hour, to lead you to the Martin Tower.

He leads on through the silent fortress, through gates and across the bailey, and, unlocking a massive clockwork lock on the door with a key chained to his waist, lets you into the tower. Up a curving flight of stairs, in through another heavy door, and into a small chamber.

"Can I trouble you for a glass of water, warder?" asks Lady Diana. He mumbles something and turns to pull a bellchain. If you have a **bottle of chloroform**, turn to **924** immediately. Otherwise, you must attempt to knock him out: make a NIMBLENESS roll of difficulty 14, adding 2 if you possess a **blackjack**, **cosh**, **club** or other blunt weapon.

Successful NIMBLENESS roll!	**937**
Failed NIMBLENESS roll!	**947**

✤ 909 ✤

Hay and Mitre Court does indeed have a much-trafficked entrance, as the Mitre pub and several other business use it for their deliveries. It is a dead end.

Turn to...	**1010**

✤ 910 ✤

The boy chatters happily. He tells you that the street boys are sure that Flat Billy and the Chief Constable have come to some sort of agreement. "See them constables ain't patrollin' in Whitechapel no more. And they ain't scared." He gives you a **Constable's logbook** that he has found and, being illiterate, has no use for.

Turn to...	**noted passage**

✤ 911 ✤

Several of the drinkers here are ratings from the nearby barracks. They always have a bit of 'lost' ironmongery to off-load, particularly in exchange for hard liquor.

To gain...	In exchange for
high pressure valve	**box of cigars**
adjustable wrench (ENG+1)	**bottle of gin**
engineer's gauntlets (ENG+2)	**bottle of whisky** and a **pork pie**
pneumatic manual (ENG+3)	two **bottles of whisky**

Roll a dice to see whether you are unlucky enough to attract the attention of the sergeant.

Score 1	Somebody blabbed...	**971**
Score 2-6	A swift agreement...	**872**

✤ 912 ✤

The King's Canal joins the Thames here after cutting its wide loop through northern London. Although the River Guild run it, the Crown owns it - the most profitable waterway in the land. Here the river-going barges of the Midlands reach the furthest point of sail for ocean-going vessels, there is a massive, mechanised transhipment dock. A wide gantry-way spans the entire dock, raising cargoes from one craft and depositing them directly in the hold of another.

	To buy	To sell
Charcoal	-	£23
Furniture	-	-
Machinery	-	£31
Pottery	£24	£21
Cotton	-	£8
Woollen Cloth	£13	£12
Coal	£10	£7
Beer	£20	£18
Wheat	-	£7
Malt	-	£6
Frozen Meat	-	-
Ice	£9	£8

If you wish to purchase **Ice**, you will need a **Perkins Machine**. To moor here, mark **moored at King's Canal Dock** on your **Adventure Sheet** and turn directly to **474**.

Steam up the canal...		**934**
Pass through the lock...	(3s)	**968**

❧ 913 ❧

Your stammered attempt at an address only causes laughter in the house. This is plainly not your field, and your words are quickly forgotten. Wright leans over as you sit. "Best leave this sort of thing to those born to it, my friend," he says. "You have your own skillset."

Return to your chambers...   **797**

❧ 914 ❧

"Oh, I didn't mean to hurt your feelings. It was worth a try, was it not? But if you are sure you want to part, then let us part as friends." She pours you a drink. "I will find my way in there, one way or another."

When you remount your velosteam, several hours later, you find that your **purse** is empty. Also remove the codewords *Curly*, *Cool*, or *Charred*, if you possess them.

Ride away...   **750**

❧ 915 ❧

The box contains a sheaf of papers, including a **Delevinne Bank Share Certificate** and **fifty guineas in banknotes**.

Turn to...   **noted passage**

❧ 916 ❧

The river turns south, and you steam past the long strand of Rotherhithe's wharves, the Imperial victualling yard and down to Deptford.

Steam on downriver...   **948**

❧ 917 ❧

Whether Mrs Roberts can help you depends on how you ask her... and what exactly you will ask.

"Does the King like oysters?" (*Contactless*)   **355**
"My party in Parliament need help."   **763**
"Would the King like to donate to an
    orphanage?" (**donors' list**)   **552**
"I am in need of money."   **815**

❧ 918 ❧

At first Sergeant Jakes is deeply unimpressed by your attempt, but a combination of flattery, liquor and your gift slipped into his pockets convinces him that he can overlook the sailor's late return this time. "After all," he grunts, "I was married once too."

"Once, sarge?" asks one of his men. "Mrs Jakes runs the laundry, don't she?"

The marine cops a heavy blow to his head, knocking off his cap. "Not 'er, you fool. Me other wife up Wapping."

The sailor is deeply grateful. He doesn't have much to give you, so he advises you to return here to talk to his shipmates if you want to trade liquor for engineering supplies. You also gain the codeword *Compassionate*.

Leave the Unicorns...   **816**

❧ 919 ❧

The expressed aim of the Compact for Workers' Equality is to bring about an absolute social revolution, destroying the power of the nobility, the guilds and the landowners in favour of direct rule by the people. Different cadres and individuals are working towards it in different ways, but there are plenty of opportunities for you to participate.

"We need to become higher profile," explains Comrade Jeffery - an ink-stained printer managing a crew designing and distributing posters. "One place we really need to have these posters is within the Crystal Palace - at the Exhibition in Hyde Park. Just think of how many people would see our statements there!"

Other aims are longer term. The Compact aim to enlist the support of key figures in the city - crime lords like Flat Billy in Whitechapel - and leaders of the various rebellions and uprisings around the nation. There is also a long-standing specific vendetta against Lord Hadrian Beaufort, the Chief Constable. Be the cause of his ruin and you will be sure to speed the people's victory.

When you complete one of these deeds, you will be instructed to turn to a particular passage where you can tally the progress of the Revolution. It will require much work and a great deal of patience but, if you act decisively, you may well end up in a significant position with a hand on the reins...
Return to the warehouse...   **489**

❧ 920 ❧

The sailor's sergeant appears just as you are concluding your deal. He catches sight of the exchange and hurries over, hand on his sergeant's baton. You push back your chair and stand, of course.

If you have a RUTHLESSNESS score of 8 or higher (including bonuses from items), then the Sergeant will decide to focus his attention on his sailors when they return to barracks and you can turn to **816** immediately. Otherwise, you must fight him - with a blunt weapon, if you have one, with your **fists (PAR 0)** or your blade. Be warned: if you draw your sword, so will he, increasing his PARRY score.

Sergeant	Weapon: **club (PAR 2)**
	or **sabre (PAR 3)**
Parry:	10 (or 11)
Nimbleness:	8
Toughness:	5

Defeat...	**931**
Victory with a blade...	**951**
Victory with **fists** or a blunt weapon...	**961**

ᔰ 921 ᘔ

Your bout with Lady Eliza Longlym pushes you to your limit: she is a fierce, dangerous opponent. The point of her blade is as sharp as her mind - and her tongue. She taunts you as you parry backwards and forwards, but in the end, you have her at your mercy.

"Very good," she says. "Just the challenge I needed." She pays for the lesson (add **£5 10s** to your **wallet**) and departs in high spirits. You bind up any **wounds** - convert them into **scars**, rolling two dice to see whether you gain any **intimidating scars (RUTH+1)** on a roll of 11 or 12.

Await the news...	**986**

ᔰ 922 ᘔ

This reach of the river is cut off from the sea by the two bridges downstream, so no ocean-going craft can reach this far. Still, the Thames is thronged with steam-lighters, carrying cargo from the docks up to countless riverside factories and warehouses. The northern bank has been built up with a fine embankment, hiding the Metropolitan sewers, and a row of plane trees give it the appearance of a country park. The south bank, however, is a welter of narrow plots, wharves, landing stages, docks and stairs. Access to the river is worth money in the city, even in this age of steam.

A short distance towards Westminster bridge, a glamourous pleasure barge slews between its buoys, lamps lit, music playing.

If you choose to put in at Bargehouse Wharf, you can buy or sell cargo here. Coal is so much in demand by the factories of Southwark that traders are willing to stretch the rules of the Coal Board's monopoly and buy from an independent captain.

	To buy	To sell
Charcoal	-	£19
Furniture	-	£25
Machinery	-	-
Pottery	-	£25
Cotton	£5	£3
Woollen Cloth	-	£13
Coal	-	£22
Beer	£12	£10
Wheat	£8	£6
Malt	-	£12
Frozen Meat	-	-
Ice	£9	£8

If you wish to purchase **Ice**, you will need a **Perkins Machine**. To moor here, note you are **moored at Bargehouse Wharf** and turn to **631** immediately.

Approach the glamorous barge...	**889**
Steam downriver under Blackfriars Bridge...	**990**
Head upstream...	**902**

ᔰ 923 ᘔ

Once on the river again, many of the concerns of the land simply dissolve. Your mate starts the engine and pours you a tankard of well-stewed tea. "Upstream, cap'n?" he asks. "Or down?"

Head upriver towards Brent Lock...	**580**
Steam downriver to the city...	**922**

ᔰ 924 ᘔ

With a few drops poured onto a pad of cloth, it only takes a moment to send the solitary guard off to a well-earned rest. You tuck the bottle away safely for later.

Continue with the robbery...	**967**

ᔰ 925 ᘔ

You bump down two steps into White Horse Alley, which is so narrow that you can touch either side with outstretched arms. Mercifully, the dished flagstones are clear of obstruction, but they have also just been washed by the proud cottagers. Make a MOTORING roll of difficulty 11, adding 2 if you have **off-road tyres**. If you succeed, you will emerge on Turnmill Street and have a clear run to Islington, by which time you should have lost your pursuers.

Successful MOTORING roll!	**151**
Failed MOTORING roll!	**969**

❧ 926 ❧

"Sergeant Jakes ain't easily persuaded, matey," replies the sailor. Nonetheless, he describes the man he should be reporting to, and a few hours later you see Jakes with a couple of armed marines enter the pub seeking late returners and defaulters. How will you proceed?

Bribe the Sergeant...
(**£10** or a **bottle of whisky**)	**918**
Attempt to intimidate him...	**941**
Forget about it...	**872**

❧ 927 ❧

You steam up the Brent, kept in the busy main channel, which has been straightened and smoothed. In the meadows on either side, the twists of the old river hide under banks of rushes. You pass the wharf of the nail factory, the brick works and the asylum, eventually turning east and between ever closer, more tightly-packed terraces, until Paddington itself approaches.

Head to the wharf...	**99**
Steam on by...	**944**

❧ 928 ❧

You ask the staff about whether they have rooms, but they shake their heads. "We're not letting rooms at the moment," comes the response. "You could try the Gun, over at Blackwall, or the Holly Bush in Hampstead."

"Or Crafton's in Lambeth, if you've a convict's ticket," says another with a look of disgust.

Finish your drink...	**noted passage**

❧ 929 ❧

"The Tariffs under discussion," you begin, "Were intended with a single aim: to support the production of the national food supply, the bushel of corn milled and baked for the daily loaf, or the stook of barley malted and brewed for the quenching of our national thirst. To ensure the fair recompense of both those devoted agriculturalists and the hands that reap, bind and thresh, it has been necessary to protect against the import of more-cheaply produced grain from across the sea by imposing an import duty, fixed yearly, in proportional response to the projected harvest."

"Get on with it," calls a moustachioed member of the opposite benches. "We all know the score!"

"Well then. Let me ask the members of the house this question: has this aim been met? Why yes, it has.

And does this need - the need to protect against the import of foreign corn, which will surely lead to the dwindling of our national wheat harvest, which is the envy of the world, together with the unemployment of countless thousands of rural folk accustomed since their ancestors' time to lean upon the staff of life, as well as upon their harvest-time earnings - does this need remain? Why yes, it certainly does. Wheat produced at four shillings a bushel in Ohio state - that distant prairie - can be shipped to Liverpool for less than two shillings a bushel, and sold at profit to its farmers, merchants and carriers at a price that can cause nothing but collapse for our domestic production, were it not for the Tariff. Certainly, there is a great need to modernise, to increase production and to meet the increasing demand of our cities for bread. But let me ask the House this third question: whose profit should it be, the feeding of the cities of this nation? The speculators of New Amsterdam? Or the honest labourers in the English wheatfield?"

The debate continues long into the night, but there is something about the balance of national interest, commercial sense and simply-followed logic in your argument that convinces many of the waverers to your position. At the final count, shortly after midnight, the House votes against repealing the Corn Laws, ensuring that food prices remain high.

Mr Wright narrows his eyes. "Do you realise what you have done? You have only reinforced the Establishment's position - and pushed the case for reform further off." Not only that, but you have also brought about a further rise in prices, as confident millers buy up future harvests. The share prices of the larger milling consortiums, like Imperial Northern Mills, will rocket. Wright walks off in disgust, shaking his head. Gain the codeword *Carling*.

Return to your chambers...	**797**

❧ 930 ❧

Among the moored steamers and packets, lighters and small river craft ply a constant trade. If you are carrying **coal**, you can sell it here to a ship's master for **£15** per unit. There are also opportunities to take cargo ashore or to bring craft downriver, if you have the right customisations or craft.

Look for tug work... (**tug**)	**1385**
Take cargo aboard... (**cargo crane**)	**1346**
Leave the moorings...	**948**

✎ 931 ✎

You are knocked down but the Sergeant seems to consider your beating punishment enough. He has a couple of the sailors drag you outside and splash water over you: one gives you a long gulp from the bottle of whisky inside his coat. Remove one **wound** from your **Adventure Sheet** without converting it to a **scar**.

Leave the Unicorns... **816**

✎ 932 ✎

Just in time, the lock snaps open, the gate swings and you steer your velosteam into the side-tunnel. The passenger train thunders past, its passengers oblivious to their good fortune.

You have found yourself in a service tunnel. It slopes steeply up towards the surface, bringing you out somewhere near Marylebone. Your pursuers are, of course, no longer a problem.

Leave the tunnel... **47**

✎ 933 ✎

Your route brings you along the Isle of Dogs, past the yard where the mighty Leviathan stands on its slips, past the drifting rubbish of the Union Docks and up to where the river turns east again. King's Canal Dock stands behind those rare things, green-leaved willows, that have rooted themselves in the silty bank.

Continue towards Limehouse... **968**

✎ 934 ✎

There is a speed limit along the canal, but you are unlikely to reach it, with the waterway so clogged with traffic, flotsam and waste. You pass a gasworks and a lime-mortar manufacturers and are forced to cover your mouth and nose against the smell. Roll a dice to see what you encounter:

Score 1-2	A floating workshop...	**1461**
Score 3-4	Little of interest...	**1218**
Score 5-6	An escape...	**1479**

✎ 935 ✎

"Was this your doing?" Reverend Highrun is desperately excited. "We have royal approval! The King has sent a pledge for five hundred pounds." Remove the codeword *Clearly*, turn to **589** and add **£500** to the current total in the box before making any other choices.

✎ 936 ✎

Your lime lantern cuts into the thick, subterranean darkness as you fly over the rail ties with a thumping rhythm. The fresh brick of the walls tell you just how recently this tunnel has been built... or begun. All of a sudden, your lime lantern illuminates a working face in the soil, where labourers' tools lie in orderly piles ready for working hours again. Shouts and flickering lights from behind announce the imminent arrival of the Constables and the navvies they have rounded up to help them corner and capture you. You have no choice but to surrender.

Turn to... **13**

✎ 937 ✎

A single heavy blow floors the beefeater before he knows what is happening. Lady Diana grimaces, then shrugs.

Enter the treasure chamber... **967**

✎ 938 ✎

Eagle Court runs behind a charity school and is used, you suddenly realise, as their playground. A mass of boys and girls kicking a ball and hopping over the cobbles turn and cheer to see you approach, but you are forced to slow to a stop. Even you are not ruthless enough to ride through a school of playing children in your desperation.

Turn to... **1010**

✎ 939 ✎

Your mate puts double lashings over the bollards. "I'll need to loosen them pretty soon," he says, "But the tide turns hard and fast here and I'd rather be too tight than banging about against these here piers." Note that you are **moored below London Bridge**.

Disembark... **1000**

✎ 940 ✎

There is a mooring alongside the iron foundry, but your mate seems sceptical. "I don't know if this is quite safe," he says. "I may shift us across the other side if space opens up." Note that you are **moored at Battlebridge Basin**.

Turn to... **129**

✌ 941 ✌

Sergeant Jakes is not going to be easily intimidated. However, he has a mortal fear of fire after years of sailing the nethundical craft. Make a RUTHLESSNESS roll of difficulty 15, adding 6, instead of 3, if you possess some **hair matches**.

Successful RUTHLESSNESS roll... **953**
Failed RUTHLESSNESS roll... **971**

✌ 942 ✌

Lady Longlym's bladework is impressive: she parries every attack and seamlessly turns them to her advantage. She leaps, dashes and turns, never losing focus or grip. She is a fearsome fighter indeed.

"The practice is appreciated," she says, tossing you a bag of coin. "I had hoped to find someone who could teach me something, though."

Add **£5 10** to your wallet and bind up your wounds: convert each of them into **scars**, rolling two dice to see if you gain an **intimidating scar (RUTH+1)** on 11 or 12.

Now roll to see the outcome of Lady Longlym's duel:

Score 1-3   A defeat for the lady...   **976**
Score 4-6   Send her victorious!   **986**

✌ 943 ✌

"It is fear. Fear of the future that keeps these tariffs in place. Fear of change. It is true, that without these taxes on imported grain, we will see our land changed dramatically, as grain bought from overseas replaces our own domestically produced corn, and thousands whose ancestors have toiled on the land, harvest after back-breaking harvest, will be left without employment." Your projections sounds dreadful. The chamber is entirely silent.

"So let us ask ourselves what we will do in such a circumstance. Will these unemployed men lie down and die in the fields they once reaped? No. Seeking a better life - a better lot - they will find new employment, among the mills and manufactories of our cities. Forced to compete with the methods of the American farmers, our agriculturalists will modernise, employing the inestimable power of steam in their fields. The mechanisation of our agriculture will be its salvation and our national opportunity, as a vast workforce is freed to work in our national industries. For this is not only possible, but necessary. As a nation we have depended on simply producing our food: yet we must now change the course of our island in a drastic and, admittedly, fearsome change, to rely not upon our ability to feed ourselves but upon our far greater ability to mechanise and trade. As the workshop of the world, our exports are worth far more than we might ever need to import. As the most technologically-advanced, our navy protect our trade from depredation and disturbance. The only thing tying us, I say, to the past, is our fear."

As you take your seat, there is a round of applause from the Wheatears. The debate continues, but your tone of national pride and scorn convinces many to vote for the repeal of the Corn Laws. At midnight, the vote is counted and found heavily in your favour. Gain the codeword *Crumb*, note passage **797** and turn to **850**, where you should correct the Parliamentary Swingometer **one point in the Progressives' favour**.

✎ 944 ✐

The canal loops around Queen Maria Park, under the overhanging rose briars of mansion gardens, little Chinese bridges to private benches and between the pleasure-boats of the rich.

On to Camden...   **1033**

✎ 945 ✐

You have arrived at the lower of the two Camden locks. The brewery stands along the canalside to the south in handsome, modern buildings. Passage through the lock is subject to a toll - unless you possess a Bargee's Badge.

Steer into the lock... (**1s** or **Bargee's Badge**) **1033**
Turn around and head east...   **962**

✎ 946 ✐

Laycock's men will hide you. Or if not his men, his cows. It is a short distance through the backstreets to the long stone sheds that house the cattle. You steam into one and find a shadowy corner behind a herd of busily-munching Herefords. The stink of their slurry and the soiled straw is enough to block out all other smells - even the coalgas of your machine. A cowherd catches sight of you, but quickly recognises the velosteam, smiles, winks, and herds more cattle into the road as the Constables' bells approach.

You hear the Imperials draw up and catch sight of the Constables' helmets over the cows backs, but then Laycock himself appears, bellowing at your pursuers and shooing them away. "Come to disturb these cows? Come to worry them and thin them out? Well, you'll be liable! I've got your numbers, yer mutton shunters, and you'll be liable for the lost earnings."

The Constables disappear and Laycock shoves his way through the animals to come and shake your hand. "Nice to see you here," he says. "Come to check on business?"

Leave the lairs...   **151**

✎ 947 ✐

The yeoman warder staggers, but does not fall. By steam, these old soldiers have thick skulls! He swings about, dropping his unwieldy pike and drawing a serviceable sabre. You must fight him!

Beefeater	Weapon: **sabre (PAR 3)**
Parry:	9
Nimbleness:	6
Toughness:	4

Victory!   **967**
Defeat!   **1500**

❧ 948 ❧

The mouth of muddy Deptford Creek reaches the Thames here. A knot of smaller lighters and river barges cluster around the dock, loading to ferry goods out to some of the moored steamers anchored on the Greenwich Reach.

	To buy	To sell
Charcoal	-	**£22**
Furniture	-	-
Machinery	-	**£28**
Pottery	**£18**	**£17**
Cotton	-	**£8**
Woollen Cloth	**£8**	**£8**
Coal	-	**£12**
Beer	**£19**	**£18**
Wheat	-	**£8**
Malt	-	**£6**
Frozen Meat	-	-
Ice	-	-

To moor here, mark **moored at Deptford Creek** on your **Adventure Sheet** and turn to **808** immediately.

Steam into the Greenwich moorings... **930**
Steam upriver towards Limehouse Reach... **933**
Head downriver... **992**
Cross the river and moor at Millwall... (*Carrot*) **1070**

❧ 949 ❧

Thick brown river water rushes beneath the ancient arches. Make a MOTORING roll of difficulty 13, adding 1 if you have a **strengthened screw**, but subtracting 2 if you are towing a **butty boat**.

Successful MOTORING roll! **988**
Failed MOTORING roll! **1008**

❧ 950 ❧

A sharp and pungent smell of vinegar hangs in these streets, the miasma seeping out from one of so many brick factories. You take a sharp left at the next junction and ride onto the pavement to avoid a trio of heavy goods wagons locked in some sort of Gordian knot. The road beyond is clear for a stretch: will you use your lead to hide nearby, or stretch out for a more distant part of the city?

Look for a hiding place at Spitalfields Market... **991**
Ride on to Bow.. **973**
Head south for the docks... **1006**

❧ 951 ❧

On seeing you draw your blade, Jakes took his sabre from his scabbard, and the drinkers and barkeep have all fled in terror. You are left alone standing over the bleeding body of the Sergeant.

You will certainly be **Wanted by the Constables** now and it will not be wise to remain around here much longer. Your faithful velosteam is warm, however, and you can trust it to get you away from this cursed house.

Make for Deptford Bridge... **833**
Race for Rotherhithe... **702**
Head for Shooter's Hill... **855**

❧ 952 ❧

You are on the King's Canal at Brentford, near where the lock joins the River Thames. From here, the canal drives a wide loop around north London, eventually reaching the river again near Limehouse. There are four locks between here and Paddington Basin, but the tolls are minimal for a craft like yours.

	To buy	To sell
Charcoal	-	-
Furniture	-	**£28**
Machinery	-	-
Pottery	-	**£28**
Cotton	**£8**	**£3**
Woollen Cloth	-	**£12**
Coal	**£20**	-
Beer	**£21**	**£19**
Wheat	**£7**	**£6**
Malt	**£7**	**£6**
Frozen Meat	**£14**	**£12**
Ice	**£9**	**£8**

If you wish to purchase **Frozen Meat** or **Ice**, you will need a **Perkins Machine**.

Steam north up the canal...
(**4s** or **Bargee's Badge**) **927**
Pass through Brentford Lock to the Thames... **580**

❧ 953 ❧

You lean into the Sergeant's face and snarl your nastiest snarl. He has, at last, met his match, and knows, with the prudence of an old sailor, when to alter his course with the wind. "Listen, you," he yells at the sailor. "Your leave is hereby extended. Get back to your warm bed and your wife!"

The sailor doesn't have a great deal to offer you in thanks, but he invites you to visit him in Shadwell when you are passing. Gain the codeword *Carpet*.

Leave the Unicorns...   **816**

❧ 954 ❧

It is obvious that your boat is about to sink. Only by desperate measures do you manage to get it close enough to the bank to get your velosteam ashore. You must remove your boat and your cargo from your **Adventure Sheet**.

Turn to...   **273**

❧ 955 ❧

At last the buildings are complete. The builders are packing away the scaffolding, carting off the last of the rubble and adding the last coats of paint. A wrought-iron sign is being raised over the gate: it reads 'High Way House'. Reverend Highrun sees you looking at it. "After all you have done," he smiles, "A little, subtle appreciation."

He leads you into the building. "The first boys and girls will be taken in tomorrow. We have nursemaids appointed from nearby for the suckling babes, several teachers, house masters and all manner of staff. This place will provide good employment, as well as a refuge for any child unfortunate enough to find themselves unwanted." He claps you on the back. "We've done well. Thankyou."

Gain **five Solidarity Points**, the codeword *Caritas* and add **Founded an orphanage** to your **Great Deeds**.

Head out into the city...   **471**

❧ 956 ❧

The canal meanders along, past Queen Maria Park, until it reaches Paddington Basin.

Put in at the wharf...   **99**
Continue on westwards...   **977**

❧ 957 ❧

You smash into the wooden trestles, knocking one aside and splitting another clear in half! The fairing covering your front wheel is badly knocked about and your lamp is damaged too: if you had a **double headlamp**, remove it now. You must also add **two damage points** to your velosteam. If it is now **critically damaged**, turn to **969** immediately. Otherwise, you manage to keep the machine going and make for Shooter's Hill, leaving the Constables in chaos behind you.

Steam on!   **855**

❧ 958 ❧

A woman complains about how she had her pockets picked by a scrawny boy down in the City. "There's a gang of them, operating out of Upper Thames Street or some such place," she says. "I've seen 'em mudlarking on the riverbank. I tell you - show them a moment's sympathy or a coin of charity, and they'll 'ave you!"

Turn to...   **noted passage**

❧ 959 ❧

The driver of the approaching train cannot steer aside and only realises too late that he might need to stop: the front buffers of the engine plough into your Ferguson with the unstoppable might of captive steam, rupturing your own boiler in a catastrophic explosion. You are hurled away like a child's rag doll, your neck broken, your skin scalded and your adventure over.

Turn to the **epilogue**...

❧ 960 ❧
☐

If the box above is empty, tick it and turn to **1119** immediately. Otherwise, read on.

Here along the western edge of the Isle of Dogs, the hulls of more than a dozen partly-built ships stand in their slips. Sparks fly and rivets ring as gangs of men go about the business of making iron buoyant through the wonder of geometry.

Steam on by to Greenwich Reach...   **948**

❧ 961 ❧

You knock the sergeant down and the gathered drinkers cheer - but your friends the sailors have already disappeared. You, however, are plied with drinks, as you have defeated the local bully and brawler, Sergeant Jakes. Gain a **solidarity point**.

Jakes is tossed out into the yard. Much later, you are allowed to leave. You had better see to your own wounds before proceeding much further!

Leave the Unicorns...   **816**

❧ 962 ❧

You pass a lumbering barge piled with scrap iron. The canal then twists on, threads under Islington through a narrow and only sparsely-lit tunnel, and kinks down towards Battlebridge Basin, where an iron-foundry and an ice warehouse stand.

Continue on along the canal... **912**
Turn into the Basin... **1218**

❧ 963 ❧

To construct a wharf on the sloping riverside, you will require the following: ☑ Casual labourers, a **measuring line**, **£15** for materials (chiefly timber and stone) and ENGINEERING score of 10 or more (including item bonuses). When you have gathered what you need, remove the money from your purse and the tick from the ☑ Casual labourers box in passage **1308** and tick ☐ Wharf.

Return to the Workshop... **1308**

❧ 964 ❧

You are taken to see a recruiting registrar. He takes your thumbprint and shuffles through a series of cards, checking for a match. "I can see that you are an individual with particular talents. Good. There is a place for each of us in the Compact, Comrade, so long as we are committed to the common good. There is no place for those who seek their own power or enrichment. All such motivations must be rent asunder by the wheels of social progress."

"How can I show my commitment?" you ask.

"A donation of twenty pounds will suffice. Or you can complete work for us. But I cannot tell you what the task will be until you commit to undertake it. The Compact demands your complete trust and obedience."

Make the donation... (**£20**) **975**
Undertake the task... **983**

❧ 965 ❧
☐ ☐ ☐ ☐

If any of the boxes above are empty, tick one and read on. If they are all ticked, then there are no longer labourers available for hire here at the Grapes, and you should return to passage **449** immediately,

There are certainly men for hire here: a gang of ten can be hired for **9s** each for a day's work. If you choose to pay the **£4 10s** in total, you can send them to your workshop in Millwall (ticking the box marked ☐ Casual Labourers in passage **1308**).

Return to the parlour... **449**

❧ 966 ❧

The damage to your craft is significant: remove one customisation from your **Adventure Sheet**. If you do not have any customisations, turn to **954** immediately.

Sail on downstream... **988**

❧ 967 ❧

With the beefeater helpless on the floor, you are able to take the **Tower Key** from his waist and let yourselves into the jewel chamber.

There a sight indeed greets you. An iron cabinet holds several crowns, each studded with diamond, sapphire, spinel and ruby. On another wall hang four jewel-encrusted swords. The orb of state glitters by gaslight on a velvet cushion, looking for all the world like a decorated grapefruit. Silver plate is stacked at one side.

Diana Derwent grins, extends her arms and spins around, taking it all in. "Here we are!" she whispers. "Now, where are those pretties?" She avoids the cabinet holding the crowns and opens a small chest standing in an alcove. "Here we are..."

From inside, she lifts a beautiful set of amethyst and emerald earrings, set in silver or some similar metal. She takes several small rings, a gold chain, several diamond brooches and other pieces you cannot see, slipping them all into velvet bags beneath her cloak. "And what have you come for?" she asks.

The value of the gems, the gold and the workmanship in this small room is impossible to count. You cannot carry a tenth of it away with you, and even if you did, how would you find a way to turn it into credit or cash? Without discreet - and utterly amoral - contacts in the world of gems, you can do nothing with these incredible treasure but find a way to melt the gold out of them and sell the stones piece by piece. It would pay for a lifetime's rich living, but it would also be a lifetime's work.

You may take any three of the following: a **golden sceptre**, a **sword of state**, a **diamond crown**, a pair of **pearl armills**, a pair of **ruby-studded gauntlets**, a **sapphire coronet** and a **ceremonial mace**.

Make your exit... **978**

❧ 968 ❧

You have come to Limehouse reach. Your front fender thumps against discarded baulks of rotten timber, chunks of floating coal, bundles of grimy cloth and drowned rats. On the northern bank are the weed-strewn gates of the King's Canal.

Enter the canal... **(3s)**	**912**
Head upriver...	**1009**
Steam downriver around the Isle of Dogs...	**916**

❧ 969 ❧

The Ferguson bucks and swerves, its tyres slipping on the filthy cobbles, and you slam to the ground. The machine slides on and hits a wall ahead with a sickening crunch. Note that it is now **critically damaged**.

Before you can get up, the Constables surround you and slap heavy manacles onto your wrists. They haul you away.

Turn to...	**13**

❧ 970 ❧

There is always rubbish floating in the river, particularly near moorings. A slick of glistening oil has spread across the surface here, smearing everything it touches with a greasy sheen. Bobbing in the filth is an unopened **bottle of whisky**.

Steam through the slick...	**1069**

❧ 971 ❧

"Who do you think you are?" roars Jakes. "I'm Water Sergeant Jakes of His Imperial Majesty's Nethundical Corps and I ain't feared o' nobody!" He and his men toss you out of the pub and into the mud. Gain a **wound** from the hard landing and if you now have **five wounds**, turn to **999**.

Return to Deptford...	**816**

❧ 972 ❧

You have taken shelter in the tomb you have adopted in the heart of Abney Park. Here you can rest, although you cannot tend your wounds as there is no water supply nearby. Nonetheless, if you wish to leave or collect anything here, use the box below for your possessions.

Note **passage 972** before making your next choice.

Open a **strongbox**...	**331**
Repair your velosteam...	**1300**
Head on your way...	**1026**

❧ 973 ❧

You tear towards Bow, bursting through a small market and leaving the tables strewn across the road in your wake. Then Constables appear ahead of you, blocking the road. There is only one chance to get away: a cart and ramp offer you the chance of jumping their blockade. Make a MOTORING roll of difficulty 15, adding 3 if you have an **improved burner**!

Successful MOTORING roll!	**1031**
Failed MOTORING roll!	**969**

❧ 974 ❧

You ride your Ferguson right up into the porch of St Mary's, through the tall doors and into the nave. "Sanctuary!" you cry. "Sanctuary!"

To say that the vicar is shocked would be an understatement. He swoops down towards you, his cassock flapping. "Sanctuary? Whatever crime you may have committed, would you compound it by bringing your infernal machine into God's house?"

You may be able to convince this man to take your side: perhaps an offering to the church coffers will do the trick. Otherwise you will depend upon your INGENUITY to make some case.

Offer the priest money...	**998**
Try to appeal for mercy...	**1015**

❧ 975 ❧

□

If the box above is empty, tick it and read on. If it is already ticked, turn to **71** immediately.

"Congratulations," says the recruiter, rising and shaking your hand. "You are now one of us." Mark your **Adventure Sheet** to note that you are a **Member of the Compact for Workers' Equality**.

"There is much for us to do. Report to Comrade Tate at the Blackwall sugar warehouse. He will give you further instructions." Remove **passdisc 32** and gain **passdisc 820**.

Leave the hall...   71

❧ 976 ❧

Despite all her prowess, Lady Eliza Longlym had not the skill to defeat the Baronet Dressley. He showed no mercy, but crippled her with several nasty cuts to her knees: she will probably ride in a steam-propelled chair for the rest of her life. Note passage **1002** and turn to **850**, where you should correct the Parliamentary Swingometer **one point in the Establishment's favour**.

❧ 977 ❧

You set off on the westward loop of the King's Canal, past the new cemetery at All Souls, under a railway bridge, past the Black Horse and on and on and on, until the city smog is far behind. The boat beneath you chugs along steadily past Southall, past the creosote works, and then you turn west again and follow the channel down to Brentford. For once, the canal is quiet and you and your mate are able to rest on the journey, watching the crows fly over the autumn fields of stubble and waiting for the rain to return.

Steam on to Brentford...   952

❧ 978 ❧

Making your way out of the Tower may not be as straightforward as getting in. If you have **Mrs Roberts' face (excellent)**, turn to **989** immediately. If not, but you possess **Mrs Roberts' face**, turn to **997**. Otherwise, read on.

Carrying your loot as carefully and quietly as you can, you leave Martin Tower and look for a way out of the fortress.

Attempt to fly out... (**winged harness**)   1039
Climb down from the battlements... (**rope**)   1007

❧ 979 ❧

The river becomes steadily busier as you meander westwards. At Brentford Ait, scores of barges lie on the mud. You pass Chiswick, Hammersmith and Putney, each smokier and filthier than the last. As you pass Wandsworth, you steam into a curtain of drifting smog that lies across the river. "It's dead slow from here on in," says your mate. "I'll light the lanterns." To moor here, mark **moored at Battersea Bridge** on your **Adventure Sheet**.

Moor here...   1132
Sail upriver...   580
Sail downriver into the city...   922

❧ 980 ❧

"Quick!" yells your mate. Together you begin to heave cargo overboard to lighten your craft. Remove one **unit of cargo** from your adventure sheet. If your barge is empty, turn to **954** immediately.

Sail on downstream...   988

❧ 981 ❧

So you settle down and write, drawing on your memories of friends and acquaintances, as well as imagined outlandish circumstances to captivate a reader. A simple tale begins to develop into the story of several generations, of love, honour, inheritance and sorrow. Re-reading your own work, the characters begin to seem more alive to you than those distant friends you once counted in the world outside.

Crucially, although you have caught the dreaded and permanent writer's disease, you stave off madness. You also now have a complete **novel manuscript**.

Turn to...   398

❧ 982 ❧

There is a sudden, resounding clang as the bow of your barge strikes something low in the water. Froth and scum rushes around you and the tower of a nethundical steamer emerges from the water.

"Mind your way," yells a voice through some sort of mechanical amplifier. "And keep to the buoyed channel! Damage to His Majesty's nethundical craft is cause for prosecution!"

Your mate puts the engine into reverse and you proceed along the river most cautiously.

Turn to...   1069

❦ 983 ❧

"What must I do?" you ask.

"The Telegraph Guild are the tool of the oppressive classes," says the recruiter. "Their communications allow the Constables to move against us. When the time comes, we will strike against them with our full force, but for now, we need information. Get hold of a **Telegraph Guild codebook** and bring it to me, here."

"How will I find that?"

"Come, are you so coy? I can suggest infiltrating their organisation - or perhaps a little burglary - but I am sure you are no stranger to desperate deals like this."

Leave the hall...   **71**

❦ 984 ❧

A circle are gossiping about the King's mistress, Maria Roberts. "She was an actress, you know? Caught the King's eye one night on stage... And that's how the world works. She has him round her little finger."

"That's right. She's got more influence than any elected politician in the land."

Another drinker snorts. "Elected politician? Elected by the two and a half voters in their crooked boroughs! A bunch of crooks."

"How do people meet her?" you ask.

"I heard she holds court aboard the *Gentilesse* - her boat on the Thames, moored down by Bargehouse Wharf. But it ain't just anybody gets an invite there: you need to be somebody or to know somebody."

"Letter of introduction would probably do it," mutters another. "As long as it were from some jakey noble."

"Oh, and then you 'as to bring 'er gold," says one more. "Or it won't swing your way."

"What a system! Now, who's for another pint?"

Finish your drink...   **noted passage**

❦ 985 ❧

You steam on into the falling dark of the evening, past Highbury corner and on towards the tenements and workshops of Stoke Newington. There is a place there where you might be able to hide.

Abney Park Cemetery is still largely waiting for occupants, but the grandiose tombs and the countless memorials scattered without plan make it a place of sombre confusion. Young trees are allowed to grow amongst the graves and it is almost a maze of gloomy, green shadows and concrete angels. If you have the codeword *Concrete*, turn to **972** immediately. Otherwise, you must make an INGENUITY roll of difficulty 13 to hide yourself and your machine in the confusion, adding 2 if your velosteam is customised with a **muffled exhaust**. If you fail, the Constables will track you for sure.

Successful INGENUITY roll!	**1005**
Failed INGENUITY roll!	**1010**

✎ 986 ✐

Does it gratify you to hear that, with your help, Lady Longlym defeats the Baronet and sends him to his final judgement? You also learned from the experience: roll two dice, and if the total is greater than your unimproved NIMBLENESS score, increase it by 1. Gain the codeword *Caltrop*, note passage **1002** and turn to **850**, where you should correct the Parliamentary Swingometer **one point in the Progressives' favour**.

✎ 987 ✐

Here is the orphanage in its slate and brick splendour. The building itself is functional and plain, but the noise of children playing in the yard has a certain glory to it - when you consider that each one of those voices belongs to a child who might otherwise be abandoned, starving or dead in the street.

Reverend Highrun has appointed staff to run the place, who are desperately trying to keep some order among the boys and girls - who are meant to be separated. There is also training for the youngsters, in an attempt to help them support themselves honestly once they are too old for this place. In truth, their struggles have only just begun.

While you are here, you can have any **wounds** or illnesses treated without charge. Simply remove the illness (such as a **stiff back**) or replace a **wound** with a **scar**, rolling two dice and gaining an **intimidating scar (RUTH+1)** on a roll of 11 or 12.

If you have a workshop in Millwall, you can choose a promising young person to train as an apprentice: tick the box marked ☐ **Apprentice** in passage **1308**.

Leave the orphanage...	**471**

✎ 988 ✐

Now that the dangerous weir of London Bridge is behind you, you are truly in the heart of the maritime city. This part of the Thames is called the Pool of London, and on either side of the channel are moored tall iron ships with anchor-chains thicker than your entire body stretching down into the silt. Countless dock entrances gape on either side and you must steer carefully to make your way between the little craft and the occasional great ship that lumbers over the tide.

Steam to the gates of St Katharine's Docks...	**478**
Steam on to Limehouse...	**968**

✎ 989 ✐

Trusting in your excellent disguises, you and Diana return to the gatehouse, where you make sign that you wish to be let out. "Will your maj... your nobility desire anything else of us?" asks the gateman abjectly.

Trusting in silence, you shake your head, step over the sill and walk as calmly as you can to the waiting steam carriage.

Leave this place...	**1014**

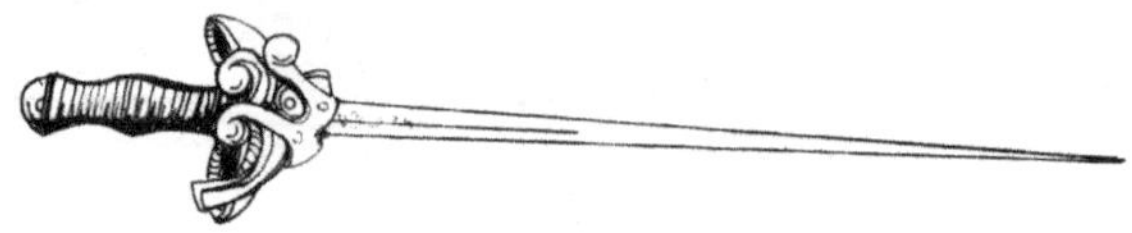

✎ 990 ✐

Your engine's chugging reverberates under the dark arches of Blackfriars Bridge and you steer between a pair of steam launches into the murky sunlight. A mist is rising on the river and swirls about the starlings and piers of London Bridge ahead. Viewed from the river, the ancient crossing seems even more ramshackle and mismatched than ever. The short spire of St Thomas' Chapel pokes up between the jettied houses like the stub of a finger on a damaged hand.

Passage beneath London Bridge is famously tricky. The narrowness of the arches creates a distinct difference in water level on either side, which the tide only exaggerates. You will have to be sure of your skill to steam through.

Pass under London Bridge...	**949**
Turn about and return upstream...	**922**
Moor beneath the bridge...	**939**

❧ 991 ❧

You have to slow your velosteam approaching the market to attract less attention. It is crowded with cityfolk, buying, haggling, delivering, carrying and calling. If you have a set of **dungarees**, turn to **1018** immediately. Otherwise you must weave into the crowd and do your best to hide. Make an INGENUITY roll of difficulty 12.

Successful INGENUITY roll!	**352**
Failed INGENUITY roll!	**1010**

❧ 992 ❧

By the time the river has come around to the east of the Isle of Dogs, it carries all the flotsam and junk of the city. You steam on through the murk, lanterns lit, listening eagerly for echoes and sound of other craft. Roll a dice to see what you encounter:

Score 1-2	A firm bump...	**982**
Score 3-4	Nothing of note...	**1069**
Score 5-6	A spillage...	**970**

❧ 993 ❧

You continue on the slow loop round towards Camden. Your mate comes over. "Best we tie up soon. Night falls quick with all this smog, as I don't want to sail smack into an iron barge."

Roll a dice to see what happens in the night.

Score 1-2	An opportunity...	**1156**
Score 3-4	A good night's sleep afloat...	**945**
Score 5-6	Flat Billy's men...	**1171**

❧ 994 ❧

After many months of thinking, distilling and reducing your ideas and convictions, reflecting on the failures of the past and present systems, you produce a slim sheaf of papers: your **manifesto manuscript**. Titles are hard to come by - particularly finding a phrase that will do justice to the universal upheaval recommended by your treatise - but the words that seem to stick to this one are *Power and Possession*.

At least it has kept you busy. Whether anyone reads it, or whether it will make any difference at all... You will have to see. Perhaps a publisher on Ludgate Hill will set the thing in type and send it out to change the world for you.

Wait out the remainder of your sentence...   **398**

❧ 995 ❧

You judder over tram-tracks and charge up the Bow Road. If you can stay ahead of your pursuers, you might manage to make it out into Essex - unless you have a hideaway somewhere closer at hand.

Head for Bow Bridge...	**1031**
Make for the Gun at Blackwall...	**1012**

❧ 996 ❧

If you have blueprints, designs or prototypes to sell to the Guild, then this is where to do it. Who knows what the result of passing such things onto the Telegraphers will be: they already have a monopoly on much of the technology of the age.

Tools and Designs	To buy	To sell
blueprints	-	**£3**
assembly line plan	-	**£8**
automatic cargo selector design	-	**£20**
mechanical elephant design	-	**£6**
airship buoyancy calculation	-	**£8**
improved bridge design	-	**£12**
calculated patterns	-	**£6**
auto-rifle prototype	-	**£25**

Return to the compound...   **878**

❧ 997 ❧

You return the way you came, but a warden catching sight of you passing beneath a gas lantern sees something he doesn't like. He calls after you. You turn in your tracks and summon your most threatening demeanour. Make a RUTHLESSNESS roll of difficulty 13. For this roll, you may not add the effect of any **intimidating scars**, since your face is entirely hidden.

Successful RUTHLESSNESS roll!	**1034**
Failed RUTHLESSNESS roll!	**1024**

❧ 998 ❧

You take out your purse and begin to count out coins, but the priest dashes you across the face. "You dare try to buy your way into this house? God's mercy is not for sale! Just and righteous is he!" The priest grasps you by your coat as the Constables pour into the church and surround you. "Take this pitiful creature away," he bids them, "Somewhere he can learn about punishment and mercy."

Turn to...   **13**

❧ 999 ❧

You are overcome by the loss of blood and collapse, unconscious, where you are. Is this the end of your adventures?

To escape being robbed, stripped and thrown in a ditch, you will need powerful - or faithful - friends here in the city. Cross an option after taking one - each can only be chosen once.

✠ If you are the **Friend of Laycock...**   1046
✠ If you are the **Friend of the
    Waterside Boys**...   1063
✠ If you are the **Friend of Lady
    Derwent...**   1080
Otherwise, turn to the **epilogue**...

❧ 1000 ❧

There is nowhere like London Bridge. The old medieval structure, with its mismatched arches and narrow roadway, has been built upon with every successive generation of Londoners, until it has become its own little world. Shops face onto the roadway on either side, their boards hanging out and displaying trinkets, greengrocery, fish, mechanisms and second-hand clothing. People are everywhere, bustling backwards and forwards, inbetween the crawling steam engines trying to make it across the river. The bridge is so narrow that a one-way system is enforced, with an hourly change, and you can clearly see how decisive men have been able to raise money for the Thames Tunnel, a quarter-mile downriver.

Halfway along the bridge stands the Chapel of St Thomas, a relic of the ancient pilgrim route to Canterbury. Parts of the stonework are crumbling, but

a steady stream of people traipse inside and over the black and white marble floor.

St Thomas' Chapel...	1038
Pick some pockets in the crowd...	1020
Go aboard your boat...	
(moored below London Bridge)...	990
Head north...	208
Head south...	631

❧ 1001 ❧

If the Thames is filthy, then the Lea is little more than a stream of chemical pollution and raw sewage. The river has a purple tinge from coke-burning waste yet, the local children pick about in the mud, collecting coals, scraps of rope and hanks of cotton, basketing them up to sell.

If you wish to moor here, mark **moored at** **Three Mill Wharf** on your **Adventure Sheet**.

	To buy	To sell
Charcoal	£18	£16
Furniture	-	-
Machinery	-	£32
Pottery	£20	£18
Cotton	-	£3
Woollen Cloth	£10	£8
Coal	£11	£9
Beer	£21	£20
Wheat	£3	£2
Malt	£9	£8
Frozen Meat	-	-
Ice	-	-

| Moor here... | 487 |
| Steam back to the Thames... | 1069 |

❧ 1002 ❧

If you have the codeword *Converse*, turn to **1017** immediately. Otherwise, read on.

"Well," says Mr Wright, "I suppose you have done your best. I cannot hide my disappointment, however. The Establishment are still in the majority and we have lost some of our staunchest allies. We shall have to look for other ways to redress the situation."

If you wish to continue helping the Wheatears seeking their democratic solution to these injustices, you will have to look out for other ways to influence the situation in Parliament. Otherwise, there may be no way forward besides bloody revolution. However, the rent has been paid on St Eanswythe Hall for some time, and they are happy to let you continue to use it to teach swordsmanship.

Turn to...   **760**

❧ 1003 ❧

To train your assistants you must have someone in your employ, as well as an ENGINEERING skill higher than theirs. You can only do this if you have **Apprentice** or **Journeyman** ticked in passage **1308**.

To hire an apprentice, you must find someone at a local pub or hiring fair who wishes to work for you.

To train an apprentice to become a journeyman, you need an ENGINEERING skill of 9 and **£20** to pay for tools and training from other local craftsmen. If you do so, you should remove the tick from the box marked Apprentice and tick Journeyman. (You may now hire another apprentice, if you know where to find one.)

To improve a journeyman to a master, you require an ENGINEERING skill of 12, a **pneumatic manual**, and **£20.** If you can do so, you should remove the tick from the box marked Journeyman and tick the one marked Master Engineer. You now have a reliable employee to manage the workshop for you.

You can only have one **Apprentice**, one **Journeyman** and one **Master Engineer** at a time working in your workshop: a maximum of three permanent employees.

Return to the workshop...   **1308**
Leave the workshop...   **431**

❧ 1004 ❧

A garrulous sky-sailor wants to tell you all about Captain Coke, the famed sky-pirate. "He flies a blue airship and strikes fear into the hearts of the Atmospheric Union. Like the Steam Highwayman of the sky!"

"Is that so?"

"It is, it is. But he's bloodthirstier, so he is. And I'll tell you what few know: he has a base in Great Wood, between Stonor and Turville, over north of Henley."

Turn to...   **noted passage**

❧ 1005 ❧

You find a grand family tomb with an easily forced door and ride your Ferguson inside. Pulling the door closed after you, you realise that this will make an ideal hideout. It is dry, roomy and utterly secret. And if coffins and cadavers scared you, then you would hardly be that ruthless road rebel, the Steam Highwayman.

The Constables only make a cursory search of the graveyard. After all, night is falling, and they may well be satisfied to have chased you off. You settle down for a night's rest on the marble floor. Gain the codeword *Concrete*.

Turn to...   **972**

❧ 1006 ❧

You steam over a swing-bridge and pause on the dockside. If you dismounted and handled the bridge-engine, you could cut off your pursuers.

If you have a **skeleton key** to unlock the controls, turn to **1027** immediately. Otherwise, make an ENGINEERING roll of difficulty 11.

Successful ENGINEERING roll!   **1027**
Failed ENGINEERING roll!   **1074**

❧ 1007 ❧

Together you and Diana rush to find a place you can climb down into the moat. You tie the rope around a handy stanchion (remove it from your **possessions**) and follow her down.

Only when your feet touch the ground do you recall that the lions live in the moat. They are easily disturbed: two have awoken and are padding towards you.

If you have any levels of **animal friendship**, turn to **1032** immediately. Otherwise, read on.

The two creatures are territorial, disturbed, and angry. You have no choice but to fight them, using whatever weaponry you might have to hand.

Lions	Weapons: **claws (PAR 0)**
Parry:	12
Nimbleness:	12
Toughness:	4

Victory!	**1126**
Defeat!	**113**

❧ 1008 ☙

A massive crunch tells you that your steering is off: you have struck one of the piers that support the bridge. Roll a dice to see how bad the damage is.

Score 1-2	Your boat is sinking...	**954**
Score 3-4	Severe damage...	**966**
Score 5-6	Too heavy...	**980**

❧ 1009 ☙

You are sailing through the Pool of London. On either bank stand a continuous wall of private wharves, each with seafaring or river craft loading and unloading, including St Katharine's Docks on the north bank. The beak-like jibs of steamcranes jut out over the decks of colliers and wool-lighters.

To pass through London Bridge, you must either wait for the tide to turn or pay for a place on the Bamford Chain, which hauls craft through one of the wider arches on a continuous loop. If you have a cargo of **ballast stones**, turn to **1284** immediately.

Approach St Katharine's Docks...	**478**
Pay for passage... (**6s**)	**1332**
Wait for the tide...	**1340**

❧ 1010 ☙

Despite all your tricks, your powerful machine and your desperate riding, the Constables have you surrounded. You have no choice but to surrender.

Turn to...	**13**

❧ 1011 ☙

"I knew I could rely on you," says Lady Derwent.

It will not be a simple exercise to fly the wings with a passenger: you will have to practice by night - and discreetly! Make an INGENUITY roll of difficulty 15, adding 3 if you possess a **velosteamer's helmet** and 1 if you own **goggles**.

Successful INGENUITY roll!	**1028**
Failed INGENUITY roll!	**1048**

❧ 1012 ☙

You can reach the Gun without too much difficulty, but to reach it and lose your pursuers is another matter. Make a MOTORING roll of difficulty 17, adding 2 if you possess a **muffled exhaust** and 1 for each possession you discard on the road.

Successful MOTORING roll!	**469**
Failed MOTORING roll!	**1500**

❧ 1013 ☙

The Coal Board are secretly working to disrupt the Telegraph Guild's dominance, you hear, even going to so far as to reward sabotage and arson with cold cash. "Them towers that went down in Kent last month, that weren't no accident. The Board put Jack Kettey's gang up to it," you are told.

"And what are the Guild doing about it?" you ask.

"Oh, just about as much. I've heard that anyone who disrupts a Coal Board delivery can claim a bounty at the Telegraph Guild compound up in Bloomsbury."

Turn to...	**noted passage**

❧ 1014 ☙

It would have never made sense to return to Derwent House, so you hide away in a small house near Hatfield that Lady Diana owns. There you remove all the paraphernalia of the job and proceed to celebrate the robbery. Gain the codeword *Crisp* and add **Stole the Crown Jewels** to your Great Deeds. You can also add 1 to an attribute score of your choice.

"What are you going to do with your share?" you ask the lady.

"Why, wear them, of course. That's partly why I chose these things. Not only are they glamorous, but only a few people would be able to identify them as belonging to the royal collection. But not around here. I'll be off on my tour before very long." She leans back in the bubbles of her bath. "I don't envy you trying to get any sort of profit out of those dreadful chunks of rock. Do you want my advice?"

"Go on."

"The gold can be melted down. Any halfway reliable blacksmith would do it. But the gems are another matter. Maybe the Brethren would handle some of them. Or you could take them abroad... Or to someone in the North?"

What will you do with these ungainly prizes? Their value is huge - but hard to access. Maybe Diana is right and melting them down is the simplest and safest option. You hardly have a kingdom of your own to rule with them. Few banks will hide them for you: you will have to keep them somewhere safe until you make a decision.

Leave directly...   **1043**
Sleep on it...   **1029**

❧ 1015 ❧

To convince the priest you must speak quickly: the Constables will soon be at the church doors. Make an INGENUITY roll of difficulty 12, adding 2 if you have a **Bible** of any kind about you.

Successful INGENUITY roll!   **1053**
Failed INGENUITY roll!   **1036**

❧ 1016 ❧

The Guild have heard that you frequent this place and have despatched several enforcers to try and capture you. They get up from their seats, holding clubs and knives, and the other patrons scatter.

Enforcers   Weapons: **clubs (PAR 2)**
Parry: 8
Nimbleness: 6
Toughness: 4

Victory!   **144**
Defeat!   **1078**

❧ 1017 ❧

The three Members come and meet you at the fencing hall. They are over-joyed.

"Well done indeed," says Mr Wright. "Our highest hopes have been satisfied."

"We may be able to avoid a blasted revolt after all," says Wheelhouse.

"Indeed," agrees Hurtbridge. "We put forward our Reform Bill imminently. With Maria Roberts' influence on the King, we will all be sitting in new constituencies within a few months."

The gentlemen are happy for you to continue using St Eanswythe's Hall: you can return to it from the lanes of Westminster at any time by adding **21** to the passage number in which you find the phrase 'slime-filled gutters'. They also arrange for you to receive some form of clemency: you can remove a single **Wanted Status** from your **Adventure Sheet**. Finally, Mr Wheelhouse takes out a fine **stossdegen (PAR 5)** and hands it to you. "I won't be needing this," he says. "Was terrified one of those chaps was going to call me out next!"

Remain in the hall...   **760**
Head out into Westminster...   **721**

❧ 1018 ❧

Your dungarees allow you to quickly meld in with the crowd of coster-mongers and porters. Leaving your velosteam parked behind a tower of crated cabbages and grabbing a tray of apples for your head, you are treated to the sight of three Constables on Imperial velosteams doing their best to beat their way through a busy and indignant market crowd. They soon give up.

Turn to...   **352**

❧ 1019 ❧

A smiling but dirty-faced man comes over to his friend at the next table. "I got the meat, Jerry," he says. "Last night at St Swithin's. Where to?"

"College o' Surgeons," replies his friend. "Bloomsbury. Them gennelmen pay good rates. Or you could even carry 'em over to Chelsea. Back of HMS Spartan."

If you want to ask the men about their occupation, you will need to win their trust. To do this, make a GALLANTRY roll of difficulty 10, adding 1 if you are **Wanted by the Constables** and 1 if you decide to spend **10s** on beer for them.

Successful GALLANTRY roll!   **1116**
Failed GALLANTRY roll or
   did not attempt...   **noted passage**

❧ 1020 ❧

In crowds like these, purses and pockets are close enough. The real skill will be in breaking through the crowd and getting away! Make a NIMBLENESS roll to see what you manage to lift.

Score 2-8   an empty moneybag...
Score 9-12 a few coins: **13s**...
Score 13-15 a wallet containing **£1 8s**...
Score 16+   a **golden bracelet** and a **silk scarf**...

Slip away...   1042

❧ 1021 ❧

"Ooh, it's like a treasure 'unt," says little Mackie excitedly. "What are we a-looking for?" After choosing any of these, cross out the option: you can only choose each item once.

✠ "A special sword."   (*Chaldean*)   1035
✠ "A book called Jensen's Statement."   1344
✠ "A set of mechanical wings."   840
Nothing else...   252

❧ 1022 ❧

You are a short distance from the village of Southall on the road to London. Much of the village's population work in the many-chimnied brickworks, but it is also an important stopping place for hauliers and travellers.

Prepare an ambush here...   1041
Ride east towards the city...   1258
Head west...   *Smog and Ambuscade 218*

❧ 1023 ❧

With the Tower Guards out of the way, you grab Marshal and begin to strap him into the harness beneath you. "You should ask permission before touching me, you know," he says.

"Where exactly are you King of?"

"High King of Sand Bank."

"Never heard of it. Or you. Until your letter."

Before Marshal has his chance to reply, you are off again, flapping hard and lifting, much more clumsily now, into the night sky. He begins to shake and moan. "I can't stand heights," he explains.

You set him down in an alleyway in the dock districts. He falls to the ground in abject relief, then seems to gather his sense of dignity and pulls himself together.

"I shall make you Duke of Sand Bank," he says, grandly.

"I would rather be paid."

He scratches his head. "You can have hundreds of Sand Bank Guineas! No? Alright. Let me give you these." He writes you a **Letter of Introduction** - whom it will impress is a question indeed - and hands you a **gold ring**.

If the King's wealth is little more than illusion, then the experience has taught you something - and you still possess the wings. Roll a dice and add three: if the total is higher than your INGENUITY, increase it by 1. You may add the title **Duke of Sand** Bank to your titles and aliases, if you like. You are also **Wanted by the Constables**, of course.

"I will make my own way back to my kingdom from here," says the King. "Farewell, noble rogue."

He slips away into the alleys and streets. Lank-haired and dressed in rags, he will excite nobody's interest in the east of the city.

Head to Millwall...   431

❧ 1024 ❧

The warden is not fooled. "You ain't the King," he cries. "Alarm! Intruders! Thieves!"

Guards pour out of the gatehouse and surround you. Lady Diana is dragged away before you can say a word. You are pinioned and heavy manacles are slammed onto your wrists and ankles.

Turn to...   1500

❧ 1025 ❧

It only takes a moment to clamber up onto the oak that reaches over the highway. You knot your rope firmly and time your leap. Make a NIMBLENESS roll of difficulty 12, adding 2 if you possess a **grappling iron**.

Successful NIMBLENESS roll!   1250
Failed NIMBLENESS roll!   1049

❧ 1026 ❧

You roll out from between the Egyptian-styled gateway of Abney Park and turn onto Stoke Newington road. Mist swirls across the cold cobbles beneath your tyres. Which way will you steer?

To Islington...   151
To Shoreditch...   308

❧ 1027 ❧

You manage to get the swing bridge turning, just as your pursuers appear at the other side of the dock. A shout tells you that the dockers have seen you, and you are quickly riding down to Millwall, where a ferry can take you across to Greenwich.

Ride away...   **431**

❧ 1028 ❧

It takes more than a dozen test flights before you feel fully in control of the wings, but with each launch and landing, you gain confidence and precision. Lady Derwent loves the sensation of swooping to and fro in the night sky, slung beneath the arching mechanisms. "This is even more fun than I expected," she says.

Proceed with the plan...   **1059**

❧ 1029 ❧

When you awake, the house is quiet. It is late in the next day and your calls bring no servants, awaken no Diana. Could she...?

Yes. A quick search of your belongings confirms it. She has taken everything you stole from the Tower and left. In its place is a letter and a burnt rose.

My dear friend,

How I enjoyed our adventure - and how desperately I appreciate your kind help. I might have succeeded without you, but your company has been quite a diversion.

Morocco awaits - and Constantinople - and Damascus. I shall think of you often, and perhaps send you a little telegraph when it seems prudent.

No-one can call me completely heartless. You seemed so glum last night - so unable to think your way out of this new fix of wealth. Let me tell you, there are ways to amuse oneself, but buying and selling dreary little blue stones is barely part of it. So I thought I'd do you a favour directly. Don't spend it all at once.

You are now the **Friend of Diana Derwent**. Add **five hundred guineas in banknotes** to your **possessions** and remove anything you took from the Tower.

Return to London...   **49**

❧ 1030 ❧

The lady is none other than Lady Serene. She smiles as she steps through the door. "So you've set yourself up in business? I thought you were going to come and visit me at Derwent House? Or have you thought better of it?"

"You don't want a fencing lesson?" you call, as she backs out of the door.

"Fencing lessons? You are wasting your time, Highwayman!"

Follow her to her mansion...   **1504**
Remain at St Eanswythe's Hall...   **760**

❧ 1031 ❧

With the long stretch of the road out to Essex ahead of you, this is your chance to use your Ferguson's speed to escape. You open the regulator, crank up the burner and accelerate. You must put a good distance between yourself and your pursuers, and that means taking every risk and shortcut you can. Make a MOTORING roll of difficulty 18, adding 1 if you have **off-road tyres**, 2 if you have an **improved burner** and 2 if you have a **gas pressuriser**.

Successful MOTORING roll!   **464**
Failed MOTORING roll!   **969**

❧ 1032 ❧

You stop and look the lead lion in the eye, and then slowly crouch to its level. It pauses, then continues to pad forwards. Diana shrinks backwards.

"Stand still," you say. "Trust me."

The lion approaches, sniffs you cautiously, and then puts its nose to your hand.

"Good lion. Nice lion. Would you like a tickle?" The hair beneath the mighty beast's neck is stiff, but like any cat, it loves to play.

"Come on," hisses Diana. You sidle to the outer wall of the moat and boost her up, then take her hand and clamber out.

Lady Diana is, for once, struck dumb in amazement. You sneak around to where your hired carriage is waiting and climb aboard.

Steam off...   **1014**

❧ 1033 ❧

At Camden the King's Canal is squeezed tightly between breweries, factories, road bridges and the swelling freight yard. Two locks guard the main quay area, where a gang of dedicated freightmen own the right to unload any cargo.

	To buy	To sell
Charcoal	-	£24
Furniture	-	£30
Machinery	£20	-
Pottery	£25	£21
Cotton	-	£2
Woollen Cloth	-	£14
Coal	£7	£5
Beer	£19	£15
Wheat	-	£8
Malt	-	£10
Frozen Meat	-	£14
Ice	£10	£8

If you wish to purchase **Ice**, you will need a **Perkins Machine**. If you wish to moor here, write **moored at Camden** on your **Adventure Sheet** and turn to **27** immediately.

Steam west along the canal...	(**1s**)	**956**
Steam east along the canal...	(**1s**)	**962**

❧ 1034 ❧

"Who under heaven do you think you are?" you bellow. "Get back to your post, man!"

With the guard successfully intimidated by, he believes, an angry King, you and Lady Diana hasten away as swiftly as you can, leaving through the postern gate held open by an obsequious helper. Once aboard the steamer, you take the controls yourself and head out of the metropolis as swiftly as you can.

Steam away...   **1014**

❧ 1035 ❧

You carefully describe Prishaw's sword and the boys set off. If anyone can find a trace of a special weapon, these boys can. They disperse into the alleyways, seeking out the rogues, the pawnbrokers, eavesdropping and feigning innocent, and return that evening with the faintest whiff of a lead.

"Gill says that he heard some folks in Limehouse were talking about some sword," explains Jerry. "Now, we could follow it up a little more, but we'd need a little coin, so's we could spread it about."

"And so we 'as sausages tomorra!" pipes a youngster.

"I'll find it myself, now."	**273**
"Go and get me that blade, boys." (**15s**)	**235**

❧ 1036 ❧

You only manage to string some desperate and wild pleas together: the priest is far from impressed. When the Constables arrive, he welcomes them in and even helps them fit the manacles on your wrists.

Turn to...   **13**

❧ 1037 ❧

You settle down to the card table. Hendon calls for sandwiches and beer and the game begins. Make an INGENUITY roll of difficulty 18.

Successful INGENUITY roll!	**885**
Failed INGENUITY roll!	**1502**

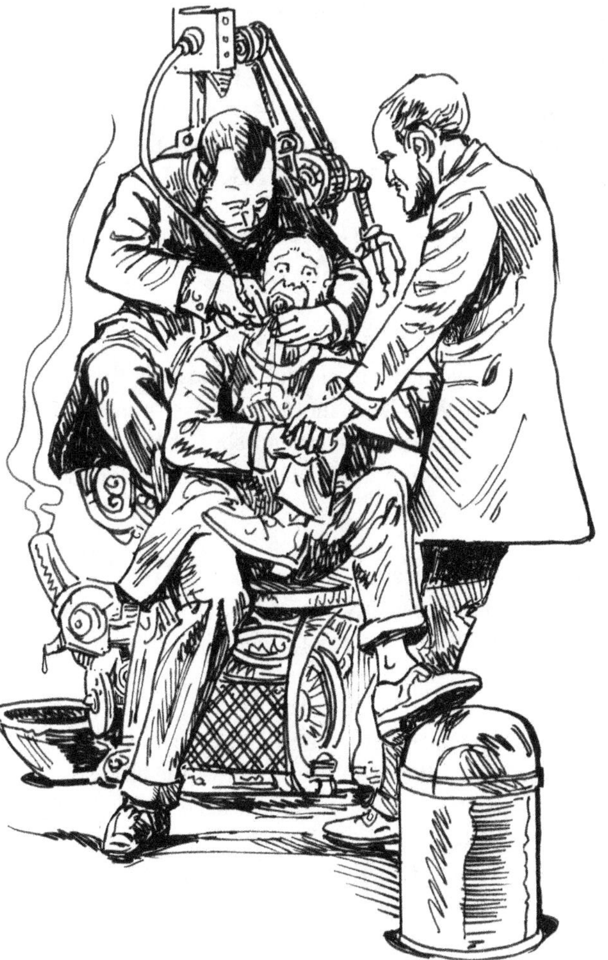

❧ 1038 ❧

St Thomas' Chapel seems to hang onto London Bridge like a birdhouse. A crypt of broad stone columns holds the building up at the level of the street, where an ancient paving of black and white marble flags welcomes the traveller. The Brethren of the Bridge minister to travellers here, as they have done for centuries, showing their store of relics, offering worship and prayer.

Look for something to steal...	**1114**
Return to the bridge...	**1000**

❧ 1039 ❧

The roof of the Martin Tower is not high, so it will take all your skill to gain height and get away back across the river. You are also carrying more weight, of course, but that was practised and part of your plan. The velvet bag is reassuring by its weight.

Lady Diana straps in beneath you and you launch yourselves off the wall just as shouts go up and the Tower Guard come pouring out of the guardhouse. Someone has spotted you! The great leather and silk wings flap once, twice, and you have gained height, twirling and circling in the night, turning south over the Thames. Now is the time to see whether your handling of the delicate, though powerful, mechanisms is up to scratch. Make an ENGINEERING roll of difficulty 15.

Successful ENGINEERING roll!	**1154**
Failed ENGINEERING roll!	**1136**

❧ 1040 ❧

You ready your weapon and prepare to fire at the approaching vehicle. A shot at the driver may bring the carriage to a halt, but a careful shot at the machinery may do the same without risking hurt. Make an ACCURACY roll.

Score 2-12 A miss!	**1357**
Score 13-14 Hit the driver!	**1397**
Score 15+ Rupture a pipe!	**1279**

❧ 1041 ❧

You ready yourself to rob whatever comes this way. This is one of the main routes out of the city, so there will be plenty of traffic. Note passage **779** and if you have a **telescope** or **binoculars**, turn to **1051** immediately. Otherwise, roll a dice to see what approaches:

Score 1	A private steam carriage...	**1391**
Score 2	The Coal Board...	**1301**
Score 3	The Telegraph Guild...	**1411**
Score 4	The Atmospheric Union...	**1456**
Score 5	The Haulage Guild...	**1444**
Score 6	An independent haulier...	**1450**

❧ 1042 ❧

A cry goes up: you have been noticed! You take advantage of a momentary gap in the crowd to power your velosteam towards the end of the bridge. Which way will you ride?

To the north end of the bridge...	**278**
To the south end of the bridge...	**614**

❧ 1043 ❧

As you mount your velosteam to return to the city, Lady Diana comes to wave you off. "I'm sure our paths will cross again," she calls. "Maybe Madrid... Damascus?" You are now the **Friend of Diana Derwent**.

Ride away...	**49**

❧ 1044 ❧

Your defeat at the table is not the end of the violence tonight at the Flask. Your opponent's vigour sends you tumbling and you knock a man's pint from his hand. He turns, but instead of seeing you, finds himself face to face with one of the ruffians, and makes a wild swing.

In a few moments, the entire bar erupts into a brawl. Glasses are thrown or smashed over heads, chairs are lifted by their legs and any minute the barkeep is bound to go for his fowling piece. It is clearly time to put some distance between you and this place.

Crawl out of the pub...	**28**

❧ 1045 ❧

The airship captain is bested. He lies bleeding onto his white jacket. You can take his **sabre (PAR 3)**, his **airship officer's cap**, a **fur collar**, **ten guineas in banknotes** and a **Union airship registry**.

Blow up the carriage...	**(explosives)**	**1127**
Ride away...		**noted passage**

❧ 1046 ❧

News reaches Laycock of your situation. For a dairyman, he has an excellent network of informers. He sends out some of his staff, who bring you back to his lairs on a stretcher borne by two jersey cows, while two others tow your velosteam.

"You poor blighter," he says. "That's what you get for standing up to the man. Let me see what can be done."

Laycock is skilled in tending his beasts, and the same gentleness and care help him to get you back on your feet. Replace any **wounds** with **scars**. However, you are not in the same shape as you once were: reduce your NIMBLENESS by 1.

It may be time for you to leave this dangerous life: total the number of **scars** that you now bear. If the total is **30 or more**, you must retire from your adventure and turn to the **epilogue** immediately. If you have fewer than **30 scars**, you can set out once more.

Turn to...   **151**

❧ 1047 ❧

A crowd this busy and distracted may well prove a fertile field for fleet fingers. Make a NIMBLENESS roll to see what you grab.

Score 2-6   Only a few shillings: **4s...**
Score 7-8   Seen and reported! Turn to **770**..
Score 9-10   A **pocket watch** and **10s**...
Score 11-12 Seen and recognised: you are now **Wanted by the Constables**. Turn to **770**...
Score 13-14 A **silver necklace** and **£2 2s**...
Score 15+   Grabbed by the Constables. Turn to **13**.

If you manage to get away with your theft, you had better mount your velosteam and get away before anyone notices what they are missing.

Ride off...   **730**

❧ 1048 ❧

A catastrophic plunge from the sky causes you a significant setback. The broken leg heals, as do the abrasions and burns, but you must reduce your NIMBLENESS by 1, as well as gaining a **scar**.

Eventually, you get the winged harness working.

Continue with the plan...   **1059**

❧ 1049 ❧

You swing down through the carriage's steam, but although your boots scrape the roof of the vehicle, you lose your footing and tumble from the rear. You hit the ground with a hearty thump and roll into a puddle. The driver, meanwhile, opens the regulator and forges ahead with a shout. Roll a dice to see if you are injured.

Score 1-3   Only bruises...
Score 4-5   A **sore back (NIM-2)**...
Score 6   A **wound**...

If you now have **five wounds**, turn to **999** immediately. Otherwise, turn to your **noted passage**.

❧ 1050 ❧

The unloading work is slow and tiresome. It takes the greater portion of the day and leaves you aching. Roll a dice to see how you are rewarded:

Score 1   Gain **2s** from a miserly overseer
Score 2-4   Gain **4s**
Score 5-6   Gain **4s** and a **stiff back (NIM-2)**

Return to the yard...   **878**

❧ 1051 ❧

Taking up position overlooking the road, you peer through your lenses and scan the road for a likely-looking target. Who will you choose for your next victim?

A private steam carriage...	**1391**
The Coal Board...	**1301**
The Telegraph Guild...	**1411**
The Atmospheric Union...	**1456**
The Haulage Guild...	**1444**
An independent haulier...	**1450**

❧ 1052 ❧

The princess smiles as she recognises you. "Oh, hello again." She looks around. "Were you about to rob me? How dastardly. Are you in need of money?" She gives you two guineas (**£2 2s**) from her purse out of pity.

Ride away...   **noted passage**

❧ 1053 ❧

"Give me a chance to show you my character, Reverend," you beg. "I would not call for God's protection if I did not hope in it."

The vicar narrows his eyes, then swings into action. He calls a verger and together they slam the doors shut and bar them with a heavy beam. A few moments later, the heavy hands of the Constables begin beating upon them.

"I cannot resist these pursuers long," says the vicar, "But if you are sincere, then you will follow my instructions. We will hide that machine of yours beneath the organ, which is being repaired. Then you will need to change into a surplice."

The vicar's scheme begins simply enough, but if you thought it was only a matter of him hiding you for a few hours until the Constables grew tired of the chase, then you were entirely wrong. He seems intent upon nothing less than your entire spiritual reformation, however long it takes. He casts you in the role of a new ordinand, explains away the locked doors to the Constables, chains up your velosteam and insists that you stay with him in the vicarage for a while. Unable to get your hands back on your machine and possessions, which are carefully locked away, you must acquiesce.

For more than a week, he teases information out of you, prying and asking and trying to pin you down. It is a fruitless task, however, as late one night, you break into his study, take his keys and regain your machine and your possessions. Leaving the surplice and a note of thanks, you climb back into your saddle and ride away.

Turn to...   **50**

❧ 1054 ❧

Your first shot ricochets off the engine's body work and hits the brass bell hanging beside the driver. That certainly gets the driver's attention. For your next, you aim at an exposed water pipe. Make an ACCURACY roll of difficulty 11.

Successful ACCURACY roll!   **1295**
Failed ACCURACY roll!   **1357**

❧ 1055 ❧

The regulation bill passes narrowly. Mr Wright is very pleased. "Your vote was crucial! With a victory like this, we increase our support in the house significantly, as well as limiting those Union dogs. I rather think a victory feast is in order."

Gain the codeword *Catiline*, note passage **797** and turn to passage **850**, where you should adjust the parliamentary swingometer **one point in the Progressives' favour**.

❧ 1056 ❧

"Halt your engine!" you cry, readying your weapons and drawing yourself up to your full height.

"The Steam Highwayman!" comes a cry from the approaching engine. You have been recognised: whether you succeed or fail, you will now be **Wanted by the Haulage Guild**. Make a RUTHLESSNESS roll of difficulty 12, adding 1 if you possess a **double headlamp**.

Successful RUTHLESSNESS roll!   **1431**
Failed RUTHLESSNESS roll!   **1277**

❧ 1057 ❧

"Well, these components need to be at the Rotherhithe, Southwark and Bloomsbury towers as quickly as possible," replies the officer, handing you three paper-wrapped parcels. "Get there before night and you'll have your pay."

The **Rotherhithe package**, **Southwark package** and **Bloomsbury package** will need to delivered urgently. Count the number of passages you move through (following this one) as you race through the city. If it takes you too long, you will not be paid.

Set out...   **878**

❧ 1058 ❧

The ladies are on their way to catch the Edinburgh airship from Parliament Hill. "How tiresome," moans one. "I suppose we will have to pick up some more cash at the station." You can take **£13 4s**, a **parasol** and a **silver necklace** from them. You will also be **Wanted by the Constables**, unless you have a **mask**.

Ride away...   **noted passage**

❧ 1059 ❧

Diana has picked the night for your robbery. You check that the wings are ready one final time and cross to the southern side of the Thames, where you scale a high warehouse to use as a launching-point. The river is dark and unreflective below you, the sky clouded and weighty with imminent rain.

You and the lady strap yourselves in and, before you have a chance to breathe, she throws her weight forward and you plummet down from the roof together. Her thrilled laughter rings through the night.

The wings respond perfectly: you swoop upwards and gain height over the water, heading directly for the ramparts of the Tower. No-one is expecting an entry from the sky. You spiral downwards, losing height, and come to a stop with a lead roof beneath your feet.

"I liked it, Highwayman," says your conspirator. "Let's fly again sometime."

The **winged harness** is unpacked and folded up before you head off, following the lady's lead. She tiptoes along the ramparts to a small barred window. Through there, she insists, are the jewels themselves. To open the window, make an ENGINEERING roll of difficulty 15, adding 1 if you have some **wirecutters**, 2 if you possess a **crowbar** and 3 if you have a **steam fist** or **mechanical arm**.

Successful ENGINEERING roll!	**1208**
Failed ENGINEERING roll!	**1235**

❧ 1060 ❧

A group of tradespeople are discussing the work of the Compact for People's Equality. "They blew up a bridge in Essex last week," says one. "And been harrying the Telegraph Guild too."

"Mark my words," replies another, "The revolution is coming. They're preparing everywhere."

Turn to...	**noted passage**

❧ 1061 ❧

"We make them," replies Diana.

She has a workshop downstairs in her yard where she tinkers and invents, much as any technologically-minded independent woman does in this day and age. Her current prototypes are close to completion, but require a little more work. You are set to, fire-welding, tensioning springs and applying layer after layer of lacquer.

Before long, the **winged harness** is complete. In the process you have learnt a great deal: improve your ENGINEERING skill by 1.

Turn to...	**1011**

❧ 1062 ❧

Mr Laycock waves you into his stableyard. "'M busy right now," he says, "But refresh yourself here."

Laycock's men will provide you with bottles of **soothing lotion** for free (they have a store they use for their cows). They will also tend to any wounds you might have (remove any **wounds** and replace them with **scars**, checking for **intimidating scars (RUTH+1)** on a roll of 12 on two dice) and keep items safe here for you.

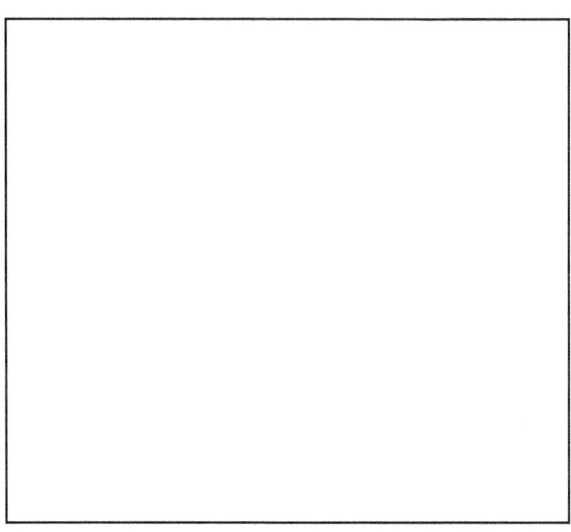

"Don't forget - I can always help you hiding from them Constables," says Mr Laycock as you set off.

Return to Islington...	**151**

❧ 1063 ❧

You come to on a dirty mattress in the Waterside Boys' attic. They have found you, broken and bleeding, and for the sake of past friendship, brought you here to recover.

Over the next weeks, they steal what you need to tend your **wounds** (replace them with **scars**, rolling two dice and replacing each with an **intimidating scar (RUTH+1)** on a score of 11 or 12) and locate your velosteam. They wheel it back to the alleyway by the stairs and cover it with a **tarpaulin**. Apart from this, all your **money** and **possessions** have disappeared. The boys are able to find you a rusty **sabre (PAR 3)**, but then you must depend on your own abilities.

Your confidence and your strength have taken some blows. Reduce each of your skills by 1. If you have **thirty scars** or more, you have no choice but to retire - and be grateful that you are still alive. Otherwise, you may manage to make your latter years even greater than your previous ones.

Head to the hideout...	**581**

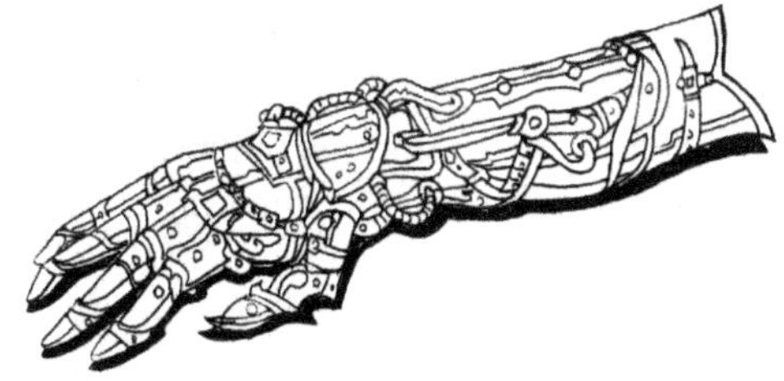

❧ 1064 ❧

The passenger is a well-known airship captain. He scoffs at you as he steps down onto the road. "I've fought Captain Coke," he boasts, "Boarding parties off Morocco and mutinies in Tahiti. You'll regret this."

Airship Captain	Weapon: **sabre (PAR 3)**
Parry:	**9**
Nimbleness:	**6**
Toughness:	**4**

Victory!	**1515**
Defeat!	**113**

❧ 1065 ❧

The constable sits back in amazement and calls in his colleague. "Do you know 'oo we've got 'ere?" he asks. "It's that'un took the Crown Jewels!"

"Yes. I am the very same."	**1076**
"The lady was responsible! Diana Derwent!"	**1085**

❧ 1066 ❧

To cause the driver to throw on the brakes you will have to ride directly in front of the engine, bluffing him into stopping to avoid an accident. Make a MOTORING roll of difficulty 14, adding 1 if you have **off-road tyres**.

Successful MOTORING roll!	**1295**
Failed MOTORING roll!	**1446**

❧ 1067 ❧

Over a pint of beer, a couple of ex-cons tell you about the welcome they received down in Lambeth, at Crafton's Cookshop. "'e's a real gent," says one. "'e was inside isself, see, so 'e knows 'ow 'ard it is gettin' on."

   "Jest show 'im yer' convict's papers," says the other, "An' 'e'll look after yer."

Turn to...	**noted passage**

❧ 1068 ❧

You ask around after anyone who might have heard of the sword. Lo and behold, a shady figure in the back room is indeed willing to sell you **Prishaw's sword** for five guineas (**£5 5s**). If you like the price, add the sword to your **possessions** and remove the money from your purse before making your way towards the Guberstein club.

Leave the Grapes...	**474**

❧ 1069 ❧

The East India Company is a mighty force in the Empire. Here, where the River Lea meets the Thames, a massive mechanised dock complex has been dug into the low-lying land. Plumes of smoke from the coal furnaces that power all the cranes, chain-tugs, gates and capstans cover the sky. Iron-hulled steamers marked with the prominent crest of the East India Company queue to enter and exit the dock on each tide.

	To buy	To sell
Charcoal	-	**£10**
Furniture	**£25**	**£24**
Machinery	**£35**	**£34**
Pottery	**£24**	**£20**
Cotton	**£1**	-
Woollen Cloth	-	**£11**
Coal	**£9**	**6**
Beer	-	**£22**
Wheat	**£8**	**£6**
Malt	**£11**	**£6**
Frozen Meat	**£10**	-
Ice	**£5**	**£4**

If you wish to purchase **Frozen Meat** or **Ice**, you will need a **Perkins Machine**. There is also a large stone-yard here, where building materials are piled high for ambitious projects. Because it is not safe for a river-going craft like yours to venture further downriver than this, this will be the furthest point of travel. To moor you must pay for the privilege, and then mark **moored at East India** on your **Adventure Sheet**.

Moor here...	(**£2**)	**461**
Head up the Lea towards Bow...		**1001**
Head upriver...		**960**

❧ 1070 ❧

Your mate steers you towards your own wharf at the Millwall workshop. The boat bumps gently against the fenders and you prepare to disembark. Note **moored at Millwall Wharf** on your **Adventure Sheet**.

Turn to...	**1129**

❧ 1071 ❧

The leader of the ruffians has a strong grip, but the combination of your road-hardened muscles, toned from handling the heavy Ferguson, and your quickness in judging your opponent's reactions mean that you can take advantage of a momentary lapse and bring his hand down painfully. You are free to make your own deal with the driver.

Work with the Brethren...   **1152**

෨ 1072 ෮

Your demonstrations go flawlessly and your comrades learn a great deal. You also increase your confidence in using these destructive materials: gain a level of **explosives expert**. Note passage **489** and turn immediately to passage **1133**, where you should tick the box marked **Comrades trained in explosives**.

෨ 1073 ෮

☐

If the box above is empty, tick it and read on. If it is already ticked, turn to **1082** immediately.

You convince the lad to hop aboard the Ferguson and speed off to the place you last saw the wandering cow. Mercifully, it isn't far away, and is munching on a late-flowering rose. The boy accepts your help in returning it to Laycock's Lairs, where you meet Mr Laycock himself. A surprisingly small man, dressed in a cowhand's woollen apron and tatty bowler, he commands the utter respect of his workforce and the local community.

He grunts when he sees the boy and cow. "Mmmph. Number 5-4-1. Nice to see you, Myrtle girl. You been feedin' her proper?"

"Yessir," says the boy.

Laycock looks the cow over quickly but carefully. "Give your mam good yield, did she? She's a gallon-and-a-half girl, Myrtle."

"Yessir. We've cream setting for butter right now. Me mam's very grateful."

As well as providing stabling for the herds that are driven down to the city for slaughter, Laycock has become very rich by providing a cow-sharing scheme for the local needy. They pay in small amounts towards a cow's feed and in return have several days a month use of the cow, when they are responsible for feeding and stabling the beast, but are entitled to the full yield of milk.

"And what about you," says Laycock, turning his attention from the cow at last. "What business is this o' yours? Unless my eyes deceive me, aren't you the one they call the Steam Highwayman?"

It turns out that Laycock is something of a fan. He has been following the reports of your robberies and rescues for some time. "Any friend of the common folk is a friend of mine." He invites you into his stables, where he shows you around and explains how his scheme works. Eventually, he waves you off, although he would clearly like to talk more. Remove the codeword *Cattleboy*, and you are now the **Friend of Laycock**.

Return to Islington...   **151**

෨ 1074 ෮

Despite all your efforts, you cannot get the swing bridge turning. All you have done is surrender your lead over your pursuers. When you get into the Ferguson's saddle again, it is too late: they have you surrounded.

Turn to...   **1500**

෨ 1075 ෮

You join a serious discussion of the politics of the day. "The Progressives should have been in government years ago," rages one drinker. "But for the Peers' Prerogative."

"What's that?" you ask.

"Immunity from arrest," he replies. "Consequently, the Members from the Establishment side of the house are consistently challenging the Progressives to duels - and murdering them on the lawns of Parliament!"

"That's right," agrees another. "I heard the other day that they're looking for someone to step in - a swordsman who can defend the interests of the people and beat the Establishment at their own bloody game."

"They are?"

"What, you're the one to do it? Well, it's Mr Wright you're looking for. He drinks at the Pineapple, in Lambeth." Gain the codeword *Chertsey*.

Turn to...   **noted passage**

෨ 1076 ෮

"Cor!" says the other officer. "Now, any chance I could get an autograph?" You are now a **Famous Lawbreaker**, if you are not already.

The amazement of the Constables does nothing to mitigate your sentence, however. You are thrown into one of the deepest cells in the Tower of London.

Turn to...   **335**

☙ 1077 ❧

The list below shows the essential materials and tools that you can create. For each one, you may require precursor materials (simple items like **copper pipe**), tools, workshop facilities (listed in passage **1308**) and money for fuel and raw materials. Materials and money are consumed by the process, but you may keep your tools and workshop facilities. Further options indicate special projects that have more complicated requirements.

To build	Materials and money	Tools and facilities
axe	1s	☑Apprentice or greater
shovel	1s	☑Apprentice or greater
grappling iron	rope, 2s	-
brass flange joint	copper pipe, adjustable wrench (ENG+1)	-
velosteamer's helmet (MOT+2)	goggles (MOT+1), mask, 10s	-
mobile telegraph	parasol, brass flange joint, punchcards (Aramanth A), £1 1s	☑Journeyman or greater, **Telegraph Guild Codebook, measuring line**
winged harness	ultra-tensed wire, roll of oiled silk, clockwork bird	☑Master Engineer, **measuring line**
steam accordion	accordion, brass flange joint, copper pipe, 18s	☑Master Engineer

Customisations	Materials and money	Tools and facilities
muffled exhaust	copper pipe, bolt of cloth	**adjustable wrench (ENG+1)**
ramming beak heavy	12s	☑Apprentice, ☑Travelling crane **wrench**
enlarged tank	£1 8s, high pressure valve	☑Journeyman, ☑Casting forge **welding tools**
double headlamp	high pressure valve, 16s	☑Journeyman, ☑Travelling crane
gas pressuriser	pocket watch, 15s	☑Master Engineer, ☑Casting forge
reinforced boiler	£3 2s	☑Master Engineer, ☑Travelling crane, **stethoscope**

Construct a wharf... 963
Construct a casting forge... 1086
Construct a travelling crane... 1123
Prepare a unit of **machinery** for river freight... 1153
Return to the workshop... 1308

☙ 1078 ❧

Once they have overpowered you, the enforcers prepare the Guild's traditional, and horrific, punishment. They take you out into the street and chop off your hand with an axe, cauterising the stump with boiling tar. When you come round, you have **lost a hand (NIM-2 MOT-2)**. You should remove one **wound** and replace it with a **scar**, and note that you are no longer **Wanted by the Haulage Guild**.

Pick yourself up...

☙ 1079 ❧

A newspaper editor is travelling to take an airship journey back to Glasgow, where his sub-editor has been filling his paper with unverifiable gossip in his absence. He scowls impatiently as you check the travelling compartment for hidden valuables. In the end you can take **£8 15s**, a **pocket watch** and a pair of **duelling pistols (ACC 7)**.

Turn to... **noted passage**

❧ 1080 ❧

Hearing of your plight, Lady Serene sends some of her people to bring you back to Derwent House. You catch a single glimpse of her before falling into deep sleep, and when you recover, some weeks later, you are told that she has travelled abroad. A letter lies on the table beside you.

My dear friend,

I had thought you immortal! But none of us are gods, or heroes of old, simply men and women of flesh and blood. Life is short, and it cannot be wasted. Do not look for me to express gratitude - do that by surviving, I beg you.

My people will give you anything you ask for, for the sake of the times we had. But do not look for me again. I will not return to London, or these awful islands. Life is too short - so I will spend it.

Your friend,
Diana

Replace any **wounds** with **scars**, and remove any **damage points** from your velosteam. Note that you are no longer the **Friend of Diana Derwent**.

Ride away...   **750**

❧ 1081 ❧

The Honourable Francis de Lankey has sent you a terse note. It reads: *What tie have you to Portsea, sir? I would demand you conclude this pretence, were your presence in the house not a greater insult than a simple resignation could wipe clean. Meet me on the lawn at dawn, if you be a person of any honour. There our blades shall decide the matter.*

So on the morrow you dress lightly, as befits a duel, and head down to the green, there to meet the gentleman.

de Lankey	Weapon: **rapier (PAR 4)**
Parry:	12
Nimbleness:	8
Toughness:	2

Victory!	**1103**
Defeat!	**1134**

❧ 1082 ❧

"Didn't I find your cow before, boy?" you ask.

"Yes, y'did, yer 'onour. But it's this Myrtle. She ain't docile like a regular cow. She won't do as she's told!"

Once again, you locate the cow and help the boy bring her back to the lairs. There, Laycock laughs to see you again. "The mighty Steam Highwayman! Rescuer of lost beasts! Pinner of Islington!" Gain the codeword *Compassionate*.

Return to Islington...   **151**

❧ 1083 ❧

A tipsy member of the Compact for Workers Equality is trying to rally the parlour's enthusiasm for what he says is the imminent revolution. "We will burst out of our headquarters with a flash, like, like a bomb!"

"Garn!" calls a drinker. "The Compact ain't got no support in London."

"How little you know," replies the speaker angrily. "The sugar warehouse at Blackwall is stuffed with guns, and printing presses too..." His companion claps a hand over his mouth and drags his friend outside. Gain the codeword *Cheered*.

Turn to...   **noted passage**

❧ 1084 ❧

To damage or destroy the Telegraph will be no mean feat. Explosives might do it, or a way of scaling the tower.

Climb the tower... (**grappling iron**)	**1283**
Fly to the top... (**winged harness**)	**1292**
Leave for now...	**692**

❧ 1085 ❧

The Constable strikes you hard across the face. "How dare you! Trying to besmirch a lady's honour! And Lady Serene, too. Why, she made a donation to the Constabulary Widows' and Orphans' Fund this last spring of such a size! You dog!"

You are taken away and thrown into a deep, deep cell in the dungeon of the Tower of London.

Turn to...   **335**

❧ 1086 ❧

Constructing a casting forge is not a task to undertake lightly. You will need considerable expertise, and even then, accidents can happen. You will need **£10** for materials and either ☑ **coal delivery** or a unit of **Coal** at your wharf (passage **1129**). Remove these, then make an ENGINEERING roll, adding 1 if you have an **Apprentice**, 3 if you have a **Journeyman** and 5 if you have a **Master** to help you.

Score 2-18   Total failure: gain a **burn (NIM-1)**...
Score 18-19   Scorched success: gain a **burn**...
              (NIM-1) and tick ☐ Casting forge
              in passage **1308**...
Score 20+   Success! Tick ☐ Casting forge in
              passage **1308**...

Turn to...   1308

❧ 1087 ❧

The leader of the ruffians slams your arm down onto the barroom table, laughing. Roll a dice to see how you fare:

Score 1-2   Shamed but unhurt...
Score 3-4   A fractured wrist: gain a **wound**
Score 5-6   A fight erupts: turn to **1044**

If you now have **five wounds**, turn to **999** immediately. Otherwise, you will be thrown out.

Turn to...   28

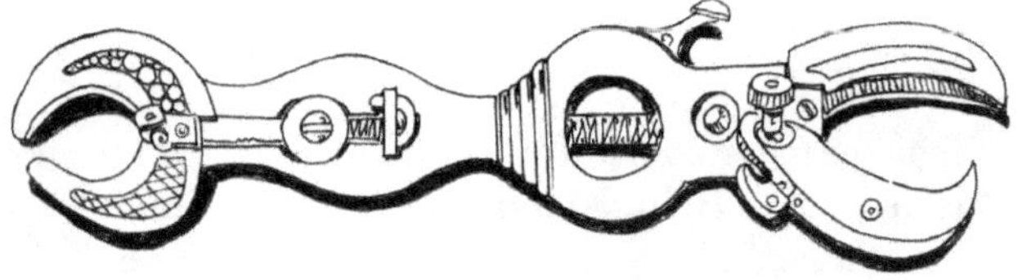

❧ 1088 ❧

☐

If the box above is empty, tick it and read on. If it is already ticked, turn to **1105** immediately.

After all your exertions, you are aboard Mrs Robert's love-boat, where she keeps court. You scout about to find her cabin and lie low until you are sure it is empty. Then you creep in, to find what you can.

And despite an hour of searching, nothing you can see indicates that she is in any way connected to the Compact for Worker's Equality. If you want to ruin her reputation, you will need to fake some sort of proof, perhaps combining her own signature with a copy of Jensen's Statement. It would take a skilled forger to bring such a thing off, however. Do you know any such person? You can take a **love note** with you, tucked carefully into a waterproof pouch, if you want. On her dresser there is also a handsome **diamond brooch** and five **gold rings** .

Swim back to shore...   **602**

❧ 1089 ❧

If you have the codeword *Commensurate, Currently* or *Constable*, turn to **675** immediately. Otherwise, read on.

The **annotated manifesto** gets considerable attention. Lord Beaufort himself is messaged, and eventually you are brought face to face. He is far less interested in you than in the book, and doesn't pay you much attention at all.

"How did you come by this?"

You describe your swim to the *Gentilesse*, your act of daring thievery, the waterproof pouch. That you knew he was on the lookout for any such thing. He opens it and his eyes widen involuntarily as he recognises - he thinks - Maria Roberts' characteristic handwriting.

Attack him...   713
Offer to work for him directly...   728
Ask for a reward...   782

❧ 1090 ❧

You find a nice broad column - there aren't any walls - and quickly moisten the self-gluing back of the poster (remove it from your **possessions**).

Note passage **741** and turn to **1133**, where you should tick the box marked ☐ Revolutionary posters posted.

❧ 1091 ❧

Your journey west is long and cold. Your shillings do not go far in the roadside inns: no landlord trusts a single rider on a dirty velosteam. Eventually, you reach the sheltering woods.

Ride towards Cliveden... *Smog and Ambuscade 366*
Head for Cutthroat Wood... *Smog and Ambuscade 561*
Ride towards Maidenhead... *Smog and Ambuscade 218*
Turn around... **50**

❧ 1092 ❧

The revolutionaries have heard about your prowess with explosives. "You did the railway near Cookham, ain't that so?" asks one in awe.

A senior comrade makes a suggestion. "We have many young hotheads here. Teach them how to use explosives carefully and you will be rewarded."

Remove the codeword *Anteater* and make an ENGINEERING roll of difficulty 14, adding 1 for each level of **explosives expert** you possess.

Successful ENGINEERING roll... **1072**
Failed ENGINEERING roll... **1107**

❧ 1093 ❧

You explain what you want to the forger. "It needs to look like this book has belonged to the woman with this handwriting for a long time. And that she believes it."

The forger isn't stupid. He knows that he is handling seditious material. Still, your money is good (as he is uniquely able to verify) and he finds a particular satisfaction in creating work like this.

After several hours' work, he returns the book to you. Remove the **love note, Jensen's Statement** and the money. In their place, you now possess an **annotated manifesto**.

Leave the forger... **221**

❧ 1094 ❧

The coupling comes undone, the road engine accelerates under the lighter load and the final wagon trundles to a halt. You quickly slash at the lashings to see what it contains. Roll a dice to see what you have found:

Score 1   a **strongbox**...
Score 2-3   four **bottles of wine**...
Score 4-5   three **parasols**...
Score 6   a pair of **golden candlesticks**...

You will now be **Wanted by the Haulage Guild** unless you are wearing a **mask**.

Ride away... **noted passage**

❧ 1095 ❧

The Duke of Innishmore is far from happy with your presence in the House. He has heard about your duel with de Lankey and wishes to redress the balance, as he sees it. His letter is long-winded, florid and old-fashioned, much like the politician himself.

He meets you in wig and waistcoat on the roof of Westminster Hall late in the evening. "The grass is too public," he says. "I wish to spare you the shame."

Duke of Innishmore	Weapon: **sabre (PAR 3)**
Parry:	12
Nimbleness:	9
Toughness:	4

Victory! **1138**
Defeat! **1134**

❧ 1096 ❧

Now that the Union steamer is stationary at the side of the road, you fling open the door to see who is travelling inside. You will have to act fast before anyone else comes this way. Roll a dice:

Score 1-2   Travelling ladies... **1058**
Score 3-4   An airship captain... **1064**
Score 5-6   A newspaper editor... **1079**

❧ 1097 ❧

"Very well," says Comrade Tate. "Surely you have something like a plan? He must be found when he is most vulnerable..."

"Aboard the *Gentilesse*," you reply.

"Of course," answers Feaver, grimly. "In the arms of his lover. Yes, why not?"

Together with the High Council, you make your preparations. Their informers keep track on the King's movements and will alert you as soon as he disappears towards his Mistress' pleasure barge. You plan your route: you will need to swim downstream with the tide, carrying the minimum of equipment.

The very next evening, the Council receives the sign: the King is going to spend a night aboard. "Now is your chance," says Comrade Reel. "You are only the blade: we are the hilt and the people are the righteous arm of judgement! Strike for each of us!"

You will only be able to carry **four items** with you: choose exactly what you think you will require to break into the heavily-guarded pleasure barge and carry out the deed. Note passage **518** and place any other items into the box in passage **523**.

Turn to... **523**

❧ 1098 ❧

"That's what them Compact were saying," agrees one of the painters thoughtfully. "We does all the work and our bosses get all the profit."

"Perhaps we need to do something about it then."

If you wish to convince the workmen of their responsibility to act, and to join the Compact for Worker's Equality, make an INGENUITY roll, adding 1 if you have a **revolutionary poster**, 2 if you are a **Member of the CWE** yourself, and 3 if you have a copy of **Jensen's Statement** at had.

Score 2-11 The workmen continue to argue...
Score 12 The workmen agree to sign up; gain the codeword *Chastise*...

Turn to... **noted passage**

❧ 1099 ❧

You listen to a woman boasting about selling stolen diamonds. She claims to have broken into a mansion and taken a lady's tiara. "How on earth did you shift it?" you ask, refilling her cup.

She winks. "Broke it dahn, didn't I? The only folks who'll buy bad stones like that are the Brethren in Clerkenwell."

"The Brethren?"

"That's right. The so-called Noble Brotherhood of Self-Denial."

Leave here... **noted passage**

❧ 1100 ❧

A familiar cattlewagon stands waiting for its turn to refuel. The farmer you helped on the Watlington road near Shirburn has made it to the city after all. He waves in recognition.

"You did me a good deed," he cries. "I made a fat profit here." He returns the **Guildsman's medallion** to you, along with **£5** in coin. Remove the codeword *Baron*.

Return to the market... **126**

❧ 1101 ❧

It will take some sort of crazed and desperate creativity to make up a tale that the Constables will both believe and reward. Make an INGENUITY roll.

Score 2-10 Uninterested... **139**
Score 11-14 Arrested... **13**
Score 15+ Rewarded: gain **10s** **139**

❧ 1102 ❧

The Union uses Atterbury engines to haul its supplies to its landing grounds and outposts. This one has a canvas-covered freight section at rear loaded with supplies. Roll a dice to see what you find:

Score 1 an **adjustable wrench (ENG+1)** and a roll of **oiled silk**
Score 2-3 a **picnic hamper**, six **bottles of wine** and a **deer carcass**
Score 4-5 a **pork pie**, a **bottle of champagne** and a **rope**
Score 6 some **welding tools** and a **mask**

Blow up the wagon... (**explosives**) **1127**
Ride away... **noted passage**

❧ 1103 ❧

De Lankey is quite a swordsman, but he has not the energy or the vigour to surpass you. He expects a more gentlemanly duel, but you beat him with a combination of ruthlessness, brute force and rage. He yields on the second blood, offering you his **rapier (PAR 4)** or a **gold ring** as a trophy. You should also gain the codeword *Clinched*, note passage **797** and turn to **850**, where you should correct the Parliamentary Swingometer by **one point in the Progressive's favour**.

❧ 1104 ❧

The designers send a cart across from the shipyards to collect your carefully-crafted machinery, packing them in newspaper and straw. The stovepiped engineer returns with the payment - thirty guineas (**£31 10s**). You can also increase your ENGINEERING score by 1.

Return to your workshop... **1308**

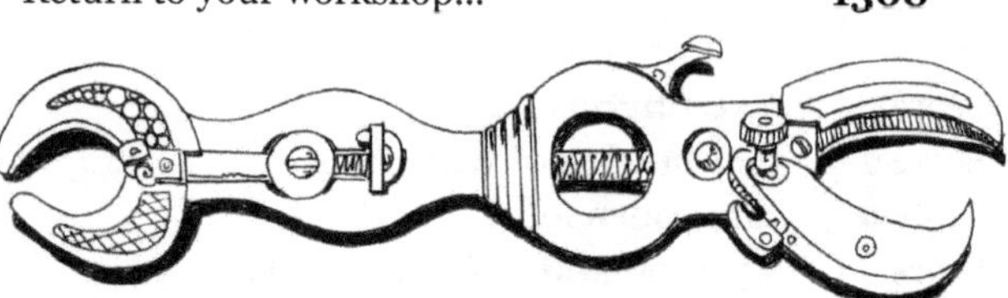

❧ 1105 ❧

What foolhardiness has convinced you to return to the scene of your former crime? Mrs Roberts has ordered a considerable improvement in her security, paid for by her regal lover. As soon as you climb onto the deck, you feel a heavy blow to the head, and all goes dark.

Turn to...   **1500**

❧ 1106 ❧

Remove all your **possessions** and **money**. You come to with a sore head and excruciating pain in your side. You are lying beneath a boardwalk on the shingle and broken brick of the river and the tide is rising around you. To survive and get yourself back to your velosteam will take a superhuman effort - or a miracle. You may simply drown in the river - an ignominious end for a hero like yourself.

If you are the **Friend of the Waterside boys**... 1110
Otherwise, turn to the **epilogue**...

❧ 1107 ❧

Something goes wrong with the delaying in one of your demonstrations and you succeed in demolishing one part of the Compact's stores. Your comrades are impressed, nonetheless. "See the power of these materials," you lecture sternly. You are lucky not to have been hurt. Gain one level of **explosives expert**.

Return to the warehouse...   **489**

❧ 1108 ❧

The Baronet Dressley is the most feared swordsman in the city: he has killed more than a dozen of the Progressive party members in the last eighteen months, and disabled many more. Behind his principles, he has an awful delight in duelling those weaker than himself. Has he at last met his match?

Baronet Dressley   Weapon: **rapier (PAR 4)**
Parry: 15
Nimbleness: 11
Toughness: 4

Victory!   1143
Defeat!   1134

❧ 1109 ❧

A steam wagon hauling furniture chugs up the slope. The driver spots you and tips his hat, plainly making a desperate prayer that he won't be your next victim. But the condition of his cargo tells you that there will be little to steal here.

Ride on...   **noted passage**

❧ 1110 ❧

The dirty river water laps around you and you slip out of consciousness again. A blur of pain and the sensation of movement wakes you intermittently and you eventually find yourself in the den of the Waterside Boys. They have rescued you once and for all.

It takes several weeks for you to regain your health in their care. They have managed to find your velosteam and bring it to the old warehouse where they hide and it will be in exactly the state that you last saw it. You, on the other hand, have had a chance to heal your **wounds** - replace each one with a **scar**, rolling two dice for each to see if you gain an **intimidating scar (RUTH+1)** on a score of 11 or 12.

You may well feel as though you have to begin your adventures again, but although you might have lost your money and possessions, you cannot lose the more intangible memories, knowledge and understanding that have seen you get this far. Faithful friends like the mudlarking urchins will stay beside you.

Set out again...   **252**

❧ 1111 ❧

Your faithful machine will never start again, and without it, you are reduced to nothing more than a common footpad. However much you have saved or lost, however skilled or feared, you cannot continue as the Steam Highwayman without your Ferguson velosteam.

Turn to the **epilogue**....

❧ 1112 ❧

"Human nature nain't likely to change," responds the workmen's gaffer. "Not this year."

The workmen are keen to make what extra money they can from their bosses, and have a few oddments to sell, if you are interested.

	To buy	To sell
tarpaulin	1s	-
grappling iron	5s	-
measuring line	2s	-
high pressure valve	10s	-

Turn to...   **noted passage**

❧ 1113 ❧

"Kids is everywhere, pinching pockets and getting underfoot," complains a drunken haulier. "I had to make a delivery down at Allhallows Wharf, by London Bridge. There was this whole gang of young hooligans out mudlarking on the riverbank. Something possessed them to start throwing mud. I would have wrung their necks if I could have catched 'em."

Turn to...   **noted passage**

❧ 1114 ❧

☐

If the box above is empty, tick it and read on. If it is already ticked, turn to **1140** immediately.

A vestry is unlocked. You slip inside and look around. There is a fine bishop's **cassock** hanging on its peg, a **bottle of wine** standing on a table and **17s** lying on a collection plate.

Leave the chapel...   **1000**

❧ 1115 ❧

"It ain't easy," says the forger. "But I've got connections, might be able to manage it." It will cost you **£60** and a set of **punchcards (Livingstone M)** to attempt to clear your name. If you want to proceed and have the requirements, remove them from your **Adventure Sheet** and roll a dice.

Score 1-2	Effort unsuccessful
Score 3-4	Remove one **Wanted Status**
Score 5	Remove two **Wanted Statuses** of
Score 6	Remove all **Wanted Statuses**

Leave the forger...   **221**

❧ 1116 ❧

The grave-robbers are intrigued by your questions. "You've a professional interest, then?" they ask. "Well, 'tis a profitable enterprise. All you need is a shovel, a lantern, and an eye for fresh graves." They share some useful tips about opening caskets, reburying efficiently and so on.

With this sort of knowledge under your belt, you are ready to give grave-robbing a try, if you like. Whenever you see the words *fresh grave*, add **45** to the **passage number** and turn to the resulting passage, where you will be able to do your own 'burking'. Do not forget to note the number of the passage you leave, as you will need to return there once your deed is done.

Turn to...   **noted passage**

❧ 1117 ❧

The High Council discuss the idea for several hours. Despite Feaver's thirst for blood and violence and Tate's hatred of law courts, they agree that a legal dethroning and execution is more likely to lead to long-term stability. Since the Progressive party have a majority in Parliament, it can be raised soon.

"I will propose the Bill."
   (**Member of Parliament**)   **583**
"We will need friends in the party."   **558**

❧ 1118 ❧

You are given some basic training in handling the top-heavy locobus. It could not be more different to your Ferguson: it is slow, steers like the Tower of London and is surprisingly unstable.

However, you are pronounced ready to drive for the Union after only a short time, and told to head off on your first route, up to Highgate and then down into the city. A clock mounted on the dashboard rings reminders of the stops you should be making - but it is far from easy to keep to schedule.

By the time you are picking up your third stop of commuters, you are several minutes behind schedule already. The passengers are becoming rude and anxious. You can attempt to calm them, relying on your GALLANTRY, cow them into quiet using your RUTHLESSNESS, or ignore them and speed up, making up the time using your MOTORING skill.

Calm them...	**1210**
Scare them...	**1224**
Make up the time...	**1234**

❧ 1119 ❧

As you approach Yarrow's Yard, you hear a cry going up. The chains holding a hull to its slip have failed, and the massive iron body is sliding down into the river, gathering speed. Workmen jump clear, but you hear the unmistakable scream of someone losing their legs. Then, before you can steer much clearer, the half-built ship rushes into the water, sending a great wake out, swamping all manner of little craft. You turn to meet the wake prow on, and your boat bucks and jolts.

Help get the situation under control...
(strengthened screw or **tug)**   1158
Sail past...   **948**

❧ 1120 ❧

You only succeed in arousing the suspicions of the landlord and his cronies. They take a dislike to you and force you to leave the inn. "We don't take to strangers with big noses," says the landlord. "You're likely to get the skin taken off of it."

Leave the Flask...   **28**

❧ 1121 ❧

You are taken to a coal-breaking house and chained up in an unlit cellar to pay for your crimes with hard labour. Backbreaking work, lack of sunlight and a poor diet saps your strength. Months pass - countless months - and you quickly lose track of how long you have been imprisoned here.

Eventually a warden takes a look at you and decides you are no longer worth your keep. They give you back your possessions and even your velosteam, but the experience has cost you dearly. Replace each **wound** with a **scar** and lower your RUTHLESSNESS, GALLANTRY, ENGINEERING and NIMBLENESS scores by 1 each.

Ride away...   **84**

❧ 1122 ❧

The fog hangs around each gas-lantern and flickering oil-flame. The white beam of your lime-lantern bounces off the myriad droplets of dew so that you are riding along in a shining cloud. The river can be heard, somewhere to your left, but not seen. You can barely see the houses along the street.

Continue on to Lambeth...   **647**

❧ 1123 ❧

To construct a travelling crane, you will need an assistant (of any level) and ☑ Casual labour, in order to erect the weighty supports. You will require an ENGINEERING score of 9 or more and **£8** for the materials. Once you have gathered all you need, turn to **1308** and erase the tick from ☑ Casual labour and tick ☐ Travelling Crane.

Turn to...   **1308**

❧ 1124 ❧

Your opponent falls to his knees and then collapses on his face in the dew. His second dashes forward as you walk away. Gain a **solidarity point.**

Return to your chambers...   **797**

❧ 1125 ❧

The ice warehouse is run by an Italian named Forsi. Along with his business shipping blocks of ice on the canal and out across the city, he runs a profitable sideline in ice-cream sales. In fact, over on the office door a notice reads 'Ice-Cream Salesmen Required.'

⊕ Apply for a position...   **1194**
Leave the warehouse...   **129**

❧ 1126 ❧

Despite your scratches and scars, you and Diana laugh as you scale the outer wall of the moat and dash towards the waiting carriage. "Now that was exciting," she grins. Surely you must agree?

Ride away...   **1014**

❧ 1127 ❧

Intent on producing as much destruction and mayhem as you can, you lay the charges around the stationary vehicle, under steam pipes and against the axles - remove the **explosives** from your **possessions**.

The resulting explosion sends sharp-edged metal whizzing into the roadside hedges and a tower of smoke up into the night. Gain the codeword *Crisis*.

Ride away...   **noted passage**

✢ 1128 ✢

There is a great deal of debate on both sides, but when it comes to the final vote, you boldly side against the Bill. Mr Wright is furious. "We didn't bring you in here to throw a spanner in the works," he hisses. "Now the Bill is lost!" The Progressive's majority is also weakened, as marginal members are convinced to side with the Establishment. Gain the codeword *Chipped*, note passage **797** and turn to **850**, where you should adjust the parliamentary swingometer **one point in the Establishment's favour**.

✢ 1129 ✢

Your very own freshly-constructed wharf is ready to load machinery and other goods aboard a barge. It is a short distance to the East India Docks and only a little further to the entrance to the King's canal at Limehouse. You have an excellent position from which to trade.

You can store **six units** of cargo here, ready to put them aboard your own boat. If you have a boat moored here, you can load and unload cargo as you wish.

Go aboard your boat ...

(moored at Millwall Wharf)	1151
Return to your workshop...	1308
Leave for Millwall...	431

✢ 1130 ✢

Loitering around the Flask with your ears to the ground will certainly risk drawing attention to yourself. Roll two dice to see if you are successful in finding what you seek, adding 1 for each **10s** you spend on drinks, 1 if you have a **Guildsman's medallion** and 3 if you are the **People's Champion**.

Score 2-8	1120
Score 9-12	1139

✢ 1131 ✢

St Gorgonia's Court is the home to the Noble Order of the Brethren of Self-Denial, known in the City simply as the Brethren. They may have initially been a religious order, but whether they retain any spiritual principles is questionable. They are known for their secretive rituals, their intense loyalty to their order and their ruthless pursuit of wealth. They are one of the key players in the city's jewel-trading game, as well as being brokers and insurance agents. If you are **Wanted by the Brethren**, there is no way you can enter unrecognized: turn to **144** immediately.

Jewellery	To buy	To sell
pectoral cross	-	**£5 18s**
emerald	**£15**	**£8**
sapphire	**£24**	**£15**
handful of small diamonds	**£50**	**£34**
bag of perfect pearls	**£90**	**£65**
bag of fine rubies	**£120**	**£80**
purple brooch	-	**£12**
locket of King Charles' Hair	-	**£12**
sapphire pendant	-	**£15**
ruby ring	-	**£30**
diamond brooch	-	**£40**
emerald jewellery	**£150**	**£85**

Try to sell a **pouch of diamonds**...	1145
Leave the Brethren...	144

✢ 1132 ✢

The bridge here is narrow - only a single engine in breadth - and keepers at either end use a relay telegraph to keep the traffic moving over the suspended roadway efficiently. When you approach, they wave you over directly, and the bridge sways as you swoop over the iron sheets of the roadway.

Head to Chelsea...	794
Ride towards Lambeth...	1122
Go aboard your boat...	
(moored at Battersea Bridge)	923

✢ 1133 ✢

Use the following list of objectives to track which revolutionary goals have met. The eventual rising of the people depends on the success of these.

☐ Wye dock workers armed (*Arithmetic*)	1
☐ Nettlebed brickmakers radicalised (*Blown*)	1
☐ Railway navvies recruited (*Boosting*)	1
☐ Comrades trained in explosives	1
☐ Dockers radicalised	1
☐ Sympathetic Royals	
(Friend of Princess Alexandrina)	2

☐ People's Champion   3

☐ Lord Beaufort poisoned, dead or imprisoned   2
     (*Currently*, *Constable* or *Commensurate*)

☐ Assistance of Flat Billy (**Friend of Flat Billy**)   2

☐ Friend of Jumbo (*Callused*)   1

☐ Cornwall united (*Definite*)   4

☐ Earl of Chester recruited (*Faraway*)   4

☐ Welsh miners allied   (*Equality*)   4

☐ Marching townspeople recruited (*Clavicle*)   1

☐ Abolishment Bill unsuccessful   -3

☐ Revolutionary Posters raised   1

For each objective listed above, add the relevant number of points to your Revolution Countdown Total. Once this total is 15 or greater, gain the codeword *Catastrophe*.

Turn to...   **noted passage**

✎ 1134 ✎

To everyone's horror, your opponent makes good his threats and leaves you lying on the red grass. If you have **thirty scars or more**, turn to **1148** immediately. Otherwise, lose a point of RUTHLESSNESS and read on.

Now you must immediately seek some sort of aid. If you have some **bandages** or a piece of **clothing**, you can discard them to staunch the worst **wound** (convert it into a **scar**) and proceed directly to your rooms. If you do not have anything to stop the bleeding, then your adventure will end here.

To your rooms...
    (**bandages** or piece of **clothing**)   797
Give up the ghost...   1148

✎ 1135 ✎

"If you ever go drinking up at the Flask in Highgate, just you be careful," advises a moustachioed stout-supper. "The landlord there's a Constables' nark." Gain the codeword *Chatty*.

Turn to...   **noted passage**

✎ 1136 ✎

There is an awful tearing sound and the wings begin to give way. You start to lose height and dive towards the river.

Diana doesn't wait. She slaps the quick-release on her harness and drops, elegantly, into the filth. You crash down a few moments later and struggle to get free from the waterlogged machinery.

The guards are on you almost immediately. They pull you into a small boat and clap irons on your wrists and ankles. The lady, however, has completely disappeared, and your captors seem more than happy to have you in their hands.

Turn to...   **1500**

✎ 1137 ✎

It will be a feat indeed to intimidate the driver of a guarded Haulage Guild road train here on the outskirts of the city. Then again, you are no common road thief, but the Steam Highwayman, feared across the land. Make a RUTHLESSNESS roll of difficulty 16, adding 1 if you are **Wanted by the Haulage Guild** and 3 if you are the **People's Champion**.

Successful RUTHLESSNESS roll!   **1214**
Failed RUTHLESSNESS roll!   **1277**

✎ 1138 ✎

The Duke is an old-fashioned duellist. He hangs back, flicking away your attacks with his sabre-tip, until he feels he has your measure. Then he attacks ruthlessly, pressing you backwards until you are pushed against the parapet. However, he has not your speed or dexterity, and fights somewhat overconfidently. After much sweat and strain, you bring him to his knees. After all you have learnt in this fight, you can add a permanent PARRY bonus of 1 to your current score. Gain the codeword *Classic*, note passage **797** and turn to **850**, where you should correct the Parliamentary Swingometer by **one point in the Progressives' favour**.

✎ 1139 ✎

Several of the garrulous regulars boast of how their pub is safe from the Constables' raids on account 'protection'. Then you notice the landlord himself keeping notes in a small book behind the bar. Later in the evening he slips out to rendezvous with a rider on an Imperial velosteam in the yard. It seems certain that he is in the pay of the Constables.

Corner the landlord and challenge him...   1147
Make an example of him...   1166

ᔐ 1140 ᔑ

The vergers are on the lookout for thieves and looters inside the chapel: you must have been very lucky before. They find you looking around and raise the alarm. You must dash for your velosteam immediately! Roll a dice to see whether you managed to grab anything beforehand:

Score 1   a gold **pectoral cross**...
Score 2   a **jewelled bible**...
Score 3-6   nothing at all...

Get away!   **278**

ᔐ 1141 ᔑ

A drift of fog comes between you and the figures. When it clears, they have gone. Perhaps the sound of your approach scared them away?

Turn to...   **noted passage**

ᔐ 1142 ᔑ

With your own casting forge, you can quickly convert items of precious metal into the small and untraceable ingots favoured by movers of bullion. You can also melt much more valuable objects...

To gain	Exchange for
gold bar	any **six** gold items (**gold ring, gold bracelet, gold necklace, golden candlesticks** etc)
silver bar	any **six** silver items (**silver ring, silver bracelet, silver necklace** etc)

Exchange	To gain
golden sceptre	two **gold bars**
sword of state	a **gold bar**, three **sapphires** and a **handful of small diamonds**
pearl armills	two **gold bars** and a **bag of perfect pearls**
ruby-studded gauntlets	a **bag of fine rubies**
sapphire coronet	**gold bar** and three **sapphires**
diamond crown	a **gold bar**, a **bag of fine rubies** and a **handful of small diamonds**
ceremonial mace	three **gold bars**

Return to the workshop...   **1308**
Leave the workshop...   **431**

ᔐ 1143 ᔑ

"A lucky and an unfair stroke," rasps the Baronet, leaning back against the railings. "Some small skill with a blade does not make you a hero." He falls silent. Gain a **solidarity point**, the codeword *Caltrop*, note passage **797** and turn to **850**, where you should correct the Parliamentary Swingometer **one point in the Progressives' favour**.

ᔐ 1144 ᔑ

It takes some nerve to come here, exactly where you are most sought-after. A sharp-eyed lookout has spotted you and alerted the Constables. The mechanics try closing the gates behind you: if you are quick, you may be able to beat a retreat. Make a MOTORING roll of difficulty 14, adding 2 if you possess a **ramming beak**.

Successful MOTORING roll!   **33**
Failed MOTORING roll!   **13**

ᔐ 1145 ᔑ

The Brother who deals in 'unhistoried' diamond trades keeps his face shaded in the hood of his black habit. He tips the stream of glittering stones from the pouch onto a swatch of velvet and peers over them.

"A delightful collection. Shall we say two hundred and fifty guineas?"

If you are happy with the offer, remove the **pouch of diamonds** from your **Adventure Sheet**, add **two hundred and fifty guineas in banknotes** to your wallet and gain the codeword *Certain*.

Leave the Brethren...   **144**

ᔐ 1146 ᔑ

Once the rain stops, you show the headman your Ferguson. He looks at it with the eye of a tinkerer. "It's only muskers ride these. Why Wills poked his gun at you, you see? But this is a lovely piece of work. Coal gas here, yes? Leaf spring on the front and back. Hmm. But I reckon I can still improve on it. If you'd like."

Lee will fit you a single customisation from the following list, free of charge, for the simple pleasure of working on your machine. If you already have these, then you will not be able to accept his help.

	To buy
enlarged fuel tank	**free**
pump and filter	**free**
gas pressuriser	**free**

When you are finished, Lee invites you to return to see them again. "We keep ourselves hidden," he says. "So remember the path that led you here."

If you want to revisit Lee and the gypsies, watch for a passage that describes "the shadow of the beeches of Ken Wood". Add **34** to that passage number and you will find yourself back with the Lee family.

Head towards Highgate...	**28**
Ride to Hampstead...	**2**

ᔈ 1147 ᔇ

You loiter until late in the evening, when the landlord begins to close up the parlour, and catch him alone near the back door. Catching him by the scruff of the neck, you tell him that you know he shops his customers to the Constables. He stutters and mumbles and protests. "I'm only trying to keep the law."

"What do they pay you?"

"Plenty. Plenty. Leave me be and you can have a share."

Let him go for a share of his payments...	**1174**
Make an example of him...	**1166**

ᔈ 1148 ᔇ

This, then, is the end of the tale of the Steam Highwayman. The damage of your wayward life upon the road has caught up with you at last: you have not the strength to recover.

Turn to the **epilogue**...

ᔈ 1149 ᔇ

You are summoned to a meeting of the Compact's High Council. Commissioners Reel and Timms, and Comrades Feaver, Tate and Snell are all gathered. Their faces are stern.

"Comrade," says Reel, "The time is nigh. Your efforts to speed the revolution, combined with the work of our cadres across the land, have tipped the balance in our favour. We are almost ready to unleash flame and retribution upon this land."

Comrade Feaver turns to you. "We need a spark to set this off. You are the one to do it: you have proved your readiness to act a hundred times."

"What is the spark you mean?"

"The King must die," she replies. "Either secretly, or publicly. His reign ends and with it, the control of the plutocrats, the Guilds and the nobility."

Are you truly ready to undertake this charge? Do you consider the Compact likely to succeed in their efforts to make this land a fairer one, for once you agree to light the fuse, there will be no turning back. You will not be able to continue your life of freedom and robbery once the barricades are up. You will either be the most hated, or the most loved, of all the revolutionaries.

"I am ready."	**1175**
"We must continue to prepare."	**1187**

ᔈ 1150 ᔇ

You join a group of furtive young men and women discussing the coming revolution. "It's coming," says one. "It's inevitable. But it won't be like in France! We'll get rid of the blamed royals for good."

"Barricades and blunderbusses," grins another.

"I've heard that the Compact have stockpiles of guns for all the factory workers in the city," says a third.

"You hold your trap about the Compact. If Comrade Reel hears you gossipping about it, he'll skin you."

"Reel's over at the Blackwall group, ain't he?"

"He's got ears everywhere, you idiot."

Turn to...	**noted passage**

ᔈ 1151 ᔇ

Your mate grins as you lash down your velosteam onto the foredeck. He tautens the tarpaulin covering and asks, "Where are we headed, number one?"

"Upriver towards Deptford."	**948**
"Downstream towards the East India Docks."	**992**

ᔈ 1152 ᔇ

If you are **Wanted by the Brethren**, turn to passage **1219** immediately. Otherwise, read on.

The job is to accompany and protect a pair of travellers on their way to Ely. They are monks, by their garb, but the muttering in the Flask identifies them as members of the Brethren: the premier jewel-traders in the city. They have hired a fast steam carriage and driver and now need an outrider to scout the road ahead of them.

"Do you expect ambushes, then?" you ask the

monks.

"Oh no, no, no. This is just prudence. Our Order routinely pays for protection on these sort of journeys."

"The profit covers it, I imagine," you reply.

"That is entirely our business. Your fee will be **£2** for accompanying us there and back." They also agree to pay for your coalgas, bed and board on the journey.

Take the job...   **1228**
Refuse it...   **12**

∾ 1153 ∾

To produce machinery in quantities suitable for the river trade, you will need an assistant ☑ Journeyman or ☑ Master, as well as a ☑ travelling crane and a ☑ wharf. Then to produce a unit of **Machinery**, you will need a unit of **Charcoal** and **£4** for raw materials.

Remove any **Charcoal** from your wharf or boat **moored at Millwall wharf** and the money from your purse, before adding a unit of **Machinery** to your wharf at passage **1129**.

Turn to passage...   **1129**

∾ 1154 ∾

The wings respond flawlessly to your masterful touch. As you lean left and twist the handles, you complete a roll over the very middle of the dirty Thames, setting Diana laughing again and the jewels jangling in their bag. Before long, you have set yourselves down on the southern bank, not far from where you originally launched. The lady has arranged for an unmarked carriage to collect you and whisk you away.

Turn to...   **1014**

∾ 1155 ∾

"Barsali? How is that old devil? Always making trouble. And his boy, now, he was in hot water, wasn't he? Any friend of his is a friend of mine - and all of ours. Right, mother?"

You stay with Lee long after the rain stops. He insists you try his damson gin and you pick up many tips about local matters. In particular, he tells you to beware the publican of the Flask in Highgate. "He works for the muskers. Anything you say in there will go straight to the Constables." Gain the codeword *Chatty*.

Turn to...   **1146**

∾ 1156 ∾

A fisherman at the riverside has caught a **top hat** and doesn't know what to do with it. He will sell it to you for a florin (**2s**) if you like.

Steam on...   **945**

∾ 1157 ∾

The man in brown pockets your contribution without ceremony. "And now," he says, "I'm sorry to say that the Constables would like a word."

A blow to the back of your head sends you sprawling on the cobbles. Everything goes dark...

Turn to...   **13**

∾ 1158 ∾

You steer close alongside the listing hull and cast a line around a stanchion. Your mate has already hung out fenders and, fully opening the regulator of your boat's engine, you manage to slow the runaway craft.

"Tide's turning," shouts your mate through the noise of the whirring pistons. "We's'll need to get this aground!"

You let the river move the ungainly weight, using your boat's powerful engine to nudge it into the riverside. The keel grinds against the mud and shingle and comes to a halt.

The owners of the shipyard are very grateful. They offer you a **bottle of whisky**, a **bargee's badge** and a **pocket watch** in gratitude.

Steam on upstream to Greenwich...   **948**

∾ 1159 ∾

You overhear two women talking about obtaining false papers. "I can't emigrate with my record, see," says one. "But that old bird at St Margaret's Court is doin' me up a whole new certiffycate."

When you find yourself in St Margaret's Court, note the passage number and double it to find the forger, who obviously keeps as low a profile as possible.

Return to...   **noted passage**

✎ 1160 ✎

To unhitch a wagon you will need to steer your heavy velosteam alongside the speeding road train and undo the coupling by hand. Make a MOTORING roll of difficulty 13, adding 1 if you possess **wirecutters**, an **adjustable wrench**, **steam fist** or **mechanical hand**..

Successful MOTORING roll!	**1094**
Failed MOTORING roll!	**1177**

✎ 1161 ✎

The footman who answers the door looks at you with nothing less than a sneer, but he lets you in and installs you in a waiting room. Remove the **Letter of Introduction**.

Eventually, another door is opened.

Enter the house itself...	**1205**

✎ 1162 ✎

The headman, Lee, is taken aback by your attempt to pay for hospitality, but he allows his wife to take the money. Plainly he considers himself in your debt, until he hits on an idea. He offers to set the sights on any gun you possess, improving its accuracy.

You can add **1 point of accuracy** to any single **gun** in your possession, marking that it has been customised like this. For example, a **blunderpistol (ACC 6)** would now be a **blunderpistol (ACC 7 improved)**. Note that this does not affect the weapon's value, should you sell it.

Once the rain has stopped, you remount your velosteam and wave to the Lees.

Head towards Highgate...	**28**
Ride to Hampstead...	**2**

✎ 1163 ✎

You drag the man clear and haul him up into the ruined street, then return to help more of your workmates, despite your own hurts.

Before long, others are here to help and you can sink into an exhausted heap. A nearby shopkeeper brings you a cup of tea and chatters with admiration for your bravery - gain **two solidarity points**.

The Metropolitan Sewer Company reluctantly pay you your **£2** for the day's work, although they now have to rebuild the sewer, not simply unblock it.

Ride away...	**139**

✎ 1164 ✎

To complete your commission for finely tuned engine parts for the massive *Leviathan*, you will require the following: **tuning calculations,** ☑ Travelling Crane, an assistant ☑ **Apprentice** or higher and **£4 10s** for materials. Once you have gathered all of these, remove the codeword *Cabin*.

Completed the engine parts...	**1104**
Return to the workshop...	**1308**

✎ 1165 ✎

The fight seems to be going in your favour to begin with, but your opponent manages to floor you several times, and eventually the beating takes its toll and you are unable to rise. The match stewards pull you to your feet and sponge you down. Remove any **wounds** received during this fight and roll a dice to see how badly you have been hurt.

Score 1-2	a **black eye (ACC-2, GAL-1)**
Score 3-4	a **missing tooth (GAL-1)**
Score 5-6	a **stiff back (NIM-2)**

Beaten, exhausted and bloody, you had better find a place to heal up before venturing into the ring again.

Turn to...	**noted passage**

✎ 1166 ✎

You are able to grab the landlord before he can defend himself. With your weapons at his throat, he is able to do little else but moan. Now you must decide how to exercise your punishment.

Kill him...	**1176**
Beat and humiliate him...	**1186**

✎ 1167 ✎

"It's a dangerous business," says the old man. "Can get you hung! But there's a mint to be made." He chuckles to himself. "We're going to need some nice thick paper... You can get that up in Bow. By the wharf, at the paper mill. And then there's one more thing?"

"Yes?"

"Every *official* banknote 'as a unique pattern on it. Calculated, they all are. So we'se going to 'ave to generate some sort of pattern with a computational engine. You'll need punchcards, see. Them Aramanth ones, I figure."

To create the forged notes, you will need the following items, together with some money to pay the forger for his time.

	To exchange
fifty guineas in banknotes	**calculated patterns**, **rag paper**, £5

Return to the churchyard...   **221**

❧ 1168 ❧

The thin man bares his teeth. "Very unwise of you." He makes to step back into the cover of his doorway.

Grab him as a human shield...   **1195**
Ride through the tunnel as quick as you can...   **1179**

❧ 1169 ❧

In your haste to get down and to avoid your pursuers, you miss a handhold and plunge to the ground. A tin roof breaks your fall, collapsing beneath you and dropping you into a hayloft. Nonetheless, the fall has injured you seriously and you are being pursued: gain **three wounds**. If you now have **five wounds**, turn to **113** immediately. Otherwise, you are able to pick yourself up and hobble to your velosteam.

Ride away!   **614**

❧ 1170 ❧

The program you run is relatively straightforward, but the patterns stippled into the long roll of paper are fiendishly complicated, each one a unique variation. Whether decorating carpets or banknotes, these will mark a final product as unmistakably computed. Remove the **punchcards (Aramanth A)**, which have been digested by the engine, and add the **calculated patterns** to your **possessions**.

Turn to...   **noted passage**

❧ 1171 ❧

A gang of Flat Billy's men have set out to see what they can win from the moored barges along this stretch of the canal. If you are a **Friend of Flat Billy**, turn to **1191** immediately. Otherwise, they will rush aboard and do what they can to make off with your cargo.

Dive overboard and abandon your cargo...   **1183**
Fight them off!   **1203**

❧ 1172 ❧

A careful shot could take out a crucial part of the steam engine's exposed regulatory system, or convince the crew that they are in mortal danger. You steady your shooting arm and pull the trigger: make an ACCURACY roll of difficulty 11.

Successful ACCURACY roll!   **1184**
Failed ACCURACY roll!   **1277**

❧ 1173 ❧

You manage to get your workmate out, but by the time you do, his crushed chest and smitten crown have given up on him: he has stopped breathing.

Others have come to help and your efforts are not ignored: gain a **solidarity point**. However, the Metropolitan Sewer Company are unsatisfied with the degree of caution your team are shown - they blame the dead worker for carrying an open flame - and only pay you **£1** for your work. After all, they now have to pay to rebuild the sewer, not simply unblock it.

Ride away...   **139**

❧ 1174 ❧

You follow the relieved landlord down to the beer cellar, where he says his cashbox is kept. However, on the final step, he tugs a cord and a heavy beam falls on your head, knocking you to the ground. Gain a **wound** and a temporary -2 modifier to your NIMBLENESS! He then turns on you, wielding a heavy club.

Landlord	Weapon: **club (PAR 2)**
Parry:	7
Nimbleness:	5
Toughness:	5

Victory!   **1186**
Defeat!   **1500**

❧ 1175 ❧

The members of the Council become yet sterner. "Then let us begin," says Commissoner Timms. "How do you choose to do this? Will you be the silent hand of the masses, or will you arrest the King and bring him to the block?"

Consider this carefully: you will only be able to bring about a public execution if the Progressives hold a majority in Parliament, and if you count on the support of key members of the Establishment. On the other hand, an assassination attempt will surely be the greatest trial your skills and prowess have ever undergone.

"I will assassinate him."	**1097**
"He must be tried and found guilty."	
(*Converse*)	**1117**
"I must prepare before making this choice."	**1187**

❧ 1176 ❧

You slit the informer's throat and leave him in his parlour in a widening pool of blood. To make the reason plain, you leave a scarlet scrawl on the whitewashed wall: *INFORMER*.

This will not go unnoticed: gain a **solidarity point**, add 1 to your RUTHLESSNESS and note that you are now **Wanted by the Constables**. You can also add an **informer's notebook** and **£15 4s** from the dead man's pockets to your **Adventure Sheet**. Erase the codeword *Chatty* and gain the codeword *Chirrup*.

Leave the inn... **28**

❧ 1177 ❧

Just as you are leaning inbetween the wagons, reaching for the coupling, a pothole jolts the gap closed, crushing your hand. You manage to pull away, but the damage is done: unless you have a **mechanical hand**, you must gain a **wound**. If you now have five **wounds**, turn to **999** immediately. Otherwise, you must call off your attack and find somewhere to tend your damaged limb as quickly as a possible.

Ride away... **noted passage**

❧ 1178 ❧

You take up a position where you're hidden and steady your aim. A few shots at the lanterns and cylinders of the Constables' steamer should worry them. Maybe a few at their feet as well. After all, you don't want to get into a shootout here. Make an ACCURACY roll of difficulty 10.

Successful ACCURACY roll!	**1226**
Failed ACCURACY roll!	**1238**

❧ 1179 ❧

As you accelerate, gunfire - mechanised gunfire - erupts from the buildings across the street. Bullets whizz over your head, spatter against the heavy mantle of the Ferguson's bonnet, and kick up from the cobbles beneath your feet. Roll a dice to see how you fare:

Score 1-2	Gain **two wounds**...
Score 3-4	Gain **two damage points**...
Score 5-6	Escape unharmed...

If your velosteam is now **beyond repair**, turn to **1111** immediately. If not, but you now have **five wounds**, turn to **113**. Otherwise, you will manage to reach the cover of the Thames Tunnel and get away.

Ride through the tunnel... **649**

❧ 1180 ❧

The footman looks at the calling card in surprise, but he admits you to a waiting room. There is a nice picture - firmly attached to the wall - and no moveable furniture other than a bowl of pot pourri. After a few minutes, you are allowed within the house itself.

Turn to... **1205**

❧ 1181 ❧

"The place you want," you hear a tipsy porter telling his friend, "Is St Margaret's Court, near the Bank of England. There's a bloke there can knock you up any paperwork you please. Even clear your record, if you were to have one."

When you find yourself in St Margaret's Court, note the passage number and double it to find the forger, who obviously keeps as low a profile as possible.

Turn to... **noted passage**

❧ 1182 ❧

The road here passes through a cutting dug by the Guild to lessen the gradient for the heavy wagon trains. At one particularly steep section, a well-placed explosive charge could set off landslide and block the road entirely. Remove the **explosives** from you **possessions** and make an ENGINEERING roll of difficulty 15, adding 1 for each level of **explosives expert** you possess.

Successful ENGINEERING roll!	**1192**
Failed ENGINEERING roll!	**1202**

❧ 1183 ❧

You leap into the water with a splash. Any paper **possession**, such as letters, affidavits, notes or tickets in your satchel, will now be ruined and should be removed from your **Adventure Sheet**. On top of this, Flat Billy's men ransack your boat and what cargo they don't steal, they spoil. Remove any **cargo units** from your **Adventure Sheet** as well.

Clamber aboard, dry off and sail on...　　**945**

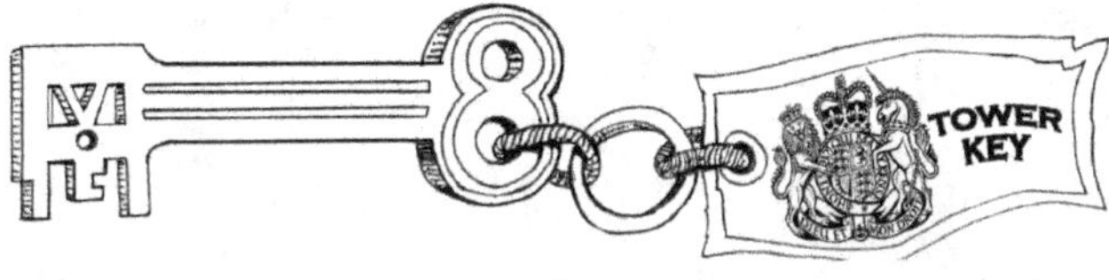

❧ 1184 ❧

Your shot strikes a valve and ricochets off into the cab. The fireman leans over his driver and hauls on the emergency steam release, bringing the engine and its cargo to a shuddering stop. You can take **£1 17s** and any of the following: a **shovel**, some **wirecutters**, a **tarpaulin**, two **ropes** and some **goggles (MOT+1)**. Gain the codeword *Cabal* and you will now be **Wanted by the Haulage Guild** unless you are wearing a mask.

Ride away...　　**noted passage**

❧ 1185 ❧

A crowd of men are lounging in Crafton's yard, eager for employment. "What'll you offer us for a good day's work?" asks their self-appointed spokesman. "We're steady lads, even if we've all been inside. None of us is scared of work."

A gang of twelve men agree on a rate of five shillings apiece: **£3** in total. If you choose to pay this, you can send them to work at your Millwall workshop and tick the box marked ☐ Casual Labourers in passage **1308**.

Return to Lambeth...　　**647**

❧ 1186 ❧

You lug the landlord's unconscious body out into the freight yard and prop him up against the door to his inn. Then you lash together a sign and sling it around his neck: *INFORMER*. The common people will be relieved to know that someone is looking out for them: gain a **solidarity point**. Returning to his cellar, you find **£13 4s** in his cash box, an **informer's notebook** and a **telescope**. Erase the codeword *Chatty* and gain the codeword *Chirrup*. Note that your NIMBLENESS will also have returned to normal.

Leave the inn...　　**28**

❧ 1187 ❧

The other members of the High Council agree to defer to your judgement. After all, you have become as influential and important within the Compact as any of them.

"But let us not delay long," warns Commissioner Timms. "Every day, more workers die in slavery and want."

When you consider the time ripe, revisit the High Council here and give them your word.

Return to the warehouse...　　**489**

❧ 1188 ❧

You leave your velosteam and creep towards the Constables' steamer. It seems that the driver is going to give in and pay up for the privilege of making his way up the road, but as soon as he brings out coinage, the Constables become greedy and start asking for more. You have a few moments to create some havoc with the road engine: make an ENGINEERING roll of difficulty 9.

Successful ENGINEERING roll!　　**1212**
Failed ENGINEERING roll!　　**1222**

❧ 1189 ❧

A convenient beech tree provides you with a perch. Lying on a wide branch over the very middle of the roadway, you lower your fishing line and wait. Roll two dice to see what you catch.

Score 2-5　　Nothing at all...
Score 6　　a wallet containing **15s**...
Score 7　　a **lantern**...
Score 8　　a **fur coat**...
Score 9　　a **sabre (PAR3)**...
Score 10　　a **mask**...
Score 11　　a **skeleton key**...
Score 12　　a **guildsman's medallion**...

Ride away...　　**noted passage**

❧ 1190 ❧

The fight begins with a cautious circling to and fro, as the sailor looks for his entry. Then he steps forward and throws a surprising long left jab at you, only just giving you enough warning to move your head. His brawny fist grazes the side of your head and he follows with a right uppercut on the step.

But that's enough to get an idea of the man's size

and speed. He relies on his reach, his power, and very short bursts of energy. He has little idea of protecting himself and as long as you keep away from those massive, heavy hands, you are able to land blow after punishing blow into his side. Misjudging for a moment, you catch his right hook with your temple, spin with the blow and only just stay upright. The crowd around you cheer appreciatively. Bets are still being made as you continue through eight, nine, ten rounds. Both panting, moving much slower now, it is as much a competition of stamina as power. You have landed far more blows, but his are heavier, and another to the head will cause you some serious damage.

Then the sailor blinks for a moment, as sweat obscures his vision, and you step inside his reach and break your knuckles open on his upper lips. Mingled blood pours over his chin. He steps back to swing but you follow him with a heavy left to the gut, followed directly by your right, leaning into the blow with all your weight. He staggers and falls backwards, groans, and lies still.

The match is yours - and with it, the prize purse of five guineas (**£5 5s**).

Turn to...   **872**

❧ 1191 ❧

"Hey there! Back off, you bruisers!"

Some of the gang members recognise you as Flat Billy's particular friend. Their leader turns the group around. "Come on, mates. There's a craft moored by the bend piled with hay. That'll make a pretty fire."

Unmoor and continue upstream...   **945**

❧ 1192 ❧

The ground shakes and, from your vantage point, you watch as the chalk and mud of the cutting tumble and cover the road. It was well-timed: the driver of the road -train, only a dozen yards distant, hits the emergency brakes and sends steam shooting out of every vent.

You dash forwards, weapons readied. After such a surprise, the guards and crew will be much easier to intimidate. To call on them to surrender, make a RUTHLESSNESS roll of difficulty 15.

Successful RUTHLESSNESS roll   **1214**
Failed RUTHLESSNESS roll!   **1225**

❧ 1193 ❧

You hear men muttering about their need for work. Asking around, you find that they muster at the Grapes near Limehouse, where dockmasters and foremen hire casual labourers on daily rates. "Though the lads at Crafton's try to undercut us," says one man. "But no-one trusts them dirty convicts."

Turn to...   **noted passage**

❧ 1194 ❧

Mr Forsi comes out to talk you through the demands of the job. "With this Exhibition, we need more staff. Leave your machine here and take this little van out to the Hyde Park. Sell as much as you can! The more you sell, the more I pay you!" It will be a short-term position only, he explains.

Drive Forsi's van over to the Exhibition...   **1221**

❧ 1195 ❧

Anticipating gunfire from the buildings opposite, you kick your Ferguson forward and grab the thin man, lifting him off his feet and putting him between you and the windows of the dreary windows.

"Hold your fire," you cry. "What do you want?"

The man laughs, despite the tightness of your grip. "We want our diamonds back, of course. Or failing that, their value. And we certainly want you, and every other road thief to realise that they cannot expect to rob the company and get away with it."

You shake him hard. "Who are you? Who is this company?"

He grins. "You'll hear from us again. Don't you worry about that."

You are getting nowhere. You throw him onto the road and accelerate towards the tunnel. Mechanised gunfire rattles out from the warehouses, but you are already on your way.

Through the tunnel!   **649**

❧ 1196 ❧

You hear a group discussing the growing influence of the Camden Brewery. "It's almost as if he wants to take over all the pubs in London!" complains a drinker.

"Who does?"

"Why, the director, of course!"

"I don't know what's the fuss," replies another. "It's good clean beer. Not your muddy home-brewed stuff. And my cousin Freddy works there. Fair

❧ 1197 ❧

To produce machinery of the quality to exhibit will be an achievement indeed. It will greatly add to your status and fame, possibly winning you lucrative contracts or sales.

Each invention can only be attempted once: when you have gathered everything you need, cross out the option below before turning to the relevant passage.

	Materials and money	Tools and facilities
⊕ an automatic cargo selector...	**punchcards (Aramanth A), brass flange joint, copper pipe £14**	☑ Journeyman or greater, ☑ Travelling crane
		Turn to... **879**
⊕ a better gun...	**pneumatic manual (ENG+3), titanium alloy, carbine £25**	☑ Journeyman or greater, ☑ Casting forge ☑ Coal delivery
		Turn to... **790**
⊕ a mechanical elephant...	**mechanical elephant design welding tools, brass flange joint, net, steam accordion, £45**	☑ Master engineer, ☑ Casting forge ☑ Coal delivery, ☑ Casual labourers, ☑ Travelling crane,
		Turn to... **1505**
Return to the workshop...		**1308**

employers, good wages. Times have got to change, that's all."

"Well, there's work there for those that want it," says the first speaker. "As for me, I'll stick with what I know," and he orders another pint.

Turn to...   **noted passage**

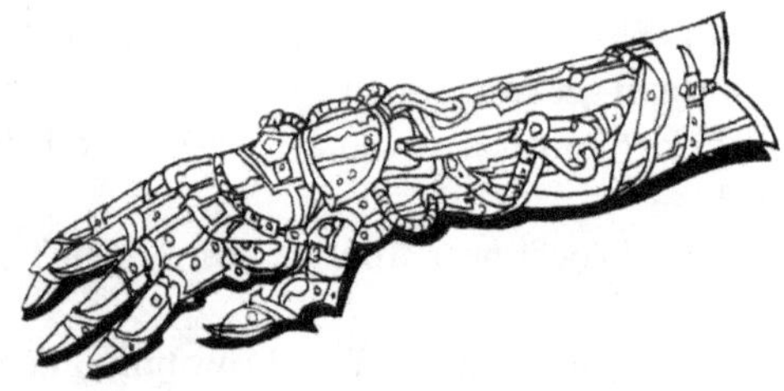

❧ 1198 ❧

The Baroness is very pleased with the proof. "So that old fart gave in, did he? Thank you." Remove the **lineage transcript** from your possessions. She writes you a fresh **Letter of Introduction**. "This should recommend you to some important people. Now let me see what else I can do for you." She gives you **ten guineas in banknotes** and offers you the choice of any two of the following items: an **ivory fan**, a **parasol**, a **box of cigars** or a **bottle of wine**.

Leave the old woman...   **151**

❧ 1199 ❧

It is late when you turn your velosteam into the yard outside the Flask at Highgate. A few lights still gleam from the parlour windows. Inside you find a seat at the bar beside a bald old man. Your few coppers buy you a dish of stew and a hunk of stale bread - and with that, your purse is empty.

"What, come to seek your fortune in the reeking metropolis of London?" asks the old man scornfully. "You won't be the last to come this way thinking that, though you're better prepared than most," he adds, eying your weaponry and road clothes.

"So what fortune can I expect to find in the city?"

He leans back and breathes out a long stream of pipe-smoke. "It depends, doesn't it? On exactly what sort of adventurer you might be. Perhaps you'll take up the cause of the common folk and deal with the gangs gripping Whitechapel, though that won't exactly be a day's work. The Chief Constable doesn't give a farthing for the poor, so perhaps you could try to right that wrong. Or are you less of an altruist than I assumed? There's opportunities to make money on every corner. You could make yourself useful to the Guilds in the City, like the Chimney Sweepers or the Brewers, or go burglarising Mayfair townhouses yourself. Trust me, there's adventure on every side."

"Tell me more about the Constabulary."   **1247**
"Who are these gangs in the East End?"   **1257**
"What about the revolution?"   **1267**

❧ 1200 ❧

All that is behind you. You are steaming through the plashy mud towards the city, with one careful eye on your boiler pressure and another on your coal-gas reserves, when you see a Constabulary steamer and a private steam carriage halted in the road. After approaching within earshot, you realise that the Constables must be stopping the travellers on some pretence. Raised, angry voices protest at their treatment.

"I've already paid the highway toll, my carriage license is in order and you've identified each of my passengers against their Citizen Numbers," argues the driver. "How can a carriage-man like myself do business? I must reach St Albans by morning."

"Just you mind your tone," says the leading Constable smoothly. "Or I'll have you on a charge. I think we're going to have a look at the luggage you're carrying. We've had a tip-off about smuggling on this route. Unless you've some reason right there that we should let you pass." He puts out his hand.

You've simply come across Constables extorting money from travellers. Is this the time for you to get involved? You can spot two Constables, but there may be others nearby, and you may not be able to count on the travellers' gratitude. Perhaps releasing the brake on their steamer would divert the Constables' attention... Or maybe you could loose off a few shots from the darkness.

Tamper with the Constables' steamer...	**1188**
Get out your blunderpistol and open fire...	**1178**
Ride on past towards Highgate...	**1199**

❧ 1201 ❧

"Well, I figure the forger in St Margaret's Court might help you out," says one beggar. "Although you'll need a fair pot of cash."

"Where's that?" you ask.

"Near the Bank of England," chortles another beggar.

Thank them... **noted passage**

❧ 1202 ❧

The charge goes off too late and the roadtrain has almost passed by. Nonetheless, the rush of chalk and earth slams the final wagon onto its side. Fearing attack from revolutionaries, the driver opens his regulator and steams on, abandoning the wagon. Roll a dice to see what it holds:

Score 1-2	Worthless bricks...
Score 3	six **bolts of cloth**...
Score 4	A **strongbox**...
Score 5	a **tarpaulin** and eight pieces of **copper pipe**...
Score 6	some **wirecutters** and a **shovel**

Ride away... **noted passage**

❧ 1203 ❧

You and the mate grab something to defend yourselves with and prepare to hold off the gang. If you can hurt them enough into hanging back, you might just have the chance to untie your moorings and head upstream.

Gang	Weapons: **clubs (PAR 2)**
Parry:	6
Nimbleness:	4
Toughness:	3

Victory!	**945**
Defeat!	**1211**

❧ 1204 ❧

You swing down from the struts and supports with a ringing laugh, hand-over-handing down a tensioning cable as the guildsmen clamber after you. A resounding crack announces the final over-stress of the beleaguered tower mechanism, and the top begins to totter, topple and fall.

You hit the ground running, leap over a pile of lumber, barrel through the gate and leap aboard your velosteam, leaving chaos and flames behind you.

Ride away! **614**

❧ 1205 ❧

"So you've found the vixen in her den," laughs Diana 'Diamonds' Derwent, Lady Serene, rising from her couch to greet you. "And here stands the Steam Highwayman, if my informers do not deceive me."

"I enjoyed our game of croquet."	
(**Lady Serene's calling card**)	**1223**
"You sent me to jail." (**burnt rose**)	**1233**
"I have been hearing tales about you..."	
(**burglary ballad**)	**1243**
"I am, indeed, that legendary figure."	**1504**

❧ 1206 ☙

You hear about the influx of tourists that the Great Exhibition has brought to the city. Apparently travellers have come from across the kingdom and even from Europe to see the wonders of industry and trade displayed in the Crystal Palace at Hyde Park.

I even 'eard," says a woman supping port and lemonade, "That the ice-cream man up at Battlebridge Basin needs more hands to sell his ice-cream, he's doing that well."

"You mean Forsi, up Pentonville way? He'll be glad of the trade. Lots of demand for his ice."

Turn to...   **noted passage**

❧ 1207 ☙

The plan is straightforward: allow the roadtrain to pass you, approach it from behind, toss your grapple into the luggage compartment and haul away whatever you manage to hook.

However, as you speed towards the Guild road train, you realise that there is a guard mounted on the final wagon. He immediately pulls an alarm cord and readies his weapon. Whether he hits you or not depends on sheer luck: roll a dice.

Score 1-2   Gain a **wound**!
Score 3-4   Gain a **damage point**!
Score 5-6   A miss!

If your velosteam is **beyond repair**, turn to **1111** immediately. If not, but you now have **five wounds**, turn to **999**. Otherwise you can make good your plan to grab something from the road train. Make a NIMBLENESS roll of difficulty 12.

Successful NIMBLENESS roll!   1229
Failed NIMBLENESS roll!   **noted passage**

❧ 1208 ☙

Inside the tower, a beefeater stands guard at the door to the jewel chamber. He is turned away from you for now, and you have a moment to strike. If you have a **bottle of chloroform**, turn to **924** immediately. Otherwise, you must attempt to knock him out: make a NIMBLENESS roll of difficulty 14, adding 2 if you possess a **blackjack**, **cosh**, **club** or other blunt weapon.

Successful NIMBLENESS roll!   937
Failed NIMBLENESS roll!   947

❧ 1209 ☙

The driver of the Union steamer spots you and increases speed. These passenger carriages are not like the heavy engines of the Haulage Guild: they can travel up to twenty-five miles in an hour on a good surface! To keep up and to force the driver to pull over, you will need to ride hard. Make a MOTORING roll of difficulty 12, adding 1 if you have a **gas pressuriser** or **reinforced boiler** fitted.

Successful MOTORING roll!   1096
Failed MOTORING roll!   1277

❧ 1210 ☙

You do your best to maintain your cool, continuing to announce the upcoming stops through the speaking tube, and projecting the best sort of authoritative calm that you can. Make a GALLANTRY roll of difficulty 13.

Successful GALLANTRY roll!   1242
Failed GALLANTRY roll!   1252

❧ 1211 ☙

With a final crack on the head, you are pitched into the canal unconscious. As a punishment for your resistance, the gang loot your cargo and sink your boat - remove it from your **Adventure Sheet**.

You won't see your mate again: hopefully he managed to get away. As for you, you drift downstream in the dark...

Turn to...   1106

❧ 1212 ☙

It doesn't take you long to find the handbrake and the regulator on the unfamiliar machine. With the wheels

released and steam easing into the pistons, the Constabulary steamer begins to move...

"Captain, the steamer!" yells the Constable to his officer. They immediately turn from the driver and dash after their vehicle, which is veering towards the ditch. Can you withold a scornful laugh? The driver of the passenger carriage jumps up into his seat and sets his own vehicle moving, throwing you a grateful wave. Gain a **solidarity point**.

Ride on towards Highgate...　　　　　**1199**

❧ 1213 ❧

"It's you, ain't it? The Steam Highwayman!" The drinkers have heard about your charitable heart and your good deeds and are proud to have you amongst them. Songs and dancing break out as they celebrate you. "The rich 'ave it coming, don't they?" cries one. "You'll see to that!"

It seems that whatever you have done, it has been remembered after all. Gain a **solidarity point** and remove the codeword *Compassionate*.

Turn to...　　　　　　　**noted passage**

❧ 1214 ❧

The crew and guards quickly surrender. "When we realised it was yer 'onour," says the driver. "It ain't worth our lives, is it, mates?" They are happy to be whole and unblooded. Roll a dice to see what you can take from them:

Score 1-2　**£1 10s** and a **strongbox**
Score 3-4　**£4 13s** and some **engineer's gloves (ENG+1)**
Score 5-6　**£5** and an **accordion**

Gain the codeword *Cabal* and note that you are now **Wanted by the Haulage Guild**, if you are not already.

Ride away...　　　　　　**noted passage**

❧ 1215 ❧

The foremen have no trouble taking you on as a day-labourer: workers willing to venture down into the stink are rare enough.

You will be paid in proportion to your ENGINEERING skill, representing your ability to help with the construction. However, there are certain risks associated with the work.

ENGINEERING score	Gain
1-4	**4s**
6-8	**6s**
9 +	**7s**

When you have been paid, roll two dice to see what the result of your work in the sewers has been.

Score 2-6　A day without injury...
Score 7-8　Gain a **fever (NIM-1 ING-2)** and the codeword *Clasp*...
Score 9-10　Gain a **wound** from falling bricks...
Score 11-12　Offered further work: turn to...　**1244**

Leave the sewer works...　　　　**471**

❧ 1216 ❧

You manage to get the barges across the river to Millwall, thumping them heavily into the mooring piles but without taking any damage to your own craft. The owner is less than pleased, but you forcibly make your point that he was taking a great risk lading them so deeply. He mutters and pays up: gain **£1 8s**.

Steam on to Limehouse...　　　　**968**

❧ 1217 ❧

The cargo selector is quite a challenge: along with the mechanical grasper that can hook, hold or heave goods, the much finer fingers that can read the attached punchcard need to be equally robust.

It takes a long time and many iterations, but eventually you have a working prototype, together with an **automatic cargo selector design**, which may in fact be worth more.

Prepare to exhibit the prototype...　　**1510**
Keep the prototype hidden for now...　　**1308**

✎ 1218 ✎

You are making your slow way through some of the narrowest and busiest parts of the King's canal. The water of the canal is filthy. On the surface floats a thick layer of refuse, straw, scraps of cloth, horse muck, dead dogs and scum.

The wharf at Battlebridge Basin, with its foundries and ice warehouse, is constantly busy: you can come alongside the wharf here to trade, if you wish.

	To buy	To sell
Charcoal	£16	£15
Furniture	£28	£26
Machinery	£32	£30
Pottery	£24	£22
Cotton	£8	£7
Woollen cloth	£11	£9
Coal	£15	£12
Beer	£22	£16
Wheat	-	£8
Malt	-	£6
Frozen meat	£12	£11
Ice	£4	-

Note that to carry **Frozen meat** or **Ice** you will need a **Perkins machine** fitted to your craft.

Steer east towards Limehouse...	**912**
Steer west towards Camden...	**993**
Moor at Battlebridge Basin...	**940**

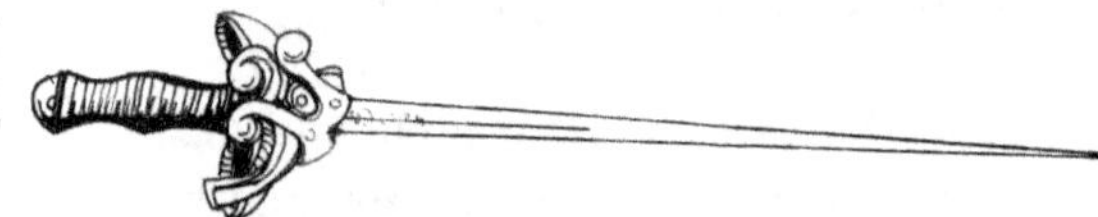

✎ 1219 ✎

The monks recognise you as one of their hated enemies. They snarl and draw long knives from their sleeves. The other customers step back to witness the fight.

"What about monkly meekness?" you ask.

"We will cut you to shreds," comes the reply. You must fight them. The monks will make two attacks for each one of yours.

Monks	Weapons: **knives (PAR 2)**
Parry:	10
Nimbleness:	8
Toughness:	7

Victory!	**33**
Defeat!	**999**

✎ 1220 ✎

They laugh. "For one o'your standing? Under a bridge is the best we can do, normalwise. But there's hotels in Bloomsbury, and rooms at some of the inns. Try the Gun in Blackwall, or the Holly Bush up in Hampstead."

Leave the beggars... **noted passage**

✎ 1221 ✎

The air grows noticeably cleaner as you drive west towards Hyde Park. Out there beneath the trees, groups of visitors picnic on the grass. It is an excellent place to sell ice-cream. The tones of the little van's carillon will call customers young and old. If you are **Wanted by the Constables**, turn to **1271** immediately. Otherwise, make a RUTHLESSNESS roll to see how successfully you proceed, subtracting 1 for each level of **musical ability** you possess.

Score 1-8	**1241**
Score 10 to 14	**1251**
Score 15+	**1261**

✎ 1222 ✎

You are struggling to release the brakes of the unfamiliar Constabulary steamer when they spot you and turn with shouts. You have no option but to leap onto your velosteam and make a getaway!

Hasten towards Highgate... **1199**

✎ 1223 ✎

Remove **Lady Serene's calling card**. It takes a moment for the lady to recognise you from that distant game on the banks of the Thames. Then she laughs, like a chime of bells. "That was a pleasant game, wasn't it?" She leans towards you. "Do you fancy another?"

"What are we playing for?"

"Oh, the Crown Jewels."

"You must be mad. I will be leaving now."	**750**
"Tell me more."	**1260**

✎ 1224 ✎

What right have a herd of commuting clerks to get angry with you? Don't they know who you are? You pull over and turn around to your passengers. Make a RUTHLESSNESS roll of difficulty 12.

Successful RUTHLESSNESS roll!	**1254**
Failed RUTHLESSNESS roll!	**1252**

❧ 1225 ❧

There is no other option left: they have had their chance. Now you must fight. You dash towards the stationary road engine and launch yourself at the guards.

Guild Guards   Weapons: **sabres (PAR 3)**
Parry: 10
Nimbleness: 7
Toughness: 5

Victory!   **1214**
Defeat!   **999**

❧ 1226 ❧

With a yelp, the Constable and his Captain dive for cover beneath their steamer. Another shot and shattered lantern glass showers over them. The driver of the passenger carriage wastes no time but accelerates up the road. You rise up out of the hedgerow and receive a wave of thanks as he speeds past: gain a **solidarity point**.

However, you had better clear out before the Constables send for reinforcements or make a serious effort to find their attacker. You aren't prepared to take on the lawkeeping forces just yet.

Mount up and ride away...   **1199**

❧ 1227 ❧

Remove the **punchcards (Habbukuk K)** and the **plan of St Katharine's docks**. It takes some time to input all the measurements from the plan of the docks, but together with the algorithm encoded within the punchcards, that is all that the powerful engine needs to tell you exactly where, and in what quantities, to place explosives for the maximum effect. You note down the readings as a **demolition sequence** and reset the machine.

Turn to...   **noted passage**

❧ 1228 ❧

You set out the same evening, up the Great North Road. The hired carriage is a weather-beaten, inconspicuous Norris engine, but it is fast, making a good twenty miles an hour even over the rutted roads. You ride well ahead, checking roadside coppices and turnings for any waiting danger, awaiting your charges at each Haulage Guild tollgate before riding ahead again.

As night falls, you pull into the yard of a roadside inn. You and the driver of the carriage, a thin man with a badly-scarred face, check over your machines before heading into the kitchen for your plates of stew.

You awake in the dusty hayloft in the middle of the night. It would be easy to out-run your employers in their Norris. If you broke into their room and found whatever it is they are carrying, you could be away long before dawn.

Go back to sleep...   **1239**
Try to steal their gems...   **1253**

❧ 1229 ❧

Your grappling iron catches in a crate and tears it open. Roll a dice to see what you hooked:

Score 1   a **telescope**...
Score 2   some **welding tools**...
Score 3   a pot of **waterproof paint**...
Score 4   some **explosives**...
Score 5   an **autogauge (MOT+3)**...
Score 6   a **mobile telegraph**...

Ride away...   **noted passage**

❧ 1230 ❧

It is only a short time until night falls and tonight is indeed, the full moon. If you have the mechanical wings that Marshal needs, you only need to find somewhere from which to launch and the game will be afoot!

Mount a rescue ...(**winged harness**) **1288**
Leave the Tower... **290**

❧ 1231 ❧

"Well, the Haulage Guild hate the railways, and the River Guild, of course. They'd love to see that fine station at Paddington go up in smoke. Or the docks down Rotherhithe flooded. But then the Telegraph Guild hate the Coal Board and the Coal Board, well, they hates everyone."

"Then there's the sweeps. You can buy a place among them - so long as you know how to work a brush."

"The Locobus drivers. They're always trying to get their licenses cheapened."

"That's true. Oh, and the Brewers."

"The Brewers 'ave an election for their new master a'coming up," says one beggar. "You could head up into the city and see about it. Their hall is north of St Paul's. Very rich guild, the brewers."

Thank them for their help... **noted passage**

❧ 1232 ❧

No matter what you do, the over-laden barges will not behave. One slams into the hull of a moored coaster and the other runs aground on a shingle bank. Their owner is furious, and promises to have you arrested. Note that you are now **Wanted by the River Guild**, fairly or otherwise.

Steam upriver... **933**
Steam downriver... **992**

❧ 1233 ❧

Remove the **burnt rose** from your **possessions**. "Maybe a little bit, yes? But I'm sure you had a pleasant time. Learnt a lot, met interesting people, hmm? So I did you a favour, really."

"I don't know if I would see it that way."

"Oh, don't hold a grudge. That really is so tiresome. And if you really wanted some portable property, I could offer you a part in my next endeavour."

"And that is?"
"The Crown Jewels."

"You must be mad. I will be leaving now." **750**
"Tell me more." **1260**

❧ 1234 ❧

There is nothing for it but to accelerate and drive like the Constables themselves are behind you. Make a MOTORING roll of difficulty 11.

Successful MOTORING roll! **1270**
Failed MOTORING roll! **1252**

❧ 1235 ❧

Your attempt to open the window goes on and on. The iron bars neither bend nor break, and their sockets are mortared iron-hard.

"Is this the best you can do?" teases Lady Diana. She takes over, using a small file in the most confident and surprising way. The bars slip out of place and you can climb through.

Turn to... **1208**

❧ 1236 ❧

"Well, you're probably looking for a *doctor*, ain't you?" laughs one of the strollers.

"There's a chap in Limehouse will stitch anyone back together," says another. "But be wary of him. There's something funny about that feller."

Leave the beggars... **noted passage**

❧ 1237 ❧

You are standing outside the house, wondering how to get in, when the door bangs open. Lady Serene herself is on the step. She has plainly caught sight of you at the window.

"So! You've summoned up the courage to come and visit me. I would still enjoy your help."

She invites you inside where she again explains her options over tea and cake. "What do you prefer? Breaking and entering - or a ruse? Those jewels are doing nobody any good there in the Tower."

"Let's do some dressing up." **596**
"I tend towards burglary anyway." **621**
"Thank you for the cake." **750**

᭝ 1238 ᭝

Your shots smack into the mud around the Constables' boots, but your carelessness has allowed them to clearly identify your hiding place. "Over there," yells the Captain, and he and the Constable rush your position with truncheon, sabre and carbine.

Meanwhile, the driver of the passenger carriage leaps back into his seat and sets his vehicle moving. You have succeeded in distracting the corrupt Constables, but have made little other gain. There is still time to clamber onto your velosteam and head off.

Ride away before the Constables get to you...   **1199**

᭝ 1239 ᭝

The next morning you set out again. The road is long and the ride uncomfortable. Just as you are tiring of the journey, something catches your eye. A short way ahead, a glint of metal reflects for a moment through a thicket. It is time to earn your payment: make a RUTHLESSNESS roll of difficulty 13.

Successful RUTHLESSNESS roll...   **1285**
Failed RUTHLESSNESS roll...   **1508**

᭝ 1240 ᭝

You don the airship officer's cap and limp out onto the road. The engine slows and the crew lean out to take a closer look.

"I say! Lend a chap a hand," you try. "I've been ambushed by ruffians. I'm trying to get back to my ship." Make an INGENUITY roll of difficulty 12 to take the crew by surprise, adding 2 if you have a **box of cigars** or a **monocle** of any kind.

Successful INGENUITY roll!   **1096**
Failed INGENUITY roll!   **1357**

᭝ 1241 ᭝

Your charming attitude and friendly demeanour, together with the tune of your little carillion, attracts many a visitor and you sell out of Forsi's excellent flavoured ice-cream in no time at all. You even share a laugh with a tourist who tells you about one of the Coal Board's celebrated machines inside the Exhibition. "They claim it is their own design, and quite new. Nonsense! The design has been stolen!" You return with an empty cart to Forsi's yard, where he pays you **12s** for the day's work.

Leave Forsi's...   **129**

᭝ 1242 ᭝

The passengers are calmed by your authority and your jokes. When you reach Threadneedle Street in the heart of the city, you are ten minutes behind schedule, but the clerks seemed cheered and ready to go about their work. They give you **8s** and a **pork pie** as tips.

Back at the depot, your manager can tell from the locobus's internal trip recorder that you missed several stops and lost time. He docks your pay and angrily informs you that you are unwelcome here. Perhaps you are not cut out to be a bus driver.

Leave the depot...   **84**

᭝ 1243 ᭝

Remove the **burglary ballad** from your **possessions**. "You mustn't believe everything you hear in this city," replies the lady.

"You deny that you stole the Duke of Sussex's ruby ring?"

"Oh that! I thought you meant something bad. Of course I took it. I have to keep my hand in, you know. What would people say about the Lady of the Burnt Rose if there weren't regular burglaries? You know all about the importance of reputation."

"And what next for you, then?"

"Well, I'm very glad you ask. There's a little place at the other end of town where they keep some pretty baubles. I don't want all of them - most of them are massive gaudy things. But one or two would be quite nice. And then there's the adventure of it." She sees your face. "I mean the Tower. The Crown Jewels. Perhaps you'd like to lend me your assistance? I could use a second, on a job this big."

"You must be mad. I will be leaving now."   **750**
"Tell me more."   **1260**

᭝ 1244 ᭝

The foreman is impressed with the way you get the dirt shovelled out of the way. "Comfortable underground, eh?" she asks. "We've need of clearers down under the Strand. Filthy work, but we'll pay you danger money."

The offer is **£2** for a day's work clearing blockages in the narrow sewers - paid at the end of the day, of course.

Take the work...   **1278**
Turn her down...   **471**

❧ 1245 ❧

You open the regulator and steam rushes into the Ferguson's driving pistons. With no flywheel to even out the sudden acceleration, it takes a skilled rider to control the power of the engine, to cope with the uneven road and to steer. Make a MOTORING roll of difficulty 12, adding 1 if you possess **off-road tyres**.

Successful MOTORING roll!	**1102**
Failed MOTORING roll!	**1357**

❧ 1246 ❧

With debts and angry customers on your tail, you will now be black-listed by the river officials: note that you are now **Wanted by the River Guild**. They are unlikely to take any direct action, but should you fall in with the Constables, it will be another damning mark.

With the river flowing out to sea, however, you are quickly able to put distance between yourself and Greenwich. In no time you come to East India Dock.

Turn to...	**1069**

❧ 1247 ❧

The wizened old drinker laughs. "Lord Hadrian Beaufort commands the Constables here. He's a nasty piece of work. Old family, as you might have guessed from the name, so not exactly in need of money. Still, a more corrupt and black-hearted soul couldn't live. He tolerates the gangs and lets the Guilds get away with their own private wars, so long as he and his men are paid." He tells you more about the Chief Constable, none of it flattering, such as the man's strange taste in entertainment and the rumours of his dungeons beneath Somerset House on the Strand.

"That's where the Constables are based?"

"Indeed. You won't find much happening in the city that doesn't lead you there."

"Now tell me about the gangs you mentioned."	**1257**
"Surely the seeds of revolution are stirring?"	**1267**
"That's enough, old man."	**1280**

❧ 1248 ❧

"Some pearls went missing," you mention to a journeyman tailor. He looks around.

"Can't talk about it now. Stand me a drink after work and I'll let you know."

Join him in the pub... (**3s**)	**1268**
Another time...	**47**

❧ 1249 ❧

The old forger licks his lips at the sight of your coins, then checks each one individually. He is, of course, uniquely able to distinguish counterfeit money. However, he seems happy with the payment and gets to work.

"You'll be wanting Lord Beaufort's name on this, I imagine," he says. "I can do a fair job of that. But what about the name of the prisoner?"

"Leave that blank," you reply. "I can fill that in."

"Right you are," he says, smoothing down the paper with a rounded blotter. "If you'll pass me that punch over there..."

A short while later you leave with the **release order** tucked carefully into your pocket.

Leave the forger...	**221**

❧ 1250 ❧

The occupants of the carriage are at your mercy! Roll a dice to see whom you have stopped.

Score 1	A family visiting the city...	**1281**
Score 2	A baker of cakes...	**1512**
Score 3	A writer...	**1343**
Score 4	A well-connected lady...	**1393**
Score 5	An old man...	**1447**
Score 6	A sculptor...	**1464**

❧ 1251 ❧

You manage to sell about half of your stock before the evening brings ice-cream sales to a close. Many a prospective customer has thought twice before turning away from your intimidating figure, and when you return, tired and frustrated, to Forsi's yard, he pays you a meagre **4s** for the day's work.

Leave the yard...	**129**

❧ 1252 ❧

Despite your efforts, you simply get further and further behind schedule. Your passengers are furious and one slams the door as he alights, bending it out of shape.

Back at the depot, the manager shakes his head. Not only have you performed miserably, but he must now charge you for the damage to his vehicle. He informs you that unless you pay for the repair, he will hand you over to the Constables.

Give him the money... (**£1 4s**)	**86**
Call his bluff...	**13**

❧ 1253 ❧

The room where the two monks are staying is a short distance away. You silently lift the latch and find where they have placed their luggage. Among it is a small, carefully locked box. Make an INGENUITY roll of difficulty 14, adding 2 if you possess **lockpicks** or 4 if you have a **skeleton key**.

Successful INGENUITY roll! **1264**
Failed INGENUITY roll! **1274**

❧ 1254 ❧

You whip up a kind of manufactured rage that quietens the rowdy passengers down. Silence reigns in the locobus, so that you are soon back on schedule.

You collect passengers in the city and bring them back to Camden and ply the route for the remainder of the day. After an entire day's driving, during which you have learnt much about the city, you are paid **6s**. You can also attempt to improve your MOTORING score: roll a single dice and if you roll higher than your ability, increase it by 1. If, however, you roll a 1, you must decrease your MOTORING score, reflecting the bad habits you have picked up from driving the locobus.

Finish the day's work... **84**

❧ 1255 ❧

The waiter pockets the crown and tells you more. He identifies her as Diana Derwent, Lady Serene, who lives in Derwent House in Mayfair. "She is fabulously rich, mon ami," he says. "So why ze likes of 'er needs to steal...?" He shrugs.

"You wouldn't make an accusation to the Constables?"

He snorts. "What would zat gain me? Probably a beating and dismissal. Zis is ze way wiz ze nobility. In my country also." Gain the codeword *Cool*.

Leave the ball... **794**

❧ 1256 ❧

You and the mate set to work with cargo crane and boathooks, dragging the now waterlogged cotton bales out of the filthy river and stacking them on the quay at Mauritius Wharf. The *Lionfish*'s mate oversees the job. "You've fairly ruined half of it," he says angrily. "So pay up: you owe me twelve pound for the damage."

Pay up... (**£12**) **948**
Unwilling or unable to pay... **1246**

❧ 1257 ❧

He smirks. "Flat Billy rules everything east of Whitechapel, north of the river. You don't want to cross him. But southside, it's Mrs Handel you have to worry about. Rob the wrong carriage and she'll want to know about it." He shows you the nub of a missing finger on his left hand. "She did that herself with a set of shears, on account of I didn't pay my dues on time. Years ago now... but she's still in charge down there."

"Don't the Constables deal with them?" **1247**
"I've heard of revolutionaries in the docks." **1267**
"Smoke your pipe in peace. I've heard enough." **1280**

❧ 1258 ❧

Beyond the village of Southall the influence of the city grows: milestones mark off your distance to the Tower, laden vans travel to the city and empty ones return, pedestrians trudge ahead of you and nary a single figure is walking back towards you. It is as though the city is a gigantic drain, swallowing anything near enough to feel its gravity. Note passage **754** and roll a dice to see what you encounter:

Score 1-2 A people's march... **283**
Score 3-4 An uninterrupted journey... **794**
Score 5-6 A stolen carriage... **300**

❧ 1259 ❧

You kneel down in the mud, the better to steady your shot, and ready your weapon. Make an ACCURACY roll of difficulty 11 to hit some crucial mechanical part and bring the engine to a stop.

Successful ACCURACY roll! **1102**
Failed ACCURACY roll! **1357**

❧ 1260 ❧

"It's quite straightforward, really. I have two plans, both of which should provide some entertainment. I am considering either some sort of impersonation - a ruse or something - or a classic burglary, maybe from the air. Do either of those appeal to you?"

Before accepting the lady's offer, it might be wise to review your ability score and **possessions**. The ruse will require high ENGINEERING and GALLANTRY scores, while the burglary will naturally favour INGENUITY and NIMBLENESS. To complete the former, you might want to be equipped with genteel disguises, **punchcards** and a fat purse for bribes. For the other option, you might want a **grappling iron**,

skeleton key and the like, and maybe your own **winged harness**, if you possess such things. Gain the codeword *Curly* and make your choice.

"Burglary is both healthy and exhilarating."	**621**
"I never turn down the chance to perform."	**596**
"I will return when I have fully prepared."	**750**

❧ 1261 ❧

There is something about your appearance which utterly terrifies your prospective customers. None will buy from you, and a group urchins begin to throw stones and horse droppings. You ride disconsolately back to Forsi's yard.

"Not a single sale? Mamma mia, you have to be the worst salesperson I have ever come across! A baby could sell this ice-cream!"

Ride away... **129**

❧ 1262 ❧

You summon your most fearsome aspect and step to the roadside, displaying all your weapons. "Stop that engine!" you cry in a voice of command. Make a RUTHLESSNESS roll of difficulty 12, adding 1 if you are **Wanted by the Atmospheric Union** and 1 more if you are **Wanted by the Constables**.

Successful RUTHLESSNESS roll...	**1096**
Failed RUTHLESSNESS roll...	**1446**

❧ 1263 ❧

Your careful shots smash the forelanterns of the carriage and force its driver to halt. You approach the passenger door cautiously and with your weapons lowered. "Step out and hand over all your valuables!" you cry.

The manufacturers have been jostled and bumped on their journey, and now they are being forced out into the darkening evening to hand over their wallets. They are far from pleased.

Their pockets and purses net you a total of **£15 3s**, and you can also take a **top hat**. However, the most alert of the passengers takes a good look at you: he certainly recognises you from a previous encounter, and you will now be **Wanted by the Constables**.

Turn to... **noted passage**

❧ 1264 ❧

The lock snaps open. Inside is a blue leather bag, containing three fine **sapphires**. You pocket the bag, creep downstairs and jump aboard your velosteam.

The night enfolds you as you ride south, back towards London. Your next task will be finding someone willing to buy these gems. However, you are now **Wanted by the Brethren**.

Ride to Islington... **151**

❧ 1265 ❧

You have managed to halt the vehicle and its occupants are at your mercy. Roll a dice to see who is inside:

Score 1	An angler...	**1293**
Score 2	An architect...	**1347**
Score 3	Minor royalty...	**1405**
Score 4	A diamond merchant...	**1435**
Score 5	The Bishop of Bayswater...	**1487**
Score 6	The Keeper of the Tower...	**1472**

❧ 1266 ❧

The men chatter about the craft on the river. "Lot of commotion down at the Nethundical moorings, off Greenwich," says one.

"I 'eard they's sailing for Spain fairly soon. Supportin' the French fleet, most like."

Another shakes his head. "Nah. Norway - the whaling fleet. I heard it from cousin Alf. You know he works in the chandlery down Rotherhithe."

Another changes the topic. "I saw that rustbucket *Tiger* moored up Blackwall way."

"Bleedin' slavers," says another angrily. "Sooner the Constables get aboard the better."

The river flow begins to slacken as the tide turns and the sea shoulders its way up into the city. "Right lads, cast off!"

Head through the bridge... **1401**

❧ 1267 ❧

"Yes, it's true. The Compact for so-called Workers' Equality have their cadres in the city. You can hear their recruiters on any street corner if your cars are open. They're always holding meetings in Pentonville. Where they're really based, I don't know. If I did, I'd sell that right on to the Constables and high-tail it with the money."

"Wouldn't you fear a reprisal after the revolution?"

He splutters, coughs and laughs. "Revolution?

Don't fool yourself. Those ratty ruffians won't ever get themselves organised enough to succeed in a revolution. They'd need someone to follow, wouldn't they? A great leader! Pah!"

"So what about the gangs?"   **1257**
"And the Constables?"   **1247**
"I'll think about what you've told me."   **1280**

❧ 1268 ❧

You buy the journeyman enough ale to be sure of getting the whole story. He tells you that there is only one woman who would dare to carry off a robbery like that. "Diana Derwent, of Derwent House. Mayfair."

"A lady?"

"By birth, maybe, but not in deed. They call her Diamond Diana, I heard."

Gain the codeword *Cool*.

Buy another drink... (**2s**)   **30**
Leave the pub...   **47**

❧ 1269 ❧

Everything seems fine to begin with, but with precious little freeboard and a mountain of cotton bales, your craft is unsteady and hard to steer. Then a screw-steamer comes churning downstream, leaving a long wake in its wings. Your boat bucks, tilts, and the heap of cotton comes crashing and splashing down.

The *Lionfish* crew are far from happy. It might be best to leave them to fish out their ruined cargo and get out of here.

Help them retrieve their cargo...   **1256**
Head downriver...   **1246**

❧ 1270 ❧

You make up the lost time, but your reckless driving, ignoring the instructions of traffic-directing Constables and cutting across the paths of other vehicles, cause several crashes in your wake. When you return to the depot, your manager is furious. "Get out of here!" he yells. "You're bringing our good name into disrepute." Note that you are now **Wanted by the Locobus Co-operative**.

Head into Camden...   **84**

❧ 1271 ❧

One of the boys looks back at you after returning the glass of his penny lick. A few moments later, you see him talking to a Constable. You have been recognised!

The ice-cream wagon is nowhere near as powerful as your velosteam, but if you are skillful and quick, you many be able to weave your way through the crowds and return to Battlebridge ahead of the Constables. Make a MOTORING roll of difficulty 10. No customisations can help you now: your velosteam is back at Forsi's.

Successful MOTORING roll!   **1382**
Failed MOTORING roll!   **1361**

❧ 1272 ❧

How the letter has reached you is a mystery. It is addressed, in fine, confident script, to 'The Steam Highwayman'.

> *To that indefatigable rogue, the Steam Highwayman,*
>
> *I find myself at a loss. You do not know me, and may not know of me, but I have watch'd your progress with interest. My name is James Marshal, High King of Sand Bank, Lord of Great Shorbury, Marquis of the North Sea, and I have been wrongfully imprisoned by the government of this land and its King.*
>
> *They have not the right, for I too am a King.*
>
> *My land, Sand Bank, is a territory to the east of the Thames Estuary, beyond the limits and the jurisdiction of this Kingdom, but in an act of war, it was invaded and I have been captured.*
>
> *They have locked me in the Tower of London. I appreciate the dignity of such a hallowed place, but my cell is small and unhealthy, and I must return to my people.*
>
> *Come and rescue me. I have heard of the winged harness that airship crews use in an emergency - that should do the trick. Meet me on the roof of the tower on the night of the full moon and carry me off. I am a rich man and you will be amply rewarded.*

If you wish to attempt the rescue, you should keep **Marshal's letter**, and will need to locate a **winged harness** and bring it to the Tower of London.

Turn to...   **noted passage**

❦ 1273 ❧

"That's a friendly bird," you say to the sailor.

"Aye, she is," he replies. "Won't bite."

The parrot hops over thoughtfully. "Kaaaawk. Lucky sweeps. Lucky sweeps."

"Make her do that trick," says another sailor. "Go on. She knows all the coal prices up and down the river."

The sailor prods the bird and asks her. "Gloria - what price coal?"

"Seven pound Camden, twenty-two South Bank! Kaaawk!"

The voice of a barge master rings out. "All right now, lads. Tides a-turn. Cast off and upriver we go!"

Head upriver through the bridge...   **1401**

❦ 1274 ❧

You cannot make any progress with the box, so you are forced to abandon your plan to rob the monks and return to your responsibilities. You creep back to the hayloft and sleep until dawn.

Ride on...   **1239**

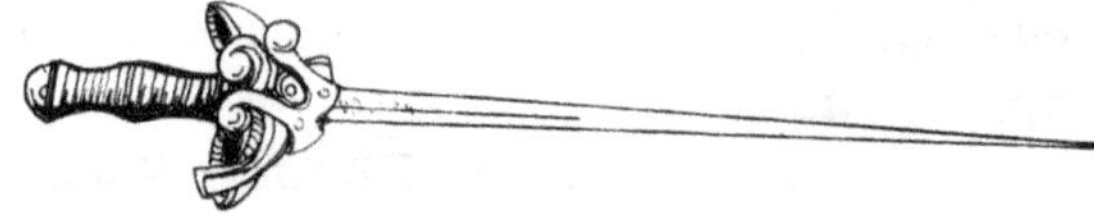

❦ 1275 ❧

Apparently, a consignment of pearls imported by a high-class dressmaker has been interrupted: the lesser quality stones were delivered in the night, along with a burnt rose, but the precious pink or black pearls have not been seen since.

"Where is this dressmaker?" you ask.

"Marylebone way," comes the reply.

Gain the codeword *Charred*.

Drink up...   **noted passage**

❦ 1276 ❧

Your fearsome appearance and reputation completely terrify the carriage driver and the passengers. You order them to climb down into the road while you rifle through their luggage. Beneath some perfectly ordinary trunks, you find a **strongbox**, sure to contain some valuables. You strap it onto the back of your velosteam and make off.

Turn to...   **noted passage**

❦ 1277 ❧

The driver is far from impressed at your attempt. You catch her goggled eye as she speeds past, laughing. She makes a deliberate swerve, trying to knock you down. Roll a dice to see how you fare:

Score 1-2   Dive into the hedge: lose a random **possession**

Score 3-4   Dodge the vehicle

Score 5-6   She clips your velosteam: gain a **damage point**

If your velosteam is now **beyond repair**, turn to **1111**. Otherwise, you mount up and ride away.

Turn to...   **noted passage**

❦ 1278 ❧

The next morning you report to the team at the Strand, where you are issued with a **shovel** and directed to an unremarkable manhole. The chap in charge ties a neckerchief across his face and climbs down the ladder.

You splash into running sewage - note that you now **stink (GAL-2)** until further notice. You begin to clamber and squeeze through the tunnels in search of blockages. Which way will you head?

Turn left towards the hotels...   **1297**
Turn right towards the park...   **1337**

❦ 1279 ❧

With a hiss of released steam and a squeal of old brake-blocks, the carriage shudders to a stop in the mud. Roll a dice to see who is inside:

Score 1   A governess...   **1289**
Score 2   A successful farmer...   **1309**
Score 3   A French manufacturer...   **1334**
Score 4   A detective...   **1354**
Score 5   A recruiting sergeant...   **1366**
Score 6   An American writer...   **1423**

❦ 1280 ❧

You leave the old man and finish your meagre supper thoughtfully. If what he says is true, then London has the potential to make you very rich - or very sorry you ever came here.

Leave the Flask...   **28**

❧ 1281 ❧

You have stopped a family who have travelled to London to visit the Great Exhibition in Hyde Park. The father, a thin and desperate man, tries to hide his six children and his wife behind him. His pale face betrays his terror.

Rob the family...   **1407**
Treat them charitably... (**10s**)   **1413**

❧ 1282 ❧

The constable turns tail, rather than deal with you and an angry crowd, and the actors are able to finish their performance. A grateful actor brings you a small share of the takings afterwards: **15s**.

Turn to...   **noted passage**

❧ 1283 ❧

Under the cover of darkness, you clamber up the framework of the Rotherhithe Class B tower, using the grappling hook to reach out onto the widely-spread subsidiary arms. You perch on a strut and look about for the best way to bring the telegraph to a stop.

You are only a short distance from the upper cabin, where operators scan the horizon for incoming messages, so you have to move stealthily. If you have any **telegraphy** skill, turn to **543** immediately. Otherwise, you must make a combined ENGINEERING and NIMBLENESS roll of difficulty 19: add your ENGINEERING and NIMBLENESS scores, together with any modifiers, and the total of two dice.

Successful roll!   **543**
Failed roll!   **591**

❧ 1284 ❧

You and the mate tie up at the little jetty below St Thomas' chapel, halfway across London Bridge, and wait for night to fall. Near midnight, a door in the lower level of the building opens, and a small group of men arrive, come to help unload your secret cargo. The **ballast stones** are moved aside (you can remove them from your **Adventure Sheet**) and the bales of silk quickly moved into the chapel crypt.

"Here's your share," says a scarred man. "But keep your mouth shut." He hands you **£5**.

Sail upriver...   **1401**
Sail downriver...   **968**

❧ 1285 ❧

At the sight of such a terrifying figure atop a powerful velosteam, the robbers scramble out of their hiding places and disperse. They don't want to risk a fight with you!

Ride on....   **1311**

❧ 1286 ❧

The bales of cotton make a tall tower, but your skill with loads and weights means that you are able to ensure it is stable, at least. Each bale is marked with a punched docket that is read by the decoding fiddle on the crane at Mauritius Wharf and hoisted directly into the waiting trailers.

"Easy work," says the mate of the *Lionfish*. "Reliable crews like yourselves are too hard to find along this stretch." Gain **15s**.

Head downstream...   **992**
Return to the moorings...   **930**

❧ 1287 ❧

With your lines made fast and the furnace stoked, you set off with the *Lilyputian*, as the steamer is called, in tow. Up around the Blackwall bend and onto Bigsby's reach, down past Woolwich, on and on, past Tripcock and Cross Ness. But when you approach Broadness, and your mate advises you wait for the tide to turn, the owner insists you steam on. There the river is a confused mass of currents: the Thames itself is trying to flow down to the sea, while the sea is pressing up into the city to the west. Your tug is swung by the mighty vigour of the river and before you realise, both you and the steamer grind ashore on the dreaded Blackshelf.

It is a full two tides later before you are able to get off, but the steamer is badly damaged and the owner refuses to pay you a penny. If you have a **strengthened screw**, you must remove it as a result of the grounding.

Steam back upriver...   **1069**

❧ 1288 ❧

Remove **Marshal's letter** from your **possessions**. Night finds you atop a tall clocktower on the roof of the Derbyshire Consolidated Investments Bank. As a sheaf of cloud covers the moon, you extend the leather and silk wings and lean into the wind.

The night breeze plucks you from the roof and sends you up on a warm draught over the chimneys. A

momentary view of the smoking city and the shimmering river... and then you dive towards the flat roof of the tower.

There is indeed a ragged figure, crouched against the leads, wildly looking up at the night. He sees your silhouette cross the sky and begins to wave. A twist of the controls sets you down beside him.

"My letter reached you," he gabbles. "I must get back to my people."

He looks nothing like a king, in attire or demeanour, but he receives your wary look with all the temper of one. "How dare you look at me like that! If you saw me in my royal robes, in the throne room, you would recognise me for who I am!" This is hardly the time to argue, but you had better hope that he is at least able to reward you.

The hesitation costs you, however. A door onto the roof bursts open and a pair of Tower Guards rush out, wielding their pikes angrily. Marshal shrieks in a far-from-regal manner and hides behind you. You must fight them!

Tower Guards	Weapons: **pikes (PAR 4)**
Parry:	10
Nimbleness:	6
Toughness:	4

Victory!	**1023**
Defeat!	**1500**

❧ 1289 ❧

The lady is a governess of a rich family in Mayfair. She has **£4 8s** in her purse, a **locket** and an **ivory fan** in her capacious carpet bag.

Ride away... **noted passage**

❧ 1290 ❧

The drivers of the Union steamers drive fast and straight and stop for nothing. Can you terrify this one? Make a RUTHLESSNESS roll of difficulty 11, adding 1 if you are **Wanted by the Atmospheric Union.**

Successful RUTHLESSNESS roll!	**1102**
Failed RUTHLESSNESS roll!	**1446**

❧ 1291 ❧

You gather several recently-printed manuals and begin to piece together what you can about the arcane art of mechanical computation. Since each inventor uses different methods and each engine is an individual piece of technical art, it is difficult to come to absolute conclusions, but there are some general principles. The majority of computational engines are worked by punchcards: four main programs are used, each designated by a name and an initial.

The card series known as Aramanth A is the simplest: it decodes or encodes, applying the powerfully repetitive ability of the engines to solves puzzles and reduce possibilities.

Another set of punchcards known in the trade as Habbukuk K allows engines to use complex mathematics to design and calculate physical models, such as machinery, structures and buildings.

A third set, Livingstone M, has the strange ability to alter other programs. It is a metacalculator and one of the most powerful programs used in the trade.

Finally, Selladore V has the properties of prediction and creativity, and is used to create data following complex principles in ways that mimic human behaviour. Who designed this program is another question entirely.

When you find yourself in a passage in which a computational engine is mentioned, look for the key word 'hopper'. Where you come across this, you will be able to interact with the machine if you possess a set of punchcards. As you have no doubt noticed, each set is given a name and an initial. Use the initial (for example, V in punchcards (Selladore V)) to identify the next word in the passage beginning with that letter after the mention of the hopper. Count the letters in that word and in the next word to create a two-digit number. Add this number onto the number of the passage in which you find yourself and turn to the resulting passage. This will give you further options or tell you what happened when you fed the punchcards into the engine.

If the passage you reach is nonsensical, it is either a mistake in your programming or the particular engine does not support that set of punchcards. You will also need to note the passage number in which you find the computational engine in case you need to return there.

Return to the library...   **269**

❧ 1292 ❧

It takes some time to plan a flight that will get you atop the Class B tower: you have to find a high point to launch from, judge the speed of the wind and your descent. It is possible, however, and that evening you are sailing beneath the stars, smog and flickering lanterns of the towers far below you, circling down to come to a landing atop the telegraph.

You are only a short distance from the upper cabin, where operators scan the horizon for incoming messages, so you have to move stealthily. If you have any **telegraphy** skill, turn to **543** immediately. Otherwise, you must make a combined ENGINEERING and NIMBLENESS roll of difficulty 19: add your ENGINEERING and NIMBLENESS scores, together with any modifiers, and the total of two dice.

Successful roll!   **543**
Failed roll!   **591**

❧ 1293 ❧

"What? What's all this?" You have awoken a sleepy, red-faced man on his way for a weekend's angling in the country. He puts up no opposition. You can take his **picnic hamper**, a **fishing line**, **ten guineas in notes** and **£2 13s** in coin.

Ride away...   **noted passage**

❧ 1294 ❧

"I was looking for Lord Prishaw," you say to the doorman. He looks you up and down and snorts. "Not a member, are you? This is where the gentry come to get away from people like you."

Leave the club...   **400**

❧ 1295 ❧

With a deadly opponent like yourself blocking the way, the driver has no option other than to stop the carriage. Roll a dice to see who she is driving:

Score 1	A seamstress...	**1320**
Score 2	An officer...	**1380**
Score 3	A barber...	**1399**
Score 4	A man with two daughters...	**1410**
Score 5	A scientist...	**1451**
Score 6	A doctor...	**1475**

❧ 1296 ❧

Over your drink, you listen to a tile-maker's tale of a jewel burglar, told in breathless awe. "The Brethren are right concerned. And I'll tell you why: it's a lady what does it. Some grand Lady out of Devon, what can't be amused with teaparties and trinkets no more."

"A noble lady?"

"That's right," interrupts a man with a sheaf of paper. "Care to buy a ballad?"

Purchase a ballad...	(**1s**)	**1316**
Finish your drink...		**noted passage**

❧ 1297 ❧

Pretty soon, the lamp carried by one of your mates begins to gutter and quieten. "Put that out!" shouts the foreman. "You'll set off the gas!" He turns to puff at the little flame, and then there is a colossal explosion.

You awake in a black tumble of brick, cobble and sewage. The sewer has been laid open to the street, about ten feet above you. There is a large **wound** in your leg (if you now have **five wounds**, turn to **999** immediately) and your ears are ringing.

Set to work rescuing the others...	**1326**
Get to safety...	**1336**

❧ 1298 ❧

You climb to the very top of the tower and unfold your wings once more. Then, like a night-borne bat or a gliding gull, you swoop off the roof and down over the roofs and chimneys of Rotherhithe. The water of the river shines silver beneath the moon. How can you suppress a laugh of delight and victory at such a moment?

Return to your velosteam...	**816**

❧ 1299 ❧

Carrying cargo may be honest, but it is slow, physically exhausting and far from profitable. Roll a dice to see how you fare, adding 1 if you possess a **butty boat**.

Score 1-2	Long shifts and hard labour: receive **18s** but gain a **stiff back (NIM-2)**...
Score 3-4	Little work to be had: gain **2s**...
Score 5-7	Fair profit: gain **£1 10s**...

Steam on...	**948**

❧ 1300 ❧

Regular checks of your machine are vital to keep it in working condition. Without the ability to steam away at speed, you would be little more than a footpad.

To repair the Ferguson you will need both tools and skill. If you have the required items indicated below, make an ENGINEERING roll. If you do not have what you need, you may return to your noted passage.

Minor damage	**copper pipe** or **brass flange joint**
Serious damage	Above item and **high pressure valve** or **pocket watch**
Critical damage	Above items and **titanium alloy** or **ultra-tensed wire** or **welding tools**

Score 1-9	Failed and gashed your hand! Gain a **wound**...
Score 10	Failed and broke a part: remove one of the **items** you were attempting to repair with...
Score 11	A fair start: remove the parts and remove **one damage point**...
Score 12+	Success: remove the parts and remove all **damage points**...

Return to...	**noted passage**

❧ 1301 ❧

A massive black road train towed by a Brewsley steamer rumbles towards you. The Coal Board must make their deliveries day and night to keep the fires and furnaces of London burning. Their road engines are built for strength, not speed, and can each tow almost two hundred tons of cargo. How will you halt this behemoth?

Attempt to frighten the crew...	**1317**
Open fire...	**1342**
Ride alongside the road train...	**1352**

❧ 1302 ❧

Having your own engineering workshop as a going concern is a great opportunity to make honest money. To set your men to work, you will need a minimum of a ☑ Coal delivery, some ☑ Casual labourers and **£4** for raw materials. If you wish to go ahead, erase the ticks from these two boxes for each of the following that you possess, add the relevant number of points to the total of two dice before consulting the table below to find your earnings:

☑ **Apprentice**   1
☑ **Journeyman**   1
☑ **Master Engineer**   2
☑ **Casting forge**   1
☑ **Travelling crane**   1
☑ **Wharf**   1

Cerise   3
Clicking   3
Century   5

Total score	Earnings
2-10	No sales...
11-12	A few hand-tools: **£4**...
13-15	Covering costs: **£12**...
16-18	Small profit: **£15**...
19-20	A businesslike return: **£18**...
21-24	Fairly good earnings: **£28**...
25-28	A good deal: **£62**...
29-30	A lucrative contract: **£100**...

Turn to...   **1308**

❧ 1303 ❧

You show yourself, throwing out your shoulders and summoning a fearsome grimace. Make a RUTHLESSNESS roll of difficulty 12, adding 1 if you have a **double headlamp.**

Successful RUTHLESSNESS roll!   **1295**
Failed RUTHLESSNESS roll!   **1277**

❧ 1304 ❧

Your lack of fear causes some of the crew to think again, but they leap down from their vehicle anyway, armed with clubs and sabres. You must fight them!

Coal Board Crew   Weapons: **clubs (PAR 2)**
Parry: 7
Nimbleness: 5
Toughness: 4

Victory!   **1368**
Defeat!   **1384**

❧ 1305 ❧

The steamer moves more quickly than you anticipated, slamming hard against your velosteam. Your tyres momentarily lose their grip as the heavier machine lifts you off the road surface and you struggle to keep control. Roll a dice to see how you fare:

Score 1-2   Gain three **damage points**...
Score 3-4   Gain a **wound** and a **damage point**...
Score 5-6   Gain a **damage point**...

Your attempted prey gets clean away, of course. The driver will probably go about boasting how he bested the Steam Highwayman. This will not be good for your reputation! If you now have **five wounds**, turn to **999** immediately. If not, but your velosteam is **beyond repair**, turn to **1111**.

Turn to...   **noted passage**

❧ 1306 ❧

If you possess a **chimney sweep's button**, the house will employ you to sweep their chimneys for a few shillings: turn to **268** immediately. "Otherwise, honest work can be found at the ash heaps in Bromley," says the under-butler with a sneer.

Leave Derwent House...   **750**

❧ 1307 ❧

The slick mud beneath your wheels provides poor grip for your velosteam and your opponent, already moving, has inertia on their side. They slam into your machine, tossing you off and into the ditch.

When you awaken, the other vehicle has long gone. You hurry to the Ferguson to assess the damage. Roll a dice:

Score 1   **critical damage**
Score 2   **serious damage**
Score 3   Remove a **customisation**, if you have one
Score 4-6   add a **damage point**

If your velosteam is now **beyond repair**, turn to **1111** immediately. Otherwise you must climb back aboard and find somewhere you can repair your trusty machine.

Ride away...   **noted passage**

❧ 1308 ❧

Your workshop is the ideal place to repair your velosteam and build complicated machinery. The list below represents the tools and resources available to you: these will make more challenging projects   possible as you invest in your setup. You can also store possessions and money here or rest in the rudimentary   accommodation, and you should note this passage (**1308**) before making your next choice.

Millwall Workshop

- ☐ **Apprentice**
- ☐ **Journeyman**
- ☐ **Master Engineer**
- ☐ **Casual labourers**
- ☐ **Coal delivery**
- ☐ **Casting forge**
- ☐ **Travelling crane**
- ☐ **Wharf**

Casual labourers can be hired at nearby pubs and yards. Each time you use them, you must erase the tick in the box, as they are only hired by job, whereas permanent employees (Apprentices, Journeymen and a Master) are not erased after use. Coal deliveries must also be erased after use.

Repair your velosteam...		1300
Open a **strongbox**...		331
Treat your **wounds**...		500
Train your assistants...		1003
Build some machinery...		1077
Do a little casting...	(☑ **Casting forge**)	1142
Go to your wharf...	(☑ **Wharf**)	1129
Work on the *Leviathan*... (*Cabin*)		1164
Create something for the exhibition...	(**exhibitor's license**)	1197
Set your workshop to work...		1302
Leave the workshop...		431

❧ 1309 ❧

The passenger is a successful gentleman farmer, heading into the city to discuss the latest in cattle breeds and fodder. He is not simply going to let you take his wallet off him!

Farmer	Weapon: **club (PAR 2)**
Parry:	7
Nimbleness:	5
Toughness:	4

Victory!	1315
Defeat!	999

❧ 1310 ❧

You approach your friend with a smile. She turns and breaks away from the French Ambassador vainly trying to impress her, and flashes you a brilliant grin. "How lovely," she says. "However have you managed to turn up here?"

You begin to explain, but the orchestra begin to play the Aether Prince Waltz and she puts up her finger. "Oh, my favourite tune. Tell me while you dance."

It is a very pleasant evening in Diana's company. She whispers to you of her plans to crack the Brethren's vault, and perhaps to take a trip around the world, or maybe to buy a new house in the country. What it is that she enjoys about your own company, who can truly say? But she dances with no-one else tonight.

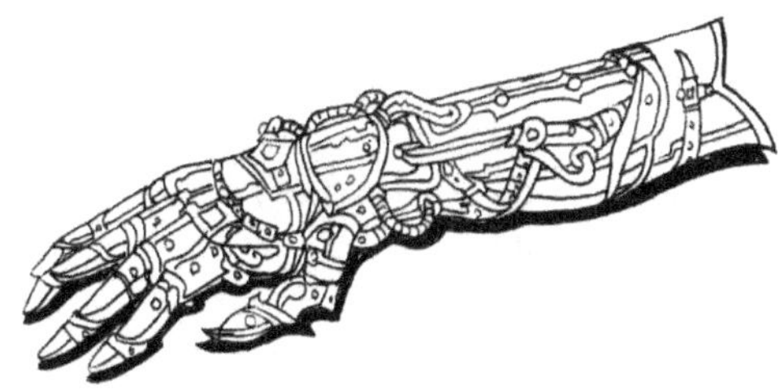

Something of her glamour rubs off on you: gain a point of GALLANTRY.

Bid her farewell...   **750**

❧ 1311 ☙

The remainder of the journey is uneventful. The monks make their delivery - out of your sight - and you return to London, weary from the long ride. Gain **£2**.

Return to the Flask...   **12**
Carry on to Islington...   **151**

❧ 1312 ☙

The Ferguson throbs with power as you release steam and accelerate towards the carriage. Very soon you have matched speed and are riding alongside, catching a glimpse of terrified faces within. You signal for the driver to pull over, but he snarls, twists his steering bar and sets the Aubrey on a collision course. He means to ram you off the road! Make a MOTORING roll of difficulty 14, adding 2 if you possess **improved brakes** or a **strengthened boiler**.

Successful MOTORING roll!   **1279**
Failed MOTORING roll!   **1305**

❧ 1313 ☙

You garner some strange looks as you step through the mechanically-revolving door into the polished hotel lobby, trailing road mud and wisps of smog. If you **stink**, or if your GALLANTRY is 5 or lower, turn to **1327** immediately. Otherwise, remove the **£3** from your purse: at least your gold is as good as anyone's. You are shown to a private room with a tall bed and, that wonder of wonders, a plumbed-in-bath.

There is a tap that spouts heated water on the simple twist of its handle, and several bottles of lotions that foam and bubble. Remove a **stiff back** or a **black eye** if you have one. For a short evening, you are able to experience the sort of luxury and privacy that your victims take for granted. You can tend to any wounds you might have, using the spare linen as **bandages**. To

do so, make an INGENUITY roll, adding 2 for each level of **medical training** you possess.

Score 1-8   A problematic injury: the **wounds** remain...
Score 9-13   Healed: replace one **wound** with a **scar**
Score 14   A dramatic result: replace one **wound** with an **intimidating scar (RUTH+1)**...
Score 15-17   Healed: replace two **wounds** with two **scars**...
Score 18   Healed: replace three **wounds** with three **scars**...
Score 19+   Healed: replace two **wounds** with a single **scar**...

You may also treat the following ailments:
a **fever**   take a hot bath, drink a **bottle of whisky** and take three **white pills** ...
a **burn**   use a bottle of **soothing ointment** and any piece of **clothing**...
a **cold**   drink a **bottle of cough medicine**...

Remove any **possessions** you have used and erase any treated ailments from your **Adventure Sheet**.

Leave the hotel...   **400**

❧ 1314 ☙

A ship's master makes you a proposition. "We've got some cargo we'd rather didn't come ashore through the taxed wharf," he says. "You could carry it upriver for us, to St Thomas' Chapel, on London Bridge."

"What's my cut?"

"Five pound. Now that ain't bad for a short run. Very little risk. We'll give you a load of ballast over it, so no-one sees anything strange."

If you want to accept the job, add a unit of **ballast stones** to your boat.

Return to the dock...   **1069**

❧ 1315 ☙

The farmer collapses on the roadside. "You've killed me! Who'll care for Bessie and my wife now?" His driver hovers nearby, quivering. You can take **£6 9s**, **ten guineas in banknotes** and a **top hat**.

Ride away...   **noted passage**

❧ 1316 ❧

Add the **burglary ballad** to your pouch. It is cheaply printed, smudgy and indistinct.

"'Tis the 'onest truth," says the ballad-singer.

> The Gem-Burgling Lady
> and her
> Fingers of Fire
> The moon was bright-shining when late she did strike,
> The gem-burgling lady with her eyes alight,
> For she knew of a ruby set square in a ring,
> That was worn at the Court before Charles, our King.
> The nobleman boasted its size and its weight,
> Dug out in Colombo and brought to this state,
> Set in rich gold of Duke Sussex's own
> Admired by all, even him on the throne.
> The ladys did simper, as he flashed it about,
> But one did not whimper, she coveted, no doubt,
> That great glimmring ruby, and she made a plan,
> To rob from Duke Sussex, that unfortunate man.
> So in the late night she did creep to his window
> When the weather was hot and the lawns like tinder.
> She lifted the latch and snuck into his chamber,
> Scorning the dogs down below and their danger.
> This gem-burgling lady did lift up the ring
> From beside sleeping Sussex, but she left him one thing:
> A rose, burnt and blackened, to replace her desire,
> This gem-burgling lady with her fingers of fire.

"On'y a few months ago. Go and ask about Duke Sussex's ruby ring: it ain't been seen since he flashed it around at court. I tell you: it caught the eye of the Fire-Fingered Lady of the Burnt Rose."

"Where did the robbery happen?"

"Why, Chelsea, o'course. At Sussex 'Ouse."

Turn to...   **noted passage**

❧ 1317 ❧

You steam out onto the highway, brandishing your weapons and looking as fierce as you can. "Halt your engine!" you cry. Make a RUTHLESSNESS roll adding 1 if you are **Wanted by the Coal Board** and 1 more if you are **Wanted by the Constables**.

Score 2-10	**1277**
Score 11-13	**1333**
Score 14+	**1364**

❧ 1318 ❧

If you have an **actor's affidavit**, turn to **787** immediately. If not, but you have the codeword *Goodwood*, turn to **799**. Otherwise, read on.

The company of actors are setting out on tour, taking their performances of *The Taming of the Shrew*, *The Golden Palm* and *Mrs Fazerlacky's Inheritance* out to the provinces. "I have hopes of a good season," says their director, an actor with a walrus moustache. "But we could do with some new stage properties, maybe a few costumes. I don't suppose you'd be willing to make a small investment?"

If you wish to invest **£10** in the company, remove the money from your wallet and gain an **actor's affidavit**, in which the director will detail your agreement.

Leave the actors...   **noted passage**

❧ 1319 ❧

Mrs Roberts has heard of you. "You were too genteel to rob Daphne, weren't you? Hmmm. She mentioned that you might drop in. Oh well, I suppose I should listen to what you have to say."

Remove the codeword *Chattering*.

Turn to...   **917**

❧ 1320 ❧

The seamstress inside is infuriated. "Don't you dare try and rob me!" she yells, before launching herself at you, armed only with her scissors.

Seamstress	Weapon: **scissors (PAR 1)**
Parry:	9
Nimbleness:	8
Toughness:	2

Victory!	**1328**
Defeat!	**999**

❧ 1321 ❧

The owner of a privately steamer demands a tow out to the estuary, against the tide and against all the advice of his crew. He promises you ten guineas if you manage it.

Take the work...	**1287**
Look for something safer...	**968**

❧ 1322 ❧

The editor of the Blucock Press is always looking for interesting manuscripts to set in type and sell to the burgeoning readership of the metropolis. Everyone seeks distraction and entertainment, whether they ride the locobus to their place of work in the city or rest their feet at the club, sit on sunny lawns or retire to faded suites in backstreet hotels. Have you anything to sell? Mrs Golding will pay an upfront fee for a good manuscript.

To sell and

manifesto manuscript £10   Gain the codeword *Critique*...

memoir manuscript   £22   Become **Famed Lawbreaker**...

novel manuscript   £50   Add **Wrote a Novel** to **Great Deeds**...

Travels of a Gentleman £14

Leave the press...   **201**

❧ 1323 ❧

The carriage occupants are not intimidated by your threats. They grasp their weapons and open fire! Roll a dice to see how you fare.

Score 1-2   Escape unharmed!
Score 3-4   Gain a **wound**
Score 5   Gain two **wounds**
Score 6   Gain a **damage point**

If your velosteam is now **beyond repair**, turn to **1111** immediately. If you now have **five wounds**, turn to **999.** Otherwise you had better scuttle back to your Ferguson and ride away.

Make a getaway...   **noted passage**

❧ 1324 ❧

The distinctive twin plume climbing from the approaching road-train identifies the locomotive as a Brewsley Leviathan - a huge, double-boilered Coal Board traction engine. They are slow, powerful and the pride of the guild's long-distance haulage network. How will you bring such a mighty machine to a halt?

Threaten the crew...   **1317**
Shoot at them...   **1342**
Ride alongside...   **1352**
Use trickery to stop them...   **1329**

❧ 1325 ❧

A Telegraph Artizan comes out and takes a look at the fittings on your velosteam. He is impressed. "Did these yourself, did you? Well, we're always on the lookout for able workers."

You are shown some machinery that needs repairing - simple stuff, not the secret coding and telegraph control machinery. "If you can get this back in working order, then we might be able to use you," says the Artizan. Make an ENGINEERING roll of difficulty 13, adding 1 if you have some **copper pipe** and 2 if you have a spare **brass flange joint**.

Successful ENGINEERING roll!   **1345**
Failed ENGINEERING roll!   **1369**

❧ 1326 ❧

You scramble over the debris and see one of your workmates half-buried in the rubble. Make a NIMBLENESS roll of difficulty 12 to haul him clear.

Successful NIMBLENESS roll!   **1163**
Failed NIMBLENESS roll!   **1173**

❧ 1327 ❧

The clerk in the foyer confronts you. "This is a respectable place," he says. "You are not welcome

here."

"Is my gold no good, then?"

He returns your three sovereigns (**£3**). "You could be carrying any manner of disease. We have a duty to protect our customers."

Leave the hotel...   **400**

❧ 1328 ❧

You manage to subdue the seamstress at last, although her sharp blades gave you some trouble. You can take her **scissors (PAR 1)**, her **fur collar**, a bottle of **soothing lotion** and **£5 10s**.

You will now be **Wanted by the Constables** unless you are wearing a **mask**.

Ride away...   **noted passage**

❧ 1329 ❧

To convince the driver and crew of the road train to halt, you will need to relay new orders from the Coal Board. If you have a **mobile telegraph**, turn to 1351 immediately. Otherwise, make an INGENUITY roll of difficulty 15, adding 2 if you have a **shovel**.

Successful INGENUITY roll...   **1351**
Failed INGENUITY roll...   **1333**

❧ 1330 ❧

There is something very, very familiar about the dark jewel pendant dangling below the lady's throat. It is, of course, the Dervish's Eye. There is no doubt about it. The woman herself - tall, slender, dark-haired and utterly self-possessed - must be the one who whisked it from your grasp at Cliveden, so long ago, leaving you to take the fall.

Ask the lady to dance...   **1356**
Watch her across the room...   **1430**

❧ 1331 ❧

You steam alongside the Brewsley, taking up a position by the coupling of the first wagon where the crew cannot clearly see or shoot at you. What will you do next?

Toss a bomb into the tender... (**explosives**) **1389**
Unhitch a wagon...   **1378**

❧ 1332 ❧

You steam over to the jetty where the Bamford Chain ends and your mate hooks on. Immediately, you begin to move against the stream. The powerful engine that winches the chain and any craft attached stands on a floating pontoon, tended by a crowd of stokers.

If you are fully laden (ie if you have no empty space in your boat), turn to **1395** immediately. Otherwise, you pass through the arch without mishap, unhook from the chain and continue upriver towards Blackfriars Bridge.

Steam on...   **1401**

❧ 1333 ❧

You have certainly caught the attention of the Coal Board crew, but they are not scared. The driver steers towards you while her crewmates ready their weapons: there is a bounty paid on robbers and they mean to have it. Either way, they have a good look at you and you will now be **Wanted by the Coal Board**.

Fight them...   **1304**
Flee...   **noted passage**

❧ 1334 ❧

The passenger is a wealthy manufacturer from the continent, come to see the latest machinery and production techniques on display at the Great Exhibition. He is far from pleased to have been delayed and sullenly throws his purse at you. "There, road-thief! In my country you would be hanged by the neck! We dealt with revolutionaries like you once and for all. How can you English claim to have a stable government when a man of industry cannot even take a business journey!" He continues in his own language, but you ride off counting his money: it comes to **£12 8s**.

Turn to...   **noted passage**

❧ 1335 ❧

You are offered the unglamorous work of towing a dredger out into the channel and minding it while the crew set anchor, lower their steam-powered shovel and begin scraping at the river bottom. You go to see their work and something catches your eye in the filth.

Score 1-3   a **chimney-sweep's button**, indicating membership of their guild

Score 4-6   a **treasure trove**: certainly of interest to the curator at the museum

When the job is finished, your mate is tired, and he insists you moor at Deptford for a little rest ashore. Note that you are now **moored at Deptford Creek**.

Go ashore... **816**

❧ 1336 ❧

You scramble over the rubble, ignoring the cry of the half-buried workers behind you, and make your way to where your velosteam is waiting. Stinking, bleeding and only-just alive, you will be sore pressed to find somewhere to recover in this state.

Ride away... **139**

❧ 1337 ❧

A massive rat runs over your foot, its raised tail tickling the back of your knee. It dodges a kick and scampers away. Then you come to the blockage.

"Here we are," says the foreman. "Let's 'ave 'im."

A mass of congealed fat, human waste, scraps of cloth, bootlaces, hair, animal bone, rotted vegetable husks and dead leaves blocks the tunnel from side to side, as high as a man. You attack it with your shovel, hacking away until it begins to break into pieces. Make an ENGINEERING roll of difficulty 11, adding 1 if you have a **crowbar**, **steam fist** or **mechanical hand**.

Successful ENGINEERING roll! **1489**
Failed ENGINEERING roll! **1491**

❧ 1338 ❧

The Haulage Guild counts thousands of roadsmen among its members. Some are reluctant, having joined the monopoly out of necessity, priced out by its tolls and license. Others genuinely believe that the Guild is providing stability and reliable employment. A group of hauliers sit around a brazier talking. One staunchly supports paying into the Guild's pension and sick-pay scheme, while another decries it. "Last autumn I came down with pneumonia and I applied for relief. Application denied, on account of some technicality. My wife's brother, up in Peterborough, lost his leg on a Guild job. His payout didn't even cover his new trousers!"

"P'raps in some instances, it ain't fairly calculated. But they compute it mechanically, you know?"

"You're simple, mate. It's a scheme. And we're just the sheep, shorn every summer. You must be woollier than most."

Each of the guildsmen wears - proudly or otherwise - a medallion that indicates their allegiance to the guild. It is their ticket to fuel and water in the Freight Yards, as well as the guarantee of certain rates of carriage they must keep to.

Show your **Guildsman's medallion**... **29**
Ask about working for the guild... **17**
Leave the guildsmen... **noted passage**

❧ 1339 ❧

You come across a young man in the blue peacoat and knitted cap of the Nethundicals. He is making his way to Deptford Creek.

"My leave's up," he says, "But I've got to get back to the Creek moorings by evening bell. You wouldn't give a sailor a lift on that velosteam of yours, would you?"

"Hop on, shipmate." **1367**
"Not tonight." **noted passage**

❧ 1340 ❧

While you wait for the tide to turn, you moor against several other craft. Their crews are sat about, playing cards or splicing worn ropes. One has a green parrot on his shoulder. If you have a **pet raven**, turn to **1469** immediately.

Chat with the crews... **1266**
Play with the parrot... **1273**
Sail through the bridge... **1401**

❧ 1341 ❧

The sort of jobs available to you depend massively on your reputation. Roll a dice, adding 3 if you have the codeword *Captain*.

Score 1   No work to be had...
Score 2-3   Only local tows: gain **2s**...
Score 4-5   Profitable work: gain **15s**...
Score 6-9   Plenty of employment: gain **£3**...

However, you must also visit the coal breaker at Greenwich to refuel after firing your tug's furnaces. Roll a dice to see how much you must spend to refill the bunkers.

Score 1-2   **10s** coal...
Score 3-4   **12s** coal...
Score 5-6   **15s** coal...

If you are unable to pay for the coal, you must sell your tug and leave the trade: you plainly aren't cut out for this work. The tug will make you **£25** and you should turn to **863** immediately. Otherwise, you will be able to continue up the river.

Steam on...   **992**

❧ 1342 ❧

It will require a steady hand to hit either the driver or a crucial part of the road engine: make an ACCURACY roll of difficulty 14 to make the shot.

Successful ACCURACY roll!   **1364**
Failed ACCURACY roll!   **1333**

❧ 1343 ❧

A skinny man in a threadbare suit steps down. "Robbery, eh? I suppose that's one way to make a living. Perhaps I should try it. Has to be more profitable than writing novels."

You can take **£3 5s** and a **pocket watch** from the down-at-heel novelist - unless you pity him enough to pass him by.

Turn to...   **noted passage**

❧ 1344 ❧

None of the boys can read, but they can all recognise revolutionary books by the way they are treated. Over the next few hours they head out filching, and return with a mound of various banned, secret or revolutionary papers. None of them are the Statement, however - the manifesto and theory that underpins the entire modern anarchist and socialist revolutionary movement.

Then Bert comes in with a tatty block of paper, pasted together and repaired several times. He says that he found it in a grocer's, behind the shopman's desk. Opening it up, you realise that this is indeed an first-edition printing of **Jensen's statement**.

Leave the hideout...   **252**

❧ 1345 ❧

The Artizan returns to find his hoist working again - if anything, better than previously - and is very happy. He hands you a sovereign (**£1**) as a one-off payment. "You plainly know what you're doing. Now, my colleague down at the Observatory is working on some complicated governing mechanisms that will help our engines run more efficiently. Anything we can do to limit our dependence on the dratted Coal Board. He will buy new machinery you design, if you show him this note." He passes you the **artizan's note**.

Leave the compound...   **400**

❧ 1346 ❧

☐

If the box above is empty, put a tick in it and read on. If it is already ticked, turn to **1299** immediately.

The mate of the paddle-steamer *Lionfish* hails you. He wants your help getting his cotton bales ashore to Mauritius Wharf.

"It looks like a job we can handle," advises your mate. "Maybe three or four trips."

"Nonsense," cries the *Lionfish's* mate. "Stack 'em up on deck. I'm not paying for four trips."

It will take some careful loading to get all the bales balanced. The crew toss them down and you, your mate and a stevedore's hook do most of the work. Fine white fibres float in the air and lie about on the water all around, setting you sneezing. Make an ENGINEERING roll of difficulty 12 to stack all the bales securely, adding 3 if you possess a **butty boat**.

Successful ENGINEERING roll!   **1286**
Failed ENGINEERING roll!   **1269**

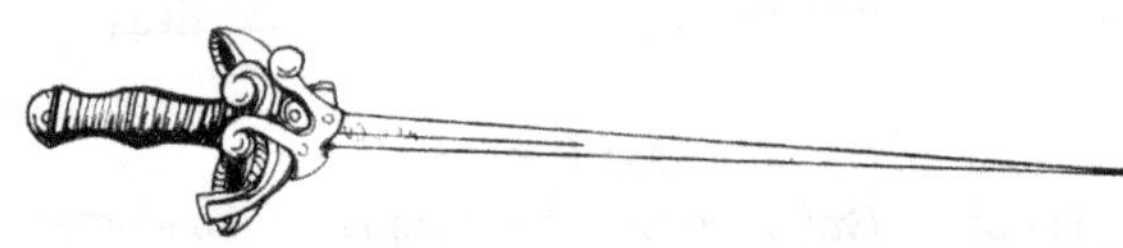

❧ 1347 ❧

You have stopped an architect, travelling to his practice in Chelsea. He mutters in frustration, but empties his purse into your hands rather than risk a confrontation. You may take **£6 5s** and his **heating blueprints**, if you like.

Ride away...   **noted passage**

❧ 1348 ❧

There is a handsome cow loose in the street. She has a full and swinging udder and a brass numberplate jangling on her neck - number 541. Gain the codeword *Cattleboy*.

Ride on...   **noted passage**

❧ 1349 ❧

A long Aubrey steam carriage approaches. It may be the personal transport of a Duke or Dame, or a licensed carrier taking fare-paying passengers on their way. You will not know until you stop them.

Threaten the driver...	**1303**
Ride alongside...	**1312**
Block the road... (**axe**)	**1375**

❧ 1350 ❧

You have succeeded in stopping the road train. Now roll a dice to see who was travelling inside:

Score 1-2	A Colonel's mistress...	**1362**
Score 3-4	A codesman...	**1370**
Score 5-6	A Guild official...	**1383**

❧ 1351 ❧

Confused by your signals, the driver hauls on the brakes and lets the steam out of the boiler in a drawn-out shriek. The road-train slowly comes to a stop. Then you leap onto the driver's plate and put your weapons to his throat.

"Take what you want," he says, throwing his hands up. "Only leave us with our lives! There's sons and daughters at home!"

You can take **£2 2s**, a pair of **engineer's gauntlets (ENG+2)** a **shovel** and a **net**.

Destroy the road train... (**explosives**)	**1389**
Ride away...	**noted passage**

❧ 1352 ❧

You launch yourself out from your hiding place, the heavy tyres of the Ferguson churning the autumn mud. The crew of the road train see you and signal to their driver to open the regulator. Make a MOTORING roll of difficulty 15, adding 1 if you have a **ramming beak** and 2 if you have a **gas pressuriser**.

Successful MOTORING roll!	**1331**
Failed MOTORING roll!	**1307**

❧ 1353 ❧

You draw yourself up and make your demand. "Alter the entry in Baronness Dimlight's family tree. She says that you have her grandfather marked as illegitimate."

"Why so he was," replies the King of Arms. "Why should I change the entry?"

Make a RUTHLESSNESS roll of difficulty 9 to convince him.

Successful RUTHLESSNESS roll!	**1387**
Failed RUTHLESSNESS roll!	**252**

❧ 1354 ❧

The detective is a thin man with a bright look in his eye. He is not about to let you take his wallet without a fight.

Detective   Weapon: **swordstick (PAR 2 GAL +1)**
Parry:	9
Nimbleness:	7
Toughness:	3

Victory!	**1359**
Defeat!	**999**

❧ 1355 ❧

The prototype is packaged up in sacking, straw and a case and a steam-cart hired for the trip across the city. You arrive at the exhibitor's entrance of the Crystal Palace and find Mr Sutter.

"So your exhibit is complete, then? We close tonight at 6. You have the night to set out your stall."

The exhibit of your self-loading rifle attracts a great deal of interest, from investors and rival inventors. The staff are forced to set a guard to watch over the prototype and manage the queues, keeping people moving. Needless to say, it will bring you a great deal of interest - as the proprietor of Millwall Engineering Works, whatever name you have been using. Gain the codeword *Cerise*.

Leave the exhibition...	**741**

❧ 1356 ❧

If you wish to speak with the lady of the burnt rose, you must claim the next dance and hold your own upon the ballroom floor. Make a GALLANTRY roll of difficulty 12, adding 1 for each named dance (such as a **gypsy dance**) you have mastered.

Successful GALLANTRY roll!	**1392**
Failed GALLANTRY roll!	**1420**

❧ 1357 ❧

Your have only managed to attract attention! The driver of the carriage quickly raises a bullet-proof shield and the occupants ready their weapons to fire back! Roll a dice to see the outcome of your assault, adding 1 for each **Wanted status** you possess.

Score 1-5   Get away unhurt...
Score 6-7   Shot! Gain a **wound**!
Score 8+   Add a **damage point** to your velosteam!

If you now have **five wounds**, turn to **999** immediately. If not, but your velosteam is **beyond repair**, turn to **1111**.

Ride away...   **noted passage**

❧ 1358 ❧

You come across a drunken nobleman searching for something. "Lost me sword," he says mournfully. "Me grandad's sword. You haven't seen a sword with a golden hilt, have you? You find it, bring it to me at the club, eh? I'll give you twenty guineas for that sword."
     "Which club?"
     "Why, the Guberstein in Bloomsb'ry."
     Gain the codeword *Chaldean*.

Give him the sword... (**Prishaw's sword**)   **1398**
Ride on...   **noted passage**

❧ 1359 ❧

The detective, sorely wounded, bows in surrender. "You have bested me this time," he says. "But I will not forget you." You relieve him of his wallet, containing **ten guineas in banknotes**, his **swordstick (PAR2 GAL+1)**, a **silk scarf** and a **Constabulary logbook**.

Turn to...   **noted passage**

❧ 1360 ❧

The travellers are a group of manufacturers returning to the cities of the north after visiting the Great Exhibition. They have been excited to observe new machinery and products and are full of ideas for improving their own factories. One is sketching out ideas on a piece of paper, toying with the layout of what is being called a 'line of assembly'. If you have an ENGINEERING score of 7 or more, turn to **4**. Otherwise you listen in politely, before noting the route these gentlemen will take through Highgate and Bishop's Wood. Gain the codeword *Clarify*.

Turn to...   **noted passage**

❧ 1361 ❧

The little steam engine in your mobile ice-cream vehicle is no match for the Constables. You are forced to ride recklessly and push the machine beyond its limits: turning a sharp corner, you topple over with a crash and a sweet shower of cold dairy products. The Constables pick you out of the mess and march you off. Forsi, keen to assist them, hands over your velosteam.

Turn to...   **13**

❧ 1362 ❧

The occupant is the mistress of a Colonel of Signals. She pretends to faint, but you haul her out into the sunlight and splash her face with a little boiler-water.
     "Take my purse, but leave me unsoiled!" she pleads.
     You can take **£5 3s**, a **gold necklace**, a **gold ring** and a **lace shawl**. You will now be **Wanted by the Telegraph Guild** unless you have a **mask**.

Ride away...   **noted passage**

❧ 1363 ❧

An overseer called Mr Stutter has charge of the exhibits. He is far from sure that you will provide the Exhibition with a display worthy of the public's attention - but he can be convinced. You can gain an **exhibitor's license** from him in exchange for a nobleman's recommendation: a **Letter of Introduction** should do it.
     "A hexhibit should be a mechanical or technological hinnovation," he instructs. "Horiginal. Hinteresting. Not stolen."

Leave the Exhibition...

❧ 1364 ❧

The crew of the massive engine are terrified: your reputation plainly precedes you. "It's the masters you want, your honour," pleads the driver, "Not the men." You can take **£2 11s**, a **silver ring**, some **wirecutters** and **Coal Board pass**.

Destroy the road train... (**explosives**)   **1389**
Ride away...   **noted passage**

❧ 1365 ❧

You attempt to make conversation with Drury to find out more about his life and circumstances, but he is very wary, and only really pausing to talk since he is hoping to get away without being robbed. His answers to your questions are terse. He looks up at the moody skies. "Looks like rain," he says. "Chap I know was struck by lightning out here on the Heath. I've got places to be."

Let him go...   **22**
Rob him...   **1376**

❧ 1366 ❧

The occupant of the carriage is a recruiting sergeant, on his way back to London after a successful trip to the counties. Mercifully, he is somewhat drunk, but still dangerous.

Recruiting sergeant	Weapon: **sabre (PAR3)**
Parry:	9
Nimbleness:	6
Toughness:	4

Victory!   **1377**
Defeat!   **999**

❧ 1367 ❧

With the Nethundical mariner clutching on behind, you tear through the City. He waves his leave pass at every checkpoint and Constable, and you reach Deptford Creek in record time - just as the evening bell is striking. He leaps off with a laugh in front of the tall barrack gates.

"Made it! Well, you're a friend to us undersea folk, then. I'll pass the word round that you're a good-un." Gain the codeword *Curdle*, if you don't already have it. You can also gain a **solidarity point** if you have **ten or fewer**.

Leave him at the gates...   **816**

❧ 1368 ❧

You subdue the crew, leaving them groaning on the muddy tarmacadam, and clamber onto the footplate of the engine. Bloodied and severe, there is now no question of the seriousness of your threat. The driver surrenders.

The crew's pockets contain **£8 13s** in coin and you can also take a selection of tools from them, including **welding tools**, a **shovel**, three **tarpaulins**, a **pneumatic manual (ENG+3)** and a **pocket watch**.

"We'll be after you," croaks a wounded coalman. "You won't get away with this." Gain the codeword *Crestfallen*.

Turn to...   **noted passage**

❧ 1369 ❧

You only manage to make the problem worse. "Some mechanic," says the Artizan. "But I think I know where I can find the spare parts I need to fix this."

When you return to your velosteam, you find that he has removed the **improved burner**!

Ride away...   **400**

❧ 1370 ❧

The passenger is a thin, nervous man. He is a specialist, paid a high wage by the Guild for his skill in writing and deciphering codes. He empties his pockets of **£4 9s**, a set of **punchcards (Selladore V)**, and a **Telegraph Guild codebook**.

Leave him...   **noted passage**

❧ 1371 ❧

You count out twenty golden sovereigns onto the King of Arms' desk while you describe Baronness Dimlight's preference to have her grandfather recognised as legitimate. He listens carefully, then takes down a book from the shelf, leafs through it, and strikes through a line with a quill pen.

"There you are." He pockets the coins.

"It's that simple?"

"For me, yes. You couldn't do that. You haven't the authority."

"But I could just walk in here and write on what I like! The door wasn't even locked."

"That would be plain vandalism, and you would be liable for the damage, as well as charged with slander or libel, if your emendations brought about any change in hereditary possession, legitimacy, order of seniority or

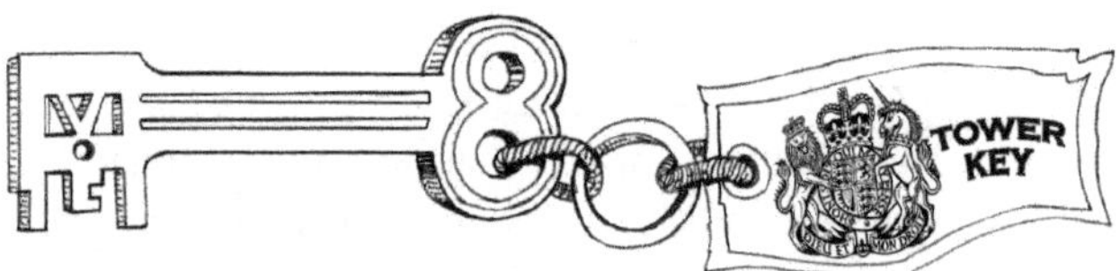

the like. But, as you say, I can simply do it with the stroke of a pen. This is what is properly called authority."

He gives you a **lineage transcript** to take to the Baronness. Remove the codeword *Canvey*.

Leave the college...   **252**

❧ 1372 ❧

Remove the **rabbit** (or whatever else you use to daub yourself with blood). You stagger out into the road, looking as desperate and hopeless as you can. You will have to depend a great deal on luck, as you have no way of gauging the passengers' attitudes towards the needy, but your appearance will count in your favour if you appear to be both hurt and respectable.   Make a GALLANTRY roll of difficulty 11.

Successful GALLANTRY roll!   **1250**
Failed GALLANTRY roll!   **1277**

❧ 1373 ❧

The beech hedge beside you is a dry golden colour, but the leaves still cling to the branches so you back in and lurk. Your patience pays off and before long you see a pillar of steam over what must be a private carriage. The overhanging trees here may help you: if you have a **rope**, you may be able to swing onto the roof of the carriage and stop the vehicle. Otherwise you can put your trust in your fearsome reputation, the accuracy of your weapon or your daring motoring skill.

Swing aboard... (**rope**)   **1025**
Attempt to terrify the driver...   **1303**
Shoot at the engine...   **1054**
Ride alongside...   **1066**

❧ 1374 ❧

A desperate boy with a prod and a floppy hat is looking for a lost cow. "Me mam told Mr Laycock we'd return it by today," he snuffles.

"You're renting a cow?"

"Ain't that normal?" he replies.

"I've seen a cow..." (*Cattleboy*)   **1073**
"I haven't seen any wandering cows..." **noted passage**

❧ 1375 ❧

The time spent waiting for a good target has allowed you to prepare. A few more strokes of the axe sends a well-positioned chestnut tree crashing into the road, scattering its spiky nutcases like green caltrops. The driver is forced to haul on the brake lever and stop the six-wheeled Aubrey with a skid. You leap out of hiding and brandish your weapons. Make a RUTHLESSNESS roll of difficulty 14, adding 1 if you are **Wanted by the Constables** and 2 if you are a **Famed Lawbreaker**

Successful RUTHLESSNESS roll!   **1265**
Failed RUTHLESSNESS roll!   **1323**

❧ 1376 ❧

"That's what I reckoned this would come to," says Drury glumly. "Me surrendering my ready cash to a common criminal on the Heath. Come on then, take it." He has **£4 5s** in his van, a **crowbar** and a set of **welding tools**. You should remove one **solidarity point** for taking advantage of him.

Ride away...   **noted passage**

❧ 1377 ❧

At your final stroke, the sergeant turns and vomits with exhaustion and drink. He collapses to the ground, leaving you to pick his fat purse - containing **£10 17s**.

Ride away...   **noted passage**

❧ 1378 ❧

You drop back towards the final road wagon, rumbling along on its twelve-foot iron wheels, and lean out to unpin the coupling. A crewmember catches sight of you and tosses a heavy lump of coal your way, but you manage to dodge it and loosen the wagon.   It immediately slows and veers to the side of the road, while the engine and crew power off up the highway.

The wagon is full, predictably, of coal, but a toolbox contains some useful items that you can take, including a pair of **goggles (MOT+1)**, a **grappling iron**, a **tarpaulin**, and a **high pressure valve**.

Ride away...   **noted passage**

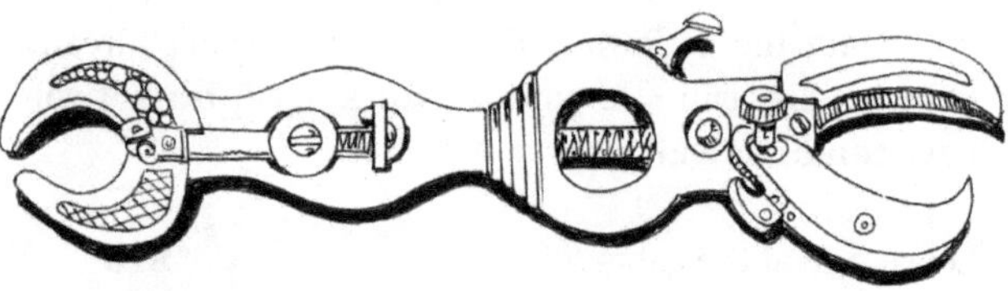

❧ 1379 ❧

A group of travellers are setting off on a journey to Wales. Their steam carriage is stacked about with boxes and hampers, camping equipment, baggage and trunks of every kind. As you watch, they set off to the cheers of their family, and one box falls off, unseen, into the gutter. Roll a dice to see what you find.

Score 1   A **strongbox**...
Score 2-4   A **picnic hamper**...
Score 5-6   A **top hat** and a **dinner jacket**...

Ride on...   **noted passage**

❧ 1380 ❧

The officer stammers and stutters. "I... have left all me weapons at home." Whether true or not, he puts up not fight. You can take a **£4 10s** and a **pocket watch** from him.

Ride away...   **noted passage**

❧ 1381 ❧

☐

If the box above is empty, tick it and read on. If it is already ticked, turn to **1109** immediately.

The steam vehicle approaching is not a guild locomotive, nor a rich nobleman on his way to his estate. It is the everyday work vehicle of a common man, doing his best to earn a living and keep his family from the poorhouse. He watches as you stand aside and throws you a wave of gratitude.

Ride away...   **noted passage**

❧ 1382 ❧

You push the little machine to its limit and accelerate through the busy streets, bumping over kerbs and corners and shedding frozen dairy products at every slewing turn. You are far too good a driver to lose concentration, even on an unfamiliar machine, and lose the Constables in Clerkenwell before heading north towards Forsi's warehouse.

He cannot believe the state in which you have returned his machine: the paint is scratched, the tyres are worn, the spokes are bent and the ice-cream... the ice-cream is melted, jettisoned or curdled. "Get outta here!" he yells. "Meybe you're some kinda race driver? So go anda enter some race!"

You climb back on your velosteam and depart.

You haven't earnt anything, but you have sharpened your skills: add 1 to your MOTORING score.

Ride away...   **107**

❧ 1383 ❧

The official is a Guild Officer, and not prepared to give up his valuables without a fight. You will have to subdue him first!

Colonel	Weapon: **sabre (PAR 3)**
Parry:	10
Nimbleness:	7
Toughness:	3

Victory!	**1386**
Defeat!	**113**

❧ 1384 ❧

You are defeated, disarmed and trussed up. Remove all your **weapons** from your **Adventure Sheet**, but you can keep your other possessions and money for now. The crew lump you into one of the coal wagons and keep watch while they jolt towards their depot. Escape is far from your mind, however, considering your spilt blood and open cuts.

Turn to...   **1121**

❧ 1385 ❧

Your small but powerful craft is admirably suited to assisting the great steamers and sail craft manouevre up and down the Thames. However, very few ship's masters will be willing to deal with an unlicensed tugboat captain. If you have a **bargee's badge**, turn to **1497** immediately. Otherwise, roll a dice to see what sort of work you manage to find.

Score 1-2	Towing over-laden barges...	**1485**
Score 3-4	Dredging...	**1335**
Score 5-6	A ship against the tide...	**1321**

❧ 1386 ❧

The Colonel surrenders eventually. "Ah've met me better," he says, offering you his **sabre (PAR 3)**. He is also carrying **ten guineas in banknotes** and a **telescope**.

Leave him...   **noted passage**

❧ 1387 ❧

"You know, I care nothing for all this nonsense," you growl. "But one thing I know. This place is a fire risk. A significant fire risk."

The wild look in your eye is enough to persuade the King of Arms. "Ah. Maybe you are right. Yes. I suppose we should look into that. A good thing that there is no immediate, risk, eh?"

He heads over to his study, scratches out a few entries, scribbles through others and draws some lines linking some parts of a family tree. And the job is done. All of that is written down for you in a **lineage transcript** to take back to the Baronness. Remove the codeword *Canvey*.

Leave the College...   **252**

❧ 1388 ❧

A Stormwright engine pulling two long country-style wagons is steaming up the slope. It is painted in the Guild colours, but they are faded and scuffed. There are no guards that you can see. Make a RUTHLESSNESS roll of difficulty 10 to , adding 1 if you possess a **double headlamp**.

Successful RUTHLESSNESS roll!   **1431**
Failed RUTHLESSNESS roll!   **1277**

❧ 1389 ❧

The explosive charge tears through the Brewsley engine, rupturing the massive boiler and sending a heavy road-wheel spinning across the road. The surviving crew are aghast! Remove the **explosives** from your **possessions**. You can also gain a RUTHLESSNESS point if you currently have 8 or fewer - and you will certainly be **Wanted by the Coal Board** now if you are not already. Gain the codeword *Crestfallen*.

Ride away...   **noted passage**

❧ 1390 ❧

You power out towards the road train and quickly take up position near the couplings. If you are very bold and ride well, you will be able to unlink the saloon wagon. Make a MOTORING roll of difficulty 13, adding 1 if you have a set of **wirecutters**, an **adjustable wrench**, **steam fist** or **mechanical hand**.

Successful MOTORING roll!   **1350**
Failed MOTORING roll!   **1357**

❧ 1391 ❧

As the carriage trundles towards you, you have a few moments to decide upon your method. How will you try to stop the driver and have the occupants at your mercy?

Trick them with a faked wound...
    (**rabbit**, **deer carcass** or similar)   **1372**
Shoot at the driver...   **1040**
Attempt to terrify the driver into stopping...   **1054**
Ride alongside and force the carriage to halt... **1066**

❧ 1392 ❧

You begin by asking an overlooked but promisingly sportive spinster to dance - and then sweeping her off her feet. You dance as a good leader should, preferring your partner and ensuring that her steps, her flights and her spins feel effortless. The others make a little room for you in admiration - everyone profits from good dancing at a ball - and as the music finishes, your partner curtseys and blushes in sincere appreciation.

After such a performance, the dark-haired lady is intrigued, and gladly accepts your invitation to waltz together. Then, as the conductor of the little chamber orchestra catches your eye and raises his baton, you begin your game.

"Aren't you ashamed to wear that stone?" you ask with a smile.

"I have a delight in gemstones. Why should I be ashamed of that?"

"Perhaps you should be ashamed of common theft."

Her laugh is like the chime of crystal chandeliers. "I would indeed be ashamed if my thefts were common," she whispers huskily. "But they are far from it. I succeed and I succeed glamourously. Would you like to hear of my next plan?"

"Your next plan?"

"I will steal the crown jewels."

It takes all your composure and knowledge of dance to stay in time, but you cannot help but bump into a dancing couple behind you in shock. "From the Tower?"

"Exactly. Quite an adventure and quite a prize. Oh, I don't want many of them. Nasty gaudy things, largely. But I have my eye on one or two. How would you like to join me?"

"I have been your patsy before."   **1453**
"Who could refuse such an invitation?"   **1436**

❧ 1393 ❧

The woman you have stopped gets down into the road. "Leave me be," she says. "I am a close friend of Mrs Roberts: I can recommend you to her."

If you choose to rob her regardless, gain a **parasol** and **£8 7s**. If you choose to let her go, gain the codeword *Chattering*.

Ride away...   **noted passage**

❧ 1394 ❧

A drunken, angry codesman sits at a table, scrawling on a piece of paper. He offers to teach you how to make a set of punchcards if you buy him a drink. If you wish to spend **2s**, gain the codeword *Coaxial*.

Turn to...   **noted passage**

❧ 1395 ❧

You scrape against the piers as the chain drags you inexorably upstream. The deep draught of your fully-laden craft means that you will need to steer particularly carefully to avoid significant damage. Make a MOTORING roll of difficulty 11, adding 2 if you possess a **strengthened screw**.

Successful MOTORING roll!   **1401**
Failed MOTORING roll!   **1442**

❧ 1396 ❧

Remove the codewords *Chuffing*, *Chapter* or *Chosen* if you have them.

There is a good chance that the crew of the approaching road train will include guards posted by the guild for protection. Whether they will have the courage to face you is another question.

Intimidate the driver...   **1056**
Ride alongside and unhitch a wagon...   **1094**
Shoot at the engine...   **1172**
Fish for loot from a branch... (**fishing line**) **1189**
Haul in a bigger prize... (**grappling iron**)   **1207**

❧ 1397 ❧

Your shot hits the driver, who collapses at the wheel and sends the vehicle careering into the ditch. With a thunderous crash, the heavy vehicle up-ends and lands solidly on its roof.

At first you only hear steam hissing out of a hundred broken pipes. Then a high-pitched scream starts. Before you realise what is happening, a second steamer comes to a halt beside the wreck and the occupants pour out, desperate to help. You had better leave the scene as quickly as possible before you are found and held responsible.

Ride away...   **noted passage**

❧ 1398 ❧

"You have it!" Prishaw is overjoyed. "Why, how very fortunate. Just as I was asking you..." He looks suspicious. "Is this a set-up?"

He is still somewhat drunk and doesn't quite trust you.

"What about those twenty guineas?"

"Err... meet me at the club," he says. "I've got money there." Remove the codeword *Chaldean*.

Turn to...   **noted passage**

❧ 1399 ❧

The barber does not put up a fight. He is neither a rich nor a courageous man: you can rob him of **£1 8s**, a **razor (PAR-1, NIM+3)** and a **pocket watch**.

Turn to...   **noted passage**

❧ 1400 ❧

The Telegraph Guild's road trains are distinctive and easy to identify. Bold green paint and brass fittings, small roof-mounted telegraph lattices and only one or two towed wagons are the norm. The one approaching you chugs steadily through the mud, its driver hunkered down in his heavy, woollen coat. It seems to be pulling a wagon of supplies for one of the Guild's outposts.

Try to intimidate them...   **1417**
Open fire...   **1415**
Wave them down...   (**green coat**)   **1449**
Leave them alone...   **noted passage**

❧ 1401 ❧

On the northern riverbank, a gang of urchins clamber about the slippery retaining walls, swinging from chains and jeering at the sailors. You chug past, pass under Blackfriars Bridge, concentrating on keeping between the channel markers.

Sail on...   **922**

❧ 1402 ❧

You step out into the road and show yourself, armed to the teeth and ready to fight. "Stand and deliver!"

Make a RUTHLESSNESS roll of difficulty 14, adding 1 if you are **Wanted by the Telegraph Guild.**

Successful RUTHLESSNESS roll!	**1350**
Failed RUTHLESSNESS roll!	**1277**

❧ 1403 ❧

Before very long water is gushing out of the pipe and pooling in the low point of the highway. By the time your prey approaches, the water is several feet deep, and the driver slows and then stops as his lime lanterns illuminate the growing pool.

Then you reveal yourself, armed to the teeth and perfectly positioned. The driver has no option but to surrender.

Find out who is inside... **1265**

❧ 1404 ❧

Your opponent is a massive, broad shouldered sailor with clubbed hair and a repeatedly-broken nose. To knock him down, you must fight him **unarmed** (using your **fists PAR 0**), relying on your NIMBLENESS and TOUGHNESS.

Sailor	Weapon: **fists (PAR 0)**
Parry:	8
Nimbleness:	8
Toughness:	5

Victory!	**1190**
Defeat!	**1165**

❧ 1405 ❧

The occupant is a young, slight, dark-haired woman with a beaky nose and an intense glare in her eyes. If you are the **Friend of Princess Alexandrina** or if you have a **purple brooch**, turn to **1052** immediately. Otherwise, read on.

The princess is not rich by royal standards, but she still has a little jewellery about her: you can take her **fur coat**, a **silver ring** and a **sapphire pendant**. However, because of her excellent memory and her influence, you will now be **Wanted by the Constables**, regardless of any disguise you may be wearing.

Ride away... **noted passage**

❧ 1406 ❧

Between them, the passengers of the locobus have **£4 8s** in coin, a **silver bracelet** and a **pocket watch**. However, you will now be **Wanted by the Constables**, regardless of any disguise, because of the number of people able to describe you.

Turn to... **noted passage**

❧ 1407 ❧

The family only have a little worth stealing: **£3 4s** in coin, a **lace shawl**, a **silver ring** and a **picnic hamper**. The husband bursts into tears of frustration. "My one holiday, you blackguard! And now we will turn home and save for another year!" His daughter spits at you before her mother scolds her sharply. Remove a **solidarity point**.

Ride away... **noted passage**

❧ 1408 ❧

The Guild's wariness means that their road-trains are better defended than ever before; you will almost certainly have armed guards to deal with if you press your attack. What now?

Intimidate the driver...	**1137**
Unhitch a wagon...	**1160**
Block the road... (**explosives**)	**1182**
Look for easier prey...	**noted passage**

❧ 1409 ❧

You prevail on the people to wait: there can be no revolution until all the preparations are fully made. "To rise now would be to invite widespread slaughter," you explain. "But that shouldn't prevent you from having some vengeance on this son of iniquity."

The crowd vent their fury on the Chief Constable, helpless and weakened in the stocks, throwing, spitting and jeering. You are looked on as the city's saviour: gain **five solidarity points.**

Soon, however, this sort of display will attract official attention. It would be best to get out of here.

Ride away... **220**

❧ 1410 ❧

A serious-looking man steps down from the carriage, drawing his sword uncomfortably. "I would not fight on my own account," he says, "But would suffer the shame of a roadside robbery. But for the sake of my two daughters here in the coach, whom I will not allow you to touch, I will fight you until my last breath." If you choose to ride away now, turn to your **noted passage** immediately. Otherwise, you must fight.

Man with two daughters	Weapon: **sabre (PAR 3)**
Parry:	8
Nimbleness:	5
Toughness:	5

Victory!	1416
Defeat!	999

❧ 1411 ❧

The Guild vehicle looks as though it is carrying passengers in a saloon wagon hauled behind the engine. This could mean profitable pickings, but if they are rich, they may be defended. How will you proceed?

Attempt to intimidate the crew...	1402
Ride alongside the road train...	1390
Leave them be...	**noted passage**

❧ 1412 ❧

There is a conveniently located waterpipe at a low point in the highway here. If you have the skill, you could set it open and flood the road sufficiently to bring the approaching carriage to a stop. If you have a **water mains key**, turn to **1403** immediately. Otherwise, make an ENGINEERING roll of difficulty 10.

Successful ENGINEERING roll!	1403
Failed ENGINEERING roll!	1432

❧ 1413 ❧

"The exhibition is a sight indeed," you say to the parents. "Educational for your youngsters and, crucially, it will broaden their minds too. You never know what potential is hidden within these little ones."

"My Mary is a musician," boasts the father. "She has been learning the pianoforte."

You ask after their plans for accommodation and recommend a cheap but salubrious boarding house while they stay in the city. Then you pass the mother a ten-shilling note. "After all your efforts to save for this trip," you comment, "It would be a shame to empty your purse entirely. Take this."

If you have fewer than **forty solidarity points**, gain one now.

Ride away...	**noted passage**

❧ 1414 ❧

Robbing the Hampstead Locobus will not make you rich, and it won't make you popular with the common folk either. Still, at least no-one will put up a real fight. If you want to go ahead, make a RUTHLESSNESS roll of difficulty 8.

Successful RUTHLESSNESS roll!	1406
Failed RUTHLESSNESS roll!	1277
Not interested after all...	22

❧ 1415 ❧

You ready your firearm to hit some critical part of machinery and bring the approaching road-train to a halt. Make an ACCURACY roll of difficulty 13.

Successful ACCURACY roll!	1426
Failed ACCURACY roll!	1429

❧ 1416 ❧

"Daddy!" cries the elder of the two girls, as he father slumps into the road. She leaps down and tries to stop his wounds with her handkerchief. You may take **ten guineas in banknotes**, two **silver necklaces**, a **gold ring** and a **top hat** from the travellers.

Ride away...	**noted passage**

❧ 1417 ❧

How will the crew respond to your threats? Make a RUTHLESSNESS roll of difficulty 12, adding 1 if you are **Wanted by the Telegraph Guild**.

Successful RUTHLESSNESS roll!	1426
Failed RUTHLESSNESS roll!	1357

❧ 1418 ❧

A woman with a case is selling gloves of various kinds. She spreads some onto the table, showing you their fine stitching and careful moulding, and seems keen to help you find a well-fitting pair.

	To buy	To sell
fine gloves (GAL+1)	£3 10s	£2
engineer's gloves (ENG +1)	£3	£2 10s
engineer's gauntlets (ENG+2)	£5	£4 10s

Leave her...	**noted passage**

⋙ 1419 ⋘

The boys return shaking their heads. "She's gone for good, she is. Last I heard, she was on an airship to Damascus. No-one in the mansion except some old uncle."

Return to the hideout..	**581**
Leave the boys...	**252**

⋙ 1420 ⋘

Try as you might, your feet will not obey you tonight. Maybe it is the free-flowing champagne or the intimidatingly glamorous ladies, but all you seem to be doing is losing the beat and tripping over yourself. You impress nobody and retreat to the buffet, where a waiter hands you little pancakes topped with sturgeon roe.

"Do you know 'oo zat is?" asks the waiter. "She is ze jewel sief."

"The lady with the roses?"

"Zat is correct. And zey all laugh and dance and show off zeir pearls, while she comes 'ere to choose 'er next victim."

Give the waiter a tip... (**5s**)	**1255**
Leave the ball...	**794**

⋙ 1421 ⋘

The approaching vehicle is the grey, silver and blue of the Atmospheric Union. It seems to be a supply wagon, probably carrying engine parts for the massive airborne machinery, or possibly supplies for the passengers and crew. Either way, the enclosed cab of the Scott-Norris engine protects the driver and his mate from gunfire and may make them hard to intimidate.

Try to scare the crew...	**1290**
Ride alongside...	**1245**
Shoot at the engine...	**1259**

⋙ 1422 ⋘

Nobody recognises the slumped figure of Lord Beaufort hanging over your velosteam bonnet: he is far too bloodied and broken. You tear through the City to the Leopard and make your rendezvous with Mrs Petty.

"Here is your traitor," you reply.

She cannot believe you, until you show her the black packet and the note Lord Beaufort wanted taken to Flat Billy (remove them both from your **possessions**). She opens the packet and sees two hundred guineas in banknotes lying on her table. It takes her no time to decipher the names and instructions in the Lord Beaufort's writing.

"You've done a great service to the nation," she says. "Rot sets in so easily. But maybe not with our next Chief Constable... You'll be rewarded. Wait here."

Mrs Petty arranges an amnesty for any crimes you have committed until now: remove all **Wanted Statuses** that you might possess. She also gives you a small **bag of perfect pearls**.

"I hope not to see you again," says Mrs Petty. "That would imply that you are not intelligent enough to profit from this opportunity."

Leave her...	**139**

⋙ 1423 ⋘

Your victim is an American writer, visiting London to promote his series of books written in an alternate timeline. He draws a blade and seems to know how to use it.

Writer	Weapon: **rapier (PAR 4)**
Parry:	12
Nimbleness:	8
Toughness:	2

Victory!	**1428**
Defeat!	**999**

⋙ 1424 ⋘

You leap up onto the bonnet of your trusty velosteam and call for attention. "Now! At last, and to reward all your patience, now is the day of revolution, friends! Lord Beaufort is here to suffer the people's justice: soon the people's justice will sweep across this land like fire on a field of winter stubble. Not the justice of the rich, but of the people. Stand with me! First we turn back these leaderless cowards, then we take the Tower! From here, we will see the whole city rise up with us!"

There is an almighty cheer from the surrounding crowds. They grasp what tools and makeshift weapons they can reach and begin to prise up cobblestones to launch at the Constables. Several engines swing out of the streets from the West and Constables clamber out, ready to quell the riot. But are they ready for a full-blown revolt?

A wild and enthusiastic charge pushes the Constables back, initially. Several go down to cobblestones and hayforks, but when they see the ugliness of the mob, their officer orders them to ready their carbines. Suddenly, the thunder and sour stench of gunfire erupts onto Tower Hill and a score of would-be revolutionaries collapse to the ground. The mob waver. A few hot-heads charge again, but this time, each one is shot or bludgeoned to the streets.

Then there is the noise of trumpets from behind you and a squad of Tower Guard come marching out from beneath the portcullises. They line up, draw their truncheons and advance.

Another volley from the ruthless Constables decides it. Before the riot becomes a slaughter, the crowd begins to melt away. Whether you attempt to ride away or to fight will not matter at all: you are marked and not allowed to escape. More Constabulary engines have arrived from Whitechapel and Shoreditch and cut off your escape routes: you are surrounded, knocked off your Ferguson and viciously kicked into submission. Then the cuffs are slapped on your wrists. This abortive attempt at revolt came far too soon. But it is not a hopeless cause: with sufficient support and planning, one day, the people will triumph.

Turn to...   **1500**

❧ 1425 ❧

The approaching steamer is a fine machine, built for carrying passengers in comfort, speed and style. It is likely to contain wealthy passengers - if you can stop it!

Flood the road... (**water mains key** or
     adjustable wrench)   1412
Shoot out the driving pistons...   1465
Scare the driver...   1455
Ride alongside...   1445

❧ 1426 ❧

You are free to take what you can from the Guild's supplies. Roll two dice to see what the wagons contain.

Score 2-4   a set of **punchcards (Aramanth A)**, a
          tarpaulin and **£2 4s**
Score 5-8   a **measuring line**, an **adjustable
          wrench (ENG+1)** and **9s**
Score 9-11 a **green coat**, a pair of **binoculars** and
          £5 17s
Score 12   a **strongbox** and a **shovel**

You will now be **Wanted by the Telegraph Guild** unless you are wearing a **mask**.

Ride away...   **noted passage**

❧ 1427 ❧

A pair of swaggering Constables are ambling along the road, twirling their truncheons and looking for trouble. They spot you and begin blowing on their whistles for reinforcement.

Steam off quickly...   **182**

❧ 1428 ❧

Your final cut slices into the writer's arm and he yelps. "Not my writing arm!" He backs away and clamps a scarf over the seeping wound. "That's unfortunate. I only just recovered from a sprained wrist." You can take **£6 7s**, a **notebook** and a **silver ring** from the writer.

Ride away...   **noted passage**

❧ 1429 ❧

The road train is protected by Guild guardsmen and they quickly open fire in your direction! You have no choice but to make a hasty exit into the dusk. Roll a dice to see whether they manage to gain a hit:

Score 1-3   Escape without a scratch
Score 4-5   Gain a **wound**!
Score 6   Gain a **damage point**!

If your velosteam is now **beyond repair**, turn to **1111** immediately. If not, but you have **five wounds**, turn to **999**.

Ride away...   **noted passage**

❧ 1430 ❧

The lady with the roses attracts a great deal of attention. From the sparkling black stone in the hollow of her throat to the very particular decorations in her hair, the wonderful colours of her dress and her demeanour of self-possession and control, she is glamour and mystery in physical form.

At the buffet, a waiter grins to see you so captivated. "You know zat she stole zat necklace," he says. "Some big 'ouse in ze country. I 'eard."

Give the man a tip... (**5s**)   1255
Leave the ball...   794

୬ 1431 ୭

With a hiss and a shriek of steam, the Guild roadtrain comes to a stop. The driver and his mate doff their caps. "Don't you worry about us, yer 'onour. Takes what you will. The Guild don't pay us enough to die for their profit."

Roll two dice to see what you can take from the roadtrain.

Score 2   a **strongbox**
Score 3-5   **£2 10s**
Score 6-8   three **picnic hampers**
Score 9-11   four **cloaks**
Score 12   six **bottles of champagne**

You will now be **Wanted by the Haulage Guild** unless you are wearing a **mask**. Gain the codeword *Cabal*.

Ride away...   **noted passage**

୬ 1432 ୭

You manage to get the water flowing, but by no means quickly enough, and when the steam carriage approaches, it simply splashes through the puddle, throwing water over the unseen figure at the side of the road. You had better mount up and find somewhere to dry yourself off.

Turn to...   **noted passage**

୬ 1433 ୭

You hand **Prishaw's sword** (remove it from your **possessions**) over to the doorman who raises a supercilious eyebrow as he hears your story. "Wait here, then," he replies.

Some time later he reappears with a note: it contains **ten guineas in** banknotes. "I was promised more than this," you reply.

"This looks like an example of his Lordship's most sincere generosity," replies the lackey. "Hardly cause for complaint."

Leave the club...   **400**

୬ 1434 ୭

Several actors have parked their wagon in the street and, unfolding its various wings and pillars, are proceeding to give a performance of *The Wanderer*. A small audience begins to gather: maids choose the moment to come and clean the front steps, boys and girls hang from windows. It is an engaging show: the head of the troupe is particularly charismatic, switching between roles of the father, an innkeeper, a recruiting sergeant and so on, while the lead is played by a striking young woman with a bound bosom and a painted moustache.

The story is just approaching the climax, when Gregor the wanderer discovers his real father, when a Constable rides up on his Imperial triwheel. "Alright, alright," he calls. "This is an unlicensed performance. You are hereby instructed to disperse immediately." The crowd begins to grumble.

Bribe the constable... (**10s**)   1454
Threaten him...   1473
Slip away...   **noted passage**

୬ 1435 ୭

An old, dark-skinned man in black bobs his head to you as he gets down from the carriage. His shabby clothes don't imply anyone important. Then two heavily built bodyguards armed with knives swing down from the far side of the carriage where they were hidden from your view. Whoever this man is, and whatever he is carrying, he is plainly able to afford the best protection.

Bodyguards   Weapons: **knives (PAR 1)**
Parry: 11
Nimbleness: 10
Toughness: 7

Victory!   1440
Defeat!   999

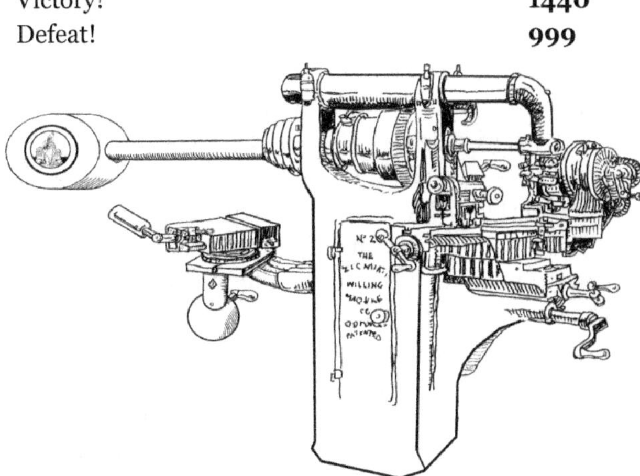

୬ 1436 ୭

"Of course," smiles the lady. "I suggest we start our plans now. We have two options open to us: simple burglary or a ruse. Each has their merits."

"A ruse?"

"Oh, some sort of performance. Impersonation perhaps. Maybe a disguise or two."

"And what would be simple about breaking into - and out of - the Tower."

She laughs again. "My dear, the place is riddled with holes like an old cheese. The river gate, the moat - let alone the glorious sky. Wouldn't it be a delight to drop from the air and make off with the gems?"

This headlong decision may throw you into a challenge beyond your ability. Without high scores in your INGENUITY or ENGINEERING skills, there is no chance of success. In such a case, you had better make a gallant excuse and improve your abilities before seeking out the Lady of the Burnt Rose again.

"Burglary is both healthy and exhilarating." **621**
"I never turn down the chance to perform." **596**
"I will meet you in Mayfair when I am ready." **794**

❧ 1437 ❧
You race towards the pedestrians and lean out to grab what you can. However, you have misjudged the distance and your hand closes on thin air. Your victims jump aside and wave their fists.

Ride away...   **noted passage**

❧ 1438 ❧
A crowd - or perhaps a mob - gathers as you approach Tower Hill. The news of the Chief Constable's downfall has travelled quickly. He has many enemies among the common people, from widows bullied by his Constables to those labelled into criminals by draconian laws. Some really are criminals, and when you dismount and haul his barely-conscious form into the ancient stocks, an angry spirit seems to possess them all.

"Rocks and turds, say I," shouts an angry voice. "Stone the bleeder and bury him in nightsoil."

"They've all got it coming!" shouts an angry woman clutching a bag of knitting. "Every son and daughter of nobility and privilege."

Now that you have brought him here, his doom is out of your control. Other hands slam the block shut and chain it tight. A hundred pieces of spoiled fruit are found in the nearby gutters and drains. Dog mess and horse manure all come sailing through the air and you arc forced to back away to prevent becoming a target yourself. Beaufort is buffetted and bruised from every side, until he is left gasping for breath.

The sound of bugles and heavy wheels announce the approach of the Constables. Someone has taken charge, it seems, and the mob are in two minds. Some wish to defy the forces of order right now and take the opportunity to revolt. Others are already slinking away.

Call for Revolution! (**Member of the CWE**) **1133**
Tell the people to bide their time...   **1409**

❧ 1439 ❧
The driver brings his engine to a stop at the side of the road and before he has discovered your trick, you have leapt aboard, weapons drawn. He and his mate immediately surrender. "Are you the Steam Highwayman?" asks the filthy engineer. "Me little boy is allus talking about you."

If you want to give the engineer a gift for his son, cross off **any item** from your possessions and roll two dice. If you roll higher than your current number of **solidarity points**, add **1** to it now.

The crew stand back as you rifle through the Guild supplies. "It's all under insurance anyways," says the driver. "And no-one can say it were our fault. We was robbed by the Steam Highwayman, no less!" Roll two dice to see what the wagons contain:

Score 2   a **strongbox**...
Score 5-7   some **ultra-tensed wire**, a **net** and
              £1 8s...
Score 8-10   a **green coat** and some **engineer's**...
              gauntlets (ENG+2)...
Score 11-12   **explosives** and **dungarees (GAL-2)**...

You will now be **Wanted by the Telegraph Guild** unless you are wearing a **mask**.

Ride away...   **noted passage**

❧ 1440 ❧
You leave both bodyguards on the floor and approach the dark-skinned man. He grins, toothily. "You won't be able to get far with these. My Company will come looking for you."

He is carrying a **pouch of diamonds**. They could be worth hundreds, if not thousands, of guineas. To sell them on you will need a well-connected fence indeed, but this could be the making of your fortune. If you survive the Company's wrath.

Ride swiftly away...   **noted passage**

❧ 1441 ❧

The mechanical elephant is a marvel. The entire city talks of what you have created and, when you proceed to walk it across the metropolis to the site of the Exhibition, a spontaneous parade of sightseers and truants forms.

From the controls in the howdah, you have a sight unlike anything you have ever seen before. Should this machine be imitated, it could change the face of transport, industry and warfare. Perhaps you have unleashed something greater than you knew.

It is, of course, a great success at the Exhibition. Add **Built a mechanical elephant** to your **Great Deeds** and add 1 to your ENGINEERING score. You should also gain the codeword *Century*.

Leave the exhibition...   **741**

❧ 1442 ❧

Your craft is slammed into the piers of the bridge, splitting a strake and twisting a frame badly. Your mate begins to toss cargo overboard to lighten the load - remove one **cargo unit** from your **Adventure Sheet**.

It takes all your effort to keep the craft afloat. However, you are still on the downriver side of London Bridge. You limp towards Limehouse, where you have a better chance of making repairs.

Turn to...   **968**

❧ 1443 ❧

The boxer you have encountered is none other than the talented Wyndham Jack, champion of the west country. To knock him down, you must fight him **unarmed** (using your **fists PAR 0**), relying on your NIMBLENESS and TOUGHNESS.

Sailor	Weapon: **fists (PAR 0)**
Parry:	9
Nimbleness:	9
Toughness:	6

Victory!	**1490**
Defeat!	**1165**

❧ 1444 ❧

While many of their members have been forced to join by simple economics, the Haulage Guild itself is powerful, wealthy and certainly able to protect its interests. The degree of protection they have decided to grant to this particular haulier and their load will decide how you are able to attack them. Make a RUTHLESSNESS roll, adding 3 if you are **Wanted by the Haulage Guild**.

Score 1-8	**1388**
Score 9-14	**1396**
Score 15+	**1408**

❧ 1445 ❧

Your attempt to ride alongside the carriage will require a steady hold on the gutta-percha grip of your steering handle. The driver is already opening the regulator and charging ahead, having spotted you on the rise in the road. Make a MOTORING roll of difficulty 14, adding 1 if you possess an **improved burner** and 2 if you possess **off-road tyres**.

Successful MOTORING roll!	**1265**
Failed MOTORING roll!	**1307**

❧ 1446 ❧

The approaching vehicle does not slow at all, but steams directly towards you, forcing you to leap aside out of the road. A scornful laugh rings out as you pick yourself out of the mud.

Turn to...   **noted passage**

❧ 1447 ❧

Your victim is a decrepit old man with long white hair and a prominently hooked nose. He looks up from a heavy book and shakes his head. "Seeking wealth, youngster? 'Tis a vain idol. Take my purse, and with it, an old man's curse." His money pouch contains **£2 4s** but you may also take his **pneumatic manual (ENG+3)**

Turn to...   **noted passage**

❧ 1448 ❧

The approaching vehicle is a customised steam lorry, plainly decommissioned from the Haulage Guild and redecorated with the name of Herbert Drury & Co., Window and Bottle Glass, Hampstead. When you emerge from the hedgerows, the driver, presumably Mr Drury himself, brakes and climbs down wearily.

Rob him...	**1376**
Chat with him...	**1365**
Ask after his wife...	**1509**

❧ 1449 ❧

Donning the **green coat** of the Guild uniform and summoning your most official expression, you signal the engine driver to stop. But does he fall for your trick? Make an INGENUITY roll of difficulty 15, adding 3 if you possess a **mobile telegraph**.

Successful INGENUITY roll...	**1439**
Failed INGENUITY roll..	**1446**

❧ 1450 ❧

The steam wagon approaching you is an underslung type with a central smoke-stack - convenient for the busy streets of London. The driver and his mate are carrying a load of plaster and stop as soon as they see you. If you have **fifteen solidarity points or more**, turn to **1462**. Otherwise, they offer you the meagre contents of their purses, which only total **4s**.

Ride away...	**noted passage**

❧ 1451 ❧

You have stopped Sir Brunter Hardwick, the famed physicist and discoverer of the planet Oceanus. He is far from pleased at being stopped, since he is on his way to make an observation at Greenwich, and he draws his rapier.

Sir Brunter Hardwick   Weapon: **rapier (PAR 4)**

Parry:	9
Nimbleness:	5
Toughness:	3

Victory!	**1457**
Failure!	**999**

❧ 1452 ❧

A brawl has broken out between rival gangs. Burly figures are flinging cobblestones and half-bricks. Several innocent citizens are cowering in doorways, trying to stay out of trouble.

Protect the citizens...	**1474**
Appeal to the brawlers...	**1484**
Ride on by...	**noted passage**

❧ 1453 ❧

"Read about it in the papers, then. But I thought you had more spirit. Anyway," she says, as the dance begins to come to a close, "If you change your mind,

look for me at my house in Mayfair. But don't make me wait. I will strike soon."

"It has been a pleasant dance, then."	**1476**
"Wait! I will join you."	**1436**

❧ 1454 ❧

"Come come," you say to the Constable. "These people are peaceable."

"It's my round," he replies. "The Sergeant won't be pleased."

"Oh, you did come round and move the vagrants on," you suggest. "But maybe in about forty minutes."

He takes the coins and starts his triwheel, ignoring the crowd and the actors, who launch back into their drama.

When the wanderer returns home to reconcile with his father and deliver up the wealth he has found on his journey, the small crowd cheer and clap excitedly. The striking actress approaches you, counting the coins in the takings cap as she walks. "We needed today's takings for coal for the wagon and for father's back ointment. Here." She hands you a **bottle of whisky**. Gain a **solidarity point** if you have fewer than 35.

Ride on...	**noted passage**

❧ 1455 ❧

The travellers in this region may fear roadside robbery, violence and degradation, but of all things they fear the uprising of the common people. Make a RUTHLESSNESS roll of Difficulty 11, adding 1 if you possess a **revolutionary poster** and 2 if you are wearing a suit of **dungarees**.

Successful RUTHLESSNESS roll!	**1265**
Failed RUTHLESSNESS roll!	**1277**

❧ 1456 ❧

The Atmospheric Union engine coming your way has the distinctive streamlining of their passenger vehicles. Will it prove to contain rich airship passengers?

Attempt to intimidate the crew...	**1262**
Ride alongside and jump aboard...	**1245**
Impersonate an airship officer...	
(airship officer's cap)	**1240**

✣ 1457 ✣

Quick-witted enough to spot a planet orbiting beyond Uranus perhaps, but Sir Brunter is not quick enough to spot your final thrust to his side. He collapses in a heap, muttering in panicked tones about unmissable conjunctions. He is carrying a particularly fine **telescope**. a **pocket watch** and **£3 8s** in small coin.

Turn to...   **noted passage**

✣ 1458 ✣

Several chimney sweeps come along the road, singing and arm-in-arm. Perhaps one of them has just got engaged, or maybe they have just been paid. If you are carrying any **chimney brushes**, turn to **1471** immediately. Otherwise they will offer you a **sooty handshake (reroll ☐)**, which you can add to your Other Notes section of your Character Sheet. It allows you a single re-roll of the dice at any point in your adventure - but it must be erased once used.

Turn to...   **noted passage**

✣ 1459 ✣

"The stalemate has been broken at last!" enthuses Mr Wright. "Well, I have some idea of how to thank you. I have an old house at Shiplake, south of Henley. In disrepair, I admit, but I never use it. Let me make the deed over to you." Gain the codeword *Caraway*.

Leave the Palace of Westminster...   **721**

✣ 1460 ✣

Lord Hadrian Beaufort has been replaced as Chief Constable by Mrs Petty - although she is still maintaining a low profile. Nonetheless, here in her headquarters you can see her remaining late into the night, working on eradicating the threat of revolution and safeguarding the empire. Does the woman ever sleep?

With a woman of this iron will and determination, there will be no further chances to break into Somerset House.

Turn to...   **139**

✣ 1461 ✣

A broad barge decked about with machinery glides towards you, towed by a pony and a long line from the path. The owner is a travelling shipwright, and he offers to improve your boat.

	To buy
cargo crane	**£10**
strengthened screw	**£12**
enlarged cabin	**£15**

Steam on...   **1218**

✣ 1462 ✣

"You're the Steam Highwayman, aren't you?" asks the driver's mate. "Well, listen here. You don't want to rob us. There's a carriage of rich folk following on just a short distance behind. They were stopping for their dinner when we steamed past."

Wait for the private steam carriage...   **1425**
Ride on...   **noted passage**

✣ 1463 ✣

"Oh, she'll be over there on the *Gentilesse*," says Burgess. "I saw her this morning. You know, on the boat moored out by Westminster Bridge."

Return to the hideout..   **581**
Leave the boys...   **252**

✣ 1464 ✣

The passenger is a renowned sculptor, accompanied by one of his muses. They tumble out of their compartment where it seems he has been having her trial various artistic poses. You allow her a moment to drape herself in a sculptural swathe of velvet, but the sculptor grabs his driver's sabre while you pause.

Sculptor	Weapon: **sabre (PAR 3)**
Parry:	8
Nimbleness:	5
Toughness:	3

Victory!   **1468**
Failure!   **999**

✣ 1465 ✣

Are you accurate enough to strike the moving couplings of the driving rods and break them apart? Or will you aim for a crucial valve and hope to release the steam skywards in a shrieking torrent? Make an ACCURACY roll of difficulty 14, adding 1 if your ENGINEERING score is 6-7, 2 if it is 8-10 and 3 if it is 11 or more.

Successful ACCURACY roll!   **1265**
Failed ACCURACY roll!   **1397**

❧ 1466 ❧

A lady brushes past you in the street. When you later look into your saddle pouches, you find that something is missing. Remove the **third possession** written on your **Adventure Sheet**.

Turn to...   **noted passage**

❧ 1467 ❧

With the **black oilskin packet** and **Lord Beaufort's note**, you will be able to prove Beaufort's corruption easily. You grab the weakened Constable by the scruff of his expensive pelisse and drag him down the stairs to your velosteam.

The fight here atop the Monument deserves to be remembered: add **Defeated Lord Beaufort on the Monument** to your **Great Deeds**. You can also take his **sabre (PAR 3)**, **golden monocle (GAL+2)** and a **gold ring** and should add 1 to your NIMBLENESS score as a result of keeping your footing up here.

Take him to Mrs Petty... (*Citrate* or
    Mrs Petty's note)   1422
Take him to the stocks at Tower Hill...   1438

❧ 1468 ❧

The sculptor quickly surrenders when he realises your readiness to hurt him. You can take **£4 13s**, a **gold ring** and a **top hat**. From his shivering lady friend you take her sole garb - a **gold necklace** - although you let her keep the curtain.

Turn to...   **noted passage**

❧ 1469 ❧

The parrot, on seeing your raven hopping about, begins to squawk angrily and nibbles its owner's ear for attention. He turns about and looks at you through narrowed eyes. "What's wrong wiv a parrot, fer all that's natural? Ravens ain't shoulder-birds."

Your raven struts about provokingly. It even hops down onto the deck and begins to peck about at the scattered crumbs. That is too much for the green parrot, which launches itself at your pet with a shriek. There is a ragged fluttering of wings, a confused pecking, a scittering of bird-claws on painted woodwork, and your raven returns to you, limping.

Your raven has been badly hurt. If you have some **soothing ointment**, you will be able to nurse her back to strength. Otherwise, the raking claws of the parrot have done too much damage and the raven will falter and give up its ghost at the turn of the tide: you must remove it from your **Adventure Sheet**.

Steering well clear of the parrot's owner and his craft, you eventually pass through London Bridge.

Steam on...   1401

❧ 1470 ❧

The traveller is a thin figure, ready to fight for the purse and utterly unintimidated by your appearance or reputation. He lets you do the work, hanging back and saving his energy. To knock him down, you must fight him **unarmed** (using your **fists PAR 0**), relying on your NIMBLENESS and TOUGHNESS.

Sailor	Weapon: **fists (PAR 0)**
Parry:	7
Nimbleness:	7
Toughness:	4

Victory!	1495
Defeat!	1165

❧ 1471 ❧

The sweeps are not impressed to see you carrying brushes. "You ain't one of us, are yer?" asks one, belligerently. "Taking work from the deserving tradesman. If you wants to train as a sweep, get on up to Pentonville, visit the 'all and get yer brass button like the rest of us!" Still, your appearance prevents them from taking it any further.

Turn to...   **noted passage**

❧ 1472 ❧

The steam carriage bears a crest with a portcullis and two rampant lions: it is the personal vehicle of the Warden of the Tower of London. He is a member of one of the old families of the land, raised in honour and tradition. He bows ironically and draws his fine rapier.

This duel has high stakes indeed. If you are defeated, the Warden will surely hand you directly over to the Constables.

Warden of the Tower	Weapon: **rapier (PAR 4)**
Parry:	12
Nimbleness:	8
Toughness:	3

Victory!	1478
Defeat!	113

❧ 1473 ❧

If you are **Wanted by the Constables**, turn to **1486** immediately. Otherwise, read on. "You're not wanted here," you growl at the Constable, readying your weapons and generally summoning your most intimidating aspect. Make a RUTHLESSNESS roll of difficulty 10.

Successful RUTHLESSNESS roll!	**1282**
Failed RUTHLESSNESS roll!	**1486**

❧ 1474 ❧

You step inbetween the fighters and some of the more vulnerable citizens cowering in doorways. A cobblestone comes sailing towards you and, despite a raised arm, it catches you a glancing blow on the shoulder that will later develop into a **stiff back (NIM -2)**. The fight broils on down the street, giving the mother and children you have sheltered the chance to dash away in the other direction. They shoot you desperate looks of gratitude: gain the codeword *Compassionate*.

Turn to... **noted passage**

❧ 1475 ❧

The occupant of the steam carriage is none other than Doctor Haven, the physician to the great and good, including to the Prime Minister. He narrows his eyes at you, clearly unimpressed by your bad manners and impatient to be about his important business.

To have such a well-connected man in your debt could be a coup indeed. You could rob him - but then again, a show of mercy or deferred judgement could be much more valuable.

Take his possessions...	**1492**
Extract a promise of help from him...	**1482**

❧ 1476 ❧

As the dance finishes, you bow to your partner. She slips you a card with a gentle sneer - no doubt in contempt - but she also flounces away, ignoring several proffered hands, proving that there is no-one else here of your calibre for her to team up with. Gain the codeword *Curly*.

"What a woman," says a red-nosed Major of Constables, watching her leave. "Count yourself fortunate! Diana Derwent, Lady Serene. How did you earn her attention, I wonder. Go on, tell me..."

You give the Major a smile and return to the buffet table. You continue to mingle and enjoy yourself at the ball before departing into the ubiquitous London fog.

Leave the ball... **794**

❧ 1477 ❧

You come across the same gang of painters and decorators on their way home from another job. They recognise you, too.

"Didn't you advise us about the causes of poverty? Well, Sandy here has it all down pat now. The unnatural possession of the methods and materials of production. According to him."

"I still say it's high prices," argues another. "And unfair taxes."

Purely out of interest, the workmen are willing to repair one **damage point** on your velosteam free of charge. "Fascinating machinery," they say, admiring the engine.

Turn to... **noted passage**

❧ 1478 ❧

The Warden staggers backwards against his steamer and falls to the road. His servants and driver hand back, terrified by your prowess with a blade and the blood darkening the puddles. You quickly rifle your victim: he is carrying a **golden necklace**, a **gold ring**, a **Tower Key** and **£8 4s**.

Speed off... **noted passage**

❧ 1479 ❧

As you steer under a bridge, a figure leaps aboard your boat and scurries towards you. "Hide me!" he cries. "Hide me! The Constables are after me!"

Let him hide in the cargo...	**1493**
Toss him overboard...	**1218**

❧ 1480 ❧

A final thrust finishes Lord Beaufort's life. Gain the codeword *Constable*.

The fight here atop the Monument deserves to be remembered: add **Defeated Lord Beaufort on the Monument** to your **Great Deeds**. You can also take his **sabre (PAR 3)**, **golden monocle (GAL+2)** and a **gold ring** and should add 1 to your NIMBLENESS score as a result of keeping your footing up here.

Head on your way... **264**

❧ 1481 ❧

Now the travellers will discover why this place is called Shooter's Hill. Vehicles heading to Canterbury, Dover and the Continent have to climb past your hiding place. You survey the road and can choose your target at will.

A private steam carriage...	**1349**
The Haulage Guild...	**1444**
The Telegraph Guild...	**1411**
The Coal Board...	**1324**
The Atmospheric Union...	**1456**

❧ 1482 ❧

"I have no need to take from you, Doctor," you begin. "You are a public servant, and the servant of public servants. Your Hippocratic oath keeps you on the right path, I'm sure. But maybe you'll remember this evening in the mist."

He replies carefully. "Veil your threats how you like, Steam Highwayman. I know who you are. Leave me be and I'll show my gratitude."

Doctor Haven is known as a man of honour. Gain the codeword *Commiserate*.

Let him go...	**noted passage**

❧ 1483 ❧

The beggars recognise you as the hero of the common people and the enemy of the oppressive Constables. "What can we do for you?" they ask.

"How I can win favour with the Guilds?"	**1231**
"I need to lose my wanted status."	**1201**
"Is there anywhere safe to stay in the city?"	**1220**
"Where can I find medical treatment?"	**1236**

❧ 1484 ❧

The fighters are mad with bloodlust and pent-up frustration. No matter your eloquence, fame or ruthlessness, they are not reasonable, and they turn their anger on you! Roll a dice to see the outcome of the hurled cobbles:

Score 1-2	A lucky escape...
Score 3	A **black eye (ACC-2 GAL-1)**...
Score 4	A **missing tooth (GAL-1)**...
Score 5	A **stiff back (NIM-2)**...
Score 6	A **wound**...

If you now have **five wounds**, turn to **999** immediately. Otherwise, you should ride away and find somewhere to nurse your bruises.

Ride away...	**noted passage**

❧ 1485 ❧

An grasping and ambitious captain has over-filled his barges with cargo - as you find out too late. They swim low and are difficult to manouevre across to Millwall. The ferryman shouts abuse as you cross his path. Make a MOTORING roll of difficulty 15, adding 2 if you have **a strengthened screw**, to keep them in control.

Successful MOTORING roll!	**1216**
Failed MOTORING roll!	**1232**

❧ 1486 ❧

"Right, that's enough of all this," says the Constable. "Clear off, the lot of you. Before you're all charged with disturbin' the peace. And as for you... don't I know you?" Quick as a flash, he slaps a pair of clock-cuffs onto your wrists: they won't open for an hour, at least. "You're coming with me, matey."

Turn to...	**13**

❧ 1487 ❧

The Bishop launches himself at you, swing his mitre at your head in a most unchristian manner. You dodge his blow, trip him into the mud and place your knee heavily into his back. The old man yowls and surrenders. You can take his golden **pectoral cross**, his decorated bishop's **cassock** and a **bottle of wine** he is carrying in a case. He also has a few shillings in his purse (**4s**).

Turn to...	**noted passage**

❧ 1488 ❧

□

If the box above is empty, tick it and read on. If it is already ticked, turn to **1477** immediately.

You ride past a group of decorators and builders who are brewing up over a portable oil stove at the side of the road. They wave you over and want to hear you opinion. "Sandy here says that money is the root of poverty. Now, how he comes to such a conclusion, I have no idea. What do you say is the root of all this poverty around us? Is it foreign trade or the lack of work?"

"You are being exploited." **1098**
"Human nature itself leads to inequality." **1112**

❧ 1489 ❧

The fatberg gives way under your dedicated assault: it cracks into several large, greasy, reeking pieces, which you then break down further and shovel back to the manhole. It takes hours of filthy work to haul it up to the surface and into a cart.

"You worked fair hard," says the foreman. "Here's more pay for a day's work than you're like to see elsewhere." You are given **£2** and told to head on your way, still trailing your own particular stench.

Ride away... **139**

❧ 1490 ❧

The ring is nothing more than beaten ground and a circle of baying audience, hot for blood and bruisings. Wyndham Jack smirks at the sight of challenger and lunges into an attack immediately on the umpire's call. It is a demanding fight. Your opponent moves quickly, attacking from any side and moving without rhythm. Blows to his body do nothing at all, so you concentrate on his face, sending in swing after swing as he steps back from an attack. When you manage to cut his brow, he begins to slow, but then surprises you with a hard fist beneath the chin, rattling your teeth and sending you to the ground. Note that you now have a **missing tooth (GAL-1)**.

Rising, you feign a greater dizziness than you really feel, and Wyndham Jack becomes overconfident. You allow him to approach, dodge his jab and then release a flurry of blows into his cheeks, eyes and brow. Blinded by the blood from his cut and confused by the sudden attack he pauses, giving you the crucial moment to ready your knock-out blow. Down he falls, hitting the ground with a heavy thud, and he does not get up.

Remove any **wounds** you have suffered in this fight and gain **£8** - the prize money for beating the champion of the West Country.

Turn to... **872**

❧ 1491 ❧

Despite your efforts, you and the team cannot break through the fatberg by hand. "We'll 'ave to crack open the street and bring in a mechanical digger," says the foreman. "The company won't like that."

They don't like it at all. You are paid a meagre **5s**, since you did not complete the work, made to return your **shovel** and sent packing.

Ride off... **139**

❧ 1492 ❧

The Doctor strips off his jacket and turns out his pockets. "Take anything you want, scoundrel. I must be about my work tonight." You can take **£2 4s**, a **catling knife (PAR 1 NIM+2)**, a **stethoscope**, a **bottle of poison** and a **silk scarf**.

Make your getaway... **noted passage**

❧ 1493 ❧

You bury the runaway under a set of tarpaulins in the cargo section. Sure enough, as you chug along, five or six figures appear on the towpath, on the bridge ahead, and on the wharf opposite, all clearly looking for someone. Once you have left them behind, he emerges and offers his thanks and, surprisingly, his name.

"I'm Michael Murley. A York man. Carrying despatches to the Earl of Chester."

"Won't the Telegraph do?"

He gives you a scornful look. "The Guild have abandoned their northern towers," he says. "Anyway, if you come North, I'll be able to thank you properly. Look for me in York." Gain the codeword *Chicken*. He scrambles ashore and disappears into the alleys.

Steam on... **1218**

❧ 1494 ❧

Count Berstedt's ball is nominally a celebration of his precocious daughter's thirteenth birthday, but really, the Imperial Russian Ambassador has a great deal of networking to do. His massive ballroom has just been refurbished and the Tsar will be picking up the bill:

everyone, everywhere, has been invited.

The buffet table contains delicacies from the East, shipped here on an eagle-headed airship, as well as dishes intended to gratify the most stolid of British palates. Roast beef, a mountain of sturgeon roe, giant jellies, set custards, pastries, turtle soup... It is a chaotic mixture.

Much like the guest list. Among the many swirling hussars, debutantes, matrons and uncles, Dukes, Earls and Scottish Barons, one figure consistently attracts your eye. A woman in a gown of strangely indefinable colour... something of pink, something of cream, beneath a smoked shade, turning to deep black as she moves. Her piled hair is pinned up with what looks like burnt-edged roses. If you already possess a **burnt rose**, turn to **1330** immediately. If not, but you are the **Friend of Diana Derwent**, turn to **1310**. Otherwise, you have a choice to make.

Ask the lady to dance...   **1356**
Watch her across the room...   **1430**

❧ 1495 ☙

The traveller goes down with a series of blows to the temple and neck, leaving you panting but victorious in the ring. Despite the damage you have suffered, you have gained a great deal of experience from these fights. Remove any **wounds** suffered in the match, add 1 to your NIMBLENESS score and add **£6** to your purse.

Turn to...   **872**

❧ 1496 ☙

If you are the **People's Champion**, turn to **1483** immediately. Otherwise, read on.

A trio of dusty and desperate beggars catch your attention. "Good evening, yer 'onour. We're hungry men looking for work. Spare a few shillings?"

Give them some coins... (**3s**)   **119**
Ride on...   **noted passage**

❧ 1497 ☙

☐

If the box above is empty, tick it and read on. If it is already ticked, turn to **1341** immediately.

You are chartered to tow a screw-paddle steamer down to Gravesend. It is a challenging job, depending on your ability to handle your craft, as well as your knowledge of the lower stretches of the tidal river. Make a MOTORING roll, adding 3 if you have a **chart of the lower Thames**.

Score 2-8   You miss the tide: delays mean a reduced payment of **£1**...
Score 9-15   A competent job: gain **£2 5s**...
Score 16+   You make great time: gain **£2 5s** and the codeword *Captain*...

Return to the city...   **364**

❧ 1498 ☙

When it is eventually time for your release, you are far from well: you have gained a **fever (NIM-1, ING-2)** and surrendered any remaining **possessions** and **money** you might have managed to bring with you. Your velosteam is, fortunately, still in the condition you left it, and the prison guards send you on your way with a **convict's pass**. "You'll need to show that to any employer," they warn. "'Tis a criminal offence to try to hide your convictions." Remove any **Wanted Statuses** you possess.

Ride away...   **253**

❧ 1499 ☙

Lord Beaufort drops his sword from a hand slippery with blood and presents himself to you. "What now, Highwayman? Am I to die at your hand?"

"Breathe your last."   **1480**
"You will face justice."   **1467**

❧ 1500 ☙

Before you are handed over to the Constables, you are carefully stripped of all your **weapons, possessions** and **money**. Erase these from your **Adventure Sheet** immediately. Your velosteam's **customisations**, however, should be left as they are.

Turn to...   **13**

❧ 1501 ☙

A busy woman is staring at a piece of paper in barely-concealed frustration. She looks up at you angrily. "I hear you're some sort of computational engineer. Well, my men have been struggling with this for days - and our calculation engine. We need to know how much cargo we can load on this German airship we're bidding for, to know whether it will make the Greenland run."

She snorts. "Barely worth our while otherwise. Calculate its buoyancy and I'll pay you handsomely."

The paper she hands you contains a mass of information about the airship: you will need access to a computational engine, as well as the correct punchcards to run on it, to do as she wishes.

Leave the office...   97

✧ 1502 ✧

Try as you can, you cannot make any headway against Hendon's play. He laughs and tosses his final hand onto the table. "I think you owe me a hundred pound," he says. "So can you pay?"

Give him the money...   (£100)   750
Handed over to the Constables...   13

✧ 1503 ✧

After weeks of tinkering and experimenting, you finally have a working **autorifle prototype.** It is not ready for use yet - the design is not robust enough - but it does display the principles you have employed. It would make an excellent exhibit at the Great Exhibition, greatly augmenting the reputation of your Millwall Engineering Works.

Prepare to exhibit the prototype...   1355
Keep the prototype hidden for now...   1308

✧ 1504 ✧

"Well, perhaps I should be asking you about some of your past deeds. Was it you that rescued Captain Coke from the gallows? I thought I heard something about that. Or duelled with Duke Barrymore in the Henley Theatre? You have quite a taste for the dramatic. Perhaps you'd like to indulge that a little by lending me a hand in my next project."

"What will you steal?"

"The Crown Jewels."

"You must be mad. I will be leaving now."   750
"Tell me more."   1260

✧ 1505 ✧

This will be the utmost challenge of your engineering skill. Even with the engine-calculated designs, the forging and manufacturing of the many parts, together with the testing and trials will take a great deal of time, and much investment. There is no guarantee that you will succeed. Remove the **brass flange joint, net,**

and **steam accordion** from your **possessions** (or the box in passage **1308**). Make an ENGINEERING roll of difficulty 18.

Successful ENGININEERING roll!   1441
Failed ENGINEERING roll!   1308

✧ 1506 ✧

If you have **Prishaw's Sword**, turn to **1433** immediately. Otherwise, if you have the codeword *Chaldean*, turn to **1297**. If you have neither, read on.

The Guberstein is an exclusive Gentleman's club of the sort that you will never have access to. Riches are only one of the entry requirements: here in society, it is all about who you know. Even if you go to the rear entrance to find work, they would turn you away.

Turn to...   400

✧ 1507 ✧

Your unsuspecting victim expects nothing, until you power past, snatching their valuables as you go. Roll two dice to see what you have managed to grab.

Score 2-3   a wallet containing **ten guineas in banknotes**
Score 4   a **fur coat**
Score 5   a **top hat**
Score 6   a **silver necklace** and a **lace shawl**
Score 7   a purse containing **£2 8s**
Score 8   a wallet containing **£3 5s**
Score 9   a **lady's wig**
Score 10   an **ivory fan**
Score 11-12   a satchel containing **chloroform** and a **stethoscope**

Turn to...   noted passage

✧ 1508 ✧

The waiting robbers are not impressed by your appearance or your threats. They burst out from the thicket as you approach, clubs and rough weapons held high. You must fight them!

Robbers	Weapons: **clubs (PAR 2)**
Parry:	10
Nimbleness:	7
Toughness:	3

Victory!   1311
Defeat!   999

❧ 1509 ❧

The tradesman turns puce with rage. "How dare you! Yes, it gets around, news about my wife, I suppose. But to think I'd live to be teased by a common hedge criminal." He grabs a spanner from his toolbox and hurls it with a lucky aim: it strikes you above the eye and puts you out cold. When you awake you have a **black eye (ACC-2 GAL-1)** and Drury and his wagon are nowhere to be seen.

Ride on...   **noted passage**

❧ 1510 ❧

The machine is a great success: it attracts much attention among the guilds and businessmen. One offers to buy the design from you for **£100**: you may either take the money or tick the codeword *Clicking*.

Return to your workshop...   **1308**

❧ 1511 ❧

Night has fallen, and for a rare moment the smog has drifted apart, allowing the moon to shine down over the narrow streets. Two figures wander through the night, hand in hand, cloaked and hooded. They peer at the locked doors of shops and houses, reading the numbers, making some sort of note with a brass mechanical recorder you glimpse. When you approach, however, they turn about and move with a strange silence into an alleyway. And disappear.

Ride on...   **noted passage**

❧ 1512 ❧

The man inside is a baker, transporting a colossal cake somewhere. He quivers in terror as you empty his pockets of **£4 15s** and relieve him of a **silver ring**.

Ride away...   **noted passage**

❧ 1513 ❧

If you have a workshop in Millwall, you can choose a promising young person to train as an apprentice: tick the box marked ☐ **Apprentice** in passage **1308**.

Leave for now...   647

❧ 1514 ❧

Leaving Beaufort clutching at his wounds, angry but weakened, you turn and dash for your velosteam. Unsurprisingly, you will now be **Wanted by the Constables**, regardless of any disguise.

Get away...   33

❧ 1515 ❧

The airship captain collapses to the ground. You can take **£3 15s**, an **Airship Captain's hat** and a telescope. You will now be **Wanted by Atmospheric Union**, unless you are wearing a **mask**.

Get away...   **noted passage**

☞ **Epilogue** ☜

So your days on the lawless road are over. Before calculating a final score to enter on the Roll of Honour, you can discover what follows your story in this book by using the table below. Did you finish your tale in ignominious execution, pain-wracked suffering or wealth and respect? Did you ever take the time to plan for your future - or was the excitement of the present enough for you?

	Dead	**Alive**
Money in purse...	0 points / £	1 point / £2
Money in bank account...	0 points / guinea	1 point / guinea
Scars	-	-3 points / scar
Wounds	-	-10 points / wound

	Dead or Alive
Ruthlessness...	2 points / point
Engineering...	1 point / point
Motoring..	1 point / point
Ingenuity...	1 point / point
Nimbleness...	1 point / point
Gallantry...	2 points / point
Solidarity Points...	5 points each
Wanted status...	10 points each
Friendships...	10 points each
Great Deeds...	20 points each
Famed Lawbreaker....	50 points
People's Champion...	100 points

100 points or fewer...	**A Nobody**
101-150 points...	**Featured in a Song**
151-200 points...	**Temporarily Respected**
201-250 points...	**Considerable Fame**
251-350 points...	**Known and Feared**
351 points or more...	**True Legend**

A Nobody

Who were you, after all? Can you lay claim to the definite article, when the shadow you left was so insubstantial? You were simply a steam highwayman, not The Steam Highwayman, and your tyre-tracks will be soon over-ridden by a hero with more vigour, more drive and more ambition.

Featured in a Song

They cannot say that you achieved nothing, so some of your more exciting deeds are retold in a ballad that enjoys a few brief years of popularity. In the next century it surfaces again and is updated by an electric folk band, shining another brief beam of attention on your nefarious career. But other than a few mentions in academic footnotes, that is it: you are forgotten.

Temporarily Respected

For some time the city continue to discuss the adventures of the masked figure on a Ferguson velosteam who wrought such vengeance on the wealthy. They wonder whether you have gone into hiding, or been caught and punished at last. The street urchins play at robbing the rich and giving pork pies to the poor in your name and an echo of your power passes down the years as a bogeyman with whom the children of the rich are threatened before bed.

Considerable Fame

Your tale is told up and down the country, aloft in the dining cabins and engine rooms of transatlantic airships and abroad wherever the rich look over their shoulder, fearing the retribution of the oppressed and ignored. Your example is used by the Compact for Worker's Equality to rally many to their cause and for a short while, a brand of beer named after your velosteam becomes a national favourite. You will never be quite forgotten, although many will take advantage of your memory.

Known and Feared

Have you really gone, or are you lurking somewhere, biding your time before striking once more at the rich and powerful? This is the fear of the guilds and the nobles of the land, and this is your legacy: you have put a spoke in the wheel of progress and a hesitation in the hand that takes in the taxes. For many years to come, the threat of the return of the Steam Highwayman will give the privileged reason to pay extra for protection on the road, and for many years, revolutionaries and common folk will be emboldened to stand up for their rights and their freedoms.

True Legend

You truly are the Steam Highwayman: your legend is as great as Robin Hood or King Arthur and your countless deeds of courage, guile, determination and style will be told and retold again and again in ballets, moving picture shows, theatrical entertainments and saccharine novels. Many lives have also been changed for the better - families lifted from poverty, rich and wealthy men forced to reconsider their selfish modes of existence and the crown itself shaken by your achievements. Your story will ring out down the ages as an example of a hero and a mystery. Who was the Steam Highwayman? YOU were the Steam Highwayman!

Acknowledgements

T his work began, a good idea,

Given from Your heart.

And I know Your nature - You are the One

To finish what You start.

Philippians 1:6

Thanks and appreciation to my wife, best friend, co-creator of all my best projects

Cheryl Anne Adamos Noutch

whose constant support and encouragement continually enables my work.

Also to:

Russ Nicholson; illustrator. It's been an honour and a privilege to work with you, Russ. Thanks for bringing my book to life with your eye on my creation!

El Jacqko De Santos; proofreader, editor and go-to voice of reason, Backer 21. Thanks for encouraging me constantly, being my partner in-crime for all these years and believing in the Steam Highwayman!

Gábor Joe Telekesi; Backer 1. Thanks for being the first aboard the velosteam - and watching the entire launch livestream!

Charles Revello; Backer 2. Welcome back - again! I hope Volume 3 takes you deeper and further into the Highwayman's life.

Kjeld Froberg; Backer 3. May Denmark fear the wrath of Kjeld Highwayman! Enjoy the adventure.

Simon Scott; Backer 4, sponsor. Thanks for your support for Steam Highwayman and all your work to bring gamebooks to the next generation. May your boiler never burst!

Graham Wilson; Backer 5, Wanted Criminal. Thanks for all your encouragement for the project and for me as a writer. Best of luck for your **Rise of the Ancients** gamebook series.

Turk; Backer 6. Thanks for returning to back this third volume of **your** adventure! Have a great time steaming beneath the southern stars!

René; Backer 7. Great to have you onboard, Rene. Your support for the gamebook community is massively **app**reciated: keep pushing the boundaries!

Kurosh Shadmand; Backer 8 and sponsor. I've really appreciated your engagement with *Steam Highwayman*, Kurosh. Best of luck with your own writing projects - particularly that open-world gamebook you're planning!

Mark Lain; Backer 9. Thanks for following and supporting the project all this time! May your **Destiny's Role** gamebook series bring you the satisfaction and success you deserve.

Ernest Bluntfist; Backer 10. Long may the Sons and Sisters of Steam (Always Geared Eccentrically) rule the roads of the South! Justice! Freedom! And a hard-boiled egg to you, sir.

Juha Rankinen; Backer 11. Thanks for joining the team, Juha. Your support means my project can continue. May you enjoy the ride!

shawndumas; Backer 12. Enjoy the adventure, Shawn! I hope you travel far and wide astride your very own velosteam.

Dave Ibbett; Backer 13. My dear friend! Thanks for your support in creative endeavours, games, and family life. Best of luck with your **Multiverse Concert Series**!

Robert Langston; Backer 14. Thanks for continuing to back the project, Robert! You've been a Day One backer again!

Kevin Abbotts; Backer 15. What commitment you've shown to *Steam Highwayman*, Kevin. I really appreciate your continued support.

Paul, Noah, Jona and Elya Brückner; Backer 16 and sponsor. Thanks for your generous pledge and your support, Andreas. May your steam pressure always remain high, and may your boys grow up to know that THEY are the Steam HIGHWAYMAN.

Bernadine Philips; Backer 17 and gamebook reader extraordinaire! Thanks for all the support you give to me and all the independent gamebook publishers. Truly, you are the gamebook writer's greatest reader!

Stuart Whitehouse; Backer 18. Great to have you backing once again, Stuart. May your tyres never slip!

Martin Ellis; Backer 19. Thanks for clambering aboard, Martin. Truly the woods and hidden places will fear you. Maybe the book will prompt you to explore some hidden parts of London too!

Michael Philips; Backer 20. Thanks for your friendship and support. I hope you enjoy this third adventure even more!

Zacharias Chun-pong Leung 梁振邦; Backer 22. Cheers for continuing to support the project, Zacky! May the roads of Hong Kong resound with the roar of your passing.

Pete Bounous; Backer 23. Thanks for joining us on this crowdfunding adventure, Pete. Your support is greatly appreciated.

Ben Cowan; Backer 24. Cheers, Ben, for your support. I hope you enjoy the ride! YOU are the Steam Highwayman!

Unai Gomez; Backer 25. Great to have your support again, Unai. May your blunderpistol never misfire and your sabre stay sharp in the scabbard!

First time backer   *Second time backer*   *Third time backer*

Graham Hart; Backer 26, sponsor. Thanks for continuing to believe in the power of stories, the power of gamebooks and the power of steam!

Richie Stevens; Backer 27, sponsor. Great to have you supporting the project again: thanks for continuing to back gamebooks and independent writers.

The Creative Fund; Backer 28.

Matt Sheriff; Backer 29. Thanks for your pledge and your keenness to get involved!

Aleksander Siatecki; Backer 30. I hope the maps lead you on many an exciting adventure. May Poland fear the Steam Highwayman!

James Terence Nelson Cleverley; Backer 31. Thanks for returning to support my project again. May your dice ever roll sixes.

Jörn Bethune; Backer 32. Thanks for your pledge and your readership. I hope SH3 makes a worthy addition to your shelf.

Godwin Matthew Teoh; Backer 33. Thanks for your continued support, Godwin. Singapore must be quaking in fear of the Highwayman by now!

Dane Barrett; Backer 34. I really appreciate your support, Dane. Best of luck with your own gamebook writing projects!

Danny Fuerstman; Backer 35. Great to have you riding with us once again, Danny. I raise my tankard to you, sir!

Oscar Andrés Schwerdt; Backer 36. Thanks for your support, Oscar. May Argentina fear the terrible Steam Highwayman!

Huckleberry Carignan; Backer 37. Great to have your support, Huckleberry. I hope you have many exciting adventures in the books.

Prof. Dr. Oliver M. Traxel; Backer 38. Great to have you backing the project once again! May Gamebooks flourish wherever you tread!

Shane Dunkle; Backer 40. Your pledge and your support is much appreciated, Shane. Enjoy the ride through olde London town...

Sam Isaacson; Backer 41. Thanks for supporting a fellow guildsmember. Best of luck with your Entram gamebook series.

Stelio Passaris; Backer 42. Thanks for returning to support again, Stelio. Enjoy the adventure and the ride.

Nathan; Backer 43. Nathan, your pledge means a lot to me. You understand why I use my gifts as I do: may you always use yours to the greater glory of God.

Fred; Backer 44. Great to have your support. I hope you enjoy the book.

Per Stalby; Backer 45. Thanks for backing my project once again! May the road ever rise to meet your wheels.

Scott H. Moore; Backer 46. Great to have your support, Scott. May the Constables never find your hideout!

Aistis Samulionis; Backer 47. Thanks, Aistis! Your encouragement in the Kickstarter comments has been particularly appreciated.

Colin Oaten; Backer 48. Thanks for your support and interest once again, Colin. I hope you'll have many happy hours in the saddle with this one.

Craig; Backer 49. I appreciate your pledge and your help in bringing this book to be, Craig. Ta muchly.

Daniel Shaw; Backer 50. Thanks for your faithful friendship, as well as your interest in the project, Dan. I hope the books are distracting you plenty!

Nils Visser; Backer 51. Thanks for supporting a fellow Steampunk author, Nils! Best of luck with your own **smugglepunk** microgenre and the Time Flight Chronicles.

Kamarul Azmi Kamaruzaman; Backer 52. Thanks for coming back for another dose of the wild madness that is Steam Highwayman. Much appreciated.

Ondrej Zastera; Backer 53. Thanks for your tenacity and making sure you were included, Ondrej! Better a later pledge than none at all.

Robert Wilde; Backer 54. Thanks for your pledge, your support and your interest. I hope you have many happy hours in the book.

Y. K. Lee; Backer 55. I really appreciate your pledge once again: thanks for climbing aboard the Ferguson another time.

Otis C Parker; Backer 56 and sponsor. Thanks, uncle Otis, for your support and belief in my project, once again! Your generosity and faith really touch me.

Simon Hedley; Backer 57. Thanks for your support again, Simon. I hope you enjoy this volume as much as the last.

Matthew Whitingbird; Backer 58. Great to have you joining us, Matthew! YOU are the Steam Highwayman.

Michael Reilly; Backer 59. Thanks for backing the project, giving advice and for all you do for the gamebook community. Best of luck with your *Tales of Quahnarren* gamebook series.

Greg Muri; Backer 60. Thanks for coming back to back me on Kickstarter again, Greg. May your firebox always burn hot and clear!

Javier Fernandez-Sanguino; Backer 61. Thanks, Javier. May the German Wald resound with the roar of your Ferguson!

Mark Lee Voss; Backer 62. Thanks for backing once again: enjoy the adventure and the smoky city.

Robert; Backer 63. You're very welcome to join the backers, Robert! YOU are now the Steam Highwayman!

Martin L Noutch; Backer 64. Thanks Dad. This book wouldn't be here without all the adventures you set me off on.

Tom Geraghty; Backer 65. Thanks for pledging your support, Tom. I hope the adventures bring you many hours of satisfaction and diversion.

Starranger; Backer 66. Thanks for pledging again, Joseph. Enjoy the midnight rides astride your velosteam.

Joseph Snape; Backer 67 and sponsor. Thanks for your generous pledge and your support for the project, Joseph. I hope you will enjoy being part of the world of *Steam Highwayman*.

Kenny Louis; Backer 68. Kenny, thanks for your part in bringing the world's most steam-powered highwayman to the Reeking Metropolis.

Hans Peter Bak; backer 69. Thanks for pledging once again and ensuring Denmark has its fair share of velosteam riders!

Matthew Lockman; Backer 70. Great to have you returning to the project, Matthew. Cheers!

A Nony Mouse; Backer 71. Thanks for your support! Squeak squeak.

Stephane Bechard; Backer 72. Merci, Stephane! Thanks for how you support the gamebook community with your **Livre Dont Vous Etes Le Heros** site

Mervyn Koh; Backer 73. Thanks for backing my work once again, Mervyn. I hope this brings you as much enjoyment as the previous outings!

Andrew Wright; Backer 74 and sponsor. Cheers, Andrew! You are (now) the Steam Highwayman! I'm sure you'll spot yourself in the book now ;-)

Rob 2.0; Backer 75. Thanks 3.0, Rob 2.0,

for once again supporting my writing. You are the Steam Highwayman 2.0!

Joonseok Oh; Backer 76. Joonseok! May Washington fear the roar of your velosteam!

Dan; Backer 77. Thanks to you and your family for backing my work every step of the way. May you choose your own adventure as a writer as God leads.

Moritz Eggert; Backer 79. Vielen Dank, Moritz! Enjoy the adventure, once again.

Ssieth Anabuki; Backer 80. Thanks for backing! May the turnpikes of Yorkshire tremble at your approach.

Ben "phantomwhale" Turner; Backer 81. Great to have you aboard, Ben. Although with your moniker, perhaps the Highwayman and velosteam would fit aboard you more easily.

Chris Trapp; Backer 82. Thanks for supporting once again, Chris. Your pledge is much appreciated.

James Catchpole; Backer 83. Great to have your support. May Norwich fear the approach of the Steam Highwayman!

Niki Lybæk; Backer 84. Tusind tak, Niki! I hope you enjoy the adventure.

Ian Hayward; Backer 85. Thanks for returning to support another Kickstarter, Ian. I hope you enjoy your rewards.

Amketch; Backer 86. Great to have your support again, Amketch. Much appreciated.

Ian Berger; Backer 87. Thanks for backing, Ian. I hope life astride the velosteam suits you!

Vladimir "The Dartmoor Dodger" Tierney; Backer 88. Cheers, Vladimir! Whether down under, or riding over the moors, you'll be the highwayman to remember with that nickname.

Melvez; Backer 89. Gracias, Melvez. I hope Spain soon comes to learn, and fear, the legend of the Steam Highwayman!

David (Lowrie) Gillson; Backer 90. Thanks for your support, David, and every success with your Black Dog Gamebooks.

Adriano Ziffer; Backer 91 and sponsor. Vielen Dank, Adriano. You sure seem to add something to the world of the Steam Highwayman: you look like a native!

Adam Mann; Backer 92. Thanks for returning to back once again, Adam. YOU are the Steam Highwayman!

Aaron Thorne; Backer 93. Your support means a lot, Aaron. Thanks for continuing to back my projects and read my books - it means the world to me.

Riccardo Pittau; Backer 94. Merci beacoup, Riccardo. Welcome to the Steam Highwayman community!

Dave Bowen; Backer 95. Great to have you aboard once again, Dave. Cheers!

Xenachick; Backer 96. Great to have your support. YOU are the Steam Highwayman.

Doug Weimer; Backer 97. Thanks for pledging and supporting the project, Doug.

Clay Skaggs; Backer 98. Thanks very much for returning to back *The Reeking Metropolis*: I hope you enjoy exploring London's secrets.

James Pearson; Backer 99. Great to have your support, James. Enjoy the book.

Rhialto; Backer 101. Thanks for your pledge and your engagement on the KS page. Your comments and support were great.

Oliver Drozd; Backer 102. Your pledge is much appreciated, Oliver. Steam right on!

TRV; Backer 103. TVM for your P, your S and your E with the SH P, TRV!

Luchino; Backer 104. Grazie, signor. Sei il Bandito del Vapore!

Bossman; Backer 105. Vielen Dank, Herr Bossman! Du bißt der Dampf Wegmensch!

Magnus Johansson; Backer 106. Tack, Magnus. I appreciate your faithful support.

Richard Harrison; Backer 107. Ta very much, Richard. May Sheffield learn to fear the rider on the green steel steed!

Deon Beswick; Backer 108. Thanks, Deon! I hope your adventure is a long and glorious one.

Michael Doberenz; Backer 109. Thanks very much, Michael. May Texas learn to fear the Steam Highwayman!

Sterling Glass; Backer 110. I appreciate your pledge. I hope the ride on the old velosteam isn't rough enough to shatter your hopes of adventure!

Cato Vandrare; Backer 111. Great to have your support again, Cato. Londinium delendum est!

Minoru Natsutani; Backer 112. Thanks very much for pledging - enjoy the adventure, Minoru.

James Drouant; Backer 113. Great to have your support for the project, James. Invest in a telescope quickly!

Ang NamLeng; Backer 114. Thanks for returning to pledge again. May your adventure in the Reeking Metropolis continue!

Nerelax; Backer 115. Thanks for backing my third project - it's massively encouraging to have such supportive readers as yourself.

JohnTFS; Backer 117. Thanks for continuing to support my work, John. I hope you enjoy the book.

Anders Svensson; Backer 118. Tack så mycket, Anders. I really appreciate your continued support.

Damon; Backer 119. Great to have you back, Damon. Enjoy the adventure!

Andy Shrimpton; Backer 120. Thanks for all your encouragement online, Andy. I can't wait to hear about your adventures in SH3!

Fabrice Gatille; Backer 121. Merci beaucoup, Fabrice. I really appreciate your support for this third time.

Alistair Davidse; Backer 122. Thanks Alistair! Have a great time adventuring as the Steam Highwayman!

Rod Hart; Backer 123. Thanks for backing again, Rod. Enjoy the aventure!

Stuart Lloyd; Backer 124. Thanks for your friendship and support - the loaned books and the car rides too. Long live education through interactive fiction, say I!

Robertson Sondoh Jr; Backer 125. Thanks for the stream of relentless positivity you release online, Robertson, as well as all you do for the readers and writers of the next generation. Keep at it!

Kozelek; Backer 126. Thanks for backing for a second time, Kozelek. Good luck on those dangerous night rides.

Ed Hughes; Backer 127. Thanks for supporting the project again, Ed. YOU are the Steam Highwayman!

Jason O' Mahony; Backer 130. Go raibh míle maith agat, Jason. Enjoy the adventure in the smoky city.

AJ Erikson; Backer 132. Thanks for your encouraging comments and appreciation of the updates, Austin. Every creator needs backers like you.

Cristovao Neto; Backer 133. Muito obrigado, Cristovao! Good luck escaping the Constables' noose... and the Guild's amputation block.

Nicola Birch; Backer 134. Birchy, I owe more of my happiness to you than I can express easily here. Thanks for being a friend to me, to Cheryl and to our marriage.

RedMick; Backer 135. Thanks for all you do for the gamebook writers of the next generation!

Simon Smith; Backer 136. Cheers, Simon! I hope you get a real scent of oil and steam from the pages.

Chris Semler; Backer 137. Cheers, Chris. Thanks for backing again.

Ed; Backer 138. Great to have your support, Ed. I hope you're more than satisfied with the book.

Nicodemus; Backer 139. Thanks, o wise Nicodemus. Stay mysterious!

James Murray; Backer 140. Thanks James, for pledging again! Enjoy the book!

mcfadds1; Backer 141. Thanks very much for supporting the project. Watch out for the Whitechapel gangsters.

Scarlett Letter; Backer 142. Thanks very much, Kristine, for backing my work once again. Your continual support means a great deal.

Demian Katz; Backer 143. Demian! Thanks for all you do and have done for the online gamebook community. The interactive fiction ecosystem would be much poorer without your enthusiasm and diligent data-basing.

Ian Greenfield; Backer 144. Thanks for backing, Ian! Your support is really appreciated.

Jonathan Green; Backer 145. Thanks for backing my project, Jon, and for the years of service to gamebook readers and writers. Not only are you the Steam Highwayman, but YOU ARE THE HERO! May you have the best of success with your **ACE Gamebook Series** too.

JJ Hapex; Backer 146. Great to have you aboard the velosteam, JJ. Enjoy the ride.

Marcy; Backer 148. Thanks for continuing to support the Steam Highwayman project and to read and enjoy my books.

Mattias Myrälf; Backer 149. Tack så mycket , Mattias! May the road rise to meet your tyres.

Peter Fuchs; Backer 150. Thanks very much for backing again, Peter.

Allan 'Goggles' Jenkins; Backer 151. Great to have your support once more, Allan. I hope you enjoy exploring London as it could have been.

Kevin Taylor; Backer 152. Thanks for returning to back again and to support my writing, Kevin.

Mel Follmer; Backer 153. Thanks for pledging, Mel! Enjoy the book!

Rebecca Scott; Backer 154. Rebecca, I really appreciate your continued support for my writing and the world of Steam Highwayman. Enjoy it!

Gareth Knowles; Backer 155. Thanks for your engagement online, Gareth, and for your pledge towards the project.

Luke Sheridan; Backer 158. Thanks for backing again, Luke. Have a great time on back on the velosteam.

Anthony Impenna; Backer 159. Thanks for supporting my project so faithfully, Anthony. I hope you enjoy this book even more than the previous ones.

Andrew Shannon; Backer 160. Great to have your support once more.

Kim, Myo, and Cho; Backers 161. Kim! Thanks for your readiness to back - and read - whatever I've done. Your friendship really means a lot in that.

Paul Jordan; Backer 162. Great to have you joining the project, Paul. May your gas line never block and your brakes never jam.

Todd; Backer 163. Thanks Todd! I hope you enjoy adventuring in the book.

Mark "Daelhoof" Johnson; Backer 165. Thanks for supporting, Mark. Now go terrify some self-righteous nobility!

Eamonn McCusker; Backer 166. Thanks for backing once again. Enjoy the ride, Eamonn.

Richard Courtney; Backer 167. Great to have your help in bringing this book to be, Richard. Have a great time in the book.

Matt Molloy; Backer 168. Thanks, Matt! May the dales fear the approach of the Steam Highwayman.

Jeffrey Dean; Backer 169. Thanks for pledging, Jeffrey, and all the best for your Road Less Travelled Gamebook projects - digital and print!

Scott Ballantyne; Backer 170. Thanks for pledging to see a third installment of the *Steam Highwayman* series, Scott. I hope you enjoy the result.

Jon and Oliver; Backers 171. Long may the Fabled Land format flourish! I'm looking forward to *The Crown and the Tower*.

Michael Hartland; Backer 172. Thanks for supporting the project again, Michael. I hope the third book is the best yet!

Peter Auger; Backer 173. Thanks so much, Pete, for backing me all this time, and believing in me. The best of success to both you and Zen in your writing - and more.

Bhajho; Backer 174. Great to have your support, o mysterious Bhajo!

D3oinncubus; Backer 175. Thanks for

pledging, Adrian! Enjoy this third book in the series!

scaryridge creative house; Backer 176. Thanks for your support.

Justin Whitman; Backer 177. Thanks for your pledge, Justin. Enjoy the adventure!

Tracey-Trace Nash; Backer 178.Thanks for your support, *Tracey*.

Stephen Chadwick; Backer 179. Thanks, Stephen. Enjoy life on the midnight road!

Amanda and Matthew Towler; Backers 180. Thanks for your support! YOU are the Steam Highway...couple, I suppose. Best of luck with all your ambushes and robberies.

Sören Beyersdorff; Backer 181. Vielen Dank, Sören. Enjoy the adventure and the opportunity to write your own adventure.

Allan Richmond; Backer 182. Thanks for returning to back again, Allan. Have fun on the velosteam!

odotus; Backer 183. Thanks for backing, odotus! Have a great time cocking a snook at those dastardly constables!

Mr. Johnson; Backer 184. Thanks Aaron! Take care, or you might end up in Parliament!

Jon Mann; Backer 185. Thanks for backing again, Jon. Enjoy exploring every corner of the city.

Levi Prinzing; Backer 186. Have a great time in the world of *Steam Highwayman*, Levi. Leave no bad deed unpunished!

Gaetano Abbondanza; Backer 187. Great to have you back, Gaetano. Thanks for all your engagement online - keep spreading the word of the Steam Highwayman.

Alan Halpin; Backer 190. Thanks for your friendship, as well as your support, Alan. I want to wish you every success with your own gamebook writing projects.

Ryan Lynch; Backer 191. Thanks for pledging, Ryan. Have a great time - and don't get caught (although some of the best experiences start in gaol...)

Adam J Purcell; Backer 192. Thanks for your pledges in each campaign, Adam. I hope you enjoy the book.

Jonathan 'Oyster bar' Lightfoot.; Backer 193. Thanks for all your support and engagement with the project, Jonathan. It's been great to share ideas and images with you - I really appreciate it.

Stephen; Backer 194. Thanks very much for pledging. Have a good time in the book!

Petale; Backer 195. Thanks for pledging! Get ruthless and get ready to rob!

Joshua Brutcher; Backer 196. I really

appreciate your pledge, Joshua. Great to have you on board the velosteam.

Adrian Jankowiak; Backer 198. Enjoy exploring the Reeking Metropolis, Adrian! Find every secret

Peter Christiansen; Backer 199. Thanks for your pledge, Peter! Have a great adventure.

Tommy Chu; Backer 200. Thanks very much for supporting my writing. I hope the book is an adequate reward.

Bobby Howes; Backer 201. Thankyou, Bobby. The best of luck on the open road!

Robert Morgan; Backer 202. Thanks for taking the risk and pledging towards my book!

Mark Buckley; Backer 203. It's great to count on the continued support of backers like yourself, Mark. Thankyou.

Stuart 'The Steam Highwayman' Miller; Backer 205. Now we all know who the *real* Steam Highwayman is... Good luck!

Nicolette Tanksley; Backer 206. Thanks for pledging towards my campaign once more.

Lorraine and Mark Jackman; Backers 207. Thanks for all your faithful support over all these years. It means a lot to me.

Simon Day; Backer 208. Thanks for being among that dwindling but faithful number of supporters for each of my campaigns - it means a lot to see you coming back for more, Simon!

permusashi; Backer 209. Thanks for your pledge! YOU are the Steam Highwayman!

Sauro Lepri; Backer 210. Great to have you onboard, Sauro. Watch out for ships named after large cats...

Guy Edward Larke; Backer 211. I hope you find the life of a roadside robber a real lark, Guy.

David Wilson; Backer 212. Great to have your help in making my book a reality, David. Thanks very much.

Tim Lawrence; Backer 213. I'm so grateful to have your support once again, Tim. The midnight road belongs to you.

Jonathan Caines; Backer 214. Never fear the Constables, Jonathan! With your attitude of generosity, you can be sure that you are on the right side of history.

Matthew Stephenson; Backer 215. Thanks for your pledge, Matthew. I hope you enjoy every minute and hour of your adventure.

Talcum Powers; Backer 216. Thanks for your pledge! The road is long, so I hope you know how to prevent saddle sores when on the velosteam!

Jim Hartland; Backer 218. Thanks for backing. I hope London is another great adventure!

Malc; Backer 219. Thanks, Malc! Enjoy the book and may your adventures long continue!

Skorpio; Backer 220. Great to have your support once more, Skorpio. Enjoy the book.

Michael Cohen; Backer 222. Thanks very much for supporting the project. YOU are the Steam Highwayman!

Sean; Backer 223. Thanks for your pledge, Seam. Enjoy the books and the ride!

Chris; Backer 224. Thanks, Chris. May California resound to the roar of the Ferguson velosteam!

Joe Tilbrook; Backer 225. Cheers, Joe! It's great to have you backing once more. Enjoy the book.

Sergio García Quiles; Backer 226. Thanks very much for pledging and supporting the project. I hope you have hours of fun with the books.

George Maicovschi; Backer 227. Mulțumesc foarte mult, George!

Andy Jenkinson; Backer 228. Thanks for your pledge and your interaction during the campaign, Andy. YOU are the Steam Highwayman!

Josh Bruce; Backer 229. Thanks for being such a legend and a stand-up man of God. You are even more than a Steam Highwayman - you are a man after God's heart.

Jules Fattorini; Backer 230. Thanks very much, Jules. Watch out for the Steam Highwayman venturing up your way in Volume VI...

Joshua Abramsky; Backer 231. Thanks for pledging for the third time. Committed support like yours means a great deal to me.

Michael Plagens; Backer 232. Thanks for your pledge and enjoy the book. YOU are the Steam Highwaymike.

luk; Backer 233. Great to have you back, luk. Thanks very much.

Andrea Maselli; Backer 234. Grazie mille, Andrea. Now go rob the rich and give to the poor!

David Gotteri; Backer 235. Thanks for backing, David! It's great to know *Steam Highwayman* will be read in Bolsover.

Paul Munday; Backer 236. Thanks for your pledge, Paul - it's much appreciated.

josandgrey; Backer 237. Thanks for pledging, Josephine. Enjoy the adventure!

Lin Liren; Backer 239. Thanks for your generous pledge, Lin, and your support for the whole online gamebook community.

Hannah Goldsmith; Backer 240. Thanks for supporting me in this, Hannah! Your encouragement means a lot to me - during the project and in life generally.

Mike Migalski; Backer 241. I'm very grateful for your pledge, Mike. Enjoy the adventure!

Florian Stock; Backer 242. Vielen Dank, Florian. Thanks for pledging and helping me build up steam.

Andy Miller; Backer 243. May the peaks and Dales resound at the approach of Andy Miller, Steam Highwayman!

James A. Hirons; Backer 244. Thanks for your pledge, Jam, and for all your contributions to the gamebook community. And the best of success for your Literally Immersive Gamebooks series.

Jim Vlahos; Backer 245. Cheers, Jim. May your tyres never puncture and your steam stay hot!

Ernest Khoo; Backer 246. Thanks, Ernest! Your pledge is really appreciated.

JC; Backer 247. Thanks for your pledge, JC. Enjoy the adventure!

Stephen Griffin; Backer 248. Thanks for pledging and supporting the project, Stephen. Enjoy the ride.

Zoli; Backer 249. Great to have your support once more, Zoli. Thanks for bringing my project to light in Hungary.

Connor Barber; Backer 250. Enjoy the adventure, Connor. Thanks so much for pledging and supporting.

James Schannep (Martin's favourite gamebook author); Backer 251. Well, I asked for that, didn't I? It's a good thing I do actually like your books. So let me thank you again for your support and your friendship and wish you the very best with your family and your **Click Your Own Poison** gamebook series.

Andrew Givens; Backer 252. Great to have your pledge, Andrew. May Maryland fear the righteous rogue on his velosteam.

Brian Schmitt; Backer 253. Thanks for backing, Brian! Enjoy your books.

Robin; Backer 254. Dank je, Robin. I hope the Netherlands doesn't prove too damp to run your velosteam!

Antony Quarrell; Backer 255. Oh for another evening motorbike ride through the Chilterns! Not too long, I hope. God bless you and the growing family.

Sibi; Backer 256. Thanks for all the support you've shown for my writing, Sibi. The very best to your family, too.

Neil Myler; Backer 257. My faithful friend! I can't forget or overlook your generosity towards me when I began this Steam Highwayman thing, or your many years of friendship. May the unjust and the selfish continually fear the sound of your steam-driven approach.

Vladimir; Backer 258. Thanks for your pledge, Vladimir! Long may you ride.

Nicole "germie" Moyle; Backer 259. Cheers! I really appreciate your pledge.

Martin Randall; Backer 260. I hope you enjoy many a ramble and many a pint in these pages, Martin. Take your time at the waterside.

Dubious Virtue; Backer 261. Thanks for your pledge. Stay mysterious!

Ken Finlayson; Backer 262. Thanks for backing again, Ken. Enjoy the adventure.

Mr Sphynx; Backer 263. Thanks for all your encouragement during and after the campaign, Goetz. Your positivity and appreciation for the updates really helped me.

Kean Stuart; Backer 264. Cheers, Kean, for coming on board and joining in.

Fabian König; Backer 265. Thanks for backing once again, Fabian.

Gábor Vitárius Dr.; Backer 266. Nagyon szépen köszönjük, Gabor Joe :-)

Raimund Ruppel; Backer 267. Vielen Dank, Herr Mantichor.

Eclectic Meeple; Backer 268. Thanks for backing the project, and enjoy the legend.

Joao Berrones; Backer 269. Thanks very much for pledging and supporting my writing, Joao.

Jared 'Pirate' Foley; Backer 270. Arr, matey. Much thanks and arrpreciation for your friendship and support.

Jeremy Hamaker; Backer 271. Great to have your support, Jeremy! Enjoy the adventure.

Steven Lord; Backer 272. Thanks for backing all three of my books, Steven. Your generosity will go before you.

Daniel Urdzik; Backer 27. Thanks for backing once again, Daniel! May your flue ever smoke cleanly!

qantrim; Backer 275. Thanks for backing once again, Quentin. Good luck in the city.

The Rangdo of Arg; Backer 276. May Arg know fear as you plunder their steam coaches, O Rangdo.

Nathan C; Backer 277. Welcome back once more: thanks so much for continuing to support my publications.

M Phelps; Backer 278. Thanks for your support and your interest in the project.

Richard Caves; Backer 279. May your coal gas ever burn hot, Mr Caves.

Richard Bunting; Backer 280. I raise a glass to your health, good sir!

Kev-La; Backer 281. Great to have your support, Kev-La.

Oliver Brettschneider; Backer 282. Vielen Dank, Oliver. Viel glück auf dem velosteam.

Travis Campbell; Backer 283. Thanks for your pledge, Travis. I hope you enjoy the world of the Steam Highwayman.

Gabriel Sandqvist; Backer 284. Tack så mycket, Gabriel. Enjoy the adventure.

Ian McFarlin; Backer 285. Once again, thanks for your generous support, Ian. I hope you enjoy the books.

Jeremy Sproston; Backer 286. T.hanks, Jeremy. Bring the steam and the glory to Italy for us all!

Stefan Anundi; Backer 287. Thanks for your pledge, Stefan. I hope you enjoy all your adventures across England.

Dean Allen Jones; Backer 288. Welcome back, Dean, and thanks for your pledge.

Hisham Barazi; Backer 289. Dankie, Hisham. May South Africa fear the approach of the Steam Highwayman!

benjebobs; Backer 290. Well, I think you'll find a use for all those pork pies, Fagin., if you search hard enough.

Anthony Christopher Hackett; Backer 291. Thanks for supporting the project, Anthony. YOU are the Steam Highwayman.

☙ ❧

Further illustration acknowledgements From British Library Public Domain Flickr account: p136 (passage 715): Title: "History of Stafford and Guide to the Neighbourhood. Illustrated with wood engravings", Author(s): Calvert, Charles, Librarian of the Free Library, Stafford [person] British Library shelfmark: "Digital Store 10352.c.37", Place of publication: Stafford (England), Date of publication: 1886, Publisher: J. Halden; P145 (passage 764-765): Title: "The Universal Mining Code for the use of mining companies, mining engineers ... The Code words specially selected to comply with the Telegraph Convention rules, by G. Ager", Author(s): Corbett, R. Sydney [person] ; Stevens, James, M.E., Corbett (R. Sydney) [person] ; Ager, George [person], British Library shelfmark: "Digital Store 7104.dd.3", Place of publication: London (England), Date of publication: 1890; P155 (passage 819/820): Title: "Where to buy at Croydon. An illustrated local review. By the Editor of the 'Agents' Guide,' etc", British Library shelfmark: "Digital Store 10368.k.24", Place of publication: Brighton (England), Date of publication: 1891, Publisher: Robinson, Son & Pike

CODEWORDS

- Cabal
- Cabin
- Caernavon
- Callused
- Caltrop
- Canvey
- Capital
- Captain
- Caritas
- Carling
- Carpet
- Carrier
- Catastrophe
- Catiline
- Cattleboy
- Causeway
- Certain
- Chaff
- Chaldean
- Chapter
- Charged
- Chariot
- Charley
- Charity
- Chary
- Charred
- Chastise
- Chatty
- Chattering
- Cheered
- Chertsey
- Chesterfield
- Chicken
- Childlike
- Childless
- Chinstrap
- Chipped
- Chirp
- Chirrup
- Chosen
- Chuffing
- Churl
- Citrate
- Clapper
- Clarify
- Clasp
- Classic
- Clavicle
- Clearly
- Clinched
- Clockwork
- Coaxial
- Collector
- Collapse
- Commensurate
- Commiserate
- Commission
- Compassionate
- Concrete
- Conglomerate
- Considerate
- Constable
- Contactless
- Contradict
- Converse
- Cool
- Corrupt
- Craven
- Crazed
- Credit
- Crestfallen
- Cricket
- Critique
- Crisis
- Crisp
- Critical
- Crumb
- Curdle
- Curly
- Currently
- Cutthroat

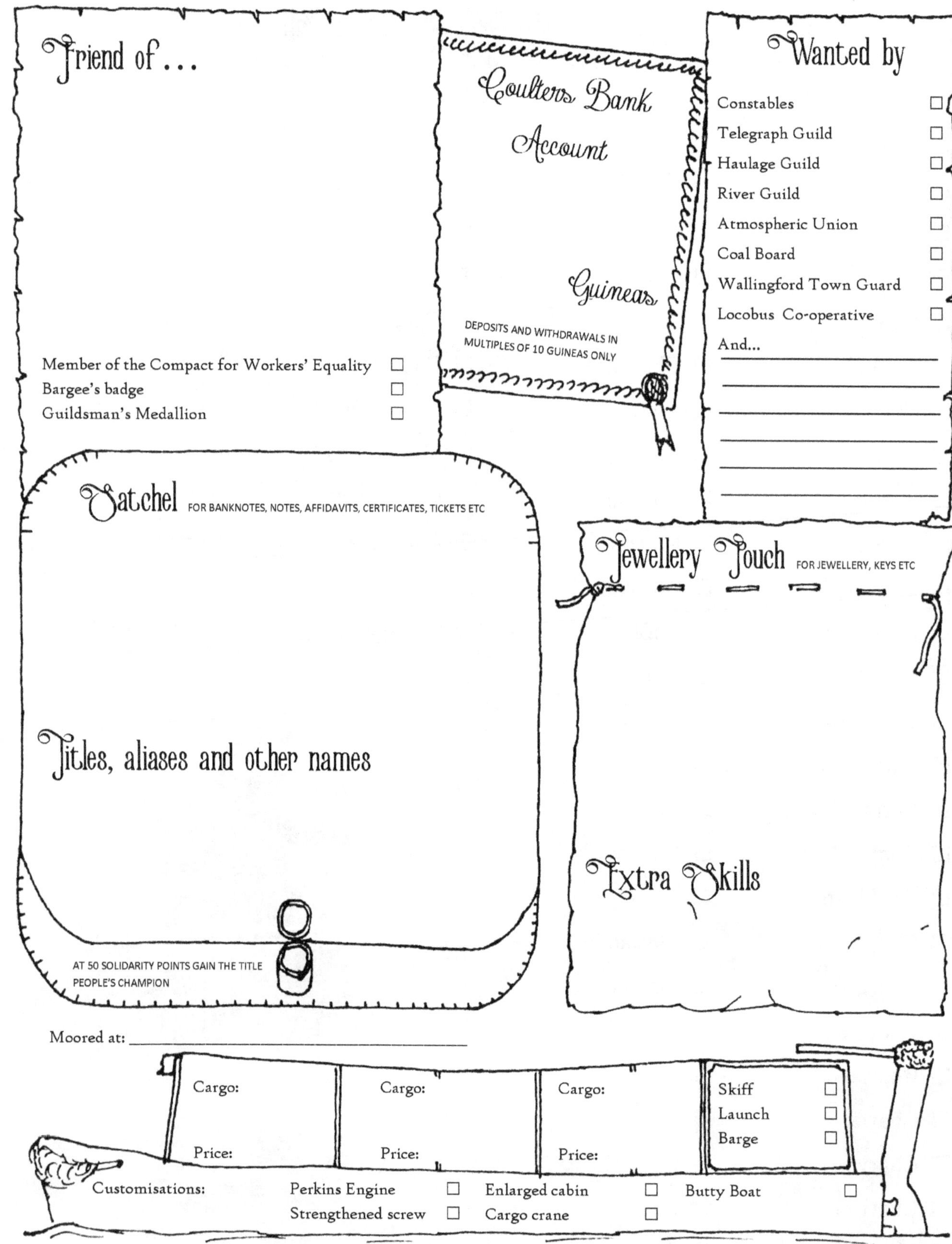

Friend of...

Member of the Compact for Workers' Equality ☐
Bargee's badge ☐
Guildsman's Medallion ☐

Coulter's Bank Account

Guineas

DEPOSITS AND WITHDRAWALS IN
MULTIPLES OF 10 GUINEAS ONLY

Wanted by

Constables ☐
Telegraph Guild ☐
Haulage Guild ☐
River Guild ☐
Atmospheric Union ☐
Coal Board ☐
Wallingford Town Guard ☐
Locobus Co-operative ☐
And... _______________
____
____
____
____
____

Satchel FOR BANKNOTES, NOTES, AFFIDAVITS, CERTIFICATES, TICKETS ETC

Titles, aliases and other names

AT 50 SOLIDARITY POINTS GAIN THE TITLE
PEOPLE'S CHAMPION

Jewellery Pouch FOR JEWELLERY, KEYS ETC

Extra Skills

Moored at: _______________________________________

Cargo: Cargo: Cargo:

Skiff ☐
Launch ☐
Barge ☐

Price: Price: Price:

Customisations: Perkins Engine ☐   Enlarged cabin ☐   Butty Boat ☐
Strengthened screw ☐   Cargo crane ☐

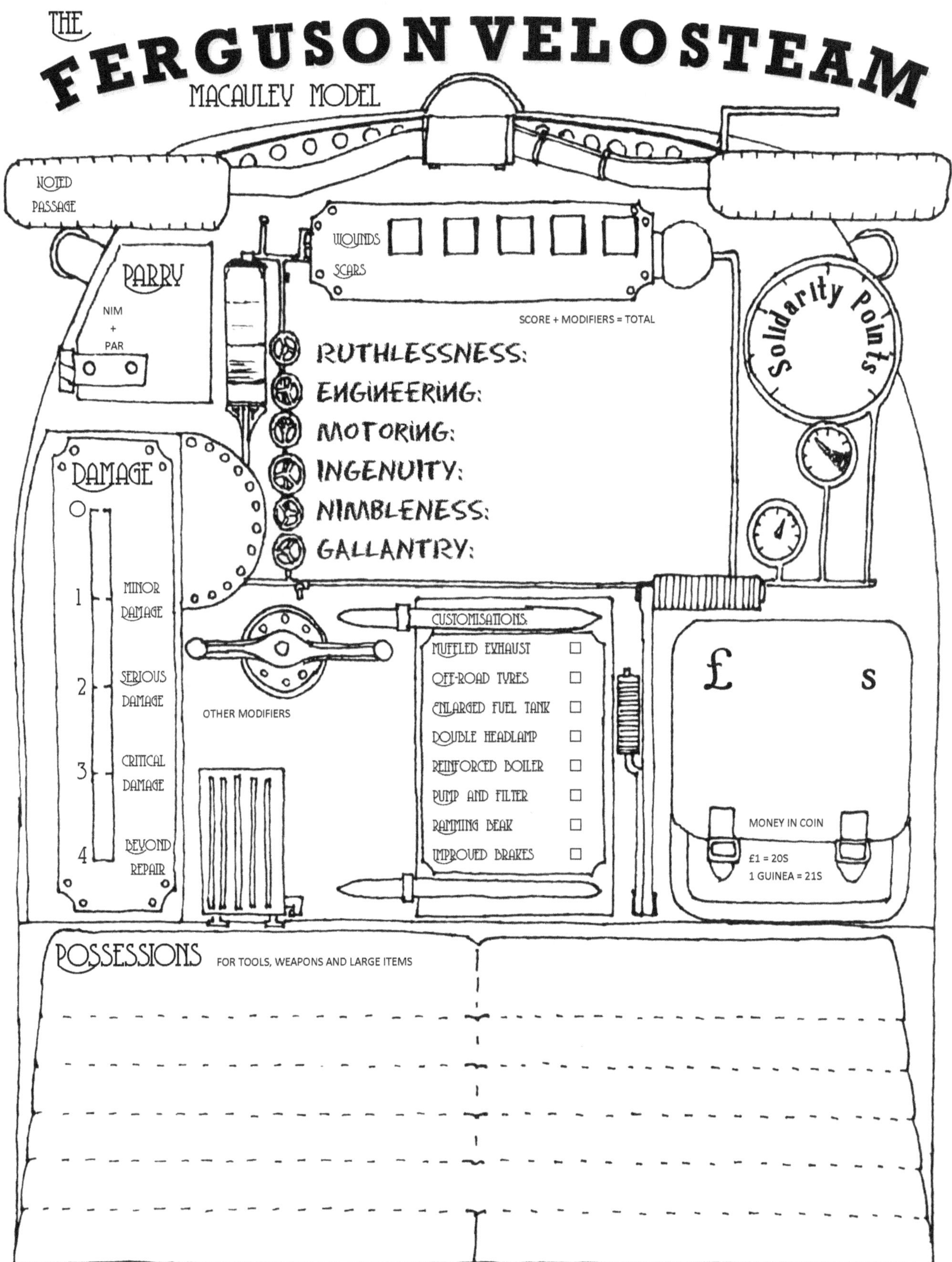

THE
FERGUSON VELOSTEAM
MACAULEY MODEL
NOTED PASSAGE
PARRY
NIM + PAR
WOUNDS
SCARS
SCORE + MODIFIERS = TOTAL
Solidarity Points
RUTHLESSNESS:
ENGINEERING:
MOTORING:
INGENUITY:
NIMBLENESS:
GALLANTRY:
DAMAGE
1 MINOR DAMAGE
2 SERIOUS DAMAGE
3 CRITICAL DAMAGE
4 BEYOND REPAIR
OTHER MODIFIERS
CUSTOMISATIONS:
MUFFLED EXHAUST
OFF-ROAD TYRES
ENLARGED FUEL TANK
DOUBLE HEADLAMP
REINFORCED BOILER
PUMP AND FILTER
RAMMING BEAK
IMPROVED BRAKES
£
S
MONEY IN COIN
£1 = 20S
1 GUINEA = 21S
POSSESSIONS
FOR TOOLS, WEAPONS AND LARGE ITEMS